*Make time for friends. Make time for **Debbie Macomber**.*

CEDAR COVE
16 LIGHTHOUSE ROAD
204 ROSEWOOD AVENUE
311 PELICAN COURT
44 CRANBERRY POINT
50 HARBOR STREET
6 RAINIER DRIVE

BLOSSOM STREET
THE SHOP ON BLOSSOM STREET
A GOOD YARN
OLD BOYFRIENDS
WEDNESDAYS AT FOUR
TWENTY WISHES
SUMMER ON BLOSSOM STREET
HANNAH'S LIST

THURSDAYS AT EIGHT

CHRISTMAS IN SEATTLE

D0242595

Dear Reader,

If this is your first visit to Cedar Cove, welcome! All the people in town are eager to introduce themselves. And if you're here for a repeat visit, welcome back. There's been a lot going on in town. Charlotte, Jack, Olivia, Grace, Cecilia and the others are looking forward to bringing you up to date on everything that's happened. You'll also discover surprises along the way…as well as some romance and a few laughs.

I promise a final resolution to the mystery about the man who died in the Beldons' B&B. After all, Peggy and Bob just want their lives to return to normal. But…there's another mystery developing, and this one involves the McAfees.

If you'd like to drop me a note, just log on to my website at www.debbiemacomber.com and sign the guest book. If you're interested in regular updates on the Cedar Cove characters, log on and click on the Cedar Cove button. As a bonus, I include the characters' favourite recipes… If you're not online but don't want to miss out, you can write to me at PO Box 1458, Port Orchard, Washington 98366, USA.

Speaking of Port Orchard… If you happen to visit, you might notice a resemblance between my home town and Cedar Cove. Not the characters, mind you, but just about everything else. Towns like this are great to visit in real life – *and* between the pages of a book.

Now, please grab something to drink (Peggy Beldon would make you a cup of tea!), find a comfortable spot and begin your visit to Cedar Cove. I'm so glad you're here.

Warmest regards,

Debbie Macomber

Debbie Macomber

44 Cranberry Point

MIRA

All the characters in this book have no existence outside the imagination of the author, and have no relation whatsoever to anyone bearing the same name or names. They are not even distantly inspired by any individual known or unknown to the author, and all the incidents are pure invention.

MIRA is a registered trademark of Harlequin Enterprises Limited, used under licence.

Published in Great Britain 2010
MIRA Books, Eton House, 18-24 Paradise Road,
Richmond, Surrey, TW9 1SR

© Debbie Macomber 2004

ISBN 978 0 7783 0339 8

60-0310

Printed in Great Britain
by Clays Ltd, St Ives plc

To Leslee Borger and
her incredible mother, Ruth Koelzer

Some of the Residents of
Cedar Cove, Washington

Olivia Lockhart Griffin: Divorced from Stan Lockhart. Now married to Jack Griffin. Family court judge in Cedar Cove. Mother of Justine and James. Lives at 16 Lighthouse Road.

Charlotte Jefferson: Mother of Olivia, widow, lifelong resident of Cedar Cove.

Justine (Lockhart) Gunderson: Daughter of Olivia, married to Seth, mother of Leif.

Seth Gunderson: Justine's husband. Co-owner, with Justine, of The Lighthouse restaurant.

James Lockhart: Olivia's son and Justine's younger brother. In the navy. Lives in San Diego with wife, Selina, and daughter, Isabella.

Stanley Lockhart: Olivia's ex-husband and father of James and Justine. Now lives in Seattle and divorced from his second wife.

Will Jefferson: Olivia's brother, Charlotte's son. Married and lives in Atlanta.

Grace Sherman: Olivia's best friend. Librarian. Widow. Mother of Maryellen and Kelly. Lives at 204 Rosewood Lane.

Dan Sherman: Grace's dead husband.

Maryellen Sherman: Oldest daughter of Grace and Dan. Mother of Katie.

Kelly Jordan: Maryellen's sister, married to Paul, mother of Tyler.

Jon Bowman: Photographer, chef and father of Katie. Engaged to Maryellen.

Jack Griffin: Newspaper reporter and editor of *The Cedar Cove Chronicle*. Recovering alcoholic, married to Olivia Lockhart. Father of Eric, who lives in Nevada with his wife, Shelly, and their twin boys.

Zachary Cox: Accountant, remarried to Rosie. Father of Allison and Eddie Cox. Lives at 311 Pelican Court.

Cliff Harding: Retired engineer and now horse breeder living near Cedar Cove. Divorced father of Lisa, who lives in Maryland. He has an on-and-off relationship with Grace Sherman.

Cecilia Randall: Navy wife, living near Cedar Cove. Accountant. Married to Ian Randall, submariner. Lost a baby, Allison.

Bob and Peggy Beldon: Retired. Own the Thyme and Tide Bed & Breakfast at 44 Cranberry Point. Have two adult children.

Roy McAfee: Private detective, retired from Seattle police force. Two adult children. The McAfees live at 5 Harbor Street.

Corrie McAfee: Roy's wife and office manager.

Troy Davis: Cedar Cove sheriff.

Pastor Flemming: Local Methodist minister.

Ben Rhodes: Retired naval officer. Member of the Senior Centre. Involved with Charlotte Jefferson.

One

Peggy Beldon walked into her newly planted garden, taking real pleasure in the sights and smells that surrounded her. This was her private place, her one true source of serenity. The fresh briny scent of the water off Puget Sound drifted toward her as she watched the Washington State ferry glide from Bremerton toward Seattle on its sixty-minute journey. This was a typical May afternoon in Cedar Cove—comfortably warm with just a hint of a breeze.

Peggy uncoiled the garden hose and moved carefully between the rows of leaf lettuce, sweet peas and pole beans. She had a strong practical streak, expressed in her vegetable and herb gardens; she satisfied her craving for beauty with the flower gardens in front. Looking back at the house that always had been her dream, Peggy smiled. She'd grown up in Cedar Cove, graduated from the local high school and married Bob Beldon on his return from Vietnam. The early years had been difficult because of Bob's reliance on alcohol. But then, to her eternal gratitude, he'd discovered Alcoholics Anonymous; it had saved their marriage and quite possibly Bob's life. Until AA, Bob had spent most nights drinking, by himself or with friends. When he drank, he became a different person, no longer the man she'd married. She didn't like to think about that time. Thankfully, her husband had remained sober for twenty-one years.

Walking between the rows, Peggy gently watered the seedlings. Several years earlier, Bob had accepted early retirement and with the severance package, they'd purchased the house on Cranberry Point. Peggy had loved it for as long as she could remember. Situated on a point of land overlooking Sinclair Inlet, the two-story structure, built in the late 1930s, had seemed like a mansion to her. Over the years, it had changed owners a number of times and had started to deteriorate, since no one had cared enough to provide the maintenance it needed. By straining their finances, Bob and Peggy had managed to buy it for a price far below its current market value.

Her husband was a talented handyman and within a few months they were able to hang out a sign for their bed-and-breakfast. Peggy hadn't known how much business to expect, how many guests would be attracted to the Thyme and Tide B and B, as they'd called it. She'd hoped, of course, that they'd make enough to supplement their retirement income—and they had. She was proud of the success they'd achieved. Their traditional home, warm hospitality and her cooking had brought them steady customers and a growing reputation. They'd even been reviewed in a national magazine, which had reserved its highest praise for the food, especially her baking. The reviewer had spent two whole sentences describing her blueberry muffins and homemade fruit cobbler. She had twenty blueberry bushes and eight raspberry canes, and she pampered them lovingly. Each summer she was rewarded with an ample supply for her guests and her family. Life had seemed about as perfect as it could get.

Then the unimaginable happened.

More than a year ago, a stranger had knocked on their door in the middle of a dark, stormy night. If it hadn't been so clichéd she might've been amused, but this was no laughing matter. The man had rented a room and then promptly locked himself inside.

A hundred times since, Peggy had regretted not insisting he complete the usual paperwork. It was late, and he'd seemed so tired that they'd simply shown him to his room. They could deal with the necessities in the morning, over breakfast.

But by morning, the stranger was dead.

Ever since, Peggy had felt as if they were caught in some kind of whirlwind, tossed about by forces beyond their control. Bad enough that the man had died in their home, but then they'd learned that he'd carried false identification. Nothing was as it seemed. By the end of that day, after hours with the sheriff and the coroner, there'd been more questions than answers.

She saw Bob pull the riding lawn mower out of the garage. At the sound of the engine, Peggy paused in watering her seedlings, one hand shading her eyes. Even after all these years of marriage, she never grew tired of their life together. They'd survived the bad times with their love intact. And their attraction, too. Bob was tall and had kept his shape, his sandy brown hair neatly trimmed. His arms were already tanned from exposure to the sun. He loved his workshop and she was genuinely impressed by what he could do with a few pieces of oak or pine. She'd fallen in love with Bob Beldon as a teenager and she loved him still.

Now, however, she was worried. She didn't want to think about the dead man, but it was unavoidable, especially after what they'd recently found out. Sheriff Davis had identified their mystery guest as Maxwell Russell. To say Bob was shocked would be putting it mildly. He'd been with Max in Vietnam. Dan Sherman, who was also dead, Bob, Max and another man named Stewart Samuels had belonged to that squadron. They'd gotten lost in a Southeast Asian jungle with tragic results.

Once the identity of the dead man was established, another shocking revelation had come to light. The sheriff, with the help of local private investigator Roy McAfee, had discovered that Max Russell's death was no accident.

He'd been poisoned.

The water bottle he'd carried with him had been laced with odorless, tasteless Rohypnol, commonly known as the "date rape" drug. The dose had been large enough to stop his heart. Maxwell Russell had gone to bed, tired from a long day of travel, and he never woke up.

Bob rode past her on the lawn mower with a quick wave, and Peggy continued to water her garden, but a pang went through her. At this very moment Bob could be in danger, but he seemed content to ignore any risk rather than admit her concerns were legitimate.

As she set aside the hose, Peggy caught sight of Sheriff Davis's patrol car coming down Cranberry Point. She immediately felt the tension between her shoulder blades. She hoped he planned to talk some sense into Bob.

Her husband must have seen the patrol car at the same time Peggy did because he cut the engine and climbed off the lawn mower. Sheriff Troy Davis turned into the driveway, then stepped out of his vehicle. In the beginning, when it looked like Bob might be a suspect in the murder case, Davis wasn't nearly as welcome here as he was now.

The sheriff, who was probably a little heavier than he should be, took a moment to hike up his pants and adjust his gun before heading across the lawn to meet Bob. Unwilling to be left out of the conversation, Peggy shut off the water and hurried across the half-mown grass.

"Peggy." Davis touched the brim of his hat and nodded in her direction. "I was just telling Bob it might be a good idea if the three of us sat down and talked."

Peggy nodded in return, appreciating the fact that he wanted to include her.

Bob led the way to the patio, and Peggy was grateful she'd taken time that morning to sweep it off. The three of them sat at the round pine table Bob had built several years earlier. He'd painted it a deep gray-blue, a color that complemented the white siding. The striped umbrella was up and the patio was awash in sunshine.

"I thought I'd update you on my conversation with Hannah Russell."

A couple of months earlier, after Max's identity had been uncovered, his daughter had asked to meet with Bob and Peggy. It had been an uncomfortable meeting, but Peggy's heart had ached for the young woman. She'd answered Hannah's questions to the best of her ability.

For her part, there was little Hannah could tell them. All she knew was what her father had told her—he was taking a short trip, although he hadn't divulged where. That was the last she'd heard. When he didn't return to California, she'd filed a missing persons report with the police. A year had passed before she learned his fate.

"I feel so bad for her," Peggy said. Hannah had lost her mother some time before and was now an orphan with no other family.

"She was pretty upset," Troy admitted. "You can imagine how painful it was to learn her father was dead. But to discover he'd been murdered..." He shook his head.

"Did she have any idea who might've done this?"

"None," Davis told them. "She asked me to thank you for your kindness. Talking with you helped her resolve in her own mind what happened to her father. Peggy, she mentioned the letter you wrote, and I could tell it meant a great deal to her."

Peggy bit her lip. "How's she getting on with her life?"

The sheriff hesitated. "I can't really say. She said she no longer has any reason to stay in California and implied that she's thinking of moving. I asked her to keep in touch and she promised she would."

Peggy could understand the young woman's feelings. With both of her parents gone, Hannah was rootless. Peggy sympathized with her desire to leave the area where she'd grown up, where she was surrounded by so many memories. Every place she turned, every place she looked, Hannah must be reminded of the parents she'd loved.

"What did you find out about Colonel Samuels?" Bob asked, eyes narrowed as he gazed at Troy Davis.

Stewart Samuels was the fourth man in Vietnam with Bob and Dan and Max. Peggy knew the sheriff had recently been in contact with him. The colonel had been cleared in Max's murder, at least as far as Davis was concerned, but her husband obviously had doubts. While Bob and the other two were eager to be discharged, back in the early seventies, Samuels had stayed in the Army and risen through the ranks.

"At this point I don't consider the colonel a suspect."

"He's some mucky-muck in Army Intelligence from what I hear," Bob muttered, as if that should be motive enough.

"Who lives in the Washington D.C. area," Sheriff Davis stated calmly. "I've had him checked out by a number of people. He's highly respected. He's been cooperative and willing to help in any way he can. Perhaps you should talk to him yourself, Bob."

Her husband declined with a sharp shake of his head. Bob wanted as little to do with the past as possible. Coping with what had happened to Dan, who'd committed suicide, and to Max, had been hard enough. The less he had to think about the past, or its effect on the present, the better.

"Is Bob in danger?" Peggy asked bluntly. Her husband might prefer not to acknowledge the likelihood of a threat, but Peggy wanted a realistic assessment of their situation.

"I think he might be at risk," the sheriff said quietly.

It wasn't what Peggy had hoped to hear, but she was grateful for his frankness. They had to face the truth, however unpleasant, and take appropriate precautions.

"Nonsense," Bob insisted. "If anyone wanted me dead, I'd be six feet under by now."

Maybe, but Peggy wasn't willing to take chances with her husband's life.

"Why don't we arrange an extended vacation?" she suggested. It'd been years since they'd been away from the bed-and-breakfast, and they could use a break.

"For how long?" Bob asked.

"Until the case is solved," Peggy told him, pleading with her eyes. This wasn't the time to put on a brave front—not in her opinion, anyway.

"No way." Bob's quick refusal shouldn't have come as any surprise. He'd been quite content to live in denial. Denial and featherbeds! *Someone* had to point out the very real possibility that he was in danger and because he was, so was she.

"I'm not leaving Cedar Cove."

"Now, Bob…"

"I won't let anyone or anything drive me out of my own home."

A chill shot up Peggy's spine. "But–"

"No, Peg," he said, and his face hardened with resolve. "How long are we supposed to stay away? One month? Two?" He paused. "More than that?"

It wasn't a question Troy could answer.

"Max was found dead over a year ago. I was supposedly in danger then, right?"

Sheriff Davis exchanged a concerned look with Peggy. "I understand what you're saying, but we didn't know then what we know now."

"I'm not running! I spent half my life running, and I won't do it again. If somebody wants me dead, then so be it."

Peggy gasped.

"I'm sorry, honey," her husband said, stretching his arm across the table to clasp her fingers with his. "I refuse to live like that, looking over my shoulder all the time."

"Then perhaps you could compromise," Davis said. "There's no need to invite someone into your home who might want to harm you."

"What do you mean?" Bob leaned closer, his stomach pressed against the rounded edge of the pinewood table. Peggy realized that despite his defiant words he was afraid. His body language revealed what he was unwilling to admit.

"I don't know how many reservations you have for the B and B, but I'd advise you to not take any more."

"We can easily cancel the ones we have," Peggy murmured. Any number of businesses in town would welcome the additional bookings.

Bob directed his gaze at Peggy. "Would that make you more comfortable?"

She swallowed and nodded.

Bob continued to look unsure, as if even this one concession was more than he felt inclined to make.

"I've been worried ever since Jack and Olivia's wedding," she whispered.

A week earlier, Bob had stood up as Jack Griffin's best man. That was just a day or two before they'd learned Max Russell had been murdered.

"All right." Bob's voice was heavy with reluctance. "We'll cancel the reservations."

"No guests," Peggy said.

"No guests," he confirmed, "until this matter is settled once and for all."

This was going to hurt financially, but it didn't matter. What did matter was having the reassurance that her husband was safe.

"I'll do what I can to solve this quickly," Troy promised them.

Peggy could only wonder how long that would take.

Two

Cecilia Randall stood on the Navy pier and watched the aircraft carrier *George Washington* sail into Sinclair Inlet. After six months serving in the Persian Gulf, her husband, Ian, was finally home. Cecilia had often heard people talk about hearts swelling and dismissed the expression as exaggerated, sentimental. Now she knew what it meant, how it felt. Her heart swelled with love, pride and patriotism as the massive ship headed toward Bremerton.

The other Navy wives and hordes of friends and family crowded the pier. Colorful banners waved in the wind, along with Welcome Home signs. News helicopters from the Seattle television stations circled the area, taping the event for the five-o'clock broadcast. The joy and excitement around her was infectious, despite the dreary, cloudy day. Even the lead-gray skies and the threat of imminent rain didn't dampen Cecilia's mood. A band played in the background, and the American flag rippled in the breeze. It could have been a Norman Rockwell painting.

Cecilia's dearest friends, two other Navy wives, Cathy Lackey and Carol Greendale, stood with her, each holding a toddler against her hip while madly waving. Cecilia hoped that before long she'd be a mother again herself.

"I think I see Andrew," Cathy cried. She screeched with happiness and waved one arm wildly above her head. Then she pointed his daddy out to her young son.

Three thousand sailors, dressed in white Navy uniforms, stood along the rail, feet apart, hands behind their backs, as they lined the perimeter of the flight deck. At this distance it was impossible for Cecilia to find Ian. The wind whipped at her face and she shouted and waved. Perhaps Ian would see her.

"Take Amanda," Carol said, heaving her three-year-old daughter toward Cecilia.

She gladly held the toddler. There'd been a time when even looking at this little girl brought her pain. Allison, Ian's and her baby daughter, was born the same week as Amanda. Had she lived, Allison, too, would've been three years old. But she'd died after clinging to life for only a few days. Her death had ripped the marriage apart. If not for a wise family court judge who ignored convention and denied their divorce, they might have ended up like so many other sad marriage statistics.

"Ian, over here," Cecilia shouted, as she thrust one arm high above her head. "Do you see your daddy?" she asked Amanda.

The little girl's arms were tight around Cecilia's neck, and she buried her face in Cecilia's shoulder.

"There's Daddy, there's Daddy," Carol said, pointing to the aircraft carrier.

Amanda looked up then, smiling, and Carol reached for her daughter again.

An eternity passed before the gangplank was lowered and the sailors disembarked, carrying their duffel bags. Soon there were reunions everywhere. Cathy spotted Andrew and ran toward her husband, weeping with happiness.

Cecilia searched frantically for Ian. Then she saw him, tall and fit and tan, his dark hair visible beneath his white Navy cap. The breath left her lungs at the sight of him and she burst into tears of joy.

Not a minute later, Cecilia was caught up in her husband's arms. They clung to each other, tears still clouding her eyes as Ian brought his mouth to hers.

Their kiss was slow, sensual and filled with six months of longing and need. By the time they'd finished, Cecilia was weak and breathless. Ian was home; her world was complete once again. The universe could have dissolved around her and she wouldn't have cared.

"I've missed you like crazy," she whispered, holding on to him, her fingers massaging the nape of his neck. There was so much to say, so much that was in her heart. None of it mattered right then, however. All she cared about was the feel of Ian's arms around her and the knowledge that he was home and safe and hers, if only on loan from the United States Navy.

"Oh, sweetheart, this has been the longest six months of my life." He continued to hold her tight against him. Cecilia closed her eyes and savored this moment she'd been waiting for.

Ian had three days of shore leave and Cecilia planned to make full use of every one of them. The days—and the nights. His return couldn't have been better planned. As far as she could tell, these next few days were her fertile period.

With his duffel bag over his shoulder, Ian reached for her hand as they walked toward the parking area. Apparently she still wasn't close enough to suit him because he wrapped his arm around her waist and drew her to his side. He smiled and his love washed over her like…like warm sunshine. That was all she could compare it to, the life-giving warmth so absent today. A light drizzle had begun and they walked a little faster, still gazing at each other.

"I love you," she mouthed.

"I can hardly wait to show you how much I love you." Then, as if the question had only now occurred to him, he asked, "You don't have to go back to work, do you?"

She toyed with the idea of letting him worry, but couldn't make herself do it. "As a matter of fact, Mr. Cox gave me all three days off." She handed Ian the car keys, and he promptly unlocked their vehicle.

"I like your boss more and more."

Cecilia did, too, especially now that Mr. and Mrs. Cox had remarried. The office became a much more relaxed place once the couple reunited. But it wasn't the Coxes on Cecilia's mind as Ian drove to their duplex. They met each other's eyes frequently but didn't speak much. Ten minutes later they were home.

"Did you bring back everything I sent you?" Cecilia asked in a husky voice when Ian parked in their assigned spot. They'd moved into military housing just before his most recent deployment, when a unit became available.

"That was very sadistic of you, wife," Ian said, his eyebrows drawing together.

Had she not known him so well, Cecilia might think he hadn't been amused by her small prank. The gleam in his eyes told her otherwise. For each of the last three weeks before he was due home, Cecilia had sent him one piece of a sheer negligee outfit. With the last piece, she'd included a note that promised she'd wear it for him when he got back. In his last e-mail to her, she could almost hear him panting.

"I hope you realize you've created a monster with that little trick of yours."

"A monster I'm eager to tame," she whispered, leaning over to kiss him.

"Oh, honey…" He broke off the kiss. "Let's get inside—fast."

"Aye, aye," she said dreamily, saluting him.

Ian slid out the driver's side and dashed around the front of the car. He opened the passenger door, helped her out and grabbed his duffel bag from the back. Giggling with excitement, they ran through the light rain toward their duplex. Ian was all thumbs as he struggled to unlock their door.

Cecilia had cleaned the place until it sparkled. The sheets on their bed were fresh and turned down, the bedroom shades drawn. After six months of separation she'd known they wouldn't want to wait to make love.

As soon as they got inside, Ian dropped his duffel and reached out for her. Cecilia came willingly, throwing her arms around his neck. He hoisted her up and headed directly for the bedroom. The second they cleared the door, Ian kissed her again, his mouth open and moist, moving urgently against hers.

He released her and immediately started undressing.

"You want me to put on that black nightie for you?" she asked.

"Next time," Ian said, his breathing shallow as he sat on the bed and quickly removed his shoes.

"One more thing…"

He gave her a questioning glance.

She knelt behind him on the bed and rested her chin on his bare shoulder. "I think there's something you should know."

"It can't wait?"

"Well, it could, but I figure this is something you might *want* to know."

"What?" he growled, turning toward her. He grabbed her around the waist, and his dark eyes bore into hers.

Cecilia smiled at her husband, smoothing her hands down his muscular shoulders, loving the feel of him. "I'm thinking this afternoon would be a wonderful time to make a baby."

Ian's eyes flared briefly. "I thought you were on the pill."

Her smile broadened as she slowly shook her head. "Not anymore. I tossed them into the garbage six months ago."

He frowned.

"With you at sea, there wasn't any need for me to be on birth control. Besides—"

"You didn't start again when you knew I was coming home?"

"Nope."

"But—but you knew when I was due back."

"I did…and I've been greatly anticipating your home-coming," she purred.

"But, sweetheart, you never said a word! I don't have any-thing to protect you from pregnancy."

"Who says I want protection? What I want, sailor man," she whispered, "is a baby."

Ian went completely still.

"Ian?"

Her husband straightened, sitting on the side of the bed with his back to her. "Don't you think this is something we should've discussed first?"

"We're…we're discussing it now."

"At the last possible moment."

"You don't want a baby?"

Ian stood then and faced her. His shoulders were bare and his pants half unzipped. He rubbed his hand over his eyes as if her question had overwhelmed him. "I do want chil-dren, but not yet."

"I thought—"

"It's too soon, sweetheart."

"It's been three years." Her desire for a child had grown progressively stronger in the months Ian had been at sea. It made sense to complete her schooling before getting pregnant again, but she'd done that and found a wonderful job. "I'm ready, Ian."

His shoulders sagged. "I'm not… I can't risk getting you pregnant." He zipped his pants and picked up his shirt, yanking it on and shoving his arms into the sleeves. He fastened the buttons with record speed and scooped the car keys from the dresser.

Cecilia bit her lip. He was right; she should've mentioned it earlier. They'd communicated almost daily via e-mail, and phone calls whenever possible. There'd been ample opportunity to discuss the matter long before his arrival home.

Ian walked out of the bedroom, then turned back at the door. "Stay right there," he said, pointing in her direction.

"Where are you going?"

His laugh was weak with impatience. "To the drugstore. Stay where you are, okay? I'll be back before you know it."

It felt as if the sun had disappeared behind a dark cloud. Perhaps, deep down, Cecilia had known this would be Ian's reaction. Her husband was afraid of another pregnancy, afraid of what it would do to her physically and what it might do to them as a couple.

Cecilia understood why he felt that way because she'd faced those same fears herself. She'd believed—or *wanted* to believe—that Ian, too, had moved past them. Apparently she'd been wrong.

Three

With a sense of joy and celebration, Maryellen Sherman carried the heavy cardboard box out of her rental house and set it in the trunk of her car. Soon she'd be living with Jon Bowman—married to him.

After all this time it hardly seemed possible. The barriers between them had been lowered. No longer could she disguise her love for him. Nor did she have to; they'd admitted their feelings for each other. The misunderstandings were over, pride and anger put aside.

Jon followed with a second box, which he set next to the first. He took her hand and gave it a gentle squeeze, silently letting her know how pleased he was that they were finally going to be together for good.

Katie, their nine-month-old daughter, slept contentedly in her crib as they brought another load out to the car, then hurried back inside the house. Maryellen realized they only had a few more minutes of peace before their daughter woke. Most of her belongings weren't even packed.

"That's it for now?" Jon asked, hands on hips as he glanced around the living room.

"I'll have more later," she promised. Maryellen had barely started packing. She'd lived in this rental house for almost twelve years and what she'd accumulated in that length of time was staggering. Sorting through clothes and books–what to keep, what to give away or throw out–had already taken weeks.

"How much more?" A note of weariness entered Jon's voice.

"Lots. Do you want to pack up a few boxes now?" She was thinking she should probably fill up the back seat of her car before they caravanned to his home.

"What I want is to get you permanently in my house." He sounded as impatient as she felt.

"I'm just as eager to get there." She stepped into the compact kitchen and tried to figure out what else they should take with them this afternoon. Moving had never seemed so complicated or frustrating.

"Did you talk to your mother about a wedding date?"

"She thinks Memorial Day is perfect." Maryellen held back a smile. She suspected her mother was just plain relieved that she and Jon had actually decided to tie the knot. Since they already had a child together, a ceremony was long past due, in Grace Sherman's opinion.

"You're sure you don't mind not having a big fancy wedding?"

Maryellen shook her head. She opened the refrigerator and took out a tall pitcher of iced tea. She'd had all the glamour and glitter with her first marriage. The wedding had been lovely, the marriage itself anything but. She'd been young and naive; the divorce, a year later, had left her reeling emotionally for a long time.

Twelve years after that, when she'd met Jon, she'd still been frightened of falling in love again. In the beginning, she'd spurned him, insulted him and did everything she could think of to keep him out of her life. She felt mortified now when she thought back on everything she'd said and done.

Jon got two glasses from the cupboard and set them on the counter. "You're not getting any bargain in the husband department, you know?"

The anger that flared in her was too hot to be denied. "If you ever say that to me again, I swear I'll…I'll make you suffer."

A smile briefly softened Jon's sharp features. He wasn't a handsome man. He was tall and long-limbed with dark hair and intense brown eyes. And he was quite possibly the most talented photographer she'd ever encountered. His work hung in one of the best Seattle galleries and his name was fast gaining recognition.

"You know everything now," he said and lowered his head, avoiding eye contact.

"You know everything about me, too," she reminded him.

They both had their secrets, painful bits and pieces from their pasts. Now they had each other and, for the first time since her divorce, Maryellen felt she could heal the unresolved griefs of that marriage. She knew it was their pasts that had kept them apart. Despite everything, they'd been drawn toward each other from the very beginning, but the secrets they'd so desperately wanted to hide had almost torn them apart.

"You're not the one with a prison record," Jon muttered.

Clasping his hand, Maryellen raised it to her lips. "I consider it one of my life's greatest blessings that I'll be your wife. Until I met you I was in prison, too—a prison of my own making." That might sound melodramatic, but she meant every word.

His smile was enough to brighten the kitchen, and she

slipped her arms around his waist and buried her face against him. "The truth is, I can't wait to spend the rest of my life with you."

His arms tightened around her as she felt a sigh rumble through his chest. "It's a little silly, don't you think, you living here until after the wedding?"

"Perhaps, but I prefer to wait." Maryellen had made too many mistakes, and with this marriage, she wanted to do everything right. When she came to him on their wedding night, she wanted it to be special.

"We have a child together, so it's not as if…" His voice trailed off.

She tilted her head to look up at him, unsure how to say what was in her heart. "Do you mind terribly much?"

"I mind like hell, but I can wait if it means that much to you."

She nodded and then kissed his jaw to let him know she appreciated his patience. Jon tangled his fingers in her dark hair as he pressed his mouth to hers. She tasted his passion and his desire, and her resolve weakened. This was all so new and exciting. Their physical need for each other had always been explosive, their hunger undeniable.

Suddenly Katie let out a wail from the back bedroom. Jon sighed and broke off the kiss.

By the time Maryellen reached Katie's room, her daughter was standing up in her crib, both arms raised to her mother. Maryellen lifted her out and, after changing Katie's diaper, carried her into the kitchen and placed her in the high chair. Her afternoon snack of juice and an arrowroot cracker was already waiting for her.

Awake now and in a good mood, Katie grabbed her juice cup and eagerly brought it to her mouth. She took a noisy slurp, then banged the cup against the plastic tray.

"Every time I look at her, I feel a sense of wonder," Jon

said and squatted down so he was eye-level with his daughter. "You're Daddy's little girl, aren't you?"

Katie rewarded him with a broad four-tooth grin.

Jon automatically retrieved his camera from the counter and started snapping pictures.

"Jon." Maryellen laughed, unable to stop herself. He was so predictable. When she'd first begun working with him at the Harbor Street Art Gallery, he'd asked her out a dozen times. Maryellen had refused all his invitations. She hadn't wanted a man in her life. Later she'd succumbed—and soon afterward she'd discovered to her shock that she was pregnant. She'd made every effort to keep Jon out of her child's life. And hers…

Like a lot of other women, she'd chosen to be a single mother. Not until Katie was born had she come to realize how much her daughter needed a father and how much she herself wanted and needed Jon's help in rearing their child. Then it seemed too late. While Jon obviously loved their daughter, he wanted little or nothing to do with her.

When he'd finished taking photographs of Katie, Jon focused the camera on her. Before Maryellen could react he'd snapped several pictures. When he'd first turned his camera on her, early in their relationship, she'd felt both self-conscious and flattered; now she simply trusted him, never protesting when he aimed his Nikon at her, no matter how unexpected the moment might be. In many ways Jon was most comfortable behind the camera's lens. It was through photography that he revealed his personality and emotions.

"I want you and Katie with me as soon as possible," he said when he'd rewound the film and removed the cartridge.

"It won't be long. Two weeks."

He looked as if he wanted to argue, but seemed to change his mind. "We've waited this long, I don't suppose another two weeks will kill me."

"The anticipation is half the pleasure."

He growled something she couldn't decipher. She could guess, though, and it made her smile.

"I thought we could ask Pastor Flemming to officiate." Maryellen didn't attend church regularly, but her mother's best friend, Olivia Lockhart, had recently married Jack Griffin, and the Methodist minister had performed the ceremony. She'd found it deeply moving.

"What about Judge Lockhart—or Griffin, I guess?"

"She's using both names," Maryellen said.

Jon nodded.

"I—I'd like a religious service." Olivia was a longtime family friend, but Maryellen had already decided against a civil wedding. When she spoke her vows, she was committing herself, before God and the community, to love Jon for the rest of her life.

Jon's eyes narrowed. "You want to be married in a church? You're sure?"

"Either at the Methodist Church or perhaps on your property, if that's all right?" Jon had inherited the land from his grandfather and had built a beautiful two-story house there. The acreage overlooked Puget Sound, with Mount Rainier as a backdrop.

"It's fine," he said. "What about the reception?"

"At the house, too." All at once she wondered if she was asking too much of him. "I don't imagine we'll have many guests, just family and a few friends. All we'd need to serve is wedding cake and champagne. If the weather cooperates, we could be married outside." With the rhododendrons, many of which grew wild on the property, and the azaleas in bloom, the place would be stunning.

He nodded. "Perhaps we should serve a few hors d'oeuvres. I can easily prepare them a day or two before."

"Jon…"

"A friend of mine can do the pictures, but I want to take the ones of you myself."

Maryellen could tell he was warming to the subject of their wedding. "Can we put all this together in two weeks?" she asked.

Jon didn't hesitate. "Of course we can." At her delighted smile, he added, "Any other requests?"

She had one, but wasn't sure how to ask.

"What?" The question was wary, as if he sensed her mood.

"The guest list…"

"How many?"

"It's not the number. Mom and my sister and a few friends, but there are a couple of people I'd like to invite and I don't know if you'd approve."

Katie squealed and dropped the heavy-bottomed cup on her tray.

Jon kissed Maryellen's temple. "You know there's almost nothing I can refuse you. Who do you want to invite?"

She leaned into him, not wanting to see his face when she told him. "Your father and stepmother." Jon had only recently revealed how his parents had chosen to protect his younger brother at his expense. They had lied on the witness stand and, as a result, Jon had been convicted of dealing drugs. He'd served seven years in prison. Not once in all those years or the years since had he spoken to either his father or his stepmother.

Jon tensed and slowly released Maryellen. "No. They are no longer part of my life. They cast me aside and—"

"You're all they have left." His brother had died a tragic death and Maryellen was convinced that his family regretted what they'd done, both in betraying Jon and in not forcing his brother to face the consequences of his crime.

Jon clasped her shoulders hard, almost hurting her with the fervor of his emotions. "We will never speak of this again, understand? I have no family other than you and Katie." Taking a shuddery breath, he let her go.

She wanted to argue and longed to help heal the relationship between Jon and his family, but she could see he wasn't ready. His parents had a granddaughter they knew nothing about. Surely that was an opportunity for new beginnings. Still, it wasn't Maryellen's place to step in, especially since Jon's feelings on the subject were this adamant.

"What about a honeymoon?" Jon asked. "Nothing fancy, but someplace we can get away for a night or two."

"You want a honeymoon?" Maryellen had been so involved with plans for her move and for the actual wedding, she hadn't given a honeymoon any thought.

"Damn straight I want a honeymoon."

"What about Thyme and Tide?" Bob and Peggy Beldon's bed-and-breakfast was said to be the best in town.

Jon shook his head. "I already looked into that, but they aren't taking guests until this murder is solved."

"Oh…" That was a disappointment.

"How about a night in Seattle? Just the two of us. Your mother will take Katie, won't she?"

Maryellen laughed softly. "In a heartbeat."

"Seattle, then?"

Maryellen nodded.

"The honeymoon will be the very best part." Jon kissed her nose, and Katie giggled as if she'd never seen anything funnier. "That amuses you, does it?" Jon said, smiling. "I guess I see your point."

"We're going to have a beautiful wedding," Maryellen

said with certainty. The prospect of it made this chaos of packing and moving seem worthwhile. Within a couple of weeks she'd be Jon's wife. The three of them would be a family.

Four

Charlotte Jefferson dressed nervously for her court appearance. She'd spent many an afternoon in the Kitsap County Courthouse, proudly watching her only daughter officiate as a family court judge. In Charlotte's opinion, her daughter was one of the wisest judges in the entire state. She got a thrill just watching Olivia mete out decisions, looking so official in her black robe.

This afternoon, however, Charlotte wouldn't be in Olivia's courtroom but in Judge Robson's. She wouldn't be alone, either. Together with several of her dearest friends, she'd be facing the consequences of civil disobedience. Still, serving time in the slammer, if it came to that, would be a small price to pay if her actions got the town council to finally bring a health clinic to Cedar Cove.

Laura, Bess and the others, including Ben Rhodes, were scheduled to meet her in the foyer outside Judge Robson's courtroom at one o'clock.

Charlotte donned her best Sunday dress, complete with the Easter hat she'd purchased back in 1966. It was a broad-brimmed yellow one with a single white plume tucked in the satin band. If Judge Robson decided to incarcerate her and the others, she intended to walk into that jail cell as finely dressed as she would've been for any church service.

Olivia and Jack didn't seem to think a prison term was likely, but Charlotte had heard rumors about Judge Robson. He was supposed to be much more by-the-book than Olivia, more of a hard-liner, and—again according to rumor—fond of making an example of the occasional miscreant.

The doorbell chimed and Harry, her cat, leapt down from the foot of her bed with an uncharacteristic display of energy and trotted into the living room. Since Olivia and Jack were out of town on their honeymoon, Charlotte wondered who it might be. Embarrassment had prevented her from asking Justine, her granddaughter, to accompany her. Olivia, of course, was well aware of the entire situation, unhappily so. But Charlotte refused to let the rest of her family and friends know, although it was impossible to keep such news completely quiet.

The peephole in the front door answered her question. Ben Rhodes stood on the other side, looking as dapper and debonair as ever. Despite her age, her heart did a tiny flip-flop at the sight of him. After all these years as a widow, she'd assumed she was too old and set in her ways to fall in love, but Ben had shown her that even long-held assumptions could be wrong.

"Ben!" She unbolted the four dead bolt locks on her front door. "What are you doing here?" she demanded, although she was more than glad to see him. "We're supposed to meet at the courthouse, remember?"

"I know, but I thought I'd escort my favorite gal into court. Are you ready?"

Charlotte straightened the skirt of her floral dress, feeling, for just a second, like the heroine in a 1950s musical.

Ben made the whole mess seem like an adventure rather than a scandal—or worse. "How do I look?"

A smile lazily crossed Ben's full mouth. At times it was difficult to forget that he wasn't really Cesar Romero, the wonderful Cuban actor. In her opinion, Ben could have been the other man's double. "You look lovely," he told her.

But adventure or not, Charlotte couldn't quite control her nervousness. "Oh, dear…I just don't know what's going to happen to us."

Ben gently patted her hand. "I don't believe the council wants that kind of negative publicity. I can just imagine what the Seattle newspapers would say about a town punishing a handful of senior citizens because we were demonstrating for health care."

"Unlawful assembly," Charlotte muttered under her breath. "I, for one, am willing to serve my time if that's what it takes to wake this town up." Just being with Ben strengthened her resolve. He made her feel brave, helped her stand up for her principles and act on the power of her convictions.

"I completely agree with you. However…" He hesitated and then forcefully expelled his breath. "I don't think we need to worry about serving jail time. We'll probably just be fined."

Charlotte just couldn't be sure. She *was* worried, especially considering Judge Robson's reputation. Would she be viewed as the ringleader? She felt particularly anxious about her friends, who'd stood loyally by her when she defied Sheriff Davis.

"I've hired an attorney," Ben informed her. Earlier Ben had agreed to represent them in court, but apparently he'd changed his mind.

Charlotte hadn't wanted to involve lawyers. For one thing, they charged an arm and a leg, and for another, whatever lawyer Ben had chosen was bound to say something to Olivia when she returned. Charlotte wanted Olivia to know as little as possible, difficult though that would be. She'd hoped to hold down the gossip.

"Sharon Castor said she'd meet us at the courthouse."

"Not Sharon Castor," Charlotte cried. The attorney was frequently in Olivia's courtroom. In fact, Sharon had recently represented Rosemary Cox in her divorce case. Charlotte had been present when her daughter had handed down one of her most controversial joint-custody decisions—a decision that, Charlotte believed, had led to the couple's reconciliation.

"Oh, dear," she said and sighed. "We might as well go." She went into the bedroom for her overnight case, which contained her medications and night cream, and reached for her jacket. Just in case... The day was cool, and from everything she'd read, jail cells were notoriously drafty. She glanced around her bedroom one last time. Once she'd received her sentence, if the worst happened, she'd contact Justine and ask her to take care of Harry.

"Charlotte," Ben said, shaking his head as she entered the living room. "You aren't going to need a suitcase."

"Don't be so sure," she countered grimly. "Suppose Judge Robson decides to make an example of me. I want to be ready." She'd long been a believer in preparing for the worst—and hoping for the best.

Ben tried to argue with her, but she refused to change her mind. In the end, he placed her suitcase in the trunk of his car.

When they arrived at the courthouse, Helen, Laura and Bess were already gathered in the foyer outside Judge Robson's courtroom. The three women rushed frantically to Charlotte's side.

"I'm telling you right now, no one's going to do a body search on me and live to tell about it," Bess declared. She raised her hands in the familiar karate posture. Their entire

Senior Center had taken self-defense lessons a few years back and Bess had faithfully attended every class.

"Have you been watching those *Karate Kid* videos again?" Charlotte muttered.

Bess glared at her. "I'm not joking, Charlotte."

"Do you think the judge will let us bring our knitting needles into jail?" Laura asked. "If you want the truth, I have several Christmas projects I'd like to start and frankly I could make good use of the downtime."

Just as Charlotte began to reply, Sharon Castor strolled up to Ben. "This is everyone?" she asked.

Ben nodded.

"Ben's hired us legal representation," Charlotte whispered to her friends. "He seems to think all the judge will do is fine us."

"That's all?" Laura sounded disappointed. "I was looking forward to prison."

In contrast, Bess folded her hands together and raised her eyes toward heaven. "God bless Ben."

Charlotte had to admit she was grateful not to have this entire matter fall upon her shoulders. She was the one who'd led her friends into trouble, and she felt responsible for whatever befell them as a result.

"We're up next," Sharon Castor announced. "Let's go into the courtroom together."

Charlotte adjusted her hat. Ben took her hand and the small party walked into the courtroom. Sharon was in the lead, with Bess, Helen and Laura marching right behind her, and Charlotte and Ben bringing up the rear.

To Charlotte's astonishment, the courtroom was packed— standing room only. The first people to catch her attention were Bob and Peggy Beldon from the Thyme and Tide bed-and-breakfast.

"We're with you, Charlotte," Peggy called out.

Justine and her husband, Seth, were there, too. Seth held on to Leif, who was almost two years old. The toddler squirmed in his father's arms, but stilled when he saw Charlotte. Justine waved, and Charlotte's eyes blurred with tears, which she furiously blinked back. It seemed half the town had shown up to offer them support.

Enjoying their celebrity status, Bess and Helen waved as if they were prom queens walking in a Fourth of July parade.

"Did you know about this?" Charlotte asked, glancing up at Ben who stood a full head taller than her five foot three.

"Not at all," he confessed, looking around. "Even Troy Davis is here."

The sheriff who'd arrested them had turned up in court to support their efforts now. Charlotte had always been fond of Troy and was willing to forgive his error in judgment. Then again, the dear boy had no choice but to arrest them when they'd declined to break up their demonstration and disperse. He'd sworn to uphold the law, whether he agreed with it or not. His presence this afternoon made his personal feelings very clear.

"Roy and Corrie McAfee are here, too," Ben whispered.

The McAfees were recent additions to the Cedar Cove community. Roy was a former Seattle police detective who'd retired in Cedar Cove and opened his own agency as a private investigator.

Grace Sherman stepped up to Charlotte and gave her a hug. "Olivia asked me to stop by this afternoon," Grace said close to Charlotte's ear. "I didn't think you'd mind if I invited a few library patrons to give you their support."

Charlotte squeezed Grace's hand. Grace and Olivia had been best friends nearly their entire lives. How like Olivia to ask Grace to fill in for her this afternoon, since she couldn't be in court herself. For a very good reason, mind you, one Charlotte fully approved of. Olivia and Jack were in Hawaii on their honeymoon.

The door at the back of the courtroom opened and in walked Maryellen Sherman, who found a seat next to her mother. Jon Bowman was with her, Katie balanced on his hip. Charlotte had taken a liking to the photographer and was pleased to hear those two would soon be married. High time, in her opinion, not that anyone had asked.

"The court will come to order," the bailiff announced. "Judge Robson presiding."

The judge emerged from his chambers and took his seat at the front of the courtroom.

Despite Ben's reassurances, Charlotte's pulse fluctuated wildly before taking up a steady beat again. This might not be pretty. Until she was asked to stand with her friends while the charges were being read, Charlotte didn't realize how frightened she was. Between Bess practicing her karate moves and Laura looking forward to knitting in jail, Charlotte wasn't sure what to expect.

Sharon Castor handled the situation in a most professional manner, Charlotte thought, her estimation of the attorney rising considerably.

"Your Honor," she said, moving halfway to the bench. "Look at this group of law-breakers and tell me what you see."

"Ms. Castor," Judge Robson said. He continued to scan the charges. "Unlawful assembly, refusing to disband—"

"Yes, Your Honor, but my clients were making a statement—a statement they felt could only be made in this manner. They feel Cedar Cove needs a health clinic and I, for one, agree with them."

"Then they should have approached the council."

"Which I did, Your Honor." Charlotte spoke before she

could stop herself. "I beg your pardon, Judge Robson," she said, feeling she couldn't let her nerve fail her now. "Both Mr. Rhodes and I attended several council meetings, but to no avail. Mayor Benson said there are no funds to establish a health clinic, but–"

"This isn't the time to discuss the merits of a medical clinic in Cedar Cove."

"Yes, Your Honor," Charlotte murmured, properly chastised. Ben gave her an encouraging smile.

The prosecutor in the case seemed disinclined to send them to jail, Charlotte noted gratefully. He made a few comments and sat back down. Sharon Castor was on her feet again.

"You can save your breath, Ms. Castor. I've made my decision."

The attorney slowly sat down.

"It appears to me that the five of you were trying to make public your case for a health clinic."

Charlotte nodded and noticed the others did, too.

"Your plan has apparently worked. Half the town is here to support you. If anyone from council is in attendance, I sincerely hope they are taking detailed notes. I don't see that anything useful will be served by fining five senior citizens who were on a mission to make Cedar Cove a better place. If I could have your word of honor that you will not assemble again without the necessary permit, then I'd be willing to dismiss all charges."

Charlotte and the others were quick to comply.

As soon as the charges were dismissed, the courtroom erupted into applause. As they walked out, Charlotte and her friends were given a heroes' reception. They were free, one and all.

Before they left the courthouse, Charlotte and Ben personally thanked Sharon and every person who'd come to their support. She was astonished their case had generated so much interest in the community. All this time Charlotte hadn't spoken about her court date because she didn't want to bother her family or friends with her problems. It was a strong affirmation of the community's affection and respect that so many people were there today.

Ben drove her back to the house. "I had no idea all those people knew about this," she told him as he held the car door for her.

"I didn't, either," Ben said.

"I suspect it was Grace who rallied everyone on our behalf."

"The next time I'm in the library, I'm going to thank her all over again."

"I will, too." Charlotte had every intention of letting Olivia know what a wonderful job Grace had done.

"You are much loved in this community, Charlotte Jefferson," Ben said as they mounted her front-porch steps. He carried her small suitcase, which he'd remembered to remove from the trunk.

"I am honored so many of my friends took time out of their busy days and came to court," she murmured, still a little overwhelmed.

"There's someone else you should include on the list of people who love you," Ben said. He sat down on the porch swing while she rummaged in her large purse, searching for the house keys.

"And who would that be?" she asked, thinking she might have stuck the key chain in her overnight bag.

"That would be me."

Charlotte froze. Ben had just declared his love—or so it seemed—and at the most ridiculous of times. She turned to face him. "Are you saying you're in love with me, Ben Rhodes?"

"I am." He looked at her directly, meeting her eyes. "The fact is, Charlotte, I'm wondering if you share my feelings."

He didn't know? He hadn't guessed? This was indeed news. With her keys clenched in her hands, she triumphantly lifted them from her purse. "As a matter of fact, I'm head over heels in love with you and have been for quite a while," she said bluntly. Having admitted her feelings, she blushed and quickly added, "Would you care for a glass of lemonade to celebrate our victory?" She opened the front door.

"Don't mind if I do." Ben followed her into the house. "I just might steal a kiss while I'm at it."

"And I just might let you," Charlotte said with a smile.

Five

The alarm went off and Grace Sherman glanced at the clock radio on the bedside table. 7:00 a.m. Her one day of the work week to sleep in, and she'd forgotten to turn off the alarm the night before. With the new spring schedule, the library didn't open until eleven on Wednesdays. But staying in bed now that she was awake seemed pointless. Sighing, she tossed aside the covers, then sat up and slipped her feet into slippers. She quickly made the bed.

Dan, her husband of more than thirty years, had been dead for some time, and she had the entire bed to herself, but she continued to sleep on one half, never disarranging the other. Old habits were persistent. Habits like waking early. Her daily routine gave her structure and comfort in a life that was increasingly out of control.

As little as three years ago, everything had seemed so normal. Her marriage wasn't particularly happy, but it wasn't unhappy, either. Her life was comfortable. Predictable. Then Dan had disappeared. For an entire year she'd lived in a state of suspension, not knowing what had happened to him, where he'd gone or who he was with. When she least expected it, just when she'd adjusted to the fact that he must be with someone else, Dan's body was discovered. He'd died from a self-inflicted gunshot wound.

Grace felt she could deal with Dan's death. At the time, he'd already been gone a year and she'd learned to live on her own and even found a certain solace in it. During those first dark, lonely months following his disappearance, she'd become acquainted with Cliff Harding, a horse rancher who lived in Olalla. Cliff had wanted a relationship, but he'd been patient, willing to wait until it felt right to her. Prior to her relationship with Cliff, the last time Grace had been out on a date was in high school. The one and only man in her life had been her husband. After she'd buried Dan, she'd finally agreed to see Cliff—but then she'd foundered and made a drastic mistake. Grace had gotten involved with another man via the Internet.

Chatting with Will Jefferson, her best friend's older brother, had started out innocently enough. From as early as she could remember, Grace had had a crush on Will. That had never gone anywhere, and after high school Will had left for the East Coast, where he attended college and then stayed. He'd written her a letter after Dan's death, and the correspondence had continued by e-mail. He'd flattered her ego, become her friend, and before she realized what was happening, she'd fallen in love with him, despite the fact that he was married.

She was embarrassed to admit how foolish she'd been. Grace knew from the beginning that Will had a wife. At first she'd pretended they were merely friends and that his marital status didn't matter. But it did. When Will assured her he was divorcing his wife, she'd wanted to believe him, wanted to be part of his life badly enough to swallow his lies. Thankfully she'd learned the truth in time to save her dignity, but at a painful price.

As a result of her liaison with Will, she'd lost Cliff Harding's love, friendship and respect. He no longer wanted anything to do with her and after months of neglect, months of misleading him—no, lying to him—she couldn't blame Cliff at all. He'd said it would be better if they went their separate ways. Twice she'd gone to him. Twice she'd asked for another chance to prove herself. Twice he'd said no.

Grace had wanted to make amends and to recover what she'd lost with Cliff. She now recognized her "love" for Will as the infatuation it was, fueled by the clandestine nature of the relationship. And she recognized the genuineness of her feelings for Cliff.

She was sure Cliff still loved her, too. She saw it, *felt* it, but he sadly shook his head. Cliff's wife had cheated on him for years and he refused to become trapped in another relationship where trust was compromised.

As far as Cliff was concerned, it was over between them.

With both Will and Cliff out of her life, Grace was lonely. Terribly lonely. Other than her work, some valued friends and her two daughters and grandchildren, she had few outside interests.

Dressed in her robe and slippers, she moved slowly into the kitchen, Buttercup, her golden retriever, at her heels. The dog ventured outside through the doggy door, and Grace picked up the local newspaper from the front porch and placed it on the kitchen table. While Buttercup did her business, Grace prepared a pot of coffee.

Her sense of loneliness was accentuated even more now that Olivia had remarried. Grace was happy for her dearest friend and yet she was afraid that Olivia wouldn't have as much time for her anymore. She was ashamed of her Internet lapse with Olivia's brother, and felt somewhat distanced from Olivia as a result.

"Well, Buttercup," Grace murmured as the dog came back inside. "Shall we see what's on the agenda for today?" She poured herself a cup of coffee while Buttercup lapped water from her bowl. A fund-raising committee meeting for the animal shelter was scheduled for that evening. One positive thing Grace had done for herself after the breakups with both Will and Cliff was to become a volunteer at the Cedar Cove Animal Shelter.

Two Saturdays a month she interviewed potential pet owners, walked and fed the animals and did whatever else she could to be useful. Janet Webb, who was in charge of fund-raising, had asked Grace to be on her committee and she'd gladly accepted.

Buttercup finished her drink and sat down at Grace's feet while Grace sipped her coffee. As she mulled over her day, she scanned the headlines, then got dressed—khaki cotton trousers, a white tailored shirt, her favorite black blazer—and drove to the library.

Grace's afternoon passed quickly. Following work, rather than race home before her meeting, Grace strolled along the waterfront. The marina was lovely, especially this time of year. In a couple of months, the Thursday-night Concerts on the Cove would start again. Cliff had often joined her for the concerts. They'd buy dinner and sit on the grass.... Grace shook her head in an effort to dispel her memories of Cliff. He'd insisted it was over and she had no choice but to accept his decision.

Before she left for the meeting, Grace went to the Potbelly Deli where she bought a sandwich, eating it at a small table by herself. Then she drove out to the shelter.

Janet Webb and the other committee members had already arrived. "I'm so glad you're on our committee," Janet said and introduced Grace to Mary Sanchez and Margaret White, both long-standing volunteers. Janet and Margaret were about the same age as Grace, but Mary was in her mid-thirties.

"We're looking for something that'll bring the entire community together," Janet explained as Grace took a seat at the table in the conference room. "For the last few years we've done the usual bake sales and car washes."

"We had a dog wash that one year," Margaret reminded her.

"Yes, and while those fund-raising events have been successful, they've been fairly small-scale. I'd like something with a little more...punch."

"What about a bachelor auction?" Mary suggested excitedly. It was clear she'd been thinking about the idea for quite some time and was nearly out of her chair with enthusiasm. "I've read about them and I think it's a wonderful idea, don't you?"

Janet hesitated. "Maybe, but I'm married and so are a lot of other women in town."

"Yes, but I'm not and, well, I know I'd certainly be willing to pay for the pleasure of having a handsome man at my disposal for an entire evening." She glanced eagerly toward Grace. "I'll bet other single women would, too."

Grace wasn't so sure, but she hated to squelch Mary's enthusiasm. "Has anyone else noticed that there seem to be more animals that need adoption lately?" she asked. "Especially dogs..." The ideas started to churn in her mind. "What about a dog auction—or perhaps the shelter could do that along with the bachelors?"

"A dog and bachelor auction?"

"Why not?" Grace asked. "We could pair up the dogs with the bachelors."

Janet seemed to be considering the idea. "That sounds promising."

"The dog would be auctioned off first, and then the bachelor. Or the other way around."

"The bachelors would need to be a variety of ages, right?" Mary asked.

"Of course," Janet said, smiling ever so slightly.

Grace could tell that she was warming to the idea.

"Be sure and ask Cliff Harding to participate," Margaret White said, leaning closer to the table. "I think he's the most adorable man I've seen in ages, and he's single, too."

"Who?" Janet asked, frowning.

"Cliff Harding," Margaret repeated. "You obviously haven't noticed him around town, but trust me, I have. He's a hunk."

Mary looked across the table at Grace. "You were going out with him for a while, weren't you?"

It was all Grace could do to nod. Cliff was a natural choice for the bachelor auction. Her enthusiasm for the project did a nosedive, but she didn't dare show her feelings.

"Can you think of anyone else who'd agree to be auctioned off for charity?" Janet asked.

"Bruce Peyton," Grace suggested with a shrug. "He's a widower who brings his daughter into the library once a week."

"Ah, yes," Mary said. "I remember when his wife was killed in an automobile accident. When was that, anyway?"

"It must've been two or three years ago," Margaret replied. "I knew her mother, Sandy. Tragic, tragic accident. I think Stephanie's death was what killed her. Sandy was gone within a year—cancer."

Grace felt terrible for the little girl who'd lost both her mother and grandmother within such a short period. She didn't know Bruce well, but he seemed loving and protective of his daughter. She didn't envy him the task of raising the little girl on his own.

"Ben Rhodes has stirred a few hearts down at the Senior

Center," Grace said, wondering how Charlotte would feel about this.

Mary nodded in approval. "Ben's an excellent choice and, seeing that he's retired Navy, he just might be able to get us a few young seamen who'd be willing to do a good deed for charity."

"That's a great idea." Janet seemed absolutely delighted now. She quickly wrote down the names on the pad. "Barry Stokes is always good about donating his time and talent to charity auctions."

Barry was the local auctioneer whose big red barn and auction headquarters could be seen from the highway.

"This is going to be just great," Mary burbled.

"It's certainly better than another bake sale."

"Why don't we talk to Seth and Justine Gunderson about letting us use The Lighthouse for the event?" Grace said.

"Perfect," Mary agreed. "We want to make this classy. The restaurant's just the right size, too."

Janet picked up a pen and pad and started writing down suggestions and assignments. "Okay, I'll see what I can do to get The Lighthouse. I'll get in touch with Barry, too." Janet made a second notation for herself. "Mary and Margaret, why don't you two make up a list of potential bachelors?"

The women nodded simultaneously.

Janet pointed her pen in Grace's direction. "How about if you work on publicizing the event—posters, newspaper ads, radio and the like?"

Grace nodded. "Of course."

"I'll ask for volunteers to work the auction at the next board meeting." Janet looked pleased with herself. "I think we're onto something really wonderful this year."

The four women continued to discuss the event and it was after eight before they ended the meeting. Margaret

White walked out to the parking lot with Grace. "I don't know about anyone else but I'd write a blank check to spend an evening with Cliff Harding."

Grace forced a smile.

"I nearly pass out every time he comes to the vet's office." She giggled like a schoolgirl. "See you next week," she said. She climbed into her car and drove off.

Grace slid into her own vehicle and braced her hands against the steering wheel. The thought of Cliff with another woman made her feel a regret so strong that for a moment she was nearly sick to her stomach. She couldn't bear it and at the same time realized she had to.

Worst of all, she was to blame for her own unhappiness.

Six

Peggy put the finishing touches on the dinner table as Bob straightened up the family room. He was pleased Peggy had chosen to serve their guests in the kitchen rather than the formal dining room. Jack and Olivia, who were back from their honeymoon, were coming for dinner, and he considered Jack as much family as friend. Olivia now, too. In some ways, however, Jack was even closer than family.

Although Bob had twenty-one years of sobriety behind him, he knew he was a single drink away from insanity. He still took it one day at a time and routinely attended AA meetings. It was through Alcoholics Anonymous that he'd met Jack Griffin. Bob and Peggy had been living in the Spokane area when Jack approached Bob and asked him to be his AA sponsor. That was the beginning of their strong friendship.

After Bob and Peggy returned to Cedar Cove and purchased this house, they'd invited Jack to visit. He'd fallen in love with the small-town community. When the editor's job opened up at *The Cedar Cove Chronicle,* Jack—a longtime newsman—had applied and been offered the position. Soon after he moved to town, he met Judge Olivia Lockhart. It'd taken some mighty fast talking on Jack's part, but he'd finally convinced her to marry him. Bob was proud to have stood up as Jack's best man.

"Honey, would you fill the water glasses?" Peggy asked as she scurried about the kitchen.

"Sure thing." His wife was a marvel, Bob thought as he dumped ice cubes into the pitcher. Peggy was a master gardener, homemaker and cook extraordinaire. The scent of her chicken cordon bleu wafted through the kitchen and made his mouth water. He knew she'd prepared his favorite broccoli salad and a special mashed-potato casserole as part of their meal. Peggy had made a habit of cooking all his favorite dishes since Sheriff Davis's last visit—as if she was determined to make his last days on earth happy ones. Not that she'd admit it, he realized, but Bob knew she was worried and he humored her.

Much of the success of Thyme and Tide was due to Peggy's skill at making people feel welcome and comfortable. Bob didn't discount his own talents. He was a reasonably adequate handyman, but it was Peggy who held everything together, including his life.

She was busy at the sink—doing what, he could only guess. He finished his assigned duty, set the pitcher aside and came up behind her, sliding his arms around her waist.

"Bob," she protested as he spread kisses down the side of her neck. "We have guests due any minute."

"Hmm."

"*They're* the ones on the honeymoon, not us."

"Does that mean you're not interested in a little hanky-panky?"

"Bob Beldon!"

"Is that a yes, you are, or a no, you're not?"

"It's a yes, but could you kindly wait until after our guests leave?" She feigned impatience, but Bob knew her far too well. Their marriage had gone through several stages, some good and some difficult, but through it all their love life had remained active. Peggy's talents extended into the bedroom and for that, Bob was most appreciative.

The doorbell chimed and Bob released his wife. Peggy made a show of tucking in her blouse. This was the first week they'd been without overnight guests, and the absence of people in the house had taken some getting used to. Bob enjoyed it for a change, but he knew that before long they'd both grow bored.

"Do you want me to get that?" Peggy asked.

"No, I will."

Peggy sighed, and Bob sensed that she was nervous. She didn't know Olivia well, and he could tell that Peggy sincerely hoped they'd all be friends. She hadn't worked quite this hard to impress someone in a very long while. Dinner in the kitchen would be more intimate, more casual, and definitely suited Jack's personality. Olivia's, too, he hoped….

Jack and Olivia Griffin stood at the front door, looking relaxed and very much in love. Jack had his arm around Olivia's waist as if he couldn't bear to be apart from her.

"Welcome back," Bob said, stepping aside to let them in. "You both look fabulous."

"We *are* fabulous," Jack said, smiling down at Olivia.

Bob had to admit they made an interesting couple. Jack was by far the more easygoing of the two. Olivia held an important position in the community, so perhaps it was only natural that she'd be more formal. Yet they were good together, good for each other in the same way he and Peggy were.

"Welcome," Peggy said as she walked into the living

room. "I hope you had a wonderful honeymoon." Jack came forward to kiss her cheek.

"We did," Olivia told her, smiling. "Unfortunately, we have to be back at work first thing in the morning."

"I've got to get out the Friday edition of the paper," Jack said, "and Olivia's due in court."

"I was lucky to get as much time off as I did," she added.

Peggy hung Olivia's jacket in the hall closet. Jack shrugged off his raincoat and threw it over the back of a chair.

"Are we early?" he asked, glancing at his watch.

"Not at all, your timing's perfect." Peggy scooped up his coat and quickly brought it to the closet. "I've got just a few things to do and then dinner will be on the table."

"How can I help?" Olivia asked as she followed Peggy into the kitchen.

"Most everything's finished, but you can keep me company."

Bob was grateful for a few minutes alone with his friend. Rather than lead Jack into the family room, he stayed in the formal living room. The last time he'd sat here had been with Roy McAfee and Sheriff Davis. That was the day he'd met Hannah Russell, the daughter of the man who'd died in his home. The daughter of a long-forgotten friend. Bob didn't want to think about any of it, but he couldn't ignore the dead man, either.

"You're looking well," Bob said. He sat in the wingback chair by the fireplace.

Jack claimed its twin, which was angled on the other side of the fireplace. "I don't know why Olivia waited so long to marry me. The woman's crazy about me, you know." He chuckled at his own remark.

"I suppose you think Peggy and I invited you to dinner because of your charming personality."

"Any other reason I should hear about?"

Bob went very still. He hadn't meant to introduce the subject quite so soon, but Jack had given him the perfect opportunity. "Listen, Jack, you're the best friend I've got. You know that, right?"

The smile faded from Jack's eyes at the seriousness in Bob's tone. "Yeah, I guess."

"I need a favor."

Jack nodded. "Anything."

"Thanks, Jack." Bob spoke quietly and hoped his gratitude was evident.

"Does this have anything to do with Maxwell Russell?"

"Yes."

"Anything new?"

"Not really, but Troy Davis stopped by for a visit last week, and he thinks I might be in...some kind of danger."

Jack uncrossed his legs and leaned forward. "*What* kind of danger?"

"He wasn't entirely sure—no one is—but with two of the four-man squad dead, it's a puzzle. Someone murdered Max. That much has been uncovered. Dan's dead, too, and although he committed suicide, I wonder about the timing. There has to be *some* connection between these two deaths."

"What about the fourth man?"

"I can't say, but when Peggy was out of earshot Troy let me know that he's warned Samuels to be careful. There are too many unanswered questions."

Jack frowned. "What did he suggest you do?"

"He thought it might be a good idea if Peggy and I went on an extended vacation."

Jack's frown grew deeper. "Then what the hell are you doing here?"

Bob sat back in his chair and attempted to look as if he wasn't intimidated by his situation. He was, though, and he hoped his acting skills were up to par. He figured he'd played enough roles in the community theater to make a passable showing. "I refuse to run away and hide. If anyone out there wants me dead, then all I can say is let him come and get me."

"I don't suppose Davis mentioned you have a stupid attitude?" Jack's scowl darkened his face.

"He might've suggested something along those lines."

Jack didn't say anything for a moment. "What does Peggy think about all this?"

Bob didn't want to discuss that. "She has her opinion and I have mine. I did agree not to take guests until this is settled. It hurts financially, but we'll survive."

"One day at a time?"

"Let go and let God," Bob said, quoting a well-known AA saying.

"What can I do?" Jack asked.

"For now, nothing, but if something should happen to me…"

"Nothing's going to happen."

Bob wasn't prepared to argue, but for his own peace of mind, he needed reassurance. He held up his hand. "I don't know what the future holds, Jack. If what Davis thinks is true, I could turn up dead, the same as Max."

"But—"

"There are a lot of things in this world that can't be forgotten or forgiven." Bob lived with plenty of regrets but none greater than his unwitting participation in a massacre during the Vietnam War.

"What do you need me to do?" Jack asked.

"I want you to look after Peggy for me." He worried about his children, too. Both Hollie and Marc lived in the

Spokane area. Peggy kept in close touch with both of them, and he talked to his son and daughter once a week.

"You know I'll do whatever I can," Jack promised.

If he were to die, Bob couldn't see either of his children moving to Cedar Cove. They loved their mother but they had lives of their own.

He reached inside his pocket and pulled out two envelopes. "I've written each of my kids a letter. If the worst happens, I want you to give them these."

Jack accepted the envelopes and nodded. "Consider it done."

Bob glanced up just in time to see Peggy and Olivia walk into the living room. "Why are you two sitting here looking so glum? Dinner's ready."

"Dinner." Bob bolted to his feet. "Why didn't you say so?"

"I'm ready anytime," Jack said.

Bob felt better than he had in days. No matter what happened, he could rest easy now.

Seven

Maryellen felt overwhelmed by everything she needed to do before the wedding. The last two weeks had passed in a whirlwind of activity and joyous craziness.

"Just look at these nails," Rachel, her nail tech, said as she picked up a cotton ball to remove the old polish. "What have you been up to?"

"Moving," Maryellen muttered, knowing that would explain everything. Her rental house was completely empty now and her belongings were all at Jon's place, but almost everything remained in boxes. With the wedding preparations demanding all her extra time, she had yet to unpack.

"So when's the big day?"

"Monday," Maryellen said.

"Memorial Day?"

She nodded.

"That's one way to help your husband keep track of your anniversary," Rachel said with a laugh. Apparently she'd forgotten that the actual date changed from year to year. "In my case, however, the first thing I've got to do is *find* a husband." The exasperation in her sigh said it all. For as long as Maryellen could remember, Rachel had wanted to get married. All the women at Get Nailed were single and, during each appointment, Maryellen could count on the main topic of conversation revolving around the lack of decent husband material in Cedar Cove.

"Did you hear the big news?" Rachel asked, rubbing furiously at the old polish.

Maryellen shook her head.

"The animal shelter's holding a dog and bachelor auction."

"With some men, it's one and the same," Terri shouted from the other side of the room. "The men I've dated have been real dogs." She laughed at her own joke, then returned her attention to her client.

Even before Maryellen's engagement, such an event would never have interested her, but she knew the girls at Get Nailed would leap at the opportunity to meet eligible men.

"I'm surprised you haven't heard about the auction. Everyone in town's talking about it."

"Just as long as everyone knows Jon is out of circulation," Maryellen teased.

"Honey, from the moment Jon Bowman looked at you, he was a goner."

Maryellen grinned. At one point—during her avoidance phase—she'd attempted to match Jon up with one of the nail techs. Her plan had backfired and as a result, Maryellen had come to realize how strong the attraction between them was. Then, a few months ago, she'd managed to convince herself that Jon was involved with someone else. The thought of him with another woman had nearly destroyed her. Only later did she learn that he was completely committed to her and Katie.

"Are you excited about the wedding?"

Right now, Maryellen was too tired to be excited. With their jobs, they'd both been working twenty-hour days in an effort to have the house and yard ready for the ceremony. Jon had spent countless hours doing yardwork and planning the reception. Thankfully the guest list was small, under thirty.

Friday was his last day at The Lighthouse restaurant, where he worked nights as a chef. He was ready to make the transition and dedicate all his time to photography. Maryellen would continue working at the art gallery until the end of the year—or until she became pregnant again. After that, she'd serve as Jon's agent, marketing his pictures and negotiating with galleries around the country.

The thought of a second baby made her feel weak with longing. They'd managed to avoid physical lovemaking, but it had been a strain on both of them. Still, she felt that waiting until they were married was the right decision—for emotional reasons rather than rational ones—although she'd never guessed it would be this difficult.

As soon as Rachel was finished with her nails, Maryellen drove to her mother's house to pick up Katie.

"Leave her with me," Grace insisted. "You've got enough on your mind."

"You're sure?"

"I love having her."

Maryellen and Katie were staying with Grace for the next two nights. "Then I think I should drive out to Jon's and see what I can do to help him get things ready."

"You go ahead."

Maryellen left, grateful her mother had been so under- standing. Just as she suspected, Jon was working in the yard, spreading beauty bark around the base of the rhododen- drons and azaleas. Both were in full bloom and shockingly vibrant in color. Jon had counted over a hundred blooming rhododendrons on his property. Of them all, Maryellen's favorites were the bright red ones.

When she pulled in the long gravel driveway, Jon walked over to the car and opened her door. "I came to help," she said and although she was tempted, she resisted wrapping her arms around his waist and kissing him.

"I thought you were getting your nails done?"

"I already did." She held out her hands for his inspection. The pale rose polish sparkled in the sunlight. "What can I do?"

"Nothing out here. I wouldn't want you to risk damaging one of those fingernails." He leaned on the shovel. "Why don't you unpack? I've got boxes shoved in every conceivable corner."

"Out of sight, out of mind?"

"Not exactly," he said with a chuckle.

Maryellen took his advice and decided to start in the master bedroom. The kitchen could wait; besides, that area was Jon's domain. He was the cook in the family, although she was willing to do her share of meal preparation. Marriage to her was a partnership, and Maryellen had every intention of being a good wife. If that meant chopping pounds of onions, well…she'd do it. In fact, she'd do *anything* to make her marriage as strong and healthy as possible.

She climbed the stairs to the bedroom, then paused in the doorway, hands on her hips, as she surveyed the room where she'd soon be sleeping. The photograph Jon had taken of her months earlier hung on the wall by the bed. It showed her in a rocking chair nursing Katie when their daughter was a newborn. He'd managed to capture the wonder and awe and love she felt, holding this tiny being in her arms. She'd hardly been conscious of Jon's presence at the time, so absorbed was she by Katie.

It gave her immeasurable joy to place her clothes in the closet next to Jon's. She carefully pushed his shirts aside and her hand lingered there. In two days' time, she would be Jon Bowman's wife. She felt a renewed sense of anticipation— and a surge of love for the man who'd fathered her child.

She opened the dresser drawers and started rearranging his things and making room for her own. That was when she found the letters. Tucked in with old receipts, maps and loose change were a number of envelopes. Most had been opened but a few remained sealed. Curiosity got the better of her and she pulled out a sheet, but then she paused. She refused to begin her marriage with an act of deception— snooping through letters that were addressed to Jon, not to her. Unsure what to do, she stacked them in a neat pile and set them to one side.

She heard the front door open and Jon calling up the stairs. "I'm ready for a break. How about you?"

She walked out of the bedroom to stand at the railing and looked down. "Be with you in a minute. I'm just finishing up here."

"Okay."

"I found a bunch of letters in a drawer. Is there any place you want me to put them?"

He frowned, hesitated and then shrugged. "Toss 'em."

"In the garbage?"

Nodding, he turned and walked into the kitchen.

"Who are they from?"

"No one important," he shouted back.

"An old girlfriend?" she pressed.

He snickered loudly enough for her to hear him all the way up the stairs. "Hardly. Just get rid of the whole bunch."

Maryellen dumped the letters into the plastic garbage bag, but then she couldn't resist. She plucked out the top one and looked at the return address. It was from the small coastal town of Seal Beach, Oregon. Years ago Maryellen had driven through it along Highway 1. She'd stopped for gas and lunch, and for some reason she'd never forgotten the town.

"Who do you know in Seal Beach?" she called down, reluctant to drop the matter. She began to descend the stairs, still clutching the letters.

Jon stepped out of the kitchen. "You aren't going to let this rest, are you?"

She slid her hand down the smooth oak banister as she walked. "I can't help being curious. You'd feel the same if it was me."

Jon shook his head, scowling. "I should've ditched those a long time ago. They're from my parents."

"Some of them haven't even been opened."

He stared up at her. "My father and stepmother are out of my life, Maryellen. They made their choice and I made mine. I want nothing more to do with either of them. Now, please just get rid of those letters, and don't mention them again."

"But—"

"Maryellen, please."

"If you insist." And this time she buried the letters in the bottom of the bag.

An hour later, her clothes hung next to Jon's in the big closet. The dresser drawers were full. At first glance it seemed as if she'd always lived with Jon, always been part of his home and his life. That gave her a feeling of contentment and somehow made their coming marriage even more real.

They ate dinner together, and sipped wine on the upstairs balcony that overlooked the water. Completely at ease, Maryellen laid her head against his shoulder. Jon's arm was around her, his long legs stretched out in front of him. The moment was so tranquil, she didn't immediately realize Jon had fallen asleep.

It was just as well. She needed to get back to her mother's house, spend some time with Katie. By now her daughter would be cranky, and Maryellen didn't want to take advantage of her mother's generosity.

Kissing Jon on the cheek, she slipped out of his arms and sneaked down the stairs, making as little noise as possible. She hated to leave, but in two days she'd be with Jon forever….

Just as she'd predicted, Katie was difficult and unreasonable that night, and her mother was exhausted. As soon as Maryellen reached for Katie, the baby settled against her shoulder, put her thumb in her mouth and promptly fell asleep. Maryellen rocked her for a few minutes, gently rubbing Katie's back.

"I can't believe one tiny baby could have so much energy." Grace sat down in her favorite chair, head thrown back, eyes closed. Opening them again, she said, "You look at peace."

"I am at peace, and so much in love."

Grace's eyes grew moist. "I hope you'll always be as happy as you are now."

Maryellen lowered her gaze.

Her mother understood her perfectly. "What is it?"

"Jon. I found a stack of letters, several of which he hadn't even bothered to open."

"Letters? From whom?"

"His parents. I badly wanted to read them but I didn't. Jon told me to throw them out." Her mother knew about Jon's situation and the way his parents had betrayed him.

"Did you?"

Maryellen nodded. "I didn't want to start our marriage off by being dishonest."

"It seems to me that if Jon has no feelings for his family, he wouldn't have saved those letters."

"I felt the same thing." Maryellen gnawed on her lower lip. "I didn't need to read them to know what they said. Jon's their only family now and they want his forgiveness. They want their son back."

"They have a granddaughter they don't know anything about."

"Yes…"

"And you, Maryellen. They'll be your in-laws."

It hurt her to think of Jon rejecting his parents' attempts at reconciliation—less for their sake than for his. Jon would never be free of the past until he could find a way to forgive his parents.

Her mother seemed deep in thought. "I couldn't bear the idea of anyone keeping me from my grandchildren," she said softly.

That was another point she should consider. Jon might not want anything to do with his family, but his parents had a right to know about Katie. And Katie had a right to know her grandparents.

That evening, Maryellen wrote Jon's family. The letter was brief. She'd memorized the post office box number and the zip code, and that was all she needed. She included a picture of Katie and a short message about how well Jon's career was going. Wanting to be sensitive to her husband's feelings, she stated that it would be best if they didn't contact her. She did promise, however, to send them occasional photographs of their granddaughter.

The next morning as Maryellen drove to the post office, she wondered if she was doing the right thing. On the one hand, she knew Jon would disapprove; on the other, she felt his parents deserved some compassion. And what about Katie? What about her future happiness?

The letter slid into the mailbox slot, and whether she was right or wrong remained undecided. Either way, it was too late.

Eight

The Dog and Bachelor Auction had already generated a lot of interest in Cedar Cove. Grace Sherman displayed a large notice in the library and Janet had asked her to deliver posters to the businesses around town. Thursday afternoon, the first week of June, Grace dedicated her lunch hour to making sure the community had all the relevant details.

The Lighthouse restaurant was her first stop. She waited at the hostess's desk for the young woman to return from seating a couple. Staring out the large windows she admired the view of the water and the Bremerton shipyard on the other side of the cove. Several people were in line ahead of her, but Grace wasn't really in a rush. She needed to speak to either Seth or Justine to confirm that she could place the large poster in the front window and to finalize some details concerning the special menu being created for the event. For now, she was simply enjoying the vista of sea and vibrant blue sky, with the snow-capped Olympic Mountains in the background. Seth and Justine had done an impressive job of reflecting their surroundings in the architecture and decor of the restaurant.

The door opened behind her, but Grace was so absorbed in the view that she didn't pay attention.

"Hello, Grace."

Her heart leapt into her throat as she turned to greet Cliff Harding. "Hello, Cliff." He was as attractive as ever, with his broad shoulders and dark eyes. He wore jeans and a tan jacket with one button fastened. His cowboy hat rested slightly forward, shading his face.

They stared at each other as if neither knew what else to say. Grace wanted to talk, but her tongue felt as if it had grown twice its normal size and refused to cooperate. It'd been weeks since she'd last seen Cliff. In that time she'd grown accustomed to being alone. Accustomed to filling her days and nights with charity projects and anything that kept her mind off what she'd done to destroy their relationship.

"You're looking well," he said after an awkward moment.

"You, too."

He smiled regretfully. "So Maryellen and Jon were married last weekend."

Moisture found its way into Grace's mouth and she nodded. "Yes. The ceremony was lovely. They held the wedding on Jon's property. My daughter was a beautiful bride." These slightly stilted, staccato sentences were the best she could do.

"I wish them both my very best."

Grace knew he did. "Katie didn't make a sound the entire time."

Cliff slid his gaze past her. "Please thank Maryellen for the invitation."

Grace didn't realize her daughter had sent him one.

He removed his hat and held it with both hands. "I didn't attend for...obvious reasons."

Grace looked away.

"I didn't want to do anything to make you feel ill-at-ease," he explained. "This was a happy day for you, as well as for Maryellen and Jon. I thought it might be uncomfortable for us both if I showed up."

He was right, of course. "That was thoughtful of you," she murmured.

The silence stretched between them. Then, as if she'd suddenly remembered the reason she was at The Lighthouse, she said brightly, perhaps too brightly, "I understand you're going to be part of the Dog and Bachelor Auction."

Cliff shifted his weight. "I was approached but I declined."

"Why?" His name had been the first one mentioned. She wondered how long it would be before she could tolerate the thought of Cliff with another woman. Not anytime soon. The ache in the pit of her stomach told her that.

Was it her imagination or did his color heighten at her question? "I didn't see much point in making a bigger fool of myself than I normally do."

"But Cliff, it's for charity."

He shook his head, and privately Grace was pleased but she recognized that her response was purely selfish.

"I figured the committee would get higher bids on a younger man. I recommended Cal Washburn."

"Your trainer?" Grace had met Cliff's trainer on a couple of occasions and liked him, although he was an intense man who seemed to see straight through her. It was unsettling. As she recalled, he spoke with a slight stutter.

Cliff's mouth moved in the barest hint of a smile. "Cal wasn't exactly keen on the idea."

"But he's willing to volunteer?"

"He didn't say, but he's considering it."

"For someone who loves animals as much as you do…"

The smile that had just begun now appeared full force.

"Are you trying to make me feel guilty so I'll agree to this, Grace Sherman?"

Grace smiled, too. "Shamelessly."

He shook his head again. "I'm too old."

"Your name came up right away. Apparently you've stirred up more interest than you realized."

"I suppose you were the one who threw my name in the hat?"

Cliff Harding was the last man she'd recommend, and all because of her own self-interest. "It wasn't me." She didn't like admitting it. "Margaret White was the one who suggested you."

He shrugged as if he didn't know the name.

"She works at the vet's office."

He gestured in a way that implied he might recognize her but he wasn't sure. "I've probably seen her then."

Silence again.

Grace couldn't imagine what was taking the hostess so long. She glanced into the dining areas, but the woman seemed to have disappeared after seating the two parties ahead of her.

"Olivia and Jack are home," she said abruptly, trying to make conversation. The silence was unbearable. She couldn't stand next to this man without being reminded of the high price her Internet indiscretion had cost her.

"So I understand."

Grace hadn't seen Olivia so happy, not in years. At the same time, she seemed to be having a little trouble adjusting to married life. A couple of recent phone calls had left Grace feeling there was some stress between Olivia and Jack, although Olivia hadn't been complaining.

"From what I hear, her ex has been visiting Cedar Cove quite a bit."

Grace froze. When Stan found out that Olivia had decided to marry Jack, he'd come to Grace, maudlin and sorry for himself. In a moment of loneliness, she'd agreed to go to dinner with him. It'd been another instance of bad judgment on her part. The last thing she wanted now was for Cliff to learn about that.

"I think Stan knows he made a mistake," Grace said tentatively. If Cliff knew about her dinner with Stan, he wasn't letting on. "People do that—make mistakes they later regret." Her eyes met his, pleading with him to realize how sorry she was. Silently she implored his forgiveness.

Cliff avoided eye contact. "Stan learned that his regrets came too late, didn't he?"

Cliff was telling Grace hers had, too.

The terrible silence was back.

"Charlotte told me what you did for her and her friends," Cliff said next, as if he couldn't bear the silence either.

Grace was furious every time she thought about Troy Davis arresting Charlotte and her group of elderly protestors. For heaven's sake, Ben Rhodes was a retired admiral! Troy should be ashamed of himself.

"Charlotte was trying to better our community. I felt the least we could do was support her efforts."

Cliff tried to hide his amusement by staring down at the carpet.

"What's so funny?"

"You," he said, raising his eyes. That little smile quivered on his mouth. "Remind me never to get on your bad side."

She *was* on his bad side, though, and the reminder instantly sobered her.

"Charlotte was thrilled with the community support and she credits you with that."

"I didn't do much."

"You spread the word."

Grace gave a careless shrug. "It wasn't much," she said again. She hadn't phoned Cliff, couldn't bring herself to do it, but in retrospect she wished she had.

As if reading her thoughts, he said. "I would've been there had I known."

The hostess reappeared just then. "Sorry to keep you waiting." She automatically reached for two menus.

Cliff looked to Grace and she saw the indecision in his eyes. It would mean the world to her if he asked her to join him for lunch. She held his gaze as long as she dared.

He stiffened, and his resolve had obviously returned. "Table for one," he said and walked away from Grace.

Nine

Roy McAfee hadn't been a private investigator for more than a few years, but he'd been in law enforcement his entire career. He was retired from the Seattle police force; after a few months, however, he'd thought he'd go stir-crazy sitting around the house doing nothing. Soon after his move to Cedar Cove, he'd hung out his shingle.

Retirement wasn't for him. Some men took to it, got involved in hobbies and interests. That kind of life was too predictable for Roy. Nothing lured him faster than a good mystery, and he didn't mean one between the covers of a book, either.

Few mysteries had intrigued him more than what was happening right here in Cedar Cove.

He sat down at his desk and reached for Bob Beldon's file. If he reviewed the facts as they'd unfolded, perhaps he'd pick up on something he'd overlooked before. He didn't think it was likely, but it wouldn't hurt to refresh his memory.

It all started the night a stranger had arrived on the doorstep of the Beldons' Thyme and Tide bed-and-breakfast. By morning he was dead.

Bob Beldon had notified Troy Davis, and the coroner came for the body. Soon afterward, it was discovered that the man had undergone extensive plastic surgery and carried false identification. For a few weeks there'd been a lot of speculation as to who he could be. Then silence—and things had died down for a while.

From the first, something about their guest had disturbed Beldon. Bob had experienced a recurring nightmare ever since his return from Vietnam. On occasion, he'd been known to sleepwalk.

Roy stopped reading and leaned back in his chair, recalling his initial thoughts when Beldon had asked him for help. Davis had questioned Beldon for the second or third time and Bob had considered contacting an attorney, but hadn't. Instead he'd come to Roy. Not too far into the conversation, Roy had realized that the other man was afraid he might have been responsible for the stranger's death.

Roy was quick to assure him otherwise, although he'd wondered the same thing in the beginning. But Maxwell's door had been locked from the inside and there'd been no sign of a struggle. The fact of the matter was that until recently, they couldn't be sure *what* had caused the other man's death. The autopsy had shown that his vital organs were in fine shape.

Not long before Bob's appointment with Roy, Grace Sherman had come to him. A year earlier, her husband, Dan, had gone missing. When Dan didn't return, Grace had sought out Roy to help locate her husband. But every lead had been a dead end.

Unanswered questions didn't sit well with him, although he'd shocked Grace with the few things he'd unearthed. One of them was the matter of thirteen thousand dollars Dan had somehow managed to keep from her. Grace had no idea where Dan could've found that kind of cash, which he'd apparently used to buy a trailer. He'd handed over his paycheck every Friday, regular as clockwork. Like most couples, they'd apparently lived month to month.

Then Dan's body had been discovered and with it a suicide note he'd left for Grace. In his last letter to his wife, Dan had described an incident that had taken place during the Vietnam war. He and three others had been separated from their squadron, and they'd stumbled into a village, which they feared was Viet-Cong controlled. Something had happened, and they'd started firing and before the smoke cleared they'd wiped out the entire village, according to Dan. They'd massacred men, women and children. The event had forever marked him. He couldn't live with himself any longer. Or so the letter had indicated.

Grace had been beside herself, not knowing what to do with the information. Roy was afraid he hadn't been much help. He couldn't really advise her; whatever became of these facts was her decision and hers alone.

Shortly afterward, Beldon had repeated the story Dan had written about in his suicide note. He'd mentioned Dan—they'd been two of the four men wandering through that jungle. He'd told Roy that afterward he and Dan hadn't seen each other for almost thirty years. When Bob had come home to Cedar Cove, they'd completely avoided each other.

It seemed too much of a coincidence that Roy would hear this grisly tale from two different people within such a short period of time. On a hunch, he'd gone to Troy Davis and suggested the sheriff check out the other two men who'd been with Dan and Beldon that day.

Sure enough, one of the men—Maxwell Russell—had been reported missing. The unidentified body had turned out to be his. Why he'd come to Cedar Cove and why he'd carried false identification couldn't be explained, though, any more than his death.

Not until later was it discovered that Max Russell had actually been murdered. Poisoned. There'd been evidence in the water bottle found in Russell's rented vehicle.

Once Russell had been identified, his daughter had visited Cedar Cove to collect her father's ashes. Davis had set up a meeting between Hannah and the Beldons, and as a favor to Bob, Roy had been at the house when she came by with the sheriff. Roy learned then that Hannah's mother had died in a car accident, the same one that had badly burned her father. The burns were the reason for Max's plastic surgery and quite possibly why Bob hadn't recognized his old friend.

The circumstances surrounding the car crash led Roy to believe it hadn't been an accident. He'd probably never be able to prove that. The accident report blamed Russell, but Hannah's father had insisted the steering had disconnected. There was nothing to verify his account.

The door to Roy's office opened and his wife walked in with a tray of coffee and freshly baked cookies. Corrie seemed intent on fattening him up, not that he was making much of a fuss. He certainly wasn't turning down homemade cookies.

"Let me guess what you're reading." That know-it-all glint shone in her eyes. "Could it possibly have something to do with the Beldon case?"

"Smarty pants," he said, grinning up at his wife.

"You're going to solve this if it takes the rest of your life, aren't you?"

Roy was close to the answer; he could feel it. He didn't know what he'd missed, if anything, but eventually his instincts would lead him where he had to go. All he needed was patience but that, unfortunately, seemed to be in short supply.

Corrie poured coffee into the mug, added cream and gave it to him. "I get suspicious when you're this quiet."

Roy leaned back in his chair, the mug in his hand. "I'm sifting all the facts through my brain."

"Do you still think the Beldons might be in some kind of danger?"

Roy didn't know how to answer. He shrugged. "Two of the four men are dead. One was murdered and the other committed suicide."

"What about the fourth man?"

"Apparently Davis has talked to Colonel Stewart Samuels. He told me he didn't think Samuels is involved—but who knows?"

Corrie looked down at the file and picked up the top sheet. "It says here he's up for a Congressional Committee assignment. If news of what happened in Nam got out, it could be disastrous to his career, don't you think?"

"True." Roy was well aware of that, but Samuels's military record was impeccable. And he lived on the East Coast. His whereabouts were accounted for during the time around Maxwell Russell's death. To be on the safe side, Roy had checked into the weeks shortly after Dan Sherman's disappearance, but Samuels had been in Europe, on a NATO assignment.

Corrie poured a second mug of coffee, black, and sat in the chair across from Roy's desk. "Linnette phoned this morning." Their twenty-five-year-old daughter had recently graduated as a physician's assistant.

Roy brightened. He adored Linnette and felt close to her. She was bright, beautiful and a source of pride. Her brother was another story. Roy and Mack were frequently at odds.

Linnette had done well in school and Mack, to put it bluntly, hadn't.

"She's applying for a job in Montana, of all places."

With the majority of physicians choosing to work in big cities, many small towns were left without medical professionals. Although she'd grown up in Seattle, Linnette had always been drawn to rural areas, so Roy wasn't surprised by her decision. She'd be filling a critical need and living in the sort of place she liked.

"Did you hear me, Roy? Montana?"

He wasn't sure what had upset Corrie so much. When Linnette had entered the medical program, they'd both known she wouldn't settle down in Seattle.

"I don't want her moving two states away!"

"Corrie—"

He wasn't allowed to finish.

"Linnette doesn't know a soul in Montana. There's plenty of small towns in Washington State that need physician's assistants."

Roy made an effort to hold back his amusement. "It's time to cut the apron strings, Mother."

Evidently not a successful effort. Corrie cast him an exasperated look. "This is our *daughter* we're talking about."

"Yes, dear."

"Don't use that tone of voice with me, Roy McAfee."

"Yes, dear."

"You're not funny. You know that, don't you?"

Roy resisted answering, although it was a struggle. "Where would you be comfortable having Linnette find a job?"

Corrie bit her bottom lip and didn't answer him.

"I have the feeling you'd like her to move right here to Cedar Cove," he joked.

At that his wife's head snapped up and her eyes widened.

She set down her coffee, then leapt out of her chair, raced around the desk and kissed him soundly.

"What was that all about?" Roy asked, pleasantly surprised.

"It's because you, my wonderful husband, are much smarter than I give you credit for."

Bewildered, Roy watched her fly out of his office.

Ten

Grace thrust her hands decisively into her garden gloves, ready to head out to the back garden to plant Martha Washington geraniums. It wasn't the way she wanted to spend Friday evening, but she refused to mope around the house. Buttercup waited for her at the kitchen door, tail wagging.

"We'll plant these now and see what we can find at the Farmers' Market tomorrow morning. That sounds like a plan, doesn't it?" The fact that Grace had begun to carry on whole conversations with her golden retriever had to be a sign of how lonely she was.

The Farmers' Market had started the first Saturday of May, and although there were only a few homegrown vegetables available this early in the season, Grace enjoyed going there each week. She almost always ran into a few friends. One or both of her daughters was likely to show up, as well.

The phone rang, startling Grace. She pulled off her right-hand glove and reached for the wall-mounted receiver.

"Hello." She forced a cheerful note into her voice, hoping with all her heart that it was Cliff. He'd weighed heavily on her mind since their chance encounter at the restaurant earlier in the week. Her hope was that he'd been thinking about her, too.

"It's Stanley Lockhart, Grace. How are you?"

Grace felt an immediate stab of disappointment. "Hello, Stan." She kept her voice cool, not wanting to encourage Olivia's ex-husband. "I'm fine."

"Me, too. Listen, would you like to go to dinner tonight?"

She glanced over at the can of clam chowder that was slated to be her evening meal. Still, she preferred to eat soup alone over a three-course meal with Stan Lockhart.

"Sorry, I already have plans."

"You can't change them?" He didn't bother to hide his displeasure.

"No." How like Stan to expect her to alter her evening because *he* needed a dinner companion.

"What if I stop by later?" His enthusiasm was back. "It's important."

"That won't work, either." She couldn't imagine what he had to tell her that was so urgent. Grace sincerely hoped he got the message, but the subtle approach wasn't always successful with Stan. Inbred politeness prevented her from being rude and telling him outright that she wanted to avoid him.

The line went quiet as he contemplated her refusal. "I see," he said, sounding depressed. "Gracie, listen, I hate to be a pest but I'd like to talk to you if we can manage it."

Gracie. From the time she was in grade school, Grace had detested that nickname. She gritted her teeth. Stan hadn't been in touch since that one dinner. Now this. She couldn't even guess what he wanted.

"Why don't you tell me what you need to see me about?"

He hesitated. "It's better if I do it in person. Is there anyplace we can meet? Drinks? Coffee? You say when and where, and I'll be there." His tone took on a pleading quality. Grace knew that Stan's second marriage had recently failed; he still seemed to be shaken. She sympathized, but she didn't want to get involved with him.

"It won't take much of your time, I promise."

She hesitated, fearing that he'd hound her until she gave in. "I plan to be at the Farmers' Market in the morning."

"Perfect." He leaped on the suggestion. "I'll see you there. What time?"

"It opens at nine."

"Make it later. Nine's a little early for me."

So now he expected her to change her Saturday schedule to suit his? What sympathy she felt for him quickly evaporated. "I'll be there at nine, Stan. If I see you then, that'll be fine and if I don't, I don't."

"All right, all right. I'll get there as close to nine as I can. Just remember I'm coming over from Seattle."

She'd forgotten that, but decided it didn't matter; he was the one who considered it so important that they meet.

Saturday morning, Grace loaded Buttercup into her car and drove to the Farmers' Market. Buttercup was a well-behaved dog who loved being around people. The animal shelter had set up an adoption center in the market. Every Saturday the shelter brought down homeless cats and kittens; once a month, Grace took her turn running their booth, which was popular with children and adults alike.

Buttercup strained against her leash in a hurry to view the kittens, and Grace sharply commanded her to heel. She'd been thinking about adopting a cat herself, since she felt bad about leaving Buttercup alone all day and a cat would be company for her.

"Mom."

Grace turned to find Maryellen pushing Katie in her

stroller. "I wondered if I'd see you here." The back section of the stroller was already full.

Grace bent down and kissed Katie, who gurgled and waved her arms. Maryellen positively glowed with happiness, and Grace was delighted. Maryellen was more confident and relaxed, more carefree somehow, than she'd ever been. And—equally important—Katie would have the benefit of growing up with two parents.

"You're out and about early," she said conversationally.

"Jon's working and won't be home until late afternoon." That meant her son-in-law was somewhere in western Washington photographing trees or birds. Or something.

"I love married life," Maryellen burst out. "Oh, Mom, how could I have been so foolish? Jon is a *wonderful* husband and father."

"Honey, I'm thrilled for you."

"I'd better get back to the house. I bought three pounds of fresh clams and I need to get them into the refrigerator."

"I didn't think you liked clams."

"I don't, but Jon does."

It seemed to Grace that if Jon indulged Maryellen, as she often claimed, her daughter catered to Jon just as much.

Grace bought a pound of clams herself and a jar of marmalade from Carol, the lady who sold homemade jelly. She glanced around and didn't see Stan and figured that was for the best. After strolling down the other aisles, she made her way toward the parking lot.

"Grace," Stan called, waving vigorously. He stood on the marina walkway. "Over here."

With Buttercup trotting beside her, Grace walked to the marina area.

"Seth suggested I sleep in his boat," Stan explained. He looked like he was ready for a tennis date, wearing white shorts and a white cable-knit sweater with a red-and-blue border.

"How's it going?" he asked, striking a relaxed pose, studying her as if he wasn't quite sure where to start.

"Good." She didn't elaborate, preferring to skip the small talk. "What can I do for you?"

His smile was strained. "You know, since Marge and I split and Olivia married that newsman, I've been at loose ends."

Grace didn't like the sound of this. She wondered if he was leading up to asking her out again, and if that was the case, she simply wasn't interested. She had to tell him before he went any further.

"Stan, I realize you must be lonely—"

"Lonely," he repeated and shook his head, a puzzled expression on his face. "No, no, it isn't that. I heard about the Dog and Bachelor Auction."

It took Grace a moment to put two and two together—and then she upbraided herself for being so dense.

"I'd like to volunteer to be one of the bachelors," Stan said eagerly.

She should've known. Stan had always enjoyed being the center of attention. The idea of women bidding on him… That would be the ultimate. In all fairness, he'd do a good job as someone's date for an evening, provided whoever won him knew what to expect.

"It's for charity, right?"

"To raise funds for the animal shelter," she told him.

"Well, you know how I feel about animals." He nodded sagely and she nodded, too, although she'd never noticed any particular liking for animals. "I'm willing to do my part," he went on, "and since I'm available, well, why not?" He cast her a practiced smile. "I imagine I could bring in a few dollars for a worthy cause."

"You don't live in Cedar Cove, remember?"

"You're right, but I did at one time and people here know me. Really, volunteering is the least I can do to help out, and I understand you're the person to talk to."

"Actually, two other women are gathering bachelors' names, but I'd be happy to suggest yours.

Stan grinned. "Thanks." Gratitude radiated from him. "I knew I could count on you."

Buttercup wagged her tail and looked up, anticipating Stan's attention. However the animal lover didn't so much as glance in the dog's direction.

"Have you already been to the market?" Stan asked.

The bags in her hands should be evidence that she had.

"How about if I buy you a cup of coffee and you can fill me in on the details about the auction? Maybe you could help me come up with a strategy."

"A…strategy?"

"Yeah, you know. How to get the ladies to bid on me. Just how many women are expected?"

"I don't know. The tickets haven't gone on sale yet."

"I just had a thought." He straightened, seeming pleased with himself. "I imagine that if the women in town knew exactly who was up for auction, the animal shelter would sell more tickets, right?"

Grace wasn't sure about that. "I suppose."

"What if you printed the names of the bachelors directly on the tickets? That might generate even more interest, don't you think?"

Stan was certainly full of ideas. "I'll make that suggestion, too," she murmured.

"Good." His eyes brightened and Grace could see he was quite taken with this bachelor auction. During their one and only dinner date, Stan had practically been crying in his soup, wallowing in self-pity. He'd regrouped fast enough, she thought wryly.

"I'll do what I can to make sure your name's added to the list," she said, eager to leave for home.

"Thanks, Gracie. I appreciate the fact that you're such a good friend."

Grace didn't consider herself that much of a friend, but she let the comment—and the nickname—slide. She directed Buttercup toward the parking lot behind the library, where she'd left her car.

"Nice seeing you again, Grace."

"You, too, Stan."

"Oh, Grace." He jogged the few steps over to her. "When you mention the idea about printing the names…"

"Yes?"

"Be sure and tell them it came from me."

"Of course." She ordered Buttercup to sit and dropped the leash for a moment so she could shift the heavy bags from one hand to the other.

"And seeing that it was my idea—" he paused and laughed playfully "—I think it's only fair that my name be one of those on the list."

"I'll make sure that's understood."

"Great." He grabbed her by the shoulders and briefly hugged her.

As if the thought had suddenly struck him, he asked, "Is there anything I can do for you?"

"Not a thing," she assured him, surprised he'd asked.

"You're sure." His hands lingered on her shoulders.

"Positive."

Just then, behind Stan, Grace caught sight of a male figure in a cowboy hat. *No, please no,* she prayed silently, *don't let that be Cliff.* Her one fear was that he'd heard about her dinner date with Stan and would think she was foolish enough to get involved in a relationship with Olivia's ex-husband.

Stan muttered something about needing to meet a friend. Before she could stop him, he gave her another quick hug and was gone.

Grace's gaze remained fixed on the man with the Stetson. When Stan freed her and left, he no longer obscured her line of vision. Sure enough, it was Cliff. He stood staring at her and even from this distance, she could see him frowning.

She wanted to tell him it wasn't the way it looked. She wasn't involved with Stan. Nor did she want to be.

After a suspended moment, Cliff acknowledged her by touching the brim of his hat. Almost immediately, he turned away.

She wanted to rush over to him and explain, but feared she'd do more harm than good. With a heavy heart, Grace headed home.

Eleven

The board meeting over, Bob Beldon left the community theater, situated just off Heron Street. He'd been active in theater since his high-school days; drama class had been his favorite and he'd starred in a number of school productions. If not for Vietnam and everything that happened afterward, he might have considered a career on the stage.

These days he got what he called his "theater fix" by participating in local productions. Currently he served on the board of directors and the group had discussed a number of potential plays for next year's season.

Bob was still thinking about the merits of *Our Town* vs. *The Matchmaker* as he drove down the winding road that led to Cranberry Point. The name of the road always amused him. As far as he knew, there weren't any cranberries growing in the area. There were cranberry bogs in Washington State, but none in or near Cedar Cove. Whistling "Hello, Dolly," he continued driving, free for the moment of the burdens that oppressed him. This was what he loved about the theater. He could immerse himself in a role—in the whole process of staging a play—and put aside his troubles. His friends in AA might call it denial, but the theater gave him a ready excuse.

Knowing Peggy, she'd have dinner started. Since it was Monday, he guessed she'd probably prepared either stuffed green peppers or her fabulous meat loaf. Either meal suited him just fine.

Still whistling as he pulled into the driveway, he found his wife watering her herb garden. Any time of year, her gardens were something to behold. The name of their B and B, Thyme and Tide, had come from both their proximity to the sea and Peggy's herbs. And of course the old saying about time and tide waiting for no man...

Speaking of time, without guests, they both had plenty of that on their hands. Money was tight, but Peggy was as skilled at budgeting as she was at every other household task. Bob couldn't imagine how they'd manage their money situation otherwise, but thankfully Peggy had it all figured out.

He drove into the garage and then walked out to greet Peggy. Garden hose in hand, she smiled as he approached. The sun was still high, although it was almost six o'clock. According to the calendar, summer would officially arrive later in the month, but as usual it would take another six weeks to show up in the Pacific Northwest. August and September were almost always spectacular. Bob had to remind himself of that in February and March, when the constant drizzle dragged down his normally good spirits.

"Hi, honey," Bob said. He stood at the edge of her garden. The fennel bulbs were flowering, and the parsley and cilantro were just peeking up from the dark, rich soil. "What's for dinner?"

"Meat loaf. How'd the meeting go?"

"Just great." He couldn't contain his smile.

"What's that grin about? Are you keeping something from me?" She jokingly aimed the hose in his direction.

"Not a thing." He chuckled, raising both hands in a gesture of surrender. "I was just thinking we'd probably have meat loaf tonight, is all."

Peggy walked over to the side of the house and turned off the water. "I'm about finished here."

Bob nodded.

"If you've got a moment, I'd like to talk."

He hesitated. When Peggy asked to speak to him in that formal way, it generally wasn't about anything pleasant.

"Is something wrong?"

"Not really."

She seemed rather closemouthed about it, which wasn't good. Now that he studied her, Bob realized he should have seen the signs earlier. Peggy was a talker, a natural conversationalist. She could—and did—talk to anyone about anything. Many of their guests were repeat customers Peggy now counted as friends.

Bob followed her into the mudroom off the kitchen. Peggy changed out of her rubber shoes and methodically put her gardening supplies on the shelf. The contrast between her highly organized work areas and his—well, sometimes it embarrassed him a little. He could be such a slob, he thought ruefully, and yet Peggy was so tolerant of his carelessness, for which he could only be grateful.

"What's going on?" he asked as they entered the kitchen.

Peggy automatically poured them each a cup of tea and set the mugs on the table. "I got a phone call from Hannah Russell this afternoon."

Bob felt the sudden need to sit down. He yanked out the chair and sat, reaching for his tea.

"I'm so worried," Peggy said, sitting across from him.

That got Bob's attention. "About what?" They'd been caught up in this nightmare for so long that he'd grown accustomed to the tension. It had become part of his reality and there was nothing to do but stand firm in the face of each new shock.

"Hannah," Peggy continued as if it should be obvious. "Her mother and father are both gone. She's like a lost soul. She's foundering, Bob." She paused for a moment. "I talked to Hollie today, and she said that in her opinion, Hannah needs a sense of security. I agree with her."

"I suppose that's only natural when someone loses both parents in such a short time." Bob envied the closeness between his wife and daughter. He knew that during his drinking years, he'd lost an important part of his children's lives.

Peggy's hands tightened around her mug. "Hannah phoned to thank me for my letter."

Bob had forgotten that Peggy had written the girl. It was just the sort of thoughtful thing she'd do.

"She wanted to tell me she's moving."

"Where?"

"That's just it," Peggy said, and her face darkened with concern. "She doesn't know. She's sold everything she can. Hollie says that Hannah's running away from her pain—that she'll carry it with her wherever she goes."

Bob nodded. "Hollie's right. I'm not sure leaving California's a good idea for Hannah. She might regret it later, selling things she'll wish she'd kept."

"That's what I told her, but she said it was too late. What she didn't sell she gave away."

Bob's own concern grew. His unease didn't revolve solely around Hannah, either. She might inadvertently have sold something that would help solve this mystery.

"That's not all," Peggy said. "I got the impression that

she's going to travel aimlessly around the country until she finds a place that…feels comfortable. That's how she put it."

Bob sat back in his chair and mulled this over. The young woman was vulnerable. Wandering from place to place wasn't what he'd want for his own daughter. "What about family? Surely she's got aunts and uncles and cousins?"

"Apparently she doesn't have anyone close."

"I see." Bob sipped his tea.

"I asked her to call us from time to time."

"Good."

"But I don't know if she will. She sounded so confused."

Bob considered what he knew about Hannah for a moment and felt a pang of sympathy. "Did you ask if there's a way for us to keep in touch with her?"

Peggy nodded. "She has a cell phone and she gave me the number. The thing is, Bob, how involved do we want to get in her life?" Her gaze held his and he understood his wife's question. She felt a certain responsibility to Hannah. After all, it was in their home that her father had died. And yet—did they want to take on the young woman's problems? That could be more than he and Peggy were really equipped to handle.

"I don't know," he admitted.

"Me, neither."

"So, what do you think we should do?" Bob asked. He trusted Peggy's intuition. Hannah aside, Max Russell's death was an uncomfortable subject. It brought up too many unpleasant memories for him and his wife, memories Bob preferred to leave buried.

"I'm not sure, but I do feel badly for her."

Bob agreed. It was hard enough succeeding in the world *with* parents, and usually much harder without. His own children had faltered, but with love and patience had eventually found their way. No thanks to the example he'd set in their early years, Bob admitted. Perhaps this opportunity to help Hannah was also a chance to make up for his missteps twenty-five years ago.

"We should phone her at least once a week," he said decisively. It didn't mean they had to become parent-substitutes, just friends....

Peggy nodded slowly. "That would help, I think," she concurred. "Then Hannah will know there are two people in the world who care about her."

"Right." Bob felt better having made the decision. This was a positive thing to do and just might help him deal with everything that was happening in his own fragile world.

Twelve

Olivia Lockhart Griffin hurried home from the courthouse. Jack had phoned earlier in the day and said he'd be late for dinner. After an idyllic but all-too-brief Hawaiian honeymoon, they'd both been inundated with work. Jack had put in late hours all week and been at the office nearly nonstop the entire weekend. Olivia hated having him gone such long hours, but when he was home, it was lovely. She hesitated—for the most part, it was lovely. Naturally, there were a few adjustments they each had to make, and some of those were more difficult than she would have expected.

After living for almost twenty years without a husband, Olivia was surprised at how easily she'd slipped back into the habit of sharing her life with a man. For the first time since her youngest son had left the family home, she put real effort into creating meals. She sat at the kitchen table now, leafing through a recently purchased cookbook, intent on luring Jack home with a healthy meal made just for him. One regular argument she had with her husband concerned his poor eating habits. Jack tended to grab whatever was quick and easy. Olivia frequently told him his diet contained far too many carbohydrates and fats to maintain a healthy lifestyle; he just as frequently shrugged off her concern.

She studied the recipes. Tofu stir-fry? Probably not, but she'd try it later on. The telephone rang, and thinking it might be Jack, she got up to reach for the receiver.

"Hello," she said cheerfully.

"Howdy, little sister."

"Will!" Her brother lived in Atlanta. It had been a real disappointment to her that he hadn't made it to Cedar Cove for her wedding. When she'd called to tell him she'd decided to marry Jack, she'd hoped he'd be able to share her special day. Apparently she'd caught him off guard, because he'd hesitated and then stuttered a weak excuse. She couldn't recall what it was just now, but at the time she'd thought something was wrong, although she couldn't figure out what it might be. Perhaps he wasn't getting along with Georgia, her sister-in-law, or maybe he had problems at work....

"So how's the happy bride?" Will asked, echoing her cheerful tone.

Olivia leaned against the kitchen wall and sighed. "Wonderful. Oh, Will, I don't know why I waited so long. Jack is so good for me."

She loved her husband's spontaneity. Her idea of a honeymoon was to laze on the beach and catch up on her reading. Jack wouldn't hear of it. Every day he had plans for them to go and see and do. Olivia wouldn't have seen any of what Hawaii had to offer if Jack hadn't coaxed her into visiting the tourist sights and activities. The nights were the best. After dinner, they danced under the stars, swam in the fabulous hotel pool and made love until they were spent.

"You sound happy."

"I am."

"I'm glad." He seemed genuinely pleased for her. "On another subject, have you talked to Mom lately?"

"Of course." Charlotte made routine visits to Olivia's courtroom, and usually brought her knitting, and often a friend or two from the Senior Center so she could brag about her daughter the judge. Her mother had shown up alone on Friday afternoon, and they'd chatted afterward, but now that Olivia thought about it, Charlotte had been mysteriously absent all week.

"What did she have to say?"

"Say? Mom?" Olivia repeated. "Well, not much, really. She did tell me that the seniors triumphed in court while I was away. Which I heard from plenty of other sources—trust me. But she's had such strong community support that she's finally got the ear of the mayor."

"Did she mention Ben Rhodes?"

"Her latest boyfriend?" Olivia teased. Her mother had spoken about Ben a number of times, but she'd never said anything out of the ordinary. Ben was retired Navy, a widower, and Olivia had assumed he was simply a new addition to her crowd of friends. Charlotte had a way of collecting lost souls.

"Exactly what do you know about Ben?" her brother pressed.

"Not a lot. Why do you ask?" Olivia mulled over what she'd heard about him and realized she didn't really know all that much. "I understand he moved to the area a couple of years ago. I remember Mom saying that Ben's a great bridge player. He apparently spends most days at the Senior Center."

"What about his claims to be a retired Navy admiral?"

Claims? Interesting choice of word. Their mother had

brought this up a number of times. "I gather Ben served in the Navy."

"So he says. Has anyone checked into that?"

"Of course not." Olivia was astonished by the suspicion in her brother's voice. "Why should we?"

"Because, my naive little sister, I don't think either of us has fully grasped what's happening to our mother."

Olivia frowned. "Why do you say that?"

Will sighed heavily. "I phoned Mom twice while you were in Hawaii and all she could talk about was Ben this and Ben that. She hardly mentioned anything or anyone else. It got me thinking that we need to find out what we can about this man who's taking up so much of our mother's time."

Now that her brother had alerted her, it occurred to Olivia that their mother *had* been seeing a great deal of Ben, especially lately. "I don't think that's a bad thing," she felt obliged to say. Ben and her mother had become good friends. Over the years, Charlotte had grown fond of a number of men, including one retired actor in the local nursing home. Because of a stroke, Tom Harding had been unable to speak, but her mother had managed to carry on long conversations with him. Meeting Tom had led to the advent of Cliff Harding in their lives, and Charlotte was friendly with him, too. And now Ben. He was new to Cedar Cove and obviously feeling a bit lost. Frankly, Olivia couldn't see any harm in the friendship.

"I don't think there's any need for alarm...yet," Will agreed with a certain reluctance, "but as I said, how much do we really know about this man?"

"Well..."

"Just what he tells us, right?"

"Well...yes." The doubts Will raised made Olivia's suspicions begin to mount. Caught up in the events of her own life, she hadn't paid nearly enough attention to their mother.

"No one's heard of Ben until the last year or two, am I right?"

"Yes," she murmured. "He moved into the area and started showing up at the Senior Center."

"No family."

"Not here." Olivia briefly recalled Ben talking about children in other parts of the country, but nowhere in Washington State.

"Don't you find that mildly suspicious?"

Olivia considered the question. "Not really."

"Then maybe you should."

She was feeling worried now but not ready to acknowledge it to Will.

"A strange man, without any connection to Cedar Cove, moves into the area. Then he seeks out our mother and before we know it, the two of them are thick as thieves."

"I've met Ben," Olivia inserted. "He's a perfect gentleman."

"Wasn't it Ben who talked Mom into this ridiculous protest rally? The man's responsible for getting our mother arrested and you think he's a good influence?"

That gave Olivia pause. "I think Mom was as much to blame for what happened as Ben."

"I wouldn't be too sure of that."

"Why not?"

"You've been on your honeymoon, Olivia. You're in love and that's great—I couldn't be more pleased for you—but you're looking at the world through rose-colored glasses."

What he said was true…to a point. "What's that got to do with anything?"

"I'm afraid," her brother said slowly, "that Mom might

be at risk. How would you feel if some man swindled her out of her life savings?"

"Ben wouldn't do that!"

"Are you sure, Olivia? Would you stake our mother's financial future on your feelings?"

She hesitated. Sitting on the judge's bench, she'd seen far too much of the pain one person could inflict on another. Her hand tightened around the receiver at the idea of anyone taking advantage of her mother.

"You're confident Ben's a stand-up kind of guy?" her brother said, his voice edged with suspicion. "Enough to risk Mom's future?"

"No," Olivia admitted reluctantly.

Will leapt on her answer. "That's what I thought. It's up to you, little sister."

"What's up to me?"

"To check out this Ben Rhodes. I've heard about men like him who prey on widows. I'm sure you've seen the same TV shows I have. We can't be too careful. I'm not there to protect Mom, but you are—and you must. We wouldn't forgive ourselves if we'd stood by and did nothing while a stranger ripped her off."

Olivia didn't know what to say. Will had read so much more into this relationship than she had. He was correct about one thing, though; she'd been preoccupied with her own life.

"What should I do?" she asked.

"Look into his background," Will answered promptly.

"But…" Olivia's mind whirled. "Mom would find out if I started making inquiries about Ben and she'd be furious."

"Then hire someone."

Going behind her mother's back went against her sense of rightness and propriety. "I'd feel better if we discussed this whole thing with Mom first."

"No way." Her brother was adamant. "She'd accuse us of interfering in her life."

"Aren't we?" Olivia didn't think they should dismiss the obvious.

"Yes, but it's for her own good. Don't do it yourself. This investigation should be handled by a professional."

Olivia was of two minds on the matter. Instinct told her she could trust Ben, but at the same time her brother was right. They knew next to nothing about this man who'd become so important to their mother.

"Do you know a private investigator?" Will asked.

"I do. Roy McAfee is a retired Seattle detective. He's good."

"Hire him and don't put it off, Olivia. This could be important."

She sighed unhappily. "All right. I'll talk to Roy."

"Good." Her brother sounded as if a burden had been lifted from his shoulders. "So how's everyone in good ol' Cedar Cove these days?" he asked, the change in his mood immediate.

"Just fine."

"How's Grace?"

Funny he should ask about her friend. "She's fine, too."

"Do you still get together every week?"

"Wednesdays for aerobics class, but that's about it. I don't see her as much as I'd like."

"How come?"

Again Olivia wondered at his sudden interest in Grace. "She's pretty involved with the Dog and Bachelor Auction, which is happening next month. Why all the questions?"

"No reason. It's just that I know you're such good friends."

Funny he didn't ask about Justine and Seth or James and Selina. She would've savored the opportunity to brag about her grandchildren.

"We e-mailed each other for a while," Will confessed.

Grace had never mentioned that to Olivia. "Really?"

"It was no big deal—we're just friends."

The conversation stopped and started after that, with a few more questions about Grace, until finally he ended it. Olivia returned to her dinner plans. Not until she was putting the finishing touches on the grilled Pacific salmon, wild rice and steamed asparagus did it hit her. Her brother was obviously concerned about their mother's relationship with Ben and perhaps rightly so; that remained to be seen. But he had another agenda. And it had to do with Grace.

He seemed awfully curious about her, Olivia mused. More than once he'd drawn the conversation back to her friend, asking her what Grace was up to and whether she was seeing anyone. If they'd been e-mailing each other, then wouldn't he know how Grace was doing?

Just as she started to put a few ideas together—very tentatively—the back door opened and in walked Jack. "You're looking thoughtful," he observed, standing in the doorway off the kitchen.

"Jack!" Not hesitating, she flew into her husband's arms and spread eager kisses across his face.

Jack locked his hands at the small of her back, smiling down on her. "A husband could get accustomed to this sort of reception." He kissed her soundly in return.

Olivia rested her head against his shoulder and sighed, loving the comfort of Jack's arms around her. "I just had the most…disconcerting conversation with my brother."

"What about?"

Olivia told him but excluded the portion about Will's repeated questions regarding Grace.

"Are you going to contact Roy?" Jack asked when she'd finished.

"I suppose I should. Will was concerned and although I think he's overreacting, it can't hurt to know for sure. I guess there's always a chance that Ben's a con man. The clever ones usually have the most convincing aliases. But the truth of it is, I hate the thought of Mom finding out what we've done."

Jack didn't say anything for a long moment. "You can trust Roy not to let any of this out," he finally said.

"I realize that."

Jack shrugged. "Personally, I don't think having Ben investigated is all that necessary."

"Me, neither," she concurred, but she'd decided to do it— if only to reassure her brother.

After dinner Olivia and Jack cuddled in front of the television for a repeat episode of *Law & Order*. Olivia had seen this particular show earlier in the year, although Jack hadn't. She didn't object to watching a rerun, but she found herself returning to the conversation with her brother.

Will had talked about e-mailing Grace. Then there was all his interest in what she was doing, whom she was seeing. Although he hadn't actually said anything, she'd sensed Will's disapproval of Grace's participation in the Dog and Bachelor Auction.

A few months ago, Grace had gotten involved in an Internet relationship with a married man. Her friend had been duped, lied to and strung along. Now, with a growing sense of horror, Olivia wondered if that man could have been her brother. Grace's heart was broken after the end of her romance with Cliff Harding, and that was when she'd told Olivia about the other relationship, accepting the blame for her role in this fiasco. Grace had never revealed the name of the married man. At the time Olivia had assumed it didn't matter, that she wouldn't have known who it was, anyway.

Now she wondered. Could it possibly have been Will?

She tried to dismiss the thought. No, of course not! Her brother would never do anything so underhanded. And if he had, surely Grace would have told her. But if what Olivia suspected was true, it explained Will's weak excuse about not being able to attend her wedding.

"Something on your mind?" Jack asked during a commercial break. His mouth was close to her ear and he took advantage of her closeness to kiss the side of her neck.

"Hmm." Olivia closed her eyes and reveled in his attention.

"This whole thing with your mother and Ben is worrying you, isn't it?"

"Not really," she muttered. She debated mentioning her suspicions about Grace and her brother, but changed her mind. If she said anything, it would be to Grace—but only after she'd had time to sort through the facts as she knew them. Until then, it would be better to say nothing, not to Jack and not to anyone else.

"Good," Jack whispered, tucking his arms more securely around her. "I'd hate to have anything disrupt our television viewing."

Smiling to herself, Olivia poked him in the ribs with her elbow. She'd been doing a lot of smiling since she'd married Jack Griffin, and she didn't think that would change anytime soon.

Thirteen

Cecilia pushed the grocery cart lethargically through the commissary's aisles. She'd been so excited about having her husband home after six months' deployment, counting the days until Ian would be with her again. She'd made elaborate plans for his homecoming and wanted their reunion to be like a second honeymoon. She'd prayed her husband would be as eager to start their family as she was. Only he hadn't been, and now it seemed nothing had gone the way she'd hoped.

"Hey, Cecilia."

At the sound of her name, Cecilia turned to find Cathy Lackey wheeling her grocery cart down the aisle toward her. "I thought that was you," Cathy said.

Cecilia managed a token smile. "How's it going?"

"Great. I left father and son to bond. I'm taking my own sweet time shopping because, frankly, I could use the break. Where's Ian?"

"Home." Cecilia couldn't disguise her misery. "Oh, Cathy, things just aren't working out between us."

"What do you mean?"

Cecilia reached inside her purse for a tissue, humiliated about breaking down in the cereal aisle where anyone might see her.

Cathy glanced over her shoulder. "Listen, let's meet in half an hour at Starbucks. Does that work for you?"

Cecilia nodded. Cathy was the one person in the world she could talk to about her most private concerns. Cathy would understand better than most people, and Cecilia realized she needed her friends more than ever.

Sure enough, Cathy was waiting for her at Starbucks. She was on the patio and had already bought them each a cup of coffee. Because the day was warm and sunny, most of the customers were sitting outside.

"All right, tell me what's happening," Cathy said when Cecilia slid into the chair across from her.

Cecilia picked up her coffee and hung her head, staring at the tabletop. "This homecoming is a complete disaster."

"How do you mean?"

"In the four weeks Ian's been home, we've barely made love." She was embarrassed to be talking about the intimate details of her marriage, even to Cathy, but she could no longer hide her unhappiness. Ian made excuses to stay away from her and it was killing her.

Cecilia looked up to see her friend frowning.

"What's wrong?"

Cecilia bit her lip to keep from crying. "I assumed Ian would want to start our family, but he doesn't. He wants me back on birth control before we make love on a regular basis."

"Are you?"

"Not yet, but my period's due soon. We've used protection, but Ian is adamant—I'm supposed to go back on the pill. Until then it's like I'm his sister. He won't even look at me and I hate it."

"He doesn't want a baby?"

Cecilia shook her head. "Every time I try to mention it, he changes the subject."

Cathy nodded sympathetically.

"Last week, when I refused to let him sidetrack me, he blew up and said he wasn't ready to be a father yet. I asked him when he would be ready and do you know what he said?" She didn't wait for her friend to respond. "Ian said he didn't think he'd ever be ready." Cecilia covered her face with both hands, distraught and weepy.

Cathy placed her hand on Cecilia's forearm. "Do you remember when I told you that I miscarried twice before Andy?"

Cecilia lowered her hands and nodded. She hated being so emotional, but she couldn't help it. She'd created a million romantic fantasies centered on their reunion and everything had gone wrong. Nothing she said or did seemed to work.

"After I miscarried the second time, I was afraid it was the end of my love life. It was as if Andrew had completely lost interest in me as his wife."

Cecilia had trouble believing it. "Andrew?"

Cathy's eyes filled with tears. "The miscarriages affected my husband in ways I didn't understand. I was so wrapped up in me that I didn't see what losing the pregnancies had done to Andrew. He was afraid to make love to me, afraid I'd get pregnant again—afraid I'd suffer again. I was convinced he didn't want me because I couldn't carry his child. And that wasn't it at all." Cathy paused and swallowed visibly. "Our minds play crazy games with us, don't they?"

Cecilia wasn't sure that applied to her situation. Ian was far more vocal about his feelings than Andrew had been, from the sound of it. Ian and Cecilia had worked hard on their communication skills and had learned to be more straightforward in expressing their needs and feelings.

Now this.

"What about that little outfit you bought from the Victoria's Secret catalog?" Cathy asked, lowering her voice to a whisper. "The one you sent him…"

Cecilia shrugged uncomfortably. "I haven't even put it on. Ian was in too much of a hurry the first night and then, well…he just hasn't been all that interested since."

Cathy laughed. "Oh, he's interested, all right, but he's also afraid. If he's in a bad temper…"

"He is," Cecilia confirmed. She couldn't remember her husband ever being as moody as he'd been this last month.

"You know why, don't you," Cathy said, smiling now. "He's frustrated."

"There's no reason for him to be frustrated. I'm ready, willing and able," Cecilia muttered irritably.

"Then let him know that."

"You think?" She hated to feel this hopeful after being disappointed again and again.

Cathy smiled. "Why don't you give that sexy little outfit a try and find out for yourself?"

The question stayed with Cecilia as she drove home, the truck filled with groceries. Her husband was working in the garage attached to their duplex when she returned. He was messing around with an old motorcycle a friend had given him, the engine disassembled and various parts laid out on a tarp. Cecilia had forgotten they even had the thing. Wordlessly he helped her unload the groceries and then went back to whatever he was doing that involved so much of his concentration. She didn't disturb him.

At six, she called Ian inside for dinner. She'd made lasagna, one of his favorite dishes, and he praised her efforts.

Cecilia glowed at his approval and waited until Ian was in bed reading before she took a long, hot shower. Heart pounding, she donned the sexy black outfit.

As well as she could, she checked her reflection in the bathroom mirror. With steam from her shower fogging up the view, it was hard to tell if she looked sexy. To be on the safe side, she liberally doused perfume on her wrists and behind both ears.

If her heart was beating hard earlier, it didn't compare with the frantic explosion going on inside her chest when she opened the bathroom door and posed there, one arm raised and resting against the doorframe.

Ian sat in bed reading. His bedside lamp cast a warm glow about the room. He seemed to be deeply involved in his novel and for a moment didn't pay her any heed. When he did happen to glance up to see her standing in the doorway, his mouth fell open.

Her husband stared at her long and hard. Seconds later the book fell out of his hands and toppled onto the carpet. He didn't bother to pick it up. "Cecilia?"

"Yes?" she whispered.

"What exactly are you doing?"

"What do you think?"

"This isn't amusing." He sat up straighter, sliding as far against the headboard as possible, as if he wanted to escape her. Yet at the same time, his gaze didn't waver from hers. His eyes seemed twice their normal size and that encouraged her.

Taking two steps toward her husband, she slowly removed the sheer black dressing gown. It took her a bit of time and she loved the way her husband swallowed convulsively as he watched.

"You like it?" She kept her voice low and sexy.

Ian didn't answer.

"I think you do," she purred seductively, unfastening the bra-style top—which revealed more than it concealed.

Ian groaned and closed his eyes. Knowing she was about to succeed she leaned over him and turned off the light. The instant she was close, he reached for her and pulled her down onto the bed.

Cecilia slipped her arms around his neck and their mouths joined in an urgent kiss. They were twisting against each other, unable to give enough or take enough. It was as though Ian had held back every bit of passion he felt for her until that moment. Their kisses grew even wilder, even fiercer. Cecilia relished his passion, which fed her own.

Moaning, she showed him in every way she knew how that she loved him and needed him and had desperately missed his touch. Ian lowered himself onto her and after the necessary adjustments to his clothing, entered her quickly. Cecilia was ready, more than ready. At their joining, they both cried out at the pure sensation, the overwhelming pleasure.

They fell asleep in each other's arms, sated and content. Once in the night, Ian woke her again and she turned willingly into his embrace. His need was as intense as it had been earlier. With their fingers locked together, he kissed Cecilia, then held her arms above her head as he sank into her. She whimpered at the beauty of their lovemaking, exulted in her husband and cried out when she reached her own fulfillment.

In the morning it was a different story. Cecilia woke to find Ian sitting on the edge of the bed with his back to her. "You did that on purpose," he said gruffly when he realized she was awake.

Cecilia sat up, clutching the sheet to her bare breasts. "Yes." She wasn't going to lie to him.

"You seduced me."

"If you want to look at it like that. I wanted my husband

to make love to me." She leaned over and caressed his back with her fingertips. "I've missed you, Ian."

He stood rather than endure her touch. "You want a baby and because I don't, you took matters into your own hands."

On that point he was wrong. "I didn't stop you from using protection, Ian."

"You didn't remind me, either."

"Is that my job or yours?" she asked, keeping her voice as level as she could make it.

Her husband whirled around and glared at her. "You made sure I forgot all about it!"

Despite the seriousness of their conversation, Cecilia smiled. "You're right, I didn't remind you. But at the time I had other things on my mind."

"A baby," he said angrily, accusing her with his eyes.

"Well, yes," she admitted. "But you know that."

Ian's eyes narrowed. "I just hope to God you don't get pregnant, Cecilia."

"That's n-not fair," she stammered, shocked by his vehemence.

"Fair or not, I don't know how I'm going to feel about any child conceived out of your deception."

With that, he stormed out of the bedroom.

Fourteen

Roy McAfee waited until late afternoon to call Hannah Russell. He'd tried earlier and learned the young woman's phone had been disconnected. When he mentioned that to Beldon, Bob had supplied him with Hannah's cell number. Apparently, for whatever reason, she'd kept in touch with the Beldons.

He dialed, leaning back in his office chair.

"Hello?" a tentative voice answered.

"Hannah?"

"Yes, this is Hannah Russell." Her response was a bit more confident now. "Who's this?"

"Roy McAfee from Cedar Cove. We met at the Beldons' bed-and-breakfast when you came to collect your father's ashes."

She hesitated again as if she was having trouble placing him. "I'm sorry, I don't recall meeting you."

Roy could understand her lapse in memory. It had been a traumatic visit for the young woman. He didn't envy her the task of dealing with her father's death and, more than that, the mystery surrounding it.

"I'm a private detective. I was at the house during your visit," he said.

"Oh, yes, I remember now. The Beldons hired you to find out what you could about my father's murder."

"That's correct."

Roy felt her warm up a bit. "What can I do for you?" she asked.

He straightened and glanced down at his list of questions. "Is this a convenient time to talk?"

"Yes, I'm not doing much of anything at the moment."

"Where are you?"

"In Oregon. I suppose the Beldons told you I've sold everything. I decided to move. The problem is, I'm not sure where I'm moving. I suppose that sounds odd. I loaded my car with everything that was important to me and took off. I'm hoping to make a fresh start somewhere."

"Bob did say something along those lines." Roy sympathized with the girl's need to escape the horrors of the past year or two. Briefly he wondered about friends and acquaintances but didn't want to distract her with personal questions when there were other, more pressing ones.

"I'd like to ask you about your father."

A short silence followed. "All right. I'm not sure what I can tell you, though."

"You can help me verify some facts."

"I'll try, but I'm as much in the dark about this as everyone else. I didn't even know he was going to Cedar Cove, let alone why. Then when he died like that..." She choked up for a moment. "That was a shock but learning he was murdered—that was so much worse. I don't know anyone who'd want my father dead."

"I appreciate your willingness to help. I promise I'll do everything in my power to find out who did this."

"Thank you," she said, her voice quavering with emotion.

While doing investigative work, Roy had discovered that family members often held crucial answers but were unaware of it. The key to solving a mystery was asking the right questions.

"What would you like to know?" Hannah murmured, recovering quickly.

"First, tell me about your father's relationship with Stewart Samuels."

Again there was a pause, as though she required time to formulate her thoughts. "Really, there's not much to tell. I never heard my father mention his name until after the car accident. Dad was badly burned and was in the hospital for quite a while. His medical insurance was limited. When it became obvious that he was going to require extensive plastic surgery, he asked me to get in touch with Colonel Samuels. Dad said Colonel Samuels owed him, but he didn't say why."

Roy made a notation indicating when Russell had contacted Samuels. He'd assumed the two men had been in communication since Vietnam, but apparently not.

"What were you supposed to ask the colonel?"

"Dad seemed to think Colonel Samuels would be able to help him get into a veterans' hospital. Which he did."

"How responsive was Colonel Samuels to your call?"

"He was…helpful." It seemed she was about to add something, but changed her mind. He'd question her later about her impression of Samuels; he had more important matters to discuss first.

"Was there anyone else your father asked you to contact?"

"No one. My father was a private person. I don't think he would've gone to Colonel Samuels if there'd been any other way."

"Did your father ever explain why he felt Colonel Samuels owed him?"

"No. He never said."

Roy made another note.

"Did you ever personally meet Samuels?" Roy asked.

"No, but I spoke to him by telephone a number of times. He was able to get my father into the local veterans' hospital. The sad part is that it was all for nothing…." She let the rest fade.

Roy was afraid she was about to dissolve into tears, but she managed to keep her composure.

"The thing is…"

"Yes," Roy encouraged when she paused.

"I don't think Colonel Samuels helped willingly. I probably shouldn't even be saying this, but whenever Dad talked to the colonel, he was upset afterward. I remember once the nurse had to give him a sedative. I was just grateful Dad would receive the necessary medical treatment."

This was interesting. Perhaps Samuels wasn't everything Roy had been led to believe. Sheriff Davis felt that Samuels wasn't involved in the murder, and Roy had confidence in his instincts, but things weren't adding up the way they should.

"Anything else you can remember about Samuels and your father?" he asked.

"Not really… They only spoke a few times, which was probably for the best, seeing the effect he had on my father. I think—no, wait." She stopped abruptly. "I do remember something. It was several months after Dad was released from the hospital. Colonel Samuels phoned the house late one afternoon. Dad took the call and immediately lowered his voice. I realized he didn't want me listening in, so I made an excuse to leave the room." She seemed to be reviewing her memories. "I went into the kitchen, but I could still hear part of the conversation."

"What do you remember?"

"I found it all rather odd. I don't know if this is any help, but as I remember it, Dad said to Colonel Samuels that he'd never told anyone. I'm not sure *what* he never told, but my father was very firm about this secret being safe with him." She finished in a rush. "I'm just wondering if I heard him correctly," she murmured. "I tried to forget it because it wasn't for my ears, if you know what I mean."

"I do." And Roy also had a very good idea what Russell had been talking about. Apparently he hadn't discussed the incident in Vietnam with his daughter. It wasn't Roy's job to enlighten her about her father's past.

"Describe the last time you saw your father."

"Alive, you mean?" Her voice rocked with emotion. "This is all so strange. Dad and I talked every day, and I was sure he'd tell me about any trips. He didn't go out a lot after the accident, and when he did he always wore a hat. He said he didn't want people staring at him, but really, it wasn't necessary. The surgery was extremely successful. Anyway, for Dad just to leave and not mention his plans was unusual.

"I happened to stop by the house to check on him and was surprised to see he had a suitcase packed. I asked him where he was going, but all he said was that he'd made arrangements to be away for a few days. I asked again, but…"

"He still wouldn't tell you?"

"No. Anytime I had a question he didn't want to answer, he pretended not to hear me."

"Can you remember what he took with him?"

"I…I didn't see him drive off, so I don't. He had the one suitcase. That much I know. And his coat and hat, of course. Like I said, he was self-conscious about his scars."

"I'm sure he must have been," Roy concurred, although

as she'd said, the plastic surgeon had done a masterful job. At first glance, one would hardly have known that Russell had undergone extensive surgery.

"That's about it."

Roy jotted down a few more notes.

"Is there anything else?" she asked.

He did have other questions, but Roy wanted to mull over what he'd learned. "Not now. Would it be all right if I called you again sometime?"

"Of course." There was a silence. "I find it hard to accept that anyone would want my father dead. Even now, it's difficult to believe he isn't here."

"I'm sorry, Hannah, for your loss," he said, meaning it. "Thank you for your help."

"If you need any further information, please call."

"I will."

The conversation over, Roy hung up the phone and tilted back in his chair, closing his eyes.

Something was still missing here.

Fifteen

"I swear this class is going to kill me one day," Grace muttered breathlessly as Olivia led the way into the dressing room. Grace used the towel draped around her neck to wipe the sweat off her face. "I'm thinking," she continued, slumping down on the locker-room bench, "that we could just meet for dinner on Wednesday nights and give up this whole aerobics nightmare."

"Come on, Grace, you love our class."

"Wrong, I love to have finished our aerobics class. It's the jumping up and down part that's a drag."

Olivia laughed out loud. It'd been the same whiny song for the last four years. Grace complained constantly about the class but Olivia was convinced that her friend actually enjoyed it. Grace just didn't know she enjoyed it. However, she was the first to arrive each week and while she might moan through the entire routine, she always admitted she felt better afterward. Not immediately, but as soon as she managed to catch her breath.

"What's that goofy grin about?" Grace's narrowed eyes focused suspiciously on Olivia.

"You." Hands on her hips, Olivia laughed again. "You crack me up."

"I'm glad you find me so amusing." Groaning, she raised her bent knee to the bench and untied her tennis shoe. "You'll be sorry one day when I'm taken away in an Aid Car."

Olivia rolled her eyes. "Would it make you feel better if I bought you a piece of coconut cream pie?"

Grace looked up. "It might. Any reason in particular?"

Olivia nodded. "I want to ask you something."

"Sure." Grace nodded as she untied the second shoe and kicked it off.

Her immediate willingness to listen and to help if she could was what made Grace such a good friend. There wasn't a single thing Olivia couldn't share with her. That was the reason this conversation would be so difficult and painful. She was afraid her oldest and dearest friend hadn't been completely honest with her—and she was afraid she knew why.

A half hour later, they sat in the Pancake Palace with large slices of coconut cream pie and coffee.

"I hope you realize this defeats the entire purpose of going to aerobics class." Grace lifted the fork to her mouth and savored the first bite.

"In certain circumstances, only pie will do," Olivia said.

"Is this one of those times?"

Olivia didn't answer her. Instead, she launched the topic that had been on her mind all week. "I got a phone call from Will a little while ago." She studied Grace, hoping to read her reaction to Will's name.

Sure enough, Grace instantly dropped her gaze. So it *was* Will she'd been involved with earlier in the year. A flash of anger, first at Will and then Grace, nearly made her lose her train of thought. Olivia squelched the urge to shake them both.

"Don't you want to know what he wanted?" she asked, trying hard to disguise her feelings.

"Sure."

Olivia sighed. "He wants me to have Ben Rhodes investigated."

Shocked, Grace raised her eyes. "Ben? Whatever for?"

"He thinks Ben's planning to swindle our mother out of her life savings."

Grace's frown revealed her disapproval. "Are you going to do it?"

Olivia hated to admit she'd caved in, but she couldn't see any way around it. "I am. I spoke to Roy earlier in the week, although I think it's a waste of good money."

"Olivia!" Grace seemed horrified, which only made Olivia feel worse. "I can't believe you actually did that."

She regretted it now, but she'd told Will she'd hire someone to look into Ben's background and so she had. "My brother made a good case. Ben doesn't have any family in the area and we really don't know much about him." It sounded ridiculous when she said it out loud. "Will convinced me we should do this. He can be persuasive when he wants to be." Again she watched Grace, studying her reaction.

All Grace did was shake her head as if she couldn't believe Olivia would agree to anything so foolish. In retrospect Olivia agreed with her. She wished she'd sat on it a day or two before calling Roy, but it was too late.

"If Mom ever hears about this, she'll be outraged," Olivia said.

"Yes, she will," Grace muttered.

"I told Will how much I like and trust Ben. I can't imagine him doing anything underhanded."

Grace lowered her eyes and sliced energetically into her

pie with the side of her fork. Olivia had the impression that her friend was concentrating on the pie in an effort to conceal her reluctance to discuss Will.

Olivia looked at her carefully. "Seems to me you haven't asked about Will in a long time," she said in a deceptively casual voice. "Any reason?"

"Not really." Grace's response was devoid of emotion.

"He certainly had questions about you."

Grace reached for her coffee, still avoiding eye contact.

"Aren't you curious about what they were?"

"Not really."

Olivia was tired of waiting for Grace to admit the truth. "It was my brother, wasn't it?" She was unable to keep the anger out of her voice. She was furious with Will and sick at heart that he'd taken advantage of her best friend—not that Grace was completely innocent in any of this.

Grace didn't answer.

"The least you can do is be honest about it, Grace. You were emotionally involved with my brother."

Tears filled Grace's eyes and she slowly nodded.

"Why didn't you tell me?" Olivia asked. Yet she realized that much of the hurt she felt was due to the fact that Grace hadn't confided in her. "We've always shared everything."

"I couldn't tell you. I should have in the beginning, but I didn't. I don't know why—no, that's not true. I do know. You would've disapproved and rightly so."

"How did it get started?" Will had visited Cedar Cove when their mother had cancer surgery, but to the best of Olivia's knowledge, Grace and her brother had barely spoken.

"It was all so innocent in the beginning." Grace stared down at the table and her voice fell to a whisper. "He wrote me after Dan's body was discovered to tell me how sorry he was. It was a lovely letter and at the bottom he put his e-mail address. I e-mailed him back to thank him. Then he e-mailed me back, and before I knew it, we were sending each other messages every day."

"My brother is married."

"Yes, I know that."

Clearly, Grace had entered into this relationship with her eyes open. Olivia was well aware that Internet "relationships" were becoming increasingly common, but she was so disappointed that someone she considered sensible and honorable would get caught up in this kind of mess. She felt the same way about Will. He was her brother and she'd always assumed he was a faithful husband, but apparently that had been a false assumption. Well, he'd hear about this.

"We managed to keep our feelings for each other under control until I spent Thanksgiving with Cliff and his daughter. I couldn't contact Will and he couldn't reach me."

"Will knew you were with Cliff?"

"Oh, yes. And when I returned from the East Coast, everything changed. He said he'd missed me and I'd certainly missed talking to him. Once I admitted that, Will started phoning me and before long he'd...declared his love." She swallowed, and fresh tears glistened in her eyes. "He kept telling me his marriage was miserable and he was getting out."

"You believed it because that was what you wanted to hear."

Grace nodded, then inhaled sharply. "Will suggested we meet in New Orleans. He sent me the plane ticket and booked us a hotel room. I nearly did it." She cupped her hand over her mouth as if to hold back a sob. "I nearly slept with a married man."

Not since Dan's disappearance had Olivia seen her friend this broken. "What happened?" she asked in a coaxing whisper.

"One night after aerobics, you casually mentioned that

Will and his wife had booked a cruise. I refused to believe it. Will told me he and Georgia had split up and that he'd filed for divorce."

This was even worse than Olivia had guessed, but she bit her tongue to keep from saying so. "Don't you think I would've told you that Will was getting a divorce?"

"Yes—no, I wasn't thinking. I was sure you didn't want anyone to know."

"I'd tell you." This was a subtle reminder that Olivia held nothing back and that she'd been hurt by Grace's silence— by her lie of omission.

"Afterward, I was so embarrassed…. I wanted to tell you, but I couldn't do it. The worst of it is that I lied to Cliff. He knew right away. He asked me if there was someone else and I told him no and feigned anger that he'd even think such a thing."

"How did he figure it out?" Grace had lied to both of them, and Olivia wondered how Cliff had been able to see through it and she hadn't.

Grace kept her eyes trained on the tabletop. "His ex-wife had cheated on him for years. He realized what was happening…. I finally admitted I'd met someone on the Internet. I said it had been innocent—to that point—but he wouldn't believe me. Cliff said he refused to be involved with a woman he couldn't trust. That's why he won't have anything to do with me now—and the truth of it is, I don't blame him."

"How did you find out Will and Georgia were still together?"

"I called the house. She answered the phone."

That must have been a shocking revelation but Olivia didn't comment. The injured party in all of this was her sister-in-law.

Grace tried to smile. The effort was futile. "I told Will I

never wanted to hear from him again and blocked his e-mail address from my computer. He tried to contact me a number of times, but I immediately deleted any and all messages. I want nothing more to do with him."

Grace had paid a high price for her indiscretion. "I'm sorry it was my brother who did this."

"I am, too." Her voice was strangled and filled with self-incrimination. "But I blame myself. Even when we were in high school, I had the biggest crush on Will. Then, when he actually claimed to love me, it was like a fantasy coming true—and I let it happen. If anyone had told me I'd willingly begin a relationship with a married man, I would've denied it. And yet that's exactly what I did."

"It could have been worse."

"Much worse," Grace said. "If you hadn't mentioned Georgia when you did, I would've met Will in New Orleans. I would've slept with him, too, despite everything I believe. I was head over heels in love with him. Thank God I learned the truth when I did."

"Does Cliff know everything?"

"Not who I was involved with, just that I was."

"You went to him, apologized?"

She nodded. "Twice. But I committed the one sin he can't forgive. It's over."

Olivia wasn't so sure. "He could change his mind, you know. Be patient. Give him time."

"I don't think time's going to make any difference," Grace confessed with heartfelt regret. "If I needed proof of that, I got it a couple of weeks ago."

"How do you mean?"

"I ran into Cliff at The Lighthouse. We talked for a few minutes and then the hostess came to seat us, assuming we were together. He made it abundantly clear that he'd rather dine alone than share a meal with me. I got the message. If he ever felt anything for me, it's dead." Tears trailed down her cheeks as she struggled with her composure.

Olivia reached across the table to clasp her friend's hand. She had some thinking to do—and the person to discuss her thoughts with was her husband.

Later that same night, dressed in her pajamas, Olivia sat on the queen-size bed, arms folded around her knees as she relayed the story to Jack.

"I can't get over the fact that all along it was my own brother." It was still a shock.

Jack frowned as if he, too, had trouble believing what she'd told him. "How's Grace doing?"

"She's brokenhearted. Cliff doesn't want to see her anymore."

Jack tossed his jacket onto the chair beside the bed.

Olivia pointed at it, silently reminding him to hang it in the closet. For a moment, Jack glanced at the jacket and then at her. Sighing, he grabbed it and found a hanger.

"What do you think?" he asked, turning from the closet.

"About Cliff?" She had to consider that for a moment. "I don't know, but I'm sure he sincerely loved Grace at one time. He doesn't seem like the kind of man who voluntarily turns his feelings on and off."

"Then there's hope."

Jack sat down on the bed as he pulled off his shoes. With a proud grin, he lined them up neatly. Shoes were actually supposed to go in the downstairs hall closet, but Olivia didn't comment. "Remember that Grace played a big role in getting the two of us back together," he said.

"I know."

Jack slid his arms around her and tugged her closer to the

edge of the bed. "Do you also remember how we met up the same day at the same movie? Accidentally on purpose?"

"Oh, yeah, that." She laughed at the memory. Their problem, in Grace's opinion, was that they were both too stubborn for their own good.

"I think we owe Grace Sherman a favor."

This perked Olivia up. "Exactly what are you suggesting?"

He was quiet a minute or so. "That benefit for the animal shelter is coming up in July, isn't it?"

"The Dog and Bachelor Auction?"

Jack nodded thoughtfully. "Just remember where there's a will, there's a way."

"Oh, Jack! What a terrible pun." She rolled her eyes. "The fact that there's a Will is exactly what got in the way." Giggling, she nudged him in the shoulder. Only Jack could make her laugh about something so distressing.

He nudged her in return and they smiled at each other.

Then she shook her head. "Cliff isn't one of the bachelors. Grace said he turned them down."

"Did he really? Maybe he needs encouragement. The right kind of encouragement."

"Jack? What are you thinking?"

Eyebrows raised, her husband stayed quiet.

"Jack?"

With a move so fast he left her breathless, Jack swept her into his arms and Olivia fell against him. "Have I mentioned lately that you ask far too many questions?"

"Not lately," she said and giggled again.

He kissed her, and soon neither one of them had a single question to ask.

Sixteen

With the television on in the family room, Peggy sat working the counted cross-stitch pattern. Bob was out for the evening; he had his regular AA meeting at six and following that, he was off to the community theater to read for a part in the latest musical production. The theater had decided to put on *Chicago*.

Peggy spent almost every Thursday night alone and had grown accustomed to having this time to herself. Two of her favorite television shows aired on Thursdays and she could count on not being interrupted.

She yawned and covered her mouth with one hand. It'd been one of those days. The rain had started early that morning and hadn't let up all day. Not a rarity for mid-June, but Peggy had hoped to work in her garden. The rain had been a mixed blessing, though, because she'd been inside when the phone rang that afternoon. It was Hannah Russell.

Apparently Roy McAfee had called her with a number of questions and she hadn't heard back from him. Hannah wondered if there was any news. Peggy hadn't known what to tell her. Unfortunately she didn't have any information for her, either, but it was unlikely that she would. The investigation into Maxwell Russell's death was out of her hands.

Hannah had sounded anxious, and Peggy had tried to reassure her. She wanted to help the young woman, but wasn't sure how. The motherly part of her longed to gather Hannah in her arms and tell her everything would be all right. The girl was hurting, wandering aimlessly to escape her pain. That wouldn't help, because wherever Hannah settled, the anguish would follow. Clichéd though it was, Peggy knew from experience that time really was the great healer.

Determined to finish the cross-stitch pattern of hummingbirds in flight so she could complete another one before Christmas, Peggy glanced down at the page and paused to rub her eyes. Either the manufacturers were making smaller patterns every year or she needed new glasses. She preferred to blame the people who printed the patterns. This cross-stitch was for her daughter and she wanted to complete one for her son, Marc, as well. Although maybe she'd better choose another pattern for Marc's… The oceanscape she'd bought might be a little too complicated.

The back door opened and she looked up. It was early for Bob to be home. "Is that you, sweetheart?"

"Are you expecting some other man?" he teased.

"Not tonight. The naked dancing men are scheduled to arrive on Friday."

"Very funny." He stayed in the kitchen. "Any of that fried chicken left?"

"I thought you'd decided not to eat at night anymore."

"I did."

"Then why are you asking about the chicken?"

"Because I'm a weak man and I'm hungry."

She smiled. "Third shelf down on the left-hand side."

"You're gonna have to do something about this refrigerator," Bob complained. "I can't find a thing to eat in here."

This was a routine complaint. The refrigerator was stuffed with food, but her husband continually claimed there was nothing to eat. Peggy didn't bother to respond.

Munching on a chicken leg, he joined her in the family room off the kitchen.

"It's getting nasty out there."

Peggy could hear the rain pounding against the bay windows in the breakfast nook. "My garden could use it."

"The grass is going to grow and then I'll have to cut it again," he muttered. "I swear it's a vicious cycle."

Concentrating on her counted cross-stitch, Peggy smiled. This, too, was one of his regular lamentations.

A branch struck the window and the wind howled. It reminded her of the night Maxwell Russell had appeared at the door, asking for a room. A chill slithered down her arms. That night was one she'd prefer to forget.

"How about a cup of coffee?" Bob asked.

"Yes, thanks."

The wind howled again and Peggy's eyes met Bob's. He didn't need to say anything; she knew he was thinking the same thing she was. That rainy night…

"Decaf?" Bob called from the kitchen.

"Please." She set her cross-stitch aside and stood, raising her arms in a stretch. "How was the meeting?"

"Good. Jack was there."

Her husband wasn't supposed to tell her who was or wasn't at his AA meetings, but there was little in life they didn't share.

"Olivia and Jack are still in the honeymoon phase," he said, sounding like a serious student of the stages of marriage. "All he could talk about was Olivia."

"It's refreshing to find a man who's madly in love with his wife, don't you think?"

Bob laughed. "That's a loaded question if I ever heard one."

"I like Olivia."

"So do I, but those two are about as different as two people can be."

"Yes, but they're well-suited, too. Jack makes her laugh. And Olivia brings balance into his life."

"He cleaned out his car for her."

"Jack?" This was a noteworthy event. Jack's car was notoriously cluttered with fast-food cartons, old newspapers and what-have-you. For years Peggy had made a joke of it.

"Apparently Olivia's something of a neat freak. Everything in its place and a place for everything."

Peggy frowned. Jack was a born slob. The only thing he'd ever organized in his life was the front page of the newspaper.

"It won't be long before Jack starts complaining," Bob said knowledgeably.

"About what?"

Bob sighed as if the answer should be obvious. "Olivia, of course. Mark my words, Peggy. Jack will give this marriage his best shot, but I don't think he'll be able to maintain Olivia's high standards."

Peggy was not amused. "That's the most negative thing I've heard you say in months."

"Don't get me wrong. I think the world of Jack—and of Olivia—but I can see the writing on the wall with those two."

Peggy was annoyed by his attitude. But before she could chastise Bob, he continued his discussion of the differences between Jack and Olivia.

"She's even got him eating healthy meals. She actually made grilled tofu and eggplant—*eggplant*—last week. I burst out laughing when Jack told me. Can you imagine a meat-and-potatoes man like Jack eating tofu and eggplant?"

"I'll bet it was fabulous." Peggy was a big fan of both and had cooked tofu a number of times. Bob had eaten it, not realizing what it was, and complimented her on dinner. She'd pass along a couple of her recipes to Olivia and explain that the secret was not to say a word.

"He made some excuse as soon as he could and drove to Burger King for a Double Whopper with cheese."

"Shame on him," Peggy murmured, although she smiled at the thought of Jack rushing out the back door, desperate for a fast-food fix.

Bob brought her the coffee in a mug. No sooner had he handed it to her than the lights flickered. "This is turning into some storm. What did the weatherman have to say?"

"I switched channels before the weather came on."

Bob scowled up at the light fixtures. "I'd better find a flashlight before we lose electricity altogether."

Peggy sipped her coffee and set the mug on the counter. "That's not a bad idea."

She followed her husband into the mudroom, where he opened a cupboard door and peered inside. "Have you heard anything on the Russell investigation?" she asked.

Bob glanced over his shoulder as if her question had startled him. "No. What makes you ask?"

"No reason. I was just thinking about everything this afternoon. Doesn't it seem mighty convenient that Dan Sherman killed himself when he did?"

Her husband didn't answer.

"I can't help wondering about that."

The lights flickered again, and this time went out. The room was pitch-black and silent without the background noise of the TV and the hum of the fridge.

"Bob?"

"I'm here."

He reached for her, his hand clasping her elbow.

There was a pounding in the distance. "What's that?" Peggy asked, jolted by the unexpectedness of it.

"I don't hear anything."

"I do."

Her husband switched on the flashlight and led the way back into the kitchen. The pounding was unmistakable now. Someone was at their front door.

"I hear it," Bob said in a husky whisper.

Panic swelled in Peggy's throat. This was like history repeating itself. "Don't answer it," she whispered fearfully.

Bob ignored her. With the flashlight guiding him, he left her and walked into the other room.

Peggy wanted to cry out, to remind him that it'd been a night like this when Maxwell Russell had come to their door. Their lives hadn't been the same since.

"Bob! No!"

"Don't be ridiculous, Peggy."

She moved behind him, trembling as he released the dead bolt. Her breath seemed to catch in her lungs as he opened the door and flashed the light on their unforeseen guest.

Hannah Russell stood drenched and shivering on the other side of the screen door.

"Hannah," Peggy cried and stepped around her husband to open the screen and let the woman in. "Are you all right?"

"I got lost," she whispered. "I thought I could find your place again on my own, but I was lost, and the rain was coming down so hard and I was sure I was going to drive off the road."

Peggy couldn't imagine why she hadn't phoned. "Come in," she urged. Bob took Hannah's coat and hung it on the hall tree to dry.

It was all Peggy could do to hide her distress when she saw how thin and pale the young woman was. "Come inside where it's warm," she insisted, taking Hannah's arm. "When was the last time you had anything to eat?"

"This morning—I think. I haven't had much of an appetite lately."

The lights flickered and came back on, and Peggy sighed with relief.

Bob clicked off the flashlight.

"I shouldn't have come," Hannah mumbled. "I told myself I wouldn't, but I didn't have anywhere else to go."

"You made the right decision. Bob, bring in her suitcase. I'll put on some soup. Hannah, you go take a hot shower and get out of those wet clothes before you catch a cold."

"I can stay?"

"Of course you can stay with us."

Tears spilled from the young woman's eyes. "Thank you. Thank you so much."

"There's no need to thank us," Peggy said, escorting Hannah to the bathroom down the hall, where there were plenty of thick, fresh towels.

When she returned it was to find her husband studying her. He didn't look nearly as certain about this as Peggy did.

"We'll settle everything in the morning," she promised.

Bob's eyes burned into hers. "That's what you said the night Max Russell arrived."

Seventeen

Rachel Pendergast checked her afternoon appointment schedule at Get Nailed as she ate her Weight Watchers frozen entrée. Jolene Peyton was down for a haircut. Rachel remembered the young girl from previous appointments. She recalled Jolene's father, too, and his uneasiness about being in an establishment frequented by females. She found his attitude fairly typical of single fathers.

Jolene was a motherless child and she'd made it clear that she was eager to have her father remarry. Bruce Peyton's wife had been killed in a car accident two years ago while driving to pick up Jolene from her kindergarten class. From what Rachel had heard, several hours had passed before anyone remembered that Jolene was still at the school. Not surprisingly, the seven-year-old was terrified of being left behind.

Despite Jolene's effort to push Rachel and her father together, Bruce Peyton amused Rachel more than he attracted her. While she enjoyed the child's company, Rachel felt that getting involved with a man so obviously in love with his dead wife had virtually no chance of developing into a healthy relationship.

Just after four, Jolene skipped into the salon, as relaxed in Get Nailed as her own bedroom. "Hi, Rachel," she said, pigtails bouncing.

The child must be going into third grade this year; to Rachel, she seemed younger than her age—again, not surprising. "Are you ready to get your hair cut?" she asked, taking out a miniature version of the plastic cape.

Bruce followed his daughter into the salon but didn't show any of her enthusiasm. He nodded briefly in Rachel's direction, then glanced nervously around as if he suspected someone would wrestle him to the ground and dye his hair blue.

"Here you go," Rachel said, turning the chair for Jolene to climb into. She adjusted the cape and secured the clasp.

With practiced ease Jolene flipped her pigtails over her shoulder. "I want you to cut it just like you did before."

"Ah, a woman who knows her own mind," Rachel murmured. She released the bands holding Jolene's hair and carefully ran a brush through it. To her surprise Bruce didn't take a seat or wander into the mall the way he had on previous visits. Instead he stood about two feet behind Rachel, watching every move.

"Do you want to sit down, Bruce?" she asked. He was making her uncomfortable, standing there like that. After cutting Jolene's hair for the last few months, she would've thought he'd trust her with his daughter.

"Dad's afraid I'm going to talk," Jolene piped up.

"Jolene!" Bruce growled out a warning.

"He told me I'm not supposed to say anything about you marrying him."

Rachel jerked around in time to see Bruce throw back his head and groan aloud.

"I don't think we need to concern ourselves with that," Rachel said, hoping to reassure him.

"You already met someone?" Jolene sounded horrified. Her big dark eyes widened with dismay.

"No, but—"

"She's going to the auction, though," Terri called out from the nail station on the far side of the salon. "We all are."

"What auction?"

"The Dog and Bachelor Auction being put on by the animal shelter." Terri pointed to the poster on the wall near the front door. "Everyone in town is talking about it."

"I'm saving every penny of my tip money," Jeannie, another nail tech, chimed in. "This could be my last chance."

"I'm more interested in the dogs myself," Rachel said for Bruce's benefit. She could just imagine what he thought of all this chatter about men.

As if the conversation had suddenly made Bruce feel awkward, he walked over to the waiting area and claimed a chair. From the corner of her eye, Rachel saw him reach for a magazine and pretend to read.

"What's a Dog and Bachelor Auction?" Jolene asked, cocking her head to one side. Her gaze met Rachel's in the big mirror.

"It's a fun event where women make bids to adopt a special pet and a date with a bachelor."

"What's a bachelor?"

"A man who isn't married," Rachel explained.

"My dad's not married anymore."

"Hey, Bruce," Terri shouted. "Have you signed up for the auction?"

Bruce lowered the magazine and shook his head. "Not on your life."

"Why not?" Terri pressed. "It's for charity, you know."

"I'm not interested in dating again, thank you very much." His steely-eyed look dared his daughter to comment.

"You said I could have a new mommy," Jolene reminded him, yelling it across the salon.

"Someday," he muttered.

"But that's what you say when you really mean no." Jolene's face fell. "You *promised*." The child seemed about to break into tears. "I'm the only girl in my class without a mommy and you said, you *promised...*"

Every eye in the salon turned to glare at Bruce Peyton.

Feeling sorry for him, Rachel helped the girl out of the chair and led her to the shampoo sink. She hoped that with a bit of distraction, Jolene would forget about her father's promises, as well as the Dog and Bachelor Auction.

When Rachel finished shampooing Jolene's hair, she noticed that Bruce had left the salon. She guessed he'd decided to wander around the shopping center, after all. That was probably for the best, considering the grilling he'd gotten earlier.

"Who else is going to be in the Back-lor auction?" Jolene asked once Rachel had her back in the chair.

"Navy men," Terri supplied gleefully. "An entire aircraft carrier full of sailors arrived last month and I hear several of the crew have volunteered."

"For the sake of charity," Rachel reminded her friends.

"I don't care why they signed up," Jeannie said, filing her customer's nails. "They're fair game."

Her friends' enthusiasm for this auction astonished Rachel. Frankly, she didn't hold out much hope of meeting anyone through a charity function. Yes, it was a clever way to raise funds, but as for meeting men, she'd been disappointed so many times she'd given up hope. Her thirtieth birthday had come and gone with barely a ripple of the calendar page. Her desire to settle into a comfortable married life was still unfulfilled, and Rachel had given up looking. If she was meant to find a husband, then it would happen. In the meantime she was content.

"Would you pay money to go out with my dad if he was in the auction?" Jolene asked as Rachel sectioned the youngster's hair.

She considered the question and shrugged. She didn't want to disappoint the little girl, but she didn't think Bruce was ready for another relationship. "I don't know."

Jolene frowned as though puzzled by Rachel's answer. "Don't you like my dad?"

"I don't know your father well enough to say if I do or not," she said honestly, hoping to ward off Jolene's persistence.

"But if you bought my dad at the auction, you'd know him."

Rachel finished sectioning Jolene's hair and reached for her scissors. She decided it was time to have a short heart-to-heart with the little girl. "Sweetheart, it embarrasses your father when you talk about him remarrying."

Jolene blinked. "That's what he said, too—that it embarrasses him. But he wouldn't say why."

"I don't think your father's ready to get involved with anyone. He loved your mother very much and I think maybe he doesn't want to fall in love again."

"I loved her, too, but I want a mommy," the girl said plaintively.

"Maybe it's just a friend you need."

"I have friends but they're my age and—" She paused and seemed to contemplate Rachel's words. "Could *you* be my friend?"

Rachel smiled. She thought it was a good idea for them both. Jolene was a motherless child and she was a woman without family. "I'd like that a lot."

"I would, too."

Rachel needed to talk to Bruce, make sure he sanctioned

this. She wanted it understood, however, that she wasn't pressuring him into any kind of relationship. This was between her and Jolene. She would enjoy playing a role in the little girl's life, but only if he had no objections.

Just as she was finishing up Jolene's haircut, Bruce returned. He walked over to Valerie, who ran the reception desk, and pulled his wallet out of his rear pocket.

"Hi, Daddy," Jolene called out.

His expression softened as he turned to face his daughter. "All right, all right, ladies," he said and shook his head, looking chagrined. "You talked me into it. I signed up for the Dog and Bachelor Auction."

"You did?" Terri was so excited she nearly leapt up from her table.

"Great," Jeannie cried, equally thrilled.

Bruce glanced at Rachel, obviously anticipating her reaction. She nodded, letting him know she approved, but she hoped he wouldn't be disappointed when she didn't bid on him.

Eighteen

During the summer months, Charlotte's favorite night of the week was Thursday. For a number of years now, the Chamber of Commerce had sponsored Concerts on the Cove, bringing in a variety of free entertainment, from pop groups to jazz quartets. Tonight was an Irish band, with fiddles and one of those Celtic drums—Charlotte couldn't remember what they were called. The concerts brought almost the entire town together once a week, as young and old alike crowded the small waterfront park, enjoying the festive atmosphere.

Before he came by to collect her, Ben had bought their dinner, teriyaki chicken and rice from her favorite take-out restaurant. Walking hand in hand, he carried their folding chairs, while she held on to their food.

"Oh, good. We have our spot," she said, looking at the place under the mountain ash where they usually sat. Some couples shared a song or a favorite movie; Charlotte and Ben had their own patch of lawn in Waterfront Park.

Ben was so thoughtful and considerate toward her, Charlotte mused as he set up the chairs and insisted she sit down.

And she loved his old-fashioned manners—the way he held doors and stood when she entered a room. The world didn't have much time or interest in those niceties anymore, but Charlotte was of a generation that still appreciated them.

They settled in their spot. It was still early, but they always arrived a good hour before the concert began in order to secure their special place.

"Oh, look," she said with the take-out container balanced on her lap. "There's Corrie McAfee. I don't think I've seen her at any of the concerts before."

Corrie glanced around as if she wasn't sure where to go.

"Corrie," Charlotte said, waving her arm. "Over here."

Corrie headed eagerly in Charlotte's direction. "Hello, Mrs. Jefferson."

"Call me Charlotte. You know my friend Ben Rhodes, don't you?"

Although he had his meal in his lap, Ben stood. Charlotte wouldn't have expected anything less.

"This is your first time here, isn't it?" Charlotte asked. "I'm sure you'll enjoy it." She wanted Corrie to know she was welcome. She hadn't had much opportunity to meet the McAfees. They were still considered new to the community, although they'd lived in Cedar Cove for several years. As a private investigator, Roy had probably learned more about this town and its people than he'd ever cared to know. It was important, Charlotte felt, to bring the couple into the fold.

Corrie gestured toward the parking lot. "I finally managed to talk Roy into coming down. He's parking the car."

"Sit here with us," Charlotte invited. "I always bring an extra blanket. It sometimes gets a bit cool in the evenings, but you and Roy would be welcome to sit on it."

"Oh, Roy's bringing a couple of chairs."

"Look, there's Grace Sherman," Charlotte said, waving

enthusiastically at the local librarian. "She has Buttercup with her. That is *such* a well-behaved dog."

Grace waved back and continued down the waterfront at a brisk pace, the golden retriever trotting dutifully beside her.

Charlotte was proud of having brought Buttercup into Grace's life. Three years ago, a good friend had moved into a retirement center and consequently needed a new home for her pet. Grace had immediately popped into Charlotte's mind. That was shortly after Dan Sherman had turned up missing, and Charlotte understood how lost and lonely her daughter's friend felt.

Roy appeared, walking along the waterfront with two folding chairs, one under each arm. He nodded when he saw Corrie.

"I don't think he's a happy camper about all this," Corrie said under her breath. "I'm the one who's fond of Irish music."

Roy walked across the soft green grass toward them. "Hello, Charlotte, Ben," Roy muttered as he set up the chairs.

Charlotte was surprised to see what a big man Roy was. She'd seen him around town any number of times, but always at a distance and hadn't noticed how tall he was.

Ben stood again and the two men exchanged handshakes. "I don't think we've met," Ben said. "Ben Rhodes."

After they chatted for a few moments, Roy settled next to his wife. They put their heads together, whispering for a moment, and then Roy excused himself.

"We were going to eat after the concert," Corrie explained, "but that chicken looks so good, Roy decided to walk across the street and pick up dinner now."

"The teriyaki is our favorite," Charlotte told her. "This is way more than I can eat. Ben and I should probably share an order but the leftovers are always so delicious the next day."

"Our daughter Linnette's favorite meal is teriyaki chicken," Corrie added conversationally. "Speaking of Linnette," she began. She fumbled nervously with her hands, and then laughed. "That wasn't a very good transition, was it?"

"I didn't realize you had a daughter," Charlotte said. She didn't know the McAfees well enough to know about their children.

"Actually, I've been looking for a chance to talk to both of you about Linnette," Corrie confessed. "She recently graduated as a physician's assistant. It was an arduous program, but Linnette feels strongly about bringing medical professionals to small towns."

Charlotte sat up straighter at this bit of news. "I suppose you've heard how hard Ben and I have worked to get a medical facility built in Cedar Cove."

Corrie nodded. "That's what I wanted to discuss. Do you have any news about what's happening with that?"

For the last two months, Charlotte and Ben had shown up for every single council meeting. They sat in the front row, as if to say they weren't going silently into that long, dark night. For her part, Charlotte had decided she'd keel over dead before she gave up her efforts to get a medical clinic in Cedar Cove.

"I don't know what to tell you," she murmured. "So far, there's been no real progress. Just a lot of talk."

Ben leaned forward. "The argument is that even if the council were to fund a clinic, the town can't afford personnel."

"Linnette applied for a job in Montana, and I hate the thought of our daughter living so far from home." Corrie waved to someone in the distance; the park was fast filling up. "I'd hoped something might turn up here in Cedar Cove. I miss my daughter and she's only a ferry ride away now. I can't imagine what it'll be like when she's hundreds of miles from home."

"A physician's assistant," Charlotte repeated. "Maybe there *is* something we can do."

"What?" Ben asked, turning to Charlotte.

Charlotte gently patted his knee. "Leave that to me."

Olivia and Jack arrived just then, and Charlotte stood and waved them over. Seeing their friends, family and neighbors was what made these summertime concerts so much fun. Her daughter waved back, but Charlotte noticed that Olivia and Jack seemed to be having a discussion before they made their way through the crowd to join her.

"There's plenty of room here with Ben and me," Charlotte told them. She moved her chair closer to Ben's. Although she'd only taken a few bites of her dinner, she'd much rather visit than eat. Closing the container, she returned it to the plastic bag.

"Hello, Corrie," Olivia said.

To Charlotte's ears, her daughter sounded stressed, although she had no idea why that would be. This was a night for relaxing, for laughter and singing and catching up with friends.

Olivia glanced at Ben and greeted him, but her tone was remote, as if she hadn't decided what to think of her mother's friend.

Her daughter's attitude troubled Charlotte, and she decided to talk to Olivia about it later, when they had a private moment.

"Sit down, sit down," she instructed Olivia. "Jack, you're looking fit these days."

He patted his stomach. "I could lose a few pounds, according to Olivia."

Charlotte smiled. So that was the reason her daughter had asked her to recommend a healthy-eating cookbook. Charlotte had bought them shortly after her cancer treatments and tried some of the recipes. They weren't bad, but over time she'd gradually reverted to eating the way she always had. Old habits were difficult to break.

"You know Corrie McAfee, don't you?" Charlotte said, wanting to make sure Olivia made Corrie feel welcome. "This is the McAfees' first time at Concerts on the Cove."

Olivia nodded to Corrie. "Good to see you again."

"You, too," Corrie said.

The two women exchanged long looks. Charlotte didn't know what that was about, either. Surely her daughter and the wife of the local P.I. couldn't possibly be colluding about anything.

"Corrie and I were just talking about a health clinic here in Cedar Cove," Charlotte continued, hoping to include Olivia in the conversation. "The McAfees' daughter is a physician's assistant, and Corrie was just saying how nice it would be if she worked in this area."

Olivia nodded absently.

"A health clinic is important, Olivia," Charlotte said, her voice a little sharper than usual.

"I agree," she muttered, frowning.

"I suppose you think a bigger jail is more of a priority."

"We could use a larger jail, but—"

"You can't be serious!" Charlotte was aghast that her daughter would think additional jail cells should take precedence over the health concerns of their community.

"We do need a bigger jail," Jack concurred. "In fact I just wrote an article this afternoon about the problems with transporting local offenders to jails in Yakima County. But, to my way of thinking, we need a medical facility more."

Olivia nodded once again, silently agreeing with her husband.

Her daughter's lack of verbal support for her cause hurt

Charlotte. Olivia was in a position to do much more and she hadn't because it wasn't important enough to her.

As if he understood her disappointment in Olivia, Ben reached for her hand and gave her fingers a gentle squeeze. She swallowed hard and managed a smile as she turned to this man she'd come to love so late in life.

Nineteen

It was a perfect day for gardening, Peggy thought—sunny but not hot, with a comfortable breeze and an almost cloudless sky.

She'd decided to visit the local nursery, inviting Hannah to join her. Now Peggy loaded a thirty-pound bag of fertilizer into the large garden cart, while Hannah wandered through the aisles of perennials.

"Let me do that," the young woman insisted, hurrying to her side. "I came with you because I wanted to help."

Peggy always enjoyed her trips to the nursery, although she rarely left without filling up the minivan. Her raspberries and blueberries could do with fertilizer. She was out of slug bait, too. Her yard was lovely, with the rhododendrons and azaleas in bloom. The lilacs were coming out, too, and she had both the purple and white varieties along the side of the house. Her small rose garden was prospering, and so was her expanding herb garden.

"We probably should talk about me staying at the house," Hannah said, staring down at the ground as if reluctant to address the subject. Peggy guessed she'd needed several days to work up her courage to discuss the matter of her staying.

"Let's do that later," Peggy suggested. "I was thinking we might go out to lunch when we're finished here." She found the best "girl talks" with Hollie always took place over lunch.

Hannah smiled. "That would be nice."

Hannah had been with them for more than a week. She'd planned to leave once, about three days after her arrival, but Peggy had asked her to stay. As she'd expected, Hannah had accepted the invitation without further argument.

An hour later, they sat on the patio at The Lighthouse eating Caesar salad with grilled shrimp and sipping iced tea.

"You and Bob have been so kind to me," Hannah said.

She still seemed frail, Peggy noted, physically as well as emotionally. "We like having you around."

Hannah looked grateful. "I don't think anyone's ever been so good to me." She reached for her iced tea and took a quick sip. "I should never have stayed this long. Originally I only intended to visit Cedar Cove for one night. But you were so welcoming, and now it's been over a week. I can't continue to take advantage of your friendship like this." She met Peggy's eyes and said earnestly, "I do think of you as my friends, you know."

"We feel the same way," Peggy murmured.

Hannah was nibbling her lower lip again. Peggy considered it a personal challenge to improve not only this girl's health but her emotional outlook. She didn't seem to have much self-esteem. Generally, Peggy thought parents worried excessively about self-esteem these days. Spend enough time with your kids, give them lots of love and reasonable amounts of responsibility, and self-esteem would naturally follow—that was Peggy's theory of child-raising. But in Hannah Russell's case... She was far too thin—to the point of being anorexic. Her clothes hung on her. Peggy had taken a lot of pleasure in tempting Hannah with her prize recipes. Ever since Troy Davis's last visit, she'd been cooking many of her old favorites. She found comfort in that and in providing Hannah with some old-fashioned mothering. Hannah seemed to blossom under Peggy's encouragement and affection.

"Bob and I want you to stay," Peggy said, wondering how many times she'd have to make this point. "We love having you."

Hannah shook her head reluctantly. "I can't do that. I'm not even sure why I came to Cedar Cove. In the beginning I told myself it was because I wanted to learn what I could about how—and why—my father died. I don't like to think about him suffering." There was a stricken look in her eyes. "You don't think he suffered much, do you?"

Peggy didn't know, but she felt a need to reassure Hannah, even if it wasn't the truth. "No, I don't think so. When Bob and I broke into the room, there wasn't any evidence of restlessness." It was as if Maxwell Russell had laid his head on the pillow, closed his eyes and never stirred again. All in all, it wasn't a bad way to exit this life.

Hannah picked at her salad. "I thought I had some questions, but I don't. I probably should. I know that Mr. McAfee seemed to have a lot—but I don't. I'm not sure I even want to know what happened. All I really want is for this nightmare to go away."

Peggy wasn't surprised by her feelings. Sometimes, for some people, uncertainty was easier to live with than a difficult truth. Hannah was obviously one of those people, preferring to simply avoid reality. Peggy had felt that temptation herself, but knew she was strong enough to cope with the truth, whatever it might be.

"I felt drawn to Cedar Cove," Hannah went on. "I was driving and driving, looking for a fresh start, and all I could think about was my first visit here."

"That's understandable."

"Why?" Hannah sounded genuinely curious.

"Well, for one thing, your father died in Cedar Cove. It's here that the mystery will be solved and although you may not want to know what happened or why, you *need* to know. That's what your mind is telling you."

"Do you really think so?" Hannah asked.

Peggy nodded.

"I…think I was drawn back here because of you and Bob." She smiled fleetingly. "When Sheriff Davis brought me to your house, you were so helpful and so nice to me. I felt…oh, I don't know, that you were just the kind of family I wish I'd had."

The young woman's words gladdened Peggy's heart, and saddened her at the same time. Obviously Hannah's childhood had been lacking in some crucial ways. Peggy felt a stab of longing for her own children. She saw her daughter so rarely that Hannah's warmth and gratitude made up for some of what she was missing with Hollie.

"I'll stay," Hannah said decisively, "but only on one condition."

"You're welcome without any conditions," Peggy assured her.

"I want to pay you rent, just as if I was any other guest. I'll need to find a job first, of course, but that shouldn't be too hard. I have lots of experience."

Peggy thought it was important for Hannah to pay rent; it would allow her to feel a sense of pride and self-sufficiency. "I understand Grace is planning to hire someone at the library for the summer," she said. "Why not apply there?"

Hannah considered that for a moment, then shook her head. "I'm not much of a reader, unfortunately. I don't know how good I'd be at helping people find books, you know?"

Peggy wasn't easily discouraged. "What jobs have you held in the past?"

"I worked all through high school at a fast-food place. I didn't really like it, but it gave me a little bit of money. My dad…" She paused and let whatever she'd started to say fade.

"What about working in a day-care center? Little Lambs recently advertised for help."

Again Hannah shook her head. "I don't have a lot of patience around little kids. I worked at a Laundromat once, too, but only briefly. I think I'd be good as a store clerk, though."

"I think you would, too," Peggy agreed and Hannah brightened immediately.

"I'll check the Help Wanted listings as soon as we get back to the house," Hannah said eagerly.

"Good idea. We'll pick up a *Chronicle* right now."

Peggy paid for their lunch, and when they arrived back at the house, Bob was there to help her unload the minivan.

"Hannah's decided to live with us for a while," she told her husband, making a point of expressing her pleasure at the girl's decision.

"I plan to pay my own way," Hannah insisted. Clutching her newspaper, she followed Bob into the garage, where he set down the thirty-pound bag of fertilizer. "First thing Monday morning, I'm going to apply for a job."

Bob nodded, but he didn't reveal nearly the enthusiasm Peggy had. She wanted to kick him for his obvious lack of interest. Peggy watched as Hannah's face fell, annoyed that her husband was so blind to how badly the girl needed their approval. Hannah was fragile and needy, and it wasn't that difficult to give her some of the attention she craved.

"I don't want to be any bother." Hannah nervously stepped back.

"You're no bother, Hannah." Bob returned to the minivan. Well, at least he'd said that much and his voice wasn't unfriendly.

"Would you like to help with dinner, Hannah?" Peggy called as she headed into the kitchen.

"Yes…of course." Hannah scurried after her. "I want to do whatever I can."

She was so eager to please and so eager to fit in. She agreed to prepare the potatoes with every sign of happiness.

While Hannah stood at the kitchen sink and peeled potatoes, working carefully and methodically, Bob walked in through the back door.

"We have a visitor," he announced.

Peggy automatically dried her hands on the kitchen towel as Pastor Dave Flemming entered the kitchen.

"Hello, Peggy," he said, smiling broadly.

Pastor Flemming and Bob had become friends over the past year or so. Max Russell's death had shaken Bob and Peggy badly, and they'd started going to church again, something they hadn't done in years. They still attended regularly. Peggy felt it had been a good decision; the services brought her a sense of peace and calm, and she was thankful for that.

"This is Hannah Russell," Bob said, gesturing toward Hannah.

"Hello, Hannah."

"Hello," she said softly, her gaze lowered.

The girl had trouble making eye contact, Peggy noticed, and hoped that with time and lots of attention she'd get over being so timid and self-conscious.

"Bob tells me you're staying here for a while."

Hannah nodded. "Mr. and Mrs. Beldon have been very kind."

"I'd like to invite you to join us on Sunday for worship service. The Beldons attend. You could go with them."

Her eyes flew up. "I don't think I'd be comfortable with that."

"Any particular reason?" Pastor Flemming asked. "It's our goal to make every visitor welcome."

Hannah just shook her head. "No, thanks."

Peggy hoped she'd eventually change her mind. It would do Hannah good, the same way it had them, but she wouldn't pressure her. When and if she attended services, it would be her own decision.

Twenty

Cliff Harding walked out to the barn to take a look at his new filly, Funny Face, born just two weeks ago. Cal, his trainer, was working with the sire in the paddock.

This ranch had been Cliff's lifelong dream. He wasn't a rich man, but he'd invested wisely through the years and cashed in his Internet stocks at precisely the right time. The profits had afforded him the luxury of buying property in the Olalla area and starting his own small horse ranch.

Cliff had known Cal Washburn for a number of years. He'd first met him when the young man worked at Emerald Downs with Thoroughbreds. Cal, who seemed more comfortable around horses than people, was far and away the most gifted trainer he'd ever known. Cliff felt fortunate to have him on a profit-sharing basis. His ability to communicate with animals was uncanny; if Cliff believed in psychic phenomena, which he didn't, he'd almost think Cal could speak to horses in their own language. Unfortunately those communication skills didn't extend to people. Cal wasn't a particularly shy man, but his stutter had been a detriment in relationships, especially with women.

"S-some...l-l-lady ph-ph—called for you," Cal said when he saw him.

Cliff frowned.

Rather than explain, Cal reached inside his pocket for a slip of paper and passed it to him. Cliff didn't recognize the name and for half a second, he experienced a sense of disappointment. A part of him had wanted, had *hoped,* the call would be from Grace.

Things had ended between them several months ago, but he hadn't been able to stop thinking about her. At one time, their relationship had held great promise. After his divorce, he'd rarely dated. He'd spent twenty years married to Susan and for the last ten, the only reason he'd stayed in the marriage had been his daughter, Lisa.

Susan had been unfaithful, not once, but more times than Cliff could count. It was a sickness with her. Cliff had left the marriage with his self-confidence in tatters, and it was years before he'd had any interest in seeking out another relationship.

When he'd met Grace, she'd immediately had a strong effect on him, one of attraction, of liking and respect. Her husband had disappeared and for financial reasons, she'd filed for divorce. He admired the way she'd dealt with the situation. Once Dan Sherman's body was found, he watched her mourn her dead husband, and he grew to love her as she slowly emerged from her grief and pain. He'd looked forward to the day he would ask her to marry him.

It came as a shock when Grace lied to him. The thing was, Grace wasn't a natural liar. She was too easy to see through. That was when he'd decided to call it quits. He'd done so, but not without regret.

After he'd checked on Funny Face and her dam, Cliff went back to the house to return the phone call. He studied the name—Janet Webb—and didn't recognize it or the number. He was mildly curious when the voice on the other end announced that he'd reached the local animal shelter. He asked for Janet and was placed on hold.

"This is Janet Webb." The woman's clipped, professional voice caught him off guard. It sounded as if he'd interrupted some important project and she resented the intrusion.

"Cliff Harding, returning your call," he said in like tones.

"Mr. Harding." Her voice softened into cordiality. "I appreciate your calling me back. I know you've heard about our Dog and Bachelor Auction next week."

"I did hear mention of it." Cliff could hardly ignore the upcoming event; there were posters all over town, frequent articles in the paper—and even in the Seattle news. Cliff would be happy to make a contribution, but he wasn't interested in participating.

"We were disappointed to learn you haven't volunteered to be one of our bachelors." Her tone grew even friendlier.

"Yes, well—"

She didn't allow him to finish. "Your name's come up more than once and from several different people."

"I'm honored, but—"

"I'm sure you won't mind if I add you to the list, then." Her voice was triumphant—as though she'd successfully outwitted him.

The woman was nothing if not persistent. "I don't think so."

His adamant refusal gave her pause. "Is there any particular reason, Mr. Harding, that you don't want to support the animal shelter?"

He opened his mouth to remind her that he did support the shelter, but, again, wasn't allowed to respond.

"One would assume that all animals would hold a place in a horseman's heart. One would assume that a horseman—"

He broke in. "I believe my trainer, Cal Washburn, is one

of the bachelors—on my recommendation." Cal wasn't likely to forgive him for that anytime soon. Volunteering Cal was supposed to serve a double purpose: to get Cliff off the hook and to give Cal some exposure to local society, specifically female society. He was a young man, after all. To Cliff's surprise, he'd eventually agreed to participate, as long as he wasn't expected to do any public speaking. Cliff assured him all he'd have to do was to stand up on stage and listen to the women fight over him.

"Yes, I see Mr. Washburn on the list," Janet said. "But what about you?"

"I'm flattered you'd ask me personally, but I'm sorry—no." Even for charity, he had his limits.

"I see," Janet said in a severe voice. "What if I told you that your participation could have a very big impact on the shelter?"

"How do you mean?"

"Someone who prefers to remain anonymous has offered to make a large donation if I can convince you to volunteer for the auction."

"What?" Cliff was sure he'd misunderstood.

"It's true. As I said, someone's offered a substantial donation to the shelter if you'll be one of our bachelors."

Cliff was both amused and chagrinned. "Who?"

"I'm afraid I'm not at liberty to say."

It could only be Grace, Cliff reasoned, but she didn't have the money to make that kind of offer. "Male or female?" he pressed.

Janet Webb laughed nervously. "As I said, I'm not at liberty to reveal the source, Mr. Harding."

"How substantial a donation?"

"Nor am I at liberty to reveal the amount."

He chuckled, completely perplexed by the situation.

"Mr. Harding, I sincerely hope you'll have a change of heart."

Cliff thought about it and sighed. "I suppose I can volunteer." He wasn't happy about it, nor did he appreciate being coerced, but he didn't want to take money away from the shelter. In any case, there was no help for it now; he'd given his word.

After a while, he wandered outside to talk to Cal. "I don't suppose you know anything about that phone call?"

The trainer shook his head.

"Someone offered a donation to the shelter if I agreed to be part of the auction."

Cal's eyes widened. "Y-you g-gonna d-do it?"

Cliff nodded, shrugging his shoulders. "Hey—you didn't have anything to do with this, did you?"

Cal shook his head again. "G-Grace?"

Grace's involvement had been his first assumption, too, but it didn't make sense, and not just because of the money. Cliff had recently seen her at the Saturday Farmers' Market, talking to Stan Lockhart, Olivia's ex-husband. The instant she'd seen him she looked guilty. Cliff suspected she'd started dating the other man. The idea of her with Stan bothered him, but Cliff had to put the matter out of his mind. If Grace wanted to see her best friend's ex-husband—well, it wasn't any of his business.

Still, he didn't know how he could have misjudged Grace this badly. She wasn't the woman he'd first believed, not nearly the honest, straightforward person he'd thought, and the realization troubled and saddened him.

He glanced up to find Cal struggling to hide a grin. "Wipe that off your face," he growled.

Cal laughed outright.

"This isn't funny."

Cal laughed again.

Soon Cliff was chuckling, too. He couldn't imagine who'd pay for him to be one of the bachelors, but it might be interesting to find out.

Twenty-One

Jon walked Maryellen and Katie out to the car and buckled their daughter into her protective carrier in the back seat. Maryellen found it harder and harder to head off to work each morning when she longed to spend the day with her husband and child. Jon and Maryellen had agreed she'd quit her job by the end of the year, sooner if they could manage it financially. Maryellen was hoping to get pregnant again, too. She wanted no more than two or three years between Katie and this new baby.

She opened the driver's side door and Jon came over to take her in his arms. "I hate seeing you and Katie leave me every morning," he murmured, echoing her own regrets.

Maryellen slipped her arms around her husband, resting her head on his chest. "I hate leaving you, too."

"It won't be much longer," he promised.

Maryellen nodded. They kissed goodbye and then she climbed into the car and drove into Cedar Cove. Kelly, her younger sister, provided day care for Katie and had done so since Maryellen's return to work the year before. The arrangement worked well for both of them. The extra income helped her sister, and Maryellen felt relieved that her daughter was with family. Kelly's son, Tyler, was wonderful with his cousin and looked after Katie as if she were his little sister. Kelly and her husband, Paul, wanted a second child; although she'd only mentioned it to Maryellen once, Kelly seemed to be having trouble getting pregnant again. Maryellen sympathized but didn't feel she could discuss the subject unless Kelly brought it up first.

There was no time to think about her family once she arrived at the Harbor Street Art Gallery. Summers were their busy season, with plenty of tourist activity and consequently lots of drop-in traffic. Maryellen preferred it that way.

A couple of years earlier she'd broken off her relationship with Jon in an effort to hide the fact that she was pregnant with his child. In order to avoid seeing her—at least before he knew about the pregnancy—he'd moved his work from the local gallery to a well-known Seattle one. His career had grown ever since. His work was back in the Harbor Street Gallery now, but it sold out almost as quickly as he could bring it in.

Maryellen knew that Jon had outgrown their gallery, although he was willing to provide a few pieces because of Maryellen and out of loyalty to the owners, who'd given him his start. The demands on his time and talent kept him increasingly busy. Maryellen was looking forward to managing his career and getting his work displayed in galleries all across North America. She had plenty of ideas, including reproductions in both poster-size and as cards.

At noon, Jon called and they chatted briefly. They couldn't be apart for more than a few hours without missing each other and craving contact, even if that was only five minutes on the phone.

"I'm working in my darkroom this afternoon," he told

her. In other words, she shouldn't call him unless absolutely necessary.

"Okay."

"What time will you be home?"

She smiled at the question because she got there within the same ten-minute period every afternoon. "Five-thirty-one," she teased.

"Cute, Maryellen."

"I can be even cuter if you want."

"What I want is you. All of you, all the time."

"That's good to know because I'm more than willing to give you all of me."

Jon laughed. "I'll be waiting for my two favorite women at five-thirty-one."

"Aye, aye, captain." Maryellen smiled as she replaced the receiver, warmed by their brief conversation.

A short while later, while her assistant was on her lunch break, an older couple came into the gallery. The building itself, more than a century old, was a historic site in Cedar Cove. As always, the wide wooden floorboards creaked as she moved out of her small office to greet the customers. The walls of the gallery displayed a variety of artwork—paintings and photographs—by several local artists, but the three pieces Jon had brought in earlier that week had already been sold.

Maryellen watched as the man and woman, arms linked, glanced about the room. They didn't seem typical of the normal tourist traffic. The man wore slacks and a short-sleeved plaid shirt, while the woman had on a rather old-fashioned shirtwaist dress. It looked as if they were on a church outing rather than visiting a small town.

"Hello," Maryellen said warmly. "Welcome to the Harbor Street Art Gallery. Is there anything I can help you find?"

"Hello." The woman smiled and turned to her husband,

apparently waiting for him to speak. When he didn't, she said, "We've heard there's a very talented nature photographer from this area whose work is displayed here."

"That would be Jon Bowman." It never failed to thrill Maryellen when a customer inquired about him. "I'm afraid the gallery has sold out of Mr. Bowman's photographs. I'll have more in later in the month."

"Oh." The woman was clearly disappointed.

"His photographs are also available in a gallery in Seattle. I'd be more than happy to give you their name and phone number if you'd like."

She nodded eagerly. "Yes, by all means."

Maryellen walked over to her desk and retrieved a business card from the gallery that displayed Jon's photographs. The man, who was quite tall and formal in his manner, accepted the card. He bowed his head in thanks and stared at it intently.

Something about him caught Maryellen's attention, but she couldn't figure out exactly what it was.

The woman moved closer to her husband. "We heard correctly then? Jon—Mr. Bowman does live in the area?"

"Yes, he does. As it happens, I'm his wife." Maryellen said this with a great deal of pride.

"I thought you might be," the man said, speaking for the first time. His tone was low, a bit gruff, as if he didn't speak often.

Again the woman turned to her husband.

"If you're interested in seeing any of his work—"

"We'd like that very much," the woman said, cutting Maryellen off. "That would mean a great deal to both of us."

Maryellen walked over to the window. "If you stop at The Lighthouse restaurant, which is just down the street, you'll see several of Jon's photographs on display." She pointed out the window. "Until recently, Jon supplemented his income by working at the restaurant."

"Doing what?" the man asked, sounding shocked.

"He was the chef."

"Jon?" The woman's tone was equally puzzled. "I... didn't realize."

This couple seemed to know Jon. "My husband is a man of many talents." Maryellen hesitated, almost afraid to ask if they were Jon's parents, uncertain what would happen if her suspicions proved to be correct.

"I–" The woman stopped abruptly and clamped her mouth shut.

Maryellen noticed how the man's arm tightened around his wife's; he seemed to be warning her that she was saying too much.

"Jon's an innovative chef. He could've made a name for himself in that field if he'd chosen to do so." Maryellen knew she was chattering, but it was the result of nerves.

"That's wonderful."

"Is there anything else I can show you?" Maryellen asked. "There are several talented local artists whose work we have in the gallery."

"We were only here about Jon's," the man said, starting toward the door. "Thank you for your help."

"You said Jon's your husband?" The woman lingered as if she wasn't ready to leave.

"We need to go," her husband insisted.

"In a minute, dear."

Maryellen studied them, wondering about the silent tug-of-war going on between the older couple. It was clear the woman had more questions, no less clear that the man was eager to be on his way.

"Do you have children?" the woman asked.

Maryellen nodded. "A daughter named Katie."

The woman placed her hand over her heart. "I'm sure she's a delightful child."

"Oh, yes. In looks she resembles my side of the family more, but she has Jon's temperament and his personality." Maryellen gently tested the waters. The woman certainly was curious. "I suspect Katie possesses her father's artistic eye, as well, but only time will tell about that."

"Marion."

The woman nodded. "We do need to go. Thank you so much…"

Maryellen nodded and returned to her desk once the couple had left. It occurred to her a moment later that she recognized the woman's name—Marion. That, combined with the pointed questions about Jon, convinced her they had to be Jon's parents. The ones she'd written shortly before her wedding. Marion and Joseph Bowman. She'd asked that they not answer her letter and they'd abided by her wishes.

Instead they'd come to Cedar Cove. Maryellen's heart leapt into her throat. She could only imagine what Jon would say if he ever found out what she'd done.

Twenty-Two

Roy McAfee was intensely curious about the news that Hannah Russell was living with the Beldons. He wasn't a man who paid attention to idle gossip, but in this instance, he knew and trusted the source—his wife.

The last time Roy had talked to Hannah, she'd been on the road in search of a fresh start. Apparently she'd found what she was looking for right here in Cedar Cove.

Deciding to look into the matter himself, Roy drove out to the Thyme and Tide. Roy didn't have many close friends—a few cops and former cops, all still in Seattle—but over the last couple of years he'd taken a liking to Bob Beldon. Corrie got along well with Peggy, too. It was rare that they found a couple whose company they both enjoyed.

Peggy had the front door open by the time Roy climbed out of the car. She was waiting for him, her smile wide.

"This is a pleasant surprise," she said as she held the screen door. "Bob's golfing with Pastor Dave this afternoon." Checking her watch, she added, "He won't be much longer, though, if you can wait."

"I should have phoned."

"Can I help you?" Peggy asked, leading the way into the kitchen. Without asking, she opened the refrigerator and brought out a big pitcher of lemonade, lemon slices floating on top.

"You might be able to do just that." Roy pulled out a chair and sat down at the round oak table. He wasn't opposed to a glass of Peggy's lemonade, especially since she made it fresh every day.

"What do you need to know?" Peggy filled two glasses and sat across from him.

Roy stretched out his arms, folding his hands on the table. "Corrie told me Hannah Russell's living with you these days."

Peggy nodded. "She came in the middle of that lightning storm we had a couple of weeks back." She shook her head. "Nearly frightened us out of ten years, arriving half-drowned on our front porch. You should've seen her when she first showed up, Roy. She was exactly like a lost kitten in search of a home."

"Where is she now?"

"At work."

Apparently Hannah was more than a visitor. Roy reached inside his shirt pocket for a pad and pen. "She has a job?"

Peggy nodded again. "This is her first day, and she was really worried about it. She's washing dishes at the Pancake Palace." Peggy frowned slightly. "I'd hoped for something better, but she was quite certain this job suited her. Unfortunately, she doesn't have much self-confidence."

Roy recalled his phone conversation with Hannah and remembered how timid her voice had been.

"She's due back any time. I'm curious as to how her first day went."

"I'd like to ask her a couple more questions if you don't mind?"

"Not at all, although Bob's going to be disappointed if he misses you." Peggy picked up her glass of lemonade and took a drink. "Did he mention he got the lead in *Chicago?* He's pretty pleased with himself, so if he has a swelled head when you see him, that's why." She smiled as she said it.

"Good for him," he murmured. Peggy looked proud of her husband, Roy thought, as well she should. "I saw him in *A Christmas Carol* last December and I was really impressed."

"He played four roles in that, including Marley with the clanking chains. The costumes were so good I didn't recognize him at first."

Roy chuckled and noticed a battered blue Honda pulling into the driveway.

"That's Hannah now," Peggy told him. She stood and walked over to the door off the kitchen.

When the girl came into the house, her eyes immediately went to Roy. She offered him a brief smile.

"How was work?" Peggy asked her. She gently placed one arm around Hannah's shoulders.

Hannah shrugged. "All right, I guess."

"Do you remember Mr. McAfee?" she asked.

Hannah's brow furrowed slightly. "You're the private investigator who called me, aren't you?"

"I am, and I have a few more questions for you. Is that all right?"

She shrugged a second time. "I suppose so, although I'm pretty tired at the moment."

Peggy got a fresh glass, filled it with lemonade and set it on the table. "I'll leave you two alone to talk. If you need anything, just give a holler. I'll be out in my garden."

It looked as if Hannah was about to ask Peggy to stay, but she seemed to find sufficient resolve in herself to face Roy on her own. She sat at the table, resting her clasped hands on the place mat. With her lank hair drawn into a ponytail and her eyes lowered, she resembled a shy schoolgirl.

"What would you like to ask me?" she mumbled.

Roy's question had to do with Samuels. Some of the facts didn't fit together in his mind. "I was wondering if you know anything about Colonel Samuels visiting California."

"To see my father, you mean?" she asked, glancing up.

Roy nodded encouragingly. "To the best of your knowledge, do you remember ever seeing him with your father?"

She hesitated. "Yes, now that you mention it, he did come to see my dad once."

Roy frowned as he scanned his notes. "I see I asked this question earlier and you claimed you'd never met Colonel Samuels."

"I didn't personally meet him," Hannah rushed to explain. "But I did see him with my father."

"When was that?"

She narrowed her eyes. "It must've been shortly before Dad left for Cedar Cove—yes, it was only a few days beforehand."

"Was your father agitated?"

"Not really. Why do you ask?"

"No reason," Roy said lightly.

"Is there anything else I can help you with?" she asked and he had the feeling she was eager for the questioning to be over.

"Not right now. I need to sort out a few things first. Will I be able to reach you here?"

"I should be around for a while. The Beldons said I could live with them for the time being. I…I probably shouldn't, but they make it so easy." She lowered her eyes again. "They really are wonderful people."

Roy agreed with her there. "Thank you for your time, Hannah."

"You're welcome."

Roy stood, ready to go, when he saw that Bob's car was turning into the driveway. Walking out of the kitchen, Roy waited until he'd parked in the garage. Bob had opened the trunk, removed his golf clubs and put them away before he noticed Roy.

"Good to see you, Roy," he said as he emerged from the garage. "Actually I'm glad you're here. I need to ask a favor."

"Ask away."

"I mentioned that my car's being worked on next week, didn't I?"

Roy nodded.

"Peggy's got a meeting with her garden club Tuesday night. Is there any chance I can take you up on your offer and borrow your car while mine's in the shop? I'll have it back first thing in the morning."

"No problem." Because Corrie and Roy worked together, her car sat at home most days.

"I appreciate it."

"I can drop it off Monday evening, if you'd like."

"Perfect," Bob said happily. "Why don't you and Corrie come for dinner that night?"

"Sounds good, but I'd better check with the boss." Corrie was the one who kept their social calendar and there'd be hell to pay if he agreed to dinner without clearing it with her beforehand.

"You do that and get back to me."

Roy left for his office a few minutes later. He collected the mail on his way in and dumped it on his desk.

Corrie generally dealt with the mail before he saw it, but she was gone for the afternoon. It was a lazy day following the Fourth of July weekend, and they weren't completely back on schedule yet.

As he sorted through the bills, flyers and letters, Roy placed the bills in one basket and the personal stuff on Corrie's desk. A postcard caught his attention. It was a plain white one, the kind available at the post office for the price of the stamp.

He turned it over and read the message twice. EVERY-ONE HAS REGRETS. IS THERE ANYTHING YOU'VE DONE YOU WISH YOU COULD DO OVER? THINK ABOUT IT. There was no signature.

Roy set the card on his desk, staring at it for a long moment. Living the life he had, there were always regrets and misgivings. If someone was asking for a list, he wouldn't know where to start.

Twenty-Three

Ian Randall was in no hurry to get home. For six months at sea, he'd counted every second he was away from Cecilia. He'd crossed off each day on the calendar until they could be together again, eagerly anticipating their reunion. Being apart from her was agony. But now that he was home, he could hardly stand to be around her because it was an even deeper agony to have her there and not make love to her.

As he neared the highway exit that would take him home, Ian slowed the vehicle to a near-crawl. He dreaded what would happen once he walked into the duplex. The tension between them had begun the instant she announced she wanted another baby, and it seemed to increase day by day.

Cecilia tried to pretend everything was as it should be, tried to ignore his bad mood. Every night it was the same: she arrived home from work and immediately set about preparing dinner. While he buried his face in the newspaper, she talked about her day in the office. She was employed by a large accounting firm in Cedar Cove and liked her job, as much as Ian liked his. Above all, they did love each other; there was no question of that. They should be happy.

Nights were the worst. He made excuses not to go to bed at the same time as his wife. He saw the hurt in her eyes, but not once did she confront him.

If Cecilia had brought the situation out into the open, it might have helped. She wanted a baby and the fact was, he didn't. Cecilia had let him know that if they were going to use birth control, it was up to him. After that one disastrous night when she'd seduced him, he decided making love to Cecilia was just too dangerous.

She made him forget. As soon as she was in his arms, he lost all thought except his need for her. The risk of getting her pregnant was just too high.

There'd been a few nights when he'd given in—and been furious with himself afterward. He'd crawled into bed, assuming she was asleep. She wasn't, and he'd surrendered every time without even token resistance. Before he knew how he'd allowed it to happen, they'd made love, and on at least two of those occasions, it was without protection.... He tried to sleep on the sofa, but Cecilia wouldn't let him, insisting she'd sleep there with him.

The only way to be safe was to avoid her. Unfortunately, his self-imposed abstinence didn't always work. Ian had never viewed himself as an undisciplined man; the Navy had drilled self-discipline into him from the minute he set foot in boot camp. But when it came to his wife, he had little resistance.

Those times he hadn't used protection—Cecilia was bound to get caught if she hadn't been already.

Ian couldn't bear the thought of another pregnancy going wrong. Losing Allison had nearly destroyed them both. Healing would come in time; he was sure of it. If only Cecilia wouldn't press the issue.

As he approached the stop sign off the freeway, Ian took a left instead of a right, going in the opposite direction from home. He drove through unfamiliar streets, dread building in him. The second he walked in the door, it would be the same thing all over again—the same desire, the same frustration. He could feel it.

By sheer force of will, he hadn't touched Cecilia in three nights. It had been torture, and Ian just knew he wouldn't be able to resist her tonight.

When he discovered that he was driving down the road to the cemetery where his daughter was buried, Ian slowed and turned in. His baby girl had died after living only a few days. She'd been born with a defective heart and there was nothing the doctors could do. As a submariner he'd been under the polar ice cap at the time and unable to be with Cecilia. In fact, he hadn't even known about his daughter's birth until he learned of her death. Upon his return, he'd requested reassignment aboard an aircraft carrier, and that request had been granted.

Parking the car, Ian climbed out. Hands in his pockets, he walked over to Allison's grave, where he stood on the grass staring down at the small marker that recorded the dates of her birth and death. Amazing, really, that so little information could involve so much pain.

He gazed down at the marker for several minutes. "Hello, Allison," he whispered. He talked to his daughter whenever he visited her grave. He'd never even seen her, never had a chance to hold her or kiss her and he felt cheated to have been denied this one small consolation. The only photo of Allison had been taken in the hospital shortly after her birth. She'd been so tiny. Her life, so short and traumatic, had been filled with pain. Each breath was a struggle.

"I see your mother's been by," Ian said. He noticed the single pink rose, a sure sign that Cecilia had visited recently. He didn't know how often his wife came to the cemetery, but he suspected it was every three or four days. "Did she tell you she wants another baby?"

Ian took a deep breath. "I don't think it's a good idea." He smiled as he said it. "The thing is, I wasn't ready when your mother told me she was pregnant with you. You took me by surprise, you know? I didn't realize a girl could get pregnant that easily." He hadn't been unhappy at the news, however; he'd been excited because it'd given him a good excuse to do what he wanted to do anyway—marry Cecilia.

His smile faded. Even when she got pregnant, Cecilia wasn't that keen on marriage. She had all kinds of stipulations. Apparently her mother had been pregnant with her when she married Cecilia's father, and the marriage had been a disaster from the beginning. Cecilia had no intention of repeating her mother's mistakes, so she'd insisted on a prenuptial agreement. It was lunacy, but he would've signed anything. The prenuptial had saved him in the end because Judge Lockhart had denied the divorce based primarily on that agreement.

"Your mother doesn't know this yet, but we might be heading back to sea." Although he hadn't told Cecilia, once orders came through, the word would be out soon enough. Under current circumstances, the Navy wasn't likely to allow him the luxury of a long shore duty. That was the bad news as well as the good. He didn't want to leave Cecilia again, especially so soon, but he knew that if he was in port much longer, she'd get pregnant for sure.

"Look after your mother while I'm away, will you, sweetheart?" he asked. "Let her know how much I love her."

He waited a moment, nearly overwhelmed by sadness. What astonished him was how much love he felt for his little girl. This was a child he'd never had the privilege of kissing good-night or cradling in his arms, and yet she was as much a part of him as his own heart.

Ten minutes later, Ian left the cemetery and drove home. He half expected Cecilia to comment that he was later than usual or ask where he'd been. She didn't. She was busy in the kitchen and barely looked up when he walked in the door.

"Did you have a good day?" she asked.

After glancing at the mail, he picked up the evening newspaper and settled into his favorite chair. "All right, I guess."

He opened the front section of the paper to block her from his sight. He found it incredibly sexy to watch his wife, walking barefoot in the kitchen in shorts and a cropped T-shirt. She dressed like that on purpose; Ian was convinced of it. The minute she got home from the office, she changed out of her business clothes and into something seductive. Half the time he couldn't keep his eyes off her.

"I had an all-right day, too," she said conversationally as she carried a large bowl to the table. "I made us a taco salad."

He nodded. "Thanks."

"Are you hungry?"

"Sort of." His appetite hadn't been good since he'd returned home. That was just another sign of the tension he'd been under lately.

"Dinner's ready," Cecilia said, sitting down at the table.

With little enthusiasm, Ian set the newspaper aside and joined her. Most nights he didn't contribute much to the conversation; Cecilia did practically all the talking. Every now and then, he'd ask her something because the silences troubled him more than the sound of her chatter.

This evening, however, she didn't seem to feel like talking, either. He was relieved when she finished dinner and brought her plate to the sink. Apparently her appetite wasn't good, either.

"Are you feeling okay?" he asked.

"I'm fine."

Ian frowned, unsure if he should believe that. But then she smiled so sweetly he couldn't doubt her.

They spent the evening in silence, each of them reading— Cecilia a magazine and he a thriller someone at work had lent him. By nine, she was yawning. "I'm going to bed."

He nodded. "I feel like staying up and reading for a while longer."

She didn't argue with him, but accepted his excuse. Then she wandered into the bedroom and closed the door. So far so good, he thought as he relaxed in his chair.

Ian made a genuine effort to read, but his mind was on everything except the words on the page in front of him. Nine o'clock was damned early for Cecilia to go to bed, he realized all of a sudden. He couldn't figure out why she'd done that. She almost always stayed up until at least ten.

At nine-thirty, he turned out the lights and walked into the darkened bedroom. It took his eyes a moment to adjust to the lack of light. Cecilia was curled up on her side of the bed, and he knew instantly that she was awake.

"Cecilia?"

"What?"

"You awake?"

"Yeah."

"Something's wrong, isn't it?"

She didn't answer him.

The mattress dipped when he sat on the edge of the bed. "You'd better tell me." His heart was starting to pound.

She pretended not to hear him. "Cecilia?"

"Are you coming to bed?"

He supposed the only way he could get her to talk was to join her in bed, so he undressed and slipped beneath the covers. Cecilia moved closer but didn't touch him. "Will you hold me?" she whispered.

"Okay." He lay on his back and Cecilia pressed her head against his shoulder. He wrapped his arm around her. She felt small in his embrace, smaller than usual.

He waited but she didn't say anything. In his heart he knew. He should've guessed right away, he supposed, but denial could be downright comfortable. "You're pregnant, aren't you?"

"Yes." She sobbed once. "Are you angry?"

He snorted softly. "No. I don't have anyone to blame but me."

"I wanted everything to be different than with Allison. I thought you'd be angry then, too, and instead you were so nice about it."

He didn't have anything to say to that.

"The news of a baby should make us happy."

"Are *you* happy?" he asked.

Cecilia didn't answer right away. "I'd be leaping up and down for joy if you were pleased."

His fears wouldn't let him feel good about this. "I'm afraid, Cecilia," he finally said.

"I am, too, but I want our baby so much. I love you, Ian. You got home almost two months ago, and this whole time's been awful. It's…it's like you hate me."

"Cecilia, no…"

"What else am I to think? You hardly talk to me and you won't even go to bed when I do. You think I don't know why? You don't want to make love to me and whenever you do, you hate yourself for it."

She certainly had him pegged. "I got you pregnant, didn't I?"

He could feel her nod.

"Yeah, well, you knew how I felt."

"You knew how I felt, too!" She sniffled, apparently trying not to cry. "I want this baby and I want my husband to love me and be excited and happy and you're not. It's tearing me up inside."

Ian expelled his breath. "I'm trying. Give me a chance to adjust to it, okay?"

Her tears moistened his shoulder.

"Cecilia, please, don't cry."

"I can't help it."

He kissed the tears from her face. Soft kisses, gentle kisses that eventually brought his lips to her mouth. "It'll be all right," he said and hoping to reassure her, kissed her again and again.

"This is our baby," she whispered, and hiccupped on a sob. "I want you to be happy…. I want you to love our baby."

"I will." He closed his eyes and struggled with his conflicting emotions.

"But you don't now?"

He dragged in a deep breath. "I'm trying. That's all I can do."

Cecilia broke free and rolled onto her side, turning away from him.

"Honey, please, do you want me to lie?"

"No."

"Then give me time." He cuddled her spoon fashion and slipped his arm around her middle. From pure habit, his palm cupped her breast. Many a night aboard ship, he'd dreamed of doing exactly this, cuddling his wife, loving her and enjoying the feel of her body so close to his own.

A sigh shuddered through Cecilia and she shifted her little butt closer to his growing arousal. She seemed to take delight in moving seductively against him. "Ian?" she whispered.

He squeezed his eyes shut and didn't respond.

"There's a nice thing about me being pregnant."

He wanted to know what it was, but at the moment the blood flow in his body wasn't headed in the direction of his brain.

"You don't have to wait until I'm asleep to come to bed anymore."

He smiled to himself. With a soft growl, he urged her onto her back. Sighing in surrender and welcome, she slid her arms around his neck and guided his mouth to hers.

"We're going to be all right," she promised him. "We really are."

Ian so badly wanted to believe her. "I know." But anything else he might have said was lost as he buried his fears in his wife's embrace.

Twenty-Four

Charlotte Jefferson couldn't stop smiling. She placed a cherry pie in the oven and set the timer, then turned to her knitting.

"Wipe that silly grin off your face," she chided Harry, her black cat, who sat on the arm of the sofa and studied her with a bemused look. "I know, I know, but this is just so wonderful I can't believe it's really happening."

When the doorbell chimed, Charlotte carefully put her knitting aside and hurried to answer it. She checked the peephole—one could never be too cautious—and saw that it was her daughter. After unbolting the locks, she opened the front door.

"What took you so long?" Olivia sputtered as she barreled past Charlotte. She was halfway into the kitchen before she stopped. Whirling around, she marched back into the living room and then sank abruptly onto the sofa, as though all her energy had drained away.

"Olivia, what's gotten into you?" Charlotte asked, concerned by her daughter's odd behavior.

Olivia bolted to her feet and almost immediately sat down again. She covered her face with both her hands. "I think I've made a terrible mistake."

"What mistake?"

Olivia dropped her hands and stared forlornly out the living-room window, her shoulders sagging. She looked close to tears. "It's Jack and me."

Charlotte gasped. "My goodness, you've been married less than three months!"

"You think I don't know that? Lately…lately it's like we can't even talk."

"You and Jack? Why? What's wrong?"

"Oh, Mom, I feel so awful. We're just so different and we irritate one another and…and…"

"There, there now," Charlotte cooed softly. Things must be bad for her daughter to show up on her doorstep in this condition. In all the years Olivia had been married to Stan, never once had she run home after an argument or sought her parents' advice.

"I love Jack so much."

"Of course you do." Olivia's feelings for him were apparent months before she admitted she was in love.

Olivia's face crumpled as she struggled to hold back tears. "I love him, but he…he's a slob. And I can't stand it."

"You have to compromise, sweetie."

"You think I haven't tried?" Olivia shook her head. "I hate myself for nagging him to pick up his dirty clothes, but really, why should I follow him around and clean up after him?"

"Wait here," Charlotte murmured. "I'm making a pot of tea." The most serious discussions required tea. For some reason, everything made more sense over a shared cup of strong tea. And whatever had happened between Olivia and Jack appeared to be serious, indeed.

Less than ten minutes later, Charlotte was back. She carried in the tray, complete with a large ceramic pot, two china cups and a plate of homemade cookies. Olivia sat on the edge of the sofa with a wadded tissue in her hands.

"Start at the beginning," Charlotte said as she poured. She handed the first cup and saucer to Olivia, then poured her own. Olivia set the cup on the coffee table, her composure shaky.

"I'm…I'm not sure how this whole thing began, but tonight when I came home and saw the mess in the bathroom, I lost it. I realize Jack doesn't care about tidiness and order the way I do, but that's no excuse for leaving wet towels on the floor. He didn't so much as pick up his dirty underwear."

Charlotte sighed.

"Maybe I shouldn't have said anything but I did, and then Jack yelled at me and…" Her lower lip trembled. "We both said things we shouldn't have. He left and then I left, and now I feel so bad."

"Of course you do," Charlotte said with warm sympathy.

"When we returned from Hawaii, he made an effort to keep the house neat, but it didn't take him long to slip back into his old habits."

"That's a man for you," Charlotte said. "With your father and me, what we quarreled about was his tendency never to throw anything out. I'd get annoyed and put ten-year-old bills in the trash and then he'd get annoyed…." She sighed again, remembering. It seemed such a small thing now.

"I know I have irritating habits, too," Olivia said. "Mother, do you think I'm compulsive?"

Charlotte wasn't about to answer but it didn't matter; Olivia barreled on.

"Just because I insist the cap be on the toothpaste and the towels hung evenly on the rack—that doesn't make me a neat freak, does it?"

"Everyone has a certain, uh, comfort level," Charlotte

said, hoping to sidestep the issue. She'd come across that useful term in a magazine article a while ago.

"I can't believe I'm running to my mother with this," Olivia cried. "It's just that I never thought Jack and I would argue so…so horribly."

"Olivia, every couple argues. It's healthy to clear the air."

Olivia nodded. "I know…. But we were both so adamant in what we said and now I think Jack's sorry he ever married me."

"I'm sure that's not true."

"He told me he'd had it with this diet I'd put him on and that if he saw another chunk of tofu he was dumping it in the garbage. But Mom, his diet is atrocious! He thinks I'm picking on him because I want him to lose a few pounds. All I want is for him to make healthier food choices."

"Of course you want him to eat properly, but–"

"He said we got along a lot better when we lived apart."

Charlotte was stunned. "He didn't mean it."

Olivia covered her face again. "I think he did, because right after that he left. I wasn't letting him walk out on me, so I left, too. Can you believe I'd do anything so childish?"

Charlotte had to admit she was somewhat amused. This must have been a humdinger of an argument.

Olivia had hated fighting when she was a little girl, too. It used to upset her to the point that she'd make herself sick.

"What should I do now?" Olivia pleaded. "Should I just go back to the house and pretend nothing happened?"

"Well," Charlotte said, gently patting her daughter's shoulder. "First of all, I'm sure Jack is feeling just as bad as you are. You both need to remember that you were single for a lot of years. Marriage is a major adjustment. Perhaps it would be best if you bought two tubes of toothpaste."

"I *did*," she said indignantly. "But Jack can't remember

which one is his. Half the time he can't find it, and mine's handy, so he uses it." She reached for her cup of tea and took a sip. "Then he gets upset when I say something. According to Jack, it shouldn't make any difference."

"I know."

"You can't possibly know. The other night I found an open jar of peanut butter on the kitchen counter. The knife was still in it."

Charlotte dropped her jaw as though shocked.

"Apparently Jack got up in the middle of the night and made himself a sandwich."

"I take it peanut butter isn't on his diet?" Charlotte tried hard not to smile.

"No, and Jack knows that. It's for his own good."

"Oh, dear."

Olivia raised her head at the sound of a car and she vaulted to her feet, dashing to the window. "Jack just pulled up out front." She squared her shoulders and looked back at Charlotte. Then, as if she were making a court decree, she declared, "Tell him I'm not here."

"Olivia, you're being ridiculous. Your car's parked in my driveway. I'm not going to lie to your husband."

"Look at me, Mother! Just look at me. I'm a sensible adult, or at least I was until I married Jack Griffin. Overnight I'm back to being a teenager. I've never come running to my mother in my life and now—now just look at me. I'm a mess! I'll talk to Jack once I've had a chance to compose myself."

The doorbell chimed. Olivia heaved in a breath. "I need to freshen my makeup…and I don't want him to know… Oh, just tell him whatever you want."

Charlotte frowned.

Olivia disappeared and Charlotte went to the front door. Jack didn't seem surprised when she answered before he'd even knocked. He had on his light raincoat, rumpled as usual, hands deep in his pockets.

"Hello, Jack."

A scowl darkened his face. He nodded. "Hello, Charlotte."

"What can I do for you?"

"Do you have a minute?"

Charlotte hesitated, then gestured him in. "Of course. Come inside."

He stepped into the house and glanced around. Charlotte noticed that his gaze lingered on the two teacups, but he didn't comment on the fact that Olivia was obviously at the house.

"I heard a rumor this afternoon and wanted to see if it was true."

"Sit down," Charlotte invited soberly, trying to hide her amusement at both Olivia and Jack. They were acting like kids—and as Olivia had said, even when she *was* a kid, she hadn't acted like this. Still, amused or not, Charlotte was worried; immature behavior could escalate and end in drastic consequences. This was a good marriage in the ways that counted. She hoped they'd give it the chance it deserved.

He chose the wing chair and stroked Harry's head as he walked past the cat. Harry remained unruffled by all these dramatics. She envied him a little.

"What did you hear?" Charlotte asked as she sat down again. She picked up her knitting, hoping it would calm her.

As if to prove this was an official visit, Jack pulled out his pen and pad. "Rumor has it Ben Rhodes met with the people of Puget Sound Medical and Dental this afternoon."

"You heard?" Charlotte was beside herself with excitement. "He went with Louie Benson."

Jack noted this information on his pad.

"I'm sure Mayor Benson will fill you in on the details."

"I don't suppose this has anything to do with that parcel

of land off Heron Street recently bequeathed to the city by the Duncan family?"

Charlotte beamed him a smile. Very little got past Jack Griffin. "It could," she murmured and continued to concentrate on her knitting for fear he'd read the absolute delight in her eyes.

"My guess—"

"I'm not at liberty to say another word, Jack. An announcement will be made by the mayor tomorrow morning."

"So Cedar Cove is going to get its health clinic, after all?"

Charlotte kept her head lowered. "That's a distinct possibility, but you didn't hear it from me, understand?"

Jack chuckled. "Sure enough."

"Is that the only reason you're here?" Charlotte asked. She wondered who'd mentioned the news about the clinic. Bess had come over earlier and Charlotte had shared it with her dear friend. Bess had been thrilled, but she never could keep a secret, no matter how much she promised.

Jack got up and stared into the kitchen. "I didn't actually stop by because of the clinic. That was a convenient excuse. Where's Olivia hiding?"

"I most certainly am not hiding," her daughter announced, moving to the kitchen doorway where she stood with her arms crossed. "I—I was taking Mother's pie out of the oven."

"Oh, dear, I'd forgotten all about it. I didn't hear the timer." Charlotte was so flustered that the cherry pie had completely slipped her mind.

"I think I should give you two a moment alone," Charlotte said, walking past Olivia to check on the pie. Never in all her life had it taken her longer to complete a single row of knitting. She couldn't quite stifle a sigh. In the last thirty minutes, she'd been up and down more times than an elevator.

Olivia remained in the kitchen doorway and it was all Charlotte could do not to push her forward. Jack wasn't standing in the living room because he liked the view. He'd come for his wife and if Olivia had a lick of sense she'd realize it.

They stared at each other and finally Jack spoke. "I promise I won't leave the peanut butter out again," he muttered.

Charlotte resisted the urge not to giggle.

Olivia sniffled. "Oh, Jack, I didn't mean any of those terrible things I said."

"I didn't, either."

"It's just that I—I guess I really am a neat freak…"

Jack shook his head. "I'm a slob. I'll try harder, I promise."

"I will, too."

Olivia flew out of the kitchen then. Charlotte peered into the living room and discovered that Jack had his arms around his wife. They hugged each other for a long moment.

Everything was going to be all right, she thought with relief. They'd have their difficulties but their commitment and love for each other was strong enough to keep them together.

"Are you ready to go home?" Olivia asked her husband.

Jack nodded and kissed the top of her head. "Do you really think I'm a sex fiend?"

"Jack!" Olivia glanced over her shoulder and Charlotte pretended not to have heard.

"Best compliment I've had in years."

"Oh, honestly." The laughter was back in Olivia's voice. Arm in arm, they walked out the door.

Sex fiend. Her daughter didn't know how lucky she was.

Twenty-Five

Bob caught sight of the other car as he rounded the corner. He'd spent the last three hours with the theater group, rehearsing his role as the attorney Billy Flynn in the musical *Chicago*. It was now after ten and this late at night, Harbor Street was nearly deserted. He noticed that the blue SUV took each turn he made, the bumper dangerously close to his own. Bob felt his heart leap into his throat just as the vehicle eased back.

He was being followed.

Bob took a left at Heron and the SUV turned left, as well. Knowing he tended to jump to conclusions, he wanted to be sure and made an immediate right. Again the vehicle behind him turned in the same direction. At least it maintained a safe distance.

Now he was convinced; he was indeed being followed. His heart racing, Bob reached for his cell phone. This wasn't an emergency and the car stayed well behind him but it was obvious the driver was tailing him. His first thought was to call Peggy, but he didn't want to needlessly alarm his wife.

Nor could he phone the sheriff's office. No crime had been committed—yet.

He'd ignored the warnings he'd gotten from Sheriff Davis and Roy. After all this time, Bob had refused to believe he was in any real danger. He'd thought everyone was over-reacting, and the only reason he'd agreed not to accept guests was to appease Peggy. All at once, he wasn't so sure about anything.

"Roy," he mumbled aloud with relief. He'd call his friend. Roy would know what to do. But try as he might, Bob couldn't remember his home number. He might be able to dig it up from the recesses of his memory, but the only number he could recall was for the office. At this time of night, Roy would almost certainly be at home.

"Great," he muttered under his breath. "Just great. Think. You can figure this out."

Then Bob remembered reading one of those "what to do in case of an emergency" articles in some long-ago publication. If you're being followed, he recalled, the advice was to drive to a police station.

With that in mind, Bob drove directly to the Cedar Cove Sheriff's Office, where he pulled into the half-circle drive-way. He stayed in his vehicle as the blue SUV drove past. It slowed briefly and then sped away.

Tension caused him to tighten his hold on the steering wheel. He sat in the driver's seat and forced his pulse to return to normal by taking deep, even breaths. When he was certain his legs would support him, he opened the car door and climbed out.

"You can't leave your car there," a uniformed officer informed him as he walked into the station.

He began to explain, then changed his mind. He might be making more of this than necessary. "I'll move it in just a moment. I need a phone book."

"You'll move it now."

Bob wanted to argue, to explain, but decided against both. It was easy enough to pull his vehicle around. He parked in the street, then walked back to the station and located a public telephone near the rest rooms.

He looked up Roy McAfee's home number and used his cell phone to place the call.

"McAfee," Roy snapped, sounding like the police detective he'd once been.

"Someone was following me," Bob said without introduction.

"When?" Roy's voice was hard as steel.

"Just now."

"Where are you?"

Bob leaned his shoulder against the wall. "At the sheriff's office."

"Good. Did you get the license plate number?"

Bob closed his eyes and shook his head. "No. I was so rattled I didn't even think to look."

"What make was the car?"

That he remembered. "A blue SUV. Ford, I think. Or maybe a Chevy."

"Doesn't narrow it down much. Are you sure you didn't get any of the plate number?"

Bob wanted to kick himself. "No, sorry."

"You okay?"

"Of course I'm all right." He hoped his voice didn't betray how badly this had unsettled him. "What should I do now?"

"Drive over to my house. I'll meet you and follow you home. We can talk there."

"Okay." He climbed back in the car and started the engine. His hand trembled as he turned the ignition key.

He checked the rearview mirror every few seconds during the drive to Roy and Corrie's. He thought he saw the

SUV once, but if so it kept a respectable distance that didn't allow him an opportunity to read the license plate. But by then he was so jumpy he would've suspected any car that came within two blocks of him.

When he arrived at the McAfees' home, Roy was already in the car. He pulled in directly behind Bob and followed him down Heron to Cranberry Point.

Peggy was standing at the back door waiting for him as if she knew something was wrong. He was only a few minutes later than he'd told her he'd be.

"What is it?" she asked as he walked from the garage to the house, Roy directly behind him.

Sometimes Bob swore his wife had a sixth sense. "I was followed."

Her eyes widened with alarm. "Just now?"

He nodded. "I called Roy from the sheriff's office. To be on the safe side he decided to follow me home."

"What's happening?" Hannah stepped into the kitchen, her expression curious—and more than a little wary.

"I think we should all sit down," Peggy suggested. Roy came into the house with Bob, and the four of them sat in the family room. Hannah, who was dressed for bed, resembled a lost waif with her long hair falling about her face and huge, frightened eyes.

"Tell us the whole story, from the beginning," Roy said.

There wasn't all that much to tell. Bob explained how the car had come right up on his bumper when he first drove down Harbor Street and then pulled back. How the driver had maintained a reasonable distance as Bob took a number of twists and turns to establish whether or not he was being followed.

"Whoever it was didn't want to be identified," Roy said.

"Did you recognize the person in the car?" Peggy asked.

Bob shook his head. "No—I didn't really look. I mean, when the car first came up behind me the only thought that went through my mind was how close on my tail it was."

"Did you notice if the driver was a male or female?" Roy asked. "One person or two?"

Bob felt like an utter failure. He should be able to answer at least that question, but in all honesty he couldn't. "One, I think. Male...but I'm not sure." Disgusted with himself, he shook his head. "I don't know. I couldn't tell."

Peggy reached for his hand and her fingers curled around his. He was sure she didn't realize how tightly she squeezed.

"Anything else you can remember?" Roy prodded.

"Nothing. But if it happens again, I'll know what to look for."

"Again?" Peggy gasped.

Bob could tell she was badly shaken, but he couldn't come up with a single reassurance. Not even one.

"Who do you think it might be?" Bob asked his friend.

"Whoever it is wanted you to know you were being followed." Roy said, "otherwise he wouldn't have made it this obvious."

"Why?"

"Why else?" Peggy cried. "He's trying to frighten us."

Bob had news for her; the attempt had worked.

"But...who would do such a thing?" Hannah asked. "What sort of person?"

"It might have nothing to do with the murder," Roy told them.

"What else could it mean?"

Roy shrugged. "That I don't know."

If Roy thought he was providing comfort, his tactic hadn't worked. Not in Bob's opinion, anyway. He was nervous and unable to hide it.

"I'm going to bed," Hannah said into the silence. "Unless you need me for anything?"

"No, no, go to bed," Peggy insisted. "Do you want me to wake you up?"

Hannah nodded. "Please. I didn't mean to sleep in this morning."

"I know. But you don't want it to happen again."

"No, I don't," Hannah agreed. "I need this job."

Their houseguest had been two hours late for work, and the Pancake Palace had phoned looking for her. Peggy had managed to get the girl up and moving, but it had been no easy task. By the time Hannah got into town, the restaurant was practically out of clean dishes. To her credit, Hannah had stayed two hours past her shift in an effort to make up for her tardiness.

"If you're all right, I should probably leave," Roy said, getting to his feet.

"We're fine," Bob lied. "You go on home. Thanks for everything." He deeply appreciated Roy's friendship and concern, which went far beyond their professional relationship.

Bob walked him to the kitchen door, then watched as Roy drove off.

"Are you tired?" he asked Peggy. She stood in the middle of the kitchen, completely still, as if she was afraid to move a single step in any direction.

"You can't be serious about going upstairs and sleeping," she said. When he didn't answer, she added, "You honestly think you'll sleep?"

"No, but that's not the point."

Peggy smiled. "I don't think I can, either. Want to watch some TV?"

They both knew they were in for a long, restless night.

Twenty-Six

Grace Sherman had been looking forward to the Dog and Bachelor Auction with equal measures of anticipation and dread. The fund-raising event had initially been her idea and Mary's, and Grace wanted it to be successful. At the same time, she was aware that she'd be sitting by while the man she loved was on the auction block. She couldn't join in the bidding herself, both because she couldn't afford it and because she knew how he felt about her now. Other women would bid on Cliff and he'd walk away with someone else on his arm.

On the evening of July tenth, the parking lot of The Lighthouse restaurant was fast filling to capacity. Women lined up outside the door, and it wasn't for dinner and drinks, Grace suspected, although the food, as always, would be exceptional. No, all those women were eager to get the best seats in the house for a close-up view of the dogs and—especially—the bachelors. Even before the auction had begun, everyone could tell it was going to be an unqualified success.

"This is just fabulous," Mary Sanchez said. She stood with

Margaret White at the entrance of the restaurant. As soon as the doors opened, they'd collect the tickets that had already been sold. The women waiting to place their bids jostled outside, peeking through the windows, chatting and laughing. The mood was jovial and high-spirited.

"The natives are getting restless," Margaret shouted to Janet Webb over the noise and laughter from outside. Janet was getting everything organized for the cashiers, who were situated at the rear of the restaurant near the bar area.

"Is there anything I can do?" Grace asked. She'd come to offer an extra pair of hands before the auction started. Her official duties, however, had been completed weeks earlier.

"Yes, Grace, there is," Janet said, her tone serious. "I want you to enjoy this event. You've worked hard and the shelter deeply appreciates all your effort."

"It was my pleasure." Grace figured that enjoying this evening wasn't remotely possible, but she was determined to try. All she could hope was that the woman who won Cliff would appreciate what a wonderful man he was.

Janet, the director of the animal shelter, walked over to the restaurant foyer, and gave the signal for the doors to open. As the crowd began to enter, Grace observed with surprise the number of young single women in Cedar Cove. She'd thought most of the people here would be familiar to her but quite a few of the women weren't. Like a crashing tide against the shoreline, people—young women, older ones and even men who were clearly there as spectators—flooded into the restaurant, tipping over chairs and scooting around tables as they jockeyed for seats.

Thankfully Grace had been able to reserve a table for friends. Olivia and Jack showed up a few minutes after the doors opened, and Charlotte and Ben followed. Grace had encouraged her daughters to attend for the entertainment value of the event, but both Maryellen and Kelly had decided to spend the night at home with their husbands and families. Grace didn't blame them.

"Can you believe this crowd," Grace commented to Olivia, looking around. It was difficult to hear over the high-decibel chatter all around them. The atmosphere of fun and excitement was as strong as the pervasive scent of perfume.

Grace could only imagine what it was like in the waiting area where the bachelors and dogs were congregated. Silently she read over the list of the bachelors, fifteen in all. Pairing them up with dogs had been a complicated task, taken on by Janet Webb. Grace wondered what breed—or mixed breed—she'd choose to accompany Cliff. A shepherd of some kind was her guess. Large, gentle and handsome...

The temporary stage, with an extended walking platform, reached halfway into the restaurant, with tables and chairs arranged on both sides. The idea was that the bachelor would walk out with the dog on a leash.

Whoever won could take the dog or the bachelor or both. If the winner only wanted one, then the auction would start over with the remaining entrant, whether man or dog. As Grace read over the rules described in the program, she hoped this novel idea would raise the funds the shelter needed, and more.

"If I'd been one of the bachelors, I bet I would've brought in top dollar," Jack boasted with a cocky grin. "Unfortunately Olivia got me first."

Olivia glanced up from her program and arched one brow. "Unfortunately? Is that a complaint, Mr. Griffin?"

The teasing left his eyes and was replaced with a slow, easy smile. "Not at all. I meant unfortunately for these other ladies." At her smirk, he shook his head. "In all seriousness, though, I think I got the better half of this deal."

"I'm not so sure I agree." Olivia rested her head against him, and Jack's arm came around her shoulders. The gesture was so romantic that Grace had to look away. Rarely had she felt lonelier or more alone, but she was finished with self-recrimination. Life goes on, as the old saying had it, and so would she.

"I see Stanley's one of the bachelors," Charlotte said disapprovingly. She pointed out her ex-son-in-law's name to Ben Rhodes. "Stanley doesn't even live in Cedar Cove."

"I know," Grace murmured, "but Stan wanted to do his part for charity."

"Did you tell him charity begins at home?"

"Mother!" Olivia mildly chastised her.

Charlotte frowned. "I only hope his ego doesn't get the better of him—for once."

In Grace's opinion, it was too late for that. Stan had volunteered under the assumption that any number of women would battle to outbid each other for the opportunity to date him.

"I can't wait to see which dog Janet paired him up with," she said, leaning close to Olivia as the waiters started to circulate with salads.

"You mean you don't know?"

She shook her head. "Janet's not deciding until she's had a chance to mingle with the bachelors and meet them."

"This could be intriguing."

Soon everyone was seated and the main course had been quickly and efficiently served, with Justine directing the waiters from the kitchen. Janet stepped up to the podium set off to one side of the platform and reviewed the rules. Next she introduced the auctioneer and Barry Stokes stepped forward.

Barry greeted everyone with a smile and a few good-natured jokes about bachelors. He managed to work the audience to an even higher level of excitement, periodically reminding everyone of the important role the animal shelter played in the community. He pointed out that the final bidding price would be separate for the dog and the man. If the bidder wanted the dog and the bachelor, the bid was actually doubled. So if the bidder wanted either the dog *or* the bachelor, the bidding would begin again. Dogs made wonderful pets, he said at the end of his introduction. And so did bachelors—which brought a roar from the crowd.

The first bachelor presented was Bruce Peyton. Grace knew Bruce through the library; the widower often came in with his young daughter. Grace recalled his wife, Stephanie, too, and was well aware that the young father continued to grieve.

Bruce was matched up with a bassett hound. Grace could tell how nervous he was by the way his gaze darted around the room. The order of the bachelors' appearances had been chosen by lottery, and she felt sorry for Bruce, whose name had obviously been pulled first.

The whispers rose as Bruce walked down the runway, the bassett hound trudging beside him. It was clear that Bruce would've preferred to hurry, but that was impossible with the slow-moving dog.

The first bid came from one of the women who worked at Get Nailed. She was immediately outbid by a woman from the local pharmacy. The bidding went back and forth between them until the last moment. Bruce—and the dog—were about to be won for the bargain price of two hundred and thirty-five dollars each when Lois Habbersmith, who worked with Maryellen at the gallery, shocked everyone.

"Three hundred and fifty dollars!"

The two women who'd been bidding stared at each other, shook their heads and sat down.

"Three hundred and fifty dollars, going once, going twice." Barry paused and pointed his gavel at the woman from the salon. "Are you sure you want to quit so soon? The bassett hound alone is a bargain at that price."

The two previous bidders shook their heads again.

"Sold," Barry announced and slammed down the gavel. "Now, which do you want? Bruce or the bassett?"

"Both!"

"Three hundred and fifty dollars each," Barry reminded her.

"Yes." Lois gleefully pulled out her checkbook and maneuvered around several chairs as she made her way to the back of the room.

Barry chuckled. "You're married, Lois. What's Don going to think when you bring home a dog and a bachelor?"

"Don approves."

Several laughs followed, along with good-natured teasing.

Lois dismissed Barry's comment with a wave of her hand. "Don and I already decided we'd get a dog. And I promised him whoever I bid on would be tall enough to reach the second-story windows on the ladder. They need a good washing, and Bruce looks tall enough to do it and young enough not to complain."

"In other words, you purchased your bachelor to relieve Don of washing the outside windows?"

"I did. Those windows haven't been cleaned in three years. Don said to go for it and I did."

"You want me to wash your windows?" Bruce Peyton asked, visibly disappointed. "Hey, is that legal?"

"Sure it is." Barry laughed, nodding his head. "You volunteered for this, and she paid good money for you."

Bruce didn't seem too happy with this turn of events. Giving Barry a disgruntled look, he walked off the stage.

The chatter diminished as the second bachelor was announced—Cal Washburn, the horse trainer Grace had met at Cliff's ranch. He was matched with a spotted gray-and-black Australian Shepherd. Again Grace thought it was a good pairing. Cal was a quiet man, gifted with horses.

Judging by the hushed whispers that rippled across the room, it was evident that Cal was a bachelor of interest. From her vantage point, Grace could see that the dog was trembling and seemed even more nervous than Cal, until Cal crouched down and whispered something in the animal's ear, which instantly quieted him. Grace watched in amazement as the pair proceeded down the runway. The bidding was fast and furious, with cutthroat competition between the girls at Get Nailed and—of all people—Corrie McAfee. In the end, Corrie won.

"Do you want the dog or the bachelor?" Barry asked.

Corrie stood while Roy remained seated with the Beldons. "I want both."

"Isn't that your husband you're sitting with?" Barry pretended to sound shocked. "What's happening to our society when married women walk off with all the eligible bachelors because they need their windows washed?"

Corrie grinned. "You've got it all wrong. The dog's for my son, Mack, and the bachelor's for my daughter."

A loud cheer of approval followed as Corrie walked over to the cashier with her checkbook in hand.

The third bachelor was Stan Lockhart, who was paired with a high-strung white poodle. Stan seemed in his element on the runway, unlike the two previous bachelors. He'd apparently been practicing and he played to the crowd, doing a fairly good impression of a model, complete with one hand in his pocket. He was obviously expecting the high bids garnered by the other bachelors. When the winner, a younger blond woman, opted for the dog and not him, his disappointment was noticeable. The bidding started over, and Stan commanded less money than the poodle.

Grace elbowed Olivia, who didn't seem to know exactly how to react; her expression was a mixture of shock, embarrassment and laughter. To everyone's surprise, Charlotte's good friend Bess Ferryman won Stan. The older woman stood up to proudly claim her prize.

"Don't tell me you're married, too?" the auctioneer demanded.

"Nope, and I'm not buying him to wash any windows, either. I've got a hot date in mind."

"Good for you," Barry said approvingly.

"Dinner, and he's buying, followed by ballroom dancing." Bess marched purposefully toward the cashier. For just a moment, it looked as if Stan might balk, but then he dutifully left the stage.

"Couldn't happen to a nicer guy," Jack whispered to the others. "I'll bet he doesn't offer his services again anytime soon."

Grace was chatting with Olivia and Charlotte when the next bachelor's name was announced.

Cliff Harding.

This was the moment Grace had been dreading all night. In an effort to prove that she was unaffected, she fixed a smile on her face and stared straight ahead, hoping no one could guess at the turmoil inside her.

Cliff was paired with a lovely female golden retriever. When he stepped onto the stage, he was greeted by loud cheers. Grace had long suspected he'd be one of the key figures at this event, and she was right.

Almost immediately, Margaret White leapt into the bidding. Seconds later, the woman who worked for John L. Scott Realty topped Margaret's two-hundred-dollar bid by another fifty.

"What about you?" Olivia asked, nudging Grace.

"I can't."

"Why not?" Olivia asked, her voice rising with agitation.

It was too complicated to explain. Now wasn't the time to try, so she simply shook her head.

"Grace, you can't just sit there and let some other woman walk away with Cliff. You have to bid."

She felt the same way, but she couldn't do it. While Margaret and the other woman continued to raise each other in fifty-dollar increments, Grace bit her tongue. Her heart pounded like crazy and her mouth went dry as she dealt with two years' worth of confused emotions. Finally she couldn't stand it any longer. Dammit, she was going to bid!

"Five hundred dollars, going one, going twice—"

"Seven hundred dollars," Grace shouted suddenly, leaping to her feet. She just hoped the animal shelter would agree to accept payments because she didn't have that kind of money in her checking account. Seven hundred dollars would put her over the maximum on her credit card, too. She couldn't go a penny higher.

There was a moment of stunned silence. "Seven hundred dollars. Do we have seven hundred and fifty dollars?"

Grace didn't dare look in Cliff's direction.

"Seven hundred and fifty dollars," Margaret White said, and her voice trembled as if to say this was far higher than she'd intended.

"Go for eight hundred," Olivia encouraged, tugging at Grace's sleeve.

Grace sat back down. "No... I shouldn't have bid when I did. I don't have seven hundred dollars, let alone eight."

"Seven hundred and fifty dollars, going once, going twice, going—"

"Eight hundred dollars," Olivia shouted, startling Grace.

Barry pointed the gavel at Margaret White, who shook her head.

"Sold for eight hundred dollars." He punctuated the sale with a bang of the gavel.

Barry Stokes's eyes narrowed as he peered into the audience. He placed both hands on the sides of the podium and leaned forward. "Is that you, Judge Lockhart?" He didn't wait for an answer. "Last I heard, you and Jack Griffin were married. Now, don't tell me there's trouble between you newlyweds already?"

"Nope," Olivia called back. "And I want Cliff *and* the dog. The dog's for my daughter, Justine, and the bachelor is an early birthday gift for my best friend, Grace Sherman."

"I can't let you do that," Grace insisted in a harsh whisper.

"You can and you will," Olivia said out of the side of her mouth. "Besides, Maryellen and Kelly went in with me." She smiled. "My orders were to bid on Cliff if you didn't—or if you dropped out. I had to bid on the dog, anyway. Justine met her backstage and fell in love with her."

"Maryellen and Kelly?"

"Me, too," Charlotte whispered, leaning across the table. "I did it for Cliff as much as you. As far as I'm concerned, you two belong together."

Grace did look in Cliff's direction then. Although he was relatively close, she couldn't gauge his reaction. All she could hope was that he agreed with Charlotte.

Twenty-Seven

Rachel Pendergast was sweeping up her station at Get Nailed. Her appointments were finished for the day, and she was ready to head back to her house. When the phone rang, she looked up to make sure Valerie, the receptionist, was around to answer it. She wasn't, but Tracey grabbed it and then held up the receiver for Rachel.

"It's that little girl," Tracey said. "You cut her hair not too long ago."

"Jolene?"

Tracey shrugged. "She says she has to talk to you."

"All right." Rachel walked over to the desk, where Tracey handed her the phone. She'd been meaning to call Jolene, anyway. "This is Rachel," she said cheerfully.

"You didn't bid on my dad." Jolene sounded as though she was on the verge of tears. "I thought you were going to bid on him at the Dog and Bachelor Auction."

"Hello, Jolene," Rachel said.

"Hi." Her voice was small and sad.

"I think your dad's very nice, but I don't think he's ready for another relationship. Remember how we talked about that? You said you need another mommy and I asked if I could be your friend instead."

"I remember."

"Is your dad there?"

"Yes, but he's in the other room and he doesn't know I'm calling you."

"Let me talk to him, okay?"

"Okay—only I want to know if you bought a dog and a bachelor at the auction."

"I did, but my friend Karen took the dog. And I'm not meeting my bachelor until Friday night."

"Who is he?"

"Well, I don't know much about him except that his name is Nathan Olsen and he's in the Navy."

"Is he in love with you?"

She wished! "No, I barely had a chance to talk to him." After the auction, the restaurant had been chaos. Rachel had only a few minutes to speak to Nate before it was time to leave.

"Oh."

"How about if you and I get together next week?"

"Will you paint my fingernails again?" Jolene asked eagerly.

"If you like."

"Can we talk about girl things?"

"Sure."

Jolene sounded happier now. "I'll get my dad."

A moment later, Bruce got on the line. "Jolene phoned you?" he said in a curt voice.

"Yes, but I was planning to get in touch, anyway. She saved me the phone call. I'd enjoy spending another afternoon with Jolene. It seemed to do her good—and me, too, for that matter."

He hesitated. "I thought you might bid for me."

Now Bruce was going to harass her about that, too? "You told me you weren't interested in dating," she said as calmly as she could.

"I'm not—just forget it, all right?"

Gladly! Talk about mixed messages. Bruce couldn't have made his feelings any more obvious; he didn't want to get involved—and that was fine with Rachel. "Can I see Jolene?"

"Yeah, sure, that would be great."

They set up a day and time, and Rachel hung up the phone, more confused than ever. She must have had a puzzled expression on her face because Terri came over to stare at her.

"What's with you?" she asked, one hand on her ample hip. "You look like a feather would bowl you over."

"Bruce Peyton wants to know why I didn't bid on him." Even as she spoke, she was astounded that he'd brought it up.

"Don't worry about it," Terri advised. "You choose your own dates."

Rachel made an effort to put Bruce out of her mind. As far as she could tell, he was a lost cause, and she was through with throwing her life away on dead-end relationships.

That Friday night, Rachel arrived at The Lighthouse ten minutes before she was meeting Nate. She sat on the bench in the foyer, waiting nervously.

She wasn't quite sure why she'd plunked down her hard-earned tip money on him. She suspected it was because the auction was almost over and she hadn't made a single bid. Terri and Jane had both bid on men, but had lost out each time. Rachel felt that at least one of the girls from the salon should "score a bachelor," as Terri put it.

But by the end of the evening, Terri was more interested in drinking Fuzzy Navels than bidding on dogs and bachelors. Jane figured she might as well save her money. And

Karen Redfern, a married friend from high school, just wanted a dog.

Then Nate Olsen had stepped onto the platform, walking a lovely and self-assured little spaniel who was destined to become Karen's dog. Nate was Navy and apparently a warrant officer, whatever that was. Although Cedar Cove was basically a Navy town, being so close to the Bremerton shipyard, Rachel wasn't too familiar with military life.

She tried to remember what she could of their brief conversation that night. He was a nice-looking man. Trim, tall with dark hair and pleasant features. She'd especially noticed his piercing blue eyes.

Rachel glanced up, and those very eyes were looking at her. He was dressed casually in slacks and a short-sleeve shirt and nothing like she remembered. Tall, yes, but blond, not dark-haired. The eyes she had right—a brilliant blue. The nice-looking part was accurate, too, as far as it went. Only she didn't recall him being *this* attractive. And so young. He must be just out of high school. Good grief, she'd robbed the cradle!

Swallowing her disappointment, she stood, came forward and held out her hand. "Rachel Pendergast, in case you'd forgotten." Her surname was easy to mispronounce.

"Hello, Rachel." His smile dazzled her.

On second glance, he might still be *in* high school. She had to restrain herself not to ask if he was over eighteen. Oh, no, what had she gotten herself into now?

"I can seat you immediately," the hostess said, carrying two menus. "If you'll follow me."

Rachel was convinced every eye in the room was on Nate and her. He was so young. How could she have missed that at the auction? It must've been awfully dark in there—or those margaritas had impaired her vision. Well, thirty wasn't that old, but at the moment she felt like she could be his mother.

They were shown to a table by the window with a lovely view. Early-evening sunlight played on the sparkling water and the lighthouse in the distance looked downright romantic. Rachel studied the menu and tried hard to think of a conversation-starter. Working with the public she'd never found that a problem. Now she felt distracted, as if she'd become a spectacle for the entire restaurant, sitting there with her date. Her young date. The guy she'd had to buy at an auction.

Finally she couldn't bear not knowing. Lowering the menu she gazed across the table at Nate. "I'm sorry if this is rude, but I need to ask you something. Just how old are you?"

Nate gave her a charming grin. "Twenty-five."

Instantly she felt worlds better. Five years—that wasn't so bad.

"How old are you?" he asked in return.

"Thirty. I've never been married, no kids and I'm a nail tech—which used to be called a manicurist—and hair stylist."

"Never been married, either. No kids." He added hesitantly, "In fairness, I should tell you I'm seeing someone else."

Okay, so she'd blown three hundred bucks on another woman's boyfriend, but that didn't mean she couldn't enjoy the evening. Still, she wondered why he'd agreed to be part of the auction if he was seriously involved with someone.

"What about you?"

Rachel shook her head. She hadn't gone to the Dog and Bachelor Auction because she had a burning desire to donate to charity. Well, she did have a soft spot in her heart for animals. But that hadn't been the driving force that had led her to the auction.

"I didn't mean to mislead you."

"You didn't." He was certainly straightforward enough. Almost the first words out of his mouth had been to inform her that there was someone in his life. They talked briefly about this woman, who was from his hometown of Fresno.

They both had the night's special, grilled Pacific salmon, which was as delicious as she'd expected it to be. Although she was technically supposed to pick up the bill, Nate insisted on paying. He escorted her back to her car and then surprised her by asking, "Would you like to walk along the waterfront?"

She agreed, and they strolled side by side toward the marina. He walked with his hands clasped behind his back.

"What's going on over there?" he asked, nodding toward the Waterfront Park.

"I don't know. Want to check it out?"

He shrugged. "Sure."

It didn't take Rachel long to realize it was a wedding party. From a distance they watched the bride and groom exchange their vows. The sun had begun to set, sinking in the glorious blue sky, casting shreds of sunlight across the surface of the water.

For reasons she didn't understand, tears filled Rachel's eyes. If Nate saw, she'd be mortified. She barely knew this man and she'd probably never see him again. Really, there was no reason for them to continue dating. He was involved. She was older. This was it, the beginning and the end of their relationship.

"Rachel?"

He turned her to face him, hands on her shoulders. His frown told her he was both confused and concerned. "What's wrong?"

"I always cry at weddings," she said apologetically, making light of her tears. They fell unrestrained down her face. And yet she wasn't actually a woman prone to tears. Not until that moment, at any rate. Lowering her head, she wiped them from her cheeks, furious with herself. "Sorry."

Without a word, Nate took her in his arms. He didn't say anything, didn't make soothing sounds. All he did was hold her. It'd been so long since a man had touched her with such gentleness, such kindness, that she wasn't sure how to respond.

Looking up at him was a mistake because she discovered that he was staring at her. Then they were kissing. Rachel had no idea who kissed whom first. One thing quickly became evident: What Nate lacked in years he made up for in experience. The man knew how to kiss. His mouth moved seductively over hers in a way that sent goose bumps shooting down her arms. He kissed her as if she were the sweetest thing he'd ever known; he savored her, relished her.

When he lifted his mouth from hers, Rachel's knees were so weak she felt she might collapse in a puddle at his feet. Caught in the sheer wonder of their kiss, she kept her eyes closed.

Thankfully he didn't apologize or make excuses, nor did he seem inclined to explain.

When she felt her composure returning, Rachel opened her eyes. "That was…very nice."

"Yes, it was," Nate whispered, then cleared his throat. "I'll walk you to your car now."

She nodded. One again she'd been wrong; she hadn't wasted her money. His kiss was worth every penny of the three hundred dollars she'd paid for this evening's date.

All the way back to the restaurant, Nate remained speechless. So did she. The truth was, Rachel didn't know what to say.

She led him to her car and got out her keys. "I had a lovely evening, Nate. Thank you."

He placed his palm against her cheek. "I did, too. But I don't think it's a good idea to see each other again."

"I understand."

"The thing is, I want to."

Rachel was careful not to meet his eyes, otherwise he'd be able to tell how badly she wanted to see him, too. "Life is like that sometimes."

"I know." His words were filled with regret.

She climbed into her car and backed out of her parking spot, hands a little shaky on the steering wheel. Driving off, she saw Nate in her rearview mirror. He stood in the lot, just stood there, watching her. Rachel felt a sense of melancholy as she pulled onto the street and headed home.

Apparently romance just wasn't for her. Damn, damn, damn!

Twenty-Eight

Maryellen's assistant, Lois Habbersmith, arrived at the Harbor Street Gallery shortly before noon. Grateful for the opportunity to escape, Maryellen grabbed the unopened letter and stuffed it in her skirt pocket.

"Lois, I'm going for a walk."

The other woman glanced at her in surprise. Maryellen almost always ate at her desk, grabbing a bite here and there between customers. With the summer half over, tourist traffic was at its peak and the gallery staff was often swamped.

"I won't be long," Maryellen promised. All she needed was a few uninterrupted minutes to read the letter. The moment she'd seen the return address, she'd known. The older couple who'd visited two weeks earlier and asked so many questions about Jon were his father and stepmother. Maryellen had suspected it then. Now she was sure.

As soon as she could, Maryellen left the gallery and walked down to the waterfront park. She slipped onto a picnic bench at the gazebo, removing the envelope from her pocket. For a long moment she stared at it, deciding that the sharply slanted handwriting was more likely a man's than a woman's.

Maryellen's hand trembled as she ripped open the envelope and pulled out a single typed sheet. Glancing at the first paragraph, she could see she'd been correct; his father *was* the one who'd written.

Dear Maryellen,

I imagine it must be a shock to receive this letter. When Marion and I got your very welcome note regarding Jon and your marriage, we were thrilled to have some way of reaching our son. You see, Jon is all we have left in the world that matters. My wife and I made a mistake, a terrible mistake, but we've paid for our sins many times over. Your letter, informing us of your marriage to Jon and the birth of our granddaughter, gave us hope. In all these years, Jon hasn't once acknowledged our letters. He's made it very clear that he desires no contact with his family.

Once we learned that he'd moved onto the piece of land inherited from his grandfather, I drove to Cedar Cove, hoping to talk to him. Marion doesn't know this, but my son threw me off the property. He refused to speak to me. Seeing the hate in him unnerved me, and I decided then that I would bide my time. I prayed that somehow, some way, he'd find his way to forgiveness. Until your letter, I'd almost given up hope.

As you probably guessed, Marion and I were the people who stopped by the art gallery a couple of weeks back. We couldn't get over our good fortune when we met you. In your previous letter, you'd failed to mention that you worked at the gallery.

Your love for Jon is unmistakable. We thank God he found you and thank God you cared enough to contact us.

Marion and I have often talked about this and are at our wits' end. We have tried every way we know to reach our son, to beg his forgiveness and to bridge this gap of pain and bitterness. You are our only hope. Would you act as a mediator? It would mean the world to us if you'd talk to Jon on our behalf. He won't listen to us but I know he'll listen to you.

Thank you.

Joseph Bowman

P.S. Marion and I did visit the restaurant you mentioned and were impressed by Jon's work. I never realized how gifted my son is. Again I have you to thank for that discovery.

Maryellen read the letter a second time. Jon's father was asking the impossible of her. Her husband was adamant that he wanted nothing to do with his parents. As far as he was concerned, they were no longer part of his life.

As she drove home with Katie at the end of the day, Maryellen was still thinking about what his parents had asked her to do. Although she knew how Jon felt about his family, she'd gone behind his back. In fact, she'd done so against his express wishes. She hated that she'd started her marriage with an act of deception. If Jon ever learned she'd contacted his parents and mailed them photos of Katie, he might never forgive her. She'd taken a terrible risk already and now they were asking her to take another—a risk that was potentially even more disastrous. Maryellen longed to help, but she was afraid of what that would do to her marriage.

When she pulled into the yard, Jon walked out to the car to meet her and Katie. He smiled as he opened the back passenger door and released their daughter from her baby seat.

Eager to escape the confines of the restrictive carrier, Katie gleefully flung out her arms and cooed at her father.

"Hi, honey," he said, kissing Maryellen briefly.

"Hi."

Despite her efforts to appear normal, her voice must have betrayed her, because Jon looked back over his shoulder. "Something wrong?"

Maryellen smiled at her husband and shook her head. He continued into the house, carrying Katie, while she followed with the diaper bag. In that instant she knew she couldn't jeopardize their secure world. They were happy. She couldn't afford to compromise their happiness, not Jon's or Katie's—or her own.

They ate on the deck that evening. Jon had poached halibut in wine and lemon, and topped it with a fresh tomato-and-basil salsa. The advantages of having a husband who was a marvelous chef were too numerous to count.

"All right," Jon said, leaning against the wooden slats of his deck chair. "That does it."

"What?" His determined words startled her.

"Turn in your two-week notice."

"Jon…"

"You clearly want to be at home."

"Jon, I can't, not yet." While it was true she wanted to be home with Katie and begin working as Jon's manager, she couldn't leave the gallery in the lurch. The owners had always been wonderful to her; not only that, she couldn't abandon Lois during the busiest time of the year.

"You're miserable," Jon said. Holding his wineglass, he frowned at her, and Maryellen tried to reassure him with a warm, loving smile.

"We were jammed this afternoon," she said, "and I hardly had a moment to myself, but that's how this business goes.

Anyway, Lois isn't ready to assume management responsibilities yet. She's learning, though."

"You aren't getting enough sleep."

"Would you stop trying to fix everything?" Although she meant to use a teasing tone, the remark came out sounding sharp and impatient.

Jon frowned more heavily. "That's what I thought a husband did."

"I'm sorry…." Maryellen didn't dare mention the reason for her mood. Standing, she collected the dirty dishes. "I guess I'm just out of sorts."

Jon brightened suddenly. "Could that mean what I think it means?"

Maryellen shook her head. She certainly hadn't had any problem getting pregnant with Katie and although they weren't using birth control, she wasn't pregnant with their second child yet.

Jon took her news with a light shrug. "I guess we'll just have to try harder. I want to experience this next pregnancy from the beginning."

Maryellen was heartened by the prospect. "That sounds good to me."

While Jon dealt with bills and paperwork downstairs, Maryellen bathed Katie and gently rocked her to sleep. She brushed the soft curls from her daughter's forehead, holding her securely as Katie sucked energetically at her bottle. Maryellen had gradually stopped breastfeeding the month before and now gave Katie a bottle early in the morning and at bedtime.

Maryellen glanced around the nursery, which always brought her a fresh surge of pleasure. Jon had drawn and painted a series of wild animals along the walls, creating for each a background that reflected its natural habitat.

Jon's parents would never see this. Maryellen closed her eyes, discouraged by the hopelessness of the situation.

"The object is to put Katie to sleep, not you," Jon whispered.

She opened her eyes to see him standing in the doorway, arms crossed. He wasn't a handsome man by conventional standards, but the sight of him stirred her emotions and her senses.

"It's been a long day," she said.

"Then take a hot bath, relax, go to bed," Jon advised.

"I've got the dishes."

"I already took care of that."

"But Jon…" she protested. Their agreement was that when he cooked, she'd do the cleanup afterward. "You spoil me."

He grinned at that. "I want to spoil you. I love you, Maryellen. You and Katie are my family. You're everything to me."

Instead of bringing joy, his words fell on her like stones. It was her own fault, her own guilt; she'd interfered where she had no right to and cruelly raised his parents' hopes.

"I think I will go to bed early tonight," Maryellen said and placed Katie in her crib. She covered her with a light blanket, waiting to be sure their little girl was truly asleep before she silently left the room.

Jon took the empty bottle downstairs while Maryellen ran hot water into the tub. She scented it with lavender salts, then got in and sank into the soothing bath.

Her decision was made. She had no choice. She'd answer Joseph Bowman's letter the next day and tell him he was asking the impossible of her. She'd mail photos of Katie from time to time and keep his parents updated, but that was all she could promise. She'd also ask them not to contact her again.

The water had cooled by the time Maryellen stepped out of the tub. She dressed in a cotton nightie and a short robe.

Jon was watching television and she sat on the sofa beside him, nestling gratefully in his arms.

"Feel better?" he asked, kissing the top of her head.

"Yes."

"Good."

"Remember what you were saying earlier?" she murmured, tilting her head and kissing the side of his jaw.

"About what?"

"Me getting pregnant."

She felt his mouth relax into a smile. "I remember that quite distinctly."

Maryellen glanced toward the television. "How interested are you in that program?"

"I can catch a rerun." He used the remote to turn off the TV, then kissed her as if he'd been waiting all day for just this moment.

Maryellen entwined her arms around his neck and opened her mouth to his exploration. Jon moaned softly, sliding his hand inside the folds of her robe, and sought her breast. Between soft kisses intermingled with lengthier ones, Maryellen reached over to snap off the lamp. They stood and began to walk toward the stairs, but didn't make it to the first step before he gathered her close and kissed her once more.

"I don't think I'll ever get tired of making love to you." He kissed the vulnerable hollow of her throat.

"I should hope not." Maryellen laughed and, walking backward, advanced one step up from him, circling his ear with her tongue. Jon groaned and she moved up an additional step. He followed, his hand again seeking her breasts. This time it was Maryellen who released a soft sigh of pleasure. If they didn't hurry up these stairs, they'd never make it to the bedroom.

As they kissed, Maryellen tore at his shirt while he re-moved her robe.

"Jon," she whispered, her voice thick with passion. They were halfway up the stairs, both partially undressed.

Still one step below her, he hugged her waist and buried his face between the fullness of her breasts.

Maryellen could feel her knees weakening. Framing his face with both hands, she gazed directly into his eyes. "Come on. I think there's a more comfortable way of doing this. It's called a bed."

Jon grinned up at her and then, in one sweeping motion, he swung her into his arms and carried her up the remaining stairs. Giggling like teenagers, they fell onto the bed and into each other's embrace.

Twenty-Nine

"Who left the milk out overnight?" Bob demanded as Peggy walked into the kitchen early Tuesday morning.

Peggy poured coffee into her favorite mug. "Good morning to you too, sweetheart."

Bob scowled. "I ended up dumping the entire half gallon."

They both realized it could only have been Hannah. Peggy wished she knew what it was about the young woman that irritated her husband so much. Bob took offense at the slightest thing; the milk incident was a good example. Hannah had worked the late shift at the Pancake Palace and returned to the house some time after Bob and Peggy were asleep. Apparently she'd decided to drink a glass of milk before going to bed and forgotten to put the carton back in the refrigerator. Yes, it was a thoughtless act, but it wasn't catastrophic. Bob had leapt at the opportunity to shriek and howl with indignation. Enough was enough.

"Stop it this minute, Bob Beldon," Peggy said calmly after her first sip of coffee. "I'll mention it to Hannah, but she doesn't need you berating her." The girl was timid as it was, and one harsh word from Bob would destroy her.

"Does she think—"

"Bob." Peggy cut him off before he could wake Hannah with his ranting. "Aren't you meeting Pastor Dave this morning?" They had a standing golf date every Tuesday. Whether they played in the morning or the afternoon depended on the pastor's schedule.

Her husband looked at his watch, frowning. He nodded abruptly. "I'll be back before noon."

"Yes, dear," Peggy murmured as she headed for her chair in the living room. Each morning she took a few moments to meditate before beginning her day. In those moments, she organized her thoughts and made mental plans of what she hoped to accomplish. Bob was often reading from the AA Big Book, and she'd gotten into the habit of claiming a little peace and quiet for herself. It allowed her to start the day in a tranquil frame of mind.

Bob paused at the door that led to the patio. "You'll say something to Hannah, right?"

"Yes, dear."

He expelled his breath loudly enough for her to hear. "Don't patronize me, Peggy."

She didn't know what had set off her husband's foul mood, but assumed that whatever was bothering him would work its way out of his system before he finished his golf game. More than likely he'd come home at lunchtime apologetic and contrite.

A few minutes later, just after Peggy had settled into her morning routine, Hannah stepped quietly into the family room. Her hair fell in thin brown tendrils about her face, which was ashen. She bit her lower lip, hesitating as if she wasn't sure she should interrupt Peggy.

"You heard?" Peggy asked softly.

The young woman nodded. "I'm so sorry…. I didn't mean to leave out the milk."

Peggy tried to reassure her with a smile. "I know you didn't."

"I'll pick up another half gallon before I leave for work this afternoon."

"Don't worry about it." Peggy gestured for Hannah to sit across from her. The girl looked shaken and Peggy hoped to comfort her.

"Did you sleep well?" Peggy asked.

Hannah's nod was tentative. "My dad used to yell, too."

The last thing Hannah needed was for Bob to do the same. "Bob didn't mean anything by it."

"I…know. It's just that when I hear a man yell, especially one who's around my dad's age, it…affects me, you know?"

"Of course it does." Peggy's irritation with her husband rose.

"My father was an unhappy person most of my life."

Hannah rarely mentioned her father. Peggy didn't know whether that was because of her grief at his death or because her memories of his accident were too painful to talk about.

"Sometimes at night, when I was a little girl, I'd wake up to the sound of my father shouting."

Peggy felt a moment's shock—and a rush of pity for Hannah. Having lived with an alcoholic for years, she wondered if Max Russell drank, too. "Did your father have a drinking problem?"

Hannah shook her head. "Sometimes he drank too much, but it wasn't a problem. Not a bad one, anyway. Some days he was mean for no reason. He used to shout at Mom and me for the littlest things."

"I'm sorry."

"He wasn't a bad person, you know. I really loved my dad."

"Of course you did." Peggy wondered if Hannah fully understood what her father had experienced during the war.

"My mom stood by him through all the times we had to move and all the fights." Tears filled her eyes. "It's so wrong that she died, so wrong."

"You moved around a lot?"

Hannah needed a minute to compose herself. She swallowed visibly. "Dad was never able to hold down a job for long. He'd be fine for a while, and then he'd drift into this…dark place."

"Dark place?"

"That's what Mom called it. He'd be happy, and suddenly it would be like someone had turned off the lights. I could always tell when it happened. So could Mom. She'd ask me to go to my room and I would because I knew what was going to follow."

"What was that?" Peggy asked.

Hannah was silent for several minutes. "Nothing pleased him. The napkins had to be put on the table just so or he'd throw them on the floor. Dinners were a nightmare. Mom always did something wrong. The meat was tough, the vegetables were overcooked, the milk was too cold. Either the silverware wasn't properly lined up or the saltshaker wasn't full enough. Everything had to be perfect for Dad. Hard as she tried to please him, it was impossible. Dad found fault with the smallest thing."

This was much worse than Peggy had realized.

"We moved at least once a year. Dad would sometimes use other names, and I had to remember what my name was because he'd change it."

"Your dad used other names?"

Hannah's head snapped up. Her eyes widened. "I never told the sheriff that. Please don't mention it, all right? Dad hadn't done it in a long time and I was afraid that if Sheriff Davis found out, he'd think my dad was a criminal or something."

Peggy sighed, but she managed to swallow the exasperated response that sprang to her lips. It would've helped had the girl revealed this earlier. Apparently, there was still a great deal they didn't know about Maxwell Russell—including why he'd come to Cedar Cove. A chill raced down her spine. They'd been on edge ever since the night someone had followed Bob home, although nothing had happened since.

"My mother was a saint," Hannah whispered.

"She put up with your father's moods all those years?"

Hannah nodded. "Sometimes I'd find her sitting on her bed reading his letters. She said it helped her remember what he was like before the war."

Peggy understood why Tammy Russell had done that. Why she'd kept on hoping, and supporting her husband and—worst of all—putting up with his verbal abuse. She'd still loved him and wanted him to become, once again, the person he used to be. No matter how hopeless that desire.

Peggy understood because she'd done something very similar. She, too, had held on to memories of the past, letting them form her hopes for the future. Before joining Al-Anon, Peggy had tried to manipulate Bob into not drinking. She'd used pressure, guilt, punishment, anger and every other behavior she could think of. None of it had worked until she'd stepped aside, forcing Bob to deal with the consequences of his drinking. But through it all, Peggy had stood by her husband, just like Hannah's mother.

"Dad was in one of his dark moods when the car accident happened," Hannah whispered. "I wanted Mom to leave him, but she wouldn't. I had a job…. I could have supported the two of us, but she wouldn't do it."

"Oh, Hannah, I'm so sorry."

"I am, too…. Mom wasn't supposed to be in the car with him that day. But he was so angry and unreasonable and he demanded that she go with him and then he had the accident—and Mom was killed." Weeping openly now, she covered her face with both hands.

Peggy came out of her chair and wrapped her arms around Hannah's shoulders, murmuring soft, meaningless words of comfort.

"If only Mom hadn't gone that day, she'd be alive now."

"I know, I know," Peggy said.

"Dad was hurt so badly in the fire and Mom…didn't have a chance. I wanted to die then, too…but the accident changed Dad."

"In what way?"

Hannah lifted her head and rubbed the sleeve of her robe over her eyes. "He was calmer, less angry afterward."

"So he was easier to deal with?"

Hannah nodded. "I think Mom's death was what did it. He was lost without her. He went through so much pain, you know, and all the surgery, and…and for the first time in my life, I felt I had a father. He talked to me and called me his little girl and said he loved me. And then…and then he was murdered." She sniffled once.

Peggy could imagine what life had been like for Hannah. Until his accident, Maxwell Russell was a harsh, bitter man who often took his anger out on his wife and daughter. It was little wonder that Hannah vacillated between grief and guilt over the death of her father.

Thirty

Grace checked her watch for the third time in two minutes and used a deep-breathing method to calm her pounding heart. Cliff would be joining her at The Lighthouse any moment now and she was as nervous as if she were fifteen again, going out with a boy for the first time.

Tonight was their dinner date, the one Jack and Olivia, Charlotte, Maryellen, Jon, Kelly and Paul had bought at the Dog and Bachelor Auction. Her friends and family had forked out a whopping eight hundred dollars to arrange this, and Grace was determined to enjoy it. If only she could calm her nerves.

She smiled as she thought of Justine's equally expensive new dog, a golden retriever like her own Buttercup. According to Olivia, the whole family adored Sadie.

And speaking of Olivia... Grace had arrived at the restaurant fifteen minutes early in order to escape her best friend.

Olivia had spent half the afternoon with her, discussing every detail of Grace's outfit, hair and makeup. Anyone might think Grace was entering a beauty pageant or attending the Academy Awards! Olivia's interest was well-intentioned, but Grace had reached her limit, so she'd left the house early and gone straight to the restaurant.

When Cliff did appear, it was all Grace could do not to jump up from her chair. Swallowing suddenly became difficult. Cliff saw her then and walked across the room, his steps slow and measured, as if he felt resigned to this evening but not pleased.

With a stiff smile, she extended her hand to him in a rather formal greeting. "Thank you for being my dinner date," she said, hoping her words were intelligible.

"I should be the one thanking you," he said as he pulled out his chair. "It's good for my ego." He paused, apparently reconsidering his comment. "Now that I think about it, wasn't it Olivia who placed the bid?"

Grace nodded. No one had paid more for a bachelor; Cliff should feel flattered by that. "Justine and Seth love the dog, and apparently Leif's quite taken with her, too."

Cliff smiled at the mention of the dog. She smiled back, more naturally this time. Cliff couldn't seem to take his eyes off her, which made her heart beat faster. Cliff looked more attractive than ever, and she gazed at him avidly. She saw him so seldom these days and when she did, it was a painful reminder of what might have been.

"How are you?" he asked, his voice low.

This wasn't a casual question; she sensed that the moment the words left his lips. He wanted the truth.

"Lonely."

Cliff lowered his eyes, although she'd noticed the worried expression he tried to hide.

His silence unsettled her, so she hurried to fill it. "I have a kitten now." She offered this information eagerly, not just to appease his concern about her loneliness but because she knew he'd be interested. "I got him at the Farmers' Market a month ago. I was doing one of my volunteer stints, and he was the last one left. I named him Sherlock because he's constantly digging into things."

Cliff grinned boyishly and his worried look fled. "What does Buttercup think of him?"

"Actually she's happy to have the company. The two of them sleep together. I have pictures." She reached for her purse and pulled out several photos of her animals, as well as her grandchildren.

"Sherlock," Cliff murmured as he studied the first photograph. "The name suits him."

"I thought so, too," Grace said. "The others are of Tyler and Katie. I refuse to let you escape without updating you on my grandchildren."

His grin deepened. "I just happened to bring a picture of April." He slid one hand into his inside pocket and brought out a photograph.

The waitress came for their drink order, and Cliff suggested a bottle of Washington State Chardonnay. Grace nodded at his choice.

She stared at the picture of Cliff's daughter and granddaughter. She'd met Lisa last Thanksgiving, when they'd flown to Maryland to be with his family. Cliff and his daughter were especially close.

After exchanging photographs, Grace looked at him. "And you?" she asked. "How are you, Cliff?"

"Busy." He didn't respond seriously the way she had; his reply was flippant.

She dropped her eyes in an effort to recover. In one word, he'd let her know she wasn't allowed access to his world anymore. Despite his earlier sincerity, that brief glimpse of caring and concern, this dinner wasn't going to change anything. Olivia and her daughters might as well have saved their money.

Grace's spirits plummeted.

The waitress returned with their wine, uncorked it and poured a sample for Cliff to approve. After the tasting ritual and the pouring, she took their dinner order.

"I'm off to Texas to buy a horse next week," Cliff said as if it was now his turn to fill the ensuing silence. "I hope so, anyway. I've had my eye on a particular quarter horse stud for quite some time." He continued talking about the qualities that made this horse important to him. Most of what he said was beyond Grace's slim knowledge of breeding and horses, but she listened attentively.

"Well, I hope your trip is successful," she said when he'd finished.

Silence again. Their whole evening seemed destined to crawl from one awkward silence to another.

"I feel I can leave the ranch now that I have Cal," he added.

"How is Cal?" she asked. Their conversations never used to be stilted like this. They always had a million things to say to each other, sharing pieces of their lives. Except for what she hadn't shared—her Internet romance with Will Jefferson. Would she never be forgiven for that?

Cliff started to chuckle, and she glanced up.

"What?" Grace smiled, too, although she didn't know why.

"The Dog and Bachelor Auction," he said. "Do you remember that Corrie McAfee bid on him for her daughter?"

"Oh—yes." She'd found it difficult to keep track of which bachelor had gone to whom, although she'd received personal satisfaction from Stan Lockhart's fate. She noticed he hadn't been around town as much lately and in Grace's opinion, that was a good thing.

"Did you read in the paper that thanks to Charlotte and

Ben, the town's worked out a deal with Puget Sound Medical and Dental to set up a clinic?"

"Speaking of Ben…" Grace closed her mouth.

"What about him?"

She shook her head, angry with herself. "Nothing… It's just that Olivia is worried about her mother and Ben."

"Why?"

"Well, no one ever heard of him until recently."

"No one had ever heard of me, either," Cliff reminded her.

"But you aren't dating a judge's mother. In her line of work, Olivia has reason to be suspicious—but I'm sure nothing will turn up."

Cliff picked up his water glass. "Nothing will turn up where?"

In her uneasiness, Grace had already said more than she'd intended. "Forget I said that." She hoped he'd simply put this conversation out of his mind.

No such luck. "Olivia's having a background check done on Ben?" he asked bluntly.

Grace felt dreadful, but she couldn't lie to Cliff again. "Yes. Please don't say anything."

"You think I'd tell *Charlotte* this?"

That made her feel even worse, since Charlotte and Cliff were friends. "No…Cliff, please, I should never have said anything."

He hesitated, then agreed with a shrug. "All right."

"I heard Linnette McAfee's been hired to work at the clinic." It was an obvious change of topic, but he accepted it readily enough and she sighed with relief.

"That's what I understand."

"Since Linnette's moving to town, maybe she'll have a chance to get to know Cal." She gestured vaguely. "More than she could on just a dinner date."

232 *Debbie Macomber*

"Cal's a good man," Cliff said casually. "I think getting out more will do him a world of good."

"I like him," Grace said although her contact with Cliff's trainer had been limited to a few short conversations. His shyness and stuttering made communication difficult. Instinctively, she wanted to finish his sentences, to spare him the embarrassment of stammering. But on honest reflection, she supposed her impulse to help had as much to do with her own discomfort as with any perceptions of his.

"He likes you, too."

Instantly Grace's heart lightened.

The waitress approached the table with their first course, shrimp bisque for Grace and Caesar salad for Cliff.

"How are Maryellen and Jon?" he asked as he set down his wineglass.

"Happy and deeply in love." In that instant, Grace wished she could withdraw the words. Talking about love was painful; under different circumstances, those words could have referred to them. "They hope to have another child," she said after a pause.

"What about Kelly and Paul?"

Grace sighed. "Kelly still isn't pregnant and she's starting to get worried."

"I'm sure there's no cause for concern."

Grace agreed, and they lapsed into silence again.

The waitress returned to collect their first-course dishes and bring their entrées. She also refilled their wine. Grace took her first taste of sole topped with a creamy shrimp sauce, and Cliff cut into his prime rib. They both made enthusiastic noises about the excellence of the food.

By the time they'd finished their meals, Grace accepted that nothing she said or did had the power to reach Cliff. So she stopped trying. There seemed little point in more small talk about the town or doings at the library or plans for his ranch; that left them with nothing much to say.

After dinner, Grace drove home, even more lonely and depressed. It was hard not to weep and to berate herself—and humbling to admit she'd failed yet again. Olivia and the girls had paid that money for one reason and one reason only. They'd hoped, as Grace had, that Cliff would have a change of heart. He hadn't.

The phone rang at eight o'clock on Saturday morning. Grace was feeding her animals. Automatically she scooped up the receiver and held it to her ear while she doled out the dog and cat food.

"Well?" Olivia demanded. "How'd it go?"

Grace resisted the urge to break into tears. "We had a very nice dinner, but that's it."

"Don't be so sure."

"Olivia," Grace said with an exaggerated sigh. "I was there. I might as well have had dinner with a statue." She switched the phone to her other ear. "The closest I got to seeing the old Cliff was when he showed me a picture of Lisa and her little girl."

"Give him time."

"No." Grace was surprised by the strength of her conviction. "I'm not going to grovel. I made a mistake. I'm sorry. If Cliff Harding can't get past that, then it's his problem, not mine."

Olivia was silent for a long moment. "Grace is that really you?" she finally asked.

"Of course it's me."

"You sound so…emotionally healthy."

"I'm glad you approve."

"I do," Olivia assured her.

Obviously Cliff had chosen to get on with his life—minus Grace. She would let him and at the same time get on with hers.

With a renewed sense of vigor, she weeded and watered her small garden.

At noon, a florist's delivery van parked outside her house. Pulling off her garden gloves, Grace walked around front, wondering if the driver had mistaken the address.

"Ms. Grace Sherman?" The deliveryman held a beautiful bouquet of roses, carnations and irises in a variety of pastel shades.

"Yes." Grace vaguely recognized the young man but couldn't remember his name.

"These are for you." He handed her the vase, turned and left.

Grace carried the arrangement into the house and removed the card. As she read the message, tears clouded her eyes. *Life has a funny way of hitting you between the eyes, doesn't it? Thank you for dinner. Cliff.*

She didn't know what he meant but she felt this must be a good sign.

Thirty-One

Ben pushed the grocery cart down the produce aisle while Charlotte sorted through the celery. The grocer tended to put the older bunches in front.

"Do you want me to pick up a few bananas?" Ben asked.

"Please." Bananas were the perfect fruit for people their age, in Charlotte's view.

Ben added a small bunch to their cart. He was so helpful in so many ways. Clyde hadn't been the kind of husband who enjoyed shopping, but Ben was more than patient about doing errands. He seemed to enjoy spending time with her. If she had a hair appointment, he drove her there and either waited in the salon or strolled through the mall. After all these years on her own, such open affection—such romantic gestures—were foreign to her. When she was with Ben she felt…treasured. True, his attention had taken a bit of adjustment on her part, since she was so used to her own company. Charlotte slowly pushed the cart ahead, watching as Ben struck up a conversation with the produce manager.

"Charlotte!"

Hearing her name, Charlotte turned to find her son-in-law strolling toward her, wearing a big grin.

"Don't tell me Olivia's got you doing the shopping," Charlotte said.

Jack chuckled and shook his head. "I came to pick up a few things she refuses to buy. Whoever heard of a house without potato chips and pretzels? Olivia said if I was going to eat fat-laden carbohydrates, I'd have to buy them myself. So here I am." He looked over his shoulder, as if he half expected his wife to follow him inside and criticize his food choices. "I don't suppose you know where they keep the microwave popcorn, do you?"

"Aisle five," Charlotte said. "I like the extra-butter kind myself."

"I'm with you," Jack muttered. "I don't know what it is with Olivia these days."

"How do you mean?"

"First she's on this low-fat kick. Okay, I admit I could lose a few pounds, but I looked like this when she married me and it was good enough for her then."

Charlotte knew her daughter's fitness plan had caused arguments between them, but she'd assumed things were better now. Olivia hadn't complained in weeks.

"Then there's this thing with Ben," he added, scowling. "It's ridiculous."

Charlotte stared at him, certain she'd misunderstood. "What thing with Ben?" she demanded. Thankfully Ben was still busy talking.

Jack looked like a man who'd inadvertently stumbled into a swampful of alligators. "Ah…that was a slip of the tongue. Forget it."

"I most certainly will not forget it," Charlotte slammed a bunch of celery into her cart. "You'd better tell me *everything*."

"Ah…" Jack faltered. "I, uh…" Finally he gave a resigned sigh. "Olivia's having Roy do a background check on him," he said grimly.

"What?" Charlotte felt her blood pressure rise.

"Charlotte?" Ben asked, joining her. He looked at Jack. "Is there a problem?"

"None whatsoever," Charlotte snapped. She smiled at Ben, who'd been nothing but a gentleman from the moment they met. Now her own daughter had gone behind her back and was having the man she loved investigated. Evidently Olivia had no faith in her intelligence or her judgment. Anyone who spent time with Ben would know he was the gentlest, sweetest, most wonderful man on earth. Olivia had met him many times. How could she *do* this? Why? The outrage turned to pain and her eyes filled with tears.

"I…I can't believe Olivia would do something like this," she said, trying to hide the hurt her daughter had caused her. Sniffling, she turned away.

Ben was at her side immediately. He slid his arm around her protectively. "What's going on here, Charlotte?"

Charlotte shouldn't have done it, but she told him. "Olivia's having you investigated. I don't know why she'd do such a thing, but apparently she has. Jack just let it slip…."

Ben's mouth thinned with irritation. "Rest assured there's nothing to find."

"Damn my big mouth," Jack muttered. "It isn't all Olivia, you know."

"What do you mean by that?" Charlotte was rigid with anger now.

"Maybe I should just pay for these potato chips and be on my way," Jack suggested, obviously uncomfortable.

"Like hell!"

Ben's eyes widened. Charlotte was not a woman who

used that kind of language. In fact, she was shocked herself. But there were times when nothing less than a swearword would do. "You tell me the whole story and I mean *now,* Jack Griffin."

Jack shifted his weight from one foot to the other. "Olivia's going to kill me for this."

"Why? She's guiltier than you are."

Jack shrugged. "You don't know Olivia the way I do."

"She's my daughter—if I don't end up disowning her over this." Charlotte had trouble accepting what her daughter had done. "Who put her up to it?" She leaned forward and glared fiercely at her son-in-law. "You, Jack? Was it you?"

He shook his head, raising his hand in a gesture of surrender. "Not me. Will."

This was even worse than she could've imagined. "You've got to be kidding."

Jack cast Ben an apologetic look.

That just made Charlotte angrier. "How dare he?" she sputtered.

"Now, Charlotte," Ben said in a soothing voice. "Let's talk about this calmly."

But Charlotte was in no mood to be mollified. "You tell my daughter that I'm in love with Ben Rhodes and I have every intention of marrying him."

Head down, Jack nodded like a repentant child.

"On second thought, I'll tell her myself."

Jack raised his index finger. "When you do speak to Olivia, I'd appreciate if you gave me a few minutes' notice first."

Ben chuckled, but Charlotte found nothing humorous in the situation. "Then consider yourself warned."

Jack clearly felt terrible, but she didn't blame him for her daughter's actions. No, she knew exactly who was responsible for this...this *insult.*

Despite his protest, Charlotte left Ben to deal with the groceries while she marched over to the courthouse. It was a good three-block walk and uphill at that, but Charlotte's indignation drove her all three of those blocks without a single pause. By the time she got there, however, she was winded. Charlotte leaned against one of the courthouse pillars and placed her hand over her pounding heart, taking slow, deep breaths.

Her expression must have conveyed her mood because no one stopped her or delayed her with conversation. After clearing security, she plowed through the crowded hallway to her daughter's courtroom. She shoved open the door decisively and...

Wouldn't you know it, the room was empty. All the better. Charlotte didn't need any witnesses to this confrontation. She went directly to Olivia's chambers. The mahogany door was closed; she knocked once and opened it without waiting for permission.

Olivia sat at her desk and glanced up, a look of curiosity on her face. "Mother?"

"How dare you, Olivia Lockhart Griffin! How dare you!" Fresh tears welled in her eyes.

Olivia set down her pen and gestured for her mother to take a seat. Charlotte hesitated, then collapsed into the visitor's chair. She reached for her lace handkerchief, tucked in the sleeve of her blouse, and dabbed at the corners of her eyes. "I'm utterly ashamed that my own children would do anything so underhanded and deceitful. How could you do this to me—and to Ben? What's he ever done to you?"

Olivia sighed heavily. "Mom, I can tell you're upset."

"Upset? You don't know the half of it!"

Olivia raised her hand. "I don't blame you. I'm sorry, but Will and I felt that in this day and age one can't be too careful."

"You don't think I'm capable of judging a man's character? Ben is decent and kind and...and honorable."

"I wanted to believe that, too, but he has no family in the area."

"No family in the area?" Charlotte repeated. "What's that supposed to mean?"

"Well, what brought him to Cedar Cove?" Olivia briefly closed her eyes, as if she were embarrassed and ashamed, as well she should be. "Will felt, and I agree, that we needed some verification of the things Ben told you."

"Like what?"

"That he's who he says he is, for one thing."

"He is!" Charlotte insisted.

"I know that now, but until I asked Roy to check into Ben's background, we only had his word for it that he's a retired admiral. He just seemed...too good to be true."

Charlotte continued to dab at her eyes and sniffle as the anger was replaced by tears. "I'm so embarrassed. I love Ben."

"Oh, Mother..."

"Don't you *Oh, Mother* me! I'm old enough to know my own feelings and I refuse to listen to a lecture from you." Using the edge of the desk to support herself, she rose to her feet. "Save those condescending little speeches for the courtroom." Having delivered her own insult–though minor in comparison–Charlotte started out of the room.

"Mom, please."

Charlotte stopped in front of the closed door, her back to her daughter.

"I'm sorry," Olivia whispered. "You're right. I should never have done this."

"It's a bit late for sorry, don't you think?"

"Yes." Again Olivia sighed. "I know how you feel about Ben."

"I sincerely doubt that, but go on." She turned to face Olivia now, her expression blank. "His sons aren't having *me* investigated."

Olivia let the comment slide.

"Ben's a companion and a friend and—"

Charlotte didn't know why she bothered. She shook her head, astonished by her own daughter's insensitivity. "I can't believe I'm hearing this from someone who was so recently married. Look at me, Olivia," she commanded, "and listen well. I'm in love. For the first time since your father died, I feel truly alive again. I wake up every morning with a sense of joy because I know that at some point during the day I'll be with Ben."

Olivia closed her eyes again, as if gathering her thoughts. "Mom, I understand what you're saying. It's the same with Jack and me." She opened her eyes, gazing straight at Charlotte.

"How would you feel if I'd had *him* investigated?"

Olivia leaned forward and braced her hands on her desk. "It wouldn't have mattered. I love Jack, and he's got nothing to hide from me."

"And you think Ben has?"

"That's just it—I didn't know."

"And now you do?"

Olivia nodded. "Roy mailed me the report last week. I sent off a copy to Will, telling him we can both rest assured that Ben Rhodes is everything he said he was."

There was a knock at the door. Olivia checked her watch and frowned. "Come in."

To Charlotte's complete shock, Ben opened the door and stepped into the chamber. Both women stared at him, although neither seemed to know what to say. For her part, Charlotte was mortified. She wanted to apologize, to ask his forgiveness on her children's behalf, but her throat closed up at the sight of him.

Olivia recovered first. "Please come in, Ben," she said. "I believe there's been a slight misunderstanding."

"That's what you're calling this?" Charlotte cried.

Olivia threw her mother a silencing look. "Would you care to sit down?"

"Unfortunately," Charlotte said, standing up and entwining her arm with Ben's, "we have to be going."

"Now, Charlotte," Ben countered. "I think it would be best if we talked this out."

"I agree," Olivia said quickly. She focused her attention on Ben. "If I've offended you, Ben, I apologize."

"If?" Charlotte shook her head. She'd always been so proud of Olivia, her daughter the judge. For the first time in longer than she could remember, she had the urge to send Olivia to her room without dinner.

"I love your mother, Olivia," Ben said boldly. "I know you do, too. We have more in common than you realize."

Olivia offered him a tentative smile. "I can see that you're good company for each other."

"Olivia, you're not listening. Ben and I are in *love*."

Her daughter stared at her.

"What I think your mother is trying to tell you," Ben said, "is that I've asked Charlotte to be my wife and she's agreed."

Olivia's gaze veered from Charlotte to Ben. "You're asking my permission to marry my mother?"

"No," Charlotte said, looking up at Ben. "We're getting married with or without your approval."

"I see," Olivia managed. She sank back into her fancy leather chair and apparently had nothing more to say.

Thirty-Two

The alarm buzzed and Cecilia opened one eye, peering at the clock radio on her nightstand. The digital readout told her it was six o'clock and time to get up. She groaned inwardly. It couldn't be six already. She felt as if she'd just gotten to sleep.

It'd been like this when she was pregnant with Allison, too. She'd felt as if she could've slept for days at a time. What made it worse now was that Ian didn't go on duty until the afternoon, so she was the only one who had to get up this early.

The minute she lifted her head from the pillow waves of nausea battered her. Moaning, she laid her head down again and closed her eyes, praying this would pass. Bolting up, covering her mouth, she raced into the bathroom just in time to empty her stomach into the toilet bowl. Still gagging, she closed her eyes again, hoping the worst of it was over.

Blindly she reached for a washcloth draped over the edge of the sink.

"I'll get that for you." Ian rinsed the cloth, wrung it out then handed it to Cecilia.

She patted the cool cloth against her face, straightened and tried to smile.

"Good morning," her husband said softly.

"Hi," she managed to respond as she wiped her mouth.

"Were you sick like this with Allison, too?"

Cecilia nodded. It was the first time he'd asked. They hadn't been married during the initial months of her pregnancy, and she'd never mentioned her problems with morning sickness. By the time they were married, the nausea had passed.

"Was it this bad?"

She nodded again. "Every morning. Until my third month."

Ian sank onto the edge of the bathtub. "Is there anything I can do?" He sounded almost guilty, as if he were personally responsible for her discomfort.

Cecilia moved to his side. "Love me," she whispered. Their relationship had been so strained since he'd learned about the pregnancy, and even before, when he knew she wanted to get pregnant. He was trying to accept this baby, but he treated her with a kind of wariness, as though he was afraid to touch her.

"I do love you," Ian said.

She turned away, and Ian put his arms around her and touched his forehead against her back. "You never told me, you know?" he protested.

"Never told you I was so sick every morning with Allison?" Cecilia asked. "Is that what you mean?" She pressed her hand over his and moved his palm to her flat stomach and held it there. "Would it have made any difference if you'd known?"

"I hear you every morning," he whispered. "You run in here and heave your guts out."

"The doctor says I should eat a soda cracker when I first wake up."

He kissed her neck, his lips lingering for a moment. "Then why don't you?"

"No time. I open my eyes and it's all I can do to make it to the bathroom."

"They can't give you a drug?"

"I won't take anything." She had with Allison and, although the physicians had repeatedly assured her that Allison's heart defect had nothing to do with the pills she'd taken for morning sickness, Cecilia couldn't completely believe it. True or not, she wasn't taking any chances with this pregnancy.

Ian sighed as if he'd give anything for her not to be pregnant. It broke her heart, but she refused to show her pain. She knew that when the baby came, Ian would love his son or daughter with the same intensity that he already loved Allison. He wouldn't be able to stop himself. Until then she'd be patient.

"Stay home today," he urged.

"And waste a sick day?" She couldn't do that. In the months to come she might need them. Besides, with Ian leaving for work in a few hours, it didn't make sense.

"Take a vacation day then."

"Why?" She turned to face him.

"Because I can't stand the thought of you going to work sick."

Little did he know that she had to pull off the road nearly every morning to vomit. "I go to work sick most days." Today wouldn't be any different. "Mr. Cox relies on me, and besides, Allison is coming by this afternoon."

Ian stiffened.

"Mr. Cox's teenage daughter," Cecilia reminded him.

"I know who you meant."

"She's a good kid, and now that her parents are back together, she's doing really well in school."

Ian's shoulders rose as he expelled a breath. "I wonder if the Coxes knew the hell their daughter would put them through when they decided to have a baby."

Despite her upset stomach, Cecilia laughed and stroked her husband's thick hair. "Babies don't come with guarantees. They grow up and turn into teenagers. When the time comes, we'll deal with it." Bending forward she kissed him on the lips. "I'm sorry, honey, but I have to get ready for work."

He grumbled for form's sake, then went back to bed while she dressed.

Cecilia put on her makeup and packed a lunch, although the sight of food made her stomach lurch. But by noon she'd be fine and her appetite would return and she'd need that lunch.

Ian appeared to be sound asleep when she left the duplex. Munching on soda crackers as she drove, Cecilia made it all the way to the office without a single emergency stop. This was progress.

According to the Navy doctor, her due date was the first week of May. May fifth. Allison had been born in June. Cecilia had gone into labor on a beautiful summer afternoon, but the perfection of the day hadn't augured a happy event. Being alone had been terrifying, even more so after her baby's birth.

Forcefully Cecilia turned her thoughts away from her first pregnancy. This time everything would be different. This time Ian would be with her and their baby would be born healthy.

Mr. Cox was already in the office when Cecilia arrived. After a few minutes of their usual easy chat, she settled at her desk and immediately began her work. The nausea almost always abated by nine. The first hour of the morning was the worst and odd though it seemed, she felt sick some afternoons once she got home. The second bout was always less intense than the first.

At noon Mary Lou, the receptionist, came into her office. "You have a visitor," she announced.

"I do?" This was unexpected. "Who is it?"

Mary Lou grinned. "Why don't you come and see?"

Cecilia walked to the front of the office and there stood Ian with a small bouquet of flowers. "Ian!" she cried. "What are you doing here?"

"I thought we'd go to lunch, if that's okay?"

"Of course it's okay. Don't you have to work this afternoon?"

"I do, but I've got time to take my wife to lunch."

She was so pleased to see him, it didn't matter one little bit that she'd brought her lunch.

They got sandwiches and drinks at the Potbelly Deli and walked to the Waterfront Park, where they chose a relatively secluded picnic table.

"I have something for you," he said as she unpacked their lunch.

Ian reached inside his pocket and brought out a plain gold cross on a chain. "I want you to wear this, all right?"

Cecilia was stunned. "Ian, it's beautiful. Thank you."

He walked over to where she was sitting and placed it around her neck and secured the clasp.

"I haven't forgotten our anniversary or anything, have I?" she teased.

"Nope."

"Any special reason you're giving me a gift?"

He shrugged and tried unsuccessfully to hide a smile. He sat back on the picnic bench and unwrapped his veggie-and-cream-cheese croissant. "You're having my baby. Isn't that reason enough?"

Tears rose in Cecilia's eyes. Because of the pregnancy, all her hormones were out of control; the smallest thing set her off. Not that this was small. No, his gift, his acknowledgement of her pregnancy, was the most moving and important moment they'd shared in months. She waved her hand in front of her face, blinking rapidly.

"You're crying?" Ian sounded surprised. "I thought this would make you happy."

"I *am* happy."

"So why are you crying?"

Then she was laughing, almost hysterically—weeping and laughing at the same time. "Because I'm having a baby, silly."

"Oh." Ian took a bite of his sandwich.

"And I love my husband."

He grinned. "Who loves his wife and his baby."

Cecilia cried all the harder then.

"Honey, don't cry. Please."

"It's just that I was so afraid you didn't. Love us, I mean." She sobbed, hiccupped and curled her fingers around the small cross. "Everything's going to be just fine this time, Ian."

His smile slowly disappeared. "I'm trying to believe that."

"I know you are. I'll do everything I can—and I *feel* it *will* be fine, but there are no guarantees."

That was one thing Cecilia understood.

Thirty-Three

Bob Beldon glanced at the menu in the bowling alley's small restaurant, although it wasn't necessary. He knew what he wanted. Two eggs over easy, bacon, cooked crisp, and two pieces of sourdough toast with strawberry jam if they had it. For two-fifty it was the best buy in town.

The waitress strolled past and without asking, filled his coffee cup. "You waiting on someone, hon?"

Bob nodded. The instant he did, Roy McAfee stepped into the crowded restaurant.

"Right on time," Bob commented as Roy slid into the booth across from him.

"Have you ordered?"

"Not yet."

Pad in hand, the waitress returned, filled Roy's mug and stood waiting for their order. Bob went first. Roy asked for a short stack of pancakes. The woman sauntered off and barked the order to the cook.

"What's up?" Roy asked. Bob had called him last night to arrange this meeting.

"Peggy told me something interesting the other day.

I've spoken to Troy Davis, but I wanted to get your opinion, too."

"Sure. What is it?"

"Seems Peggy and Hannah had a little heart-to-heart."

"Did you learn anything?"

"Yes." Bob added sugar and cream, then stirred his coffee. "Hannah let it slip that her father sometimes used false names. Peggy asked her about it, and I gather that through the years Max had amassed a whole slew of names and identifications."

Roy's eyebrows lifted. "It didn't occur to her to bring this up earlier?"

"Apparently not."

Bob reviewed what had led up to this confession. "She left the milk out all night and I got a little upset because it spoiled. After I went to play golf, Hannah came out of her bedroom and started talking to Peggy. From the way she described it, life with her father was no bed of roses, for her or her mother."

"She's never said anything negative about him before, has she?"

Bob needed to think about that. He shrugged. "Not that I can remember. It's like she's been living in a fantasy world. In the beginning she painted a picture of the three of them skipping through the years as happy as can be. Turns out life wasn't quite as blissful as she let us believe."

"Makes sense, I guess," Roy said, cupping his mug with both hands. "She lost both parents within a short period. In tragic circumstances people tend to recall the good times instead of the bad."

Bob supposed his friend was right. "Didn't Troy ask her if she knew anything about her dad using fictitious names?"

"I'm sure he did. Did she explain why she lied?"

"Peggy asked her the same thing. Hannah claimed she was afraid that if anyone found out, there'd be trouble and she couldn't deal with it. From what she said—and didn't say—trouble seemed to follow Max wherever he went."

Frowning, Roy sipped his coffee. "Did she happen to mention any of the names he used? Or where he got the various pieces of ID?"

"No, but if Peggy asks, Hannah will probably tell her." Bob didn't think Hannah trusted him enough to confide that information, but she had a close relationship with his wife.

"Have Peggy ask her and I'll find out what I can. It might give us a lead."

Bob nodded. He'd hoped Roy would volunteer to do exactly that.

"Did Hannah know anything about the fake ID her father carried when he died?"

"She says she didn't."

Roy studied him. "Do you believe her?"

Bob had considered that question carefully and the fact was, he couldn't be sure. He wasn't especially fond of the girl and couldn't account for it, even though he had no real reason to dislike her. Peggy had taken to her fast enough, and heaven knew the young woman needed his wife's affection. Hannah's nervousness and her jittery manner made him uncomfortable. If Bob raised his voice even slightly, she cowered as if she expected him to pounce. Of course, what she'd told Peggy explained a great deal.

"Anyone following you these days?" Roy asked just as the waitress delivered their breakfasts.

"Not that I can tell. Nothing since that night, anyway. I'm beginning to wonder if I imagined it. But I know I didn't. Maybe it's not even connected to Max. Maybe it was some random wacko."

Roy poured hot maple syrup over his pancakes. "You sound disappointed."

"I am. It's ridiculous to live the way Peggy and I are living. I want this resolved, one way or another. I'm also thinking it's time we started taking guests again. This whole mess has cost us thousands of dollars." He took a gulp of coffee. "If someone was really after me, wouldn't he have done something by now?"

Roy nodded. "I tend to agree with you. If someone was going to make a move, it probably would've happened already."

Bob grunted agreement through a mouthful of toast and jam.

"On second thought—"

"Come on, Roy," Bob protested, not giving the other man a chance to finish.

"You want my advice? Then I'll give it to you, and seeing that it's free, you should appreciate my generosity."

"All right, all right." He broke the egg yolk with a corner of his toast. "Share your wisdom."

Roy grinned. "Only accept reservations from people who've stayed at the B and B before. People you know."

"In other words, turn down strangers who arrive in the middle of a dark and stormy night."

His friend chuckled. "You got that figured out."

Bob finished his breakfast and reached for his recently refilled mug. "I have a theory I want to bounce off you."

Roy relaxed, leaning against the back of the booth. "Shoot."

"You know everything—what happened in Nam, right?"

Roy nodded, his expression serious.

"You remember that I didn't have an easy time after the war. I did everything I could to bury the memories. I sought oblivion. It was bad for everyone, especially Peggy and the kids." He paused. "Outwardly Dan Sherman seemed to adjust to civilian life. That's what I assumed, anyway. I didn't see him for decades. And even when I moved back to Cedar Cove, we tended to avoid each other. So I didn't know he struggled with demons, too."

Roy waited while Bob sorted through his thoughts. "From what Hannah told Peggy, Max didn't cope with life after the war any better than I did."

"He drank?"

"Some, I gather, but I don't think that was his only problem. He pretty much became an obsessive-compulsive, although that wasn't the term Hannah used."

"Remember how neatly everything was packed inside his suitcase?"

Bob nodded. They'd all been struck by it.

"What are you thinking?" Roy pressed.

"When I came back from Nam, I realized that someday, some way, I'd have to pay for what happened in that village. If I've learned anything about life these fifty-odd years, it's that there's a symmetry to things." He lowered his voice. "I...took lives, and now it seems someone wants to take mine."

With the words out in the open, Bob felt better. He'd been thinking about this ever since Max's death, but hadn't found the courage to verbalize it.

"Go on," Roy urged.

"I think Dan realized this, too. He preferred to take his own life, choose his own time."

"I—"

"Hear me out," Bob insisted. "I wonder if it's possible that a family member of one of our...victims has hunted the four of us down. He might have confronted Dan, forced him to take matters into his own hands. For that matter, what else would send Max rushing to Cedar Cove? I think whoever's responsible is looking for revenge."

Roy considered his theory. "I don't know. It could be, but I doubt it."

"Why? Plenty of Vietnamese have immigrated to the United States since the war."

"I think it's a bit far-fetched to believe one of them has a vendetta against four American soldiers after all these years. Why wait until now?"

Bob shrugged. "I don't know." Roy could be right; this scenario was probably a fantasy, something he'd invented in his own desperation.

But nothing else made sense, either.

Thirty-Four

Walking into the mall parking lot on Friday evening, Rachel hummed an old Eagles song, trying to get her mind off her pathetic love life. Her one date with bachelor Nate Olsen had been exactly that. One date. One expensive date. It depressed her that she hadn't heard from him in the two weeks since.

Well, so be it; he'd told her he was involved with a girl back home. She could have accepted that, would have without a qualm, but then he had to go and ruin everything by kissing her. Damn, he was one good kisser. As far as Rachel was concerned, he should be arrested for possessing a lethal weapon—his lips. The way he'd kissed her had been so spectacular he'd left her in agony. That single kiss had made her ache even more for a romantic relationship.

Not that she was desperate. Not like some of the women who came into the shop. Only that morning she'd had a client, a working wife and mother, and listened to a litany of woes. The husband drank, was unemployed, hung around the house and was seeing another woman. The really crazy thing was that Rachel's client was mad at this jerk's girlfriend! In Rachel's opinion, this client was so worried about the trees, she didn't see the forest. Yeah, it was a cliché, but clichés were useful sometimes. Anyway, if her client did toss the bum out on the street where he belonged, he'd soon find some other woman to support him. Rachel had seen it happen again and again.

She was so involved in her thoughts that she almost didn't hear someone call her name.

"Rachel."

She turned around and discovered Bruce Peyton walking rapidly toward her. "Oh, hi," she said, her hands tightening around her car keys. Jolene had spent the previous Sunday at her place. She'd picked up the little girl and dropped her off four hours later, with only a minimal exchange of words with Bruce.

"Hi." He grinned. "Jolene had a really good time last Sunday."

"I did, too." They'd shopped, eaten pizza, watched videos, painted their toenails and chatted.

"She hasn't stopped talking about it."

"I'll give her a call soon and we'll bake those chocolate chip cookies I mentioned."

"She said something about that. I hope you'll send a few of them home with her."

"Of course." Rachel moved toward her car. It'd been a long week, and although she didn't have any special plans, she was eager to get home.

"Are you doing anything tonight?" Bruce asked.

"Not really. Did you want to drop Jolene off?"

"No, no," he said hurriedly and shook his head. "She's spending the night with a friend. It's a slumber party."

"What about this Sunday afternoon?"

"Sure, she'd like that."

"I'll see you then."

"Rachel." He stopped her again, looking decidedly uncomfortable. "Listen. Are you doing anything right now?"

"Now?" she repeated in a puzzled voice.

"I mean, do you have a dinner date or something like that?"

"No."

"Do you want to have dinner with me?"

Bruce was asking her out for dinner? "You and me? Like a date?"

He nodded. "Not an actual date, just dinner with a friend. If you want to. If you've got other plans, that's fine. No big deal. I was thinking of the Taco Shack."

Rachel hesitated.

"You've got plans." A defensive edge sharpened his words.

"No, it's just that I'm not sure this is a good idea."

"How come?"

She had a few questions of her own. "Why are you asking me? Why now?"

His head reared back as if her questions were unexpected. "Why not now? Jolene's with her friends for the night, and the truth is I'm not all that interested in my own company."

It certainly wasn't any fun to sit in a restaurant alone. Rachel knew that because she'd done it herself. And really, what would she do tonight other than watch TV and eat a microwave dinner? "All right."

A smile smoothed out the frown lines on his face. "That's great. Do you want to go with me or just meet there?"

Rachel looked at her car and decided to meet Bruce at the restaurant. With anyone else, she would've suggested she go home, shower and change clothes. But Bruce seemed to be in a rush. It was already nearly seven. Rachel had done a perm late in the afternoon, which had taken longer than she'd expected.

By the time she arrived at the Taco Shack, Bruce had

found a place at one of the picnic tables. The menu was posted on the wall above the counter. Rachel knew everything listed on it, since she stopped in at least once a week for takeout.

"What would you like?" Bruce asked when she joined him. He gazed up at the menu.

"I'd like the enchilada platter," she said. "One chicken and one cheese with extra salsa."

Bruce smiled, nodding. "That's my favorite, too, but I prefer two beef enchiladas." He removed his wallet from his back pocket as he approached the counter. The line wasn't too long for a Friday night, although Rachel suspected that in another ten or fifteen minutes, there'd be a wait for a table.

Bruce placed their order and carried a tray with sodas to their table. He unloaded their drinks and pulled out the chair across from her.

Rachel suddenly realized that Bruce had come to the mall just to see her, since he'd been walking in as she was walking out. Still, she found it hard to fathom that after all this time, after their numerous conversations, he actually wanted to take her to dinner.

"Jolene told me you went out on your date with the bachelor," he commented, then sipped his cola.

"I did."

"How'd it go?"

She shrugged and reached for her diet drink. "All right, I guess."

"Are you going to see him again?"

He was mighty curious about her time with Nate Olsen. "Probably not."

He studied her, frowning slightly. "You sound disappointed."

"I am. I like Nate. He's a little young for me, but—"

"He's younger than you are?"

Rachel burst out laughing, attracting the attention of those sitting close by. "You sound like my father."

"Sorry." He lowered his head as though embarrassed. "Forget I said anything."

Bruce seemed jealous, which shocked her. "Bruce?"

He looked up.

"What's all this about?"

"What do you mean?"

Rachel narrowed her eyes. "You know what I mean. Let's not play games, all right? When you came to the mall this evening, it wasn't because you had some errand. It was to seek me out, wasn't it?"

"Anything wrong with that?"

His defenses were up again, but so were hers. "Well, no, but why pretend otherwise? Just be honest, would you?"

He raised his hands, palms up. "I am being honest."

"To yourself, I mean," she elaborated.

The waitress, a high-school kid judging by her appearance, brought their enchilada platters. Rachel glanced down at hers and Bruce looked at his and in a perfectly synchronized movement, they switched plates.

"Do you mind if we eat before we continue this inquisition?"

She gave him a quick grin. Sliding her fork over the cheese enchilada, Rachel cut off her first bite. "I didn't intend to give you the third degree."

"The thing is," Bruce admitted between bites, "I'm not exactly sure why I asked you to dinner. I dropped Jolene off at her friend's house and here it was Friday night, and I didn't feel like spending the evening alone. I got a hankering for enchiladas, but I didn't want to take up an entire table just for myself."

"I usually order mine to go."

"I tried to think of someone who might be interested in

coming with me, and you were the first person who popped into my head. So I figured I'd see if you were available."

Rachel wasn't sure she should be flattered. At the moment she was too perplexed to figure it out.

"Jolene likes you a lot," Bruce said halfway through their meal.

Rachel was fond of the little girl, too, but her feelings about the child's father weren't quite as straightforward. Might as well find out what was going on here. "Do you like me, Bruce?" she asked bluntly.

"Obviously. I didn't stop to analyze it. I thought you might be available and I was right. I'm glad."

"I am, too," she said. "I was headed home for reruns of *NYPD Blue.*"

"You don't go bar-hopping with your friends?"

She shook her head. "I learned a long time ago that a bar isn't a good place to meet men." Not decent men, anyway, she amended to herself. Problem was, she didn't know *where* to meet men. She was wary of the Internet and not a club-joiner. She enjoyed crafts but she had yet to meet a single guy hanging out at a quilting bee.

"Have you had many serious relationships?"

She shrugged. "A few." She'd dated a guy back in her early twenties, discovered he was already married and dropped him instantly. That kind of grief she could live without. Ever since then, she'd been careful. Perhaps too careful… "What about you?"

His gaze fell to the table. "There's never been anyone but Stephanie."

The way he said his dead wife's name led Rachel to believe there never would be anyone else.

"I'd like to give this a shot," he said unexpectedly.

"This?"

"Us."

She opened her eyes wide. "Are you saying you'd like to go out with me?"

"Is that so surprising?"

Rachel needed a sip of her soda to ease the sudden dryness in her throat. "Frankly, yes."

"Would you be willing to see me now and again?"

"To what purpose?"

Bruce's mouth narrowed. "You're the kind of person who reads the last page of the book before you buy it, aren't you?"

That was precisely what she did. She laughed. "As a matter of fact, I do."

"I thought so. I don't know to what end. We can agree to play this by ear. Is that okay with you?"

"I guess." She considered it for a moment. "Tell me something first."

"All right."

"Asking me out tonight—did it have anything to do with Nate Olsen?"

The question seemed to trouble him, because he didn't answer immediately.

"Probably," he said at last.

At least he was honest about it.

"If he asks you out again, would you go?"

Now it was her turn to think matters over. "He won't. He's involved with someone else." She was gathering up her purse as she spoke.

"You're sidestepping the question," he said. He held the restaurant door for her and they walked into the parking lot.

"I know."

"Either you don't want to answer it or you're afraid to."

"I'd rather not discuss Nate, okay? You know," she said

confidentially, leaning toward him, "it would've been a perfectly wonderful night if he hadn't kissed me."

"Excuse me?"

"Never mind." She waved her hand dismissively. "It's too hard to explain."

"I guess I shouldn't try to kiss you, then."

"Don't be too hasty," Rachel said with a mischievous smile. He smiled back.

But he didn't kiss her. Standing in the well-lit parking area outside the restaurant, it would have been awkward to do anything more than exchange pleasantries.

"Do you still want Jolene to come over on Sunday?" Rachel asked.

"Sure. Can I see you then, too?"

Rachel nodded. Bruce opened her car door and she slid into the driver's seat. "Thank you for dinner."

"I'll give you a call sometime tomorrow afternoon."

"Okay."

Rachel pulled onto the highway and drove toward her own neighborhood, feeling more than a little confused. As soon as she got home, she saw that she had a telephone message.

Setting down her purse, she began to slip off her shoes and pushed the play button on her machine.

Nate Olsen's voice stopped her cold, one shoe off, one foot raised.

"Rachel, hi… I'm sorry I missed you." His words were followed by a short pause. "I'm still thinking about our dinner and was just wondering if you were, too. I'll talk to you later, okay?"

Thirty-Five

On the first Monday of August, Grace Sherman opened the library and posted the sign for the free movie that would be shown Saturday night. This was a new feature the library had begun in June. It'd been Grace's idea, and the popularity of the event had surprised and delighted her. She believed the library should be part of the community, that it should be responsive to people's needs and interests and attract patrons of all ages. She always chose a movie families could watch together. That often meant a classic; this week's was *The African Queen*.

Mondays were always busy and the morning passed quickly. Loretta Bailey returned to her desk and Grace realized her assistant was already back from lunch. It seemed she'd left only a few minutes ago. If Grace was going to have lunch, she had to take her turn now.

She reached into the bottom drawer for her purse and when she straightened she came face-to-face with Lisa Shore, Cliff Harding's daughter.

"Lisa," she said, recovering quickly. "What a pleasant surprise!"

"Hello, Grace."

She was a lovely young woman who reminded Grace of Cliff in a dozen different ways, although she didn't resemble him physically.

"I can't tell you how happy I am to find you. I took a chance coming into town like this, since I wasn't sure you'd be here. I felt we should talk." The look in her eyes implored Grace.

"What are you doing in Washington?" That was a silly question; she was visiting her father, of course. Grace had no idea how much Lisa knew about what had happened between her and Cliff.

"Rich and I are here to see Dad. I don't suppose you could squeeze in a quick lunch, could you?"

Grace struggled with her composure but managed to respond graciously. "Of course I can. Why don't we sit down for a few minutes first? How's April?"

"Growing by leaps and bounds," Lisa said, obviously proud of her daughter. "Dad and Rich took her into Seattle." She glanced away guiltily. "I told them I had a bad case of cramps, which is actually true, so they suggested I stay home. I wanted to come into town to see you—but that part I *didn't* share with my dad."

Grace understood how difficult it must've been for Lisa to mislead her father. What she had to say must be important.

Grace slung her purse over her shoulder, waved goodbye to Loretta and walked out of the library with Cliff's daughter.

They were barely out the door when Lisa spoke with a quiet intensity. "I just had to find out what went wrong between you and my dad."

Grace sighed, unsure whether or not she should be grateful that Cliff hadn't said anything to his daughter. Then again, maybe he had. It was clear that Lisa knew something, or that she sensed it, anyway.

They bought crab salad sandwiches—the Potbelly's special of the day—and sat down on a park bench near the marina. Tourists and locals alike strolled past.

"Dad won't tell me a thing," Lisa said as soon as they'd unwrapped their sandwiches. "All I know is that you're not seeing each other anymore."

Grace focused her attention on the boats gently bobbing in the marina. She simply couldn't look Lisa in the eye and explain what she'd done.

"Everything's my fault," Grace said, her voice trembling.

Her confession was followed by a short silence. "That's not what my dad said."

"He's wrong," Grace insisted. "I misled him—no, it's more than that, I deceived him." She refused to minimize her role in their separation. If not for her Internet relationship with Will, she suspected she'd be engaged or even married to Cliff by this time.

"How?"

Grace realized there was no help for it. Lisa had a right to know the truth. "I was seeing Cliff and at the same time involved with another man." There it was—the plain and horrible truth.

Lisa gasped. "But that's what my mother did. Now I understand…"

"I know, I know," Grace whispered. Her betrayal had been unforgivable in Cliff's eyes, a repeat of the betrayals he'd endured during his twenty-year marriage. Grace understood that she'd committed the one unpardonable sin and she accepted responsibility for it.

"Are you still involved with this other man?"

Grace shook her head. "It was quite a while ago."

"Then why aren't you seeing Dad?" Lisa finished the first half of her sandwich. Grace hadn't started hers; she put it in her bag to eat later.

She clasped her hands together. "Cliff won't have anything to do with me. I can deal with that now but it's taken me a long time to reach this point. You have a wonderful father, Lisa. Although we aren't part of each other's lives anymore, I'll always love him."

Lisa wrapped up the remaining half of her lunch, then crossed her arms and leaned back on the park bench. "I find that interesting, because Dad said almost those identical words to me. That he isn't part of your life anymore but he loves you."

"He loves me? He said that?"

"He was crazy about you when he brought you out to meet me last year—and he still is."

"But…"

"You have to understand my father. He's a complex man. He doesn't give his heart easily, nor does he stop loving someone just like that." She snapped her fingers for emphasis. "Look at all the chances he gave my mother."

Grace rejoiced at Lisa's words, but that joy was virtually shattered by Cliff's adamant response. He loved her, despite what she'd done, and yet he refused to forgive her.

"I've tried to reach him," Grace said in a low voice. "I was such a fool and when I discovered the other man intended to stay in his marriage…"

"He was married?"

Grace felt her face heat with humiliation. How easy it had been to rationalize her behavior at the time. Now, it mortified her even more. She had no excuse, no justification to offer, other than her own schoolgirl fantasies.

Lisa took her hand and squeezed it gently. "That explains why Dad's acting this way."

Grace hung her head. "You don't know how much I regret everything."

"I'm sure you do," Lisa said gently. "Still, you bid on my dad in the Dog and Bachelor Auction."

"How did you hear about that?" she asked, surprised that Lisa knew about the charity event.

"From Cal. How much did Dad cost you?"

"Your father was my birthday gift from my friends and my daughters, and they paid a whopping eight hundred dollars."

Lisa let out a low whistle.

"No one paid more for any bachelor."

Lisa grinned and gave her a thumbs-up. "Have you gone on your date already?"

Grace nodded and decided she didn't want to discuss their evening out. There really wasn't much to say, which was depressing in itself. "He sent me flowers afterward," she added sadly.

"That sounds like my dad. You're probably the only woman other than my mom and me he ever sent flowers to."

If Lisa was hoping to encourage her, she'd failed miserably.

"How long are you in town?" Grace asked, changing the subject.

"Only until tomorrow—that's why I had to speak to you this afternoon. It was now or never."

"I'm so glad you did."

Lisa sighed. "Dad has your picture in his bedroom. Did you know that?"

Grace shook her head.

"It's on his bedside table. He doesn't know I saw it, but I did. It's one of you and Midnight."

"He probably just forgot to take it down." Grace didn't want to get her hopes up, not after the disappointment of their dinner together, and the fact that she hadn't heard from him after receiving the flowers. "Or," she said deject-edly, "he's just very fond of that horse."

"Well, he is, but that's not why he kept the photo in his room."

Grace remembered the day Cliff had taken the picture. It'd been October and her first trip to his ranch. This was before he'd torn down the old barn and replaced it with the bigger, more modern stable. Cliff had given her the "grand tour," and as they walked around his property, he'd shared his vision of the ranch. He spoke of the improvements he hoped to make, the breeding programs he'd planned to institute. She hadn't understood a lot of it, but she'd felt his passion and his love for horses. That same day, he'd shown her his stallion and then stepped back to take her picture as she stood by the corral fence. At that very moment, Midnight had trotted toward her and poked his head over the top rung, curious about this stranger. Grace had turned to admire him and to stroke his sleek black neck. It was that image Cliff had captured on film. He'd shown her the snapshot, but he must have enlarged and framed it.

"I'm worried about my dad," Lisa confided.

"Why? How do you mean?"

"He's working too hard and he doesn't seem nearly as happy as he was the last time I saw him. I didn't notice it until this summer. He's been trying to hide it, but I know my father."

Grace wasn't nearly as happy, either. "I wish I could help, but there's nothing I can do."

"But there is, don't you see?" Lisa said with such fervor that tears sprang to her eyes. "Win him back, Grace. He loves you and you say you love him."

"I do!" Her love for him was real; she wanted Lisa to be-lieve that. "But he doesn't want to see me."

"That's not true. Even Cal said my father's a different per-son since you two broke up."

"What should I do?" Grace couldn't think of a single

thing she'd left unsaid or undone. Despite Cliff's repeated rejections, she'd tried again and again, until it became obvious nothing would change his mind about her.

"Fight for him," Lisa pleaded.

"Who do I fight? Cliff himself? How?"

"Wear him down," Lisa said. "Send him cards and letters."

"E-mails?" she suggested, eyebrows raised.

"Yes," Lisa cried. "Do something—anything—and don't give up until you've broken through his defenses." She twisted sideways on the bench, sitting so she could face Grace. "But only if you sincerely love my father."

"I do," Grace assured her again. "I truly do."

"I felt you must—but I had to find out. I had to know for sure."

The two women hugged. Grace was so moved by the honesty and hopefulness of Lisa's words, she felt like weeping. "Oh, Lisa, I can't thank you enough."

"Don't let me down."

"I won't," she promised.

That very night, Grace wrote Cliff a long e-mail. She began by thanking him for the flowers and then told him how much their dinner date had meant to her. She said, in simple, straightforward sentences, that she missed him and thought of him often.

When she finished she reread the e-mail. In it, she shared her concern for Kelly and Paul and their struggles to have a second child. She wrote humorously about her trials with Sherlock, and how the kitten refused to be ignored, describing the inventive ways he pestered her until Grace lavished attention on him. This was Grace's own less-than-subtle way of telling Cliff she wouldn't go away, either. Not this time.

The next afternoon, during lunch, Grace walked down to the corner drugstore and purchased a handful of cards, some clever, a couple that had dramatic photos of horses, and a few romantic ones.

As soon as she got home from work, she hurried to her computer, animals in tow, and logged on to the Internet, hoping for a response from Cliff. Her heart fell when she found none.

"Did you think this would be easy?" she said to Buttercup. Sherlock scratched at her leg until Grace lifted him onto her lap. She petted him with one hand and typed with the other while she considered the possibilities. It could be that Cliff had deleted the e-mail without even opening it. Or decided to ignore it. Or perhaps he hadn't checked his messages lately.

She e-mailed him a second time and mailed off a card the following morning. Eventually she'd wear him down, as Lisa had said. Eventually he'd see she wasn't going away. She loved Cliff. He was the best thing in her life and she refused to give him up.

Thirty-Six

"Bob!" Peggy shouted from the foot of the stairs. "Phone!"

Bob laid down the script of *Chicago*—he'd been memorizing his lines—and walked to the top of the stairs. He'd been so intent on the scene, he hadn't even heard the phone ring.

"Who is it?" he called.

Wearing her "Kiss the Cook" apron, Peggy stood there looking up at him. "He didn't say."

Mumbling under his breath, Bob hurried to the master bedroom and picked up the phone. "Hello," he muttered impatiently.

"Robert Beldon? This is Colonel Stewart Samuels."

The crisp military tones went through Bob like an electrical charge. It was the voice of a man he'd hoped never to hear from again. The voice of the man who'd led him into battle. A soldier who'd stood with him in a Southeast Asian jungle. Who'd saved his life and then, at the same moment, robbed him of it.

"Yes." With difficulty he managed to respond.

"I'm going to be in the Seattle area in the next few weeks. We need to talk."

It'd been more than thirty years since Bob had last spoken with his commanding officer. He could go another thirty years and it would suit him just fine. So far, the only person in contact with Samuels had been Troy Davis. Bob would've preferred to keep it that way.

The colonel continued, giving the details of his trip to the Pacific Northwest. Bob stood rigid until the other man announced he intended to visit Cedar Cove.

"Is that necessary?" Bob demanded. Seattle was too close for comfort, but having him in Cedar Cove for any length of time was downright intimidating.

"I believe it is. There's a matter between us that requires resolution."

How formal he sounded. So cold-blooded and hard.

"Two of our comrades are dead, one a suicide and one murdered," he said. "I'm hoping we can figure this out, once and for all. Agreed?"

"Yes, I—" Bob wasn't given a chance to finish his sentence.

"Good. I'll have my assistant make the arrangements."

Before Bob could comment further, the phone went dead. Bob stood there unseeing, his hand still on the receiver. After a moment, he replaced the phone and slowly, almost as if he were in a trance, walked down the stairs.

Peggy was in the kitchen with Hannah preparing dinner. When she saw him she abruptly stopped mashing the potatoes.

"Who was that on the phone?" she asked, walking toward him.

He stared at her, still numb inside. "Colonel Samuels."

"Stewart Samuels?" Hannah repeated, moving closer to Peggy.

Peggy glanced at Bob and then at Hannah. "What did he want?"

"He's coming to Cedar Cove."

Hannah let out a small cry of alarm and quickly covered her mouth. "What's he coming for, did he say?"

Peggy wrapped her arm around the young woman's shoulders. "Why are you so afraid?"

Bob wasn't sure if the question was directed at him or Hannah, but their guest was the one who answered.

"He's just so…military."

"I thought you were grateful to him for all his help with your father," Peggy said, looking at Hannah.

"I was…I am. Dad never would've gotten the medical care he needed if it hadn't been for Colonel Samuels. But…he frightens me." She trembled as if a chill had overtaken her.

"Bob?" His wife turned to him for answers he couldn't give. "What's going on?"

"I don't know. He said he had business in the area and felt we should talk. He asked that I set up a meeting with Roy and the sheriff, too."

Peggy frowned. "Does he think Dan Sherman's death and Hannah's father's are linked?"

"I don't know." But it was more than that. Samuels had indicated that he had business with him, too. Bob didn't want to see Stewart Samuels, didn't want to be reminded of the past, and yet it was there, confronting him, and had been every day since his return from Vietnam.

That night, unable to sleep, Bob lay in bed and stared at the ceiling. The digital clock by the telephone told him it was after two, but he was wide awake. Peggy slept peacefully beside him, oblivious to his anguish.

A full moon cast shadows on the walls. With the window open, the scent of the cove, of seawater, wafted toward him. He usually found it relaxing, but tonight his mind refused to let him rest. Every time he closed his eyes, all Bob could see, hear, taste and smell was Vietnam. Tension filled him. He didn't want to go back to those memories, didn't want to think about them, didn't want to feel.

Suddenly he heard the glass door off the kitchen sliding open. Bob's eyes widened with fear. He lay perfectly still as the noise drifted up the stairwell—a noise so slight Bob was sure he must be mistaken. As he strained to hear, the sound of muffled footsteps sent fear shooting through his veins. His adrenaline kicked in and he folded back the sheet and sat on the edge of the bed. Sweat broke out across his forehead. Leaning forward, he closed his eyes to listen more closely, hoping this was his imagination, after all. But the warnings Roy had given him rushed through his mind and he remembered the car that had followed him.

Bob looked around for something he could use to defend himself.

He found nothing. His golf clubs were in the garage, and the sturdiest thing he could take with him was a work boot.

Peggy stirred. Even in her slumber she must have sensed his fear. "What's wrong?" she whispered.

He brought his finger to his lips. "Someone's downstairs."

Bob felt his wife stiffen. She grabbed his arm and scrambled to a sitting position.

"How did they get in?"

"The patio door."

"Did you lock it?"

He nodded.

"Should we phone 911?" Peggy whispered.

A board creaked at the bottom of the stairs. Whoever was in the house was coming after them. It was too late to call the sheriff's office. Both Bob and Peggy froze in horror.

Nothing.

In that one beat of his heart, Bob acted. He refused to sit and wait. If someone had come to kill him, he wasn't going to die without putting up a hell of a fight. Roaring off the bed, he stormed out of the room.

Peggy cried out in an effort to stop him. Fumbling with the light, she lunged for the phone as Bob flew out of the bedroom and into the hallway. He smacked the light switch with his palm.

There, standing at the foot of the stairs, was Hannah. She gasped at the sight of him.

"Hannah!" he cried, furious with her for the scare she'd given him. "It's Hannah," he shouted back at his wife.

"What the hell are you doing sneaking around the house at this time of night?" he demanded.

She cowered before him, quaking, with her head bowed. Her long hair spilled over her shoulders and hid her face.

"Hannah, for heaven's sake, what are you doing?" Peggy ran down the stairs, tying her robe as she did.

"I…I–"

Bob found a folded sheet of paper on the downstairs hall carpet and leaned down to pick it up. A glance told him it was a farewell note from Hannah.

"I…I thought it was time for me to go," the young woman said, her voice so low it was hard to distinguish the words.

"But why would you sneak away in the middle of the night?" Peggy asked.

Hannah shrugged one shoulder.

Apparently the I-don't-know shrug was supposed to explain everything.

"I'm afraid!" she wailed. Seconds later, she broke into sobs.

Peggy immediately slipped an arm around Hannah and guided her into the kitchen. Hannah's suitcase sat in front of the patio door. Apparently she'd opened it and then decided to leave a note at the foot of the stairs.

Bob collapsed at the kitchen table, so badly shaken he couldn't stop trembling. He wanted to scream at Hannah, frighten her the way she'd frightened him, but he knew he dare not.

"Why are you afraid?" Peggy asked gently once she'd sat Hannah down. She filled the kettle and put it on the stove for tea.

"I don't know… I lost both my parents. I can't bear the thought of losing you, too."

"Why do you think you would?" Peggy asked quietly.

"Because…"

"Does this have to do with Colonel Samuels's visit?" Peggy asked next.

Hannah didn't answer, but Bob suspected Peggy was right. For her own reasons, their guest was as worried about the man's visit as he was himself.

Thirty-Seven

Olivia hung her robe in her chamber closet and collected her purse, preparing to leave the courthouse at the end of another long day. Couple after couple stood before her with their lives in shambles, eager to tear apart their homes, willing to destroy their children's security. Each partner seemed intent on proving that he or she was perfectly capable of surviving without the other. There was so much anger and bitterness, so much false pride. Some days she found her task of deciding the fate of these families overwhelming.

She glanced at her watch as she headed toward the parking lot. She was meeting Grace for dinner that evening. It was the first time since Olivia's marriage that Grace had asked to see her outside of their aerobics class on Wednesday night. They phoned each other fairly regularly and occasionally met at the Farmers' Market on Saturday mornings, but her marriage had changed their relationship. They were each discovering how to proceed under these new terms.

Olivia welcomed the opportunity to talk to her lifelong friend. There were things she wanted to discuss—things she couldn't really talk about with anyone else. And something in Grace's voice told her she had concerns of her own.

Once in her car, she drove the short distance between the courthouse and The Lighthouse restaurant. Her daughter and son-in-law had done a marvelous job and she was proud of their success. Still, as a mother, Olivia worried. Justine was working too hard; she was a young wife and mother, in addition to managing the restaurant's books and occasionally filling in as hostess.

As luck would have it, Justine was working that night. Her face brightened when she saw Olivia. "Hey, Mom," she said with a quick hug. "It's good to see you."

There'd been a time in the not-so-distant past when their relationship had been strained. Justine had been seeing a much older man, and she'd felt defensive and angry at the world. Olivia had wanted so much more for her. She knew that, in some ways, Justine was still grieving over the death of her twin—Jordan had died in a tragic accident at the age of 13. But Justine had finally come to a more peaceful acceptance. Olivia felt that was because of Seth. In fact, everything had changed when Justine fell in love with Seth Gunderson.

"Where's Jack?" Justine asked, looking past Olivia.

"The office, where else?" Jack worked far too many hours, but nothing Olivia said convinced him to delegate some of his tasks. He was involved in every aspect of the newspaper and loved his job. Now that *The Chronicle* had gone to five editions a week, his hours were even worse than they'd been before their marriage. They'd argued about it repeatedly, but Olivia supposed she might as well get used to having a part-time husband. Jack had promised this wouldn't last much longer, but she suspected nothing was going to change until he retired. *If* then…

Justine seated her at a window table, then returned to the front of the restaurant and talked to one of the waitresses. It was still early in the evening and the restaurant was only about a third full. As soon as she had someone to cover for her, she walked back to Olivia's table.

"Got a moment?" she asked.

"Of course." Grace wouldn't arrive for at least ten min-utes.

Her daughter pulled out the chair across from her. "How are things with Grandma?" she asked.

Olivia sighed and wondered how much of the story her daughter knew. Probably all of it. "We're talking again."

Justine smiled, obviously relieved. "Grandma's going to marry Ben, you know?"

Olivia was well aware of that. "She sent me a letter." It hurt that her own mother had written instead of telling her face-to-face. "I didn't mean to hurt her," she admitted. "Will and I had Ben investigated for her own protection, but our concern backfired."

"I know." At least Justine sounded sympathetic.

"Mom was upset about our lack of faith in her," Olivia said. She must have known instinctively how her mother would feel because she'd found it necessary to hide their in-quiries from Charlotte.

"What else did she say in her letter?"

"She said everyone deserves to be happy, regardless of age, and reminded me how pleased she was when I mar-ried Jack."

"She's right, you know," Justine murmured.

"Of course she is." Olivia had no disagreement with that. "She wants Will and me to treat Ben fairly and with respect. The same goes for his sons, of course." She frowned. "I don't think she's met them, though, at least not yet." With a quick shrug, she added, "Naturally I intend to respect Mom's wishes. It's been a bit difficult, thinking of my mother with another man, but it's her life and I want her to be happy."

Justine agreed. "I never said anything when you decided to marry Jack," her daughter said softly. "But deep down, I wanted you and Dad to get back together. I knew it would never work, but the little-girl part of me wanted my parents to love each other again."

Olivia was shocked to see tears in her daughter's eyes. Justine blinked furiously, as though embarrassed. "I still think about Jordan," she whispered.

"So do I."

Justine nodded. "Do you remember what day it is?"

Olivia realized with a jolt that she'd been so preoccupied with what was happening in her own life she'd let the date slip. On this day, August tenth, eighteen years ago, her son had drowned. Her entire life and those of her two surviving children had been divided by that date. The time before Jordan's death and the time after.

Wiping the tears from her face, Justine forced a smile. "I didn't mean to get all maudlin. Let's get back to Grandma, before we both dissolve."

Olivia agreed and swallowed past the lump in her throat. "I stopped at Mom's house earlier in the week and we hugged for the first time since she found out, and she forgave me. I'm sure she'll tell you herself, but they've set the date for their wedding."

Justine grinned sheepishly. "I know all about that. Grandma came in earlier today and booked the restaurant for the reception. She talked to Uncle Will, and he said he's coming out for the wedding."

Olivia was glad to know that, because she wanted to give Grace ample warning. When Will arrived, Olivia planned to have a long talk with her brother about his Internet relationship with her best friend. He'd taken advantage of Grace and betrayed his wife, Georgia. Olivia was furious whenever she thought about it.

"Hi, you two," Grace said, coming toward them. "Am I interrupting anything?"

"No, no," Justine said, rising gracefully from the chair. "I was keeping Mom company until you got here." She looked at Olivia, winked and was on her way.

Funny how just a few minutes with her daughter could mean so much. Olivia felt close to Justine and to her son James, too, and considered herself fortunate to have such wonderful children.

"Sorry I'm late," Grace said as she sat down across from Olivia. "It took forever to finish up at the library."

"Don't worry about it. Justine and I had a chance to talk and we don't get to do that nearly often enough."

"I know how she feels," Grace muttered. "You and I have barely any time together these days."

"I'm sorry," Olivia told her friend, and she was sincere. She *had* been neglecting their friendship, but was determined not to let that continue. "How's your week been?"

Grace shrugged noncommittally. "It was the best of times, it was the worst of times. What about you?"

Olivia smiled. "The same. Jack and I are still adjusting to living together, which hasn't been as easy as I'd hoped, but you know most of that." She'd complained often enough during their aerobic workouts on Wednesday nights. "Mom and I are talking now and she's forgiven me. Oh, and before I forget, Will's coming out for the wedding."

Grace paled visibly but didn't comment.

"Now, what's new with you?" Olivia asked.

To her surprise, Grace grabbed a tissue from her purse. "I have something to tell you, but I'll probably cry."

Olivia was aghast. "What is it?"

"Last week I got a letter from Mike Sherman, Dan's cousin in Oregon." She paused a moment to collect herself before continuing. "He wrote after Dan's death and we've talked a couple of times since, but this came out of the blue."

"What did?"

Grace nervously folded the edges of the linen napkin. "Mike really feels bad about this, but he thought it was time I knew that Dan borrowed thirteen thousand dollars from him. Apparently he asked for the loan a year or so before he vanished. Mike didn't want to say anything after Dan disappeared."

"Oh, no—he wants the money back now?"

Grace nodded. "He hated to ask, but he provided the paperwork and sure enough, that's Dan's signature on the promissory note. Mike said it's been over four years and he needs the money. He seems to think I got some life insurance settlement after Dan's body was discovered."

Olivia knew she hadn't. Her opinion of Grace's dead husband had never been high but she considered the fact that he'd burdened Grace with this loan unforgivable. Especially since Dan had to know that Grace wouldn't be able to collect on his life insurance if he committed suicide. Furthermore, the trailer he'd purchased with that money—the trailer he'd killed himself in—was a total loss.

"What are you going to do?"

Grace wadded the tissue in her hand. "What else can I do? I'm refinancing the house and paying him back the money, plus interest. It isn't Mike's fault that Dan chose to end his life."

"Aren't you going to tell him you didn't get any insurance money?"

"No." She shook her head. "It would only make him feel

worse about asking for the money back, and he doesn't deserve that. Frankly I'm grateful he waited as long as he did. If he'd hit me with this any sooner, I don't know how I would've dealt with it."

"What's that going to do to your finances?" Olivia knew things were already tight.

"I'll survive. I've made it through worse times than this."

"I know. Did you tell Sheriff Davis and Roy?"

"Roy said it was another piece of the puzzle falling into place," Grace told her. "He was the one who originally found out about the trailer. We always wondered where Dan got the money...."

Olivia was proud of Grace for taking this latest blow in stride and refusing to let circumstances overwhelm her. She was about to say that when Grace changed the subject.

"On a brighter note," she said with a big smile, "I heard from Cliff."

"You did?" Olivia knew her friend had made a concerted effort to win back the rancher.

Grace almost squirmed in her chair with excitement. "I have to tell you I'd nearly given up hope."

Olivia leaned toward her. "Well, don't keep me in suspense. Tell me what happened!"

"I drove out to his ranch with a batch of chocolate chip cookies ten days ago."

Olivia nodded approvingly. "And?"

"I wanted to weep with frustration when he wasn't home, but I talked to Cal and he was so encouraging. I like him a lot. He said he'd make sure Cliff knew I'd stopped by."

"I like Cal, too." Olivia had only met the trainer once and briefly, but she'd taken an instant liking to him. Although he was quiet, even solemn, she sensed a deep reserve of strength and character.

"Did Cliff call you?" Olivia leaned closer, eager to hear the details.

"No…actually I haven't talked to him yet." But Grace showed no sign of being discouraged. "I received an e-mail."

"What did he say?"

The waitress stepped up to the table, and Olivia realized they'd been so intent on their conversation they hadn't given any thought to food or drink. The young woman took their order for wine spritzers and left.

"Well?" Olivia pressed.

"Cliff thanked me for the cookies. He was very polite and he didn't write anything else, but, Olivia, I feel like there's a crack in this wall he's erected between us. He can't ignore me anymore. I won't let him."

"That's great!"

"I'm not fooling myself. I have a long way to go, but that one message cheered me so much I've been walking on air ever since."

"Have you sent him other messages?"

Grace nodded. "Every evening. I mail a card twice a week but Cal told me Cliff's started collecting the mail himself. When I don't send a card, I write an e-mail. He hasn't blocked my name, so I know he's getting those messages, too."

Olivia reached for her menu. For the first time in months, she had the feeling that everything was going to work out between Grace and Cliff Harding.

Thirty-Eight

Maryellen tucked the latest photograph of Katie into a business-size envelope, along with a short note to Jon's parents. She left it unaddressed and slipped the envelope in with the rest of the mail she planned to drop off at the post office Monday morning. She'd fill in the necessary information later rather than risk having Jon find an envelope with his parents' address.

He'd been gone since early morning, and Katie was napping. Maryellen rarely had uninterrupted time these days and she relished these private moments. She was pregnant again, although she hadn't said anything to Jon. All in due time. She wanted the situation to be perfect when she told him.

The front door opened and Maryellen walked out of the bedroom and looked over the upstairs railing. Jon was home earlier than she'd expected. He'd slipped out of the house before dawn for a day trip to the Olympic rain forest.

"Jon." She didn't bother to disguise her delight at having him home. When he'd left, he'd kissed her goodbye and whispered that he didn't know when he'd return.

Now, seeing her upstairs, he smiled, set aside his camera

equipment and hurried up the stairs, his energy undiminished despite his long day.

Maryellen met him at the top of the staircase and he threw his arms around her waist. "Where's Katie?"

"Asleep."

He wore that special smile of his. The one that told her he'd had a good reason for rushing home. "When did you put her to bed?"

Maryellen gave a coy shrug. "About half an hour ago. What do you have in mind?"

Jon's throaty chuckle sent shivers of excitement down her spine. "First things first. A shower, followed by something to eat and then…" He hesitated, still smiling, and brought her close. "On second thought, I'm not that hungry."

"Oh, honestly," she chided, but she relished his strong sexual appetite.

"Want to take a shower with me?" he whispered.

"Not now. You go, and I'll put together a couple of sandwiches. I wouldn't want you to faint from hunger."

He nuzzled the side of her neck. He held and touched her often. After so many years of living alone and avoiding relationships, Maryellen hadn't been entirely comfortable with his need for frequent physical contact. But the longer they were together, the more accustomed she became to his caresses—and the more she craved them.

"How did your day go?" he asked as he headed into the bedroom, still holding her by the hand.

"Actually it was pretty quiet. Katie and I spent some time outside and then I paid a few bills." For obvious reasons she didn't mention she'd also written a letter. "Did you get the photographs you wanted?"

Jon pulled her into the room with him. "I got several that should work, but the whole time I was trudging through the forest I kept thinking how much more enjoyable it would be if you and Katie were there, too." He released her hand, then sat on the edge of the bed to remove his shoes.

"I've got leftover meat loaf," she said.

Jon looked up at her blankly.

"For your sandwiches."

"Sure, whatever."

Maryellen grinned.

"What's so funny?" he growled, jumping up and catching her around the waist again. He brought her down onto the bed with him and rolled over, trapping her beneath him. He ran his fingers through her hair and his eyes softened as he gazed down at her.

In that moment, she felt his love so strongly she wanted to weep. Pregnancy made her overemotional; she remembered that from before.

Sliding her arms around her husband's neck, Maryellen drew his mouth down to hers. Their kisses were slow and tender. After Katie's birth—when Maryellen realized how much she'd come to love Jon—he'd refused to make love to her. Those months had been agonizing, but now it seemed there was no satisfying him—or her.

"Come into the shower with me," he said between tantalizing kisses.

"It's the middle of the afternoon."

"So?"

"Jon…" Her protests were growing weaker by the moment.

"All right, all right…I'll take my shower." He stood up and walked into the bathroom, shedding clothes as he did. The haze of desire didn't dissipate immediately. Maryellen got slowly off the bed and went downstairs. Times like this reminded her how fortunate she was to be loved by Jon Bowman.

She'd just finished making the meat loaf sandwiches when Jon skipped down the stairs, his shirt unbuttoned and his hair still wet from the shower. She froze when she saw that he was carrying the envelopes she'd left upstairs. Watching him carefully, she hoped he'd set them on the edge of the counter, where they usually put the mail, and leave it at that.

Her heart nearly stopped when the envelopes slipped from his hand and scattered across the floor. They both leaned down to retrieve them.

"I'll get these. Your lunch is ready," she said, hoping to distract him.

It didn't work. "Who's the letter to?" He straightened and held the unaddressed stamped envelope in his hand.

"A friend."

He stared at it for several seconds, frowning.

"Do you want your lunch or not?"

He ignored her question. "What friend?"

"No one important," she said, trying to squelch her panic.

"Maryellen, what friend?" he asked. "You look like a cat with feathers in your mouth. Is there something you're not telling me?"

"What's the big deal? Just someone who stopped by the gallery recently."

He studied her, eyes narrowed. "Do you mind if I take a look?" She knew he probably suspected another man; the truth was even worse.

She pressed her back against the counter, feeling her pulse hammer in her neck. She couldn't answer him.

"Maryellen?"

She turned away. "It's to your parents."

"What?" he exploded.

"Don't be angry," she pleaded, her eyes closed.

He was silent for so long she couldn't bear not knowing his thoughts. Tentatively she turned around, biting her lower lip, afraid her deception was about to destroy her happiness.

"What have you done?"

"I—"

"Is this the first time?"

She shook her head.

He groaned with frustration. "I told you how I felt about my family."

"I know…."

He clenched his fists. "And you decided you knew better? You felt it was your duty to go against my wishes?"

"I—"

"How did you know where to reach them?"

Maryellen took a calming breath. "I found their letters."

"Didn't I ask you to throw them out?"

"Yes—and I did." But until then, he'd kept the letters and that told her he still felt an attachment to his family.

"My father chose to offer me up as a sacrificial lamb. He betrayed me."

"He's so sorry, Jon. If only you'd talk to him, you'd see for yourself."

"Talk to him?" he shot back at her. "*Talk to him!* I spent seven years in hell because of my so-called father. I'll rot before I say one word to him again."

"You don't mean that! You can't have that much hatred in you."

"Obviously you don't know me as well as you think." He whirled around and dashed up the stairs.

Maryellen couldn't leave things as they were. She raced after him. "Please listen," she begged. "Your father isn't well. He's aged and he's frail and—"

Jon sat on the bed and jerked on his shoes. At her words, he grew still. "You've seen him?"

This was possibly a worse offense. She clasped her hands behind her and nodded. "They came into the gallery.... I didn't know who they were but your father wrote me afterward and asked me to act as a mediator between you."

"What did you tell him?" he demanded.

"I said no—all I did was mail them a letter to let them know about Katie and me and—"

"That's bad enough." He stood and brushed past her.

"Where are you going?"

Already halfway down the stairs, he glanced over his shoulder. "It seems I can't trust you, Maryellen."

"Can't we talk? Please don't do this."

Jon paused at the foot of the stairs. "There's nothing to talk about. I need time to think."

With that, he slammed out the door.

Brokenhearted, Maryellen slumped to the floor on her knees and hid her face in her hands. If Jon couldn't forgive his parents, it was unlikely he'd forgive her, either.

Thirty-Nine

"Peggy," Bob shouted from the patio. "We're going to be late." He wasn't that keen on attending church this morning and would've gladly stayed home had Peggy agreed. However, he knew better than to ask.

His wife hurried out the back door and cast him an exasperated look. "I tried to talk Hannah into coming to worship service with us, but she isn't interested."

As far as Bob was concerned, Hannah was the lucky one. Peggy didn't want to hear it, though, so he attempted to console her. "Until recently, I wasn't interested in church, either, remember?"

Peggy nodded and climbed into the passenger seat. "I don't know what it is with the two of you."

"The *two* of us?" For the most part, Bob avoided Hannah, which wasn't that difficult. She worked odd hours at her dishwashing job at the Pancake Palace. She was rarely home for dinner and frankly Bob preferred it that way. He'd tried to get along with their guest. Two or three times he'd made a genuine effort to talk to her, but Hannah was like a frightened rabbit; she ran for cover the moment Bob approached. He'd given up and settled for hoping that she'd leave soon.

Peggy frowned as she set her Bible in her lap. "Ever since Colonel Samuels phoned, both of you have been edgy and out of sorts."

"That's an exaggeration if I ever heard one," he snapped.

"No, it's not," Peggy insisted. "Hannah's as bad as you—worse, even. She isn't sleeping well. I know because I hear her roaming from room to room at all hours of the night. Of course, you're not much better."

Bob didn't argue; he'd been sleeping fitfully ever since the conversation with his former commanding officer. Bob couldn't explain the reason. It remained as much a mystery to him as his attitude toward Hannah. He'd tried to like the girl, but his negative reaction to her was visceral. Instinctive. Maybe it came from some innate revulsion to cringing, fearful personalities. He hated her clinginess with Peggy and he couldn't seem to change her aversion to him. Well, there was nothing he could do about it.

"Church would be a big help to Hannah." Clearly Peggy hadn't finished worrying about their guest's refusal to attend Sunday morning services.

Bob made a noncommittal grunt. The truth was, he'd had to drag himself out of bed that morning. Just as Peggy asserted, he hadn't been sleeping well. Little wonder. He was afraid that the moment he closed his eyes, the nightmare would return. It often struck without warning. Life would be perfectly agreeable if he could turn in for the night and have simple, pleasant dreams. Unpredictably he'd be thrust back into a Vietnamese jungle, gripped by terror. He hated every aspect of the dream. For years, he'd tried to drown out the noises of that day. The voices. Screaming. Shouting.

Crying. Alcohol had only made it worse. If anything, the voices had gotten louder.

Sobriety wasn't helping all that much, either. The voices continued in a low drone that he ignored as much as possible. He'd been fairly successful until Maxwell Russell died in his home. Then the nightmare came back full force.

"Thank you so much," Bob muttered under his breath, angry with his old army buddy.

"Did you say something?" Peggy asked.

Bob shook his head.

Peggy glared at him. "You're certainly in a fine mood this morning."

He didn't bother to answer because she was right. And feeling the way he did, the last place he wanted to be was church.

"Bob," Peggy cried.

"What?"

"You just missed the turnoff."

Damn, she was right. "Let's skip church this morning, okay?"

"Not you, too?" Peggy whined. "First Hannah and now you."

"I don't feel like it today."

"We're almost there. Please, don't be difficult."

Not wanting to get into an argument, Bob sighed and found a place to turn the car around and head back toward Briar Patch Road. Within five minutes, he slipped into an available space in the crowded church parking lot.

Organ music drifted out the open doors. Thankfully they were late enough to avoid all the handshaking and friendly chitchat. In case Peggy hadn't guessed, he wasn't in a sociable mood.

Of course, being late also meant they couldn't get a decent seat at the back of the church. Those who arrived early set claim to the back five pews. He and Peggy ended up sitting in one of the middle rows. That was acceptable, since at least they'd missed the "meet and greet."

Following the music, Dave Flemming stepped up to the pulpit and opened his Bible. Bob had left his at home. Peggy flipped to the book of Matthew, chapter six, the reference listed in the bulletin she'd picked up on the way in. Bob crossed his arms and closed his eyes. He had no intention of listening. He was here to keep the peace at home and for no other reason. For all he cared, the pastor could be talking about the inflated price of dot.com shares.

Then it hit him—one word in particular. *Forgiveness.* He opened his eyes and sat up and started to listen. It was as if Pastor Flemming knew his innermost thoughts and had written the sermon specifically with him in mind. The idea unsettled him.

At the close of the service, the congregation stood and sang together. Normally Bob enjoyed the singing. He had a good baritone and at one time had considered joining the choir. His commitment to the community theater took up most of his free hours, however. It was the theater or the church choir. He'd chosen the theater.

At the end of the song, the service was over and the pews began to empty. Still deep in thought, Bob remained seated.

"I need to talk to Corrie," Peggy announced, then got up and scurried off. Apparently she was afraid he'd argue with her and was gone before he had a chance to tell her to take her time. He had some thinking to do.

Usually Bob resented being left to twiddle his thumbs while Peggy did her socializing, but just now, he was grateful for a few moments of solitude.

He didn't know how long he sat there, alone in the

church. Peggy would come and get him when she was ready, he figured, letting his thoughts drift where they would.

"Hello, Bob." Pastor Flemming stepped into the pew and sat down next to him.

Bob knew Dave, liked him well enough to play golf with him every week. They hardly ever talked about God, which suited Bob just fine. To him, a man's faith was a private matter.

"Pastor." Bob smiled in his friend's direction.

"Something on your mind?" the other man asked.

Bob shook his head. The pastor knew some of the story. He'd been the person who'd recommended that Bob contact Roy McAfee in the first place. He trusted Dave. At the time, he'd been desperate, half-afraid he was losing his mind.

"Well, maybe I do need to talk." Bob paused and drew in a deep breath. "What you said about forgiveness kind of hit home, you know?"

Pastor Flemming nodded. "It's in the Lord's Prayer. We recite it so often we tend to forget what it means."

Bob agreed. He'd said the prayer at every AA meeting for years, and had never truly understood the part about forgiveness. "You said this morning that we can only accept forgiveness to the extent that we're able to forgive ourselves." Those were the words that had struck him with such intensity.

The pastor nodded again.

"Some people require a lot of forgiveness," Bob murmured.

"We're all sinners."

"But like I said," Bob continued, "there are sins, and then there are sins. Some of us will never find forgiveness. In certain circumstances, it just isn't possible."

The pastor said, "In such cases, you do what you can and then you forgive yourself."

"That isn't possible, either," Bob said, unable to keep the despair from his voice.

"Remember what else I said, Bob. Your willingness to forgive others is directly related to your willingness to forgive yourself."

That wasn't news Bob welcomed. It had never occurred to him that the two were linked.

He heard a sound at the back of the church and turned around to see that Peggy had appeared. She hesitated when she saw him talking to Pastor Flemming. "You've certainly given me something to think about," Bob mumbled, eager now to escape.

The only way he could figure this out was by himself. He had to stop resisting the memories. Maybe then he could lay them to rest.

Forty

On the last Saturday morning in August, Grace was scheduled to work the animal shelter's booth at the Farmers' Market. On her last stint there, she'd netted Sherlock, who was the remaining kitten in the litter and the only one left without a home. The whole day, she'd had the feeling she'd end up with one of the six kittens that had been placed for adoption. Sure enough, she'd come home with eight-week-old Sherlock.

She always enjoyed the market, especially on days like this—bright and sunny yet not really hot. In the rainy months of winter, she often found it hard to remember how lovely summers could be in the Pacific Northwest.

Today, as usual, the market teemed with activity. The variety of products sold there always impressed her—everything from fresh oysters, plucked only hours earlier from the beach, to knitted afghans.

Grace had her hands full with the animal shelter booth. She'd left Buttercup at home; she was too busy to watch the dog and, besides, Sherlock would keep her company. All morning long, Grace answered questions and talked to the children who crowded around, instantly attracted to the kittens. She had ten this Saturday, plus several mature cats, and hoped to arrange adoptions for at least half.

Grace was grateful she was busy, which helped keep her mind off the fact that Will Jefferson was in town. Olivia had phoned shortly after Will's arrival to let her know. He'd tried to call her once, but she had Caller ID, and when she saw Charlotte's name, she let the answering machine pick up. Sure enough, it was Will. Grace feared Charlotte might inadvertently mention that she did volunteer work with the shelter and would be at the market this weekend.

Just when she finally felt she was safe, Grace glanced up and nearly swallowed her tongue. Standing a few feet away from her was Will Jefferson, the man she least wanted to see. Her heart seemed ready to implode. For one crazy moment, all she could do was stare. When her senses returned, she looked sharply away.

Unfortunately, all the children who'd gathered to admire the kittens had drifted off. It was apparently the opportunity Will had been waiting for. He walked toward her, his steps determined and his gaze focused relentlessly on her. He'd always been handsome, and his attractiveness, combined with her schoolgirl fantasies, had blinded her. But Grace wasn't the same woman she'd been a few months ago.

She squared her shoulders, decided there was no avoiding a confrontation, and scooped up a kitten. The heat of embarrassment reddened her face until she realized she had nothing to be embarrassed about. She wasn't entirely blameless, but Will was the one who'd lied.

"Hello, Grace." His greeting was as soft as a caress.

"Hello, Will." It demanded all her strength to keep her voice even and unemotional.

Grace knew his presence would make her uncomfortable at the wedding unless they cleared the air. She suddenly wondered if Will had sought her out because he wanted to apologize. Like her, he understood that they'd both be at Charlotte and Ben's wedding. They'd have to make peace—even a superficial peace—or the whole event would be too awkward, not just for themselves but their families and friends.

Grace needed to let him know two things: that she was willing to put the matter behind them and that she wanted nothing more to do with him. For Charlotte and Ben's sake, she'd be civil.

"You look wonderful," Will said smoothly.

A sick sensation hit her directly in the stomach. She held the kitten draped over her arm and close to her side, as if for protection. "Olivia told me you were coming for the wedding."

"Yeah, I figured she would." He slid his hands in his pockets and struck a casual pose. "I'll be here for several days." He let that information fall, apparently expecting a response. "I hoped we could get together."

"Get together?" She couldn't have heard him correctly. He couldn't possibly be suggesting they see each other socially.

"Mom and I are going to dinner tonight, but I'm free on Sunday."

"You're asking me to have dinner with you?" The man's audacity was unbelievable. "You can't be serious, Will. You lied to me!"

"You're right, that was unfair, but I've always been fond of you, Grace. I'm here—"

"Where's Georgia?"

He didn't even blink at the mention of his wife. "Home. We each have our own lives."

"I'll bet you do." Grace couldn't disguise her sarcasm. She wondered if Georgia knew she was supposed to have her own life. And how about their cruise? Did they have separate lives there—and separate rooms? Not that any of it mattered.

"I arranged my flight to come in early so you and I could talk. Do you realize what you did? You didn't give me a single chance to explain. You cut me off without listening to a word I had to say."

"Are you or are you not married?"

He sighed heavily. "Married, but this is important, Grace, for both of us."

She shook her head. "I don't have anything to say to you, other than that I don't care to see you or speak to you ever again."

He frowned as if saddened by her lack of understanding. "We both know you don't mean that. You *can't* mean it after everything we've been to each other." He took a step closer. "I've missed you, Grace. These last few months have been hell without you. Don't you feel that, too?"

She was careful not to answer him. "I'm grateful for the lessons you taught me," she said instead.

He nodded impatiently.

"The thing is, I came so close to—"

"You love me, Grace," he interrupted. "You did when you were in high school and you do now."

"I was a teenager then and I'm a woman now. I'm glad to say I occasionally learn from my mistakes."

"We're not a mistake," he said urgently. "Don't you see that what we had was special?"

He was good; she'd give him that. "What we had was a very big mistake. If you arrived early for the wedding because you wanted to see me, then I'm afraid you're in for a major disappointment. If I never see you again, I'll be a happy woman."

He shook his head firmly. "You can't mean that," he said with the same intensity as before.

"I mean every word. Now please…please leave me alone."

He frowned and turned away, but took only a few steps before he turned back. "I'm staying with my mother, so if you change your mind…"

"I'm not going to. Please don't contact me again."

He smiled—a smile obviously calculated to melt her stony heart. "I refuse to believe you're serious. Okay, you have a right to be angry, but I can't divorce Georgia. It would devastate her. But if that's the only way I can have you, then—"

Grace raised her hand to stop him. She'd heard enough, more than enough. "Go. Just go."

He frowned again, like a petulant child, but finally left. All of a sudden Grace started to shake. Her knees felt like they were about to give way and she sank into the folding chair in the animal shelter booth. Gently stroking the kitten on her lap, she closed her eyes and took in several calming breaths.

"Grace."

She opened her eyes to find Cliff standing there. "Are you all right?" he asked. "You look pale."

"I'm fine," she lied. She'd hoped he'd come here today, wished for just this moment, but not immediately after a confrontation with Will.

"No, you're not fine," he said bluntly. "That was Will Jefferson, wasn't it?"

So Cliff had seen her talking to Will. Her first thought was to defend herself, to explain that she wanted nothing more to do with Olivia's brother. Instead, huge tears filled her eyes and trailed down her cheeks.

"You cared about him, didn't you?"

"No," she cried, and knew that was a lie. "Yes…fool that I was. I did care at one time, but not anymore. Oh, Cliff, don't you know? It's you I love. I can't give up on the two of us. I tried to and I'd almost succeeded but then Lisa—"

"You spoke to Lisa?"

Grace winced; she was only making matters worse.

"You and Lisa talked?" he repeated.

Grace nodded, swallowing hard. "She came to see me at the library, and I'm so grateful she did."

"What did she say?"

Grace stared down at the sleeping kitten in her lap. "She said you loved me, too."

He dropped into a crouch so they were at eye-level and tucked his finger beneath her chin. "That was when you started this e-mail campaign, wasn't it?"

She nodded again. She wondered if her barrage of messages had succeeded. This was the first time they'd actually talked face-to-face, and she wanted to throw her arms around his neck. Well, except for the kitten, of course...

Cliff held her gaze for the longest moment before looking away.

"Did it work?" she whispered.

At first she didn't think he was going to answer, but then he gave her a lightning-quick smile. "You're a difficult woman to ignore."

"I am?" Her heart was jumping inside her chest. "Really?"

"Before I knew it, I was hurrying to the mailbox every day and logging on to my computer, hoping there'd be a note from you."

The Internet was part of what had gotten her into this mess. It was only fitting that it should be a means of getting back what she'd lost.

"Are you willing to give me another chance?" she asked, holding her breath for fear of what he might say.

"We can begin slowly."

She bit her lower lip. "Thank you."

Cliff wiped the tears from her cheeks. "How about if we have a cup of coffee and talk once you're finished here?"

Grace nodded, so happy she was afraid she'd start crying again. Maybe they could attend Charlotte's wedding together. She hardly dared hope....

Forty-One

Cecilia knocked lightly on her employer's open door. Mr. Cox glanced up from his paperwork, smiling when he saw her.

"I wanted to remind you that I have a doctor's appointment this afternoon," she said.

Zachary Cox's gaze went to his appointment calendar. "Ah, yes, I see that now. As it happens, Rosie and I are taking the afternoon off ourselves."

Her employer had escaped with his wife for several afternoons this summer. Cecilia suspected they were rediscovering the excitement of being in love, the passion of their early years. "Will Allison be coming in today?"

Mr. Cox nodded absently. "Rosie's teaching her how to knit. Her first project is a blanket for your baby."

Cecilia had proudly shared the news of her pregnancy with Allison a week earlier. "That's so sweet of her."

Mr. Cox smiled again. "You've been very good for my daughter, and this is something she wanted to do for you."

All Cecilia had really done was listen to the girl. She'd been going through a difficult time after her parents' divorce, but she seemed to have made a complete turnaround.

"Leave whenever you need to, Cecilia."

"The ultrasound is scheduled for two-thirty."

"Is your husband going with you?" Zach asked.

Cecilia nodded. "He wouldn't miss it for the world."

"Good. I'll see you in the morning then."

Cecilia returned to her desk, her spirits high. Every day was special. The dreaded morning sickness had slowly disappeared, just as it did the first time.

Now that he'd accepted her pregnancy, Ian was a hundred percent supportive, his attitude one of eager anticipation. She felt more confident than ever in her husband's love.

At two-thirty, Ian was waiting for her at the Navy hospital, pacing the hallway outside the technician's office.

"I'm here," she said.

Ian hurried over to her. "How are you feeling?"

"All right. Just as important, how are *you* feeling?"

His grin was so sexy, it was all she could do not to kiss him right then and there. "Excited. We're going to see a picture of our baby."

"I'm excited, too."

He started to open the office door, but Cecilia stopped him. "We should decide now if we want to know the sex of the baby or if we want to wait."

"Do you want to know?" he asked.

"It doesn't matter to me either way."

He agreed. "Me, neither." He held open the door for her and they walked into the reception area. Several other expectant mothers, at varying stages of pregnancy, were already waiting.

Cecilia went up to the counter and handed over the necessary paperwork, along with her Navy identification. When she'd finished, they sat down next to each other. Ian held her hand and gently rubbed it with his thumb in a soothing, comforting motion. He was nervous, she realized, but then so was she.

It seemed to take forever before her name was called. With a full bladder, she'd found it hard to sit still for that long. But finally it was their turn. Ian entered the inner office with her, after which they were led into the ultrasound room. Once Cecilia was lying on the table, her belly covered with cool gel, she noticed how pale Ian had become. He'd asked to come with her, but now she wondered if this was such a good idea.

"Ian?" Cecilia held out her arm to her husband. His grip was tight as he linked their hands. "Everything's okay."

He nodded. "Of course it is."

The technician, a woman who wore a name tag that identified her as Jody, directed their attention to the monitor. "We should be able to see the baby in just a moment."

As the tiny fetus came into view, Ian rose to his feet to get a better look. "That's our baby?" His voice was filled with surprise and awe.

"That's your baby," Jody said softly, moving the paddle over Cecilia's stomach.

"Is everything all right?" Ian asked. "I mean the baby seems awfully small."

"She'll grow."

"She?" Cecilia repeated.

"I always refer to a fetus as female. Were you hoping for a son?" The question was directed at Ian.

"Either," he answered, staring at the monitor.

"Is this your first child?"

Ian pulled his gaze away from the screen long enough to look at Cecilia. His eyes darkened with pain.

"Our first baby died shortly after she was born," Cecilia explained. "That's the reason Dr. Chalmers ordered the ultrasound. He wants to be sure there aren't any problems with this pregnancy."

Jody patted Cecilia's hand. "So far everything looks perfectly normal."

It had with Allison, too, Cecilia recalled, but she'd only had the one ultrasound in the early stages of her pregnancy and there hadn't seemed to be any need for another. Who could have known? Who could have guessed that her baby would be born with a defective heart?

"I'm so sorry about your first baby." Jody's voice was sympathetic.

Cecilia glanced at Ian and saw that just talking about Allison had stirred painful memories. "We're both a little nervous this time around."

"All we want is a healthy baby," Ian added.

"Of course you do." Jody manipulated the paddle a bit more. "Would you like to know the sex of your child?"

"You can tell this soon?" Ian squinted at the screen, as if that would help him decipher what she saw that he didn't.

"A trained eye can."

Ian squeezed Cecilia's hand. "Should we?" he asked.

"You don't want to be surprised?" If it was solely up to her, she'd prefer to wait, but there were definitely advantages to learning the baby's sex in advance.

"I've decided I do want to know," Ian said eagerly.

"All right, all right, tell us," Cecilia said, laughing.

Jody grinned. "It looks to me like you're having another little girl."

Ian let out a deep, heartfelt sigh. "A girl," he repeated. His hand tightened around Cecilia's to the point that it was painful.

"Ian!"

"Sorry," he said when he realized what he'd done. "A girl. We're having a girl."

Cecilia nodded. She was so excited that she could hardly hold back her emotions. After Allison's death, Cecilia had given away all her daughter's clothes, with two exceptions. She'd saved the outfit she'd planned to bring Allison home in, and a favorite baby blanket she'd purchased shortly before the birth. That was it. The two things she'd saved because it was too emotionally difficult to give everything away.

Following the ultrasound, they went to a movie. Ian held her hand all through the show, as if he needed a constant connection with her. They went out to eat afterward, but because they were saving to buy a house, all their budget would allow was a meal at the Pancake Palace.

This was a rare night out and Cecilia chatted lightheartedly during dinner. Only when Ian reached for the bill did she realize how quiet and somber he'd grown over the course of the evening.

"Ian, you're not worried about the baby, are you?"

His denial came far too quickly. "No, the technician said everything was fine. Why should I be worried?"

"I don't know. Why should you?" she pressed, unwilling to drop the subject.

Her husband looked away and when he returned his gaze to her, his eyes were brimming with pain. "It's just like before."

"What is?"

"First, the pregnancy's a surprise, just the way Allison was a surprise."

"But this is a happy surprise."

Ian agreed willingly enough. "I was ecstatic when you told me you were pregnant with Allison."

"You're happy now, too, aren't you?"

He brought her hand to his lips and kissed her knuckles. "It took some adjusting, but I'm pleased about the baby."

"It *is* different this time," Cecilia insisted.

"Is it? Has the morning sickness been different?"

He had a point. "No, that was the same."

"With Allison, the ultrasound didn't show anything abnormal, either."

Again all she could do was agree. "We're married now," she said.

"I married you in my heart the first night we made love. Even before that, I knew I wanted to spend the rest of my life with you."

"Oh, Ian." At times he could be the most romantic man in the world. At others…well, he was a man.

He sighed. "I'm trying not to worry."

"I know, but it really is different with this baby. For one thing, you're home now and you're not scheduled to go back to sea until after my due date."

He sighed, more loudly this time. "No guarantees on that."

"I know, but they won't send you out so soon, especially after you were away for six months. The Navy wouldn't be so heartless."

"I want everything to be perfect for you and the baby," he said hoarsely. "I'm trying not to worry, Cecilia, but I can't help it."

"Wait and see. We're going to have a perfectly healthy baby girl."

He closed his eyes. "I pray that you're right."

So did Cecilia, but she had no guarantees to give him, either.

Forty-Two

Colonel Stewart Samuels was coming to Cedar Cove sometime in the middle of September. During their telephone conversation, the colonel hadn't been able to give Bob an exact date. Soon, though, he'd be here and as the time crept closer, Bob grew increasingly uneasy.

After the last performance of *Chicago,* Bob removed his makeup and changed clothes. Usually he hung around with the rest of the cast. Tonight, in particular, was a festive occasion, since the wrap party would take place once the set was struck. But the last thing Bob felt was festive, so he made his excuses and left after the show.

In addition to not feeling sociable, he was nervous. Ever since he'd arrived at the theater, Bob had the feeling someone was watching him offstage as well as on.

As he walked into the dark parking lot, an eerie sensation shuddered down his spine. The temptation to whirl around and confront whoever might be following him was nearly overwhelming. He resisted, half hoping that his nemesis would do him the favor of killing him and be done with it.

No such luck.

Since he'd been allowed to live, Bob climbed into his car and started the engine. The headlights shot twin beams across the mostly empty lot. Bob stared out the windshield and, to his disappointment, saw nothing out of the ordinary.

His depression had begun shortly after Pastor Flemming's sermon, but it had been simmering from the time Maxwell Russell had died in Bob's home. Even before the body had been identified, Bob knew this dead man was somehow connected to him. Max Russell had haunted him, reminded him of sins long past. They'd never learned his reasons for coming to Cedar Cove—to the Thyme and Tide. Bob guessed it had something to do with Dan's suicide, but that was only speculation. They'd never know for sure.

Bob pulled out of the parking lot and onto Harbor Street. From town, the road wound along the waterfront. Normally Bob followed it down to Cranberry Point, but as soon as he reached Harbor, a pair of headlights came up behind him.

Bob smiled to himself. So his instincts were right. He'd been watched and whoever was watching had decided to follow him. Surprisingly he experienced no dread or fear; instead he felt a sense of vindication. This proved he'd been right all along.

The car turned off Harbor and onto Cedar Cove Drive, which Bob hadn't expected. Apparently his stalker knew he'd been caught. For reasons he didn't want to analyze, Bob made a sudden decision to follow whoever it was. He found a convenient spot to turn around and speeded after the other vehicle. Bob flicked his high beams on and off and felt a certain satisfaction in letting the follower know he was being followed.

This was all a bit silly, but he stayed behind the car, eager to find out what he could. The vehicle slowed and turned into The Pink Dog tavern. A pink neon French Poodle flashed on the bar's sign. If Cedar Cove had a seedy area, this was it. Workers from the shipyard stopped in for a beer on the way home; they were The Pink Dog's regular clientele. On Saturday nights, the parking lot was nearly full. Bob turned in and watched as the other car claimed one of the few empty parking spaces.

Riveted, Bob sat in his vehicle, staring as a man climbed out of the car and headed for the front door. Bob strained for a better look, but the light was too weak and all he got was a general impression. Tall, with a thick waist, the guy had a beer gut that hung over his belt, faded jeans and a grease-smudged shirt. He didn't so much as glance in Bob's direction. Bob suspected this guy hadn't been tailing him, after all. He looked more interested in a cold beer and a good time than anything to do with Bob.

He waited and then parked facing the front door so he could check out everyone who came and went. Still, Bob didn't know what he should do if he saw the man again—or if he'd even recognize him.

He hadn't been anywhere close to this kind of establishment in years. He knew better. He'd been sober since 1983. For several minutes all he did was stare at the flashing sign. It hypnotized him, that sign, reminding him of days when his best friend in the world was a bottle of beer.

His mouth started to water and the urge for a drink was so strong that he held the steering wheel in a death grip. He could *taste* a beer. He remembered how, on a hot day, there was nothing that satisfied him more.

It felt as if he were in a trance. He was shocked by how powerful the pull was, and he knew he was no more immune to the lure of alcohol now than he'd been the day after his first Alcoholics Anonymous meeting twenty-one years ago.

Bob took out his cell phone. He needed help, and the first person he thought of calling was Jack. He pushed the speed dial button and waited. Jack had a cell that he kept in his car but constantly forgot to recharge. No answer. With increasing desperation he called the house.

After three rings, Olivia picked up.

"Oh, hi, Bob," she said after he'd asked for Jack. "He's on his way home from Bainbridge Island. Did you try his cell?"

"I did. No need to tell him I phoned, I'll catch him later." All Bob wanted was someone to tell him not to go inside that bar. Anyone. He had to *hear* it, because the pull toward that front door grew stronger and more compelling with every breath he drew.

"Of course," Olivia said. After a moment's hesitation, she asked, "Is everything all right?"

"Sure," he lied but realized he must have sounded as desperate as he felt. "On second thought, have him call me, would you?"

"The minute he walks in, I'll let him know. You want him to call your cell phone?"

"Please." Bob didn't bother to say goodbye. He ended the call and put his hand on the door handle. He'd tried. If he walked into the Pink Dog, it was because Jack hadn't answered his phone. He'd been there for Jack countless times over the past fourteen years, but now—when he needed a friend, someone to talk sense into him—Jack was nowhere to be found. Typical. When he needed help, his good friend Jack was unavailable.

As Bob opened the car door, a cool breeze blew inside. He breathed in the scent of the night and closed his eyes, knowing full well that if he walked into that bar, it would be the end. He'd go right back to the hell his life had been twenty-one years ago. Right back to the insanity, the madness that had controlled him.

He placed one foot and then the other on the ground outside the car. He blamed his golfing partner, Pastor Dave Flemming, for this. In his frame of mind, it was easy to cast blame. All this talk about healing and forgiveness. What Dave didn't understand was that some sins couldn't be forgiven. Yeah, he talked about forgiving yourself, but that wasn't an option for Bob, not with what he'd done. Some acts defied forgiveness. A man couldn't slaughter women, children, old people, and ever be the same again. It just wasn't possible. Maybe he should've died that day.

Bob remembered returning from Vietnam. He'd landed in San Francisco, grateful to get home alive. When he was granted leave, he'd been warned against wearing his uniform into town. Returning soldiers were called "baby killers" and had blood thrown at them. Bob defied the order. He would have welcomed the attack. Then the whole world would know what he'd done; he wouldn't have to hide it any longer.

Rocking slightly now, Bob stabbed his fingers through his hair. He wanted a drink. One. He'd stop with one. That was all he needed. After twenty-one years, he knew what he could handle and what he couldn't. One beer would satisfy this need and then he'd turn around and walk out.

Blindly he grabbed the cell phone on the seat next to him. As he stared at it, he knew that if he walked into that tavern he was as good as dead. He might as well blow his brains out the same way Dan Sherman had. Drinking would take longer to actually kill him; that was the only difference.

Death wasn't such a bad thing, he reasoned. People died every day and the people they left behind mourned them, but life continued.

As if in slow motion, Bob hit speed dial for Roy McAfee's home number; fortunately, he'd programmed it in after that other incident. He'd try one last time, reach out.

Roy didn't need to know his dilemma, but he could provide human contact, a human voice. Bob gazed up at the heavens, deciding that if his friend didn't pick up, he had his answer. He'd know it was useless and he should just give in and have that beer. Hell, he'd buy the whole tavern a round. But if Roy answered, then God was telling him to get back in his car and drive away. It'd be God's fault if he started drinking again, he thought, hysterical laughter bubbling up in his throat.

The phone rang four times, and Bob swore that each ring lasted ten seconds longer than the one before. When the answering machine clicked on, he bolted upright at the unexpectedness of it.

"You've reached the home of Roy and Corrie McAfee. We aren't available to take your call right now...."

Bob severed the connection and stared down at the phone.

Then he looked up at the night sky again. "That wasn't the deal," he shouted. Roy had answered, all right, but it wasn't really Roy, just his voice on an answering machine. In other words, God had given Bob a half-assed answer.

Bob felt the torture of indecision. He longed to test his strength and prove he was strong enough to have one drink and walk away. But he knew... Everything he'd ever learned in AA told him otherwise. Still, he didn't care. He wanted that drink. Needed that drink. Craved that drink.

The sound of his cell phone ringing jolted him badly. He grabbed it with both hands and fumbled at the keypad.

"Yes," he snapped.

"Where are you?" It was Peggy.

"Why?" he demanded. He didn't want to talk to his wife. Didn't she realize he had a life-altering decision to make?

"Something's wrong. I could feel it. Where are you?"

Bob opened his eyes wide. Could Peggy be the answer to his prayer? He slid back inside the car.

"I thought you'd be home by now," she continued. She sounded troubled. Almost afraid. "This isn't like you."

"I'm all right."

"Are you sure?"

He was now. "I thought there was someone following me again."

"Was there?"

"No...I'm on my way home."

"I'll be waiting."

Bob started the engine and backed out of the space.

He was going home.

Forty-Three

Maryellen stepped out of the shower, hair still wet. It was the afternoon of Charlotte and Ben's wedding. She'd mentioned the ceremony to Jon, but they weren't exactly on good terms. The one time she'd asked, he refused to attend the wedding with her.

He also refused to discuss his parents. He remained civil, but distant and guarded. Every night they slept side by side without touching, without talking. Her beautiful home felt like a prison and Maryellen couldn't bear it.

Being pregnant didn't help. She hadn't told Jon yet. She'd planned to, knowing she should, but as time went on and his attitude didn't change, she realized it was a hopeless situation.

After dressing and blow-drying her hair, she got out an overnight bag and packed as much as it would hold. She added several extra pieces of clothing to Katie's diaper bag, as well. When she was finished, she carried both to the car.

Maryellen was on the verge of tears. She loved Jon and hoped they would be able to resolve their problems, but she'd begun to fear that wasn't possible. Her husband no longer trusted her. He felt she'd betrayed him. He couldn't understand or accept that she'd only been trying to help him reconcile with his family—for his own sake and his daughter's.

With a sleeping Katie over her shoulder, Maryellen gently tapped on the door of the darkroom where Jon was developing film. Whenever he was in the house at the same time as she was, he found a way to avoid her. If she was upstairs, he had some reason to linger downstairs. Meals were a painful experience. They sat across from each other and made polite conversation, but Maryellen simply couldn't connect with him.

"What is it?" Jon called impatiently.

"I'm leaving for Charlotte's wedding now."

"All right."

Maryellen hesitated. "Are you sure you can't come with us?"

"I'm sure."

"Okay." Disappointment settled heavily on her shoulders. "Give the newlyweds my best."

"I will." Maryellen swallowed painfully. "Listen, Jon, I'm thinking I won't come back after the wedding."

"What?"

"I talked to Mom earlier, and Katie and I are going to spend the night with her."

"Hold on a minute," he said and opened the door.

Maryellen stepped back nervously as Jon's gaze held hers. "You're going to your mother's place for the night?"

She nodded.

"Why?"

Maryellen shrugged. "I need time to think."

"About what?" he challenged.

"I can't live like this," she whispered, breaking eye contact.

He didn't respond.

"I'm sorry, Jon, sorrier than you know." Her voice cracked, and she turned away and left the house.

To her surprise, he followed her to the car. When she'd placed Katie in the car seat, she straightened. Jon stood with his hands in his pockets, staring down at the ground.

"Are you coming back tomorrow?" he asked as she walked around to the driver's seat.

"Do you want me to?"

He didn't answer.

"That says it all, doesn't it?" She climbed in the car, started the engine and drove to the end of the driveway. Her heart was about to break. Hands clenching the steering wheel hard, she lowered her forehead and drew in a deep breath.

The minute Maryellen arrived at her mother's house, Grace knew something was wrong. "You'd better tell me," her mother said as Maryellen carried in her bags.

"We'll discuss everything after the wedding," Maryellen insisted, managing a smile. "It's all right, Mom. Everything's going to be fine."

Her mother looked as if she didn't believe her, and rightly so. Maryellen didn't believe it herself.

The wedding was lovely. Standing beside her mother, Maryellen battled tears. Only five months earlier, she'd stood before Pastor Flemming and vowed to love Jon for the rest of her life. It had only taken her five months to screw up her second marriage. Five months. That had to be some kind of record outside of Hollywood.

The church was nearly full. Charlotte's dearest friends crowded the front pews, wearing red hats and purple boas. Olivia and her family took up two pews. So many people had wanted to share in the couple's happiness. Unfortunately, neither of Ben's sons had been able to come; both he and Charlotte must have been disappointed.

Despite the jubilant mood, Maryellen felt a sense of hopelessness and inner turmoil. The church seemed to get hot and stuffy and the room began to sway. Maryellen sat down, taking several deep breaths, fearing she was about to faint.

"Maryellen?" Grace sat down beside her.

She offered her mother a feeble smile. "I'm pregnant."

Her mother smiled from ear to ear and squeezed her hand.

"Jon doesn't know."

"I think it's time for you to tell him, don't you?"

Maryellen couldn't answer.

The music started then, and Pastor Flemming came to the front of the church. Charlotte and Ben joined him and gazed up at each other with such adoration that Maryellen had to blink back tears.

She heard footsteps behind her and hope leapt into her heart. She turned around, thinking, hoping, desperately wanting the late arrival to be Jon. Instead, Cliff Harding slipped into the pew beside her mother. She watched as they looked tenderly at each other and then Cliff tucked her mother's arm in the crook of his elbow and smiled over at Maryellen and Katie.

Somehow Maryellen made it through the rest of the day. The reception at The Lighthouse was elegant, with vintage wines and the best champagne—neither of which she touched—and a selection of delicious hors d'oeuvres. Several people asked about Jon, and Maryellen invented a convenient excuse. He was busy with a photographic commission and couldn't come; he sent his best wishes. He had, in fact, given the newlyweds a framed photograph of the lighthouse, one that Charlotte had long admired.

Knowing her mother wanted to spend time with Cliff, Maryellen drove back to the house on Rosewood Lane. Katie was cranky and hungry by then, so Maryellen hurriedly heated her dinner. She was giving Katie a bath when she felt the first painful spasm. The sharpness of it caught her unawares and she nearly doubled over.

Kneeling on the floor in front of the bathtub, she watched as her daughter splashed joyfully, unconscious of the turmoil in Maryellen. No, please God, not the baby. Nothing else happened and she breathed easier.

After a few minutes, Maryellen lifted Katie from the tub. The pain shot through her and she gasped as the blood rushed between her legs. Holding Katie against her, Maryellen sank to the floor.

The front door opened a moment later and Maryellen sagged with relief. "Mom…help…oh, Mom."

Grace was in the bathroom in an instant; Cliff was with her. Her mother's eyes were wide with alarm.

Maryellen was weeping by then. Katie was screaming.

"I've lost the baby…I've lost the baby," she wailed in grief and pain, sobbing openly now.

After that, everything happened so quickly, Maryellen had trouble making sense of it. The next thing she knew, she was at the hospital in Bremerton and a doctor was telling her she'd suffered a miscarriage. As if she hadn't figured that out for herself. Maryellen barely heard a word he said, crying as hard as she was. He asked about her husband, but she shook her head. Jon didn't even know she was pregnant.

It was decided she should spend the night in the hospital and after the D&C, she was wheeled into a private room. A lone figure stood in the shadows. Jon. Apparently her mother had called him. Or perhaps Cliff had; it didn't matter. He was with her.

Maryellen looked at him and fresh tears coursed down her cheeks. She turned her head away.

"Maryellen," he whispered, moving to the bedside. "Why didn't you tell me?"

She had no answer for him.

"I am so sorry." Each word was carefully enunciated.

Deeply depressed, Maryellen could only shake her head. She was sorry, too. Sorry about everything.

Jon sat down beside her and after a moment, reached for her hand and kissed it. She realized then that his eyes were bright with tears.

She started to sob again and stretched out her arms. Jon wrapped her in his embrace and together, with their arms securely around each other, they wept.

Forty-Four

Roy McAfee always checked his answering machine when he arrived at the office. There'd been a number of hang-ups recently. In light of the mysterious postcard he'd received a few weeks back, these hang-ups troubled him. He expected a few occasionally—any business got its share of wrong numbers—but his office had received more disconnected calls than usual in the last six weeks.

Corrie was making coffee after collecting the day's mail on her way into the office. Sitting down, Roy opened the drawer on the left-hand side of his desk and pulled out the cryptic postcard. He still didn't know what to make of it.

He heard Corrie moving around the outer office and realized she was about to deliver his coffee and the mail. Not wanting her to fuss over the postcard, he slipped it back inside his desk drawer.

Sure enough, Corrie entered his office, handing him a fresh mug of coffee. "There wasn't much mail this morning," she said as she placed a stack on the corner of his desk.

Usually she was the one who stopped at the post office.

It was pure coincidence that Roy had collected the mail the day that postcard arrived.

Corrie remained standing on the other side of his desk; she seemed to be waiting for something.

Roy anticipated a comment that didn't come. "Anything else?" he asked.

"Look it over," she said, gesturing to the few pieces of mail.

Roy reached for them and leaned back in his chair while he shuffled through the usual flyers, bills and—he hesitated when he caught sight of the postcard. He stared at the picture of the Space Needle.

"Read it," Corrie said.

Roy turned it over. The message was in the same block lettering as the first one. Only this time it read: THE PAST HAS A WAY OF CATCHING UP WITH THE PRESENT.

"What does it mean?"

Roy stared at the card, as perplexed by this message as he was by the first. "I haven't got a clue."

"There's no signature."

Roy set the card down on his desk. "People who send these kinds of messages generally don't sign their names."

Corrie walked over to the far side of the room and looked out the window. "This isn't the first one, is it?"

At times Roy swore Corrie should be the private investigator. She had real instincts about people, and a reliable sense of what was true and what wasn't.

"Is it?" she demanded, turning to face him.

Roy reluctantly shook his head. Slowly opening the drawer, he brought out the other postcard.

Corrie walked quickly to his desk and picked it up.

He watched her read the short, cryptic message and saw that she was as mystified as he was.

"When did this arrive?"

He couldn't recall exactly. "A few weeks ago."

"Why didn't you say anything?" she cried, throwing down the postcard. "I'm your wife. I have a right to know."

Roy shrugged halfheartedly. "What was the point? Why should you worry because someone's getting their kicks mailing me silly postcards?"

"You're being threatened and you don't feel it's important to let me know?" She raised her voice. "I'm not only your wife, I'm your business partner!"

"Now, Corrie…"

"Don't talk to me as if I'm a child."

"Then stop overreacting. It's just a postcard and if you read it again you'll see it isn't threatening."

Corrie picked up the card they'd received that day and read it aloud. "The past has a way of catching up with the present." She leveled her gaze on Roy. "That sounds ominous to me."

Roy shook his head. "Not necessarily."

"I hope you're taking this seriously." Restless now, Corrie started to pace.

Roy didn't want to upset her any more than she already was—but, in fact, he hadn't taken the threat seriously. Not really. Until this morning. One postcard he could dismiss, but two? The earlier message had been something vague about regrets. Sure he had regrets. Every police officer did. It came with the territory.

"Think!" Corrie insisted. "This must have to do with one of your old cases. So you should review your old cases and narrow it down to someone capable of…this."

Roy shook his head again. "I was on the force for more than twenty years and handled thousands of cases. Do I have regrets about any of them? Damn straight I do, but I always did what I believed to be right."

Corrie refused to let it go. "Could it be someone who was released from prison recently?"

"I don't have a clue." Over time he'd helped put quite a few men behind bars. A whole lot of suspects weren't particularly grateful for his detection skills.

"What about threats? Did anyone threaten you while you were on the force?"

There'd been some; convicted felons often looked for someone else to blame for their bad luck. He was a convenient target, but no one case stood out in his mind.

"Forget it," Roy urged, snatching up a pen, pretending to get to work.

"I can't," Corrie murmured, but she returned to the outer office.

Roy could tell how shaken she was. He wanted to reassure her but didn't know how. He'd wasted time mulling over the first postcard and hadn't come up with anything. If some nutcase wanted to mail him a message on the back of a postcard every few weeks, what could he do about it? Apparently, whoever was doing this derived a bizarre sense of satisfaction from it. In Roy's opinion, his mystery correspondent didn't seem intent on causing him harm.

After a few minutes, he went to check on Corrie, using the excuse of refreshing his coffee. He found her kneeling in front of the filing cabinet, sorting through old police files. He'd always kept a personal notebook about every major case he'd worked, as well as newspaper articles and other information. Corrie, an inveterate organizer, had made files for each year. She had two or three on the floor beside her.

"What are you doing?" he asked as he poured coffee into his mug.

"Checking out our old Cedar Cove cases, plus some of your notes from the Seattle PD."

Roy sipped his coffee and turned to take a look at one of the names. "Parker," he read slowly.

"Harry Parker," Corrie reminded him. "Three years ago. He befriended a neighbor, and was supposedly helping the old man with yardwork and such."

It sounded familiar.

"The old man's daughter, who lived back east, said she suspected Harry of stealing her father blind and asked us to look into it. The woman had good instincts."

"I remember." Roy said. Harry was currently serving time at the men's prison in Shelton for forging checks and theft.

"As I recall, Harry swore you tricked him into a confession."

"I didn't have anything to do with his statement to the sheriff," Roy countered.

"Nevertheless, Harry blamed you."

Roy doubted it was Harry who'd mailed him those two postcards. He suspected this went back to his days in the Seattle Police Department.

"It's none of our Cedar Cove cases," he said.

"What makes you so sure?" his wife demanded.

"I just am. Whoever this is, whatever it's about, it goes way back." The tone of this latest card said as much. Something from his past was about to hit him square between the eyes.

They spent the morning looking through old files and journals, some cases going as far back as twenty years. He ended up with a short list of people to check out, but didn't feel hopeful. This afternoon he planned to make a few phone calls.

Corrie went out to lunch with Peggy Beldon and came back in lighter spirits. While they were at the mall they'd run into a sale of some sort. Roy had stopped counting all the money she'd supposedly saved them by shopping at sales. Interestingly, she found it logical to spend money in order to save it.

"Peggy said something interesting at lunch," Corrie said

as she stepped into Roy's office. "Bob thought someone was following him again a little while ago."

This was news to Roy. "He never mentioned it to me."

"That's because after a few blocks, the car went past him. Bob turned around and followed the other car for a short distance, but in retrospect he doesn't think he was being followed, after all."

"I guess that's why he didn't tell me about it."

"Do you remember the night Bob phoned you in a panic because he was convinced he was being followed?" Corrie asked casually.

"Sure. He drove over to the sheriff's office."

"While we were at lunch, I realized something else. Something I'd completely forgotten until Peggy mentioned it."

"What's that?"

Corrie leaned against the doorjamb. "Bob's car was in the repair shop that week."

"That's right," Roy whispered slowly. He was beginning to connect the dots.

"In other words, Bob was driving our car that night and not his own."

Roy nodded. That possibility had never occurred to him and he suddenly felt a little foolish. Once again, Corrie had proved herself a natural detective. "In other words, whoever was following Bob might've been looking for me."

"Do you still think those postcards don't mean anything?" Corrie whispered.

Forty-Five

Grace was meeting Olivia for lunch midweek. So much had happened in both their lives and Grace wanted—no, *needed*—time with her friend. She was dying to talk about Cliff and the way he'd come to sit with her during Charlotte and Ben's wedding. The ceremony lingered in her mind; she'd been moved by its simple beauty and by the love Charlotte and Ben so obviously shared. Tears had blurred Grace's eyes, but she wasn't the only one who'd reacted emotionally. When she'd been able to look up, she saw that several other people were wiping tears from their cheeks. Even Cliff seemed touched by the vows Charlotte and Ben had written, vows that acknowledged love for their dead spouses and love for each other. Currently the newlyweds were off to Victoria, British Columbia, for a short honeymoon.

Naturally Will had been there for both the ceremony and the reception, as had Stan. Grace had avoided them as much as possible, but she was more concerned about Will. However, Cliff seemed to understand how difficult the reception would be for her, and had remained close to her side. Several times Grace had noticed Will heading in her direction, but he stopped when he saw that Cliff was nearby. Grace assumed he'd return to his wife after this, which was just as well.

Grace valued Cliff's protectiveness at the wedding and, even more, the way he'd helped her with Maryellen. His calm presence had kept her focused as they comforted Maryellen and waited for the Aid Car. Afterward he stayed with Katie until Grace could come home.

Maryellen had been released from the hospital the next day. Jon had insisted on taking her and Katie home. Grace sensed that things weren't right between them. Now wasn't the time to pry, though, not when they were grieving over their loss. Still, Grace had every intention of finding out what had gone wrong in her daughter's marriage.

The miscarriage had devastated both Maryellen and Jon, but they were young and there'd be other children. Yet she knew it was difficult to think rationally after such a painful loss, and in her own way Grace grieved for her grandchild.

Grace was looking forward to her visit with Olivia, who'd just had a new grandchild—her third. When Olivia phoned that morning to confirm lunch, she'd jubilantly announced that James and Selina had a baby boy, born early on September eighth. Mother and son were doing fine, and James was one proud papa. They'd named the baby Adam Jordan. Three-year-old Isabella was said to be excited about becoming an older sister.

Grace had good news of her own, most of which had to do with Cliff, of course.

Before he left her on Saturday night, he'd made a point of letting her know he'd be in town on Wednesday and would come to the library. She was pleased and so relieved that they were resuming their relationship and that he was willing to give her another chance.

Just after noon, when Loretta returned from lunch, Grace retrieved her purse and small lunch bag. She decided to wait for Olivia by the totem pole outside the library. They each had a limited lunch break, and Grace didn't want Olivia to waste time looking for her in the library.

They'd already planned to bring their own lunches and eat in the waterfront park. With the refinancing of the house, Grace's tight budget was even tighter. In an indirect way, re- paying Dan's loan had been a financial help, however; Grace had gotten a much lower rate of interest and arranged to pay off the house in half the time that'd been left on the origi- nal mortgage. She had to keep a close watch on her spend- ing, but she'd manage. The fact was, she'd done a fairly good job of it ever since Dan's disappearance.

Grace loved Cedar Cove's waterfront. She looked out over the marina and across the cove to the Bremerton shipyard. She could see the massive aircraft carrier *George Washington* in the distance and remembered the joy of the wives and families when it finally returned from the Per- sian Gulf.

"Grace." A man's voice interrupted her musings.

A sense of dread struck her and she turned slowly to dis- cover Will Jefferson. She'd assumed he'd left town by now, assumed she wouldn't see him again, assumed everything had already been said.

"I had to see you one last time before I went home." His eyes pleaded with her.

Grace peered down the hill, hoping to see Olivia. No such luck. She was trapped with Will, and although this was usu- ally a crowded area, there was no one nearby right now.

"I can't believe you no longer care about me," he said in a voice that throbbed with sincerity.

Grace refused to meet his gaze. So far she'd been polite,

but that hadn't worked. "Believe it," she said sharply. "You're married. I don't mean to be rude, but I don't want anything more to do with you. I thought I made that clear."

"Okay, fine. I'll divorce Georgia if that's the only way I can have you."

Grace shook her head. She wanted to yell at him to stop harrassing her, to go home to his wife, but the polite little girl she'd been wouldn't let her. Where was Olivia? Grace scanned the street, desperate to find her friend. What could possibly be taking her so long?

"Grace, listen to me." Will sounded hurt and confused. Then, as if overcome with emotion, he gripped her by the shoulders, forcing her to look at him.

"Leave me alone," she cried, jerking herself free.

"I can't! I love you."

Sure he did. Grace might have been a fool once, but she wasn't going to play that role twice, especially with the same man.

"I wanted to talk to you at the wedding, but you stuck to your bodyguard all day long."

Obviously he was referring to Cliff.

"Just hear me out," he said.

"No!" She could hear the desperation in her voice. "The best thing you can do is just go."

"Who is he?" Will demanded. "Is it the guy you were with last Thanksgiving?"

"Cliff is twice the man you'll ever be." Cliff knew the meaning of honor and decency. Even though he wasn't happy in his marriage, he'd stayed for the sake of his daughter because it was more important to him that her world remain secure. Grace could only imagine how difficult that had been.

"I'll prove to you how much of a man I am." Will glanced

over at the hotel across the street from Mr. Wok's, the Chinese restaurant, as he placed his hand on her shoulder a second time.

"Leave me alone!" she said, almost shouting. Outraged she slapped his hand off her shoulder.

"At least talk to me. We can spend a quiet afternoon together and discuss this like reasonable adults."

"There's nothing to discuss!" She shook her head vehemently. "Just go. Olivia will be here any minute."

Will heaved a sigh. "I can't leave until you promise to meet me. What about tonight?"

"No!"

"We need to talk," he insisted again.

"I believe the lady said she wasn't interested."

Grace whirled around to find Cliff standing behind her. He'd come into town earlier than she'd expected. He had his checkbook in his hand and she realized he must have stepped out of the bank.

"The bodyguard?" Will asked her in a whisper.

"I would appreciate it if you left," Grace said calmly and clearly although her heart was pounding crazily.

"I believe the lady would prefer it if you left *now*," Cliff said. He slid his checkbook in his hip pocket, taking a protective step toward Grace.

Will glared at him for a long intense moment. "Frankly this doesn't involve you."

"If it involves Grace, then it involves me," Cliff said coolly.

"I asked you to stay out of this," Will muttered, moving closer to Grace.

Placing himself in front of Grace, Cliff stood shoe to shoe with Will and eye to eye. They scowled at each other, neither willing to back down.

Then, for no apparent reason, Will swung wildly at Cliff.

"Cliff!" Grace cried out a warning. She needn't have worried; Cliff could take care of himself.

He easily sidestepped the punch and delivered one of his own, catching Will in the jaw. The force of the blow sent Will Jefferson staggering backward. He lost his balance, collapsing onto the asphalt. Almost immediately his jaw started to swell, and blood trickled from the corner of his mouth.

Grace brought her hand to her mouth, unsure what to do. Thankfully she saw that Olivia was rushing toward them.

"You saw what happened," Will shouted, pointing at Cliff. "He attacked me!"

"I saw everything," Olivia cried, running the last few steps.

Will's eyes blazed with righteous indignation. "I'm suing you for every cent you own. Olivia, call the sheriff. I want this man arrested on assault charges."

Olivia had her arm around Grace's shoulder. "As I said, Will, I witnessed what happened."

Will stood and brushed himself off. "Stay here so the sheriff can take your statement. I want this…this bully prosecuted."

Olivia frowned at her brother. "You might have a change of heart when I testify that I saw you throw the first punch. From where I was standing, Will, it seemed Cliff was protecting my friend from your unwanted advances."

"I…I—" Will clearly didn't know what to say.

"Go home, Will," Olivia said sadly. "You've behaved atrociously and I'm ashamed of you."

Will stared openmouthed at his sister.

"Let's have our lunch," Olivia said and slipped her arm through Grace's. "Will, I'll talk to you later. I have a few things to say." She smiled at Cliff, but Grace could see that it cost her an effort. "Cliff, would you care to join us?"

"No, thanks." He shrugged carelessly. "I'm heading back

to the ranch." His gaze briefly held Grace's before he started toward the parking lot.

"Will I see you later?" Grace called after him.

Cliff turned and shook his head. "Another time perhaps."

Will smiled despite his torn lip. Grace could tell exactly what he was thinking—he might not have her for himself, but he'd done what he could to keep her from Cliff.

Forty-Six

The phone call came when Bob was least prepared to deal with it. He was still shaky; the need for a drink lingered, as intense now as it had been in his first week of sobriety. All that held him together was his love for Peggy, his determination and his AA meetings.

The call let him know Colonel Stewart Samuels was on his way to Cedar Cove and would arrive within the hour. He'd made hotel reservations at the local Holiday Inn Express near the waterfront.

"Are you all right?" Peggy asked when Bob replaced the receiver.

He didn't answer because he couldn't. At first Bob felt numb, but once his blood started flowing again, he felt a deep sense of dread. He wanted this entire mess to vanish, to go away once and for all. This was what he'd feared since leaving Vietnam. Everything he'd struggled to forget, everything he'd hoped would remain forever buried, was about to be exposed. Never had he experienced such vulnerability. The sins of his past were about to tear his life apart. But not only his—Peggy's, too.

Two of his fellow soldiers were dead and that left him and Colonel Samuels. It was a distinct possibility that his life was at risk and that the other man could also be a target. He felt almost fatalistic about it; in a way he'd been expecting retribution for those killings in the jungle since the day it all happened.

By the time Bob returned to the States following his stint in Vietnam, he was already drinking heavily. When he married Peggy, he'd managed to keep away from alcohol for a while. But that control was short-lived and within months he'd found solace in having a few beers with his buddies after work. It hadn't taken him long to progress to the hard stuff.

After Vietnam he'd vowed never to speak of that terrible day again. With one exception, he'd kept his word until recent events had made that impossible. He hadn't found it easy dredging up those memories, voicing them. God help him, he'd like to forget Vietnam ever happened.

"Bob." Peggy placed her hand on his arm, breaking into his thoughts.

"I'll be fine," he said hoarsely.

She continued to stare at him doubtfully. He'd never told her how close he'd come to having a drink that night or how her phone call had saved him. Bob didn't consider himself an especially articulate man and certainly not a poetic one, but he thought of Peggy as his harbor, his place of safety.

"Stewart Samuels is on his way," he said as casually as he could. "He'll be here within the hour."

Peggy stiffened.

Bob nodded and realized his wife was as ill-at-ease as he was himself. "When he arrives, I think it'd be best if the two of us talked privately."

Peggy bit her lip. "I'll put on a pot of coffee and make an excuse to leave."

"I'd appreciate it." He brought his arms around her and hugged her close. "I appreciate *you*." Closing his eyes, Bob breathed in the scent of her hair and the light fragrance of her cologne. Peggy was his life; without her he was nothing. He only hoped she knew how deeply he loved her.

When the white rental car pulled off Cranberry Point and into their driveway, Bob's stomach was twisted into knots. The man who stepped out from behind the wheel bore little resemblance to the officer Bob remembered. Samuels was tall and lean with salt-and-pepper hair cut in a close-cropped military style. Although he wasn't in uniform, he moved in a manner that suggested a soldier's discipline.

Bob walked out the front door to greet him. His heart felt like a sledgehammer pounding against his chest as he moved slowly toward the man he'd once known. The man who'd been his squad leader.

They met halfway and for a long moment stared at each other as if unsure of what to say. Finally Stewart Samuels extended his hand. "Hello, Beldon."

Bob nodded and thrust out his own hand, replying formally. "Colonel Samuels. Welcome to Cedar Cove."

"Thank you."

Neither moved. Samuels broke eye contact first, glancing around at the large two-story house with its brilliant green lawn and flower beds vibrant with color. Peggy's garden was still in bloom, her herbs scenting the air.

"I'm glad you came," Bob said, although that was a patent lie. Samuels was the last person he wanted to see, but it was either face the truth now or regret it for the rest of his life.

Samuels laughed as if he recognized Bob's words for the falsehood they were. "It's time we figured out what's going on here."

Bob agreed as he led the other man into the house. "Past

time." He held open the screen door and let Samuels precede him. "Peggy's got coffee on. I thought the two of us should talk privately."

Samuels made no comment. As soon as they reached the kitchen, Bob introduced him to Peggy, who smiled graciously and welcomed him to their home. She poured their coffee and left.

Bob carried their coffee to the oak table in the breakfast nook. He stretched out his arms and cradled his mug with both hands. "The years have been good to you."

Samuels sat across from him, facing the cove. "To you, too."

"Things didn't go so well with Dan," Bob murmured, staring down at his coffee.

Samuels nodded, still gazing out at the water.

"And from what Hannah told us about Max, he didn't fare much better." So much had come to light recently; her life with her father had gradually been revealed, and it was a life that made Bob want to weep with pity. Every day Peggy seemed to have something more to tell him. Hannah continued to avoid Bob, but he now saw that he wasn't the only one. Frightened and shy, the girl kept her distance from most men. He felt equally awkward with her, to a degree he didn't really understand, but he made a greater effort to be tolerant.

"We've both had a lot of years to think about this. Time hasn't made it any easier, has it?"

Bob shrugged. "I tried to forget. The bottle didn't help. Without AA and my wife, I'd be dead by now."

"How long have you been sober?"

"Twenty-one years."

"Good."

"How about you?" Bob asked. Each man had dealt with the tragedy in his own way. Bob had relied on alcohol, Dan had gone deep within himself and Max had drifted for years, never settling in one place or one job.

"Nothing I could say or do has the power to change what happened," Samuels admitted. "I blamed myself. I was the one in charge, the one responsible. I couldn't bring those villagers back from the dead, but I could dedicate my life to my country. I've served the military to the best of my ability."

Bob slowly raised his eyes to study the other man. Looking at him closely he saw haggard features that revealed the torment of the years. His mouth thinned and he swallowed hard.

"I know what you mean," Bob said quietly.

"I'm glad you suggested we talk, but for another reason." Samuels paused long enough to sip his coffee. "After I learned about Max's death, I decided to find out what I could. Two men dead within such a short time made me wonder whether you and I were at risk, too."

Bob considered mentioning his own fears, but remained silent.

"I felt it was important to finally confront the past. I'd spent all these years living with what I'd done. I was up for a Congressional Committee appointment, and I knew that my background would be investigated. What I discovered shocked me and it'll shock you." He gazed out at the cove again. "The massacre was documented in the files of Army Intelligence."

Bob's mouth fell open. "How could it have been? We were alone—no one knew. Someone talked?" Bob refused to believe it. Dan hadn't, and he'd kept his own mouth shut all these years.

"No. A reconnaissance group was there, hidden in the jungle. Snipers had been deployed to the village because of reported Viet Cong activity."

"Just a minute." Bob held up his hand, stopping the other man. His mind was racing, and he actually felt dizzy. This was more than he could take in all at once. "Are you saying someone actually saw everything that happened and reported it?"

Samuels nodded. "A sniper and his lookout. And," he added, "they're both dead. One died later in a helicopter crash, and the other had a heart attack about five years ago."

"The army knew all along what we'd done?"

Again the other man nodded. "As you can imagine, the authorities were eager to bury it as deep as possible, although the army's Criminal Investigation Command had the details." He still hadn't looked at Bob but kept his eyes focused on the water view.

Still Bob didn't fully comprehend everything Samuels was telling him. "The village *was* controlled by Viet Cong?"

Samuels forcefully expelled his breath. "In some ways I think it might've been better if I'd been killed that day. I've never forgotten what I did, or the sight of the women and children I murdered."

"I haven't forgotten, either," Bob added, struggling to retain his composure.

Samuels brushed a hand over his face. "We were doomed the moment we set foot in that village."

The murders of those men, women and children had shaped all four men forever afterward. They could no more go back into the jungle and alter the events of that long-ago afternoon than he could shrug off this load of shame and remorse. Knowing there'd be no official reprisals didn't make any difference to how he felt. Bob sipped his coffee and let it moisten his dry mouth.

"For years I suffered from flashbacks," Samuels confessed. "I was on antidepressants and sleeping pills. I didn't sleep through an entire night for ten years after I got back from Nam." He shrugged. "Often I still don't."

"For me it was nightmares," Bob said.

They were both quiet for several minutes after that, and Bob thought about those other two men, the sniper and his lookout, and what they'd seen. They'd reported it to army intelligence but obviously had never gone to the press. Was that on orders? Or out of loyalty to soldier comrades? He wondered how that experience—and that secret—had affected them. Bob decided he couldn't think about that anymore, not right now.

He broke the silence. "A friend of mine has a couple of questions regarding Russell. I'm hoping you wouldn't mind talking to him."

Samuels's eyes narrowed, and Bob saw his hands clench. "Who is it?"

"A private investigator I hired shortly after Max died. For a while there, I was afraid I might somehow have been involved with his death."

Samuels relaxed his hands. "If I can help, I will," he said simply.

Bob knew Roy was counting on that.

Forty-Seven

"Rachel, phone! Line one," Valerie shouted from the reception desk at Get Nailed.

Smiling apologetically at her client, Rachel reached behind her and grabbed the phone. "This is Rachel."

"Rachel, it's Nate."

Instantly her heart flew into her throat and she blinked wildly, trying to stay calm. "Hi," she said as casually as she could, but her voice was barely more than a whisper. They'd seen each other twice in the last month, at the same time she'd been seeing Bruce. She enjoyed Bruce's company and adored Jolene, but he was more of a friend than a love interest. With Bruce she remained cautious; he seemed to enjoy their dates as much as she did, but there wasn't any deep romance between them and they both knew it.

"Can I see you tonight?" Nate asked urgently.

Rachel frowned. "This isn't a good time for me. Could we talk later?"

"It can't wait. Word just came down that we're shipping out."

The aircraft carrier *George Washington* was leaving the Bremerton shipyard!

"When?"

"Soon. Listen, I know you told me you're seeing this other guy."

"It's not that—"

"I'm involved with someone else, too, but I couldn't leave without at least saying goodbye."

Rachel closed her eyes, not knowing what to say. Before she could decide, her heart answered for her. "All right. When and where?"

He hesitated, and she leapt into the silence.

"Meet me at my place at seven, and we can figure it out then," she said and immediately wanted to kick herself. Was she crazy? This man made her feel weak with longing every time he touched her. Now he was about to leave for what could easily be several months, and she'd just invited him to her home. Even as she spoke, she knew that once Nate was in her front door, neither of them would want to leave.

"Seven. I'll be there," he said, sounding relieved.

"Okay." The line was disconnected.

Rachel's co-workers knew something was up and started questioning her. When she told them Nate was being deployed, it seemed all the girls had advice they wanted to impart.

"Don't do anything stupid," Jane said.

Rachel rolled her eyes. "I'm not going to bed with him, if that's what you think."

"It's exactly what I think," Terri said as she sidled up to Rachel's station. "You're nuts about this guy."

"I don't know what I feel," she insisted, and it was true. Okay, there was a mutual physical attraction, but a relationship needed more than sex. If all she was looking for was physical, she could have it any night of the week. Even in this age of frightening consequences, she knew women who changed sexual partners as often as they changed their shoes. Rachel didn't want casual sex; she wanted an emotional connection and a sense of genuine intimacy.

By the time she finished at the salon, Rachel was totally confused, torn between caution and wild desire. Her last appointment showed up late, so she didn't get home to her small town house until almost six-thirty. The first thing she did was jump in the shower and then change clothes. Her hair was still wet when the doorbell rang. As quickly as she could, she added styling gel to her curls, ran her fingers through them and dashed to the door.

Nate stood there waiting. His eyes widened with appreciation when he saw her. "Hi."

"Hi," she said. "Come on in." Before he could move, she held out a hand, stopping him. "Maybe that's not such a good idea. What do you think?"

Nate grinned. "I'm thinking if I come inside, it could be dangerous." He stared down at his feet and sighed. "To tell you the truth, I don't know if I should be here, but I couldn't stay away."

Rachel had no answer to give him, but she silently rejoiced at his words.

His eyes held hers. "I've got a girlfriend back home. You know that."

She nodded.

"You're seeing that widower guy."

"I am." They'd been honest with each other from the beginning.

He continued to stand there, his eyes directly on hers.

"I'll miss you when you go to sea," she murmured.

"I'll miss you, too." He jerked his fingers through his

hair in a nervous gesture. "Listen, we could go to dinner if you want. Talk."

"Sure." He seemed as aware of the sexual energy between them as she was. It was best to avoid temptation, she told herself, but she could still enjoy an evening with him—which seemed like a reasonable compromise. "Let me put on a pair of shoes and get my sweater."

"Okay."

He waited by the door as Rachel hurried into her bedroom, got what she needed and returned a moment later. Locking up, she followed him out to his car.

They ate at the Taco Shack and fed each other pickled jalapeños. Nate was the only man she knew who liked food as spicy as she did. They laughed and talked and seemed to have a million things to say to each other. The evening flew by and before Rachel realized it, the restaurant was closing.

"I guess I'd better take you home," Nate said.

She reluctantly agreed. When she'd told him she was going to miss him, she hadn't been flirting; she'd been telling the simple truth. They drove back to her place in silence.

"I'll e-mail you, all right?"

"I don't have a computer," Rachel said. She'd never dated a guy in the Navy before, so this was all new to her.

"Oh. That might make it difficult to stay in touch." He was clearly disappointed.

"How long do you think you'll be away?"

"No idea. The Navy doesn't let me help with the decision-making."

She smiled at his sense of humor. They arrived at her house, and he pulled alongside the curb but kept the engine running.

They sat for a few minutes, neither speaking. "Rachel, I

really enjoyed tonight. Every time I'm with you, I come away wanting to see you again and then I remember..."

She turned and pressed her finger to his lips. "Don't say it."

Nate hugged her and leaned his forehead against hers. "I've never wanted to kiss a woman more than I want to kiss you right now. I can't, though, because I know what'll happen next."

Rachel knew it, too.

"But I don't think I can stop myself." Groaning, he closed his eyes, then gently, sweetly, touched his mouth to hers. His arms tightened around her and he sighed. Slowly he withdrew his lips from hers before their brief kiss could develop into anything more. "I'll walk you to your door," he said in a low, husky voice.

"You don't need to. I can see myself in."

"No," he insisted. "My mother would have my head if I didn't."

"Okay." He certainly wasn't making this easy.

He held her hand as they walked to her door, which he unlocked. When he'd finished, he handed her back the keys.

"I'll wait to hear from you," she said.

He nodded.

"Be safe, Nate."

He nodded again, his expression somber.

Rachel lightly touched the side of his face and, unable to resist, brought her lips to his. Like him, she didn't give the kiss a chance to become anything more than a quick farewell. She walked hurriedly inside.

Nate returned to his car and once she'd heard him pull away from the curb, Rachel opened the front door and stood looking down the street. The tears that burned her eyes shocked her a little. She hardly knew Nate Olsen. They'd gone out a grand total of three times, and at the end of every one of these dates, she'd had the impression she wouldn't see him again.

Sniffling, Rachel went into the bathroom and grabbed a tissue. If she was going to fall in love, the least she could do was be smart about it. Oh, no, not her. She had to complicate everything and fall for a sailor who was as good as engaged to another woman.

Sitting in the dark with her bare feet on the coffee table, she continued to bemoan her pathetic love life. The light over her door shone dimly, but it didn't really illuminate the room, despite the uncurtained windows. If she had any sense, she'd get up and turn on the lamp, but in her present frame of mind she preferred to sit in the dark.

Someone knocked on her door, and through her window she could see the shadowy shape of a man. Her breath caught in her throat as she ran to answer it. There, on the other side, stood Nate with his hands shoved in his back pockets.

At first all they did was stare at each other. Then, as if magnetically drawn to him, she stepped closer.

"I don't know what's happening to us," he whispered, "but I couldn't just leave you like this."

Rachel felt the same way.

"For the first time since I joined the Navy, I don't want to go to sea."

Rachel didn't want him to leave, either.

"Come with me."

"Where?"

"I don't know. Let's sit on the beach and watch the stars."

She wanted to shriek and sob with joy. "Are you going to kiss me?"

He grinned boyishly. "Probably. Are you going to let me?"

She smiled, too. "I'm thinking about it."

He threw back his head and laughed. "Don't think too long."

Forty-Eight

The alarm buzzed and with a frustrated groan, Ian rolled over and cuddled Cecilia close. Slipping his hand over her waist, he lightly pressed his palm to the ever-so-slight bulge.

"Hmm," Cecilia purred softly as the radio played a Carly Simon tune. "Don't tell me it's time to get up."

He kissed the top of her head. "Afraid so."

She laid her hand over his. "Baby says good morning, too."

"Morning, baby," Ian whispered. The words nearly stalled in his throat. This was the last morning he'd be with Cecilia until after the baby was born. The *George Washington* was being deployed to the South Pacific for the next number of months. Six was what they'd been told, but it could be longer.

Cecilia rolled onto her back and looked up at him with her dark brown eyes. "Everything's going to be okay. Stop worrying."

Ian wasn't sure whether she was trying to convince him or herself.

"I'll be fine. I have friends this time." She rested her head against his bare shoulder.

"Does that mean you won't miss me?" Ian attempted to make a joke out of it, but failed.

"Oh, honey, you know I will."

"Some husbands and wives get into big fights about now. Makes it easier to leave."

Kissing his jaw, she whispered, "I'd rather make love than argue."

"Me, too." He never was much good at arguing with her, anyway. He loved Cecilia beyond reason. And, in spite of his fears, he'd come to believe that if they continued to put off having another child until he felt "ready," it would never happen.

"How much time do we have?" Cecilia whispered as she stroked his upper arms.

He nibbled on her ear. "Enough."

Her smile was slow and sexy as she tucked one silky leg between his. Their lovemaking was hot and urgent. Afterward they held each other for a long time, neither willing to release the other. It meant they had to rush so he could make his quarters, but Ian didn't care.

Cecilia hurriedly dressed to drive him to the shipyard. While he gathered up the remainder of his things, she walked out to the parking area to start the car. Although she'd tried to hide it, Ian had seen the tears in her eyes. She wasn't the only one who felt emotionally shaky; in all the years he'd been with the Navy, he'd never dreaded going to sea the way he did now. His attitude must have shown because the minute he slipped into the car, Cecilia offered him an encouraging smile.

"Everything's going to be fine," she assured him again, but he read through her bravado.

Ian desperately wanted to believe her. But he couldn't quite overcome his doubts. Dread almost overwhelmed him as she backed out of the parking area.

"It really is all right, Ian." She gently touched his knee.

"You know this, do you?" He didn't mean to sound so sharp, but every fear caused by the death of their first child was staring him in the face with this second one. The knot in his stomach refused to go away and wouldn't until he knew for a fact that she'd delivered a healthy baby girl.

"I'll send you updates every time I go to the doctor."

"Promise?" Mixed in with his fears was the suspicion that Cecilia would try to protect him from the truth. But he wanted to know every detail of her pregnancy. *Needed* to know.

"I promise," she vowed.

They rode in silence for a short while. All the time Cecilia was driving, Ian worried that when the moment came to leave, he wouldn't be able to do it. His gut told him this deployment was history repeating itself. They'd known Cecilia was pregnant with a girl when he'd left three years ago. She was pregnant again with a girl.

He'd been at sea when Allison was born.

He'd be at sea when their second child was born, too.

Cecilia's ultrasound had looked perfectly normal the first time.

This ultrasound revealed nothing abnormal, either.

Now he was leaving, and the weight on his chest was almost more than he could bear.

Forty-Nine

Maryellen sat on the balcony outside the master bedroom and stared out over the calm waters of Puget Sound. She could see Mount Rainier clearly in the distance. It seemed close enough to touch.

Katie slept peacefully, curled up on Maryellen's lap. The little girl's hand clutched her favorite blanket, her other thumb in her mouth.

Closing her eyes, she breathed in the briny scent of the sea and listened to the muted sounds of late afternoon. It'd been nine days since she'd miscarried her baby. Nine days since she'd slept a whole night, and nine days since her heart was torn to shreds.

Jon had been attentive and thoughtful, anticipating her every need. Yet they lived as polite strangers. He was worried about her, and Maryellen suspected he'd talked to her mother because Grace had been by to visit nearly every day.

At the sound of her husband's footsteps behind her, Maryellen glanced over her shoulder.

"Did I wake you?" he asked.

She shook her head.

"Do you want something to drink?"

She declined with another shake of her head.

Jon sat down in the rocking chair beside the swing. "We haven't talked in a while."

Maryellen cradled her sleeping daughter. "There hasn't been anything to say."

"I'm sorry about the baby." Jon's words were hoarse with emotion. He said it so often, and each time it made her want to weep all over again.

"Do you mind if we don't discuss the miscarriage? There is no baby."

Jon wiped a hand over his face. "I blame myself for this."

"You did nothing, Jon. You have nothing to feel guilty about. These things happen." She repeated what the physician had said, but his words had been of little comfort then and were of less comfort now. However, that was all she had to offer her husband.

"I was angry and stupid."

Maryellen didn't respond.

"You didn't even tell me you were pregnant. You couldn't—because I wouldn't let you."

"Jon, don't. Please don't." She was too depressed to hear him punish himself over this.

"It's because of the pregnancy that you decided to stay with your mother, isn't it?"

Maryellen refused to answer. So many things had gone through her mind the day of Charlotte and Ben's wedding. Jon had been so angry with her and so unforgiving. He'd refused to even talk about it. When she'd left for her mother's, he'd let her go without uttering a single word to stop her. The only reason she was at the house now was that he'd brought her here from the hospital.

Jon got out of the chair and started pacing back and forth. "Maryellen, please just say something."

She looked up at him, puzzled by his outburst. "What do you want me to say?"

"I don't know. Anything. Just don't sit there staring off into the distance. I can't stand to see you like this."

"I'm grieving…"

"For the baby?"

She nodded. "And for us."

Jon leaned against the support column, as if he didn't have the strength to stay upright.

"Less than two weeks ago, you were willing to let Katie and me walk away. Remember?"

Jon didn't answer.

"I know what I did in contacting your parents was wrong," Maryellen whispered, "but I never set out to hurt you. All I wanted to do was help."

"I didn't want your help," he shouted, startling Katie who jumped and began to fuss until she found her thumb again.

With Maryellen's steady hand on her back, Katie quickly returned to sleep. "Let's talk about this another time."

"No." Jon was pacing again, back and forth, like a man possessed. His mouth thinned. "I told you before I don't need my parents, don't want them in my life. You and Katie are the only family I have."

If what he said was true, then he wouldn't have let her drive away that Saturday afternoon.

He held out his hands in silent pleading.

As she continued to watch him, he plowed his fingers through his hair, then straightened and seemed to come to some resolution. "Do you want a divorce?" he asked suddenly.

"No, but I wonder how long our marriage will last."

Her remark obviously shocked him, and Maryellen felt

she had to explain herself. "You so easily cast aside people who love you. If you can cut yourself off from your father and stepmother, then you can do it with Katie and me. In time you probably will."

"That isn't true." He fell to his knees in front of her, clasping her hands and gazing up at her intently. "Look at me, Maryellen. You and Katie are everything to me."

"Until I do something that upsets you."

He stood and put distance between them. "That's not true."

Maryellen didn't have the will to argue. She knew otherwise.

"Do you want me to tell you I'm willing to forget what my father did? Is that what you want me to say?"

"No."

"Then what?"

"I want you to have peace," she whispered.

"Peace?" He repeated the word as if he'd never heard it before. "You want me to *have* peace or you want me to *make* peace with my parents?"

"Both," she said, "but until you find peace within yourself, you won't be able to deal with your parents."

"I was perfectly happy with my life until you came along."

Despite herself, Maryellen grinned. "You only thought you were."

"I don't need them."

"You kept their letters," she said softly.

"I meant to throw them away."

"But you didn't. It must've given you some kind of emotional gratification when they wrote letter after letter, and you never answered."

He narrowed his eyes. "You don't know what you're saying."

She shrugged. "Perhaps not."

"You want me to make peace with them and I can't. I won't. I'm sorry, Maryellen, but even for you I can't do it."

Such a lack of forgiveness was frightening to Maryellen. "I don't expect you to forget what they did, but forgiving is something else," she said.

He shook his head vehemently.

"You must feel a real sense of justification and righteousness knowing how badly they wronged you—and knowing that you're punishing them now."

His eyes blazed, but he held his tongue.

"I don't think I'll ever fully understand the full extent of your pain. Your family betrayed you. They chose your brother over you and you're angry."

"You're damned straight I am."

"You have every right to be. Perhaps they don't deserve your forgiveness, but don't you see what this bitterness has done to you? Don't you understand that until you can let go of this pain, you're incapable of experiencing real joy?"

She could tell he wanted to argue with her, but she didn't give him the opportunity.

"Now you're angry with me," she said, "and I admit it was wrong to go behind your back. But you let me walk away because that sense of righteous indignation was more valuable to you than your love for me."

He opened his mouth to challenge her, but apparently changed his mind. He paced, his steps speeding up, then slowing as he went through some internal argument. "What should I do?"

"Look in your heart. Work on your attitude, your unwillingness to release all this pain."

Jon shook his head, hopelessly this time, as if she was asking the impossible. "You make it sound so easy."

"I know it can't be."

He sighed deeply and his shoulders sagged in defeat. "You're welcome to keep in touch with them if you want."

"What about you?"

His jaw tightened. "I'll wait a while, but I'll try, Maryellen. For you and Katie, I'll try."

In that moment, the cloud of depression that had hung over her since the miscarriage lifted. She held open her arms to Jon and was quickly engulfed in his embrace, with Katie between them.

"I can't ask for more than that," she whispered.

Fifty

Bob had been prepared to dislike Stewart Samuels, but in the days since he'd arrived in Cedar Cove, he'd had ample opportunity to gain a healthy respect for the other man.

Because of a meeting with some old friends from the police academy, Roy had been out of town. As soon as Corrie notified him that Samuels was in Cedar Cove, Roy had altered his travel plans and was due to get back late Monday morning.

By unspoken agreement, Stewart Samuels and Bob didn't discuss Maxwell Russell. For the most part, Hannah had stayed out of sight during Stewart's visits to the house. When Bob asked Peggy about it, his wife was eager to make excuses for her. For some reason, Samuels frightened the girl, but that didn't really surprise Bob. He supposed it was because of Hannah's wariness around men. She preferred her own company and often stayed in her room, where she read or watched television. Peggy was the only one with whom she seemed to feel comfortable.

Roy arrived a little after one on Monday afternoon, and to Bob's surprise Troy Davis, the local sheriff, showed up with him. Stewart Samuels was already at the house when Bob answered the door. He led the two other men into the living room.

"Sit down," Bob instructed everyone when the introductions had been made. Peggy quickly distributed coffee, then sat down next to Bob. He took her hand and they entwined their fingers.

Roy reached inside his pocket, pulling out a small notebook. "I have a couple of questions, if you don't mind?" He looked at the sheriff as if seeking his approval.

"I'll answer them if I can," Samuels assured him, leaning forward slightly.

Roy nodded, his pen poised. "Tell me about the first time you met Russell after his accident."

"We didn't meet. Everything was handled over the phone."

"That can't be," Peggy said and then instantly shrank back as if she wanted to retrieve the words. "I'm sorry. Go on."

Samuels shrugged, obviously a little puzzled at the outburst. "I'm sure I'm right about this, Peggy. Max had the physician contact me to ask for my assistance in getting him into a veterans' facility. He needed extensive plastic surgery. Apparently he had only limited health insurance."

"You never went out to California to see him following the surgery?"

"Never." Samuels was adamant. "I did speak to him a few times, however."

"When was that?" Troy asked.

"I can't recall the exact dates, but it was after he'd undergone surgery, which I understand was successful."

"What did he want to know when he phoned?"

"Actually I was the one who called him," the colonel explained. "The hospital social worker reported on his progress and suggested Max get some counseling. He suffered from post-traumatic stress syndrome. I urged him to sign up for the sessions."

"Did he agree?"

"Yes. The doctor told me later that Max had a number of appointments and they seemed to be going well. I was encouraged the next time I talked to Max himself. I only spoke with his counselor once, but she seemed pleased with his progress."

"Do you know of any reason he'd want to visit Cedar Cove?"

"None, except…" He hesitated and gazed down at his folded hands. "It might've had something to do with the therapy sessions—some desire to reconcile himself to what happened in Nam." Samuels paused. "As I recall, he was tight with Dan Sherman back then."

"Did he mention that he intended to visit Dan?" Roy asked.

"No. Like I said, I only talked to him two or three times."

The sheriff spoke next. "When did you learn he'd been murdered?"

"When Mr. McAfee contacted me," Samuels said, nodding toward Roy. "I've received intermittent communications since then, from Mr. McAfee and from you."

"Peggy," Troy began, turning to her. "You said something earlier."

She shook her head nervously. "I'm sure I misunderstood."

"Misunderstood what?" he pressed.

"Hannah," she said, rubbing her index finger over her cuticles. "We were discussing her father recently, and she told me she saw Colonel Samuels talking to Max shortly before he left California."

"That isn't possible," Samuels told her. "I was in Washington D.C. on assignment nearly all of last year. The only trips I made were to England and Belgium."

"That would be easy enough to verify," Roy said to Davis.

"Let's do it right now," Samuels insisted. "If you have a specific date in mind, I can have my assistant pull up my calendar and we'll go through it online."

Troy Davis accompanied the colonel into the other room, where Bob kept a computer on his desk. Bob had already turned it on, since he'd been using a bookkeeping program earlier. Now, as they waited, Roy sipped his coffee. Bob loosened his hold on Peggy's hand. This wasn't nearly as intimidating or awkward as he'd feared.

"Is Hannah here?" Roy asked.

"She's in her room," Peggy said, "but I'd like to keep her out of this as much as possible. Anytime someone mentions her father, she gets upset."

Roy looked from Peggy to Bob. "We'll need her to verify the facts."

Peggy still seemed uncertain. "She's been through so much already, I hate to drag her into this. As you can imagine, Hannah's easily upset, especially when it involves anything to do with her parents."

"In the long run, this will help her," Roy said.

Peggy turned to Bob. "I agree with Roy," he said. "The only reason she's living with us is because we want to help her. This discussion might put some ghosts to rest for her."

Peggy left and returned to the living room before Troy and Stewart Samuels came back. Hannah resembled a frightened child about to be called to task. She stayed close to Peggy's side, her head bowed. After a brief nod in Bob's direction, Hannah sat on the ottoman beside Peggy. In a gesture of reassurance and comfort, Peggy placed her hand on Hannah's shoulder.

"You never told us that your father was in counseling," Roy said, speaking to Hannah.

"I'm sure I did. Didn't I?" she asked Peggy.

Peggy shrugged. "I'm sorry, I don't recall if you did or not."

Hannah laughed weakly. "What's the big deal? He saw a counselor."

"You said he often carried false identification, too," Bob added.

"We certainly could have used that information earlier," Troy muttered, straightening.

"My father was never able to hold down a job for long," Hannah rushed to explain. Her eyes darted between the sheriff and Roy. "He…he sometimes used a different name in a different town."

"That isn't what you told me before," Troy said. "When I asked you about it, you claimed you couldn't imagine your father doing such a thing."

"I…I was in shock," Hannah whispered, staring at the carpet. "I can't remember everything you asked me. I'd just learned that my father was dead and that he might've been murdered." She buried her face in her hands and Peggy gently patted her back, glaring at the sheriff as if he were purposely intimidating the poor girl.

"Sheriff Davis, is this necessary?" she asked when Hannah started to sob.

"This is a murder investigation, Peggy."

"You think I murdered my own father?" Hannah cried, leaping to her feet. "He was the only person I had in the world! Why would I want him dead?" She gestured wildly at Samuels. "He's the one who's up for some important promotion—he's the one who led those men into that village and killed all those women and children."

Peggy gasped. "How…how did you know?"

"My dad told me all about it while he was in counseling. He was a murderer, and so are Bob and him." She pointed a shaking finger at the colonel. "I think he killed my father, too."

"I was in Europe at the time of your father's death," Stewart Samuels said evenly.

"Sure you were—he was drugged, remember?" she said viciously. "You came to the house and gave him that water bottle and then you left."

"The dates of Colonel Samuels's travel record state otherwise, Hannah," Sheriff Davis said calmly. "If anyone was with your father before he decided to drive to Cedar Cove, it was you."

She shook her head in denial. "I didn't even know he was leaving."

"That's not what you told me," Roy said.

"Then…then there's been some misunderstanding." Hannah began to back away, easing toward the kitchen one small step at a time.

"Stop hounding the girl," Peggy insisted. "Can't you see you're frightening her?"

"I've always found it curious that the drug used to kill Maxwell Russell is commonly seen in date rape situations," Roy said. "It's generally considered a young person's drug."

The room went quiet as everyone stared at Hannah.

"I first noticed the inconsistencies in your answers the afternoon I spoke with you on the phone, Hannah," Roy continued. "I talked it over with the colonel and was able to verify his statements, but not yours. Perhaps you can explain yourself."

"Of course I can," Hannah said.

"You said your father was a good man."

"He was," Hannah cried.

"But he couldn't hold down a job?"

"He tried…."

"He abused your mother?"

"Yes!" the young woman screamed. "Nothing was ever

good enough for him. I hated him. I loved him." Her face twisted into a mask of pain and fear. She stood with her hands in tight fists. "He deserved to die. He should've been the one killed in the accident, not Mom."

"Hannah." Peggy was instantly at her side. "You don't know what you're saying."

Shoving Peggy aside, Hannah faced the others. "You're all alike, aren't you?"

"What happened to your mother?" Troy asked.

"She died. My father was the one who was supposed to be killed, not my mother. I paid my friend Davey to put air in the steering column of Dad's car. He'd lose control of the car and it would crash. It was supposed to be so easy, but then Mom decided to go with him.

"I tried to get her to stay home, but she wouldn't listen. Dad wanted her to come along and she refused him nothing." The words were spat out with such anger that her face was contorted. Bob had never witnessed anything like it.

"He suffered, you know. That was good. It made everything better when I saw how badly he'd been burned. Still, it wasn't enough. I could have killed him in the hospital. I wanted to, but when I saw that he was in agony, I thought death was too good for him."

"Hannah," Peggy cried, "don't say any more. You don't mean any of this."

"Yes, I do," she cried. "I mean every single word. My father was a bastard and I hated him for what he did to my mother and me. I could never have friends, bring them to the house. Every time I had a friend we moved. Dad would lose his job again or the neighbors would hear him beating on Mom. He broke my arm when I was six, you know." Her eyes narrowed. "No, you don't know because no one knew. I couldn't tell the doctors what really happened. I was supposed to have fallen down the stairs." She shook her head, her voice rising. "I made him pay for that, too. Davey helped me. He bought me the roofies and told me how to do it. He said I wouldn't get caught!"

"Hannah Russell, you have the right to remain silent," Troy said, standing. He advanced toward her slowly. "Anything you say can and will be used against you in a court of law."

"Shut up," she screamed so loudly it hurt Bob's ears.

"Hannah, please," Peggy pleaded.

"No…not this time," she screeched. "Then Dad started talking to that shrink and he changed. He wanted to start his life over and be happy. I couldn't let him be happy, not after the hell he'd put me through. He deserved to die. I wanted him dead. Dead," she shouted. "Dead and burned and gone forever."

Troy walked over to Hannah with a pair of handcuffs and when she realized she was about to be arrested, she fell to her knees and broke into deep sobs.

Peggy moved to comfort Hannah, but Bob stopped her. Hannah had murdered her own father. All these weeks, they'd been housing the killer and not known it. Peggy turned to Bob, burying her face in his shoulder.

"It's over now," he whispered soothingly.

"Did you know?" she asked, looking up at him.

He shook his head.

Davis led a sobbing Hannah out to his patrol car. The young woman glanced over her shoulder at Peggy as if silently pleading for help. Peggy held her hand over her mouth. This was difficult for her, Bob knew, but she stood silently beside him.

Then Hannah let loose with a string of swearwords that shocked them all. Even from inside they could hear her clearly. The room went completely still after Troy had driven off.

Roy left soon afterward and only Peggy, Bob and Stewart Samuels remained.

"I'm sorry it came to this," Stewart said. "Sorry I didn't confront the past sooner and deal with these issues."

"We each buried that day as deep as we could," Bob said. "Now it's been unearthed...."

"And now maybe the two of us can get on with our lives."

For the first time since he'd returned from Vietnam, Bob felt that was possible. There would always be guilt, but perhaps he could find a way to expiate his sins.

Fifty-One

The aerobics class seemed easier this Wednesday evening, despite the sweat Grace could feel on her brow. Lunging left, then right as the loud music vibrated through the room, she followed the instructor's lead, using every ounce of energy she had.

Perhaps this surplus of vigor was due to her mood. She was still furious with Will Jefferson. She hadn't seen or heard from Cliff in a week. Once again, his faith in her had been shaken, and somehow she doubted she'd hear from him again. Will's express purpose was to destroy any possibility that Grace might find happiness with another man, but she refused to let him succeed. She didn't understand any of it—his willingness to betray his wife, his insistence on a relationship with Grace or his apparent vindictiveness at her rejection. But, dammit, she wasn't letting him ruin her chances with Cliff!

"Good luck, buster," she muttered under her breath and with a burst of energy finished the program. She hadn't come this close only to lose Cliff without a fight. If he didn't call her soon, she'd go back to sending him notes and e-mails.

"What was that you just said?" Olivia gasped as the music ended. Her reddened face glistened with sweat.

"Never mind," Grace whispered. The cool-down exercises started, her least favorite part of the workout. Grace retrieved her mat from the corner of the room, and placed it next to Olivia's. Perhaps it was her age, but it was becoming increasingly difficult to do some of these stretches. Especially the one in which she had to bend one leg and cross it over the other and then turn to the side. She always seemed to be facing in the wrong direction.

"You've been in a bad mood all night," Olivia said when they'd completed the class and walked to the dressing room. "What's gotten into you?"

Grace shrugged.

"Cliff?"

She didn't answer. "Do you have time for coffee?" she asked instead.

"I can't," Olivia said regretfully. "Jack's still at work, and I know if I don't literally drag him out of that office, he'll be there half the night."

"Poor Jack."

"Poor Jack nothing. I feel like a widow! We should still be in our honeymoon phase," Olivia complained. "I wish the management would let him hire an assistant editor."

"They should," Grace agreed.

"You're telling me." Olivia reached for her towel and wiped her face. "I can't apologize enough for my brother. I'm so angry with him."

Grace dismissed her friend's concern. Olivia wasn't responsible for Will's behavior. Neither was Charlotte. The best excuse or explanation they'd come up with was some kind of midlife crisis, but neither she nor Olivia had much sympathy with that.

"What are you doing Saturday?" Olivia asked. "Maybe we can go to brunch or the movies or something?"

"Why don't we go to an afternoon show?" She was working at the animal shelter in the morning, and planning to have dinner with Kelly and Paul that evening.

"You're on," Olivia said as she headed to the showers. "I'll call you later and we can pick a movie."

Grace smiled in agreement.

Still feeling out of sorts, Grace returned to the house. Buttercup, ever faithful, was waiting for her when Grace unlocked the door. She turned on the lights and found Sherlock curled up nose to tail, sleeping on her sofa.

"Hello to you, too," she chided as she brought her exercise gear to the laundry room.

The blinking light on her answering machine caught her attention, and she grabbed a pen and paper, then pushed the play button. At the sound of Cliff's voice, a huge smile broke across her face. She hadn't heard the whole message before she punched out his number.

Cliff answered on the second ring. His hello was gruff, which was typical.

"Hi," Grace said. "I wondered if I'd hear from you."

"I've been busy."

"I know. Me too. How are you?"

"Okay. You?"

"Better now that I've heard from you." Even over the phone line, Grace felt his smile.

"Lisa called this afternoon. She wanted an update on what's happening between us."

"What did you tell her?" Grace carried the phone into the living room, sat on the sofa and moved Sherlock into her lap. The cat didn't like being disturbed, but settled down quickly enough.

"The truth."

"Which is?" Grace asked, stroking glossy black fur.

"That I can't seem to stop loving you, despite my best efforts."

Grace felt tears prick her eyes. "I can't seem to stop loving you, either."

Cliff exhaled softly. "I know it's a little early, but I was hoping you could join me for Thanksgiving again this year."

"Are you flying out to be with Lisa and her family?"

"No. Since I spent time with her this summer I'll probably just stay here."

"Alone?"

He sighed. "Not if I can help it."

"Would you like to have dinner with me and the girls?" Grace didn't know yet what her daughters' plans were, but it would be easy enough to find out.

"Can I invite Cal, too?"

"Of course." Grace remembered that Cal was one of the bachelors who'd been on the auction block. "Speaking of Cal, has he gone out with Linnette McAfee yet?"

"Nope. I don't think she's too thrilled with her mother setting this up," Cliff said wryly. "And Cal's blaming me, since I encouraged him to participate."

"Is Linnette already living in Cedar Cove?" Grace had been too busy to keep up with the latest regarding the clinic. She knew Linnette had accepted the job of physician's assistant. The lot had been cleared and the structure was going up so fast, it was hard to believe that just a few weeks earlier there'd been absolutely nothing in that location.

"Not yet. I gather she'll be moving here next month to help set things up. According to Charlotte, the clinic should be in full operation by the first of the year."

"That's great. And I guess it means Cal will have his date soon."

"Seems that way," Cliff said. "Frankly I think it'll do him good."

"I think so, too."

"Will I see you before Thanksgiving?" she asked.

"Probably."

"I'll take that as a yes."

"Do you want to come out here Friday afternoon after work?"

"I think that can be arranged," Grace said.

They spoke for a few more minutes and by the time Grace hung up, she felt more hopeful than she had in days.

Buttercup walked over to the sofa to receive her share of attention. Sherlock, still reclining on Grace's lap, lazily opened one eye but didn't object to Buttercup's presence. Grace stroked her dog's head, smiling. She'd worked hard to regain Cliff's trust and was determined never to give him reason to doubt her again. This was one lesson she'd learned and learned well.

Fifty-Two

Corrie McAfee looked up from the playing cards in her hand and sighed as she tried to remember which suit went with which. Giving up, she stared helplessly across the table at Peggy, sending her a silent plea.

The two couples had spent a delightful evening together and after dinner had decided to play pinochle. Corrie hadn't played in years, so her skills were weak, and unfortunately Roy took such games far too seriously. Peggy had been more than willing to be her partner, although Corrie could tell her friend's mind wasn't on the game. For that matter, neither was hers.

"What's your bid?" Roy helped himself to a pretzel as he studied his own hand. Her husband and Bob Beldon had walked away with the first three games and gloried in their triumph a little too much.

"You guys have already won three in a row," Corrie said. "I think Peggy and I could use a break."

"Ah, it's just getting good," Bob protested.

"I'll make some popcorn," Corrie said, hoping the two men would be willing to put the game aside for that long.

"All right, all right," Roy muttered, not concealing his disappointment. He could be so competitive sometimes.

Peggy followed Corrie into the kitchen and leaned against the counter as Corrie set up the hot-air popcorn popper. She took a stick of butter from the fridge and cut a generous cube to melt in the microwave. "I can't bear to eat popcorn without real butter," she explained. With the machine making its usual racket, Corrie joined her friend at the counter.

"I still can't believe it…" Peggy let the words fade.

"You're in shock about Hannah, aren't you?"

Peggy nodded. "Not for even a second did I suspect she was capable of murder."

"Have you been to see her at the jail?"

Peggy shook her head. "She's refused all visitors, including me."

That must be hurtful to Peggy, Corrie thought as she dumped the popcorn in a large bowl and poured on the melted butter.

"I talked to Troy Davis earlier in the week and he told me Hannah's decided to take a plea bargain. Once all the legalities have been dealt with, she'll be transferred to the women's prison in Purdy."

"I can only imagine how difficult this must be for you," Corrie said sympathetically. Peggy had grown close to Hannah over the last few weeks. The horror of learning that the young woman was responsible for her parents' deaths had, needless to say, distressed her. At this stage, Peggy couldn't influence the girl's situation at all. The authorities in California had been notified and were in the process of arresting the friend who'd tampered with her father's car and bought her the drug. Extradition papers would be filed against Hannah soon. Unless a deal could be made, she'd stand trial in her home state of California.

"I'm so sorry," Corrie whispered, touching her friend's arm.

"I know. I am, too. She's ruined her entire life." Peggy bowed her head for a moment, then looked up. "What I want to know is when Roy and the sheriff figured it out."

Not sure what to tell her, Corrie shrugged. "I can't answer that. Although we work in the same office, my husband usually keeps his suspicions to himself. Half the time I don't have a clue what's going through that thick head of his. What I *can* tell you is that he and Troy discussed the case now and then and compared notes."

Peggy's expression was pained, as if she was reliving the moment of Hannah's arrest.

"My guess is that Roy and the sheriff went over their ideas together and came to the same conclusion," Corrie said.

"Are you talking about me and my brilliant mind again?" Roy asked as he stepped into the kitchen, Bob directly behind him.

"Obviously we've so outplayed you women that you're ready to admit defeat," Bob said smugly.

"We could always put on a DVD," Roy suggested, scooping up a handful of buttered popcorn. "Nothing goes better with popcorn than a movie."

Bob yawned. "I don't know if we should. It's getting to be the witching hour for me."

"Me, too," Peggy said reluctantly. She turned to Corrie. "Dinner was wonderful. An evening out was just what Bob and I needed to get our minds off this mess."

"It was our pleasure," Roy said. He slipped his arm around Corrie's waist and they accompanied their friends to the front door. When Corrie had retrieved their jackets from the hall closet, Roy politely held Peggy's for her.

"Look," Peggy said when they opened the door. "Someone left you a gift."

A beautifully arranged fruit basket stood on the porch. Filled with apples, oranges, bananas, grapes and a variety of nuts and chocolate, it was wrapped in silvery cellophane and decorated with a large plaid bow.

"Who would send us something like this?" Corrie asked, surprised and pleased, but when she bent to reach for it, Roy stopped her.

"A more important question is who'd drop it off without ringing our doorbell?" His arm restrained her from lifting the basket. "Leave it where it is," he said, frowning.

Corrie stared at her husband. "Do you think it's the same person who mailed us those postcards?" she asked, her voice low.

"I don't know."

"It looks like there's a card with the fruit," Peggy said.

Before Roy could object, Peggy pulled it from the basket. Corrie blinked, half-afraid something might explode in her friend's face. She sighed with relief when nothing happened.

"Maybe it's an early Thanksgiving gift." Peggy handed the card to Roy. "We'd better go."

Bob nodded and after another round of thank-yous and farewells, they headed toward their car.

"Open it," Corrie said even before the Beldons had pulled away from the curb.

"In a minute," Roy muttered. He stepped into the house and Corrie followed him. Roy examined the envelope. It was addressed to the McAfees at 50 Harbor Street, so the fruit had been delivered to the right house. Roy held the small envelope up to a light before he tore it open.

Inside was a single piece of typed paper.

"What does it say?" Corrie asked urgently. She didn't want Roy hiding anything from her. It was only by chance that she'd learned about the postcards.

Roy scanned the letter and gave it to her.

I don't mean you any ill will. I just want you to think about what you did. Don't you have a single regret?

Corrie quickly read the note and looked up at her husband with frightened eyes. "What does this mean?" she asked.

Roy shook his head. "I have no idea. I guess we'll have to wait for the next message."

He placed his arm around Corrie's waist. He didn't have the answer yet, but he would soon. He'd cleared too many cases not to succeed at solving this one.

Whoever was doing this, it was personal. Sending the fruit basket to 50 Harbor Street had breached the sanctity of his home. But he'd find out who'd done this.

His instincts still told him that he and Corrie weren't in physical danger. But there were other dangers, less obvious ones, and Roy knew they could cause just as much harm.

He wasn't prepared to let *anyone* risk the haven he and Corrie had found in Cedar Cove.

Watch for
50 HARBOR STREET
in March 2010!

*Discover what Roy eventually learns about the person who's
sending him and Corrie these "messages." You'll want to
keep up with your other friends in Cedar Cove, too.
How do things go for Grace and Cliff? What about
Olivia and Jack? Will Cecilia's baby be all right?
And Rachel — will she choose Nate or Bruce?*

Read on for a look at the first chapter…

One

Corrie McAfee was worried. And she knew that her husband, Roy, was too.

Who wouldn't be? Starting in July, Roy—a private investigator—had received a series of anonymous postcards, and while the messages weren't overtly threatening, they were certainly distressing.

The first communication, which had been mailed to the office, spoke of regrets. During the intervening weeks, there'd been several others. Corrie had read each postcard so often she'd memorized them all. The first one stated: EVERYONE HAS REGRETS. IS THERE ANYTHING YOU'VE DONE YOU WISH YOU COULD DO OVER? THINK ABOUT IT. There hadn't been a signature then, or on any of the other cards. They'd arrived at infrequent intervals and been mailed from different locations. The cryptic messages kept playing in her mind. The passing of time hadn't helped; she was as much in the dark now, in October, as when she'd seen that first postcard.

There was a final gasping, gurgling sound as the coffee drained into the glass pot. The noise distracted Corrie from her worries for a moment—long enough to glance out the wide office window that overlooked downtown Cedar Cove, Washington. Serving as Roy's secretary and assistant had its advantages, and in this instance, disadvantages. Sometimes ignorance truly was bliss; the current situation was definitely one of those cases. She'd sleep better if she'd never learned about the mysterious postcards.

And yet...even if Roy had managed to keep them hidden from her, she would still have known—because the last message had been hand-delivered, at night, to their front door. Not to the office like the others, but to their home. Late one evening, someone had walked up the sidewalk and onto the porch of their house. As it happened, Roy and Corrie were entertaining dinner guests that night—and had opened the door to discover that an unknown person had left a fruit basket and an accompanying note. Chills raced up Corrie's spine at the thought that this person knew their home address.

"Is that coffee ready yet?" Roy called from inside his office. Apparently she hadn't delivered it fast enough.

"Hold your horses—it's coming." Corrie didn't mean to snap at her husband. Normally she wasn't short-tempered. This uncharacteristic outburst revealed how upset she was by everything that was happening to them. Sighing, she filled a clean mug for Roy and carried it, steam rising, into his office.

"Okay, that does it," she said, putting the coffee on the corner of his desk. "We have to talk."

As if he didn't have a care in the world, Roy leaned back in his chair and locked his fingers behind his head. They'd been married for twenty-seven years, and Corrie found him as attractive now as she had in college. Roy had played football for the University of Washington and been a "big man on campus," as they used to say. He was tall and broad-shouldered, still muscular, his posture as straight as ever. He stayed in good shape without apparent effort, and Corrie envied, just a bit, the fact that he'd never gained any weight. His dark hair had thinned and was streaked with gray, which only added a look of dignity to his appearance.

Of all the women he dated during college, he'd fallen in love with *her*. Theirs hadn't been an easy courtship, though. They'd broken up for more than a year, and then reunited. Once they were back together, they realized how much they loved each other; there'd been no uncertainty about their feelings. They were married shortly after graduation and their love had endured through trials and tribulations, through good years and bad. They'd had plenty of both.

"Talk about what?" Roy asked casually.

His nonchalance didn't fool Corrie. Her husband knew exactly what was on her mind. "Does THE PAST HAS A WAY OF CATCHING UP WITH THE PRESENT tell you anything?" she murmured, sitting down in the chair normally reserved for clients. She wanted Roy to understand that she wouldn't be put off easily. She was afraid he knew more about these postcards than he'd let on. It would be just like him to try to protect her.

Roy frowned. "Those messages don't have anything to do with you, so don't worry about it."

His answer infuriated her. "How can you say that? Everything that happens to you affects me."

He seemed about to argue, but after all these years, he recognized that she wasn't going to be satisfied with glib reassurances. "I'm not sure what to tell you. I've made enemies and, yes, I have regrets, but who doesn't?"

Roy had reached the rank of detective for the Seattle Police Department and been forced into early retirement because of a back injury. In the beginning, Corrie had been excited to have her husband at home. She'd hoped they'd be able to travel and do some of the things they'd always planned, but it hadn't worked out that way. Roy had the time now, but their finances had been adversely affected when he'd had to take early retirement. Their income was less than it had been by at least twenty percent. In a money-saving effort, they'd moved from Seattle and across Puget Sound to the community of Cedar Cove. The cost of property was much more reasonable in Kitsap County, which also offered a slower pace of life. When the real estate agent showed them the house at 50 Harbor Street, with its wide front porch and sweeping view of the cove and lighthouse, Corrie knew immediately that this house and this town would become their home.

Welcome to Cedar Cove –
a small town with a big heart!

Local private detective Roy McAfee and his wife Corrie have been receiving anonymous postcards with messages asking if they "regret the past." What does it mean?

And it looks like the romance between Cliff at the horse farm and Grace Sherman is back on. Could a wedding be on the cards?

www.mirabooks.co.uk

They had closed a case and stayed on to analyse the results, catching up, enjoying each other's company. It was what they always did, their way of starting afresh. Everyone knew that. John had left the building first, abandoning his insomniac partner.

'Who's conducting the search? They'll have to verify—'

'The fire department's first priority is to make sure it's safe,' said Liberty. 'Of course they'll report their findings as quickly as possible. Anything I hear, you'll know. John's right, you should go home, there's nothing you can do.'

May stared up at the building, suddenly unsure of himself.

Longbright watched the column of rusty smoke rising fast in the still grey air. She felt disconnected from the events surrounding her. It was the termination of a special partnership; their names had been inextricably linked, Bryant, May, Longbright. Now she had left and Bryant was gone, leaving May alone. She had spent so much time in their company that the detectives were more familiar than her closest relatives, like friendly monochrome faces in old films. They had been, and would always be, her family.

Longbright realized she was crying even before she registered the shout, as though time had folded back on itself. A fireman was calling from the blackened apex of the building. She couldn't hear what he was saying, would not allow herself to hear it. As she ran towards the ruins with the fire officers at her heels, the familiar codes started passing through the rescue group.

A single body, an elderly white male, had been located in the wreckage. For Arthur Bryant and John May, an unorthodox alliance had come to a violent end. They were her colleagues, her mentors, her closest friends. She would not allow herself to believe that Bryant was dead.

An immolation had joined the end to the beginning, past and present blown together. John May had always sensed that routine demise would not be enough for his partner. They had just closed a sad, cruel case, their last together.

There were no more outstanding enemies. Bryant had finally started thinking about retirement as the unit headed for a period of radical change, sanctioned by new Home Office policies. He and May had been discussing them only the Friday before, during their customary evening walk to the river. May thought back to their conversation, trying to recall whether they had spoken of anything unusual. They had strolled to Waterloo Bridge at sunset, arguing, joking, at ease in each other's company.

John and Arthur, inseparable, locked together by proximity to death, improbable friends for life.

2

CRIMINAL PAST

'You mean to tell me that amateurs are being invited to solve murders?' asked Arthur Bryant with some surprise. 'Have a pear drop.'

'Is that all you've got?' May rattled the paper bag disappointedly. 'They kill my mouth. A study published by the Scarman Centre had apparently found that trained investigators are no better than non-professionals at telling whether a suspected criminal is lying.' The centre was a leading crime-research institute based at Leicester University. Politicians took its findings very seriously.

'Surely the Home Office and the Association of Chief Police Officers won't endorse the scheme?' Bryant squinted into the bag. 'I thought there was some Winter Mixture left.'

'I don't know where you get those sweets. I'm sure they don't make them any more. HO's already endorsed the plan. They reckon any respected person with common sense and an analytical mind can be recruited. Civilians are going to be given unlimited access to evidence and records. I thought you'd be pleased. You suggested the same thing years ago.'

'Well, the general public have a distinct advantage over us.' Plastic carrier bags floated around the traffic lights at the end of the Strand like predatory jellyfish. The hum of traffic around them was like the drone of bombers. The air was acrid with exhausts. Bryant leaned on his walking stick to catch his breath. The stick was a sore point; May had bought it for his partner's birthday the previous year, but Bryant had been horrified by the suggestion that he was facing mobility difficulties. It had remained in his conservatory for several months, where it had supported a diseased nasturtium, but now the elderly detective found himself discreetly using it. 'Civilians aren't limited by knowledge of the law. I've been employing members of the public ever since the unit opened in nineteen thirty-nine.'

'Looks like HO has finally come around to your way of thinking,' May remarked. 'They've got a new police liaison officer there, Sam Biddle.'

'No relation?'

'His grandson, I believe.'

'How odd. I was thinking about old Sidney Biddle only the other day. So sensible, solid and efficient. I wonder why we all hated him? Do you remember, I once tricked him into shaving his head by telling him that German bomber pilots could spot ginger people in the blackout. I was terrible in those days.'

'The grandson is forwarding candidates to us. We could do with more recruits like DuCaine. It'll be a fresh start for the unit. I rang you last night to discuss the matter, but your mobile was switched off.'

'I think it broke when I dropped it. Now it keeps picking up old radio programmes. Is that possible? Anyway, there's no point in having it turned on when I'm playing at the Freemason's Arms.' They stepped through the scuffed gloom of the buildings hemming Waterloo Bridge. 'I once took a call while I was going through the Gates of Hell, hit one of the pit-stickers and nearly broke his leg. The cheeses weigh about twelve pounds.'

'Am I supposed to have any idea what you're talking about?' May asked.

'Skittles,' the detective explained. 'I'm on the team. We play in the basement of a pub in Hampstead. The discus is called a cheese.'

'Playing children's games with a bunch of horrible old drunks isn't my idea of fun.' He tended to forget that he was only three years younger than his partner.

'There aren't many players left,' Bryant complained.

'I'm not surprised,' replied May. 'Can't you do something more productive with your evenings? I thought you were going to tackle your memoirs.'

'Oh, I've made a healthy start on the book.' Bryant paused at the centre of the bridge to regain his wind. The pale stone balustrades were dusted with orange shadows in the dying sunlight. Even here the air was musty with vans. There was a time when the stale damp of the river permeated one's clothes. Now the smell only persisted at the shoreline and beneath the bridges. 'They say there are fish in the river again. I heard another human torso was washed up by Blackfriars Bridge, but there was nothing about salmon. I'm looking up old contacts. It's rather fun, you should try it. Go round and see that granddaughter of yours, get her out of the house.'

'April had a breakdown. She can't bear crowds, can't relax. The city gets her down.'

'You have to make the best of things, fight back, that's what Londoners are supposed to be good at. You really should go and see her, encourage her to develop some outside interests.' Bryant looked for his pipe but only managed to find the stem. 'I wonder what I've done with the rest of this,' he muttered. 'I've just finished writing up our first case. Did I tell you I went back to the Palace to look over the files? They were still where I'd left them in the archive room, under tons of old photographs. The place is exactly as I remember it.'

'Surely not,' exclaimed May, amazed.

'Oh, theatres don't change as fast as other buildings.'

'I thought some of the finest halls were destroyed in the sixties.'

'Indeed they were, music halls mostly, but the remaining sites are listed. I watched as they put a wrecking ball through the Deptford Hippodrome.'

'How many other files have you got tucked away?'

'You'd be surprised. That business with the tontine and the Bengal tiger, all documented. The runic curses that brought London to a standstill. The corpse covered in butterflies. I've got all our best cases, and a register of every useful fringe group in the capital.'

'You should upgrade your database. You've still got members of the Camden Town Coven listed as reliable contacts. And do I need to mention the Leicester Square Vampire?'

'Anyone can make a mistake,' said Bryant. 'Look at that, a touch of old Shanghai in London.' He pointed as a fleet of bright yellow tricycles pedalled past, dragging bored-looking tourists around the sights. 'Do you want to buy me a cup of tea at Somerset House?'

'It's your turn to pay.'

'I didn't think you'd remember.' Bryant squinted at the fading sun that was slipping behind the roof of the Savoy, as pale as a supermarket egg. 'Not only were the files on the Palace Phantom still in the archives, but I discovered something interesting about our murderer. I've often thought of him over the years, poor old bugger.' Ahead, the Embankment was picked out in neon, fierce reds and blues, part of a Thameside festival. It looked like a child's drawing of the river finished in crayons.

'What did you find out?'

'I was thinking of paying a visit to the Wetherby tomorrow morning,' Bryant announced, not quite answering the question. The Wetherby was a sister clinic to the Maudsley on Southwark's Denmark Hill, and housed a number of patients suffering from senile dementia.

'Are you finally going to have yourself checked over? I'd

love to join you, but I'm having lunch with an attractive lady, and nothing you say will persuade me to do otherwise.'

Bryant made a face. 'Please don't tell me that you're entertaining the notion of *relations*.'

'I have every hope.'

'I must say I find it rather grotesque that you still have a sex drive at your age. Can't you just use internet porn? How old is this one? She must be younger because you don't fancy women as old as you, which makes her, let me guess, late fifties, a post-war child with a name like Daphne, Wendy or Susan, a divorcee or a widow, a brunette if your track record is anything to go by. She probably considers you the older child she never had, in which case she'll be mooning over you, wanting to cook you meals and so on, and won't mind waiting a little longer for the pleasure of finding one of your vulgar off-the-peg suits hanging in the other side of her wardrobe.'

Irritated by the accuracy of his partner's predictions, May dug out his lighter and lit a cigarette, which he wasn't supposed to have. 'What I do in my free time is no concern of yours. I'm not getting any younger. My cholesterol's through the roof. This might be my last chance to have sex.'

'Don't be revolting,' snapped Bryant. 'You should pack it in, a man of your age, you're liable to pull something in the pelvic region. You're better off taking up something productive like wood carving. Women cost a fortune, running up restaurant bills and trawling shops for a particularly elusive style of sandal.'

'They still find me attractive. They might even consider you if you smartened up your act a bit.'

'I stopped buying shirts after they went over six quid. Besides, I like the trousers they sell at Laurence Corner, very racy, some of them.'

'They sell ex-military wear, Arthur. That's the lower half of a demob suit you're wearing. Look at those turn-ups. You could park a bike in them.'

'It's all right for you, you've always been able to impress women,' Bryant complained. 'You don't have the demeanour of a bad-tempered tortoise.'

May's modern appearance matched the freshness of his outlook. Despite his advanced age, there were still women who found his attentiveness appealing. His technoliteracy and his keen awareness of the modern world complemented Bryant's strange psychological take on the human race, and their symbiotic teamwork dealt them an advantage over less experienced officers. But it still didn't stop them from arguing like an old married couple. Their partnership had just commenced its seventh decade.

Those who didn't know him well considered Arthur Bryant to have outlived his usefulness. It didn't help that he was incapable of politeness, frowning through his wrinkles and forever buried beneath scarves and cardigans, always cold, always complaining, living only for his work. He was the oldest active member of the London police force. But May saw the other side of him, the restless soul, the gleam of frustrated intellect in his rheumy eye, the hidden capacity for compassion and empathy.

'Fine,' said Bryant. 'You go off with your bit of fluff, and I'll go to the clinic by myself. There's something I want to clear up before I close my first volume. But don't blame me if I get into trouble.'

'What sort of trouble could you possibly get into?' asked May, dreading to think. 'Just make sure you wear something that distinguishes you from the patients, otherwise they might keep you in. I'll see you on Sunday, how's that?'

'No, I'll be in the office on Sunday.'

'You could take some time off. I'll even come and watch you play skittles.'

'Now you're being patronizing. But you can come to the unit and help me close the reports. That's if you can tear yourself away from . . . let's see, Daphne, isn't it?'

'It is, as it happens,' admitted May, much annoyed.

'Hm. I thought it would be. Well, don't overdo things.' Bryant stumped off across the bridge, waving a brisk farewell with his stick.

That had been on Friday evening. May had no idea that Sunday would be their last day together in Mornington Crescent.

3

FULL CIRCLE

Five days later, Longbright stood in a private, neglected section of Highgate Cemetery, watching as a simple service placed a public seal on Arthur Bryant's life. Behind them, journalists and Japanese tourists took photographs through the railings. Arthur had no surviving relatives. His landlady Alma was the only non-official in attendance. She had threatened to talk to the press if she wasn't allowed at the graveside. Alma was privy to most of the unit's secrets, via her indiscreet tenant.

Longbright remained beside the wet rose plot containing her colleague's urn as members of the unit trooped by, awkwardly pausing to offer their condolences. Liberty DuCaine led the new generation of unit employees. It felt like the passing of an era.

Longbright was strong. She preferred to stand alone, and refused to cry. Her fiancé offered to drive her home, but she told him to wait in the car. The cemetery grounds were still waterlogged from the recent torrential rain. Briars and nettles drooped over fungus-stained stone, nature anxious to hide all signs of earthly disturbance. Arthur Bryant had arranged to be buried here sixty years earlier, after the death of his greatest love. The retired detective sergeant found it hard to appreciate that a man of such peculiar energy could be so totally obliterated: the forensic lab had identified his body by the melted set of false teeth Bryant had been fitted with during the year Margaret Thatcher came to power.

Some kind of songbird was making a fuss in the tree behind her. Longbright turned towards it, and found May standing silently in her shadow. 'I guess that should be a symbol of hope,' she said, 'but I wish I had a gun.'

'I know how you feel,' admitted May. 'I don't know what to do without him, how to begin going on. What's the point? It's as though someone tore up the world.'

'Oh, John, I'm so sorry.' She took his hands in hers. She felt angry, not sorry. She wanted to accuse someone and blame them for the loss of their friend. She had seen more of life's unfairness than most people, but it did not stop her from wanting revenge. Alma Sorrowbridge came over and stood quietly with them. The West Indian landlady wore a large silver cross on her black-lace bosom. She was very old now, and shrinking fast.

'John, I wanted to speak to you earlier, but they' – she pointed back at the journalists – 'they were watching me. I have something for you.' She pulled a newspaper-covered oblong from beneath her coat. 'I found this in Mr Bryant's flat. It's addressed to you. Not that I've been touching his things, you understand.'

May accepted the slim folder and tore off the wrapping. His breath condensed around the cream linen cover as he studied it. 'This is Arthur's handwriting,' he said, tracing an ink indentation with his finger. 'Has anyone else looked at it?'

'I showed it to Detective Sergeant Longbright earlier.'

'I took a section of the binding for forensic testing,' Longbright explained. 'Just to make sure it was his.'

May examined the gilt edge of the paper. 'I've certainly never seen it before. Might be the first chapter of his book.'

'It was stuck down the back of the wardrobe,' said Alma.

'I moved it to hoover. He told me he was going to write his memoirs, and wanted to borrow my old fountain pen because it had a broad italic nib.'

'Why would he want to write with that?'

'You know how he had these funny ideas. Never let me clean under his bed in sixty years. He had things growing.'

'I'm not surprised.'

'No, in round glass pots.'

'Ah, Petri dishes, yes, he did that sort of thing all the time. Thank you for this, Alma.'

Bryant's landlady made her painful way out of the cemetery. May wondered how long she would cope without her tenant. He watched her go before returning his attention to the book. His numb fingers carefully parted the pages. Inside was a single loose sheet covered in dense scrawl. 'He never kept case notes like this,' he told Longbright. 'Arthur wasn't organized enough. He couldn't even find his dry-cleaning tickets.' Despite Bryant's lack of proficiency with laundry collection, it appeared that he had indeed written something in the last weeks of his life. Unfortunately, it wasn't readable.

'It's in shorthand,' explained Oswald Finch when May talked to him later. The unit's staff had been temporarily rehoused in storage rooms on the top floor of Kentish Town police station. Finch was, strictly speaking, a retired forensic pathologist but knew a thing or two about indecipherable writing, as anyone who had seen his own handwriting could testify. 'Definitely shorthand. Not the most recent kind either, an older version. This is tachygraphy of the type that Samuel Pepys used in his diaries. Before the nineteenth century it was popular among lawyers and naval officers. Hopelessly arcane now, of course. Be interesting to see how he copes with modern vocabulary. Analogous nouns and phonetic spelling, probably. That's why he wanted the broad nib, to place emphases.'

'But can you transcribe it?' May asked impatiently.

'Good heavens, no. But I might be able to download a program that can. Could you leave it with me for a few days?'

'I'd rather read it myself. Can you forward the program to me?'

Finch had almost forgotten that May had once trained as a codebreaker. 'I don't see why not. It won't be very user-friendly, though.'

'How typical of him not to write it in plain English. I'll call you with a new email address and security reference. I'm going to be on leave for a while. I have to get out of London.'

Finch understood. Arthur Bryant was virtually a symbol of the city. There were memories of the man and his cases almost everywhere you looked.

A few days later John May drove down into the Sussex countryside, and it was there, on the rich green downs above Brighton, seated in the attic room he had rented above an unpropitious pub called the Seventh Engineer, that he downloaded the translation program and set to work.

At the start of the document was a note from Finch:

John – I've tried to give you a head start by programming substitutions for the most frequently used words, but some of it's still a bit wonky. Bryant appears to have used a very peculiar writing style. It's rather rambling and all very indiscreet, the only good thing being that many of the people in his account are presumably dead and therefore unavailable to pursue lawsuits. I hope it throws some light on what has happened. Perhaps DS Longbright can help you fill in the gaps. From the way Arthur hid it, he seems to have anticipated that something disastrous might occur. If you think this has any bearing on the blast, we'd better put together a report for RL.

RL was Raymond Land, the unit's impatient and unforgiving new acting head. May's eye was drawn to the postscript: '*By the way, you might be interested to know that Longbright's mother features in the case. I'd forgotten she once worked at the unit. I think Arthur had a crush on her.'*

May set about copying the pages of the notebook into his laptop. After typing in a few hundred words, impatience got the better of him, and he ran the translation program. His fingers idled against the keyboard as he tried to make sense of what he read.

He was looking at an account of their first case, the start of a memoir. Through the fractured text he began to hear Bryant's voice. Pouring himself a gin, he began typing again. He transcribed the single loose sheet and ran the translation program, watching as the letters unscrambled themselves.

An uncomfortable sensation began to take hold of him. The loose page was a fresh addendum, a confidence not intended for publication. Its final line acknowledged a failing: *'I know I will go back, because I cannot leave the past alone . . .'* May was suddenly sure that Bryant had done something to cause his own death. You didn't work with a man for sixty years without gaining an insight into his behaviour. Arthur had disturbed the past, and somehow it had killed him. The idea was preposterous, but stuck fast.

He stared at the words on the screen and thought back to their first meeting in the Blitz. That strange, exhilarating time had also ended with a consignment to flames. It was as though events had somehow come full circle. Bryant had known that his actions could place him at risk. Why else would he encode the memoir and hide it?

The elliptical translation wasn't enough to provide an explanation. May knew he would have to rely on his own elusive memories in order to appreciate what had happened. As the sun slipped below the trees and the shadows became scented with damp earth, he closed his eyes and allowed his thoughts to drift across over half a century, to a time when

London's character was put to a test few other cities could have hoped to survive.

He tried to remember how the seeds of their future had been sown. It was 1940. It was November. A nation was at war, and the world had blundered into darkness.

29

4

SKY ON FIRE

Viewed from the far perspective of world terrorism, the wartime bombing of London now seems unimaginably distant. But the blossoming white dust clouds, debris bursting through them like the stamens of poisoned flowers, contained the same moment of horror common to all such events.

The conflict had been so long anticipated that in some perverse way its arrival was a relief. The people of Britain had methodically prepared their defences. This time the island did not wait to recruit its forces. Conscription created armies, and attacks were launched by sea and sky. For those who remained behind, daily life took strange new forms. Children carried their gas masks to school. Public information leaflets explained the rules of the blackout. Rationing made the nation healthier. An aura of orderly common sense settled across the city of London.

As the fittest men were conscripted, the streets grew quieter, and an air of becalmed expectancy prevailed. It felt as though a great change was drawing near. More civilians found a purpose in war than in peace. Nothing could be taken for granted, not even an extra day of life. For those who were as old as the century, it was the second time to fight.

In 1939, London was the largest city in the world. The riches of the British empire still poured through its financial institutions. Memories of the depression had faded. Good times, boom times, had arrived. Despite the false celebration of 'peace in our time', rearmament paved the way to prosperity. One still saw reminders of the Great War on the streets: one-armed liftmen, blinded match-sellers, men who stuttered and shook when you spoke to them. During that earlier conflict, German airships had bombed the city but managed to kill only 670 people. Surely, everyone said, it would not happen again.

Even so, the Committee of Imperial Defence had begun a study into air-raid precautions as early as 1924. They calculated how many bombs could be dropped by Germany should hostilities recommence, and how many people they would kill. Every ton of explosive would cause fifty casualties, a third of them fatal. Three thousand five hundred bombs would fall on London in the first twenty-four hours. It would be essential to maintain public order, to prevent the city from descending into a living hell. For the first time in a war, the reinforcement of morale at home became a priority.

The first bomb to explode in London was not dropped by the Germans but planted by the IRA, and aimed at the most prosaic of targets – Whiteley's emporium in Bayswater. German bombers could not reach their target, and the city had become an impregnable citadel. The country's prime minister had seen active military service, and was experienced in the way of warfare. The King remained in Buckingham Palace. The government, the monarchy, the people were seen to be moving in one direction. The shops remained open. The deckchairs were set out in Hyde Park, and the band played on.

But by November 1940, the uneasy anticlimax of the Twilight War had been over for six months, and the Blitz had become a way of life. After the fall of France, the nation was braced for imminent invasion, and Londoners were so used

31

to living under the constant threat of air attack that they simply went on with their business. 'Taking it' became part of the fight, as important as attacking.

Bombs were particularly devastating when they hit crowded stations. One hundred and eleven people were crushed and blown apart at Bank station. Sixty-four were drowned in cascading mud at Balham. Everyone knew someone who had died, or who had narrowly escaped death. The thin newspapers were filled with vague news of victories, but personal experience suggested only misery and endurance.

Images etched themselves in John May's mind and remained there throughout his life: a bus standing on its end, a warden hugging a silent, terrified child, a bright blue hat at the edge of a blood-spattered crater. One night, audiences emerged from *Faust* at Sadler's Wells to find the sky on fire. If London was the centre of the world, the world was burning. It was a violent place in which to discover a purpose. It was a good place to forge a friendship.

5

SANDWICHES ON THE BRIDGE

On the morning of Monday, 11 November 1940, after a weekend of sirens, booming anti-aircraft guns, distant bombs and droning aircraft, nineteen-year-old John May was most concerned about getting to work early, because it was his first day in a new job and he was anxious to make a good impression.

He jumped from the rear platform of the bus as it slowed on its turn from the Aldwych, and searched the ashen pavements of the Strand, wondering if he had somehow missed an air-raid warning. It was still quite dark, too early for a daylight assault. The blackout ended half an hour before sunrise, when the greatest danger to commuters was the 'silent peril', trolley buses that glided by with a whisper of sheened steel. The clear weather of the last two days had allowed heavier bombing raids than usual, but the morning was mild and overcast, a healthy sign; German bombers were unable to follow the river into London's heart when the cloud base was so low.

May wasn't sure where the nearest shelter was, and had yet to make his way to Bow Street. He kept his shirt-tail hanging out below the hem of his jacket as a white flag to motorists; over four thousand people had been killed in blackout accidents during the first few months of the war. It was safer to take an overseas posting with the British Expeditionary Force.

The shops and restaurants of the Strand had been boarded up from the Kardomah to the Coal Hole, but a sign nailed beneath a shirtmaker's 'Business As Usual' banner pointed the way to a shelter. May made a mental note of it. The street lamps were off, and only strips of white paint on the kerbs marked out his route. He passed a large branch of Boots fortified with sandbags and, near the top, when those had run out, old telephone directories.

May wondered if he was over-keen, turning up so early on his first day. There had been several raids the previous night and few Londoners had managed more than four hours' sleep, despite the protestations of patriots who insisted that their slumber was undisturbed by falling bombs. This morning it seemed as if the entire city had decided on a late start. He passed a pair of sleepy-eyed girls walking arm in arm, their matching homemade hats pinned with luminous brooches. An ARP warden paused in a shop doorway to draw guiltily on a thin roll-up. An elderly man in a cap and a heavy wool coat checked the gutter for dog-ends. The grey street smelled of rolling tobacco and charred wood.

Sixty years later, John May would amble along the same route and see more people sleeping rough than he had during the war, but at the moment, on this anaemic Monday, all he cared about was reaching his office before someone decided that they had made a terrible mistake and didn't actually need a new recruit to work in an experimental police department, especially not a kid who had been prematurely thrust into his profession by the outbreak of war.

He found the police station at Bow Street with ease – he'd spent enough mornings in Covent Garden with his father to know his way around – but could not locate the entrance he had been instructed to use. Carfax, the bulldog-faced desk sergeant, sent him out of the front door, past the hand-printed sign to the public that read: 'Be Good – We're Still Open', and into a side alley where he discovered the unmarked blue door. Failing to find a bell, he was about to knock when it suddenly opened.

'Are you the new chap?' asked a statuesque young woman whose cockney accent emerged through carmine lips. 'Blimey, you're a bit eager, aren't you?' She opened the door wider. 'You'd better come in, you're making the street untidy.'

May pulled off his cap and stepped into a narrow corridor. The young woman's protuberant bust was alarmingly close to his face in the darkness, but she didn't seem to notice. 'Go up the top of them stairs and take the first right. Mind you don't trip on the treads, some of the rods are gone, and there's textbooks everywhere. We only just moved in.'

May reached the linoleumed landing and found himself standing before a faintly lit office door. Radio music played inside. On the panel in front of him was tacked a sheet of paper reading: 'KNOCK AND WAIT'. He did so, lightly, and when nothing occurred, more heavily.

'You don't have to bash the thing in,' called an irritated voice. 'Just open it.'

May entered a cluttered sepia room with a sloping floor. A pair of green glass desk lamps threw cones of light against the blackout curtains, where a young man with chestnut hair and a purple scarf knotted round his throat was trying to see something through a magnifying glass. 'The Home Office insists on the "Knock and Wait" signs,' he explained, not looking up. 'They're meant to give us time to clear away sensitive papers. As if we had any in the first place. Here.' He thrust the glass at May, together with a sheet of butcher's paper covered in hand-drawn illustrations of butterflies. 'See if you can spot a hidden message on that.'

Taken aback, May turned his attention to the drawing and studied it carefully. 'They all have the same pattern, red admirals,' he said, 'but the colours are wrong. They rather look like naval code. You know, signal flags. Admirals, I suppose that's the tip-off. I think I can read it.' He squinted at the page. 'W-E-R-E-O-U-T-O-F-T-E-A.'

'I see.' The young man snatched the sheet of paper back from him. 'It'll be from the tailors downstairs. They were both in the navy. We have to share the kettle and the gas ring. Bit of a smartarse, are you?'

'No,' stammered May.

'Jolly good,' said the young man, holding out his hand. 'I'm Arthur Bryant.' He tugged his fawn cardigan over a pudgy stomach and smiled conspiratorially. 'You must be Mr May. What should I call you?'

'John, sir.'

'Don't call me "sir", I've not been knighted yet. You look fairly sturdy. We could do with someone like you.' Bryant was the indoor type, shorter and fleshier than his counterpart. May boxed and played football. He had a long reach, wide shoulders and thick thighs, a look women liked. In decades to come, the difference in their heights became more noticeable as Bryant shrank and May's posture stayed firm.

'Did you meet our glamorous DS?'

'Rather.' May nodded enthusiastically.

'She's a hoot, isn't she?' Bryant's smile unclouded into a grin. 'One of the first female detective sergeants in the country, thanks to this mess.' May assumed he was referring to the war and not the room. 'Idolizes American film stars, wears make-up and high heels to work against the rules, not at all frightened of looking like a tart. Gladys Forthright. She's engaged to a sergeant called Harris Longbright. Do you think she's just doing it for the assonance?' Bryant barked an extraordinary laugh. 'I must say I thought they were going to send me someone older. You're what, twenty?'

'Nineteen.'

'Nineteen, eh?' Bryant rolled his pale blue eyes. 'That's a bit young for this lark.'

'Not at all,' May bridled. 'There were lads younger than me lost at Scapa Flow.'

'You're right, of course. Eight hundred on the *Royal Oak*. It makes one doubt the existence of a grand plan. Still, all hands to the pumps at home, eh? I hope we'll be able to do something useful together. I hear they're making you a detective.'

'Apparently.' May tried to sound nonchalant. 'I was on a one-year intensive but I wasn't able to finish the course. It's impossible to get into Hendon, and our place was closed down. They've run out of instructors.'

'So they just bumped you up? Very decent of them. I'm twenty-two and absolutely forbidden from participating in investigations unaided because they think I'm irresponsible, but there's no one else available to head the unit, ha ha. They probably sent you here because you look sensible. Good trick, that.' Bryant peered round the edge of the blackouts, saw that the street was growing light and opened the curtains, hastily switching off the desk lamps. 'We can't afford to get fined again,' he explained, looking down through the X-taped windows. 'I'm hopeless at remembering to turn things off.'

'You didn't get called up?'

'Well, I did, but I've a bit of a dicky pump.' He gave his chest an exploratory tap. 'And there were other factors that prevented me from going,' he added mysteriously. Years later, May found out that Bryant's brother had died on a Thames barge, and because their mother lived alone in Bethnal Green without financial support, the Port of London Authority had arranged a special dispensation for her surviving son. There was another mitigating circumstance that protected Bryant from conscription, but it was not something he felt comfortable speaking of. 'What about you?'

'Essential industry. I'm waiting for a post to come up. I've been recommended for cypher-breaking. Shortlisted for a special unit intercepting codes coming from the Atlantic.'

'They're putting something together in Hertfordshire, aren't they? If they don't get a move on it'll all be over. Do you want a pipe? We've still got some tobacco, but it's a bit ropy.' Bryant waved a wallet of foul-smelling shag past him and dropped it into the chaos of the desk.

'I don't, thanks,' said May, removing his coat and looking for somewhere clean to put it. 'There's a very good code station already running, but they're stocking it with the best of the Oxford grads. I'll just have to wait my turn.'

'You probably want to know what this is all about,' said Bryant, pushing a chair at him. 'Sorry no one could tell you much, but the MoI and the Home Office are very big on public morale at the moment.'

'I've noticed,' said May. 'The block on information is a bit stiff. Part of Hyde Park near Marble Arch was roped off at the weekend. They reckon an underground shelter was blown to bits, heads and arms and legs everywhere. The only way they could tell the girls from the men was by their hair. But I didn't see anything about it in the papers.'

'No, you wouldn't. I can understand that, but some of the other directives are driving us barmy.' Bryant sucked noisily at his pipe. 'This business with lifts having to be kept at the bottom of shafts during raids, except in tube stations where they have to be kept at the top. I suppose it's sensible, but all transgressions have to be reported, and it makes so much paperwork. Not that you'll have had any paperwork on us.'

'No, they wouldn't even tell me what PCU stood for.'

'Peculiar Crimes Unit, isn't it frightful? I think their perception of the word "peculiar" and mine differ somewhat. I've got some bumph here you can read through.' He rooted around among his papers, sending several overstuffed folders to the floor, but failed to locate anything specific.

Thinking about his first impression of Arthur Bryant some years later, May was reminded of a young Alec Guinness, bright-eyed and restless, distracted and a little awkward, filled to exhaustion with ideas. May was less excitable, and his habit of keeping a rein on the more excessive reaches of his imagination pegged him to others as the reserved, serious one. After their deaths, it was said by their biographer that 'Bryant said what he meant and May meant what he said'. May was the diplomat, Bryant the iconoclast, a decent combination as it turned out.

'They meant "peculiar" in the sense of "particular", but the damage is done, and the name is attracting some very odd cases. We had a report last month of a man sucking blood out of a Wren in Leicester Square. It's hopeless. The Heavy Rescue Squads are busy trying to locate people who've been buried alive under tons of rubble, most of the central London constabulary remaining at home have left to join the ARP, the ATS and the AFS, and we're expected to go chasing around after Bela Lugosi. Morale again, you see. They don't want people to think there's a bogeyman roaming around in the blackouts, otherwise they won't head to the shelters. Panic in the streets; it's an image that scares the hell out of them. You'd think we were more of a propaganda unit than a proper detective squad.'

'How many of us are there?' asked May, moving a stack of handwritten music scores from a chair and seating himself.

'Half a dozen, including you. Superintendent Davenport's the most senior DI, spends all of his time haunting the HO and the Met, or playing billiards with Sergeant Carfax, who's married to his ghastly sister. She comes creeping around here on the scrounge for salvage donations, got a face like a witch doctor's rattle. No, we don't see too much of Davenport, luckily. Then there's Dr Runcorn, rather ancient and not much cop but the only forensics wallah they could spare us. We have a young pathologist called Oswald Finch, tragically born without a sense of humour, we use him for the serious stuff. DS Forthright is also a part-time member of the WVS. Then there's us two, and finally a couple of utterly vacant PCs, Crowhurst and Atherton. Crowhurst has something wrong with his depth perception and falls over a lot, and Atherton used to be a greengrocer.'

'My father is a greengrocer,' said May indignantly.

'No offence, old man,' apologized Bryant, whose own father had abandoned his family to earn drink money in Petticoat Lane peddling rings for blackout curtains at a shilling a dozen, 'but poor old Atherton really would be better employed shifting sprouts. Oh, and we're getting one more today, a former copper called Sidney Biddle. I've got his details around here somewhere. Davenport was very keen about taking him on. I get the feeling he's coming in as a bit of a spy, though I'm not sure what he'll find to report on. We're rather a dead-letter office. To date we've had a hand in a couple of prosecutions, but nothing that can be made public.'

'Why not?'

Bryant rubbed his nose ruminatively. 'The sort of cases that pass through here are a bit of an embarrassment for everyone concerned. The regular force can't handle them, so they end up on these desks.' He indicated the overflowing surfaces of the two desks that had been shoved back to back beside the window. 'I'll have a clear-up while you get settled. Have Forthright find you a tea mug, and hang on to it. You never know when there'll be a shortage. We can get most things, but you hear rumours and everyone goes mad.'

May knew what he meant. With each passing week, a household item, so taken for granted before the war, would vanish from the list of available home comforts. Last week there was a run on toothbrushes. The smallest rumour was enough to spark panic buying. Foods were fast disappearing from the daily menu. Oddly, the commonest items seemed to cease first, so that sugar, butter and bacon were rationed while milk chocolate remained available.

At lunchtime, Bryant took his new partner for a walk down to the Thames. The city was turning itself into a fortress, barricaded, sandbagged and patrolled in imminent expectation of invasion.

40

'What topsy-turvy times we live in,' laughed Bryant, striding across the windy reach of Waterloo Bridge, his scarf flapping about his prominent ears. 'I've stood here after the alert has sounded and watched the German bombers flying low along the river, dropping their loads on the docks, then I've gone back to the unit to investigate a theft of cufflinks from some diplomat's quarters in Regent's Park as if it was the most important thing in the world.'

'What's your speciality?' asked May, pacing beside him.

'Mine? Academic studies, really. Classics. Abstruse thought. The HO thought the war might throw up a few cases that need sensitive handling, and realized that there were no brainboxes in the field of detection.'

'Who decides which cases we get?'

'Well, Davenport likes to pretend he does, but the orders come from higher up. He's not a total dunderhead, of course, just ineffectual. I think being placed in charge of this unit is a bit beyond him. He's rather strait-laced. The RAF wouldn't have him because he's short-sighted, and he's still miffed. My word, I don't like the look of that.'

In the distance white clouds were breaking, and shafts of sunlight glowed above patches of oily water.

'They're trying to restrict movement around the city, putting up a lot of barricades, something about not wanting too many people out on the streets, but I managed to flannel a couple of passes out of Davenport that should get us any-where we want to go. Where do you live?'

'I'm staying with an aunt in Oakley Square,' May explained, leaning on the white stone balustrade and looking down into the water. 'Camden Town. I'll be able to walk in if the services are disrupted. I was born in Vauxhall, not a very salubrious area, but my mother managed to get me into a decent school.' He laughed. 'They've shifted all the children from our local Mixed Infants down to Kent for the duration. Poor people of Kent.'

'I heard a country woman on the wireless say that she

would rather take a savage from Fiji than a child from Birmingham,' said Bryant. 'Those kids will probably give the countryside a good shaking up.'

'I take it you're a town man, then.'

'Lord, yes. I went on a hop-picking holiday once and was never so miserable in my entire life, although I did learn how to poach rabbits. I'd hate to be out of the city and miss all this. Everyone's so friendly all of a sudden. I think it's because we're part of something at last, not pulling in different directions. Can't you feel it? Things are shaking up instead of sticking where they've always been. Remember how everyone used to hate the ARP wardens before Christmas, going on about how they did nothing except play darts and cards all day? Look at them now, being treated like heroes. I think some good will come of it. The old sangfroid is starting to melt, don't you think? Lords and layabouts sharing the same misfortunes.'

'Spoken like a communist,' joked May.

'I believe in liberty but I'd fight for it, I'm not a conchie,' said Bryant hastily. The wind was watering his pale eyes. 'I'd like to have fought in the Spanish Civil War but I didn't know anyone else who was going. There aren't too many people in Whitechapel who've heard of Franco. I think it's mostly the upper classes who can afford to support their ideologies, not us proles. And you don't have to be politically astute to know that Neville Chamberlain behaved like an arse. I was sixteen when I saw newsreel footage of Hitler's Congress of Unity and Strength, and I remember thinking, nothing good will come of this. All those fervent torchlight parades. If I could see it, why couldn't politicians? Are you a Catholic?'

May was taken aback. 'No, C of E. Why?'

'You have the unperplexed attitude of a boy raised by priests. Practising?'

'Not terribly regular.'

'So what's your take on all this?'

42

May looked gloomily into the shadows beneath the bridge. 'I suppose we're being tested.'

'Think you'll come out of it with your faith intact?'

'I'm not too sure about that.' He shook his head sadly. 'Very possibly not.'

'Interesting. A war to shake the faith of the Church. Combat is supposed to strengthen one's resolve. Well, we'd better be getting back. There's not much on at the moment, but I'm expecting Sidney Biddle after luncheon. Davenport wants me to make him feel welcome.'

'I've got some sandwiches,' said May, pulling a square of greaseproof paper from his jacket pocket. 'Egg and mustard cress, do you want one?'

'I've got ham and beetroot, we can have half each. Let's eat them here. We might see a plane come down.'

'It's a deal.'

The two young men stood in the middle of the bridge exchanging sandwiches as the first of the Luftwaffe's bombers appeared low over the Thames estuary.

6

ACTS OF VIOLENCE

May closed the transcribed files on the laptop and shut its lid. Beyond the bedroom window above the pub, a car stereo was playing hip-hop at a deafening volume, the bass notes shaking the glass in its casement. The elderly detective rose and watched the vehicle fishtail rubber streaks on tarmac. His partner Bryant had always liked noise, thriving in the dirt and chaos of the city streets.

May's instinct, when away from Bryant but thinking of him, was to pick up the telephone and call for a chat. The day before the funeral he had absently done just that, and had been disconcerted to hear Bryant speaking – in that confused tone he adopted with all technological devices – on his office voicemail line.

Now he rang the unit and asked to be put through to Liberty DuCaine.

'We've got no incendiary evidence matching the blast pattern yet,' Liberty told him. 'It's hard to say what sort of device caused it. There was a piece of shell casing found in the next street, but it's still being analysed.' He sounded harassed and distracted. There was a lot of noise in the background.

'But you have a team on the case, don't you?' asked May.

44

'Sort of. There's a lot going on here at the moment.'

'This was a bomb attack that killed a senior police officer, for God's sake. It should receive the highest priority.'

'I'm aware of that, Mr May.' Liberty's voice was filled with patience. 'But right now we have a full-scale drug war on our hands. Two gangs of fifteen-year-old wannabe Yardies running around the streets of Lambeth armed with AR-15 laser-sighted armour-piercing rifles that fire nine hundred and fifty rounds a minute. Damned things are accurate to six hundred yards, not that any of them can shoot straight. The little bastards are buying them from American websites. We've got two civilians dead and one of our men down. You must have seen the newspapers.'

'Forgive me, no, I haven't picked up a copy. The unit's not supposed to get involved with stuff like that.'

'Under these conditions everyone has to help out. I'm sorry, Mr May, I understand how upset you are, but things are bad here. I promise we'll have someone call you as soon as there's any news.'

May thanked him and hung up. He felt obsolete. The new crimes infecting the crowded city streets were almost beyond his comprehension. People were being shot – shot! – for the most trivial reasons: a jumped traffic light, an altercation in McDonald's, simply being in the wrong place at the wrong time. When had it started to go so wrong?

May thought back to the war, and his first meeting with Arthur, and that led him to the murder. The first one, his first sight of a dead body. That had changed everything. A fall from innocence, and the start of a lifelong fascination with violent crime.

7

FINAL STEPS

The lights. The wings. The devil's face. She saw them again and again, until she was dizzy, until she felt sick. The slender woman, her arms raised tightly above her head, spun on the empty stage until she began to fall.

Tanya realized how tired she was when her pirouette nearly toppled her into the orchestra pit. It was Sunday, 10 November 1940, and she had been rehearsing the whole of the afternoon. Angry with the failure of her limbs, she continued to work on her solo long after the rest of the company had grown tired of competing with her. Now the cast had gone across to the Spice of Life pub, hoping that an air raid would force them all down to the cellar, where they could stay, hurricane-lit and vintage-fed, for the remainder of the evening. They had left her alone with her restless energy, a solitary figure marking out her steps in the penumbral auditorium.

This time she had only just managed to stop at the edge of the stage. As she walked off into the wings to collect her towel, the muscles in her calves trembled with exertion. Stan Lowe, the stage doorkeeper, was supposed to wait for her to leave, but even he had gone off to the Spice. Her stomach was unsettled. She found a foil-wrapped chunk of marzipan chocolate in her bag, and chewed it. London theatres were beautiful but claustrophobic, designed to present the tableaux of traditional plays, and although the stage of the Palace was deep, it was not wide enough to be occupied by a cast of their size. Choreography had to be reined in, grand gestures expunged from Tanya's repertoire of movement.

This was not to be a late nineteenth-century production of the kind usually associated with Jacques Offenbach; there were no monobosoms, trains, boned corsets and fans to restrict the movement of the dancers, leaving them with only the jumps and lifts of a traditional ballet corps. Instead their gestures were to be free and unrestricted, but this created problems in the finite space, especially now that the wings had been deepened. Tanya wondered how she could augment her moves without antagonizing everyone. The wings, necessary to hide the ranks of dancers from the audience's view while they were queuing to go on, ate into the performance space, reducing the area in which they could operate.

It was while she was sponging the sweat from her long neck that she heard the noise. It sounded like someone coughing, or barking hoarsely. The pitch was low and indistinct, emanating from the chest, like the racketing of the homeless man who bedded down behind the protective canopy of the theatre after it closed. He always arrived as the last of the players left, and scrunched himself up behind a section of board in the corner of the main entrance, beyond the reach of the ARP patrols. He was not like the young men she used to see sleeping rough in Soho Square before the war. He reeked of the night's dark recesses, reminding her that the lost and the lonely were easy prey in a time of hostilities. He smelled, she noticed, how the whole of London was starting to smell, of uncleanliness, of fatigue, of death.

Tanya allowed her towel to fall and tilted her head. The sound was usually deadened in here, but tonight she sensed

47

something else. The house lights were down and only the stage remained illuminated, a miasma of emerald and crimson. She wondered if the homeless man had managed to find his way in somehow, and was waiting for her to leave the warmth and safety of the set.

It came again, the strange coughing noise. A muttered phrase, a warning. She could almost make out words, but where were they coming from? The triple-decked theatre was a whispering gallery; you could tell where sounds originated because the air was so dead and echoless.

'Who's there?' she called at last. 'Geoffrey, if that's you it's not amusing.'

She knew most of the others didn't like her. There was very little dancing in this production, and of the three classically trained ballerinas featured, only she had a solo. The others watched her working hard, thinking that she was trying to steal the limelight, and resentment accumulated like storm-clouds; she was used to that. She was damned good and she had the solo, and if the rest of them didn't like it they could go to hell.

She realized that she had been rehearsing alone for over three hours, only breaking for half a sandwich. Like all dancers, so much of her body fat had been converted to muscle that she needed to eat regularly. Tanya enjoyed the solitude of practice, but now her body was resisting her commands.

She left from the upstage right exit. One part of the set was fixed, the carmine cretonne mask of a gigantic demon, its lips arched wide in the rictus of a satanic scream. The mouth was so large that several dancers could enter through it at once. The designs were too grotesque for her tastes, inappropriate to the times. People were scared enough. The artist was newly exiled from Eastern Europe, and it showed.

Tanya was dressed in a sweat-soaked blouse and slacks, but decided not to suffer the cold water of the dressing room. Most of the backstage corridor lights had been turned off

48

hours ago in order to comply with government restrictions on electricity, and she didn't want to stay any longer than necessary. She felt even queasier now, and wondered if she had eaten something that disagreed with her.

As she looked up at the darkened tiers, she felt the building closing in. Something about its shape induced a sensation of claustrophobia. Although the corridors burrowing through its brickwork had been repainted a cheerful yellow, they were still cramped and confining after the expanse of the stage. The sides and understage areas were a nightmarish maze of columns and tunnels, with wiring strapped in loose bundles along the ceilings and walls. There was nowhere to store anything. It was all too elaborate, even for the grand opera it had been built to contain. The electricians were forever leaving boxes and cables lying around. Her supple limbs were her greatest asset, and needed to be protected from such dangers. It would take only one fall to end her career. She wasn't getting any younger. Who knew how many seasons she had left?

At least the Palace was still open. Other theatres were going dark. Bombs were keeping the audiences away. Hardly any of the central playhouses had adequate emergency exits. If the war lasted much longer she doubted there would be a play left running in the entire West End.

As she made her way up the centre aisle she heard the voice again. This time it was more distinct. A stream of muttered nonsense, like the rambling of a fever. It could only be coming from the back of the stalls. The rear seats were arranged beneath the dark saucer-shaped overhang of the dress circle. To reach the exit she had to pass through to the back. No other door on this level was open.

Tanya was not easily intimidated. She was fit and strong, and more than a match for any crazy drunk who had wandered in from the street. But suppose it wasn't a drunk? What if someone meant her harm? She had enemies. All successful people did, it was the underside of victory. Some of the adulatory fan mail she received bordered on obsessive. Suppose she had a secret admirer who turned out to be mad, like that girl she had worked with in Milan?

Tanya paused at the shadowed edge of the centre aisle, unsure what to do.

But there was really no choice. She had to leave through the rear stalls doors or remain in the building, retracing her steps and passing through the labyrinth of unlit corridors that led to the dressing rooms. It was time to remember who she was, the star of the only big production to be opening in the West End since war broke out, the show's number one dancer, not some gutless chorine. She marched forward into the red plush darkness, and found the rear doors padlocked.

Her nerve did not fail. She returned to the proscenium and climbed up into the wings, making her way around the slip and following the few lights which, oddly, appeared to have been left on for her. They provided her with a runway, a direction back into the building.

If there was another exit apart from the stage door, which Stan always locked as he left, Tanya had yet to discover it. She'd heard that there was a separate side entrance especially reserved for royalty, but was not sure how to reach it. The air grew colder the further she ventured from the stage, and the trickle of sweat between her shoulder blades dried like a sliver of frost. She could no longer hear the voice, and began to wonder if she had imagined it. This part of the building ran below ground level, but a goods lift waited just ahead of her. The cage was up above, and as she summoned it she fancied she heard a fresh movement in the flies, like the dragging of a sandbag.

The cable wheel trundled into action. The lift creaked and started to descend.

Darkened theatres did not usually frighten Tanya. She had spent half of her life in them, and the stories of ghosts walking across balconies after the audience filed out were just colourful fables that enhanced the reputations of their houses. Even so, tonight seemed different. Her stomach was tinged with the poisonous acidity she usually experienced before the first public performance of a new piece.

It was then that she felt the touch, cold fingers on her right shoulder, a light tap that caused her to cry out in alarm. But there was no one to be seen. From somewhere above her came a distinct footfall – thump – then silence. Tanya pulled back the trellis door and jumped into the lift cage. She had just managed to shut it when the muscles in her legs stopped holding her up, and she fell heavily forward.

Her head brushed against the wooden side wall as she dropped onto her knees. She wondered why she was having such difficulty moving. She felt too tired to reach up and press the ground-floor button. Trying to control the tic of a rogue nerve in her calf, she lay sprawled across the floor of the lift, her mind pitched into panicked possibilities. Suppose it was a stroke, like the one her mother had suffered? Her career would be obliterated in a heartbeat. She forced herself to consider her options. Could she crawl over to the brass button panel and find the alarm?

Her legs were insensate, as if they had been injected with cocaine. What now? It became hard to think, or to feel anything at all, just numbness, blessed numbness. Someone was touching her useless limbs. She could definitely feel something cold gripping her ankles, but what was it? How could anyone touch her without opening the trellis door? She listened to the rasping breath and longed to turn her head, but her muscles failed to respond. Something was clutching her hard now, pulling at her feet. A feeling came at last, cold metal scraping her toes. Her legs were being moved, her body pulled and twisted so that her head slid onto the floor, forcing her to look up at the ceiling. What the hell was wrong with her feet?

They were sticking out of the cage. Whatever it was that had taken hold of her had pulled her feet between the staves of the trellis, so that her ankles were resting on the crossbars.

She was alone now, left in this graceless position, trying to imagine a way out of an absurd predicament.

This is how people die, she thought. A bomb falls on the building, the bricks close in around you and you're trapped until someone can dig you out. This is my worst fear made real. My mother alone in her kitchen, trying to call for the maid, attempting to reach the telephone in the hall. I should have been there for her instead of rehearsing, always rehearsing. Now it is too late.

She heard a new noise.

The click of a button being pushed was followed by the familiar whirring of oiled gears. The lift was being summoned on the floor above. She forced her head up and watched in horror as the concrete level of the floor descended to her sightline, down to her ankles, brushing, then touching, then pressing, then crushing.

The audiences of the Palace Theatre, Cambridge Circus, had delighted in a thousand lingering kisses, a thousand cruel deaths, a thousand emotional farewells. But there was no audience here tonight to witness the end of a dancer, to see the terrible cleaving of bone and flesh, the steam of blood, not lurid Kensington Gore but something real and dark and intimate, to hear the agonized screams of a woman in mourning for the end of her career as much as the loss of her feet.

8

THE ARRIVAL OF THE CUCKOO

Sidney Biddle had never been in trouble with the police, so
he joined them, and then the trouble began. At the outbreak
of war, he entered training with a determination to be the
scourge of the criminal world, anxious to change the ways of
people he considered corrupt, stupid, lazy and weak. Any
officer will tell you that a person entering the force with such
a mentality is doomed to a lifetime of disappointment.
Triumphs are transitory, failures painful, gratitude rare and
grudging. Policemen and nurses are yoked together under the
category of social services, but nurses bond with their
patients. Policemen get no thanks from those they arrest.

Not that Biddle expected appreciation, but he had been
hoping for more concrete results from his zealous approach
to the law. At school he had been hardworking and humour-
less, possessed with a religious fire. His parents were at a loss
to understand him, and blamed themselves for having produced a child so determined to be a model citizen that they
were forced to hide newspapers from him, in case he discovered new enemies within their pages.

After police college, Biddle found himself inexplicably on
the beat. He had expected to start in a position of greater
responsibility, but his attitude had bothered his seniors, who

wisely decided to drum a little humility into him before allowing their star pupil to turn his searching gaze on a sinning populace.

Biddle hated life in the constabulary, manning inquiry desks to deal with old ladies who had lost their dogs, walking freezing patrols, scouring the rough parts of Islington for troublemakers, assigned the gaslit thieves' walks that no one else would touch. It appeared to him that the police were fighting a losing battle. Recruitment standards were in freefall. The police were taking whoever they could get, and they couldn't get much.

In his eyes, there was a far deeper malaise eating into modern society, a moral turpitude that allowed slum children to die in squalor and innocents to be coshed in the streets. He considered most of his colleagues to be more stupid than the lads they were trying to catch. What kind of a world was it that allowed thieving to become more of a vocation than policing? He hated the lapel-thumbing swaggers, the beery airing of prejudices, the backslapping arrogance, the barely veiled contempt for civvies.

Displaying an excessive devotion to duty is no way to make friends. Biddle's colleagues singled him out for all the worst tasks. When he finally managed to get a transfer, it was to a unit so invisible to the rest of the force that he felt sure he would be safe at last. Nobody seemed to know what the new job would entail, but Biddle figured it had to be better than staying where he was.

He was told that the new unit operated under independent financial status, and was answerable only to the Home Office. He had heard rumours: that a series of special squads was being set up to deal with crimes of terrorism, treason and misconduct, acts that were likely to cause social unrest, panic and the loss of that indefinable but essential wartime quality – public spirit. There were already the best part of a dozen services in place to cope with the physical needs of a nation at war. One unit was studying the psychological aspects of propaganda and misinformation, and another was to gauge the effect of continuous bombing on public morale.

The PCU did not publicly recruit and had very few permanent staff. No one inside it was allowed to mix with regular members of the force for reasons of security. There were other stories: of an ongoing feud between the unit and the City of London police, and of a row with the Home Office over the cost of hiring a group of white witches to help with an investigation.

Not since the country's civil war had the rumour-mongering machine worked so adroitly. Adolf Hitler, many said, was consulting an astrologer called Karl Ossietz to help him formulate his invasion plans. There was a belief among shop girls in the north of England that German paratroopers were landing in Norway disguised as parsons, that they were coming for healthy English girls and would force them into German baby farms. When sensible folk started believing nonsense like this, clearly something had to be done, but solid information was hard to come by. Mail was censored. All sensitive details were excised. No weather forecasts were issued. Every time an offensive was launched the newspapers sold out in minutes, and you had to find yourself a wireless.

Biddle expressed his views to Superintendent Farley Davenport at a lecture on law enforcement, and was invited to apply to the unit. A few days later, he was notified that his application had been accepted. He couldn't stay where he was because his colleagues were making his life hell, and the PCU seemed to be the only other place left for him. He was exempt from conscription because the police recognized his zealotry as a useful tool in troubled times, so long as it could be controlled. And Davenport aimed to control it well.

Which was how Biddle found himself in the chaotic offices above the tailor's, in the alley beside Bow Street station one murky Monday afternoon in November 1940. He felt uneasy from the moment DS Forthright invited him to step inside. The unit didn't appear to be attached to the police station, or anywhere else where real officers gathered. There were no incident, briefing or custody rooms, no communal areas of any kind. There appeared to be a secure property room and some kind of makeshift crime lab, which was odd, because they were usually tucked away in separate offices far from public view, or buried inside much larger buildings where protection could be assured. Such places were primed with red steel alarm bells because tons of evidence, including cash, jewellery, guns and narcotics, passed through them. This unit was beside a busy police station, right on a crowded public thoroughfare, and didn't appear to be protected in any way that he could see.

'You won't have seen a place like this before because we're an experimental unit,' Forthright explained, reading his mind, 'and at the moment it's a one-off. We're a bit short of space but at least we've still got a roof over our heads. I'd take you to your office, duckie, but it's full of tea chests.'

The detective sergeant seated herself on the edge of Bryant's battered desk and studied Davenport's latest recruit. Tough-looking, sturdy, hair cropped too close to the head. It gave him the appearance of being carved from solid bone. She'd heard a lot about this young chap. He sounded too good to be true, or at least, too good for the unit. He didn't say much but his small grey eyes took everything in, and he was already starting to unnerve her.

'I'm sure your mates have warned you about Mr Bryant,' she said, more to break the silence than for any purpose of imparting information. 'He's the unit's big thinker. You've probably heard he's a bit potty.'

'Is he?'

She paused to consider the idea. 'Well, I suppose it depends upon your attitude towards clairvoyants, spiritualists, table-tappers and the like.'

'Cranks and crackpots, society's wastrels,' said Biddle without hesitation.

'Then yes, I reckon you'll find he is a bit eccentric.' Forthright sighed and looked at the floor, wondering if Bryant was on his way back yet.

'I'm told he works long hours.' Biddle crossed to the mantelpiece and studied the books piled there. *Common Folk Remedies. A Comprehensive History of Occult Practices. The Complete Mythology of the British Isles. The Everyman Book of Wartime First Aid.* The last one had several pages place-marked with playing cards, and in one case a haddock bone. He looked further along the shelf. *Unnatural Vices – Their Causes and Cures. The Third Sex. Fifty Thrifty Cheese Recipes. Nachtkultur and Metatropism. How to Spot German and Italian Aircraft.* A picture of a beautiful, melancholy woman looking out across the Thames at sunset, and a sepia print of a crazy-looking old lady, possibly Bryant's grandmother, were balanced on top of a copy of *Whither Wicca? The Future of Pagan Cults.* What kind of madman read stuff like this?

'He's young, Mr Biddle. He doesn't sleep much because he has a lot of energy and doesn't want to miss anything.'

'How old is he?'

'Twenty-two, but don't let his age fool you. When he's awake and at the office he expects everyone else to be as well. You'll soon get used to his funny ways.'

'I was employed directly by Mr Davenport and ultimately report to him.' Biddle looked around the shabby room and sniffed. Stale tobacco and something unhealthily perfumed. He sniffed again.

'Incense,' Forthright explained. 'He reckons it helps him to concentrate.' She folded her arms across her ample bosom. 'If you think this is a step up to promotion, Mr Biddle, you can forget it. It's a bleeding dead-end job.'

'I'm not looking to make my name. I just want to see results achieved,' Biddle told her.

'Well, we all want to do our bit, I'm sure,' Forthright agreed. 'But if you keep an open mind, you can learn a lot.'

'And Mr Bryant's new partner is starting today? I'm surprised not to see him here.'

Forthright found herself not wanting to volunteer any more information. She already liked John May. He looked logical and uncomplicated. Arthur was hoping he would handle the technical side of assignments, deal with the labs, tests, collation of evidence, procedural work. The DS raised her head at the sound of footsteps in the corridor.

The door opened to reveal Bryant, wrapped in a huge, partially unravelled brown scarf, with his new partner in tow.

'Stone the crows, Gladys, are you still here?' Bryant pulled ineffectually at the scarf. 'I thought you'd be gone by now.' It was Forthright's afternoon for working for the WVS in the Aldwych.

'I was settling in your new colleague.' Forthright rose from the desk corner and straightened her serge jacket.

'Not ours, surely?' asked Bryant, glancing vaguely at Biddle. 'This can't be the fellow. He's as fit as a butcher's dog. I thought we only got the halt and the lame. Welcome to the unit, Mr Biddle.' Bryant held out his hand. 'I hear you've proven a bit too smart for your local constabulary. This is another new teammate, Mr John May.' Bryant peered down into his scarf to find the knot, then glanced up at Biddle, studying his colleague with undisguised interest. 'We're certainly getting some young blood today. How old are you?'

'Twenty-one, sir.'

'We'd better find you a place to hang your hat,' said Bryant airily. 'I understand you're Davenport's man.'

'I report to him.'

'So am I right in assuming you're here to keep an eye on us?'

'I wouldn't put it like that, sir.'

'Really?' Bryant smiled cheerfully. 'How would you put it?'

Biddle had never taken such an instant dislike to anyone in his life. There was something about Arthur Bryant that made him want to punch him in the face. The other, taller man had not yet said a word. Perhaps he felt the same way.

'Mr Biddle will need to be released for his forensic course,' Forthright reminded him.

'Oh yes? What are you studying?'

'Blood and tissue typing, gas chromatography, perishable evidence,' Biddle replied.

'Hm. Anything more – intuitive?'

'Sir?'

'Interested in forensic psychology at all? Like to get inside the perpetrator's mind rather than studying the mud he leaves behind on his boots?'

'Not sure about that, sir.'

Bryant grunted disapprovingly. 'Well, with Mr Davenport's permission, we'll have to see if we can whip you into shape. I suppose you've been hearing a lot of rubbish about the unit.'

'No, sir.' Biddle stared blank-eyed at him. He appeared to be studying a point on the wall somewhere above Bryant's head.

'Don't worry, I've heard the rumours too. All I ask is that you're here when I'm here. If your classes clash, we'll have to work something out.'

'I'd prefer to let Mr Davenport decide my priorities, sir.'

'Oh, I see,' said Bryant, seeing all too well. He thought for a moment, then brightened up. 'In that case, you can start by making us all some tea. Sweet and strong. I won't ask where you get the sugar from although there's a shifty-looking chap on the corner of the alley who does a nice line in demerara, and use my mug, not a cup, they're for visitors. Make one for Mr May as well. Do you take sugar, Mr May?'

Biddle glared more fiercely than ever at the spot on the wall. 'That's not a duty covered in my job, sir.'

'Nor's cleaning the lavatories, but that's what you'll be

doing if you don't learn to make decent tea. I'm timing you. Tick tock, tick tock. Off you go.'

Biddle reluctantly retreated, and Bryant booted the door shut behind him.

'So, it seems we have a cuckoo in the nest,' said Bryant with a sigh. 'He looks a bit of a Jerry, don't you think? It must be the haircut. Oh, bugger.' A siren had begun to wail in the street, rising in tone, then dropping. 'We have to go down to the cells next door. Biddle can bring our teas over, but he'd better not spill any.'

9

PECULIAR CRIMES

'I wouldn't make too many jokes about Davenport in here if I were you, Arthur,' warned Gladys. She glanced at John May hovering awkwardly beside them in the cell, anxious not to appear to be listening. 'I won't always be around to protect you.'

The green and cream corridor of the underground cell sheltered the entire staff of Bow Street. The PCU personnel were granted their own cell during air raids, either out of respect for their privacy or because Sergeant Carfax had been saying unpleasant things to the others about them. The lights were off, and the acrid stench of the hurricane lamps made everyone's eyes water.

'You're not talking about marrying old Longbright again, are you?' asked Bryant with a grin. 'I thought you'd put your wedding plans off until after the war.'

'Not wishing to sound morbid, Arthur, I could be an old maid or a widow by then. Eight years I've been at Bow Street, eight years of late nights and ruined weekend plans, and what happens? Hitler invades Denmark and all leave is cancelled. Not only do I have to do my job, but I also get to be your nursemaid, placate your landlady, arrange for your laundry to be collected, fend off reporters and lie to everyone who's trying to have this place closed down. Now I've been given one weekend in which to get married and sort out the rest of my life. Is it too much to want a little happiness before we're all blown to smithereens?'

'Perhaps you have a point,' Bryant admitted. 'I wish you a long and happy marriage to the bounder Longbright. Listen.' From somewhere above them came the muffled thump of a bomb. The next one would reveal whether bombers were heading towards them or away, like the forking of thunderstorms. 'We may emerge from here to find the unit gone. Give us a cuddle.'

'I most certainly will not, you dreadful man.'

Bryant was going to miss DS Forthright. He had felt a passion for her from the morning he had seen her standing in the queue of the Strand Lyons, adjusting her stockings in plain view of the staff. As she hitched up the hem of her skirt, he had become so distracted by her shiny dark thighs that he had emptied a jug of milk down the front of his trousers. When Gladys looked up and saw Bryant staring at her she seemed genuinely surprised. 'What?' she had asked loudly in Bow Bells elocution. In the manner of British gentlemen across the centuries, everyone had looked away, embarrassed.

There was something peculiarly unselfconscious about Gladys. She didn't seem to care what anyone thought of her. Bryant was aware of other people every second of his life. What women thought of him mattered to a punitive degree. It was to do with being young, of course. After he adjusted to the idea of being undesirable, life became easier. By the time he hit forty, he no longer cared about the effects of what he said or did, which was good for him and bad for everyone else.

Forthright had put a highly promising pathology career on hold in order to gain field experience in the unit, and planned to continue her studies at night, but the war had come along and changed everything. The last thing she had wanted was to have some lovesick young man mooning over her, especially one as callow as Bryant. She knew it was only infatuation, and told him so. Worse was to follow when it became apparent that she was in love with a much older man. Utterly fed up, Bryant had allowed work to fill his waking hours, and tried not to think about Forthright and her fiancé spending their weekends locked away in some bedroom retreat, at it like knives while bombs fell around them. Now she was going, to hearth and husband and probably loads of children, leaving them stuck with the ghastly sneak Biddle. Was it any wonder he felt frustrated?

'I can't imagine why Longbright wants to get married at his age,' complained Bryant. 'Harris is old enough to be your father.'

'Not in the legal sense. Thirteen years, if you must know. We can still have children.'

'Vile thought. I'm surprised he still has the ability after working in the radiography department for so long. They all get tired sperm. And you'll be working for him, which won't be healthy.'

'I've worked for him before. He's the best there is.'

Bryant pulled his scarf over his ears and threw it onto the bunk by the door. Atherton, Crowhurst and Runcorn were seated glumly beside one another, reminding May of a Victorian souvenir brought back from an unfashionable resort. 'Do sit down and relax, John. You're going to be seeing a lot of this place.' Bryant turned to Forthright. 'You'll have no one to take you to the flicks, old sausage. I hear Longbright hates picture palaces.'

'You might as well face the fact,' she ran a crimson fingernail over the permanently windswept tufts of Bryant's hair, 'you've run out of ways to stop me leaving.'

'You're the only one who knows how I like things,' Bryant wheedled.

'Mr May will soon learn to cope with your foibles. He can be the other half of your brain from now on, can't you, Mr

May?' She patted a smudge of soot from Bryant's collar. There was a dull smokiness to the afternoon air of London that hung in the clothes these days, as though someone was constantly lighting bonfires. 'It's about time you treated yourself to some new shirt cuffs. I'd have sent you a formal invitation to the wedding, but it's in a register office and I know you don't approve.' Forthright's eyes twinkled. 'It's a pity. There wouldn't have been anything nicer than to see your funny little face peering over the top of a hired morning suit.'

Bryant flopped back his hair and gave her a helpless look.

'He's all yours, Mr May.' Forthright pulled off her police sweater, and nearly took their eyes out. 'I have to get changed. That's the all-clear. Arthur, why don't you go and keep an eye on your other new recruit?'

Bryant brightened a little. 'Making his life a living hell might cheer me up. He's taking a long time with that tea. You don't suppose he's been flattened? This is for you, by the way.' He produced a badly wrapped package from his coat and passed it to her. The red ribbon slipped from the brown paper the moment Forthright touched it.

'Oh, Arthur.' She looked down at the dog-eared copy of *Bleak House*. He had brought it with him from the office, the only item he felt was worth protecting. It was Bryant's favourite book, the ancient edition his father had bought for him in Paternoster Row, the one he always kept above his desk. She knew how much it meant to him. Curling the ribbon round her fingers, she slipped the roll into a pocket without thinking. 'I am going to miss you, you know.' She reached over and tugged the top of his ear.

Atherton had a camera with a flashbulb, and suddenly took a picture. Everyone looked surprised.

'Go on now, bugger off,' said Bryant, reaching for his pipe as the others started to file out. 'Mr May and I have a lot to discuss. Someone has to explain what's expected of him.'

Forthright went to her WVS meeting. Biddle sullenly

reappeared with mugs of tea just as they were leaving the cell. Back in the unit, the young detectives settled themselves in chairs opposite one another. Bryant opened a window and tamped down his pipe.

'Shall we risk it?' he asked May. 'The sun's come out. I bet they're copping it out in Essex.' He cleared a small patch of his desk. 'Everything gets so dusty.' He held up a brochure. 'Now this', he pointed to the title page, 'is your bible. Davenport wrote it, so of course it's gibberish, but I can give you the gen. The unit was originally planned years ago as part of something called the Central London Specialist Crimes Squad, but they received unhealthy publicity after they failed to solve the Paddington trunk murder of nineteen thirty-five. The squad never really flourished, and was finally disbanded three years later.

'The following year our superintendent persuaded West End Central and the City of London police that their more troublesome cases should be siphoned off to a renegade group. Davenport's no diplomat, and he upset them right from the outset. Whenever we're criticized I send a letter to the HO reminding them that we handle only the files no one else knows how to tackle. I've been granted powers to develop my own specialist team, the brief being to deal with fringe problems, but in reality this means becoming a clearing house for everyone else's rubbish. The unit was defined by the Home Secretary as London's last resort for sensitive cases, but it's becoming a home for dubious and abnormal crimes. It's also acting as a resource for officers seeking to close long-term unsolved murders. London's regular forces have their hands full with looting, not to mention the assaults and robberies they're getting in the blackout, although of course we're not allowed to talk about those.'

Bryant sucked hard at his pipe, made a face and relit it. 'We've been given autonomy, but the problem lies in the types of witnesses and materials I attempt to have included in our cases. The lawyers kick up a fuss about admission of

65

evidence. They're not open to new ideas.' He decided to spare his new partner the details of how the testimony of a spiritualist proved the last straw for a Holborn judge, who refused to hear any more from the unit's witnesses until Bryant could assure him that they were all technically alive and in human form.

The PCU worked on unaided, unappreciated and unloved in rooms above Montague Carlucci, the bespoke tailor's next to Bow Street station, holding the front line against all that was malevolent and profane, until war broke out and their casebooks suddenly filled, at which point Davenport saw a chance to please the Home Office. The unit had started to draw crazy people like moths to a flame. It was the war, everyone said; the war was to blame for everything that could not be explained.

For the time being at least, it suited the purposes of those in power to use the unit as a clearing house for unclassifiable misdemeanours. London faced an accelerated crime rate. It was to be expected in a place where everyone thought that each day was to be their last. Nobody wanted the city to get a reputation as a centre for spies, crime syndicates or murderers. It was important now, more than ever, to show the world that Britain could cope. Privately, though, Bryant wondered how long the line would hold.

'We had a lot of fuss about a man who was frightening the wife of the Greek ambassador. She said he appeared in their garden walking strangely, and that it looked as though his head was on back to front. Naturally it turned out to be an Italian, putting some kind of curse on the poor woman by wearing his coat the wrong way around. Silly, you'd think, but dangerous too. Given the current situation between Greece and Italy, we had to be very careful. The Eyetie eventually led us to a man who supplied Mussolini with cheese, and the War Office immediately started developing plans to poison him. They're working on something similar with Hitler and watermelons. Or was it bananas?'

66

As the afternoon waned, Bryant described his favourite case histories, even acting some of them out, and revealed the nonconformist methods he was keen to introduce into standard investigative procedures. He left the barmier-sounding ones for May to discover in his own time. For Bryant, the important thing was to make sure that he had an ally against the cuckoo, Biddle, whom he suspected of making mental notes against him.

By the time John May left the alleyway in Bow Street it was night and the traffic had virtually ceased, leaving him alone once more in the disconcerting darkness of a city under siege. As he groped his way home, the case file of a murdered dancer was making its circuitous way towards the unit.

10

COLD FEET AND ROASTED CHESTNUTS

'Can't you tell him I've already left, John?' It was early on Tuesday morning, and Arthur Bryant had just been informed that Farley Davenport was on the telephone for him.

'He knows you're here. He says he can hear you in the room even when you're not saying anything.'

'For someone who appears to be deaf most of the time, he has very acute hearing when he needs it.' Bryant searched his jacket pockets, looking for his pipe. He was forever losing it, especially when it was lit, and had a habit of setting fire to things. 'Is he still holding on?'

May gingerly returned the heavy Bakelite receiver to his ear, then covered the mouthpiece. 'I can hear him breathing.'

'Oh, for God's sake give it here.' He held out his hand so that May could pass him the telephone before busying himself on the far side of the office. 'What can I do for you, Davenport? I was just on my way out.'

'Alvar Lidell mentioned that business with the Leicester Square Vampire on the wireless this morning, Mr Bryant.'

'I know. I found his report fanciful in the extreme. He's in danger of developing a sense of humour. One can't help feeling it would be detrimental to the war effort.'

'Be that as it may, I believe I had expressly instructed you

68

not to attract any publicity to the matter. We shall have to issue denials.'

'Someone from the *Daily Sketch* came creeping around asking questions. I told him the absolute bare minimum. I didn't think for a moment that he'd pass the information on to anyone else. I can't for the life of me imagine how the BBC got hold of it.'

May waved his hand at Bryant, requesting the receiver. 'Ah, our Mr May would like a quick word with you.' He threw it as though it was burning his fingers.

'Mr Davenport? That account was treated as a jocular endpiece to the news. It couldn't possibly be taken seriously, provided no further information is released. To refute the report now would only validate it.'

There was a pause on the line. 'I didn't realize you were an expert on the subject, Mr May.'

'I'm not, sir, but a fire can't burn without oxygen to feed it.'

Another pause. 'Perhaps you're right. Let me have another word with your colleague.' May hastily passed the telephone back.

'I'll let the matter lie there, Mr Bryant, provided there are no further security breaches of this sort,' warned Davenport. 'These are the kind of propaganda victories Goebbels is praying for.'

'Fair enough, point taken,' said Bryant. 'I'm in receipt of your new boy, by the way.'

'Ah, Mr Biddle,' said Davenport cagily. 'Thought you could use an extra hand.'

'I now have the perspicacious Mr May, for whom I thank you. Biddle is rather over-egging the pudding, don't you think?'

'Don't push your luck, Mr Bryant. He's there to keep an eye on things.'

'I'll make sure he spells our names correctly in the reports he prepares for you.'

There was a small, deathly silence on the other end of the line. 'As long as you're spending government money, you must be made accountable to the public.'

'I wonder that they don't have a right to know at least some of the things that go on.' Bryant winked at May across the cluttered desks.

'The news must be managed correctly if it is to have the right effect on the morale of the nation,' barked Davenport. 'You will not let this happen again.'

'Righty-ho, message received and understood.'

There was a pop and the line went dead.

'I say, thanks for getting me off the hook,' said Bryant, replacing the receiver.

'What's Davenport like?'

'He can be a bit of a stick. He's incredibly old, of course, and I've seen a happier face on a pilchard. I hope I never get to be like that when I'm past forty. He's utterly convinced that Goebbels is watching our every move.'

'They say Goebbels has a cloven hoof,' said May, 'did you know?'

'Oh, *that*, it's a club foot. He was exempted from fighting because of it.'

'It's a strange feeling, not being involved in the physical battle when so many others are.'

'I know what you mean. We saw an internal memo about the number of dead. Fourteen thousand civilians have been killed in the last two months, with another twenty thousand seriously wounded, and four-fifths of them are Londoners. They're keeping that quiet.'

'One looks at the sheer scale of the suffering and feels so useless. I would like to have taken part in Dunkirk.'

'You're here to use your brains, John. The government knows how to put its good minds to work. The boffins will win the war in other ways. You'll see.' He grinned mischievously. 'Something rather odd has just come in, as a matter of fact. Come and join me in about an hour, will you?

70

I'll be – let's see,' he checked the address he had scribbled down, 'at the corner of Shaftesbury Avenue and Cambridge Circus, opposite Marks and Co. You'll have to go the other way round from here, cut over to Long Acre and work your way up. They've closed the top of Bow Street for bomb clearance.'

'Well, what do you make of this?' asked Bryant, glancing at the chestnut stall parked at the edge of the road. They were standing outside Marks and Co., the bookshop later recognized by its address, 84 Charing Cross Road. 'The gentleman here found something unusual on his chestnut stand last night, and called the police. They had a look and passed it on to us.'

May looked at the nervous young man of Mediterranean descent who stood beside his brazier. There was a sharp chill in the morning air, and very little traffic. Frost glittered on the rooftops of the houses in Shaftesbury Avenue, silvering the tiled turrets.

'This chap started heating up his brazier and noticed something that shouldn't be there among the chestnuts. Two somethings, to be precise. A pair of women's feet, very small. Heavily calloused, toes quite deformed.'

'Good Lord.'

'I always think anyone who eats pavement food deserves an upset stomach, but this is beyond the pale. There were a few raids reported after dark last night but they soon stopped, and no enemy aircraft managed to reach this far into the city, so I don't think we're looking at body parts from an explosive device. Besides, take a good squint at them.' He poked at the discoloured feet with the end of an HB pencil, carefully turning them over.

'Do I have to?' asked May squeamishly.

'Oh, you'll get used to sights like this. See here, the flesh at the edge of each ankle is neatly torn. Bombs leave limbs and appendages ragged. The skin's quite dry and hard to the

71

touch. No blood. Look at that, clean bone. So we're looking at death earlier than discovery, perhaps twenty-four hours before. Do you want a boiled sweet?'

'No, thank you.'

Bryant rustled the bag. 'Warm you up,' he said, 'Bassett's Winter Mixture. I've mislaid my pipe.'

'I'm fine, thanks.' May blew on his hands and briskly stamped his feet.

'You must get yourself a decent winter overcoat. There's a lot of standing around in this job, and that suit isn't warm enough. If you're short of cash or coupons I can sort something out for you.'

'I'm sure I can find something,' May promised, eyeing his partner's eccentric choice of apparel. Today Bryant was dressed in a suit of large green checks, over which he had thrown a fawn cashmere coat clearly manufactured in the nineteen twenties for someone much larger. He had topped off the ensemble with another unravelling hand-knitted scarf of indeterminate length, shape and colour.

'Now that you've had a look at the feet in situ, I suppose we should pop them into a bag and offload them.' Bryant produced a pair of red rubber gloves and slipped them on. He lifted the feet from the pan of the chestnut stall. 'Mercifully not scorched. Our vendor here had the good sense to leave everything just as he found it. He should really be taken in for questioning, but he hardly speaks any English. I think he's an Ottoman, and rather frightened of losing his work permit, if indeed he has one. I should make a friend of him. I've always wanted to sail up the Bosphorus.'

Bryant produced a cloth bag from his pocket with all the flair of a magician, opened the zip that ran along one side and dropped the feet in. He offered May another chance to study its contents.

'So what's this chap's routine?' asked May. 'I imagine the vendors store their braziers in a lock-up overnight.'

'Just off Soho Square near the Henry Heath hat factory.

They don't bother to clean them out very often, although they're supposed to, they just lock the lids. He hasn't let the brazier out of his sight since he wheeled it from the lock-up this morning. The holding bay was shut by the last man to leave, and remained sealed until this morning.'

'So the feet must have already been in the brazier last night. How could he not have noticed?'

'He was in a very nervous state when he closed up. The air raid, remember?'

'Did he leave the stand unattended at any time?'

'He went for a wee in Moor Street earlier, but didn't want me to know. I spoke to a couple of the other sellers before you got here. It's a sackable offence, leaving your stall un-attended. They're meant to get another stall runner to cover for them but obviously they can't during the raids. He'd just got back when the sirens started up, so he had to leave the cart and head for a shelter. That time, he was gone for about an hour.'

'Do you need someone to translate for him?'

'He's proved to be a pretty good mime so far. I think he's told us all he knows. Besides, we can't get any decent translators. They're all working for the War Office.'

'I wonder if the rest of the body will turn up. Let's see if anything's been reported overnight, and check with the river police.'

'God, it's cold,' complained Bryant, who had hands like ice even in midsummer. 'Good idea. There's a box in Charing Cross Road, save us going back to the unit. Take this chap's name and address.'

'Aren't you worried he might do a bunk?'

'I'm not going to drag him back to Bow Street for questioning. The bully Carfax will simply frighten the life out of him, and then he'll tell them nothing.'

The pair made their way along Charing Cross Road, past bookshops that stacked salvaged paperbacks on tables out-side their shops, and chemists advertising a peculiarly furtive mixture of products for gentlemen: trusses, contraceptives and nudist health magazines. They passed the old match-seller who stood on the corner of Newport Street, his blindness and missing leg testifying to an earlier conflict. Finally they reached the blue police box, and Bryant used his key to unlock it. He talked to a woman on the switchboard, and after a few minutes she called him back.

'Seems they've already got the rest of her,' he told May cheerfully. 'At least, they've found a body without feet. They're waiting for formal confirmation, but she's already been identified informally. A dancer named – hang on, I've got to write this down somewhere – Tanya Capistrania. Rather exotic. Being taken out of the Palace Theatre right now, *sans pieds*. The cleaners found her with her legs wedged into the trellis of the goods lift. Suggestive, isn't it, when you consider that the chestnut man left his stall in Moor Street, which runs alongside the theatre? Come on, let's go over and take a look. There's a woman who works in the box office who's waiting to show us around. Smile nicely and she might give us the kind of tidbits she wouldn't divulge to some ox in a police uniform.'

'Shouldn't we see where that chap left his chestnut stand first?'

'Good idea.' Bryant was still dangling the cloth bag containing the pair of feet. 'I wouldn't mind getting rid of these as soon as possible. I don't want anyone thinking I've nobbled a couple of black market pig's trotters.'

They slipped back through the early morning traffic, crossing Cambridge Circus, and passed under the side canopy of the Palace Theatre. May bent down and checked the gutter. He touched his index finger to the cobbles. 'Look at this. Someone has tipped coals out. I'm surprised they haven't been nicked. There's quite a bit of dust around. No footprints, which is odd.'

'The coals could have come from any one of the houses over there.'

'You're right.' He rose, brushing his hand on his coat. 'But this is where the Turk must have parked while he went for a Jimmy. It's a very short street.'

Bryant cricked his knees to take a closer look at the coal dust in the gutter. 'It's like hunting in reverse, isn't it?'

'How do you mean?'

'Finding the spoor from an act of cruelty, and trying to perceive the fading traces that lead away from it, following the dispersal of the participants rather than their convergence.' He thought for a moment, then leaned on May's shoulder to raise himself up. 'There's something out of joint here. What's that German word? *Unheimlich?*' He pulled his scarf protectively about his protuberant red ears. 'A cold wind. And a rather forbidding building. Definitely sinister.'

They stepped back into the road and looked up at the theatre. The exterior of the Palace was one of the most impressive examples of late Victorian architecture left in London. Standing alone on the west side of Cambridge Circus, finished in soft orange brick with peach-coloured stone trims, it sported four domed pinnacles, matching sets of stone cherubs, complex frescoes and decorative panels, with a peaked central pediment topped by the delicately carved figure of a god (miraculously intact, given the bombing that had taken place in Shaftesbury Avenue), and below it, nearly fifty arched front windows, currently boarded up to protect its patrons against flying glass.

'A suitably Gothic building in which to begin a murder investigation,' said Bryant, relishing the thought. 'But our duty is to the innocent. For that reason we must enter the realm of darkness.'

11

FORGOTTEN PEOPLE

. . . *A duty to the innocent*, thought John May, as he paid the miserable landlord of the Seventh Engineer and made his way back to rainswept London, the London of the new millennium, a place that bore only a superficial resemblance to the dark city of the Blitz. He felt old and tired, because Bryant was no longer alive to keep him young. Throughout his career he had been treated like the junior member of the team, even though there was only a three-year age gap between them. Now he was finally alone, and so bitterly miserable that there seemed little point in going on. But he had to, he decided, at least until he knew how his partner had died.

He stared through the train window at the cumuliform dullness blurring the horizon of the city, and tried to imagine what had been going through his partner's mind. Second-guessing Arthur Bryant had never been easy. A few days before his death, Bryant had returned to the site of their first case. The memoir's addendum suggested that he had been hoping to shed further light on the events of the past. Could he have upset someone so badly that he had placed his life in danger? Surely there was no one left to upset. The case had been solved and sealed. The characters it involved were as deeply buried as London's bomb rubble, and just as forgotten.

In 1940 the pair of them had been little more than precocious children. They had stumbled through their first investigation, and had somehow discovered a murderer. It had been a very different world then, more private, more certain. Nearly everyone they knew from that time was dead. Who was there left to question? Who would even remember? He knew he could expect no help from the unit; they were too busy confiscating Chinese-made assault rifles from the hands of drug-addled teenagers.

May's taxi pulled up outside his flat in a spray of effervescent drizzle. He had recently sold his house and moved to St John's Wood, to a small apartment with bare cream walls and a marble balcony that very nearly over-looked Regent's Park, if you stood on a chair. The old house had become hard for him to manage. Now he had a lift and a porter, and invisible neighbours who arrived and left with-out so much as a shoe squeak or latch click. Here he could sit and dream, and wait for death. Without Bryant, there seemed to be no alternative. It was as if the future had suddenly been walled off. He had always known that his partner would die first. Dreams of loss had disturbed his sleep for more than a decade. Bryant had laughed when he had described his nightly fears. Arthur had always been the stronger one. There was something callous in his nature that protected him from pain. Now the nightmare had sprung to life, and with it a new enemy. He wondered how he would cope alone.

May paused in the hall and sifted through the pizza deals on the mat. Beneath them he found a folded sheet of plain paper posted from the flat next door.

Dear Mr May,
I thought you ought to know that someone has been looking for you.
– Mrs R. Mamoulian

May rang the doorbell of number 7, and it was answered by a tiny old lady with unruly grey hair knotted in a bun as big as her head. She beckoned him inside with a wave of her noodle ladle. Around her slippered feet scampered a kickable dog with bug eyes. May inched his way through a blue corridor lined with fragile china animals, into an obstacle course of a sitting room. Every available inch of space was taken up with occasional tables covered in doilies, glass ducks, ceramic fish, glazed birds, antelopes, tiny gilt cups and, above the fireplace, a large porcelain bear in the coils of a snake. He wondered how the dog managed not to smash anything.

'I wouldn't have put a note through – we keep ourselves to ourselves,' explained Mrs Mamoulian, 'but he was loitering in the corridor with the lights out, and frightened the life out of Beaumont' – the dog yipped at the sound of his name – 'so I called my husband. Maurice spoke to him, but the man refused to give a name or explain what he was doing outside your door.'

'What did he look like?' asked May, carefully unsnagging himself from a china okapi.

'Creepy, with these awful glaring eyes and huge fangs, like a werewolf.'

'Oh, really?' May's assessment of his neighbour expanded to include the option that she might be insane.

'My eyesight's not that good but I'm sure he was trying to force open the latch. I wanted to call the police but, well,' she eyed the neat arrangements of china ornaments as if they contained secret mysteries, 'you don't want everyone to know your business, do you?'

May opened up his flat, leaving his wet bags in the hall, and seated himself in the lounge to make some calls. Ringing the Wetherby clinic, he managed to locate the doctor Bryant had seen the day before he had been blown up, and explained the situation.

'Of course I remember him, he walked straight through

into the private ward without stopping to get permission from our duty officer.' Dr Leigh sounded distracted. He was trying to talk to someone else in his office while fielding the police call. 'At first I thought he was one of the patients.'

That sounds like Arthur, thought May. 'Did he tell you what he was looking for?'

'Yes, eventually. He seemed to be in a great hurry. He wanted to check our files for long-term residents, but he wanted records going back sixty years. I told him we didn't keep them for such a length of time, and anyway, they were incomplete because we'd had a fire here a few years ago, so he left.'

'Did he give you the name of the person he was looking for?'

'You'll have to hold on.' The receiver was dropped, to be picked up half a minute later. 'That was the odd thing. He told me the patient was male, probably suffering from deep trauma, and would have been admitted without a name. I tried to help him but didn't know where to begin looking. What could I say? Those who enter the clinic as residents usually have a history of treatment. Their cases are heavily documented. Mr Bryant seemed to think that we might have taken in war victims who'd lost their memories, or at least their identification documents. I told him if we had, they'd be deceased by now. I'm afraid he became rather abusive.'

'Yes, he does that,' May sympathized. 'But were you able to help him?'

'Look, I'm really not sure. We're very busy here.' Dr Leigh was not prepared to admit that one of their patients had set fire to the ladies' toilets and was now locked in a cubicle, threatening to swallow his tongue if his demands weren't met, and as these demands included the reinstatement of the Great Hedge of India and a meeting with the late singer Freddie Mercury to discuss the hidden meanings in his lyrics, they were all in for a long day.

'He was going around questioning the nurses,' said the

doctor impatiently. 'Wanted to know when various patients had arrived, how long they were staying, that sort of thing. But I don't think we were able to help him.'

'Why not?' asked May.

'Well, when my staff tried to answer his questions, he ignored them and went off to talk to someone in the day room.'

'Do you know who?'

'I have no idea. But he was making notes on some kind of a list.'

Alma Sorrowbridge put down her squeegee and gave him an odd look. She was the only woman in the Battersea street who still washed her front step, and was proud of the fact. 'What sort of a list?' she asked.

'Names of people – patients. Something from the Wetherby clinic. In his room, perhaps.'

'I've disinfected his floor but I left everything where it was,' she said dolefully. 'I couldn't bring myself to throw nothing away. There's a lot of boxes.'

'Fine, then that's where I'll look,' said May.

Alma folded her arms across her chest. 'There is seventy-two of them.'

'Good God, where have you put them all?'

'I'm an old woman, Mr May, I got no strength left to start moving stuff about. They're where he kept them, in the basement. Besides, I been Mr Bryant's landlady on and off since the war. I'm not going to start touching his things now, just 'cos he's with God.'

'Would it be all right if I had a quick look through?' asked May.

'I suppose so,' Alma sniffed, 'but remember,' she raised a fat finger at the ceiling, 'he can still see you.'

'He always did like watching me work. Take me to the boxes.'

May spent several fruitless hours wading through the files

and papers in the cartons, but they were arranged according to the workings of Bryant's disordered mind. The human male possesses a powerful urge to collect things; Bryant had collected books, papers and magazines that revealed a lifetime of idiosyncratic behaviour. As May rummaged through the photographs of forgotten faces, the absurd news clippings, the abstruse monographs of disbarred lawyers, maverick scientists and mentally unstable professors, he knew he would find little of use. Sixty years of tangled memories; there was simply too much to decipher.

A papery cloud of moths fluttered out of a carton containing nothing but old razor blades. One box contained several hundred keys, another held only seed packets and raffle tickets.

May raised himself from his knees and dusted down his trousers. Perhaps Bryant had thrown the list away. His partner had, to his certain knowledge, visited one other place in his final days. The archive room of the Palace Theatre.

He dug out his mobile and rang ahead for an appointment. It felt good to be doing something, however uncertain. Positive action was the only way to keep his mind from sinking back.

12

INTO THE PALACE

Dr Runcorn had already instructed the Palace not to open its doors to the public that morning. The last thing he wanted was for customers to tramp any remaining evidence through the magenta pile of the foyer carpets.

Theatrical rehearsals were under way for *Orpheus in the Underworld*. The production was due to open without previews on the coming Saturday night. The unusual step of premiering on a day when the critics had normally gone to the country was deliberate. Nearly all of the first week's performances were sold out, thanks to shocked stage whispers along Shaftesbury Avenue that the production would not survive for more than a few performances before the Lord Chamberlain closed it down. Nobody knew exactly what had been altered in this radical reworking of Offenbach's operetta, but the scenery going in depicted all the damnations of Hell, including several freshly invented for the occasion. The carpenters were telling their mates in the public bars that they had never heard such dirty language recited on the London stage, and there were tales of skimpy costumes on the girls that put the Windmill in the shade and left nothing to the imagination.

Bryant knocked at the theatre's main entrance. PC

Crowhurst nodded to him through a gap in the boarded-over glass, and hastily unlocked the door. The interior of the Palace was mock-Gothic, with a central marble staircase that offered views back on itself like a recurring image from an Escher etching. Its steps and walls were worn pale, scoured by their nightly brush with more than a thousand bodies. Dusty electroliers hung down through the stairwell, their crystals gleaming dully like ropes of low-grade pearls.

'Hm. Nobody home.' Bryant peered into the frosted-glass lozenge of the box-office booth. 'Let's try the floor above.' He enthusiastically took the stairs in pairs and triples, forcing May to trot beside him. 'We're not going to give the press anything on this one. Davenport wants us to screw the lid down tight because of the victim's background.'

'Which is what?'

'Apparently her parents are Austrian. She trained in Vienna, mother's dead, father's Albert Friedrich, the international concert organizer. He's a pretty well-known chap, worked with C.B. Cochran here in the twenties, but Friedrich has lost a lot of good faith lately over his attitude towards the Jews. He has enough right-wing connections in neutral territories for the FO to keep files on him. He's also a professional litigant. I imagine he'd be prepared to make trouble for everyone if anything unsavoury leaks out about his daughter. Do you have a girl?'

'I'm sorry?'

'I was wondering if you had a girl. You know, a sweetheart. I don't, more's the pity.' Bryant sighed and shook his head with incredulity. 'It's not through lack of trying. I don't understand it. There's supposed to be a shortage of decent men. You just don't seem to meet the right ladies in this job.'

'I don't have a girl at the moment,' May admitted. 'I was seeing someone, but she's been posted to Farnham and isn't keen on writing letters.'

'Oh well, we anchor in hope, as the sailors say. Our contact here is a woman called Elspeth Wynter, supposed to be a mine of information.' He held up the cloth bag and checked that it was still dry. 'I must walk these feet back soon so that Oswald can get started on them.'

'Which one is Oswald?' asked May.

'Finch, our pathologist over at West End Central. Keen as mustard but such a stick you can't help winding him up. At least, I can't.' He stopped and studied the framed posters arranged along the corridor ahead. 'Thank God *No, No, Nanette* came off. All those performances of "Tea For Two" would turn anyone into a murderer. I don't understand it; America gets Ginger Rogers and we get stuck with Jessie Matthews. Nobody up here. Let's try again.'

Bryant turned on his heel and dodged past the confused May, rattling back down the stairs to pass into the theatre's centre foyer. 'I used to be quite a fan of the theatre,' he called over his shoulder, 'but I haven't been since the war began. They're all variety halls now, of course. People have lost the taste for anything serious. Who can blame them?' He looked about and sniffed the air. 'Theatres have a particular smell, don't you find? Mothballs and Jeyes fluid. It's so gloomy in here with the windows boarded up and all this cold marble, like a morgue. I wonder what D'Oyly Carte would make of the place now.'

'Wasn't this where Carte set up his national opera house?' asked May.

'Oh, it was to be his crowning glory. Nearly one and a half thousand seats spread across four floors, five bars, unrivalled backstage facilities, a modern mechanical marvel with room for more scenery than any other house in London. Poor chap opened it with Sullivan's *Ivanhoe* in 1891. The thing ran for a while, but it was a real plodder by all accounts, po-faced, arse-numbing, no good tunes, riddled with self-importance. Audiences wanted the bouncy songs and jokes of *The Mikado*, not wailing British epics about duty and fortitude. They tried a few more serious operas, then gave up the ghost and turned the place into a variety hall.'

He rapped on the box-office window with the handle of a furled umbrella he had spotted leaning against the wall. 'I say, are you in there?'

The frosted glass slid back to reveal a small tired-looking woman in a shapeless brown jumper and skirt. Knitted into the jumper was the title of Offenbach's operetta, the capitals picked out in blue wool. An overpowering smell of 4-7-11 cologne assaulted the detectives. The woman had an old-fashioned marcel wave, her hair held in place with kirby grips, and wore a pince-nez. May guessed that she was nowhere near as old as she appeared to be. She had nice eyes, large and rather sad.

'Ah. You must be Mr Bryant. I was wondering when you'd get here.'

'Miss Wynter? I see you're already advertising the show.'

'Oh, this.' She pulled at her jumper, embarrassed. 'Isn't it awful? Insistence of the new management.'

'John, this is the front of house manager, Elspeth Wynter. My partner, John May.'

'I'm pleased to make your acquaintance, Mr May.'

'A pleasure to meet a lady of the theatre,' said May, in the charming tone he unconsciously reserved for women.

'We looked in once but couldn't see anyone.'

'No, you wouldn't. I was on the floor with Nijinsky.' Elspeth opened the door of her office and emerged carrying a tortoise in a straw-filled cardboard box. 'I keep him under my stool because of the electric heater,' she explained, 'but I can't leave him alone because he chews through the wiring. Nijinsky's supposed to be hibernating but he's an insomniac. It's the bombs, they're enough to wake the dead. Do you want to go down and meet the company? They're about to start today's rehearsals.'

Bryant looked surprised. 'Have they been told what happened?'

'Only that Miss Capistrania went missing yesterday and will be replaced.' She walked ahead of them with the tortoise box under her arm, leading the way to the stalls. 'The artistic director is a lady, Helena Parole. This is a bit of a comeback for her. She's been away for a while, if you know what I mean.' She made a drinking gesture with her cupped right hand. 'Problems mixing grape and grain. The insurers aren't allowing her to touch a drop for the entire run.' She pointed down to the group standing in front of the bare stage. 'Not all of the sets have arrived, and everyone's getting nervous because they can't finish blocking.'

'Forgive me – blocking?'

'Fixing their physical movements, Mr May. Talk to me if you want to know anything. I'm always here, and I keep tabs on them all. The one in the yellow bandanna is Helena. The coloured gentleman with the artistic haircut is Benjamin Woolf, Miss Capistrania's agent. The confused-looking fellow is Geoffrey Whittaker. He's the stage manager. The girl beside him is Madeline Penn, the ASM, she's on loan from RADA because our other girl got bombed out and had a nervous breakdown. The man sitting down on the box steps in the snappy cardigan is Harry, he keeps the peace around here. They'll introduce you to the company.'

'Is it necessary to meet them all?' asked May, who was not at home in theatrical surroundings.

'It might throw some light on Miss Capistrania.' Bryant shrugged. 'We need to know if she was close to anyone, that sort of thing.'

Helena Parole had a handshake like a pair of mole grips and a smile so false she could have stood for Parliament. 'Thank you so much for taking the time to come down and see us,' she told May, as though she had requested his attendance for an audition. Her vocal cords had been gymnastically regraded to dramatize her speech, so that her every remark emerged as a declaration. May felt the hairs on the back of his neck bristle with resentment. 'I haven't told them a thing,' she stage-whispered at him. 'The spot where we found the corpse has been made off-limits, but they think it's because of repair work on the lift. Everybody!' She clapped her hands together and waited for the members of the company to quieten down and face her. 'This is Mr May, and this is Mr . . .' She leaned over to Bryant. 'I'm sorry, I didn't catch your name.'

'Mr Bryant.'

'Oh, like the matches, how amusing. Is that a *nom de plume*?'

'No it's not,' snapped Bryant.

Helena turned back to her cast. 'Mr Bryant,' she enunciated, thrusting her tongue between her teeth in an effort to extend the name beyond two syllables. 'They're going to be asking you a few questions about Miss Capistrania. It shouldn't cut into our time too much, should it, Mr May? We do have rather a lot to get through. Perhaps you can conduct your interviews out of the sightlines of my principals. It throws them off. I'll have a folding chair put out for you over there, and do try to keep the noise down, thank you so much.'

Having put May publicly on the spot, she accepted his silence as agreement, thrust her hands into her baggy khaki trousers and went back to directing her cast. Bryant felt as though he had been dismissed from the auditorium. Helena's eye rested easiest on men she found attractive, and clearly John May was in her sights. With a grimace of annoyance, Bryant stumped off to the side of the stage.

He found the goods lift separated off by wooden horses with warning boards tied to them by bits of string. The lift couldn't have drawn more attention if Helena had given it a part in the production. The electrics had been switched off at the mains, but Bryant dug a torch from his pocket and shone it into the shaft, quickly spotting the vertical brown streaks that marred the concrete barrier between the floors. On the other side of the stairwell, another slim beam of light illuminated a crouching figure. It turned and stared at him.

'God, Bryant, you frightened the life out of me,' said

Runcorn. 'Must you creep about like that? I could have dropped this.' He held up something in a pair of tweezers.

'What is it?' asked Bryant.

'Muscle tissue by the look of it, probably torn from the victim's ankle as it shattered. Don't these lifts have fail-safe devices to halt them if a foreign body gets caught in the mechanism?'

'It's half a century old. Safety wasn't a priority then. The Victorians lost a few workers in everything they built, rather like a votive offering.'

Dr Runcorn, the unit's forensic scientist, was one of the top men in his field, but his air of superiority, coupled with the punctilious manner of a civil servant, made him disliked by nearly everyone who came into contact with him. That was the trouble with a unit like the PCU: it was destined to be staffed with the kind of employee who had been rejected from other institutions in spite of their qualifications. Dr Runcorn was especially irked by Bryant, whose intuitive attitude to scientific investigation seemed at best inappropriate and at worst unprofessional.

'I haven't finished here yet,' he warned, 'so don't start walking all over the area touching things.'

'I wasn't going to,' said Bryant, affronted. 'You surely don't think it was an accident, do you?'

'A damned odd one, I agree, but stranger things have happened.'

'Hard to see how her feet ended up on a chestnut brazier, with that hypothesis,' Bryant pointed out.

'Oswald Finch took receipt of the cadaver from West End Central and has already run a few tests on it, reckons she might show positive for some kind of drug, possibly self-administered. These artistic types are noted for it.' Runcorn sniffed, rising from his crouched position and cracking his back. 'I don't know why he can't test for more obvious causes of death first like any normal person: heart failure, stuff like that. I just know that her feet were cut off and she didn't struggle. There are a couple of scuff marks here on the landing, the heel of a shoe, nothing particularly out of the ordinary. Suggestive, though.'

'Why?'

'Oh, I don't know.' Runcorn tugged at his ear, thinking. He was awkwardly tall and so thin that he looked lost inside his clothes. 'It's a backward scuff, but it faces forward to the lift. Like this.' He adopted an angular pose, something that came easily to a man who was six feet three and pigeon-chested. 'As though you were bracing yourself against the trellis. You might make it if you were pulling something through the bars of the lift. As if you were trying to drag out a heavy box. Or pull something through the cage. Legs, perhaps.'

That was the good thing about Runcorn, thought Arthur. Like Finch, he operated on a secondary set of signals, pulses that passed invisibly beneath his rational senses.

'There's another mark on the linoleum several feet away. It looks like it could be a match. If we can place someone out-side the lift with the victim inside it, then you might have a murder case. But why cut off her feet?' Runcorn stared gloomily down into the lift shaft.

'She was a dancer,' Bryant replied.

'Meaning what, exactly?'

'Suppose she had somehow survived,' said Bryant. 'Can you think of a better way to guarantee that she'd never perform again?'

13

LIVES IN THE THEATRE

Elspeth Wynter had spent her whole life, or rather the thirty-two years she had so far experienced, in the theatre. She came from a long line of theatre folk. Her grandfather had been a Shakespearean, once spoken of in the same breath as Burbage, Garrick or Keane. His wife had been cast in his shows as a perennial parlourmaid, and in true theatrical tradition had borne him a son in the rear of the stalls. Eight years into the new century, that son fathered his only child, Elspeth. Although his wife survived a pelvic fracture when she fell from the stage of Wyndham's Theatre, she ignored her doctor's warnings about the perils of motherhood in order to bear a daughter. The birth killed her.

Elspeth's father took the King's shilling for the Great War, but grisly memories of Ypres wrought changes in his life from which he never fully recovered. Prevented from returning to the front by the state of his nerves, he resumed the family profession. In the twenties he delivered a shaky baritone in countless threadbare Gilbert and Sullivan revivals, but the shows closed as unemployment began to bite and the cinema became affordable to the lower classes who had filled the music halls.

Elspeth's father could not look after himself, let alone a

teenage girl. He had no family beyond his colleagues in the theatre, and drink coarsened his acting. Elspeth was raised by sympathetic ushers and nursed from fretfulness while her papa performed in the twice-nightlies. As they trooped from one cold auditorium to the next, shivering in damp dressing rooms, shaking the fleas from lodging-house beds, playing in faded costumes to dwindling audiences, this daughter of the stage looked about her moth-eaten, mildewed world and began to wonder if the possession of theatrical blood was really the gift that her father's boozy friends claimed it to be.

Elspeth knew from an early age that although she was not destined for the boards, she would always be a part of the theatre; watching her father declaim each night from the box kept empty and permanently reserved for royalty – there seemed to be one in every playhouse – she watched the painful changes time wrought on his performances. The twenties were uncertain years, but not as lean as the thirties. Her father drank more as the audiences dried up. He, too, dried on stage, nightly forgetting his lines, relying on prompts, booed by an unforgiving audience weaned on cinema newsreels. The new medium had no truck with forgetfulness. Celluloid eradicated variable performances. To no one's surprise, he finally died in make-up and costume, during a trouser-dropping farce in which he had already been dying nightly.

Elspeth did not attend his funeral; there was a matinee. She had graduated from programme seller to bar cashier to ASM, through the various stressful stages of management until she suffered a nervous collapse and returned to front-of-house work. She was a West End girl, one of theatre's dedicated personnel, invisible to audiences but essential to everyone who worked there. As one show closed, another began rehearsals, and each run marked the periods of her life more completely than any calendar notation.

She had experienced a moment of passion just once, at the age of fifteen: pushed into a dressing room at the Palace and thrust into by a man she had only ever seen from the aisle of the stalls. He was playing the villain in a revival of *Maria Marten, or The Murders in the Red Barn*, and had barely paused to peck her on the cheek and pull up his trousers before returning to catch his entrance cue. While her seducer ranted across the boards, twitching his moustaches, his shirt-sleeves flecked with Kensington Gore, she too bled and suffered, and burrowed away in the crimson darkness to forget the world outside.

The theatre held no terrors for her. It was home, and filled with secrets, just like any family. It encompassed every happy moment in her life. As Elspeth paced the indistinct aisles of the Palace, its pervasive calm seeped into her. She could tell when the half-hour call was coming without looking at her watch. She sensed the rising tension of backstage activity, even though she was stationed in the front of the building.

Geoffrey Whittaker was also dedicated to the theatre, as invisible and essential as a spark plug to a car. He too was the latest – and the last, it turned out – in a long theatrical line. As stage manager to the incumbent company, he was in charge of the administration, the set, the lighting, the props, the health and safety of his audience, the scene changes, the laundry mistresses, the wardrobe people and the carpenters. He knew how to get scorch marks out of a starched collar, how to fix a cellulose filter over a follow-spot, how to unjam the springs on a star trap, and how to keep bills unpaid until the receipts were in.

Like Elspeth, he was unmarried and probably un-marriageable, because his career constituted a betrothal of sorts. Unlike Elspeth, he had a sex life, rather too much of one. In addition to dating girls in the shows, he made visits to a private house in the East End, where for a reasonable fee his needs were taken care of. This abundance of sexual activity allowed him to concentrate on his job without becoming distracted by the dancers' bodies during rehearsals. He had grown up in the Empires and Alhambras, helping his parents prepare for the night's performance, and could imagine no other world. Colours were duller outside, and the skies were not painted but real, which made them untrustworthy. In the theatre, you always followed the script. Beyond this world there were only unrehearsed moves, mistimed entrances, lines spoken out of turn.

The start of the second great war brought unwelcome transitions to Geoffrey's hermetic world. Venues were changing hands, falling empty, getting bombed. Philanthropy had been replaced by the desire for quick profit. Boxing matches and coarse variety acts moved in to entertain a new type of audience: commoner, louder, one that lived from moment to moment. Now there was something less comforting in the atmosphere before a show, something contaminated by the urgent, hysterical laughter that nightly rang from the stalls. Theatres were more frenetic, and companies diminished as the most able-bodied men went off to war. The Shaftesbury was bombed, the Strand and Sadler's Wells went dark. It was like a game of musical chairs, and nobody knew when the music might suddenly stop.

But Elspeth and Geoffrey still heard the audiences of their childhoods above the sound of hot water gurgling in the pipes, still listened to the ticking of the warm-air conduits, the backstage footfalls of departing painters. They were still the sounds of home.

And something had irreversibly changed. Elspeth had sensed it first at the outbreak of the war, a creeping disquiet that felt wholly out of place between the gaudy vermilion aisles of the Palace Theatre. She was alive to the smallest changes around her, and could detect any eddy of emotion in the silent building.

Late one night, closing up after a performance, she had suffered a terrible premonition, and her life had passed before her eyes. She told no one about the dark, scarred thing that stalked behind her in the rufescent rows of the dress circle, creeping down the vertiginous steps of the balcony. She experienced a sense of panic more with each passing performance, never knowing at what hour it might strike, for there is no day and night in a theatre. She only knew that it was there, watching and waiting, that it meant harm, and that something wicked had to happen.

Anxious to escape, she slipped out of the building and into the blackout, following the white stripes that had been painted on the paraffin lamps hanging from the protection boards around the front wall of the theatre. The Palace was her habitat, but she was lately being driven from it. She stopped and looked up at the entresol windows, and glimpsed the terrible visage, a pale oval peering out of the smoking salon at her, its features so distorted that it could barely be considered human.

Geoffrey had seen the faceless creature too, scurrying between the rows of the balcony, loping across a distant corridor, but he had not believed his senses. It was the war, he told himself, shaking his head. The constant fear played tricks on you. Last month a bomb had fallen through the roof of St Paul's Cathedral, destroying the high altar. For many it had seemed like a blow struck against God himself. If Hitler was the devil kept at bay, perhaps his acolytes were already here, moving among them, and wouldn't they choose such a godless place as a theatre from which to corrupt the innocent?

Geoffrey Whittaker sat in his office on Sunday evening and smoked, but his hands shook. Nothing could drive him from the only world he understood. He told himself that, at forty-six, he was too old for an attack of nerves. There were men out there less than half his age fighting to preserve his freedom, even though he did not want to be free. He was a willing prisoner of the theatre, its plans and strictures. His life was patterned on the stage directions of a dog-eared script. But something had crept inside his world that had no place in the production. His trembling fingers pulled another cigarette from the pack and inserted it between his lips.

Outside the Palace, Elspeth Wynter ran on into the blackout, through the empty city streets, her breath ragged behind her ribs, daring herself to go forward into darkness, frightened to return. But the home that had nurtured her for so many years could not be left so easily. It, too, was her domain, and beyond it, beyond the blackouts, there was no structure, no control, only the terrible light of freedom.

For Elspeth and Geoffrey, and hundreds like them, theatres were the last repose of stasis and sanity in a world hurtling beyond sense. But even they would be touched by the bloody hand of madness.

14

DOUBLE ACT

'What the hell are you talking about, keep it out of the press?' asked Benjamin Woolf. 'I've already had a call asking why she didn't keep an appointment with a photographer this morning. What am I supposed to do?'

'This is a tragedy for all of us, Ben,' said Helena Parole, whose earnest attempts to empathize with others was undermined by the fact that she didn't care about anyone else. 'I understand your feelings entirely.' She compounded the hypocrisy by rolling her eyes at May coquettishly.

That Tuesday morning, the mood at the Palace Theatre was fractious. Thanks to a night of bright moonlight there had been bombing raids until dawn, and no one had slept well. Sloane Square tube station had been hit, killing many. In the morning's papers, questions were being raised about the efficacy of public shelters. Not enough people were using them, and there were rumours among those who did that infection was rampant. Sanitation remained haphazard, and there was a general feeling that the unchanged air spread all manner of germs. Most Londoners preferred to stay at home, tucked inside cupboards, under the stairs, sleeping in ground-floor rooms or outside in an Anderson shelter: fourteen arched sheets of corrugated iron bolted together and half buried under earth that flooded in wet weather but could survive everything except a direct hit.

The stage was still empty. Few of the cast had yet arrived, but members of the orchestra were seated in the pit, patiently waiting to resume rehearsals. They usually practised in airy rooms behind Waterloo Station, but those had been requisitioned by the War Office, and now the musicians were crammed before the stage in a dimly lit theatre instead of playing in a sunlit space overlooking the river. The most able-bodied among them had been taken by conscription, and they had been forced to fill up their ranks with fiddle-scratchers from the twice-nightlies and even a couple of Leicester Square buskers.

Luckily their conductor, Anton Varisich, like many great conductors, was as adept at diplomacy as he was at extracting mellifluous harmonies from his motley crew. He had topped up the percussion and woodwind sections with exiled Spanish and French players, lending the arrangements a jaunty cosmopolitan air in keeping with Offenbach's play, but previously unheard in London. The nation's music still owed more to the palm court than the boulevard, and consequently the players were having a whale of a time because they were doing something new. Quite how they'd manage to rehearse when the cast turned up and wanted to practise their lines would remain to be seen.

'Will you understand when I tell the next person who calls that your star dancer might be a little late for rehearsals on account of not having any *feet*?'

'You can't be serious.'

'That's what they're saying.' Woolf threw his long body back down onto seat C15 and smoothed a hand across his brilliantined hair. There was an ever-present aura of sarcasm about him that no one responded to positively. 'The police are crawling all over the building, you won't tell any of us what's going on and I'm supposed to act like everything's tickety-boo.'

Helena glared up into the darkness beneath the roof. 'Benjamin, please, you're an agent, lying is a professional qualification for you, like a merit badge or something. You can tell the press she's joined the WAAFs and flown to Timbuktu on a mercy mission if you want, and they'd have no choice but to believe you. She's frightfully upper class, and her reputation will need protecting.'

Their conversation was punctuated by the noise of the wind section practising scales. Woolf had to raise his voice to be heard, but Helena did not wish to shout back. She knew how easily panic could infect a cast facing a deadline under already difficult conditions, but she was going to make sure that the Windmill wasn't the only theatre to stay open throughout the war.

'It's difficult for all of us,' she explained with feigned sufferance. 'You'll just have to do the best you can. I'm out of gaspers, darling, would you light me?' Benjamin touched a match to a Viceroy and passed it to her. 'These gentlemen are detectives, and hope to have the whole thing quickly sorted out. You know how easily these girls fall in with the wrong types.'

'Perhaps we should continue this discussion in Miss Parole's office,' May suggested. 'I think we're in the way here.' He looked back at Bryant and followed his partner's gaze to the stage. Bryant's attention had been drawn away by the arriving dancers, half a dozen long-legged girls who stood whispering and giggling in the shadows of the wings.

Bryant was captivated by what he saw. The theatre held a special fascination for him. When John looked at posturing actresses angling their best sides to the audience, he saw nothing but mannequins and painted flats. Arthur saw something fleeting and indefinable. He saw the promises of youth made flesh, something beautiful and distant, a spontaneous gaiety forever denied to a man who couldn't open his mouth without thinking.

In Helena's office May raised the window behind the

battered oak desk and looked down into Moor Street, where men in black heavy rescue and white light rescue helmets were clearing sections of charred wood from a blackened shop front.

'Am I right in thinking that, as the company's artistic director, the production's success lies in your hands?' Bryant asked.

'Absolutely.' Helena looked tense and angry. She brushed at the cigarette ash smudged in the cleavage of her tight white blouse. 'I have a board of directors to answer to if *Orphée aux enfers* fails. I tried to keep Offenbach's French title. They felt it would put people off. I said, "It shows solidarity with the people of France, and it's the cancan, how much more accessible can you get?" Eighty years ago this was considered a trifle, an after-dinner joke. Now the English think it's high art because three words are French. They're such peasants. They'll queue to see a mayoress open a fête but only fall asleep in opera houses. It's not like this on the continent, you know. The French have more respect for their artists.'

The thin November sunshine threw slats of light across her make-up as she unfurled a plume of cigarette smoke into the coils of her coppery hair. The exhalation softened her harshly painted eyes. Bryant realized that she was probably his new partner's type, firm-jawed, full-busted, full of life. She had presence, like an expensively upholstered piece of furniture, a reminder of more luxurious times.

Helena knew that it was important to care about the members of her cast. They weren't actors, Benjamin had once told her, they were her children. But she had no children. What she had was a failed three-year marriage to her agent which had foundered over the argument of raising mixed-race infants in a land where black skin was still seen as a peculiarity. Now, because of the war and the lack of jobs in the theatre, she and her former husband had been forced into each other's company again.

'We have to find a way of keeping it out of the press.' Helena joined May at the window. 'Although the story would do wonders for the box office.' She closed the window. Smoke still loitered in her hair, momentarily recalling an image of the Medusa. 'This show represents a massive commitment of time, energy and money. It's going to brighten up London and raise the morale of thousands of people every week.' She turned to the detectives. 'The board has been planning it for years, setting *Orpheus* up as a public company, raising finance on an international scale, waiting for cast availability. The war has made us redouble our efforts. None of us can afford a flop. We're putting our futures on the line. If *Orpheus* fails to recoup its costs, the insurers will step in, and one of our greatest theatres will fall dark for the remainder of the hostilities, perhaps for ever. So, does anybody have to know what happened? They're more concerned with their own safety than hearing about some dancer's misfortune. We open in four days.' Helena felt safer when others considered her incapable of kindness. 'As far as we knew, she was working late on Sunday night and went home. Couldn't she have decided the role wasn't for her and left the country?'

'Don't you think you owe her something, Helena?' asked Benjamin. 'Suppose somebody has a grudge against the performers? What about the safety of the rest of the cast? The safety of the audience?'

'You know as well as I do that the audience is always separated from the stage.'

'Is that really true?' asked May.

'Backstage and front of house are two entirely different worlds. You can get from one to the other only by going through the ground-level pass doors. There are just two of those, and one has been locked for so many years I don't think anyone knows where the keys are.' She ground out her cigarette. 'It was probably someone from the cast of *No, No, Nanette*, driven insane by Jessie Matthews.'

100

'I can make a case for press restriction if you really think the play is in the interests of the city's morale,' Bryant offered.

'It'll be tough keeping things quiet this end. So long as an actor's near a telephone, word always gets out. Death poisons the atmosphere in a place like this.' Helena knew that performers were sensitive to the slightest undercurrents rippling the still air of an auditorium.

'How are we going to explain that our dancer has disappeared?'

'She had no friends.' Helena stole another cigarette. 'Nobody who pushes that hard ever does. She told me she was getting weird letters, Mr May. Sex-crazed men wanting her to walk on them with stilettos, that sort of thing. People were drawn to her aggression. It could be any one of them. They follow the movements of performers in the papers and turn up in the front row every night applauding in the wrong places, and there's nothing you can do about it.'

'There is something,' said May. 'The telephone bookings for which you mail out tickets, we can cross-check the addresses of all the reservations so far.'

'And what are we supposed to do in the meantime?' asked Benjamin.

'Resume rehearsals,' said Bryant, taking his partner's cue. 'Behave as if nothing untoward has happened.'

'You could make an announcement to the effect that Capistrania has been taken ill and has been placed in quarantine,' added May. 'Scarlet fever perhaps.'

'Thank heaven someone around here is ready to take charge.' Helena gave May a reassuring smile. 'I already feel safer in your capable hands.'

Bryant made a face behind Helena's back, and was caught in the act when she turned round. He transformed his grimace into a cough as, somewhere far below, an oboe hit a warning note.

'I thought you were jolly impressive with La Parole back

101

there,' said Bryant, bouncing along the corridor to the box office as they left. 'We make a bloody good double act. Perhaps we should take to the stage: Bryant and May, detective duo, some juggling, a patter song and a sand dance, what do you think?'

'I think you're completely loopy,' answered May truthfully. 'It's a murder investigation. I don't have the training for this.'

'You're young enough still to have an open mind,' said Bryant, laughing. 'That's all the training you need.'

15

SOMETHING POISONOUS

'Hello, Oswald, something's different in here, have you had the place decorated? I'm rather partial to the smell of new paint.'

'Very funny, Mr Bryant.'

Oswald Finch, the pathologist, sat back from his desk notes and cracked the bones in his wrists. His team had been forced to disinfect the department at West End Central after Arthur had presented him with a cadaver so slippery with infesting bacteria that it had reacted with their usual chemical neutralizers, causing the entire floor to reek of ammonia and rotting fish. This was no problem for Finch, who had the occupational advantage of being born without a sense of smell, but Westminster's health officer had threatened to shut them down unless they did something about it.

Apart from the nuisance factor of dealing with council officials, Finch couldn't see what all the fuss was about. He found the process of bodily decay fascinating. Bryant had suggested that, as a longtime supporter of Tottenham Hotspur, he was used to seeing things slowly fall apart.

'At least we got you a nice fresh one this time,' May pointed out cheerfully. There was something so depressing about being in Finch's presence that people adopted an air of forced jollity around him. He had the suicidal expression of a Norwegian painter and the posture of a unstuffed rag doll. No one in the unit had been surprised when Oswald's glamorous wife had left him for a dashing RAF officer. Rather, they were amazed that he had managed to marry anyone at all.

'She's been dead since Monday evening. Come and take a look.' He rose and led the detectives through to a windowless green-tiled chamber behind his office. Scrubbed wooden workbenches and ceramic sinks alternated along opposite walls. One table was in use, its occupant covered with a white sheet more to reduce temperature change than to spare feelings.

Unlike most autopsy rooms, this one had variable light settings instead of bright overhead panels. The reason became apparent when May studied the laboratory's centrepiece, a mass of counterbalanced mechanics so advanced for the time that, as yet, the results it yielded could not be considered as admissible evidence. Having developed the system exclusively for the unusual demands of the PCU, Finch was now testing the prototype in the hope that it would become the new industry standard. The unit was so close to the discovery of computer technology that, years later, John May wondered how they had not managed to stumble upon the invention of binary code. But on that day, he had been so fascinated and horrified by the sight of a dead body that he saw little else.

'I assume you've definitely ruled out some kind of bizarre accident?' asked Bryant.

'I'm not so sure. According to your man Runcorn, she didn't fall down in the lift, she passed out. No fibre snags on the lift wall or something; you'll have to speak to him about it. And I don't think loss of consciousness was caused by anything natural like a narcoleptic fit. Her medical files indicate that she was in perfect health.'

'You've already raised her records?' asked Bryant. 'I'm impressed. We don't even have a typist.'

'We don't hang about here, Arthur,' said Finch pointedly, 'not when you can lose half an afternoon from an air raid.'

'Do we now have a formal identification of the body?'

'The theatre's registered doctor knew her. She has no family living here. We think her father's in Vienna. We're trying to notify him now. Look at this.' Finch drew back the sheet to expose the body's right shoulder, then pressed the end of a nail file against the inside of Capistrania's upper arm. 'Ignore the lividity. The flesh clearly retains any indentation marks you make on it. In my book that's a sign of infected tissue. The introduction of something poisonous. My first reaction was to check for evidence of a narcotic, stuff a dancer might possibly use to improve her performance.'

'Is that what they do?'

'I don't know,' Finch admitted. 'I don't know any dancers.'

'You go to that hoochie-coochie place in Clerkenwell. Forthright used to see you queuing up outside as she was going home. Anything come up in the blood samples?'

'This equipment's faster than most, but there's an awful lot to test for. I started by looking at cardiac glycosides, oldendrin, nerioside, toxic carbohydrate groups, but there's no evidence of vascular distress, no common signs of poisoning.'

'How can you be sure?'

'I can't, but convulsions in such a confined space would cause bruising on the limbs and some kind of organic material deposit at the site, which Runcorn has yet to find. There's no indication of haemorrhage, diarrhoea or vomiting. I checked the stomach contents. She'd eaten a sandwich about three-quarters of an hour before death, some kind of poultry in the filling, nothing unusual, and a type of chocolate bar, something with nuts in – don't Barker and Dobson do one? I don't think it's an allergic reaction of any kind. Still, the gastric juices are disturbed, and if we assume that assimilation was rapid, causing her to fall down shortly after she'd entered the lift, I'd say we were looking at something that paralysed her muscles. There's a lot of clenched tissue in her limbs.'

'So you know what she didn't die of. What's your initial reaction?' Bryant had come to trust Finch's instincts, even though they were unlikely to find their way into official reports until the appearance of corroborative evidence.

'There's some slight inflammation and discoloration on her right knee. Dancers bruise all the time, of course, but this one's very fresh, consistent with falling in the lift. I think she just dropped suddenly in her tracks, which suggests a fast fall in the supply of blood to the brain or some kind of synaptic disruption, but I'd still expect more electrical activity.'

'What do you mean?'

'Limbic convulsion. Aberrant behaviour from the nerve endings. Cuts on the hands, something to indicate a bit of thrashing about.'

'You realize what you're saying – it's possible that she collapsed and got her feet caught.'

'I have to say that because of the trace evidence.' Finch moved down to the base of the table and rolled back the sheet. 'You can see the avulsive trauma here in tissue dragged right from bone, separated from all of its connective materials. That's how we know the skin and musculature around the ankles have been torn, not cut. These parallel scrape marks are actually scored deep into the cartilage, and the bones are severely compacted to a depth of an eighth of an inch. That's consistent with the concrete ledge hitting the feet and breaking them off. You can get Runcorn to look along the ledge for vertical striations that include bone particles. Obviously the pain must have been appalling, and for a young lady to remain still while something like this happened, I just think it's unlikely that she would have been conscious. There's another thing. She's very short, slender, very small-boned, virtually no body fat.'

'A lot of dancers are tiny,' May pointed out.

'Small people are easier to poison, although there are exceptions to the rule. Women get drunk more quickly than men because they carry more fat. Dançers are a different kettle of fish, though. A fast-acting muscular poison, possibly something naturally occurring, would have taken care of her. I just ran tests for a substance called coniine, which paralyses the body in pretty much the same way as curare.'

'Curare? I thought that caused heart failure. One has images of blowpipes being aimed in the jungle.'

'That's because it was used by Orinoco Indians. A plant resin. But I believe there's a prescribed clinical version available in America. It's not unheard of for doctors to inject it into pre-op patients in order to reduce the amount of anaesthesia needed. The point is, we've got a positive match for coniine, but not for curare. Something was definitely introduced into her body, but I'm at a loss to understand how. There are no visible puncture marks of any kind.'

'What about in the feet?'

'Obviously I've yet to examine those.'

'But you don't think it likely that she was injected.'

'I didn't say that. I said there are no *visible* signs so far. Hypodermic injection sites can heal very quickly and disappear completely within two days.' He tapped a pencil against his long yellow teeth. 'There is something here, though. Take a look at this.' He pointed to the small radiophonic monitor angled above the cadaver. 'One of our new gadgets. I'm not sure how reliable it is yet. It's taking subcutaneous readings from different levels in her body tissue. This is the balance of acids that occurs at cellular level. They should all be about the same height.' The screen showed a number of bright green lines, but some were much taller than others.

'And what does that mean?' asked May, looking up at the chartreuse-tinged face of the pathologist.

'That's rather the problem.' Finch narrowed his eyes as he studied the drifting pulsations. 'I haven't the faintest idea.'

16

OFF THE RADAR

Janice Longbright was seated on a stack of Tampax boxes trying to type with two fingers. Outside, on the steps of Kentish Town police station, a gang of teenagers were screaming at each other. The former detective sergeant forced herself to block out the noise and concentrate. With the Mornington Crescent offices blown to smithereens, the unit's surviving personnel had been evacuated to the nearest annexe, but with the force on full alert, no chairs or desks were available for them to work from. The Tampax boxes had been found in the boot of a boy's car, cushioning a number of rifles and stolen army pistols, and made a passably comfortable seat.

The sounds in the street were becoming more confrontational. Longbright looked around the overcrowded office at men and women barking into phones, and was unsurprised that no one had the energy to go outside and stop the fight before someone got hurt. The gang members would be at each other again the second the police departed. Trying to help them was like sticking a plaster on a cut throat.

With John May still off on leave, Longbright had reluctantly agreed to return to the unit for a few weeks.

Balancing the telephone on her knee, she tried Sam Biddle's number. This time she got through to him. The Home Office's new police liaison officer was supposed to be providing them with relocation plans and news of emergency funding, but was proving evasive.

'I can't give you anything concrete at the moment,' he insisted. 'There are too many other priorities.'

'So I keep being told,' replied Longbright impatiently. 'Presumably we all have to be firebombed before we get your attention.'

'We have to make sure the police can protect civilians first. Yesterday we had tourists getting caught in crossfire at Stockwell tube station. Once this situation is under control we can take a look at the unit's future.'

'What's happening in this city isn't a "situation", it's an epidemic, things are out of control. And who said the unit's future was in question?'

'Your building is gone, Longbright.'

'We still have our staff.'

'No, you have one of your two directors left alive, and he's beyond retirement age.'

'We have DuCaine and the other new recruits.' Longbright was stung by Biddle's reversal of attitude. Only days ago he had been talking about recruiting amateurs, in accordance with the Scarman Centre's findings.

'The minister's position on this is that Mr Bryant was caught up in some kind of internecine feud that resulted in his demise. We don't have the manpower or the money to investigate all of the surrounding circumstances. Obviously what happened is unfortunate, but it's our position that Bryant was acting alone and knew the hazards of doing so. We're concerned about the dangers to the public posed by the collapse of the building, but as mishaps go these days, it's pretty much off our radar.'

'Your grandfather was a great friend of Arthur Bryant's. He would be ashamed of you now, Mr Biddle.' Longbright slammed down the receiver just as the stack of boxes slid away beneath her.

To calm herself she went to her car for a cigarette. A young girl with a sharp face and scraped-back blond hair challenged her.

'This your motor? You gonna give me a tenner for saving your stereo?' Her hands were thrust defiantly into the cheap cotton of her jacket. Longbright presumed she was carrying a knife.

'I'm a police officer. Fuck off before I arrest you.'

'You can't arrest me, bitch.' The girl stuck out her chin. She was all of fifteen. Longbright knew without looking that she had track marks on the backs of her legs.

'I'll think of a reason if I have to.' Longbright moved her aside and climbed into the car, quickly locking the door. She watched the girl walk back to her mates, feeling almost sorry for her.

A cigarette soothed her nerves. She exhaled smoke and sat back in the seat as sirens started up in the police station car park. Poor John, she thought. Wherever he is, he'll have to figure this one out by himself.

17

IMPRESSIONS

'There is no precedent for what we're trying to create here, Mr Biddle,' explained Bryant. 'There are no superior officers correcting our mistakes. The last thing I need is you going to Davenport and informing him of our progress.'

Bryant had received another scalding telephone call from the unit director about the amount of time the detectives had spent at the theatre, and he could have found out only through his newly appointed agent.

'I'm just doing my job,' said Biddle hotly. 'Mr Davenport wants the matter cleared up quickly, and for the law to be observed. How else can he report back to the victim's father? Your absence from the office contradicts—'

'You don't decide how I choose to work.' Bryant ran his hands through his floppy fringe and thumped down behind the desk, then dug about in a drawer for a packet of 'Nervo' fortified iron pills. Bryant did not enjoy the best of health, and was forever testing new cold remedies. In this case his cold symptoms were more to do with the resentment he felt at losing DS Forthright to something as pointlessly career-damaging as the state of matrimony. He studied Biddle resentfully. He had seen the type before. Thin-skinned, competitive, angry with the world. School had been filled with boys who saw everyone else as a threat. Half of them became so confrontational that they lost their friends by the time they left and ended up in the Territorials, where the war would take them.

'We can investigate this case in any way we see fit,' explained Bryant. 'We have none of the prejudices of the regular police force.'

'You have none of the resources. No equipment. No manpower. They've given you nothing at all,' muttered Biddle. 'That's why they leave you alone, you don't cost anything.'

'We have our minds, Sidney, the most powerful weapons we possess.' As far as Bryant was concerned, his office was a monk's cell, a sanctified if incredibly untidy billet where acolytes concentrated on their devotions to the cause. It was not simply a cheap place to dump dead cases.

'You'll see I'm using a blackboard,' Bryant pointed out. 'I gave Mr May a chance to explain his audiophonic filing system and it failed to impress me, so I'm falling back on a tried and trusted method.'

'You didn't give it a chance, Arthur,' May pointed out. 'It'll work if you just learn how to use the deck.' He had borrowed the cumbersome tape machine thinking it might help, but Bryant had managed to wipe the tape clean and irreparably damage the recording heads, although quite how he had managed to do it remained a mystery. It didn't help that he kept magnets in his overcoat pockets.

For Arthur this was the start of a lifelong stand against technology that would one day result in his crashing the entire central London HOLMES database and part of the air traffic control system at Heathrow. The young detective possessed that peculiar ability more common to elderly men, which produces negative energy around electrical equipment, turning even the most basic appliances into weapons of destruction. The more Bryant tried to understand and operate technical systems, the deadlier they became in his hands, until, at some point in the nineteen sixties, just after

112

he had set fire to his hair by jiggling a fork in a toaster, man and machine had been forced to call a truce.

'So,' Bryant brandished a chunk of chalk, 'Runcorn's mysterious footprints suggest a second person at the death site, but not much else.'

'We can't be sure who was in the theatre at the time,' said May, pulling on the overcoat he had borrowed from his uncle. The office was freezing. The radiators had packed up again.

'Everyone is required to sign in with – what's his name?' asked May.

Bryant consulted his notes. 'Stan Lowe checks members of the company through the rear stage door. Elspeth Wynter keeps an eye on the front of house. Geoffrey Whittaker sees everyone in the auditorium. Between the three of them they usually know who's in the building. We'll have a roll call by the end of the day.'

'She was a beautiful girl,' May pointed out. 'Too beautiful for others to get close to.' The cast at the theatre had proven reticent on the subject of their friendships with the dancer.

'But somebody did, though, didn't they?' said Biddle fiercely. 'Maybe she led her boyfriend on, drove him to attack her. It happens all the time.'

'No, Sidney, ordinary murders do not happen like this. Most occur at home, within the family unit, where the perpetrator is a spouse, sibling or friend. War changes that. Crimes start to happen without reason, because people are upset, or angry, or just frustrated. Acts of violence are squalid, casual, mundane. Contrition, misery, fingerprints everywhere, children in tears. This death was absurdly theatrical, to mutilate someone in the home of Grand Guignol. That's what makes it unique, that's why the case has come here.'

'You think someone in the cast is trying to stop the production?'

'It's unlikely to be anyone involved with the show, because

113

they're the ones with the most to lose. If you were working with Capistrania and had a violent grudge against her, why not wait until she left the theatre for the night? Why draw attention to your own workplace?' Bryant's eyes were bright with enthusiasm. 'There's enough danger out there on the streets right now, what's one more casualty? Go on, whack her over the head with a brick and dump her on a bombsite, who would know? Anything can happen in the blackout if you've a mind for it – a calculating, egotistical, opportunistic mind. One thinks of the Rosicrucian Robert Fludd and his theories of anti-magnetism, brilliant and deranged. The greatest dangers come from the man without a conscience. Look at the photographs of Hitler at Nuremberg two years ago, the deadness behind the eyes that denies humanity, just as it betrays the true darkness of the soul.'

May felt exhilarated around Bryant. He had always imagined that somewhere out there, away from suburban dullness, ardent young people were allowed to give freer rein to their thoughts. He felt as though he had arrived at a place he had always wanted to be.

'How can you concern yourself with the mind of the murderer when it's the victim who's been done wrong?' asked Biddle hotly.

'Because we can do nothing for the victim. John, surely you must agree?'

'I suppose so, but it's difficult to set aside sorrow for the death of someone young.'

Over the years, the detectives argued so much that eventually their polarized altercations mellowed into the kind of bickering that passed for daily conversation in married households. Bryant was more receptive to unusual paths of thought. May's attitude was flexible, but he seemed in a permanent state of surprise. He was warmer, more approachable. He empathized with victims. Bryant was the opposite. He hailed from a sphere of arcane textbooks and borderline beliefs. There was something mad about him, as if he had lived in the city for centuries. Biddle couldn't imagine how his mind worked, or what had made him place his trust in John May so quickly. Bryant appeared untouched by the horrors of war, except on a level of academic interest, and showed no capacity for kindness. May's mental processes were easier to follow. Bryant just frightened people. He smelled of some weirdly pungent aftershave and looked like a distracted, misanthropic student. He trusted books more than other human beings.

Biddle was an observer. He stayed silent and noticed the things others missed. He could already feel the undertow of loyalties that might pull the two detectives in different directions. It was worth making a note of. In terms of career advancement, it could prove useful.

'Sidney, we seem to have lost you.' May pointed at the blackboard. 'Points of correspondence in these footprints.'

Biddle studied the photographs pinned at the top of the board and tried to concentrate. 'The design is similar in shape and dimensions, and there's what looks like a faint worn area on the instep common to both,' he pointed out. 'The moulded sole probably means plimsolls, which is good, given the distinctive patterns produced by different companies.'

'I noticed that many of the cast members wore a specifically styled stage shoe with a rubber sole like that,' added May.

'What would you suggest we do with these prints, then?'

'They were made on lino and concrete respectively, so I'd try to raise a more detailed image with an electrostatic mat.' May knew that you could pass an electric charge through a sheet of foil layered between two sheets of acetate, photograph it at an angle that contrasted the surface, and it would reveal details of the shoe that might otherwise be lost.

'No need. I was informed that such shoes come from a specialist shop in St Martin's Lane. That's your job sorted out for the rest of the day, Sidney. Till receipts.' Biddle looked uncomfortable. 'What's the matter?'

'We should be looking for her enemies.'

Bryant's face clouded. 'What does forty-eight mean to you, Mr Biddle?'

'The first forty-eight hours are the most important in any murder investigation,' he mumbled.

'And would you mind telling us why that is?'

'The evidence starts to deteriorate.'

'Exactly. The physical surroundings of violent death become muddied. The people who knew this unfortunate young lady will still be around after those barely visible heel marks have gone.'

'I think what Mr Bryant is trying to point out', said May, 'is that no matter how hard we try to preserve the site, someone or something will stir the air, touch the floor, imperceptibly change the scene. The city we live in now is not the city we lived in five minutes ago.'

'Oh, but it is, John,' stated Bryant, annoyingly. 'The growth circle sees to that.'

'I'm not sure I follow. Growth circle?'

'Natural forces create order out of chaos in specific sites, and there's nothing you can do about it.'

'I hardly think this is the time for an argument in semantics,' said May.

'It's not semantics, it's psychogeography. Ask yourself to name the most soulless and depressing central thoroughfare in London. New Oxford Street would be high on your list. Why? Because it's a forced nineteenth-century creation; it was noted to be atmospherically dead when it was built, and it always will be. Natural growth fails in a spot that was artificial to begin with.'

'I must agree with that,' said Biddle, then quickly shut his mouth.

'Fine,' said May, surrendering. 'Would you like me to check out the number of murders in nineteenth-century

Cambridge Circus, or shall we go back further, to the age of the Black Death, say?'

'Where we need to go is back to the theatre,' said Bryant. 'You and I will take Miss Wynter's tour of the building. We shall sense the impressions left behind on the air. The auditorium of the theatre, that's where the drama is playing itself out.' He waved a warning digit at Biddle. 'And not a word to Davenport, you, or I'll put pinholes in your gas mask.'

18

GRAND TOUR

Elspeth Wynter replaced the receiver and made a note in her theatre order book. Many of the *Orpheus* opening-night guests were unable to attend because of war commitments. Even so, word of mouth had provoked enough intrigue to sell out most of December. Audiences scented a success in the making. They recalled snippets in newspapers, heard wireless reports, remembered names, gradually assembled facts. The director was suitably infamous, the cast was on loan from the finest companies in the world, including Offenbach specialists from Lyon, and a strong whiff of scandal hung over the show. The play's ribald new script had incurred the suspicion of the Lord Chamberlain; there was a rumour that he might have it banned.

Elspeth suspected that Helena Parole wanted to court controversy. She knew what would happen once word reached the censor's office that this production featured virtual nudity, simulated sex and a salacious translation. There would be demands for its immediate closure. But the owner of the theatre company had apparently made contingency plans, though nobody knew what they were.

Elspeth climbed down off her stool and studied the figures. The production was to be the most spectacular depiction of

Pluto's Underworld ever attempted. The designs for Hades and Olympus were sure to provoke outrage – and generate welcome column-inches. But part of the original cast had been lost to ENSA commitments, most of the chorus girls were inexperienced and under eighteen, and good actors were scarce.

Across from the booking office, downstairs in the auditorium, she could hear the orchestra limbering up as rehearsals got under way. It was a special sound, unique to the theatre. Those tentative first chords told her that a new production had started, and that the public would soon be on its way.

It was cold in the foyer. In the last few days the close dampness of autumn had dissipated, to be replaced by diamond skies and too many freezing clear mornings. It meant that daylight raids could be carried out, and bombers had been sighted brazenly venturing deeper into the city. Messerschmitt 109s, fighters equipped to dart in and drop small-calibre incendiary bombs, were being seen more frequently. Everyone now recognized different aircraft by their outlines and the sounds they made. The Heinkels were German bombers, rearguarded by Junkers during night raids. Hurricanes and Spitfires were ours, and provoked cheers. Sometimes pieces of plane fell right into the road. Oxford Street had been knocked flat, as had the whole of Stepney.

On the first night of the Blitz, the East End fires had burned so fiercely that you could read a newspaper by their light in Shaftesbury Avenue. 'Get-You-Home' booths had been set up around town, staffed by officials who could explain alternative routes. Commuter trains were being bombed and strafed with machine-gun fire. A direct hit had killed twenty in a Marble Arch subway. A group of teenage girls had been buried alive in a busmen's canteen. Parachute bombs drifted through the dust-filled skies like deadly jellyfish, frightening the life out of passers-by. A bomb had destroyed a London perfumery, filling the air with the scent of tropical flowers. A sixteen-year-old boy had appeared in court charged with lighting fires to guide German aircraft inland, Nazi paraphernalia having been discovered in his bedroom. These were disturbing times.

Elspeth felt a draught across her legs and looked up, thinking that someone had opened one of the doors, but the entrance hall was empty. She was waiting for the detectives to return for their tour of the theatre. She instinctively knew when someone was in there with her – the foyer of the Palace was more familiar than her own bedroom – but now it felt different, tainted by death.

At the stage door, Stan Lowe set aside his newspaper and listened. The pastry girl in Maison Bertaux swore she had seen a body being carried out to an ambulance parked in Greek Street. Now Stan had been informed that Tanya had gone – you didn't need a sixth sense to figure out that something wicked had happened to her. Dancers suffered falls that could wreck their careers in a single mistimed step, but to take someone out in silence suggested that she was dead.

Although he had barely met her, it was the idea of bad luck befalling someone in the theatre that disturbed him. Acts of betrayal and revenge unfolded nightly beneath the proscenium arch, but something like this, with police and doctors spiriting away a covered body, felt like an ill omen.

As the sound of the orchestra died away, the balding velvet curtains tied back above the entrance to the stairs shifted slightly, as though a theatrical ghost had just brushed by them. Could somebody have come in and slipped past the window? The buzz of the stage intercom made him start, but he was thankful for something to occupy his mind.

'The theatre first opened as the Royal English Opera House on the thirty-first of January eighteen ninety-one, five years before the first films arrived in London.' Elspeth Wynter pushed open the rear door to the stalls and led the detectives

120

down the centre aisle. 'It was the fulfilment of a lifelong dream for Sir Richard D'Oyly Carte, but the dream lasted only a year. Sullivan's grand opera *Ivanhoe* was not the great success everyone had hoped it would be, and as no one else stepped forward to write an English opera, this magnificent building became the Royal English Variety Theatre, then the Palace of Varieties, and finally just the Palace.'

Elspeth had clearly conducted the tour before. Dressed in shapeless brown cardigan and skirt, she marched between the rows, pointing out details as she passed, keeping her voice in a practised low register. 'We've lost the key to the left-hand pass door, and it's been painted over so many times I doubt anyone could get it open without a chisel, so we have to use the right one. Stan Lowe keeps the key to that and won't lend it out to anyone he doesn't know. Follow me.'

Bryant watched Elspeth's wool-clad bottom as she walked ahead and wondered what it was that attracted him to older women. He speculated on the idea of asking her out. 'Is there any way of turning more lights on?' he asked.

'This is as bright as it gets, I'm afraid. Parts of the theatre are always in darkness. It gets worse beneath the stage and up near the roof.'

May peered up into the gloom, but could discern little more than the vague outlines of four boarded upper windows. The interior had once been green and gold, with red draped curtains, but had subsequently been painted a depressing chocolate brown because a job lot of railway paint had become available at low cost. The sepia walls were rubbed through to the original gilt where members of the audience had paused to touch the plaster cherubs in the friezes, as though they had the talismanic power of saints.

'Theatres are much more artificial than most people realize,' said Elspeth, leading them down a passage beside the stalls. 'Much of the auditorium decoration is built from painted papier mâché. The marble panels you see around the proscenium arch are false. There are no pillars blocking views because the whole structure is made from steel cantilevers, like Tower Bridge. The bricks are mere cladding. Along this side used to be the entrances to the cheaper seats. There were several kiosks selling drinks and cigars, and here is the royal entrance, nine steps up to the royal box, which is partitioned and has its own retiring room, the idea being to keep the classes quite separate. There are other boxes, ten in all. The sightlines are poor, but of course they're for being seen in, not for seeing from. The company office is to the right of the stage door, as is dressing room 2. All the dressing rooms are on this side, along with the front-of-house changing room and a number of quick-change areas, but it would take a week to discover all the hidden spaces.'

'You'd have to find a way of gaining access to the building before you could hide yourself,' Bryant pointed out.

'Quite,' agreed Elspeth, opening the door that led to the lift where Capistrania had died. 'We'll take the stairs if it's all the same to you. The entresol floor has three dressing rooms, a smoking lounge and salon, and the booth for the projectors.'

'Projectors?'

'The music hall would show a short silent film as part of the variety bill,' Elspeth explained. 'In nineteen twenty-two they premiered *The Four Horsemen of the Apocalypse* with a live orchestra and a staff of thirty making the sound effects.' She led them higher. 'Next is the dress circle, more dressing rooms, then the upper circle, also the wig room, and finally the balcony, formerly the amphitheatre. The casting offices are right at the top, along with the conference room, the archive rooms, storerooms, the fly gallery and the loading gallery, and a ladder leading up to the grid that I've never seen anyone use.'

'I had no idea the place was so enormous,' said May.

'Five floors no member of the public ever sees.' Elspeth pulled back a curtain leading through to the balcony. 'Be careful here, it's so steep that some people become sick. Please use the handrails.'

Bryant took one look down and put his hand over his eyes. 'I can't,' he admitted. 'How could anybody sit up here?' Some fourteen rows of seats were arranged in plunging descent to a low parapet over the auditorium. 'I don't think we need to see this, do you, John?'

'You've seen the public and business side of the theatre. Now I'll show you the mechanical areas. We'll have to go single file.' She led the way into a musty narrow corridor filled with boxes and wiring, and pointed through an archway. 'I can't get you across without returning to the pass door, but you can see from here. There are three gantry levels, a carpenter's bridge, five stage bridges, two hanging bridges. The slopes and bridges raise scenery, and there's a flying counterweight system that's hardly ever used. At the top is a drum and shaft mechanism capable of lifting half a dozen backcloths at a time. There are a further three floors under the ground,' explained Elspeth. 'I hope neither of you has a problem with confined spaces.'

If Bryant had discovered that he suffered from vertigo, May found the backstage areas claustrophobic. It was impossible to imagine what these areas were like when they were filled with staff and actors. They were now inside an *Alice in Wonderland* arrangement of wooden columns and twisting corridors, their tracks crossing over each other like ghost-train tunnels. There was nowhere to move except slowly forward. The lights, hanging from bare wires and wedged into corners, only disorientated May even more. He felt beads of sweat breaking out on his forehead.

'As you can see, the lower levels are crowded with chariot cuts and sloat cuts. Sloats are cut-out pieces of scenery. There's a chariot and pole system for the wing flats, but it's all too elaborate even for grand opera, and no one has ever really used it to the full extent for which it was designed. There's the grave trap and the revolve, the star raps, and lots of other little doors. It's terribly over-elaborate.'

'What powers it all?' asked May, peering uncomfortably into the darkness.

'In nineteen hundred and seven they started producing their own electricity from three coal-fired boilers which drove the steam turbine engines.'

May tried to imagine the hellish scene below, with stage-hands stoking glowing furnaces, and felt sicker than ever.

'I wonder how they managed to top up the engines with water,' Bryant mused, fascinated by the chaotic machinery of beams, cogs, wires, pulleys and rods.

'Oh, there's an artesian well down here too,' Elspeth explained, pointing out the eerie green shimmer of water reflected on the distant bricks opposite. 'The pump is under the orchestra pit. They're supposed to keep the hatch cover on the well because it's very deep and hard to see in the dark.'

'Can we go back up?' asked May, wiping his forehead.

'I say, are you all right?' Bryant shot him a look of concern. 'Feeling shut in?'

'I hope it's helped you get the lie of the land,' said Elspeth, returning to her box office.

'Absolutely,' Bryant told her enthusiastically, but all she had shown him was how easy it would be for a murderer to hide in such a building and never be found.

19

THE WEIGHT OF THE WORLD

'Ten minutes, everyone,' warned Helena Parole. 'We've still got a lot of work ahead of us tonight.' She rose and gathered her notes from the seat next to her. 'Harry, where are you?'

'Over here, Helena,' called her assistant. 'I wonder if I could talk to you for a moment.' He was standing at the back of the stalls with Olivia Thwaite, the show's costume designer. Olivia's wardrobe designs had graced enough Noel Coward productions to inspire new fashions at the Café Royal, but the Blitz had forced her family back to their country home in Wiltshire, and she was now thinking of retiring. She intended to make *Orpheus* her swansong, and would not settle for anything less than perfection. Consequently, the costume manufacture was running late, which at least kept this aspect of the production in step with everything else, even though it was giving Harry heart failure.

'It's about Eurydice's first-act costume,' he explained as Helena strode up to him. 'Olivia would like to double the amount of flowers sewn on her dress.'

'I know the material's in short supply,' said Olivia. 'I promise you it's entirely necessary. The bodice is transparent, and since you specified no undergarments, her breasts and buttocks will clearly be seen beneath the lights. I'm sure I don't need to remind you that the Lord Chamberlain's rules forbid nudity except in motionless tableaux under special lighting arrangements and a special licence, a licence I understand we do not have.'

'I assure you there will be no vulgarity,' promised Helena. 'The semblance of nudity is entirely as I intended.'

'But not as Miss Noriac intends.' Harry spoke for Olivia. It was something he was in the habit of doing whenever possible. It allowed him to defuse tension between stage personnel by rephrasing overheated arguments into the semblance of reasonable conversations. 'She is concerned that as a woman with a voluptuous figure, she will not look her best if the audience can see her entire body.'

Eve Noriac had joined the production on loan from the Lyon Opera House, and represented a heavy investment as their Eurydice. It was important to keep her happy in order to maintain courteous relations with the prestigious French company.

'She's somewhat on the portly side, but she has a marvellous *poitrine* and should be proud of it. Olivia, can't you make her see that?'

'I don't see that it's my job to tell your female lead that she has to appear in the buff before one and a half thousand people every night,' reasoned Olivia.

'I think Olivia would like to add flowers in the top half of her costume for the sake of decorum,' said Harry gently.

'I don't want her to go on looking like a walking advertisement for the Kensington Roof Gardens, thank you, Harry. Go and talk to her, would you? Tell her I'm not having daffodils sewn over her nipples just because she can't leave spuds alone.'

'I'll suggest she speaks directly to you about your perception of her appearance, bearing in mind her reservations about the décolletage.' Harry didn't mind liaising between the director and her cast, but it had reached the point where he was acting as an interpreter.

He left Helena and Olivia arguing about the wardrobe and

made his way backstage. The scenery for the opening tableau had arrived, and he squeezed between freshly painted scrims depicting sheaves embroidered with hand-sewn cornflowers, courtesy of the ladies of the Bank, Holborn and Aldwych underground stations, who had wanted something to do in the evenings.

Above his head hung a great globe painted a rich cyanic blue and topped with a set of opened steel compasses, a symbol of cartography and freemasonry denoting the mapping of the earthly world. The globe had been manufactured for a Glyndebourne production of *The Magic Flute*, then junked after the production was cancelled on account of the site's proximity to the exposed Sussex coastline.

The shepherds and shepherdesses of the chorus had returned to the flies. The principal players were familiarizing themselves with the finer details of their roles, having taken musical direction at rehearsal rooms in Covent Garden. At this stage of the production, when the librettist was belatedly putting the finishing touches to his new translation of Offenbach's work, it seemed that nothing would ever come together, but this was how it always was. The production would not coalesce into a performance until the dress rehearsal on Friday.

'Corinne, I don't have you in my diary until late this evening,' said Harry. 'You're not due on for another two hours.'

'I'm recording a talking book for the blind over in Greek Street,' explained the diminutive comedienne who had been cast in the role of Mercury, a tenor role usually played by a male. 'The producer's called a break while they sort out their wiring or something, so I thought I'd come and see how everyone was coping with La Capistrania's mysterious disappearance. I'm dying for a snout, love. You haven't got one on you, I suppose?'

'You know you're not supposed to smoke back here,' said Harry.

'Don't give me that. I've seen you creeping out the back for an oily rag. Go on, chuck us a Du Maurier. Has anyone dared to mention Tanya today?'

'God, no. You can cut the atmosphere with a knife. I've only got a Woodbine, but you can have it. Helena's still waiting to see if her replacement is up for tonight's run-through.'

'There'll probably be an air raid and we'll all spend the evening under the stage trying to play whist by the light of a forty-watt bulb again. I suppose you know they're saying she's been murdered?' Corinne airily brandished Harry's proffered cigarette. 'Working as a spy for her father and assassinated by fifth columnists, apparently.'

'I've heard rumours,' admitted Madeline Penn, the skinny, nervous ASM. 'Stan's been putting the fear of God up everyone as they sign in, but there's been no real news. She's walked out of jobs before, hasn't she?'

'He reckons she was carried out of this one in the dead of night,' offered Charles Senechal, a chubby Anglo-French baritone who, like their Eurydice, was on loan from Lyon. 'Slaughtered by a lover. Body parts missing.'

'Well, if that's the case, somebody made a jolly good job of cleaning up the blood,' said Corinne.

'If I had a franc for every story I heard circulating around a theatre I'd be rich by now.' Charles had been assigned the role of Jupiter. It was a part he had performed so many times before that his performance was in danger of becoming petrified, but audiences loved him.

'Apparently she was having a torrid affair with someone right here in the theatre,' whispered Madeline.

'I haven't heard about that.' Harry looked shocked. 'I'm sure I would have seen her with someone.'

'The trouble with you, Harry, is you never notice flirting between the sexes,' snapped Corinne. 'She was being rogered by someone in our esteemed cast. I should know, because I caught them at it. Walked into her dressing room thinking she'd gone for the night and there she was with her heels in the sink and her bloomers hanging from the light. She didn't even make the effort of trying to look embarrassed.'

'Who was it?'

'That would be tittle-tattle, Harry, and I know you don't approve. Besides, I was fascinated by the sight of his hairy bottom poking out of his shirt-tails.'

'You should tell the detectives.'

'What, and have them hanging around all week ogling the chorus girls? You know how I feel about outsiders. Elspeth, put that thing down, love. It weed all over the stage yesterday.'

Elspeth Wynter had been watching from the wings, where she had gone to retrieve Nijinsky. The tortoise refused to stay in its box, and regularly headed for the dim warmth of the backstage areas. 'Sorry,' she called, picking up the animal and putting it inside her cardigan. 'Is that another air-raid warning?' She cocked her head and listened to the distant rise and fall of the siren.

'Bugger, does that mean we all have to go down to the understage again?' Corinne complained. '*Quelle* bore. I'll have to get another coffin nail from somewhere, I can't do Woodies, they slaughter my throat. Doesn't anyone smoke Park Drives or Kensitas these days? Charles, have you got *un clope*, love?' Nearly all of the French contingent smoked.

'I only have roll-ups,' said Charles. 'Three Nuns or Dark Empire Shag, take your pick.'

'God, no thanks, I want some voice left.'

'Then try the sparks.'

Corinne pushed past Jupiter and the young assistant, crossing to the far side of the stage, where Elspeth stood. Harry looked over and saw her searching for an electrician. As he idly watched, he noticed something was wrong. The stage had been cleared but the spotlights were still on, and the house lights had been dropped. The spots should have been off and the stalls lights raised. He could barely see beyond the edge of the stage.

'Charles,' called Corinne, her gravelly voice absorbed by the sound-deadening backcloths of the Hades set, 'there's nobody over here – ask someone on that side, would you?'

Harry turned in the direction of the shepherdesses, but they had gone down to the section of the basement that had been designated a shelter. He looked back over at Corinne, who was waiting in the flies, but could barely make her out. He felt Charles brush past him, and saw an unlit cigarette in his hand. Either he had asked someone for Corinne, or had decided to palm her off with one of his homemade specials.

Harry noticed that Charles was halfway across the stage when he heard something rip – later, he recalled the sound as being like someone tearing a sheet, which was also the noise a bomb made as it fell – and glanced up just in time to see the great blue planet break loose of its moorings.

He wanted to call out, but the words were stuck in his throat.

Charles had not noticed. The globe was swinging towards him in a graceful arc. Harry heard the impact that lifted the Frenchman off his feet. The sound was followed by a dull crack as Senechal's head was slammed into the brick wall at the rear of the set. When Harry looked again he saw that the sphere had come to rest on the floor. It took him a few moments to realize what had happened.

As he lurched towards the giant prop he heard other shouts in the auditorium. Blood the colour of crushed black-berries pumped across the floorboards. A thick dark puddle was soaking into the backcloth. One end of the compasses had speared the baritone through his ribcage, just below his heart. Charles coughed loudly in the sudden silence, and sprayed the stage with blood. His left foot beat a reflexive tattoo on the floorboards before falling still.

He was dead before Harry, or anyone else, could reach his side.

20

SOMETHING IN THE ARCHIVE

'Two deaths in the same theatre,' said Bryant, rubbing the chill from his hands as they descended the stalls staircase of the Palace. 'I'd call that a bit more than coincidence.'

'You sound sorry you didn't see it,' May remarked.

'Well, I am. Of course I am. From a professional point of view it would have been instructive.'

'Two talented people just had their lives cut short,' said May hotly. 'You might be able to put their relatives at peace as to how and why they died.' He was growing tired and irritable. The air-raid siren had proven to be a false alarm, and had caused them to miss the real drama. Bryant's heart-lessness bothered him. 'People are suffering all around us, and there's nothing one can do except try to keep the lives of their survivors in some kind of order. One must heal wounds by providing answers to questions.'

'Quite, old chap. Still, two extreme acts of violence in a public auditorium.' Bryant lightly tapped his partner's arm. 'They feel like symbolic rites, don't you think? Signs that the mad illogic of the war is entering places of sanctuary. After all, British theatre is a bastion of common sense, civilized, safe, middle class, old-fashioned. Theatrical performances are structured on the principles of cause and effect. The auditorium exists outside of time or place, and only comes alive with the rising of the curtain.'

'I really don't see your point,' said May.

'My *point*, dear fellow, is that these murderous acts went unwitnessed by any audience, in a place where people come expressly to revel in sensation. Come on, let's see what we've got.'

Charles Senechal's body had been removed to an ambulance parked in Romilly Street. The stage had been cleared of all flats and cloths except the cotton duck and hessian frames that stood in the up-centre area against the gaudy crimson cyclorama of Hades. The great blue globe lay where it had fallen, sparkling beneath a profile spot and a pair of par lights.

'What's it made of?' Bryant asked Mr Mack, the head carpenter, whose first name nobody seemed to know. Bryant walked round the globe, his fingers trailing lightly across its surface as if trying to divine some inner purpose from its topography.

'Plaster, built around a central wood core. It weighs a bloody ton. Took three of us to get it up there. I hope it ain't cracked.'

May followed the arc of the planet back up to the raised iron platform on the right side of the flies, the area above the stage where much of the scenery and lighting equipment was suspended. 'How was it held in place?'

'Two steel cables attached at forty-five-degree angles, locked in by bolts. One of the wires must have broken at the top end. The rest of the cable is still attached.'

'So the right-hand wire snapped, leaving the globe to swing down on the left wire like a wrecking ball. Ever seen an accident like this before?'

'Never, and this is my forty-third production,' Mr Mack replied. 'Those cables can take a lot of weight. Go up there and take a look.'

Bryant wasn't thrilled by the idea of climbing along the

gantry. He ascended the narrow steps leading to the first of the stage bridges like a man condemned. From where he stood he could see a large steel hook screwed into the wall. About two feet of wire hung limply down from it. 'In order to be sure of catching someone, you'd have to keep them on their mark from when the wire was cut until the globe hit,' he said absently.

'What do you mean, their mark?' asked May.

'The prearranged spot you reach onstage, where you stand in any scene. All stages are divided into nine squares: up right, centre right, down left and so on. Sometimes there's a front extension, an apron that makes a tenth area. Performances are spatially three-dimensional, and have to be learned accordingly, like chess moves.' Taking a deep breath, Bryant reached over the catwalk railing and pulled up the wire, examining the end. 'Tell me about the compasses, Mr Mack.'

'They're just pieces of pressed tin,' the carpenter explained, 'but each arm is four feet long, and we had to put a sharp point on the end of one because it didn't look like a real set of compasses without a needle.'

'Who told you to do that, the set designer?'

'No, I answer to Geoffrey Whittaker, the stage manager. He takes care of my practical needs. Raymond leaves the materials up to me. He's only concerned about the look of the stage once it's lit, although he'll tell you the difference between hardwood and composition board by the way light bounces off it.'

'Raymond Carrington is the lighting chief,' May pointed out.

'The only access to the wire is from this gantry,' said Bryant. 'And you saw no one.'

'No. This stage is narrow as working areas go, but it's deep and we're capable of producing a lot of mechanical effects. That's why it gets the big song and dance shows; there are more scene changes in musicals, and more scenery has to be flown in. You can bring someone up from any part of the floor, lift whole sections of the stage, do revolves, put in a lot of filler flats and wing divisions, drop dozens of backdrops, scrims and props from above. The lighting is handled from a master board in one of the dress boxes, so there's more room backstage for physical effects. Even I get confused up there sometimes, trying to figure out where each part of the scenery is.'

'It's not your job to fly them in and out?'

'No, the stagehands do that, but I have to check and repair them all the time. Scenery gets damaged after virtually every performance.'

'Had you repaired the globe recently?'

'We've had no dress rehearsals yet, so there's been no need to.'

'You don't think a stranger could have come in from the street after the siren sounded, climbed up the right-side gantry and waited for Mr Senechal to walk across the stage?'

'I don't see how,' said Mr Mack, scratching the top of his head. 'The only time the side bay doors are open is when we're bringing scenery into the dock, and there's always someone manning the stage door whenever the theatre's being used. Besides, the gantries are in virtual darkness. There's no way of easily climbing along them unless you know exactly where the footholds are.'

'So, Miss Betts was in the wing looking for an electrician with a cigarette. Miss Wynter was there with her retrieved tortoise. Miss Penn, Mrs Thwaite and Miss Parole were all in the process of heading to the basement, as were Harry, Mr Woolf and Mr Varisich. Up until the siren sounded, Mr Woolf had been watching the front entrance from the box office, and the stage door keeper—'

'Stan Lowe. He has an assistant called Mouse. I s'pose he has a real name but I don't know what it is—'

'—was still in his booth at the base of the stairs, and neither of them saw anyone enter or leave. You were by the bay doors, which were locked. And there's no other way in or out.'

'I wouldn't quite say that,' said Mr Mack. 'There is a pair of exits on to the roof, and they're unlocked from the inside because of the current ARP regulations.'

'You can get out of the building via the roof?'

'Yes, but you can't get in from them, and you can't go very far once you're out. Sometimes we have firewatchers stationed out there, but not today. They have to prop open the door with fire buckets when they go up because we've not enough keys.'

The Palace Theatre was one of the few London theatres standing in grand isolation. Its facia overlooked Cambridge Circus, but its sides were separated by Shaftesbury Avenue and Romilly Street. Only the rear section touched any other buildings, a short row of houses in the lower part of Greek Street, and the Palace roof stood considerably higher than those.

'So no one entered or left during the rehearsal. See here, John.' Bryant held the end of the wire aloft. 'Even with my hopeless eyesight I can tell this was cut. A clean shear. There is no way that you could arrange it in advance.'

He carefully made his way down onto the stage to examine the wires that had been drilled into the globe. Corinne Betts, the comedienne playing Mercury, had been sedated by her doctor. Chorus girls were talking in shocked whispers in the wings.

'Where would I find a copy of the design for the globe?' asked Bryant.

'The prop designs and stage plans are all in use,' said Helena Parole, walking into the light thrown by one of the fresnel spots. 'They're changed and updated all the time, so they'll be scattered about in different offices. We mimeograph copies of everything and work from those.'

'What do you do with the originals?'

'They go up into the archive room. They'll be clearly

labelled.' The lack of concern in her voice bothered May. 'Do you want me to send someone for them?'

'John, I wonder if you would oblige?'

'Of course.' May left the stage and went to the company office for the keys. He took the lift to the fifth floor, pulled open the trellis doors and stepped out into a dingy hall. The boarded-up end windows prevented light from entering, but the pairs of defunct gas mantles at either end of the hallway would have done little to dispel the creeping gloom, which was deepened by chestnut walls and threadbare brown carpets.

May flicked a brass switch at the head of the corridor, but nothing happened. According to Helena, there was barely a time when the electrics functioned correctly. The faint glow from the electroliers in the main stairway allowed him to make out the doors to his left, but none of them was labelled. He checked the first door but found that it had been fitted with a Yale. The key he had taken from the company office was a long-handled Victorian affair, scabbed with rust.

He located the theatre archive in a room at the darkest turn in the corridor. Within the cramped suite were dozens of overstuffed boxes and damp cardboard files cataloguing productions and stars. Dim light was provided by the bare bulb overhead. He glanced across the titles on the lids of the boxes and pulled out some of the Palace's monochrome publicity photographs. Buster Keaton performing with his father, the pair of them bowing to the audience in matching outfits. The jagged profile of Edith Sitwell, posturing her way through some kind of spoken-word concert. A playbill for W. C. Fields starring in a production of *David Copperfield*. Another presenting him in his first appearance at the Palace as an 'eccentric juggler'. The four Marx Brothers, gurning for the camera. Fred Astaire starring in *The Gay Divorcée*, his last show before heading to Hollywood.

The dust on the lower boxes betrayed an even earlier age. The infamous Sarah Bernhardt season of 1892; Oscar

Wilde's *Salome* was due to have been performed at the theatre, but had fallen foul of the Lord Chamberlain's ruling about the depiction of religious figures. The legendary Nijinsky, seen onstage just after his split with Diaghilev. According to the notes, he had left the Palace after discovering that he was to appear at the top of a common variety bill. Cicely Courtneidge in a creaky musical comedy, her dinner-jacketed suitors arranged about her like Selfridge's mannequins. The first royal command performance, in 1912. Anna Pavlova dancing to Debussy. Max Miller in his ludicrous floral suit, pointing cheekily into the audience – 'You know what I mean, don't you, missus?' Forgotten performers, the laughter of ghosts.

An accordion folder labelled *Orphée aux enfers* lay on the nearby desk. May pulled it out and began sifting through the floor plans and set blueprints. He found the design for the second tableau, Mount Olympus crowned by clouds, its great azure sphere pinned in the heavens, and carefully folded it into his jacket pocket.

The anguished cry that tore its way along the corridor made his scalp tingle. It was the call of a human in terrible pain. May jumped to his feet and ran outside, but there was nothing to be seen. He heard it again, softer and more in sorrow this time, but the acoustics were so dead that it was impossible to pinpoint the location of the sound. The other doors along the corridor were all sealed. Some looked as if they had not been opened for many years. Panic crawled over his skin, sending him back to the lift and the light.

He had just pulled the trellis door shut when he heard the cry again, a miserable low bellow that reverberated in the lift shaft. May jammed his thumb on the descent button and the cage dropped down through the building, recalling him to life and safety. He was nineteen and impressionable. The city was blacked out every night, and the dark held hidden terrors. In years to come, his dreams would vividly recall his haunted week at the Palace.

'You imagined it,' said Bryant, poking about in the pockets of his battered gaberdine raincoat for a Swan Vesta. 'Nothing to be ashamed of, old chap. We're all a bit jumpy. This building hasn't seen daylight since the start of the war.' He lit his pipe while May unfolded the sheet of paper he had removed from the archive. 'So this is the original design for the globe and compasses?' Bryant asked Mr Mack as May smoothed the stage plan flat on a workbench.

'It looks the same as the finished model,' commented May distractedly. He was still thinking about the deep cry echoing in the corridors.

'Does it? Would you say that the compasses occupy the same position as they do in the drawing, Mr Mack? Do you have a first name?'

'Mr Gielgud always calls me Mr Mack because of his memory,' explained the carpenter. 'We used to talk about table tennis.' He spat a mouthful of chewing tobacco into his handkerchief and examined the plan. 'Blimey, you're right. The point of the needle is higher on the full-scale version by about a foot.'

'Who told you to raise it?'

Mr Mack studied the drawing in discomfort. 'It's not like me to make a mistake. There should be a master diagram. This is one of the earlier sketches. Someone must have moved the globe.'

'I don't know how much more evidence you need to prove a case of premeditation,' Bryant told his partner.

'The carpenters reckon accidents happen all the time in the theatre,' said May.

'That's right,' agreed Mr Mack. 'You've got a lot of people jumping about in a very small space, surrounded by moving mechanical objects, some of them weighing tons. Feet get crushed, arms broken, ankles shattered. Arthur Lucan fell through this very stage.'

'But they don't normally die, do they?'

'That's true, sir, they don't.'

'And the problem with these two deaths is that we lack any kind of a link between them,' whispered Bryant.

May consulted his notebook. He felt that someone should keep a record in case Davenport decided to question their tactics. 'Well,' he pointed out, 'they were both represented by the same agent, weren't they?'

21

FREEDOM FROM MEMORY

He was searching for something in the files. John May sat in
the archive room of the Palace Theatre and rested his aching,
aged bones.

He was perched on a canvas stool with a mildewed cardboard box on his lap. Many of the photographs, plans and
notes beneath his fingers were stuck together with time. They
bore marks of damp, tea, candle grease. He wished he knew
what he was looking for. He knew only that Bryant had been
here before him, just days before he died.

In the years following the investigation, more photographs
had been added to the files of the Palace: Jimmy Cagney, tap-
dancing in a USO camp show; Betty Grable singing;
Laurence Olivier grinning gap-toothed in Osborne's *The
Entertainer*; John Tiller's Girls, high-kicking their way through
the 1958 season; a thousand forgotten variety acts armed only
with funny walks and silly catchphrases; the cast of *Les
Misérables*, changing yet changeless across the years. And a
grey police file on the Palace Phantom, dated November 1940,
left to be rediscovered over sixty years later.

Here were the typed interviews they had conducted with
the cast and production crew of *Orpheus* at the onset of that
terrible season. The last pages of the file were missing. Only

the interviews remained. But there had clearly been other pages here. The freshly torn staples at the top of the file attested to that. He looked through the interview list again. Corinne Betts, Miles Stone, Eve Noriac, Geoffrey Whittaker . . . he could barely put faces to the names. Elspeth Wynter, Arthur had fallen for her, but had it been out of love or pity? Who knew now, and what did it matter? He imagined the faces of Londoners, photographs pinned to an immense police board stretching hundreds of miles back into the past, across two thousand years of continued inhabitancy. So many dead, so many yet to come . . .

The ring of his mobile phone startled him. He pulled the Nokia from his pocket and answered it.

'John? It's me, Alma. I hope I'm not disturbing you.'

'Me? No, how are you?'

'My legs are wicked, no change there, just getting old. Janice said you were back, and I was worried because someone's been in Mr Bryant's flat.' She called him John; she always referred to Arthur as Mr Bryant.

'How do you know someone's been in there?'

'There was some stuff left out and now it's gone. I know because I did the dusting. I told you I didn't like to throw anything away. I don't want to let the rooms out no more.'

'Was the door forced?' asked May. 'Did they break in?'

'No, nothing's damaged, the front lock's in one piece. They must have got them skeleton keys.'

'I don't think that's very likely, Alma. But it's a standard lock, it isn't too hard to open. I've done it before now. What did they take?'

'Just some pieces of paper from the table.'

'You don't happen to remember what they were, do you?'

'I know because I typed them out for him myself,' explained Alma. 'They were Mr Bryant's dental records.'

May walked down Charing Cross Road and cut through to the back of the National Portrait Gallery, carefully avoiding the junk-food swill of Leicester Square. He detested the swirling scrum of the pedestrianized zone, the latent danger, the shoving, dislocated crowds that filled a once-beautiful space. It was hard to imagine, but the area had been pleasanter to stroll through when traffic had traversed it. Now, the tourist hot spots of the city were the very parts that made it like everywhere else. Was it possible to imagine those buildings without inhaling the animal-fat stink of McDonald's or KFC? He never thought London would cease to appeal to him, but the little faded glory it still possessed was being scuffed away by the dead hand of globalization. On his down days he saw London as a crumbling ancient house, slowly collapsing under the weight of its own past.

As he pushed his way through a herd of name-tagged visitors in matching baseball caps, he wondered if he had left it too late to retire to the continent. France seemed a good bet, more at ease with its history. Crucially, he had never visited the place with his old partner. Perhaps he could be freed from memories there. He thought of his embittered son, recovering from years of addiction in a French commune, of his wife and daughter, and how he had survived them both, but even then he remembered Nathalie, how Bryant had loved her and lost her . . .

Damn you, Arthur, he thought, let me go.

He knew there was only one way he could stop himself from subsiding into the silent past: he needed to settle the murder of his alter ego. Without the truth, there would be no rest. Not now, not ever.

22

BLOCKING

'I'm offended that you should even ask,' Benjamin Woolf bristled. He never looked more suspicious than when he was trying to appear injured. 'I represent a great many artists.'

'I'm not saying you had anything to do with their deaths, even though no one actually saw you at the time of Senechal's impalement,' Bryant snapped. 'You're very touchy for an agent.'

'We don't all have hides like rhinos, Mr Bryant.'

'How many other performers in the company do you represent?'

'Oh, quite a few.'

'*Exactly* how many?'

Woolf made an effort to look innocent and failed. 'I'd have to work that out and get back to you.' The detectives had set up a base in the company office, and were seeing everyone who had been present in the auditorium when Charles Senechal had met his death.

'Do you have some kind of special deal going on with the cast members you represent?' asked Bryant.

'Something like that.' Woolf ran a finger along his thin moustache.

'Are you on friendly terms with them all? How close were you to Miss Capistrania and Mr Senechal, for instance?'

'I keep a respectable distance from all my clients. I'm there when they need me. I give them advice and support, I listen to their problems, nothing more.'

'But it's a twenty-four-hour job, isn't it? You take their calls when they come off stage at night, cope with their insecurities, assuage their doubts?'

'Of course. All theatrical agents worth their salt do.'

'Do you know much about their personal lives? Who they were closest to, who they were amorously involved with?'

'Some are forthcoming, others aren't. I don't pry, if that's what you mean. They have to tell you some things, obviously.'

'What did Tanya Capistrania have to tell you?'

'You must understand she had very few friends in this country. She told me she was seeing someone in the company. I don't know much about Charles except that he's married and has a flat in Paris. His wife and son are on their way here right now.'

'So Miss Capistrania was having an affair and Charles wasn't.' Bryant sucked hard on his pipe, trying to keep it lit.

'For all I know he could have been. Performers become very tight-knit during the course of a run. They form liaisons that last only while they're working together.'

'Would you care to divulge the identity of the man Miss Capistrania was seeing?'

'I suppose it won't do any harm to the young lady now,' sighed Benjamin. 'But you mustn't say I told you. It was Geoffrey Whittaker.'

'The stage manager?' Bryant was surprised. He didn't look the type to conduct a torrid affair.

'It's not the first time he's got up to this sort of thing. He's pretty well known by the Piccadilly commandos.' He was referring to the squad of prostitutes who brazenly worked

144

around the Circus, stepping out of doorways to accost servicemen on leave.

'He's a bit old to be a Lothario. What about Miss Capistrania?'

'Tanya was famous for upstaging her fellow players. She was very driven to succeed. The usual story, pushed by her family from an early age. Nobody's got much good to say about her.'

'And Charles Senechal?'

'The opposite. Everyone thinks – thought – he was wonderful. He's played all three of the baritone roles in *Orpheus* before, a consummate professional and a wonderful singer.'

'I see. What about some of the others who were there when it happened, Harry – what's his surname, Cowper? And Corinne Betts?'

'Corinne's seeing one of the shepherds. A boy in the chorus. I don't think it's anything more than mutual convenience. Harry, well, he's a bachelor. Let's leave it at that.'

'So there are a few *amours* in the background. Any risk of blackmail with Harry?'

'I suppose there's always a risk, but the theatre's safer than most places. Outside the Palace, people keep asking if I'm a visiting calypso player. In here, nobody cares about the colour of my skin. Why are you interested?'

'The globe could have been intended to hit anyone, couldn't it?'

'Oh, I see. Harry's well liked. There's often someone like him in a theatre company, born to be a den mother to the rest. Runs around after people making them feel better. Nurses the bruised egos. Corinne's got a bit of a mouth on her, but I don't know that she's made any real enemies. Some of the cast went to Café de Paris to see her perform her comedy routine a couple of weeks ago, and she bought them all drinks afterwards. It won her a lot of friends.'

'So there are no real connections that you can see, apart from the fact that Miss Capistrania and Mr Senechal were both performers represented by you.'

'May I remind you that I'm the one losing out here.' Woolf made a further effort to look pained, but appeared to be suffering from heartburn. 'They were more than my clients. They were investments.'

'I'd say everyone's investments are in danger of disappearing now, wouldn't you?'

'No,' replied Woolf, 'no, I wouldn't. Don't you know the show always goes on?'

'If I find reason to suppose that anyone else's life is in danger, I won't hesitate to close down the production.'

'Aren't you a bit young to have that authority?' asked Woolf, alarmed.

'I'm not sure,' Bryant admitted, giving up on his pipe, 'but it would be interesting to find out. Let me get this clear in my head. While the globe was being cut loose, there were four people actually on the stage: Mr Senechal, Miss Betts, Miss Wynter and Mr Cowper. Mr Mack was further back in the wings, Miss Parole was in the stalls with Mr Whittaker, Miss Penn, Mrs Thwaite and Mr Varisich, heading in the direction of the pass door. Stan Lowe was manning the stage door, and you were out in the front box office. What were you doing before the siren sounded?'

Benjamin thought for a moment. 'I was talking to Elspeth. I left the auditorium, but then I heard the commotion and ran back in.'

'To your knowledge, was there anyone else near the stage or in the stalls?'

'I don't think so – wait, Anton was still in the orchestra pit. Eve and Olivia were arguing about something as they came out, a problem with a dress, so they must have been nearby.'

'Do you think it likely that any of them could have climbed the gantry to the globe and cut it loose?'

146

'I don't see how,' interrupted May. 'The gantry is clearly visible from the stage.'

'Then there's someone we haven't accounted for,' said Bryant, prodding his partner in the shoulder. 'Someone else in the theatre. Someone up there, in the dark.'

23

OFF TO THE REALM OF DARKNESS

'Have you heard? They're killing all the poisonous snakes and reptiles at London Zoo, in case the cages get bombed,' Betty Trammel, one of the *Orpheus* chorus girls, told John May that afternoon. Like most of the other female dancers, she had long legs, a tiny midriff and shapely breasts that the detective found himself covertly watching. 'And they've had to put sandbags around the pink flamingos because they're suffering nervous breakdowns.' She smiled at the detective and rolled her enormous eyes. They were set in a heart-shaped face, framed with blond curls. 'I used to cut home through Regent's Park to my place in Camden, but they've closed the public path past the zoo. It's getting so a girl doesn't know what's safe any more.' Betty spoke with more refinement than the other chorines. She had a smile that could put a froth on a cup of coffee, and she knew it.

'I'm in Camden. I can walk you home if you like,' May offered gallantly.

'I might just take you up on your proposal.' She placed her hands on spangled hips and grinned. 'Give me two minutes to get changed.'

Bryant watched in disgust as Betty bounced off into the wings. 'What is it', he asked, 'that makes girls go so damnably gooey-eyed over you? I don't understand it. You only have to stand next to them and they start rolling bits of themselves about like Betty Boop.'

'I think they just feel, you know, comfortable around me,' said May, surprised by his own powers.

'Well, they don't do that with me,' Bryant complained, scratching the back of his ear in puzzlement. 'I can't see why not. I'm a bloody good catch. I have prospects. I have an enquiring mind. You'd think that would be appealing.'

May stared at the aisle carpet, embarrassed. He could not tell his new friend that there was something about his fierce energy that disturbed people. The more Bryant tried to be sympathetic, the less believable he was. It was an unfortunate effect that was to bedevil him throughout his life.

'And the types that go for you,' Bryant continued, 'well!'

'What's wrong with their "type"?' asked May, offended.

Bryant searched the air, almost at a loss for words. 'You can't see it? My dear fellow, they're so – obvious.'

'Look, if it bothers you that much, I don't see why you don't find a date of your own. Go down to the box office and ask Elspeth out, she's keen as mustard. I've seen the way she looks at you.'

'Oh, I don't know about that.' Bryant poked his pipe-stem down into his top pocket, considering the idea. 'Do you really think so?'

'I'm sure of it. Go on, ask her. She'll be glad to get out of here.' The blackout made houses stuffy and airless at night. Even in a building as large as the Palace, the still atmosphere weighed heavily in the lungs.

'All right,' vowed Bryant, grinning bravely, 'I will. I'll go and ask her right now.' And he did.

She turned him down. It didn't take her long either. He was gone for only two minutes.

'She has to look after a sick relative,' said Bryant on his return. 'I wasn't convinced.' He grumpily kicked at the ground. 'Here's your bit of fluff.'

Betty had rouged her cheeks and changed into a fox-fur coat. Divested of her blond wig, she was revealed as a mousy brunette. She waltzed into the company office and seized May's arm as though it was a lifebelt. 'Are we going for a drink, then?' she asked cheerfully, pinching May's cheek.

May was almost pulled through the doorway. 'I'll see you in the morning, Arthur,' he volunteered. 'Stay out of the light.'

'Yes, you go and have fun. I still have a police investigation to run.' Bryant shoved his trilby onto his head. 'I think I'll go back to Bow Street and ruin Biddle's evening.'

By the next morning, the mood of the company had become morose and belligerent. To have a member of the cast killed by a stage prop was not unheard of, but after a long night of bombing raids that frayed the nerves and lasted until dawn the idea of it panicked everyone. Performers were at the mercy of stagehands when there were a large number of scene changes to incorporate in the action. Three years earlier, two members of a Belgian dance troupe had been fatally injured at the Albert Hall when a vast steel wheel had collapsed on them. The scenery at the Covent Garden Opera House, with its newly overhauled hydraulic system, had nearly decapitated one of its principal players in front of a horrified first-night audience. Recently, a trapdoor in the Palladium stage had opened without warning, dropping a chorus girl down a dozen steps, breaking both her ankles. Players were superstitious and productions easily made bad reputations for themselves.

Helena Parole was aware of the cast's sensibilities, but hoped they would be cheered by today's arrival. Their Orpheus was landing, fresh from a triumphant American tour of *The Tales of Hoffmann*, the opera wrongly regarded as Offenbach's only serious work. Miles Stone had hit the big time, but his *Orpheus* contract pre-dated his rise in stock, and he had not managed to wriggle out of the agreement in time to seize his Hollywood break. MGM was offering him a role in a screwball comedy that would help to cement his image as the smart girl's sex symbol, but unless something went wrong with *Orpheus* and the production was cancelled, Miles knew that he would be forced to remain in bomb-strewn London throughout the winter. The film would be recast with someone else, and his window of opportunity would slam firmly shut.

Consequently, the company's leading player found himself in an ambivalent mood when he arrived to find that Jupiter was dead. It was a tragic loss, of course, but if the cast were so demoralized that the production could not continue, he would be freed.

'Everybody back to their positions and we'll take it from Eurydice's invocation to death.' Helena Parole rubbed her eyes. The cast was nervy and out of sorts. Anton Varisich, the conductor, was particularly bad-tempered, and seemed unable to control his orchestra, who were coming in late on their cues. On stage, Eurydice lay in the cornfield as Aristaeus stood over her, feeling her pulse.

'*La mort m'apparaît souriante, qui vient me frapper près de toi,*' sang Eve Noriac.

Helena threw her script over the seat in front of her. 'For Christ's sake!' she shouted. 'What the hell do you think you're doing?'

'I'm sorry,' called Eve, rising on one elbow and squinting down at her. 'I'm used to singing in French. It's easier for me to remember my lines this way.'

'The management has decreed we're to use our sovereign nation's native tongue,' snapped Helena. 'They want a popular hit. The only people who can speak another language in England are foreigners. Let's go again from the top.'

'*Death appears to me smiling, coming to strike me while I'm near you . . .*'

Helena sat back and listened. Eurydice had a remarkable soprano range. The plot was of no consequence to a modern audience, a once-saucy parody of classicism that held little meaning for anyone now, and yet Eve invested her words with such conviction that you would listen if she sang addresses from a telephone directory.

Helena was suddenly aware that the music had stopped. 'What now?' she cried, sitting up.

'Someone's taken my fork,' complained Aristaeus. 'It was here a minute ago.'

'Will somebody find his bloody fork?' called Helena. 'Harry, go and look for it, would you?'

'Can he just mime it for now, Helena?'

'Helena?' Aristaeus had walked to the front of the stage and was shielding his eyes from the key lights. 'Is this a practical?'

'You know it's not. I told you that earlier.'

'So the trapdoor's not going to open when I reach "Off to the realm of darkness"?'

'No,' she replied wearily. 'We won't start using the drops and lifts until the end of the week. No sense in wishing more accidents on us, is there?'

'I can see you're busy,' said John May quietly. 'I'll wait here until you're ready for me.'

Helena checked her watch in alarm. 'I'm sorry, I didn't realize it was time for our meeting, Mr May. We're running behind this morning.'

'That's quite all right,' said May. 'I'm enjoying the rehearsal.' He felt like sitting in the dark for a while. Betty had kept him out later than he had intended, and the AA guns stationed in Regent's Park had been booming for most of the night. On top of this, he had now spent his entire first week's wages on a girl, and he hadn't been paid yet.

'We're still interviewing everyone who was with Miss Capistrania and Mr Senechal on the days of their deaths,' May reminded her as they seated themselves in Helena's arched office above the balcony. 'I need to talk to your assistant.'

152

'Harry, yes, he was there when Charles was killed.'

'And Corinne Betts, who I'm told actually saw the globe fall.'

'She's not on today's call sheet but Harry has her landlady's telephone number.'

'Mr Bryant reckons that casts grow into extended families during the run of a production,' said May. 'Is that true?'

'For better or worse, yes.' Helena opened the window behind her chair and lit a cigarette, waving the smoke out. The management had asked the company to reduce their daytime smoking because the new auditorium upholstery absorbed the smell. Nobody had bothered to point out to them that the whole of the city stank of burning varnish and brick dust. 'We've got a cast of real troupers. Normally a deranged German sniper could burst in and machine-gun the audience, and they wouldn't miss a line. I know many of the boys and girls from previous productions. They've been doing scenes in groups for a while. They've received musical direction and attended rehearsals with the same choreographer. Now it's just a matter of keeping them calm.'

'So it's still going smoothly?' May felt as though he should be taking notes, but wasn't sure what to write.

'I wouldn't say that. The thing never fits perfectly from the outset. Steps get in the way of recitative, cues come in the wrong places and have to be rearranged. You get a lot of masking and scissoring, but nothing that can't be worked out.'

'Scissoring?'

'Actors crossing each other's paths onstage. We're over the worst. I shout at them, but it doesn't mean anything. By opening night we'll be a big happy family.'

'Then why do Mr Bryant and I feel shut out?' asked May.

'Because you're outsiders, darling,' laughed Helena. 'You expect backstage to be a hotbed of gossip and intrigue, but this one's not. There's too much riding on the production for anyone to behave in an unprofessional manner.'

'Perhaps you're right,' May admitted. 'I suppose I was expecting histrionics. Highly strung actors, the usual clichés.'

'So long as you realize that they are only clichés,' said Helena reproachfully.

Just then the door to the artistic director's office burst open and a tall, angular woman of about forty flew in.

'I'm not going to work with that dreadful bitch for one more minute!' she cried before chucking herself lengthwise onto Helena's sofa. 'He's ruining my entrance. I said to him, "Darling, I wouldn't let any man step across my entrance, let alone an old cow like you," and he said, "I can't see how you would know, dear, you've never been with a man in your life," waving his whip at me in front of the shepherdesses. I said, "I've played bigger houses than this," and he said, "Only when you were working the back passage of the Alhambra, love." He said, "I've played the Duke of York's, Her Majesty's, the Queen's," and I said, "The Queen's is an ice rink, dear, no wonder you're so frigid." Oh, you're not alone, I'll come back later.' She threw herself back onto her feet. 'So I'll leave you to sort that out then, if you would.' And she was gone in a cloud of Arpège, slamming the door behind her.

'You were saying?' said May gently.

'Well, there are a few exceptions to the rule,' Helena admitted, blanching.

'Who was she, by the way?'

'Valerie Marchmont. She's playing the role of Public Opinion, God help us,' said Helena.

Down in the foyer, Arthur Bryant knocked on the window of the box-office booth. Elspeth Wynter looked up from her booking forms and smiled vaguely. 'Hello, Mr Bryant. A pleasure to see you again.'

'I'm glad you feel that way,' said Bryant, tugging his scarf straight. 'We're conducting interviews—'

'Of course, I understand,' she said hastily. 'Can we do mine here?'

'We're supposed to record them at the unit.'

She looked hesitant. 'We're absolutely frantic, what with the schedule running behind.'

'Perhaps I could arrange something.' Bryant attempted a smile, liked the effect and widened it. 'On the condition that you have a bite to eat with me.'

'I don't know, it's our busiest day so far for bookings. I can't be away from the telephone.'

'Half an hour,' said Bryant. 'A bowl of soup somewhere nearby. I won't take no for an answer.'

Elspeth was flustered. 'All right, but it will have to be just over the road. The little Italian place in Moor Street?'

'It's a deal.' He pulled on his hat and flicked the brim of it nonchalantly. May was right. Persistence paid off after all. While his partner had been out with Betty Boop, Bryant had passed a miserable evening filing reports and being covertly studied by Sidney Biddle, who appeared to have nothing better to do than watch him and surreptitiously scribble notes in a diary. Biddle's visit to the St Martin's Lane shoe shop had proved disappointing. Although shoes matching the prints were sold only to theatres, they went to nearly every theatre and variety hall in the country.

Bryant stepped outside the theatre foyer and back into the natural light of the morning. Across the road, workmen had barricaded the pavements and were digging holes, searching for cracked gas mains. The Pioneer Corps were salvaging furniture from a bombed office in Shaftesbury Avenue. In schools across the city, children were swapping souvenir incendiary bomb fins from the night's raids. At this point in the war, over two hundred tons of high explosive were being dropped on London every night.

He took a deep breath. The burning smell lingered in the air even on the freshest days. He wondered whether they were mad, trying to discover how just two people had died, when all around them men, women and children were being killed violently and unexpectedly. The AFS men had been putting out oil bombs in the next street all night long.

Some theory, he knew, would have to reveal itself soon or he'd be for it. With a sigh of resignation, he stepped back into the chill shadows of the theatre.

24

READING SIGNS

Sidney Biddle was getting angrier.

From what he had seen so far, the Peculiar Crimes Unit was aptly named. The place was a total shambles. There was no excuse for it, war or no war. Everything was just as Farley Davenport had predicted. Procedural policy appeared to be non-existent. There was no chain of command, and members of staff were allowed to do exactly as they pleased. True, Arthur Bryant was the last to leave each night, after diligently entering the day's activities into the unit's logbook, but he kept it locked up in his office, so it was impossible to guess whether his entries were accurate or fanciful.

More bothersome was the fact that he, Biddle, appeared to have been excluded from Bryant's circle. He had been identified as the enemy in the camp and was shut out of all conversations, notes, briefings and interviews concerning the events at the Palace.

And the black-marketeering that was going on! All around him, all day, everyone was on the fiddle. Runcorn and Finch bartering tea, sugar and armfuls of rhubarb with the boys in the tailor's shop, PC Atherton, Crowhurst and the Bow Street constables coming in with buckets, kettles, clocks, tin openers, gardening tools, boots, pencils and tins of furniture polish. Everyone seemed to know that a potato peeler in good nick was worth two spanners.

Once again, he was an outsider. Sidney sat in the window of the office behind Bow Street station and morosely sipped his tea, watching the clearance boys at work. The empty offices beyond the Royal Opera House appeared to have been commandeered as fire-alarm stations and first-aid posts. Perhaps he should have taken a job with the Press and Censorship Bureau. At least they were performing an essential duty. Last month, the corner of Leicester Square had been bombed flat, and holes had been blown in the District Line railway tunnel at Blackfriars; right now the bureau would be busy suppressing the truth, retouching photographs, stemming negative information, tucking away all morale-damaging reports until after the war.

With a twinge of annoyance he realized that he would rather have been accepted by the others in the unit than marked out as someone to avoid. Even Runcorn, the miserable forensic scientist, ducked back into his office whenever he saw him approaching.

Everyone associated with the unit appeared to hold Arthur Bryant in high regard, although what Bryant had done to earn their esteem was far from obvious. And the other new chap, May, was creeping around in his partner's footsteps, clearly filled with awe.

Biddle checked the spelling in his report and recapped his fountain pen. By the end of his first week he hoped to have a dossier on Bryant that would draw a constricting ring of common sense around the unit. Davenport had made it clear that he wanted them closed down before the month was out. He'd clearly had enough of boffins being allowed a free hand while everyone else had to buckle down.

Biddle knew something else the others didn't know, because he had taken the call himself. DS Gladys Forthright would soon be on her way home, because her fiancé had backed out of the wedding. All they needed now was an unstable woman moping about the place. He smiled to himself as he blew on the page and closed it. She might just prove to be the straw that broke this peculiar camel's back.

'I'm so glad you could spare the time to have lunch with me,' said Bryant awkwardly. He never knew what to say to women. Consequently his behaviour around them was formal and slightly unnatural.

'I've always had a soft spot for the police. My brother's a crown court duty officer, not that I ever see him. I have to be getting back in a minute.' Elspeth pushed away her soup plate. The café was steamy and crowded with customers queuing for tables. 'There's a dress rehearsal this afternoon. Helena feels that several of the scenes aren't working so she's changing them. There are no out-of-town try-outs, and unless you tour first, the team only has rehearsals and previews to get it right.'

'Do shows change much before opening night?' asked Bryant, scooting a fork around the remains of the suspiciously unmeaty gravy on his plate.

'Oh, some of them become unrecognizable, especially the musicals. Of course, I'm strictly FOH so I'm not privy to everything that goes on, but you hear it all from the front of house because stages are designed to project sound forward. Do you think Helena will be able to keep the show running?'

'I don't know,' Bryant admitted. 'Westminster Council will have to be given our crime reports because of the Palace's status as a public building, but they've already got their hands full, so it's pretty easy for me to stall them. Their final decision will be swayed by the Lord Chamberlain's attitude. If he decides that it's a threat to public morality, there's nothing I or anyone else can do to keep it open. An appeal to Churchill might work, I suppose. I understand that when he was young he used to champion the ladies of the music hall.'

'All this talk of the chorus girls appearing nude is sending

159

the box office through the roof,' said Elspeth. 'We'll soon have the Christmas season fully booked. If the Lord Chamberlain does shut us there'll be nothing else to put in after it. We'll go dark for the first time in thirty years. It doesn't bear thinking about.'

'If the Lord Chamberlain objects, couldn't a compromise be reached?'

'Yes, if Miss Parole would just agree to cover up the girls' . . . you know . . .'

'What?'

'Nipples,' she mouthed at him, looking down at her chest. She dabbed a napkin at her forehead, embarrassed. 'It's so hot in here, Arthur. That scarf must be strangling you. We never overheat in the foyer, even in the middle of summer. So much marble.'

'You're all very loyal to the theatre,' Bryant conceded. Just being outside the building made Elspeth uncomfortable. He wondered how she would cope if the directors closed the show down and fired the permanent staff. Theatre management seemed a separate breed from the acting companies, one of the oldest and least recognized London tribes, working long hours for low salaries, never in the limelight themselves, unable to imagine any other life apart from the stage. 'Mr Whittaker's like you. I'm surprised you aren't . . .'

'What?'

'Well, together.'

'Me and Geoffrey?' It was good to see her smile. 'God, no. The theatre would always be in the way. We'd never talk of anything else. Besides, he's a terrible womanizer.'

'Are there really no problems between Helena and members of the cast?'

'None that I know of. The only row is with the stage-hands, because of these accidents. I mean, we're all assuming the rumours are true about Miss Capistrania suffering something similar. Everyone's wondering who'll be next, but they all get on with their work. It's incredible how the press has managed to twist the whole thing around. Have you seen the article by Gilbert Riley in this morning's edition of the *Evening Standard*? He's suggesting we're the victims of some ancient theatrical curse. And then there are those photographs.' Elspeth was referring to the fact that someone had managed to take several shots of semi-naked chorus girls through the door of a rehearsal room several days earlier. 'Where's Mr May today? He seems ever so nice.'

She fancies him, thought Bryant immediately. Well, why not? He had the same effect on every woman he met. Presumably it was some kind of chemical reaction, scientifically quantifiable and easily explained. Some men had it, he decided, and others didn't.

'He's finishing the interviews,' said Bryant, pushing his plate back and picking up the bill. 'I have to submit a report to my superior by tomorrow. The process would normally take longer, but the war is speeding everything up.'

'The last fourteen months have passed so quickly,' agreed Elspeth. 'So many horrors, so many changes. I just celebrated my thirty-second birthday. Not a good age for a single woman.' Her hand absently brushed her cheek. In the dusty light from the restaurant window she suddenly looked much younger, as if she had been kept all her life within the walls of the theatre, untouched by the ravages of the outside world. Bryant felt a sudden pang of desire for her. 'It's rather ironic still to be working in a shrine constructed for a man who made merciless fun of spinsters.'

'Oh, Gilbert, you mean. Yes, he was a bit hard on the ladies. But Sullivan balanced him. He loved women too much. It must have been an interesting alliance.'

'I daresay you see the parallels with your own partnership,' said Elspeth carelessly.

Bryant pretended to bridle at the thought. 'Crusty curmudgeon and laconic ladies' man, whatever can you mean?' he said.

Elspeth's eyes sparkled with mischief. 'Oh, I don't think

you're such a curmudgeon. You have the heart of someone who's been in love. Trust me, I know the signs.'

'Well, once was enough.'

'You're young. You have plenty of time yet, provided you can manage to stay out of harm's way.' She checked a tiny gold watch. 'I need to get back. Perhaps we can see each other when I get out.'

'And perhaps we can eat somewhere other than here,' said Bryant, paying the bill. 'Their meat sauce tasted as though it had been boiled up from the innards of a horse.'

'If they keep reducing our rations, I imagine that's what we'll end up eating.' Elspeth rose and straightened her hat as a woman shoved past her to claim her seat.

The young detective laid a gentle hand on Elspeth's shoulder. 'I've overlooked something. You know the theatre better than anyone . . .'

'I know it well, but so does Geoffrey. And Stan Lowe, and Mr Mack.'

'Am I making mistakes? What have I missed?'

'I think perhaps . . .' She hesitated for a moment, studying his wide blue eyes. A connection tingled as she opened herself to him, then quickly cooled as she remembered her place. 'I think you should talk to the owner of the theatre company. You might learn more than you imagine. Everyone has secrets.' She pushed open the restaurant door and glanced guiltily at the theatre. 'I've said enough. I really must go.'

For the briefest of moments Bryant had read something in her eyes that he could not interpret: fear, mistrust, the pain of hidden knowledge. He was young, and still had much to learn about people, especially women.

25

THE NATURE OF ILLUSION

Every time May passed near the footlights of the Palace stage, chorus girls would peer round the wings at him and start giggling. He wondered what Betty had told them. The evening had been a lot of fun, though bloody expensive, and the pretty chorine had made it obvious that she would welcome entertainment again at the weekend. Knowing that Bryant had returned to the unit the previous night, May felt an odd sort of disloyalty to his partner. It was only the end of his third day, and he was fraternizing with potential suspects instead of working late.

'I thought I'd find you down here,' he said, spotting the unruly fringe of chestnut hair that stuck above the back of a row of stalls, six rows from the orchestra pit. Bryant was sprawled with his legs hooked over the seat in front. The stage was partially lit with fresnel spots to reveal a hellish scene. Crimson caverns of oil and fire glittered with droplets of lava, and the petrified purple bodies of demons jutted from priapic stalagmites. The effect was, if not quite obscene, very near the edge of public toleration in 1940.

May pushed down the seat next to his partner and leaned over. 'Did you know that while the theatre company is occupying the Palace, it owns the stage, the backstage area and all rights of access, but not the front of house or its offices? Those are in the control of the theatre's owners. Each of the companies is placing the responsibility on the other, so now we're not allowed to talk to staff on the premises. I'm trying to make arrangements to continue off site.'

'We should have done that from the start,' said Bryant grumpily. 'It'll shake them up to be questioned in official surroundings. I wish I hadn't tried the mystery meat pie at luncheon, I feel most uncomfortable.'

May pointed at the semi-naked women cavorting with each other onstage. 'I suppose all of this offends your purist sensibilities.'

'Not a bit of it,' said Bryant. 'Offenbach was far from pure. In fact, he outraged the purists of his age, so he'd probably approve of the nudity, although he might think some of the sex scenes are going a bit far, even in our supposedly enlightened times.'

'Perhaps you could tell me what's supposed to be going on' – May waved a hand at the stage – 'all this operatic hellfire and brimstone.'

Bryant unbuttoned his waistcoat and massaged his podgy stomach. 'For a start it's not an opera, it's an *opéra bouffe*.'

'What's the difference?'

'It has mythological, supernatural elements. It's fanciful. It's intended as a comic diversion.'

'So there's no fat lady singing at the end?'

Bryant swivelled his head and studied his partner coolly. 'You're not much of a music lover, are you?'

'Oh, I don't know, I like a bit of a dance to Glenn Miller. I'm always willing to learn.'

'I know a numbers-and-fractions merchant when I meet one. You're a science bod. I saw you listening to Oswald Finch when he was going on about body fluid ratios. Your ears pricked up.'

'I just thought I should know a bit about all this.' He bounced his fingers in time with the music.

'I must say, it's suspiciously appropriate.' Bryant un-knotted a few feet of his scarf and sat up. 'Jacques Offenbach was a forerunner of Gilbert and Sullivan. He's the reason they started writing together. He had huge successes with these romps in Paris, even though the critics were sniffy. *Orpheus in the Underworld* is over eighty years old. Back when it was first performed, everyone who could afford to visit the theatre had a decent working knowledge of the classics, so Offenbach could make fun of Greek legends and everyone would get the joke. Here, he's taken the most famous part of the Orpheus myth and reworked it. Orpheus was the son of a muse who saved the Argonauts from the Sirens. He ventured into the Underworld to get back his beloved nymph, Eurydice, who had been bitten by a snake.'

'Oh, I remember that bit. Pluto let him have Eurydice back on the condition that he didn't look behind him at her until she reached daylight, but he did.'

'Well done. Offenbach's version breaks with traditional mythology. He cynically parodies the characters and makes the story a social satire. He turns Orpheus into a salacious violin teacher, makes Eurydice a tart and has her old man moaning about having to go off and save her.'

'Who's that, then?' May pointed out a statuesque woman in vast grey crinolines. He had last seen her throwing a histrionic fit in Helena Parole's office.

'That's the figure of Public Opinion. In Offenbach's version of the myth Orpheus is pleased to see the back of his wife, and goes down to Hades only because Public Opinion threatens him with exposure about his own dalliances. Eurydice lusts after a shepherd called Aristaeus, who is really Pluto in disguise. She gets bitten, and is taken down to Hell, but finds it more boring than she expected. Meanwhile, on Mount Olympus, the gods are grumbling to Jupiter about

165

their rights, he gets hot for Eurydice and they all go down to Hell.'

'I think I get the idea,' interrupted May. 'Presumably it all ends in tears.'

'No, it ends with the cancan. A real trouser rouser, sends you home with a song on your lips and a lump in your drawers. In those days, the stage used to be lit with floats, oil wicks that were floated on water to reduce the risk of fire. It was an effect designed to show up the dancers' thighs, so you can imagine the excitement it caused with a lot of saucy high-kicking. The ladies of the Paris chorus rarely bothered to wear knickers, and performed all kinds of athletic motions to reveal themselves to the wealthy patrons in the front rows.

'As well as stuffing his recitative with knowing jokes, like Morpheus being the only god awake when all the others are sleeping, Offenbach filled his entertainments with references to other nineteenth-century operas, so the trio of the last act of *La Belle Hélène* is lifted from the *William Tell* Overture, and in this opera there's a direct pinch from Gluck's version of *Orpheus* that got screams of laughter from the audience. The ending's topsy-turvy too, because Eurydice doesn't want to go back with boring old Orpheus, and he doesn't want her, so Pluto's condition of not looking back at her on the way out of Hades is really an escape clause for both of them. Eurydice ends up as a bacchante, one of Hell's call girls, merrily high-kicking in the inferno.'

'Sounds rather immoral.'

'That was the whole point. What interests me', Bryant continued, warming to his subject, 'is Offenbach's capacity for deceit. Here was a man who used tricks and jokes, paradox, caricature and parody, who lied about when and where he was born, a man who was not French at all but probably a German rabbi, who conned his way into the Paris Conservatoire despite the fact that foreigners were banned from attending, who was a published composer at nineteen, a virtuoso on the cello and, bizarrely, the toy flute, who had five children and became a Roman Catholic, whose success was so great that *le tout Paris* had to be nightly turned away from his theatre. He was a conundrum, a shamelessly charming scoundrel. He had what our Jewish friends call "chutzpah".' Bryant folded his arms across the back of the seat in front of him, lost in admiration. 'Offenbach's been out of favour for the last few years. But he was capable of scandalizing in his time.'

'People really take offence at this sort of stuff?'

'Not any more. Classical Greek scholars find the whole thing particularly amusing.'

'So we're not dealing with a deranged Greek?'

'Oh, I wouldn't rule out anything at this point.' Bryant turned his attention back to the stage. 'But I wonder if someone wants to stop the production for another reason.'

'You have one in mind?'

'Actually, yes. Elspeth told me I should talk to the owner of the theatre company.'

'I don't see what the owner could have to do with this.'

'Somebody's spending an awful lot of cash, several thousands of pounds, to get the show to opening night.'

'When the country needs money for manufacturing weapons? That's almost treasonous.'

'Not if you strengthen the spirit of the people. And sell the production to other countries, of course. These days plays are like motion pictures. A production can be simultaneously staged around the world.'

'You can't strike prints like you can a film.'

'No, but you can license other companies. *No, No, Nanette* is probably still going strong in Addis Ababa.'

'I don't see what someone would gain by stopping the show from opening.'

'That's where it gets murky. Rival businesses could be searching for a way to lower the value of their enemies' stock. Or the backers themselves could sabotage their own production because it has to be insured to the hilt. If they found they'd misjudged the market, or sensed that the show was shaping up badly, they could halt it and claim the insurance. It depends on the equity structure, how the deal is underwritten.'

'They'd have a tough time convincing the insurance company in this climate,' said May. 'War damage must be bankrupting them. Can we check out the backers?'

'I've already briefed the pen-pusher Biddle on that.'

'I take it you're not intending to do any more work today, then.'

'Look here, I had four hours' sleep last night. There was a frost this morning, and my bedroom ceiling has a hole in it that's open to the sky. I actually felt like kipping down in the tube, just for warmth.'

'I don't know how people can do that. The smell of unwashed bodies on the platform of Covent Garden this morning was terrible.'

'John, people can get used to anything. Our job is to make sure they don't get used to murder. I'm going up to place some telephone calls.' Bryant hauled himself from his seat. 'Enjoy the rehearsal.'

'Wait,' said May. 'Tanya Capistrania's role in the show. The method of death. A dancer loses her feet. And the performer assigned to play Jupiter—'

'Is hit by a planet,' said Bryant. 'Yes, the idea had occurred to me that perhaps there's some grander plan. It's just so odd that it should happen on a stage.'

'Why?'

'Oh, the illusory nature of the theatre, I suppose. The whole thing about the stage is that it's a huge trick, a visual paradox. If you could see the set from overhead, you'd realize that the scenes you see from the stalls only exist as a series of angled flats, with actors slipping between them. The perspectives are far more false than you realize. Designs have an almost Japanese sense of construction, layer upon layer.'

168

'I'm not sure what you're getting at,' said May.

'I'm not sure I'm getting at anything,' Bryant conceded. 'I need to sleep on the problem. If indeed any of us are allowed to get some sleep. We'll have to see what the moonlight brings.'

26

REPAIRING THE PAST

What did the moonlight bring? John May walked to the centre of Waterloo Bridge and stopped. Behind him, the suspended wheel of the London Eye stared out along the line of the Thames. May adjusted the nylon Nike backpack strapped between his broad shoulders. He liked modern clothes; they had freed an older generation from constricting suits and ties and tight-fitting toe-capped shoes. He wore trainers and jeans without embarrassment. He was too old to be concerned with the strictures of fashion.

The river had the flat grey dullness of a plastic groundsheet. There were hardly any boats to be seen in either direction. If he closed his eyes he could see the wartime fire barges. The sound of traffic faded from his ears, and the city fell silent. Those Blitz mornings were so quiet and still that one could slip further back in time, to an age of cart-tracks and wooden slums. Now, the past and the silence were gone for ever. The city survived in fragments, as though it had been painted on glass and the glass had shattered.

He was on his way to meet Janice Longbright. He had found a yellowed picture of her mother in the archive at the Palace Theatre. It had been taken by PC Atherton in 1940, clowning around in the cell at Bow Street, just before she had supposedly gone off to marry Harris. Their wedding had finally taken place at the end of the war, in disastrous circumstances – but that was another story. He wanted to be with Longbright, even if there was nothing to say. She was his only remaining connection to the past.

He had to find out who was stalking them, and why Bryant's dental records had been stolen. Could someone have wanted a souvenir of the dead detective? It was the first thing he asked her when they met.

Longbright was sitting in the corner of a black-and-white-tiled fish restaurant in Covent Garden, tearing the claws from the sockets of a crab shell. She had a cigarette sticking from the corner of her mouth, and was squinting through the smoke at the eviscerated crustacean. 'I'm sorry, John, I was starving and started without you,' she apologized. 'You've lost a bit of weight.'

'They say bereavement does that to you.'

'Well, don't lose any more. You're half an hour late.'

'Am I? I didn't mean to be.' May slid onto the bench seat opposite and poured himself a glass of wine from her carafe.

'I suppose you were standing in the middle of Waterloo Bridge, staring into the filthy water and thinking bad thoughts.'

'You know me too well.'

'You can't bring him back that way.' She wielded a vicious-looking pair of pliers, cracked open a claw and dug out its flesh.

'I realize that. I was wondering if someone else is trying to bring him back.'

'By nicking his dental records? I hardly think so. I called the dentist, by the way, but it's a new bloke. Bryant's regular man has gone on holiday, nobody seems to know where. They're going to call me back. Did it cross your mind that the bomber might have been trying to get the both of you?'

'I don't think so. If he'd figured out how to get into the unit, and knew about Arthur's habit of working on a Sunday

171

night, he must also have known that I rarely stay late at the weekends.'

'I've got people checking the station CCTVs, but there's a lot of coming and going around that place because of the club next door, and they're nearly all wearing hooded jackets. You can't see a bloody thing.'

May watched Longbright disembowel the crab. 'My neighbour told me someone tried to break into my apartment. She said something about teeth. The man had huge fangs.'

He studied the former detective sergeant. Her make-up looked thick in the pale morning light. She reminded him of her mother, not least because she styled herself on the forgotten film star Ava Gardner.

Janice dropped the crab claw and stabbed her cigarette into a tin ashtray. 'God, I miss him, don't you? Stupid question. I've been trying to find out too, you know. One hundred and forty-two major cases between nineteen forty and two thousand and three, not counting the thousands of small unsolved dramas the pair of you waded through. It could have been anyone.'

'But it wasn't,' said May. 'I'm sure it's connected with the Palace.'

'You can't know that. There's no one left. Stone, Whittaker, Wynter, Noriac, Parole, that poor creature who committed the murders, even Mouse, the stage door boy, they're all dead. I've checked all the records and made all the calls.'

'Then we've overlooked someone,' said May simply. 'Just as Arthur did all those years ago. Here, this is for you.' He took out the photograph and handed it to her.

'My God.' Janice touched the edges of the faded monochrome picture. 'I could be her.'

'You are.' May touched her hand. It was hard to believe that Gladys Forthright's daughter was in her fifties. Looking at her he felt the present shift into the past. He was forced to shut his eyes and wipe them clear. 'Tell me, do you think we wasted our lives?'

Janice looked shocked. 'What do you mean? Of course not. All the people you helped, all the—'

'I'm not talking about work, I know what we did. I mean us, Arthur and me. He loved Nathalie and lost her. He was infatuated with your mother, but she didn't want him. He waited years for Gladys. I married the wrong woman, lost her and my baby girl. My son has a daughter who can't even leave her house any more. What was it all for? Sometimes I think Arthur and I worked so hard because there was nothing else for us to do.'

Longbright picked up the photograph and dropped it into her shoulder bag with an air of finality. 'Well, there's something for you to do now,' she said, taking up the crab once more and splintering its legs into pieces. 'If you want to save the future, you have to repair the past.'

'And how am I supposed to do that?'

'I may have found a way. Alma remembered another sheet of paper lying on Bryant's dining-room table, beside the dental records. She thinks it was from a hospital. It also went missing. I'm assuming it was his list of patients released from the Wetherby. The nurse who compiled it for him says there were over fifty names on it. But he might have made a mark against one of them.'

'I don't see how we'll find that out now.'

'It took me years to get him to keep copies of everything.'

'You think it was a copy?'

'Yes. And I imagine he would have left the original at the office.'

'Then it's gone. The unit was obliterated.'

'Your partner was an untidy man. He never put anything back in its rightful place.'

'You don't think it would still be in the photocopier?'

'If it is, it's between a sheet of glass and a layer of heavy heatproof plastic. I can't think of anything that would preserve it better.'

May dug for his mobile phone.

'Relax,' said Longbright, biting into the soft flesh of the claw. 'I've already called Finch. We're going through the remains after lunch. Bash in a crab first, I promise you'll feel a lot better for it.'

27

THE MASK OF TRAGEDY

'I've never seen anyone die before,' said Corinne Betts distantly, twisting a curl of hair at her ear, 'not actually go from living and talking to suddenly lying on the ground covered in blood, like a stage prop. You'd think you'd see something leave, a wisp of air.' The little performer was being interviewed by John May. They were seated in the tiny white-tiled dressing room that Mercury had been sharing with Jupiter.

'We have someone who can talk to you about the psychological aspects of witnessing death, if you'd like,' May offered. 'It's something they've set up for people who've been bombed out. It hasn't proven very popular so far, but it's supposed to help.'

Corinne dug out a bottle of Scotch and a pair of enamel mugs. 'I'm not bothered. Call me cynical, but I suspect institutional comforting is designed to give nosy people something to do. My sister was killed during the first week of the Blitz. She was working in a maternity hospital near the Guildhall. We weren't close; she didn't approve of the way I live. Even so . . . I feel all right now, a little strange, like I did when I heard about Maisie. As though something has shifted. At least they found her body, and I know why she died. Everyone is much more upset than they're letting on, you know. There's talk of spies, all sorts of rubbish. There's a theory that Tanya was just picked out at random and murdered. Was she?'

'It's certainly possible.'

'And Charlie? That wasn't an accident either?'

May shifted uncomfortably in his seat. 'Someone aimed at Mr Senechal and cut the wire attached to the globe.'

'Blimey. You think it's an inside job, someone trying to stop the production?'

'I don't see how anyone could have entered the theatre unseen.'

'I suppose you're waiting to be handed names. We're all meant to turn informer and blame the people we don't get along with.'

'Do you want to nominate someone?'

'Me? I've no axe to grind with anyone here, except perhaps Little Miss Perfect, and that's only because she gets on my nerves for being so gifted.'

'Who do you mean?'

'Eve Noriac. You only have to look at her. Haven't you met her yet? She's young, she's beautiful, she's rich and she's French so of course all the men adore her. She has the starring role and she deserves it. It's just that it all seems to come so easily to her. She's been rehearsing in splendid isolation with her own tutor, away from us commoners. She turned up late for this afternoon's rehearsal, and hardly concentrated at all while the rest of us were floundering around. She's touched by the muses. And I've heard she's set her sights on Miles Stone, our Orpheus, so they'd rather be living out their roles in the play.'

'What about Tanya Capistrania? Did she have talent?'

'She worked hard, but was never more than proficient. The parts you take on have to sit comfortably with you, otherwise your awkwardness transmits itself to the house. The audience is always aware that it's watching "acting".

Real stars make you believe in them because they believe in themselves. The audience is on their side from the moment they arrive on stage.' Corinne leaned forward conspiratorially. 'I'll let you in on a secret. Acting is a confidence trick. You don't attract good roles without exuding confidence, and you only have that if you already know you have talent. The two go hand in hand, and without one, the other spirals out of control.' She knocked back her Scotch and grimaced. 'Tanya wasn't seeing just Geoffrey Whittaker. She was also having an affair with John Styx.'

'Someone from outside the production?' asked May.

'No, that's his *Orpheus* role. His real name's David Cumberland – you know, like the sausages. He doesn't get going until act three, basically gets one decent number to himself and joins in with the others for some melodramatic dialogue. But perfect for Tanya.'

'Why?'

'Darling, you can't have an affair with someone if they're always on stage the same time as you.'

'You say an "affair".'

'Yes, he's got a civilian wife tucked away somewhere. It was probably a matter of mutual convenience. There's nothing like a good tension-releasing fuck after you've been singing at the top of your lungs all day, pardon my French.'

'Any link between her and Charles Senechal that you can think of? Did they spend much time together offstage?'

'I don't think they even knew each other. In the early stages of a production you can address the most intimate dialogue lines to a stranger and not get to have a real conversation with them at all. Particularly if there's a celebrity performer among you. They make the less experienced members of the cast nervous. The stars have to break the ice first. Protocol, my dear. I'm not from a stage background like the rest of them, so it doesn't wash with me.'

'How did you get the part, then?'

'Mercury is a pretty physical role.' Corinne topped up

their mugs. 'Lots of charging about on winged feet. I saw someone do it on roller skates at the Blackpool Tower Ballroom. Helena came to one of my humorous monologues and asked me to attend a casting session. They were seeing lots of other short fat people. Comedy women, you know the sort of thing. If they're fat they must be funny.'

'Will you do me a favour, Miss Betts?'

'Corinne, please. Theatres are intimate places. We should be on first-name terms.'

'You seem to have a fairly objective outlook. Would you tell me if you hear anything unusual?' He looked up at the posters of demonic heads lining the walls, different productions of *Orpheus* around the world. 'I mean, unusual by theatrical standards.'

'You can't ask me to spy for you, Mr May. They're my friends.'

'I appreciate that. But Mr Bryant thinks something is happening here that goes beyond the scope of normal criminal investigation.'

'And what do you think?'

'I'm not sure. This is my first actual case.'

'They've sent a boy to do a man's job.' She gave a dark chuckle. 'Isn't that the war all over.'

'We don't have the facilities to protect everyone. We don't even have the means of finding out who else might be at risk.'

'I see your problem,' said Corinne. 'It's like acting. You don't get very far with a role until you've established your motivation. If you can't find anything to relate to, you never get a grip on the piece.'

'Then perhaps we understand each other,' said May, smiling gently.

'You're a nice man, John.' Corinne brushed his jaw with the back of her hand. 'Don't let anything happen to the rest of us.'

* * *

Corinne Betts waited twenty minutes for a 134 bus, but it was raining and the first two were completely full, so she decided to start walking. She liked John May a lot. She had always been drawn to younger men. They had a sense of innocence that she no longer had the strength to muster.

She wondered if there was a link between Tanya and Charles that she had missed. It was fun in a Conan Doyle-ish way: an old, dark theatre, a murderer on the loose. Except that Conan Doyle had been dead for a decade. His *Strand* magazine stories now belonged on the bookshelves of elderly aunts, and the war had stolen away the vicarious pleasures of murder.

It set her wondering about motives again. You'd have to be pretty angry with someone to plan their death, particularly at the moment when there was every chance that they might disappear under a bit of falling masonry. And to be annoyed with two people as different as Charles and Tanya made no sense at all. If someone was trying to stop the production, why not just set fire to the theatre? It wasn't as if there were any likely suspects. In fact, the more she thought about it, the stranger everything became – an air of Greek tragedy, the severing of limbs, the compass falling from the sky. Something began to prick at her skin. She resolved to take a long bath and have a smoke before going to bed.

She had reached the top of Tottenham Court Road before another 134 came along, and although she waved at it, the damned thing refused to stop. The rainswept corner of Euston Road had become one of the bleakest and most exposed points in central London, now that so many craters of brick and stone had transformed tarmac into the surface of the moon. They said an old woman had been blown out of her house in her iron bedstead, and had not woken up until the rescue squad reached her. 'They' said a lot of things. It was becoming impossible to know who to believe.

The few people she passed were carrying bags and

suitcases, heading to stations, or to houses that had roofs. A hearse passed her with perhaps a dozen children in it, their faces pressed against the windows, evacuees being taken to their train. The distant plane trees of Euston Road were just visible in the downpour, the tops of their branches rustling and twisting in the rain-laden wind. Here the street was preternaturally empty, the boarded-over shop fronts as dull as the terraced houses set back from the road. She hated the blackout, the dead carapaces of buildings, their rooftops darker than the sky.

Corinne was about to cross the road beside the tiled wall of Warren Street tube station when she became aware of someone else moving on the street. Grey veils of rain fell ahead of her, blurring the view, but a figure appeared to be waiting on the opposite pavement. It was dressed in a black rubber raincoat, with the hood raised. There was something wrong with its face, she thought: too white, too still. The figure twisted back and forth, clasping itself, its head bouncing from side to side, as though it was laughing, or in terrible pain.

Corinne walked to the striped traffic island in the centre of the road. From the corner of her eye she saw the figure shift again, passing across the dimmed lights from the station ticket hall. She watched as it reached the edge of the pavement, and found herself staring into a distorted face as pale as porcelain, the crying tragedy mask of traditional theatre. A passing truck churned its way through a lake of rainwater. When she looked up once more, the figure had vanished.

It had seen her alarm, she was sure. Angered and frightened, she ran across the road, moving past the taped crosses of shop windows, until she realized that she was running in a hard panic, and forced her pace to a walk.

She could not understand where the fear had come from. She was only aware that she had felt it, a chill prickling between her shoulder blades, a primal warning that someone or something meant her harm or, worse still, wanted her.

28

VENOM

'Mr Bryant, wait, I'd like a word with you.'

It was late on Wednesday evening when Oswald Finch came running after the young detective, who was backing a black Wolseley out of the half-flooded car park behind Bow Street police station. He had requisitioned the car from the pool in order to visit his aunt in Finchley. She had trouble getting about, so he was taking her a joint of beef. Bryant affected to ignore the pathologist and almost ran over his foot. Exasperated by the obstruction that had placed itself between his vehicle and the exit, Bryant jemmied open the window with the end of a soup spoon set aside for the purpose, and eyed him brightly. 'Oh, Oswald, it's you. They still haven't fixed this window. What do you want?'

'Mr Bryant, there's an enormous plant in my office. Your constable told me you put it there.'

'Well, I didn't personally move it, it's far too heavy for me to touch, with my back.' Bryant searched about for the hand-brake. 'I had Atherton bring it up. Do you like it?'

'Well, frankly no, I don't.' Finch bobbed down to look at him. 'It's six feet tall and blots out all the light, and it smells strange.'

'That's just a bit of root rot. It's been sitting in

contaminated water, a broken sewage main, I imagine. A house in St Martin's Lane got bombed out and they were clearing the site. There are insects of some kind living in its soil, I thought you might know what they are. They've got a bite rather like a mosquito, brought me up in livid red lumps, some kind of tropical necrosis. I once found something similar in a flat belonging to an Ethiopian student in Tufnell Park. We still don't know what killed him. I thought you'd be interested.'

'Floral virology's really not my field, and it's in the way. I can barely get the door open.' He rocked hesitantly back and forth in front of the automobile as Bryant throttled impatiently.

'I'd keep it open for a few days if you can, Oswald, just until you're used to the smell. It's quite overpowering. The buds shed a sort of purple pollen, very sticky, gets everywhere. I knew you'd be fascinated. Don't get any on your shirt, it seems to burn.'

'Look, I really don't think—'

'Jolly good. How are you getting on with the tissue samples from Tanya Capistrania?'

'Er, well, that's just it. I've carried out some more detailed analysis, and I think poison was ingested. In fact I'm sure—'

'Ingested? That could be anything, couldn't it? I mean, you can die from having water injected into your spine, or air into your brain or anything. Can't you be more specific?'

'Well, er, something she ate.'

'You mean the chicken? The chicken sandwich?' Bryant released the handbrake and the car hopped forward.

'It wasn't chicken. It was quail.'

'I don't see a difference.'

'Ah, but there is. You remember I got a positive test for coniine. Well, there's a plant rather like parsley or London rocket in appearance, *Conium maculatum*, not at all uncommon, springs up on waste ground, especially around bomb sites. Causes the kind of muscular paralysis I described. There's no real antidote beyond gastric lavage, and only if it's performed moments after ingestion. It's a long-recognized poison, most commonly known as hemlock.'

'Hemlock? It supposedly killed Socrates, didn't it?'

'I really have no idea. The thing is, some birds are immune to the plant. Quail eat the seeds without suffering any damage, but their flesh becomes highly toxic. It's feasible that the victim just got a bad quail. The perils of a rich diet.'

'Wouldn't she have experienced symptoms?'

'Yes, any time from half an hour to three hours after consumption, but she might not have recognized them as such. Dancers suffer muscular pain all the time.'

'You're telling me she may not have been murdered at all, Oswald?'

'That's right. She may simply have become paralysed, fallen down and been unable to move when the lift started up.'

'Well, thank you, that makes my evening.' Bryant ground the gear lever forward, forcing Finch to jump out of his path. Blithely ignoring the horn blasts from behind, the Wolseley thumped up the kerb in front of the station as Bryant beckoned to his partner. John darted towards the vehicle with a late edition of the *Evening News* held over his head as Arthur threw open the passenger door.

'John, Runcorn is going to conduct some kind of tension test on that prop globe, isn't he?' said Bryant, trying to clear the condensation from the windscreen with his sleeve. 'Can you run the wire ends under a microscope and check the shear?'

'I'll do it, but the waiting time for equipment isn't good. The samples will probably have to go over to Lambeth.' John smiled. 'I saw you talking to Mr Finch. He's very upset about that plant.'

'He works faster when he's upset about something. I'm annoyed about his chemical theory.'

'You should be pleased to hear about Miss Capistrania,' said May, puzzled. 'It may mean we've just stumbled upon an unfortunate series of circumstances.'

'Very unfortunate when you consider that her feet managed to turn up in the possession of a chestnut vendor. Who is entirely innocent, by the way. His movements are fully vouched for. If we're not looking for a murderer, somebody out there must have a pretty black sense of humour.'

'There's a lot of it about. None of Tanya's colleagues liked her very much.'

'How much do you have to hate someone to hide their feet? I'll tell you, John, right now the unit could do with a renewed funding pledge, and we'll only get that if we find a culprit quickly.'

May peered through the windscreen. 'Don't pull out just yet, there's a lot of traffic.'

'Well, I don't believe it,' said Bryant, twisting the wheel hard and stamping on the accelerator to a chorus of screeching tyres, 'it's all too absurd, quails and hemlock and falling planets. The chances of two people undergoing such colourful ends in close proximity is positively Jacobean, and I don't swallow it for a moment.'

'Strange things happen all the time,' May felt compelled to point out. 'Do you have something against the laws of chance?'

'I do, as it happens. I think while we're under bombardment, all sorts of peculiarities might emerge, just not in this fashion.'

'I say, you're driving awfully fast without lights. Why are you in such a rush?'

'After I've visited my aunt I'm taking Alma out tonight, and I'm running late.'

'Your landlady? You're taking your landlady out to dinner?' A traffic policeman loomed out of the dark at them, and jumped from harm's way like a startled hare. Bryant was a terrible driver. His priorities corresponded to none of the ones mentioned in the Highway Code. Nor did his signals, for that matter.

'Nobody mentioned dinner. She happens to consider me companionable.'

'Still, it's a date. I thought you were working on Miss Wynter.'

'Miss Wynter is already spoken for. Her first love is the theatre. I suspect she enjoys her status as a spinster. Alma knows how to enjoy herself.'

'Don't tell me you're planning a night of love.'

'If you'd met her, you'd know you were being disgusting. Alma is religious and respectable. We have a couple of shilling seats for *Gone With the Wind*. She has an unfathomable obsession with Clark Gable, and can't find anyone else to go with her.'

'Well, at least you can watch with an easier mind.'

'Far from it,' said Bryant, 'I'm going back to the theatre afterwards. They'll be rehearsing late because the weather's too bad for bombing. I want to make sure nothing else happens.'

'You mean you want to be there if it does.'

Bryant swerved the vehicle over to the side of the road. Horns honked and tyres screeched in the darkness. 'How's this for you?'

May reluctantly opened the door. 'It's not at all where I'm going but never mind, I'll get a bus, it's safer.' He pushed his long legs out into the rain. 'Try to have a relaxing evening with Alma. You know where your nearest shelter is?'

'Alma will, she's very practical. I won't take anything in, you know, I shall be thinking about severed feet. I daresay you're off to enjoy yourself with your busty sexpot.'

'Actually, I'm taking a night off to recuperate,' said May. 'From what you've told me, your landlady sounds most keen. Perhaps you should consider the benefits of matrimony.'

'It seems an awful lot of effort just to get regular sex and someone to wash your socks. I mean, she already washes my socks.'

'Which still leaves the sex. I bet you can't remember your last time.'

'Oh yes I can,' called Bryant, pulling away from the kerb. 'Saturday night.' He indicated left and turned the wheel right. 'It could have been perfect, but for one thing.'

'What's that?' May hopped onto the pavement and squinted through the rain.

'I wasn't with anyone,' laughed Bryant as he plunged back into the unlit traffic.

29

THE REFLECTED INFERNO

Eve Noriac loved the smell of an old theatre.

It was something no amount of carpentry or repainting could remove, a richly human odour. She had grown up on the south coast of France, in a small town outside Nice called Beaulieu, so sun-caressed that the area around it was known as La Petite Afrique, and her arrival in England had coincided with the most prolonged period of rainfall the country had seen in a decade. Within a fortnight she had resolved to go home, but then in May her homeland had been invaded, and she had been forced to stay.

It was then that she discovered the theatres. The Lyric, the Apollo, the Fortune, the Criterion, the Cambridge, each had its own stamp and style, but they all exuded the same sense of shared life. The diurnal passage of each play brought platoons of awestruck schoolchildren and seasoned veterans, locals and tourists, suffering spouses and devoted worshippers. The challenge was to unite them all and win them over.

No two shows were ever the same, even though they appeared identical from the front of the stage. A nightly war was waged for the hearts and minds of those watching. Ground was gained and lost as each evening peppered itself with small victories and defeats. Much-rehearsed movements were swallowed up or skimmed past unnoticed. Flaws were observed or concealed. Each script was a recipe for pleasing the crowd; moments rose perfectly to the intention of the text or fell flat. The subtle ebb and surge of the performances made for different emphases that could alter the total effect of the entertainment within the batting of an eye.

Eve's role as Eurydice was the essence of the piece, but for a young soprano it was also a stepping stone for career-making roles to come. Some sopranos were technical virtuosos who honed their skills through ceaseless training. Others were born with a natural undisciplined talent that merely had to be shaped. The second type was rarer, but more thrilling to experience. Technical singers never bared their souls. Naturals were destructive, dangerous, even doomed. Their voices could create an extraordinary atmosphere of tension.

Actors can believe strange things; Eve Noriac knew she was a natural, and that her gift was granted by the gods of the theatre. They looked down kindly upon her, and protected her from harm. On the previous Saturday she had walked from St Paul's to Blackfriars during a daylight bombing raid, while the wardens shouted at her to get off the street. Who you had faith in wasn't important; it was that you had faith at all.

Eve's only failure was in her choice of lovers; she knew she would have to do something about Miles. He had barely set foot in the theatre before they had fallen upon one another in an urgent, sweaty embrace. Thinking about him now, Eve knew he wasn't her type. Miles would cling. She would have to wait until after opening night to tell him it had been a bad idea. She had no wish to damage his confidence before the critics had their chance.

Miles Stone was Eve's counterpart, Orpheus to her Eurydice, and right now he was trying to keep the voice on the other end of the line from fading, but the building's acoustics were playing tricks on him. It was as if the theatre frowned on the outside world, and interfered with the line connected to the ancient two-piece telephone in the hall outside the company office.

'I don't understand what you're doing in London,' he shouted, pressing his finger into his free ear. 'I thought you were staying in New York. What do you mean, I invited you? I said don't come. Yes, I did.'

Rachel's reply was damaged by a searing crackle of static. This was all Miles needed right now, his mother staying in town. While everyone else's mothers were heading for the comparative safety of the countryside, his was coming to the city.

'Why don't you let me check you into a hotel?' he asked. He knew Rachel would prefer to stay in his damp apartment building. She distrusted English hotels, with their erratic service and weird plumbing.

'No, not in the centre, it's not safe,' said Miles finally. 'I'll find you something further out, but you can't just waltz along to rehearsals.' He was through taking Rachel's advice. She always promoted Becky, his ex-wife, acting as if he was still married to her. Getting divorced was one of the few good ideas Miles had ever had. Changing his name from Saperstein to Stone had been a less successful move. He'd liked the mnemonic sound of Miles Stone; at least, until he overheard his agent referring to him as the Millstone. He knew he would have to ask Eve to stay away for a few weeks. Although the decree absolute had been settled a year ago, he was sure that Rachel still considered him married in the eyes of God, and he had not helped matters by occasionally sleeping with Becky when he was in New York. Rachel would only get into an argument with Eve if they met, and she would ensure that there was a meeting because she would turn up at the theatre whether he liked it or not, and report back to Becky. He had been caught in the velvet trap all his life, betrayed by his love of difficult women.

He settled the receiver back on its hook and walked down to the stage, a fiery riot of red, gold, purple and indigo flats and skycloths. There was so much set-dressing that he wondered whether the audience would be able to see anyone at all. On Saturday night they would have a full house plus the critics, the police, the St John's Ambulance brigade and the odd ARP warden to add to the confusion.

An extraordinarily high note reverberated through the auditorium: that note was meant for him. Eve Noriac was standing at the front of the stage, stretching her throat and impatiently swinging her arms. As Miles set off down the stairs once more, he wondered how Orpheus had managed to avoid visiting Hell to save her in the past, seeing that she was not a woman to be kept waiting.

It was half past nine, and the few remaining performers were tired. Helena was slumped in a seat six rows fom the orchestra pit, sipping her hundredth cup of tea. On stage, Eurydice was having trouble adjusting to her new Jupiter in their duet, the '*Duo de la mouche*'. The understudy baritone was now transformed into a bluebottle, and was finding it difficult to hit his mark while managing the celluloid wings of the costume.

'All right, everybody, we'll resume this at ten o'clock to-morrow morning,' Helena called, clapping her hands. 'If anybody needs to share a cab, please let Geoffrey or Harry know.' She rose and walked up the aisle, lighting a cigarette.

'Helena?' Harry came hobbling up beside her. He had twisted his ankle in a pothole at lunchtime, and had spent the day on his feet. 'We haven't heard sirens yet, but the searchlights and sound locators have gone back up in Charing Cross Road. I was wondering if you'd prefer to have the cast stay over in here. We could open up a couple of the old practice rooms. I think there's some bedding lying about.'

'You can discreetly ask the girls,' Helena suggested, sucking blessed smoke into her lungs, 'but the boys can go home.

190

There's enough hanky-panky going on without putting the girls in temptation's way.' She loosened her bandanna and shook out her hair. 'If any member of the audience complains about having to sit for two hours on a narrow horsehair seat I shall ask them to try it for a fortnight.' She grabbed Harry's hand. 'Come on, you. Let's lose the others, I don't want to talk about work tonight. I'll buy you a Scotch in that nancy-boy bar you like so much. If we get in before the raids start, they might lock us in all night.'

Betty Trammel awoke with a dry mouth and a throbbing head. After the rehearsal, the ladies and gentlemen of the chorus had retired to the Spice of Life for drinks, and had stayed until closing time. The bombing raid had made travel impossible, and she had decided to sleep on a canvas camp bed in the upper circle practice room on the condition that her friend Sally-Ann slept in the room next to her. She had no intention of staying alone in the theatre. Not that it frightened her, it took a lot to do that these days, but she wanted someone to talk to. She knew she had chosen the wrong time to return to England, but her course was set, and now she had to make the best of it. She decided to lie awake and listen to the night city while planning her next move. Instead she fell asleep almost instantly, and only woke because she found herself desperately thirsty.

The room's single window was blacked out, and the street far below was so silent that she thought for a moment it must have snowed. Rubbing warmth into her goosefleshed arms, she swung her legs from the bed and made her way slowly towards the door, where she had left a torch. She knew there was a bathroom at the end of the corridor, and presumed she would find some potable water. The torch threw a dim yellow circle onto the brown walls. She paused before the room in which Sally-Ann slept and listened to her light snoring, then made her way through the darkness.

'*Chante, belle bacchante,*' she sang under her breath as she walked, '*chante-nous ton hymne à Bacchus.*' Too much bloody Bacchus, she thought, twisting the torch beam onto the bathroom door. Her head was killing her, and she had nothing to take for it. Behind her, the faint light of the candle she had deposited at the top of the main staircase flickered and shifted.

Betty shone her torch around the bathroom, checking that it was empty, then shut the door and locked it. To do so was an act of habit; at home she had three brothers. She set the torch down on the edge of the sink, beneath the bathroom mirror, with its thin beam pointing up. They weren't allowed to turn on the lights when they used the lavatory up here because the windows weren't covered, and Helena had warned them that any more fines would come out of their own pockets.

She ran the cold tap, listening to the ghostly sound of clanking pipes, then filled an enamel mug with water and drank deep. The water had been standing too long in the cistern, and tasted brackish. She made a face, then noticed the chiaroscuro effect of the torchlight on her reflected flesh.

Detective May was rather a dish, she thought, but obviously penniless, which was a pity because she'd been saving herself for a wealthy man. There was something appealing about the fact that he was so young and unsullied. He clearly found her attractive. Betty stuck out her tongue and examined its pale coat. Then she drew in a deep breath, and held it.

But someone continued breathing behind her.

She still had her mouth open in surprise when the great white mask of a face unfurled itself over her right shoulder. Its mouth was a tortured red gash, like an angry cut from a sword, the teeth unnaturally large and distorted. The eyes were wild and cloudy, scarred with shiny stretches of skin. Above his hairline she saw a scraped knob of gleaming, cracked bone. His sore red hands clawed out for her in a

192

mannered pose, captured in the torch beam like a frame from some forgotten Chaney film, or a scene from the Inferno – Dante's version, not Offenbach's. He had the shape of some poor limbless creature from the First War, more mutilated than any of the old soldiers she still saw on the streets selling pencils.

She screamed so loudly that the sound of the torch being knocked over into the sink was lost. Her last sensation before losing consciousness was one of anger, that she could be so foolish as to strain her vocal cords in this manner, just days before her big night.

Bryant heard the scream and ran towards it with his hurricane lamp raised, but was forced to stop and retrace his steps when he realized that he had come out near the left-hand pass door, the one that was glued shut by years of paint. It took him another minute to climb the stairs to the rooms of the upper circle. Betty's friend Sally-Ann was awake and shrieking and clutching her shoulders, and waving her hands at the bathroom.

Bryant opened it and helped Betty to her feet. As he turned on the tap and splashed some cold water on her face, Sally-Ann grabbed his shoulder.

'Something ran up the stairs,' she yelled, pointing.

Bryant realized that he was meant to dash off after the villain, but didn't much fancy it. He trotted to the bottom of the staircase and looked up into the pitch black. 'What, up there?' he asked.

'Yes, yes, hurry, get him!' Sally-Ann's panic had infected the revived chorine, and now they were both jumping up and down, flapping their arms about.

Bryant reluctantly mounted the stairs. The landing was so dark it gave him claustrophobia. With his lantern held high he walked cautiously forward, and found himself in the deserted brown corridor of the balcony offices. He raised the lamp in the opposite direction. Nothing that way either. But when he returned to his original position he was startled to see the broad back of a man disappearing round the bend in the corridor, no more than fifteen yards away.

Where the hell could he have come from? Bryant asked himself. The corridor was empty. How can he see in the dark? He set off in pursuit of the retreating form. He reached the turn, stopped and gingerly held the lamp out further, half hoping that whoever was up there would be scared away by the light. He wished May was here, lumbering along beside him, big and sensible and brave.

Having waved the tin lantern for long enough, he finally peered round the corner.

And found himself inches from a white staring face. He yelled, the face yelled, and he dropped the lamp in terror.

Luckily the lamp had a safety wick, so it didn't splash burning oil everywhere, but it went out all the same. It took Bryant a full minute of fumbling in the dark with trembling fingers to get it lit again, and then he found himself sitting on the floor next to a full-length mirror.

From somewhere up near the roof he heard boots scraping on iron rungs, then the slam of a steel door. Whoever he had been chasing was now locked outside on the roof with no way down. Thank God for that, he thought, smoothing his hair and straightening his clothes into a more ordered appearance. I can tell the girls I scared him off.

30

THE THREE HUNDRED

Thursday morning brought evidence of the previous night's bombing, but the streets of central London were mostly quiet and unscathed. John May was alarmed to discover that he had somehow used up his week's rations of everything except lard. He hadn't the faintest idea what to do with lard beyond trying to swap it for something edible. On the second to last page of his ration book was a list of mysterious serial numbers and a government message that read: DO NOTHING WITH THIS PAGE UNTIL TOLD WHAT TO DO. It summed up the official attitude to everything.

But nobody seemed to mind. In 1939 it had been estimated that at least a quarter of the population of Britain was undernourished. Now, families were thinking carefully about nutrition, discovering vegetables they had hardly ever seen or used before.

May prided himself on his youthful fitness but had begun to put on weight. His aunt had taken the war to the kitchen front with a vengeance. Overnight she started presenting her favourite nephew with unappetizing combinations of shredded cabbage, spinach, beetroot and turnips. She rustled up scabby-looking potato pancakes and fish-head soups seasoned with sorrel and grated nutmeg, baked purées of bile beans with celery and chestnuts, liberally lubricated with dripping or stiffened with suet. One night she boiled something experimental with slippery elm and condensed milk that took the finish off the dining-room table so completely she was using Karpol on it for weeks after to restore the shine.

'Why don't you go and buy us a couple of coffees while I finish up here?' instructed Bryant as his partner arrived for work. 'We're out of tea, and the Carlucci brothers have traded all theirs. Get a couple of Bath buns while you're at it.'

'It's a bit embarrassing,' May admitted, 'but I'm afraid I'm low on funds. I've already spent my first week's salary.'

'Too busy impressing the girls. I suppose I'll have to give you an advance.' Bryant dug into the pocket of his voluminous woollen trousers. 'Here's ten bob. Don't worry about getting into debt. I'm spending wages I'm not due to earn until about six years after my death.'

'Thanks awfully. Biddle says you saw the Phantom last night.'

'Indeed, but I do wish you wouldn't call him that. I trapped him on the roof, actually. When I got up there I found a surprised firewatchman sitting on a ventilation flue. He told me he'd seen someone come flying out of the door, only to rush at the side of the building and vanish over it. When he ran to the ledge and looked down, there was no sign of anyone. It was as though he'd simply flown off into the night air. Poor bloke was beginning to think he'd imagined it when I turned up.'

'Where on earth could he have gone?'

'Buggered if I know. There aren't even any windows he could have dropped through. Nothing but a sheer brick wall and a long drop to the street. I've sent Crowhurst up there this morning to take a look around. What bothers me more is that your chorus girl locked the bathroom door from the inside when she entered, and yet this creature materialized right behind her.'

'You're telling me it has the ability to walk through walls and vanish over the edges of buildings like a vampire bat.'

'No, you're telling me. I can see your lips moving. Go and get the coffees.'

May went and got the coffees, but the image of someone sinister materializing in the bathroom next to the semi-naked girl stayed with him.

'I feel it's my duty to offer Betty police protection,' he said when he returned.

'Hm. I thought you might say that. I'm studying you for tips, you know. Your manner of dealing with the opposite sex could form the basis of an anthropological study. The most annoying part is, you don't even realize you're doing it.'

May was anxious to change the subject. He was staying with his aunt because his father's philandering had destroyed their family, and May lived in fear of taking after him. He set down the coffees and looked over Bryant's shoulder. 'What have you got there?'

'Zurich. They came back to us overnight. Damned efficient, the Swiss, although not to be trusted, of course.'

'What's in Zurich?'

'We've been tracking the money,' Bryant explained. 'The finance to stage the show. From Lloyd's of London, across to the continent and into neutral territory.'

'And you can find that out from here? I'm very impressed.'

Bryant studied the teleprinter paper for a moment and isolated a number of addresses. 'The production is being presented by a financial group registered in Victoria under the name of Three Hundred International.' He unravelled another foot of paper and carefully folded it. 'Listen to this. Three Hundred International Banks is registered in Zurich but is Greek-owned. Central European office, Athens. Other companies in the group include shipping, automotive accessories, property, blah blah, ah, here, a chain of theatres. Shipping and theatre, odd bedfellows, don't you think? I wanted a profile of the whole group but all I've managed to find so far is a general prospectus, and that tells me nothing. I spoke to some jobsworth in the Victoria office, but he wouldn't give me any information. What would make a shipping magnate diversify into the theatre?'

Shortly before he died, Arthur Bryant was interviewed about his earliest case. He told his interviewer, 'After the hostilities ended in nineteen forty-five, over a fifth of London's theatres had been destroyed or rendered unusable by bomb damage. The rest were bought up by a single consortium. The old theatrical families and their peculiar way of life, the life we briefly experienced, vanished almost overnight.' The interviewer had pretended to take notes, but he had only been interested in hearing about the murders . . .

'How many companies do these Three Hundred people own altogether?' asked May.

'I haven't counted them all. I was endeavouring to do so when you tipped up. It's rather hard to keep track of.'

'Here, let me give you a hand.' May pulled up a stool and began glancing through the text.

'Fine,' said Bryant, fishing in a top pocket for his spectacles. 'My eyes aren't too good this morning. We arrived late at the Gaumont last night and had to sit right at the front; it nearly blinded me. Stay and help.' He grinned. 'We can send Biddle on all the horrible running-about jobs.'

The checking process took over an hour. After a while, Bryant grew irrationally annoyed that May was more proficient with the new teleprinter keyboard than he would ever be, and went off to scrounge a packet of tea from the station next door.

'So, how many have you found?' he asked when he returned.

'I should have guessed.' May gave him a meaningful look. 'Exactly three hundred.'

'They own *three hundred* companies? Are you sure?'

'Some of them are very small. There's one listed here in

Scarborough, a theatrical talent agency called Curtain Call Productions. I just rang them and spoke to the managing director. He was delighted to talk to me.'

'Could he tell you anything?'

'Only that Andreas Renalda, the big boss, lives here in London.'

'Handy. Ever hear of the Club of Rome? It's supposed to be an Anglo-American cabal of business managers and planners. It was first secretly assembled in the late nineteen twenties to form some kind of one-world government. That was based on something called the Three Hundred Club, which gets its title from a biblical passage, Romans, chapter three, verse three hundred. Just before the Great War, Germany's Jewish foreign minister announced that the economic future of the continent was in the hands of three hundred men who all knew each other. They're also called the Olympians, following on from the Illuminati and the Cathars. It's one of those paranoid theories that suggests a small elite group runs the financial empires of the world.'

'I wouldn't go looking for conspiracies where there are none,' May advised, reading through the printed addresses.

'You've got to agree it's a bit of a coincidence that the group controlling the theatre company should be named after them.'

'It's a coincidence that doesn't make any sense,' said May heatedly. He was beginning to see where Bryant was going with the idea. 'Why would the owner of such a company wish to kill the cast of a play that's costing him a fortune to stage?'

'That's the question, isn't it?' Bryant smiled annoyingly.

'Don't you think there are enough crazy rumours about Nazi infiltration in British business without us adding to them?'

'If any lesson from war is to be learned, John, it must be always to prepare for the unexpected and face the unthinkable. There is no orthodoxy to follow now. Everything is in a state of flux.'

As if to emphasize Bryant's warning, a pebble knocked sharply against the windowpane. When May peered down into the street he saw Betty Trammel looking up at him imploringly. 'Your lady sergeant won't let me in,' she explained. 'I told her I simply had to see you.'

One look at her darkly swollen eyes warned him that the stifling dream world of the Palace was taking its toll on those who depended on it.

31

THE STRENGTH OF DAMAGED SOULS

Arthur Bryant sat in the flesh-chilling gloom of the marble foyer and wondered whether he should tackle the receptionist again. He had been waiting to see Andreas Renalda for forty minutes, and no one had appeared. The reception room of Three Hundred International, Horseferry Road, Victoria, was a dingy mausoleum filled with paintings of continental lakes, their frames criss-crossed with strips of tape to prevent injury from flying glass. Filling the entire wall opposite was an immense Victorian bookcase, the contents of which appeared to have been chosen by the yard. He had heard about companies buying up the stock of bombed-out booksellers. It irritated him that they were being used merely to suggest erudition. Bryant was considering the problem when the receptionist received a call and beckoned to him.

'Please go to the fourth floor, Mr Bryant, and someone will meet you.'

The young detective straightened the knot of his tie in the lift mirror. It had been his partner's idea to interview the head of the theatre company. May made a good impression on strangers, whereas Bryant's interview technique managed to be both obtuse and hectoring. In an attempt to learn from his affable partner, Bryant had insisted on handling the appointment, and had scribbled out a scrappy list of questions a few minutes before setting out from Bow Street. He wasn't sure what he expected to find, but something told him it was best to start at the top.

John May had his hands full comforting his chorus girl, who had not yet recovered from her encounter in the theatre. Her lurid description of her assailant was exaggerated, no doubt, by an attack of blackout nerves and too much to drink. Bryant had suggested as much to May. He had not meant to sound callous; it was all too easy to joke about being scared nowadays. Everyone was scared. Nobody was given enough information. The newspapers were short of paper and short of news. Too many heart-warming stories about horses being dug out of collapsed stables and not enough analysis of the nation's long-term prospects. Perhaps that was the idea, Bryant decided; if people suspected the cold truth, they would give up right now.

Andreas Renalda's assistant was encased in a black wool dress and black stockings, and looked more like a theatrical performer than anyone he had met at the Palace. He was shown into a plush cream-shaded office overlooking a block of Edwardian apartments. It must seem odd, he thought, that pyjama-clad couples could find themselves separated from company executives by ten yards and two panes of glass.

'Peculiar, is it not?' came a strongly accented voice behind him. 'On my first day I arrived early and walked to the window to find a startled woman with no clothes on just a few feet away. Such a thing would never happen in my country. People have more respect for themselves.'

Bryant turned to face a stocky man in his mid-thirties with shoulder-length black hair and fierce dark eyes. As he set a lurching pace across the room, the detective realized that the man facing him was wearing steel calipers on both legs.

'I am Andreas Renalda.' The tycoon held out his hand. 'You must be Mr Bryant. Please take a seat. You will forgive me if I stand.'

Bryant tried to explain his look of surprise. 'I'm sorry to see you've been injured.'

'No, I was born this way. My legs are useless, but my brain is in perfect working order. So, you were expecting someone in good health and I was expecting someone older. Well, nothing lives up to expectations.'

'I assure you I meant no offence.'

'Of course you did not, and none has been taken.' Renalda waved aside the apology. 'I am at a loss to understand how I can help you, though.'

'I just wanted to learn a little about you,' said Bryant, shrugging with what he hoped was a look of healthy curiosity.

'There is nothing here to interest a policeman. The company belonged to my father, and he left a long shadow.' He gave a crooked smile, wagging his finger at Bryant. 'I have seen you before.'

'Oh? Where?'

'At the theatre. I am often there, watching the rehearsals.'

'Nobody told me.'

'That is because no one else knows. I do not want them to feel they should be on their best behaviour just because the man to whom they all owe their jobs is in the building.'

'Are you financing the entire production?' asked Bryant.

'One hundred per cent,' Renalda answered, leaning against the rear wall of the office in a position he presumably found comfortable. 'You have a particular question in mind?'

'What can you tell me about the Club of Rome?'

Renalda's smile cooled a little. 'Ah, that. Rather an embarrassment to us all. The Three Hundred.' He made a little gesture with his hand, as if to say, you understand. 'My father was not the most tolerant of men. For a while he kept an office in Berlin, and he created the name while it was there. We closed that branch in nineteen thirty-six. The company's history is rarely recounted with any accuracy.'

'Well, I'm a pretty attentive listener,' lied Bryant.

'We are Greeks, Mr Bryant. To be a success in Greece, you are connected with the sea. My father, Sirius, made his money in shipping. He understood the sea, and trusted no one but his immediate family. He had a son whom he considered worthless, and then his beloved wife gave birth to me. From the day I was born, I was chosen to run the business. Sirius was half blinded in the Boer War, but his handicap only made him fight harder. When he saw my withered legs, he took it as a sign that I would grow up to be a fighter too. He believed in the strength of those who were damaged, saw it as a test of man's nature. My father was very superstitious. Sirius never understood women, but he valued his wife enough to take her advice. I remember a conversation he once had with William Randolph Hearst. "Grant the women some of your power," Hearst said, "they will always surprise you." He did not say whether he regarded it as a good thing.'

'And your mother took over the running of the company when your father died?'

'She held the reins of power in his lifetime, and maintained them until I was strong enough to make decisions.' Renalda winced, shifting his balance from one steel scaffold to the other. The device that granted him mobility was also the source of great pain.

'Why did he not consider your older brother worthy of taking control?'

'Perhaps he saw too much of his younger self in him.'

'But after your father died, your mother presumably could have shared his empire with her other son?'

'I really do not see that this can have relevance to your problems, Mr Bryant.'

'They're your problems, too. Two people died in your theatre this week. I'm sure you appreciate that where the loss of human life is concerned, we have to expand our investigations into areas we would not normally enter.'

'Indeed. And on a personal level, I must insist that you include me in your list of suspects. After all, I was in the building when Mr Senechal was killed.'

'You weren't on my list.' Bryant hated being caught out. 'Nobody told me you were there.'

'I have my own key to the royal entrance. It's more private. If I attempt the stairs with these things,' he banged the side of his leg, 'I clank like a steam train. People can always hear me coming.'

Bryant picked up his hat and rose to leave. 'You realize I'll have to ask you to close down the theatre if anything else happens.'

'You must understand the scale of our undertaking, Mr Bryant. This is not some little play that can weather bad reviews and closure after a week. Global capital is invested in this production. *Orpheus* has been designed to run for years around the world, changing the financial stakes for future productions everywhere. It is a golden goose that will lay eggs for years, in spite of your archaic censorship laws. Shutting down the production is not an action I would be well disposed towards.'

'Perhaps not, but if I thought it would protect lives, I'd order it.'

'I think you will find yourself with an interesting battle on your hands.' Renalda displayed an alarming array of teeth. 'The days of the British owning everything on their terms is coming to an end. Future fortunes will be made with the involvement of international cartels such as ours.'

'I understand very little about the workings of the business world,' Bryant admitted, remembering his father in Petticoat Lane. 'What do you intend to do about Charles Senechal? You've lost a first-class baritone.'

'I am sorry for his family, but there are plenty of other good voices. I understand you wish to place an order restricting access to the theatre's backstage areas.'

'That's correct. From now on nobody comes in or leaves

without signing with my men. You'll appreciate that we need to know who is in the building at any time.'

'We have many people who need to hold meetings with Helena Parole and the production staff.' Renalda swung out his left leg and moved forward, standing free in the middle of the floor. The callipers gave his body a fragile sense of stability.

'Then they'll have to sign in with the front-of-house manager or be arrested.' Bryant stuck his hat on his head and tipped it back at a rakish angle. 'I've taken up too much of your time already.'

'If there is anything more that I can tell you, perhaps you will let me know?' Renalda's courteous smile closed over his teeth.

Bryant turned at the door and looked back across the room. This was Renalda's inner sanctum. Bare walls, glass coffee table, mahogany desk, cream blinds. No photographs, no plaques, no papers. Not a scrap of personality showed. There was damage in the family's history, enough to make a man hide his feelings. 'I'll make sure you're kept in the picture once our information has been verified.' He paused, thinking. 'Are you close to your mother, Mr Renalda?'

'My mother is dead, but yes, we were very close.'

'And I suppose your relationship with your brother—'

Renalda cut him off. 'I see no reason to provide you with further personal details unless you intend to charge me with an offence.'

'I'm sorry, I was thinking aloud, it's a bad habit.' He smiled, brushing his fringe back from his high forehead. 'I'll see myself out.'

'Mr Bryant.' Andreas Renalda swivelled to face him. 'I would prefer it if you would obtain all the information you need about my company directly from me in the future. It will save you telegraphing Zurich.'

Renalda was still smiling when he made the offer, but as he left the building Bryant couldn't help feeling that it had been a threat.

32

INFERNAL MORTALITY

For the next five decades, the two detectives made it their habit to walk along the south bank of the Thames around sunset, from the Houses of Parliament to Blackfriars, and if the weather was especially fine, all the way to Tower Bridge. After this the river grew too wide to cross as it made its way to the sea.

They argued about criminal psychology, endlessly revising their conclusions, but sometimes, when the sky was lower and the colours were drained from the Embankment buildings, they talked of women they had loved and lost, of plans made and abandoned, of outlandish ideas and unrealized dreams; often they just walked in comfortable silence, enjoying the lightness of air across the water, letting the sunlight fall on their faces.

On days like these they set each other questions about the city that, for all its faults – and there were an increasing number – they still liked best. Their second visit to the river took place on Thursday, 14 November 1940, and it was John May who came up with the first question, setting a course for years to come.

'Look at that.' May pointed to the damaged dome of St Paul's, fires smouldering behind it like the distant horizon of a forest. 'Still standing.'

'Only just,' said Bryant sadly. 'Most of the bookshops in Paternoster Row have been burned out. I spent many happy hours browsing there as a child.'

'I bet you don't know where you can see a second St Paul's Cathedral, a replica in miniature.'

'I do, as a matter of fact,' replied Bryant, who had dandified himself today with a silver-topped umbrella, a gift from his landlady. 'There's a big architectural model made of wood in St Paul's crypt.'

'I was thinking of another one,' said May with a grin. 'We've walked past it. Give up?'

'You've got me there, old bean.'

'It's held in the arms of one of the bronze female statues on Vauxhall Bridge.'

'Well, I never knew that.'

'I'll point it out to you next time.'

Bryant paused and looked out over the water, pretending to watch a boat, but May knew he had stopped to catch his breath. He had first noticed the problem when they had climbed the stairs together at the theatre. His partner had been panting with exertion by the time they reached the landing, and had made an effort to hide the fact. He charged about in a mad rush, refusing to give in to his heart.

'Two flamboyant deaths, the first without an audience, the second on stage before several people. Murders are prefaced by violence, John. They don't just come out of the blue. It makes no sense.'

'Does it have to make sense?' asked May kindly. 'Take Miss Capistrania. Whoever killed her must have wanted to humiliate her, carting off the feet like that. With Senechal, perhaps the killer just saw his chance and seized it.'

'Without a motive we have nothing. There can be no witness appeals, no knocking on doors, no one to pull in for questioning apart from the theatre staff and cast. The interviews I've dumped in Biddle's lap so far are among the most unedifying I've ever heard. We have a murderer acting in

freefall, panicking, not caring who he strikes. I hate not finding a pattern.'

'There is a bit of one, though,' said May.

'Well, I'm damned if I can spot it.'

'Have you not noticed? He has only attacked during air
raids. There was one around the time of Capistrania's death,
another just before the globe fell, and another last night,
when Miss Trammel frightened him away. Crowhurst took a
look around on the roof this morning while you were in
Victoria, and found absolutely nothing. Perhaps he can get
into the theatre only during blackouts, or when everyone is
off the street. Judging from Betty's description, people would
certainly notice him if he was walking about in broad
daylight.'

'You've a point there,' agreed Bryant. 'Was it windy late
last night?'

'I can't remember. I can easily check. Why?'

'Just an idea I had about our ghost who walks through
walls. Let's find some shelter, I don't like the look of those
clouds.'

The rain funnelled into iron gutters and rattled through
drainpipes. The sky had a bare, washed-out look, as though
the darkened world beneath it had been finally forsaken. The
café that stood beneath the brick railway arches of Waterloo
Bridge looked closed until they saw that the lights had been
turned low.

'When I was a child I used to believe that bad people
always acted for a reason. Now I'm starting to think criminal
behaviour is inexplicable,' said Bryant, disconsolately
stirring his tea. 'There have always been individuals who are
prone to murder. They're methodical, but not logical. Look
at Crippen, Wainwright, Seddon, Jack the Ripper, they
weren't driven by quantifiable needs but by aberrant
impulses. And now the world has become an irrational place.
That's why the Sherlock Holmes method of detection no
longer works; logic is fading. The value system we were

raised by in the thirties has little relevance. Beneath this stoic attitude of "business as usual" there is madness in the very air.'

'I don't know how you can think that.' May wiped a patch of window clear with his sleeve and watched the sheets of obscuring rain slide across the road like Japanese paper screens. 'Throughout history, human nature remains unchanged. The world's oldest questions are still being asked. Medea, Oedipus, we're not adding anything that the Greeks didn't already know. If you believe our knowledge has no relevance, why have you become a detective?'

'I thought I could be useful, so long as I could prove it to Davenport and the Home Office.' Bryant carefully set aside his teaspoon. 'You clearly have other interests apart from your work. I'm not sure I have anything else. I think about what's going on all about me until my brain feels as though it might rip itself apart.'

'Then you should find something else to concentrate on. If you imagine that without your job you have no purpose, you must find one.'

Bryant appeared not to have heard him. He absently tore at a Bath bun. 'Have you ever been to the Lower Marsh market in the middle of a workday morning? It's filled with old people. Half of them can barely walk, and so many are alone. It's like an English seaside town in winter. Everyone looks so cold and frail, as if death is already touching them. I wonder how they can be bothered to go on amid such devastation. It's a kind of courage, and I'm not sure I'd have it if I was in their shoes. When the war ends they'll have lost our generation again.'

'Oh, this is sheer morbidity. Don't spend all your time in the unit. Have you considered the option of regular sexual intercourse? I can't recommend it highly enough.'

'I'm no longer mentally equipped for spousal duties. My interests are too arcane. The Met boys all talk behind my back, you know. They think I'm obnoxious. They're waiting for our funding to be pulled away. They'll all have a good laugh then. I don't make friends.'

'Rubbish, Arthur. DS Forthright told me that you've made tons of friends, it's just that, well, you've befriended the kind of people nobody else talks to. Or even goes near.' He had heard about Bryant consulting the Deptford medium Edna Wagstaff and her flat full of stuffed tabby cats. 'In fact, from the sound of it you've made friends with people many others would cross the road to avoid.'

'You'll be able to adapt with the times, John. I'm already going in the opposite direction. At the age of seven I was reading Plato and Aristotle. By the time I was fifteen I had finished *A la recherche du temps perdu* in French. Academic enlightenment is a curse. It's certainly held me back with the fair sex. Forthright is the only woman I feel truly comfortable around these days, and that's because I tend to think of her as a man.'

'Maybe you should try a good nerve tonic.' May looked down at the brown Formica tabletop, resting his broad hands on the cool surface.

'I've tried them all. The unit is being given the difficult tasks to keep it out of the way. It's easier to separate out the problem cases than to explain to the Home Secretary why they aren't being investigated. We're a government expediency.'

'You think investigating murder is a waste of time?' asked May. 'Why, we could have great successes ahead if we learn to apply your ideas. All those listings in your contact files for spiritualists, clairvoyants, covens, cultists. Could they really be of use?'

'As much use as anyone so rational that they can eventually become a judge and sentence an innocent man to death. If we're going to run the unit together, you'll have to agree at least partially with my methods, otherwise you'll never sanction their use.'

'I already trust your instincts, Arthur, even if I don't understand you.'

'I don't believe in the innate goodness of people any more, John, if I ever did to begin with. Are you a Christian?'

'I was raised as one. I'm not sure what to believe now. I know you've got a theory about the theatre. Why don't you tell me?'

Bryant looked as if he was about to, then changed his mind. 'It's hard to explain. I think we're being presented with a challenge. I keep coming back to the Greek gods, the capricious ways they exacted revenge on mortals. We've been chosen to make certain that something happens, but I'm not sure what. There's a Greek god on the roof of the Palace, did you notice? Right at the pinnacle, a fragile-looking thing, still in one piece despite the bombing. I wonder they don't remove it. I can't place who it is, but there's something very odd about it. I believe somebody's playing a cruel game.'

'To what end?'

'I'm not yet sure. To spark an investigation into the workings of Three Hundred International, or to decimate the theatre company. Or perhaps the killer simply can't help himself. What is it that guides his murderous impulses? How can we know?'

'There are plenty of practical steps we can take,' offered May. 'Start by tightening security, putting men in the building round the clock. We need to be firmer with Stan Lowe, the stage door chap. Will he take notice of us, do you think?'

'He should do. They all should. I mean, we have government authorization, and you're over six foot.' Bryant bucked up. 'I suppose I'd better talk to Davenport about bringing in officers from another division. When I joined the unit I was promised a staff of twenty. We're down to half a dozen, and two of those are constables.'

'Let's finish the interviews so that Biddle can see if there's anything anomalous in their stories. Runcorn and Finch can liaise with Lambeth and pull in results from the rest of the forensic samples. We have to locate every entry point in the building to prove that nobody entered the theatre immediately before Senechal's death.'

Bryant dug a florin out of his coat pocket and placed it on the table. He admired the way in which May came up with plans, making everything sound ordered and rational.

'So, what did you make of the managing director of the Three Hundred?' asked May once they were outside.

'I found him rather intimidating.' Bryant unfurled his umbrella and raised it. 'I wouldn't like to be his enemy. But he does have a certain menacing charm.'

'What do you mean?'

'I don't know. There's something odd about him. I'd like to dig up some more on his background. Of course it'll be hopeless trying to get information out of Greece, but an old chum of my uncle's spent a couple of years in Athens as a correspondent for *The Times*. I'll give him a call. Are you around for a drink tonight?'

May looked at his watch. 'I'm sorry, Arthur, I can't tonight. I'm seeing Betty again. She was a bit shaken up, and doesn't want to spend another evening in the theatre.'

'Oh, right.' He sniffed and looked out at the water as they recrossed the bridge. 'Well, I should go back to the Palace, give Lowe a talking-to.'

'You don't have to,' said May, feeling guilty. 'Look here, you're welcome to join us tonight.'

'No, it's fine. I have my notes to catch up on, anyway.'

May watched as Bryant turned away and walked back along the Embankment, ducking beneath his umbrella as he skirted the stippled puddles. He would always see him like this, walking ahead, walking alone.

33

AS BAD AS EACH OTHER

Always ahead, always alone, thought May. If only I'd been friendlier from the outset . . .

He returned his attention to the retired pathologist.

'I haven't finished yet. I'm eighty-four,' continued Oswald Finch. 'I'm slowing down. When you get to be this old, it seems like everyone else is on rollerblades.'

'I appreciate that, Oswald,' May insisted, 'but you must have removed most of the intact material by now.'

'Oh, we've removed it from the building, all right. Not that it's my job, you understand. I'm just here because, well, I have an interest in finding out what happened.' He pushed open the door of the evidence room. 'Nobody's had a chance to go through it all.' In front of Longbright and May were around thirty large clear plastic bags filled with chunks of charred wood, blackened files, sticks of furniture, bricks, pieces of broken glass and twisted metal.

'This is all that's left of the unit?'

'Pretty much so.' Finch lowered himself into a chair and grimaced. 'Stinks, doesn't it? Wouldn't be surprised if there were still bits of Bryant in there.'

May ignored his remark. The pair of them had never really got on. Even so, he was surprised and rather touched to find

214

Finch in the building. 'Did you find any of our office equipment in one piece?'

'Not actually in one piece, but there are surviving chunks that were shielded by closed doors. Raymond Land thinks the explosion was caused by old hand-grenades, you know. Something about cordite striation patterns.'

'Surely grenades couldn't have done so much damage?'

'Well, they weren't all the same size, some were more powerful than others. The Mills grenade was really a small-barrelled missile containing up to three ounces of amatol. Modern blast sites smell different because they use more sophisticated chemical compounds. This was pure stuff. We found powder burns on the walls. The remains of your photocopier should be over there somewhere.' Finch pointed into a corner, and May and Longbright clambered across the bags in that direction.

'He was always playing tricks on me, you know,' called Finch as they went through the bags. 'Gluing my furniture to the ceiling, putting fleas in my briefcase, weeing into my rain gauges, getting my keys recut so that they only fitted the ladies' loo, replacing the fish in my tank with piranhas. Remember the tropical plant that made us all sick? A tarantula fell out of it and bit my wife. He had a very strange sense of humour. I suppose I'll miss him.'

'Over here.' May unzipped the top of a sack and peered in. 'This looks like it.'

'Let me give you a hand.' Longbright was as strong as her mother had been. Together they lifted out the buckled grey panels of the photocopier and set them on the floor. The quarter-inch plate-glass square was cracked, but had not shattered. Unfortunately, the plastic lid had melted tightly over the top of it, like Cheddar on a piece of toast.

'Give me your penknife.' May took the Swiss blade from Longbright and inserted it into a corner of the lid.

'You're tampering with evidence,' complained Finch, turning his chair round. 'I'm not a part of this, I'm not looking.'

He couldn't stop himself from glancing over his shoulder. 'Aaah, you're not even wearing plastics, you're as bad as Bryant.'

May sawed the blade through the melted cover and gingerly pulled it away from the glass sheet. There beneath the cover was a single scorched sheet of paper. With the tips of his fingers he lifted it away from the glass.

'Looks like we've got it,' he told Longbright, grinning.

'You're not taking evidence away, it's illegal,' cried Finch. 'Sixty years I've had to put up with this kind of behaviour. Why me?'

'Oh, stop moaning, Oswald, you can just pretend you never saw us,' said Longbright.

'You're on the CCTV, I'm not going to lie for you and risk my job.'

'You're eighty-four, this is no time to worry about being passed over for promotion.' Longbright rose and carried the sheet to a bench by one of the side sinks. 'This is odd,' she said, after examining the scorched page for a minute. 'It's got Arthur's notes scribbled in the margins, but it's not a list at all.'

'What is it?' asked May.

'I think it's an architectural plan,' she said finally. 'Look at the stamp on the bottom. "Palace Theatre Revised Edition September 19 . . ." Can't read the rest of the date.'

'He must have taken it from the archive room when he went back to the Palace. Then what did he do with the list of patients from the Wetherby clinic?'

'Maybe it was of no use, and he threw it away. He told you he'd been to the theatre, so he was either looking for this, or stumbled across it while he was researching his memoirs.'

'But what is it?'

'Dunno,' Longbright admitted. 'Oswald, is there a light-box anywhere?'

They laid the scorched sheet on a fluorescent panel and May studied it. 'Looks like a layout of two long corridors, bisecting at one end. These shadings ... the wall cross-sections look completely circular. What's he written down the side?'

'Looks like a circumference measurement. You wouldn't normally build a corridor with round walls, would you?'

'I wonder if it could be part of a theatrical set design. It would help to have a complete date. The Palace might keep records of the struck sets.'

'We could check it against them,' said Longbright. 'That's what Bryant would have done.'

'We don't know what he was looking for. Anyway, I have a better idea.' May dug out his mobile. 'Arthur had an architect friend called Beaufort. I think we should get an expert opinion.'

'Wait a minute, you're not leaving here with evidence,' warned Finch, barring the door.

'Don't be daft, Oswald. No one will know unless you tell them.' May moved him gently aside.

'What you're doing is illegal,' Finch called as they left with the evidence. 'You're both as bad as him, you realize that, don't you?'

34

JUNO'S SON

It was still raining hard in Charing Cross Road. The deluge vibrated across the roof of the auditorium. Somewhere, water was dripping onto metal, like the beat of a drum. It was impossible to keep the weather out of a theatre as old as the Palace. There wasn't a Victorian building in London that didn't have a damp patch somewhere, and the cracks caused by the continuous bombing made it worse.

Stan Lowe and PC Crowhurst sat inside the Greek Street stage door, at the rear of the theatre, watching the rain fall. Spatters of water leaked over a handwritten sign that Bryant had made Lowe place on the wall. It read: 'NO VISITORS AFTER HALF-HOUR CALL OR DURING SHOW. DO NOT LEAVE THIS DOOR OPEN FOR ANYONE YOU DO NOT RECOGNIZE.'

For the first few weeks of the Blitz Stan Lowe had allowed the well-protected stage door area to be used as a first-aid post, but now he had been forced to add chains and a padlock. Most of the cast, orchestra and backstage crew had been signed in for the technical run-through. Crowhurst had taken names and addresses from everyone. He had heard the same piece of music, something Jack referred to as the 'Sleeping Chorus', echo through the backstage areas over a dozen times now, and was growing mightily sick of it.

'I suppose you know there's a ghost,' said Stan matter-of-factly, knocking out his pipe on the emulsioned brick wall at his back. 'You ain't got any tobacco to spare, have you?'

PC Crowhurst poked about in his jacket and produced a half-ounce of St Bruno Flake. 'You can have that and welcome,' he said. 'What sort of ghost? Not Dan Leno?'

'No, he haunts Drury Lane. Only time Leno's ever appeared here is in a newsreel.' He pushed a wad of tobacco into his pipe and returned the packet with a nod. 'This is some old Shakespearean actor. You know them bleeding great china dogs on the stair landing? They was his. This old cove was playing Polonius, and he gets to the arras scene, only the Dane's sword is missing its button, see, and when 'Amlet runs him through, he really runs him through, only nobody realizes because he's behind the bleeding curtain, isn't he, so they play out the rest of the scene, and it's only when he's supposed to get off the stage that they notices. Well, a'course by that time it's too late to do anything for the poor old bugger, so every time there's a new play coming on, he turns up as Polonius in a bloodstained doublet and hose, wandering about backstage putting the willies up the carpenters.'

PC Crowhurst looked sceptical. 'Miss Trammel says he looked deformed, like he'd done something terrible to his face,' he pointed out. 'She said it was like a mask of tragedy, you know, like a Greek mask. She was in a right state this morning.'

'His face was contorted 'cos he'd been run through with a bleedin' epinard,' said Lowe sagely. 'Actresses suffer with their nerves. That's why so many of 'em take to the drink.' He flicked out a match and drew hard on the pipe. 'Anyway, he was a bleedin' awful Polonius. I could shit a better lecture to Laertes than that.'

Onstage it was the beginning of act two, and the gods slumbered on Mount Olympus. Venus, Mars, Cupid and the chorus went through their paces, but there was no Jupiter. Geoffrey Whittaker, the stage manager, was on the company office telephone trying to organize transport to collect their new head of Olympus, who was stuck on the wrong side of a bombed railway line in East London.

Helena was tired and irritable. She wanted a break and needed a whisky, but Harry and Elspeth were tailing her around the building to make sure that she didn't find a way of breaking her contract. The technical run-through was necessary at this point because an unusual amount of scenery had to be flown through the tableaux, and Mouse, Stan Lowe's boy, had been appointed to transcribe the complex stage manoeuvres in a movement programme as they progressed.

It didn't help that the performers were having to work around a central hole in the production. Few of the cast had known Charles Senechal very well, but his absence was acutely felt. The understudy baritone had been approved and cast at the same time as Senechal's appointment, but he didn't have the diction quality Helena required for the recitative passages, so she was anxious to give him extra coaching. Senechal's wife and child were holed up in a quiet Holland Park hotel, and had been visited by Andreas Renalda, who had dispensed with pleasantries and instructed the distraught woman not to talk to journalists. Luckily for him she spoke little English, and her interpreter was employed by the company.

With the arrival of the auditor, the company secretary and the treasurer's wife, Stan Lowe gave up trying to keep the area restricted. Happily, Helena remained professional. She'd coped with ranting producers, cheating financiers and lying managers, compared to which the gripes of cast members who found their dressing rooms too far away or their fellow performers impossible to deal with were frankly small potatoes. But, God, she wanted a drink.

* * *

Rachel Saperstein was just starting to cope with the idea of her son's success. She was proud of him, even though the Saperstein family name was apparently not good enough for Miles any more. She had been up to the apartment the company had rented for him, and had found the meat safe in his scullery completely empty except for a bottle of vodka, which would only ruin his stomach in later life. Now she was seated at the front of the upper circle, watching him perform on the London stage, and her heart swelled with pride as he sang each note.

In the balcony of the theatre, above her, a young man named Zachary Darvell fidgeted in his seat and refined the tip of his hand-rolled cigarette with finger and thumb. 'Of course I'm proud of her,' he whispered across the seats. 'I couldn't do what she does, night after night. Trouble is, she doesn't think I can do anything.'

'So where's your father?' asked his best friend Larry.

'He buggered off ages ago. He was selling defence bonds until the war started, and now he's a black marketeer. She rehearses all the time, so they were never together. I saw more of the baby-sitter than either of my parents.'

'Lucky boy.'

'Yes, it was pretty damned good.' He held sharp smoke in his lungs, then exhaled. 'Have the rest of this, I know you're down to your last Woodie. Try not to cough, I don't want her looking up and seeing me.'

'What do you care?' asked Larry, accepting the cigarette.

'If she sees me up here she'll throw a tantrum. Especially if she finds me with you.' Zachary was supposed to be in medical college, but he and Larry had cut classes, not that there were many to cut at the moment. Every student with the ability to hold a scalpel had been seconded to the local hospital unit, where their tasks largely consisted of helping to clean up bodies. Sometimes identifying marks had been so neatly blown off that the only way to tell if the victims were male or female was to check for a sciatic notch. Everyone

221

smoked because it was the only way to get rid of the smell of dead bodies. Today the students had decided to hang out in the West End, cooling their heels on counter stools in a few bars, looking out of the windows, watching stockingless girls in tight business skirts dart through the rain.

Larry had asked where Zachary's mother worked, and Zachary had suggested going to see her. He wanted to show Larry how he could breeze into a major theatre and be recognized. The pair had gone up to the balcony, standing at the rear, so close to the top of the building that you could hear the rain. Now they were sitting in its front row, smoking and watching. Below them, Barbara Darvell, soprano, wife of Jupiter, waited for her cue as a pair of stage-hands struggled hopelessly with a prop cloud.

'Must be peculiar, always being in buildings with no windows,' said Larry, drawing on the last inch of the cigarette. 'No night or day. You can't even hear the traffic outside. At least there's more room than in the shelters. I don't know how people can be bothered to go down there. All those mewling infants. You've just as much of a chance staying under your stairs.'

'My mother used to say that fire engines were the curse of the performer,' said Zachary. 'Now she's had to add dog-fights, bombs and sirens to her list of interruptions. She goes all over the world, but I don't think she sees much outside because she's either rehearsing or performing.'

'Strange job.' Larry checked his watch. 'Let's go.'

'You haven't heard her sing yet.'

'I know what opera singers sound like, it's unbelievably horrible, no offence to your dear mama. Come on.'

'I just want to stay until she does her piece.' Zachary didn't want to make a grand thing out of it, and tried to sound offhand. 'I'll catch you up. Go over to the Spice and order me a gin and French. I'll meet you in the saloon bar.' He watched in annoyance as Larry threaded his way along the steep row to the exit. Back onstage, Juno rose to join in at the end of Mercury's song, but the sight of her was obscured by a gauze-covered purple cloud.

Zachary pushed the seat back up and stood in the shadowed aisle at the front of the balcony. He wanted her to know he was there, but the idea embarrassed him. His mother preferred the company of her own friends, theatricals who talked endlessly about themselves to the exclusion of everyone else, behaving as if nobody else was worth a damn. He would come home to their overheated house in Chiswick and find the place filled with thespians slugging her whisky and getting excited about Euripides. Surely it was meant to be the other way round, with her accusing his friends of being layabouts? In a few months' time he would be able to get to the front, then perhaps she would take notice of him.

Below, Juno was singing about making room for Mercury, a bouncy song but not exactly Henry Hall, and if Zachary leaned forward he could see his mother rolling her eyes at the rest of the cast and overacting wildly, except that it was an operetta so nobody seemed to mind.

Miles Stone's mother thought the woman was overacting too. Why didn't the director do something about it? It wasn't fair that she couldn't sit in the stalls. She had been told not to, because onlookers in the sightlines put the actors off. Juno was still shrieking away and waving her arms about like a demented windmill. Rachel felt like going down to the stage and giving her a slap. She was putting her son off his stride, anyone could see that. Rachel squinted back into the seats behind her, to see if anyone else had noticed, and her eye caught a glint of sharp light from the balcony above her head.

Zachary heard a sound behind him, a seat creaking, and turned as the occupant rose. At first he thought Larry had returned. Then he saw the hulking, twisted figure. The poor chap was deformed, and was trying to speak. His face was like something from an amusement-park mirror, a badly made-up villain from a melodrama. A terrible face, like one

223

of the demons from the production below, hideously brought to life. Big hands, young hands.

'What's the matter? How can I—'

Zachary was going to ask him who he was. He wasn't afraid, until he saw the slim shine of the cut-throat razor as it folded open. Then he jumped back. He raised his hands in protest when the blade flew past. For a moment nothing happened. Then the skin of his palms split like opening eyes. By now the razor was returning at a higher level, passing his left cheek, the bridge of his nose, slicing flesh and muscle and bone, stinging across his throat, cutting deeper at his thyroid cartilage. Other red mouths were opening all over his face and neck. He could not see. A thick caul of blood dropped over his eyes, obscuring his vision. The hand darted forward again, and Zachary felt a far more terrible pain at his throat. A three-pronged fork had been pushed into his windpipe, sealing it. He stumbled forward but was pushed back, over the step, and over the low wall of the balcony.

Miles Stone had half expected Rachel to turn up at the theatre, but he hadn't counted on seeing her seated at the front of the upper circle watching his every move. It was enough to put him off his stride. They were halfway through the technical and Juno was upstaging him all over the place, and there was nothing he could do but ignore her and go on with his lines. Eve was watching from the wings. She knew that his mother was coming to town, although she had no idea that he had slept with Becky as recently as his Carnegie gala night in New York three weeks ago. It made sense for Miles to keep his mother and his new girlfriend apart – they would either be instant enemies or, worse still, form an alliance against him.

Stone could see his mother fidgeting in her seat. It didn't help that she was wearing a preposterous hat. He tried to ignore her and carry on with his recitative, but from the corner of his eye he saw her twist round and look up. She didn't appear to be watching the stage at all. Was it a criticism of his performance? He glanced back at Juno and realized that she had followed his glance to the upper circle. As he waited for the technicians to clip the cloud scrim back on its rollers, he looked over at his mother once more. She was still turned away from the stage. He was so intent on watching her that he missed his cue.

'Miles, when you're absolutely ready,' called Helena. 'I appreciate it's been a long day but I hate to keep everyone waiting longer than necessary.'

'Of course, sorry.' They had cut Eurydice's scene with Jupiter at the end of the third tableau and had skipped to the flight from Hell, but Public Opinion's rowing boat was now stuck in the flies, and the orchestra seemed confused about their entry point.

Between the late arrival of two woodwinds and the total disappearance of Jupiter, who had been replaced in the run-through with a hobby horse tipped on its end, Anton Varisich was close to walking out. The sudden noise in the balcony made the conductor cut his orchestra off in mid-note, although someone had trouble stopping, because there was a piercing howl from one of the instruments. For a moment he thought that somebody had thoughtlessly banged the seats up again, and in an afternoon of stops and starts, Varisich's legendary temper was about to make itself felt.

'*Miss* Parole,' he called to Helena, referring to her so formally that it showed disrespect, 'would you be so good as to join me at the podium for a moment?'

Helena Parole allowed a beat of defiance to pass before complying with the conductor's request, then made her way to the side of the stage. She had worked with Varisich before and had survived his angry outbursts often enough to know that he was relatively easy to mollify. It was a matter of letting him see that she appreciated the subordination of the stage performance to the music. Text was updated and retranslated at regular intervals, but the music remained sacrosanct. So long as she respected this rule, they would work well together. She tried to imagine a tall glass filled with Glenfiddich, and donned her most quenching smile. Varisich was going to complain about the presence of outsiders at the run-through, and about the levels of noise they were creating, but now somebody was yelling. On stage, several members of the chorus were pointing into the centre of the building.

It wasn't until they ran towards the screaming woman in Row A of the upper circle that they looked up and saw the man, now a twisting, bloody blur, flail and fall from the edge of the balcony.

MANIFESTATION OF GUILT

Zachary Darvell's nose had been pushed into his skull by the fall. His face was a crimson mask. The segmented flesh was efflorescing with bulbous bruises, pink jelly the colour of an infected gum protruding through slashed skin. His jawbone was exposed in a shockingly severe white line. The iron fork was sticking out of his gullet. He looked like a prop demon removed from the set after a particularly arduous run. His left arm hung at an unnatural angle to his body. There was a member of the St John's Ambulance Brigade in attendance, uselessly armed with a tin box full of crêpe bandages, calamine lotion and smelling salts. Barbara Darvell had rushed up from the stage and was cradling her son's head.

'What happened?' asked Bryant, who had just entered the auditorium in time to hear Juno's son plummet noisily from the balcony.

'He's dead.' Barbara Darvell swallowed thickly. 'I looked up and saw him. He had his back to me. Someone was standing behind him. A tall man. I could see his arms moving. I couldn't make sense of it from where I was.' She pointed feebly down at the illuminated set of Hades. Droplets of blood had spattered the artificial carnation that still stuck from Zachary's jacket lapel.

'What's that?' Bryant pointed to the fork handle protruding from Darvell's throat.

'Aristaeus' fork. It went missing from the prop box.'

'I've just been up in the balcony. It's deserted.' Geoffrey Whittaker dropped to his knees and tried to catch his breath. 'Let's get everyone back to their dressing rooms for a few minutes,' he suggested. 'There was no one else up there, no one at all.'

'How do you know?' yelled Barbara Darvell. 'How could you look everywhere? We can't see in this damned gloom!'

'I was in the stairwell and ran in,' Geoffrey explained.

'I certainly didn't see you,' said Harry.

The assistant's remark took Whittaker by surprise. 'What are you saying?'

'Just that I know who was in the stairwell and you weren't there.'

Whittaker was angered by the idea of having to defend himself. 'If you must know, I'd gone upstairs to get something from my office, and stood at the back of the balcony for a moment. Mr Darvell was sitting in the front row by himself. I left the auditorium and was coming back down the central staircase when I heard a shout and a crash from the floor below. Then I ran down to him. He only just missed landing on that lady over there.' He pointed at Miles Stone's shocked mother.

'He landed a seat away,' gasped Rachel. 'I nearly died.'

'Then the person who pushed Mr Darvell must have passed you on the staircase,' Harry insisted.

'No one passed me.'

'I don't see how you could have missed him, Geoffrey.'

'My son is dead, could you show some restraint?' cried Barbara Darvell.

'Perhaps we should leave the matter until the police have finished searching the building,' Harry suggested.

'You can manage here, can't you?' Bryant strode along the row of seats and raced down the stairs to the stage door. There he found Lowe and Crowhurst looking puzzled.

'Has anyone left in the last few minutes?' he asked, trying to get his breath back.

'No, sir. Only the gentleman Mrs Darvell's son came in with. What's going on?'

'There's been another one,' Bryant explained. 'You'll let me know if anyone tries to leave?'

'Of course, sir, I – hang on, that's the royal entrance.' Beyond them came the muffled slam of a door.

Bryant stuck his head out into the street and saw a broad figure in a shiny black raincoat divorce himself from the shadow of the royal entrance. He turned and saw John May walking from the other direction, towards the stage door.

'John!' he shouted. 'That's our man! Stop him!'

The dark figure started and broke into a run, instantly followed by May. Night had fallen and the blackout was once more in full force. Shaftesbury Avenue, blurred and smeary with rain, was almost deserted as they turned into it.

I've got him, thought May, watching the figure ahead as it hit a thicket of parked motorcycles belonging to the army despatch riders. There was something round the man's neck, a raised collar or hood that obscured his head. He looked to be around six feet tall, but in the gloomy drizzle of the early evening it was hard to make out any further detail. To May's horror, the raincoated figure vaulted the first motorbike and landed hard on the kick-start, firing up the engine. The army engineers kept their Matchless bikes in racks beside the road, ready to take them to emergencies. May grabbed the nearest machine and mounted it. He knew how to ride, but with the lights of London extinguished and the roads wet, he wasn't sure whether he would be able to give chase. The engine barked into life on first kick, and he released the handlebar valve lift as he took off, slamming into the road so closely behind his quarry that their wheels almost touched.

The motorcycle in front fishtailed sharply and skittered across the oncoming traffic in the direction of Piccadilly

Circus. May felt his back wheel slip as he followed, and was able to keep the bike upright only by hammering his boot along the tarmac and forcing the machine into a vertical position. He concentrated on the black square of the numberplate in front, LR109. The figure hunched low as he throttled up, the engine's roar deepening as he passed between a pair of unlit taxis. May forged ahead too, trying to draw alongside, but the bike was pushing beyond a safe speed. They passed the side of the London Pavilion and the darkened cinema opposite, hitting the Circus traffic at such speed that buses were forced to brake and swerve. The electric advertising hoardings that had become such an area landmark were extinguished, lending the buildings a drab, derelict air. LR109 cut the wrong way round the boarded-over fountain and shot into Piccadilly with May in pursuit. A policeman, visible only by the white stripes on his cuffs, raised his hands and ran towards them, then backed off when he saw that neither bike was going to stop. The sound of his whistle was quickly lost as the pair raced on past the Royal Academy into oncoming traffic.

Bryant's going to kill me if I don't catch him, thought May as he accelerated. The young detective felt chill rain pitting his face as the wheels lost their purchase on the slippery road, found it again and pushed him on. The buildings on either side were great grey blocks, no light showing anywhere. Ahead, just beyond Green Park, a bomb had heavily cratered the middle of the road, and rubble-removal trucks indistinctly lined its edges. As they came closer, May saw that the entire causeway was cordoned off. He can't get through, he told himself, watching in disbelief as LR109 pounded up over the kerb and into the long portico under the Ritz. May felt the kerb slam his tyres as he followed, the back wheel juddering as he shot beneath the arches, his engine reverberating in the tunnel as he scattered the shrieking evening-gowned women who were exiting the hotel.

At the end of the colonnade, the bike in front swung

sharply to the right off the main road and thundered into the maze of narrow streets that constituted Mayfair. May tried to close the gap between them, but was forced to slow in order to turn the heavy machine. He could hear LR109 revving and braking, but caught only glimpses of its brake light as the machine raced ahead of him. At Curzon Street the lead bike was forced to slow as pedestrians ran for safety, and May gained a few yards. As they turned into the dark chasm of Bruton Street, the detective saw the thick brown earth and bricks strewn across the road, and knew that his tyres would not cope with them. The other bike had bypassed the mess by mounting the pavement. He hit hard, the Matchless's handles jumping out of his hands as the machine jerked from his control. He knew that if it went over now it would trap his leg beneath the engine, and forced himself to roll backwards, leaving the bike seconds before it toppled and slid along the street in a shower of sparks, to vanish over the side of an unfilled pit.

Bryant ran round to the foyer and checked on the FOH box office. He doubted that May would be able to track their man for long in the blackout. Elspeth was almost asleep when he knocked on the glass, startling her so badly that she nearly fell off her stool.

'Did you see him come past here?'

'No, no one's been through.' She straightened her cardigan, embarrassed. 'I'm afraid I was having forty winks. The phones are down. Seamus told me they've found an unexploded bomb across the road and the Heavy Rescue people have severed a line getting to it.'

'Who's Seamus?'

'Our milkman. He was dropping off some rhubarb from his allotment.' She held up a paper bag full of purple stalks. 'I said it would be nice to see a banana again but there are limits to his powers.' She patted a stray lock of hair into place and smiled vaguely. By the entrance doors, a heavyset woman in a pinafore rose from her mop bucket and came over to the detective.

'Did you just wake her up? Poor lady was trying to have a rest.'

'She's been here with you?'

'All the time. You're one of them detectives, ain't you?' she asked. 'Several of the chorus girls are talking about a phantom roaming the theatre, have you heard? Apparently it's got hands like claws and eyes that glow red in the dark. And Miss Betts said it followed her up Tottenham Court Road, wearing a mask.'

'I need to use your phone,' said Bryant.

'I just told you, the lines are cut. And you don't want to listen to her silly gossip,' warned Elspeth, raising the tone of her voice by half a social caste. 'Actresses get such first-night nerves, it always shows itself in silly stories.'

'Where's the nearest call box?' asked Bryant.

'That'll be the other side of Cambridge Circus. Oh, it's quite the norm, lurid imaginations working overtime. During the rehearsals for *No, No, Nanette* one of the saxophonists dropped dead, and rumours went around that he'd been cursed by Negroes because he played late-night sessions in a jazz club and owed them some money. People get such funny ideas.'

'Yes,' agreed Bryant uncertainly, heading for the door. He nodded to the cleaner. 'If you hear any more talk about a Palace phantom, you'll let me know, won't you?'

'He'll be back,' she said cheerfully. 'Not that he worries me. I've got nothing to fear.'

'Oh? Why not?'

'He's not real,' the char explained, hitching up her bolstered bosom. 'It's just guilt. These young girls, they're a bit loose, a bit wild, living for the moment, running around with boys and getting up to God knows what in the dark. Extroverts and introverts, it's all in their collective unconscious, a manifestation of guilt, if you ask me.'

'Well, your manifestation of guilt just killed someone with a cut-throat razor,' he snapped.

Bryant had not expected an earful of Jungian theory from the charlady. He stepped carefully over the wet marble and stood on the step outside, looking up at the sky. A pall of brown smoke hung over the buildings to the east, most likely dust from building clearance. The clouds were starting to break now, giving the bombers a clear path into the city. He wondered what terrors the night would bring this time.

Poking the last of his tobacco into his pipe, Bryant headed off in the direction of the phone box, a theory shifting uneasily at the back of his brain. The globe, the compass, the flute, the wind, the mask of tragedy, the statue on the roof of the theatre, Stone's mother, the flower in Darvell's lapel, things he could not make sense of without sounding deranged.

If he was wrong, it would not just be the finish of a promising career, it would end the credibility of the unit for good.

36

THE BROADER PICTURE

'What on earth happened to you?' asked Bryant. His partner was covered in streaks of mud, his jacket torn from shoulder to waist.

'Came a bit of a cropper on an army motorbike,' May explained, examining himself. 'Our man moved like a bat out of Hell. I lost him in the back streets, didn't Biddle tell you?'

'He said you stole an army emergency vehicle and smashed it up. Don't worry, I'll square it with them later. Are you all right?'

'Took the skin off my hands, no real damage. What are you doing?'

Bryant was standing on an upended metal milk crate in the car park of Bow Street magistrates' court, preparing to throw a muslin-wrapped leg of pork onto an iron sheet that was balanced on a pile of masonry rubble. 'I'm testing out a theory,' he explained, swinging the leg and letting it go. 'Bloke fell out of the balcony. I suppose they told you. Slashed to bits with a straight razor. Not one of the cast, though.' He climbed down from the crate and bent over the joint of meat, which had landed squarely on the metal sheet. 'It's all right, condemned black-market pork, quite inedible, but it's about the same weight.'

'As what?' asked May, bemused.

'As a pair of feet, obviously.' Bryant threw him an old-fashioned look as he hoisted the leg for another swing.

May had no time for such foolishness tonight. He was starting to wonder if his partner was all there. 'Mr Davenport's waiting for us in your office,' he warned. 'At least, I assume it's him.'

'Raw-boned, red-faced man, tufts of grey hair coming out of his ears, staring eyes, lots of broken veins in his nose, reeks of chewing tobacco?'

'That's the one. I hope he doesn't see your plant.'

'What plant?' asked Bryant, his eyes widening in innocence.

'Don't pretend you don't know. That one with the serrated leaves. Chinamen dry them out and smoke them. Reefers. Used by Limehouse dope fiends.'

'Are you accusing me of being a dope fiend? Actually, it's an old herbal remedy.'

'Well, I've hidden it under your desk just in case.'

'Thanks, old man.' Bryant grinned. 'You're a sport.'

Farley Davenport stared with distaste at the mouldering Tibetan skull surrounded by African juju charms that inhabited Bryant's bookcase. 'Perhaps one of you can explain what's going on at the Palace Theatre? Someone just wrote off an army bike, another one is still missing.'

'Mr May here was in pursuit of our murderer. We're lucky he's still with us. I've asked for an apprehension on the other number plate.'

'Who was this bloke who died?'

'He shouldn't have been allowed inside the building,' Bryant explained, in that way he had of not answering the right question. 'I requested an access restriction, but the company's director overruled me.'

Davenport was finding it hard to make the detectives understand why he was so angry with them. He ran his hands through his thinning grey hair and made a frightening face. 'I asked for all visitors to be signed in and out. That should have been enough.'

'That's exactly what we did,' said Bryant, 'but somebody still got hurt. We shouldn't have been allowing any visitors in at all. There are people wandering about all over the place. It's like Hyde Park on a bank holiday in there.'

Davenport grunted with disapproval. 'I had a phone call from some mad harpy named Parole, typical bloody show-business type, complaining to me about areas of the theatre staying shut. She couldn't seem to tell the difference between a real-life murder and a staged drama.'

'I'm sorry, sir. I told her we needed exclusive access to certain areas for forensic examination, but she refused point blank to close off the rest of the building. Apparently it's beyond her control because there are two separate companies involved, hers and the management who own the theatre.'

'This bloody war is giving everyone an excuse to defy the law.' Davenport's nose looked redder than ever. 'I tell you, when it's over all these women will go back to being bloody housewives and we'll be able to get on with running the nation again.'

'Miss Parole answers to a board that's determined not to allow anything to hamper the production.'

'It's going to be hampered a bloody sight more when Westminster shuts it down,' snapped Davenport. 'If this had happened in peacetime the building would have been cleared without question. Good Lord, three people dead, ghostly sightings and what have you, people frightening one another with stories about phantoms that walk through walls. It's the Palace Theatre, not Borley Rectory. Do you want to tell me how it happened?'

'I'd like to, sir, but we're not sure ourselves. Mr Darvell, the boy who was attacked in the balcony, is the son of a member of the cast. He and a friend were watching the run-through. The friend left, Darvell was seen to stand up at the front and turn his back to the stage, he was cut and fell over the parapet. It's a low rail, and the floor slopes steeply. The fall broke his nose, his jaw and his collarbone, he lost too much blood and died. The person he nearly landed on, Miles Stone's mother, glimpsed his attacker from below, and what she saw matches the description of the man Miss Trammell gave last night. This is the man who got away on the stolen bike.'

'What a bloody nightmare. It wasn't Darvell's friend?'

'He was already in the pub when it happened.'

'I suppose you know that the press has got the story now.'

'We kept it back as long as we could,' said May, 'but the chestnut vendor was discovered by the *News of the World*. Luckily that particular rag only comes out once a week.'

'You really are a dunderhead, Bryant,' Davenport complained. 'Half their stringers do double duty with the *Daily Sketch*. There's bound to be something in tomorrow's paper.'

'I think you're overestimating the *Daily Sketch*'s interest in theatre,' Bryant protested. 'Coverage of *Orpheus* is too intellectual for their readership.'

'You think a murderer loose in an old music hall is too intellectual? "Hellfire Show Summons the Devil", that sort of thing, a bit too brainy for the masses? You may be academically on the button but you're not much good at understanding people, Bryant. I suggest you go down there,' he slapped his hand against the window, 'and see how the ordinary man in the street is passing his days. There's a typing pool sitting out on the corner of the Aldwych in the pouring rain, working under a makeshift shelter of corrugated iron because the roof's been blown clean off their office. You're telling me they don't want to have their minds diverted by a juicy murder?'

Chastened, Bryant fell silent. It seemed to May that their superior might have a point.

'The partially digested meat in Miss Capistrania's stomach

showed positive for hemlock,' he pointed out. 'There was an empty sandwich tin in one of the wings, and hers are the only prints on it. Nobody seems to know where she got her food. Quail is not the sort of item you often find outside of Simpson's in the Strand these days. We've checked with all the butchers' shops in the area. There's a place in Brewer Street that sells quail, but they don't recall serving her, and besides, they're noted for carrying out stringent quality checks on their meat.'

'Anything new on Senechal?' asked Davenport.

'The cable ends were examined under a microscope and came back with an open verdict on them.'

'What do you mean? Either the wire was cut or it wasn't.'

'Dr Runcorn thinks there's a possibility that it sheared under its own weight. He reckons the cable had been reused so many times that it was probably full of stress fractures. But if it was cut, the person who cut it had to be standing on the gantry at the time in order to judge the moment for the globe to hit Mr Senechal.'

This news made Davenport far from happy. He liked the unit's cases to be tied up neatly so that he could present them to his superiors as solved and closed, another job well done. He wanted someone to blame. He would have put everything down to sheer bad luck if it wasn't for this latest attack. And, of course, there were the feet.

'How the hell did they get onto a chestnut stand?' he asked again. 'Come on, Arthur, you must have an idea by now.'

'I do, but you won't like it much.'

'Try me.'

'I think they were thrown into the cart from the canopy of the theatre.'

'What on earth makes you say that?'

'The evening was dry, and the vendor had griddled his fire before the air-raid siren called him away. On the morning of the discovery, PC Crowhurst noted that the coal dust on the pavement was unmarked by any footprints. Mr May and I saw it for ourselves. There are several sets of small mullioned windows above the canopy. One on the second landing has a pane missing, and another has a broken hasp. They're not big enough for a person to climb through, but you could stick an arm out of them. I think somebody dropped the feet out of the window, intending them to land on the canopy. Instead, they rolled off and fell onto the chestnut stall, which happened to be standing by the kerb below.'

'You mean the Turk just left it there and scarpered?'

'He was obeying the law, sir, getting himself to a place of shelter. Obviously, the blackout was still in effect when he returned, so it's feasible he didn't notice that anything had been disturbed.'

'Have you checked the canopy beneath the window for blood spots?'

'We didn't find anything swabbable, but it has rained since then.'

'I'd like to be able to tell Miss Capistrania's father that his daughter's death was a bizarre but unfortunate accident.'

'I don't see how you can do that.'

'In case it's escaped your attention, Mr Bryant, there are no motives. Capistrania hardly knew anyone in London. Senechal was universally admired. This last chap isn't even directly connected to the production, for God's sake.'

Davenport lowered himself into Bryant's chair and attempted to straighten his legs beneath the desk, but something was in the way. He peered under the desk. May gave his partner a grim look.

'Worse still, if Capistrania's death could have been mistaken for food poisoning, why would someone make it look like a murder by throwing away the bloody feet? And why attack a boy who's got nothing to do with the theatre? There's no sense in it, is there? I bloody give up with you lot.' He reached beneath the desk and pulled up Bryant's marijuana plant. 'What on earth's this?'

'Ah,' stalled Bryant, 'so that's where it is. Evidence. I'll bag it.'

'What evidence?' asked Davenport suspiciously.

'Ah, the Leicester Square Vampire. Dr Runcorn wanted some items removed from his house for examination.'

Davenport was thrown off guard. 'I didn't know we'd caught him,' he said.

'We haven't,' countered May as he gently drew the plant away from Davenport. 'He's a suspect. A, um, Lithuanian botanist experimenting on rare plants with, er, horticultural grafting techniques. I'll get rid of that for you.'

'You're telling me the Leicester Square Vampire is an experimenting Lithuanian botanist?' Davenport rose and walked to the door, vaguely troubled. 'Do you think I'm completely stupid? I've been fielding hourly calls from Albert Friedrich, Capistrania *père*, who, you'll be pleased to know, is staying at the Austrian ambassador's house this weekend, where he'll be receiving no less a personage than George VI himself for tea. I'm seeing the Home Secretary on Saturday morning. I want your written conclusions about this investigation presented to me no later than six o'clock tomorrow night. And give me rational solutions, none of your psychological supernatural mumbo-jumbo.' He slammed the door behind him.

Bryant stuffed the plant into the top drawer of his desk. 'I think that went quite well, don't you?'

'No, I don't, frankly. Have you come to any conclusions?'

'Well, there's a madman on the loose, obviously. Someone who hated Capistrania enough to have her mutilated, who had Charles Senechal killed in full view of his peers, who slashed a young man to death just because he was close to a member of the cast. We'll test the bike for prints when it turns up but I don't suppose we'll get anything.'

'He was wearing gloves.'

'Then there's the Greek aspect of all this. Which reminds me, we need to find out who gave Zachary Darvell the flower.'

'What flower?'

'The silk carnation. Stan Lowe says he'd never seen the boy wearing a buttonhole before. Not his usual style. Don't those gypsy women in Piccadilly press them on you as you pass? I'm sure they're not made of silk these days, though, unless someone's cutting up parachutes. And then there's the business with the flute.'

'You've completely lost me,' said May, exasperated.

'Anton Varisich halted the orchestra when the accident occurred, but his first flute released a high-pitched note of alarm. Except of course he couldn't have, because two of the woodwinds, of which the flautist was one, had failed to turn up that morning – so who played the note?'

'Arthur, I have absolutely no idea what you're talking about.'

'I'd like to tell you,' said Bryant, 'but I think I'd better make sure I'm right first. While I'm doing that, you might pause to wonder why Davenport's so anxious to keep this out of the newspapers.'

'I imagine he doesn't want the unit made to look foolish.'

'Nobody knows about the unit,' said Bryant. He raised his voice. 'Come in, Mr Biddle. Don't hover outside.'

Sidney Biddle looked defiant. 'I wasn't listening,' he said at once, thereby confirming he was. 'I was coming to see you.' He warily ventured into the cluttered sepia office.

Bryant threw his partner a questioning look. 'Oh? What's on your mind?' Biddle's tie was knotted so tightly under his collar that it appeared to be choking him.

May stretched back in his chair. 'Why don't you take a seat, Sidney?' he prompted.

The young man twisted awkwardly round to look at each of the detectives in turn. 'I want to transfer out of the unit, Mr Bryant.'

'You've only just got here. Can we ask why?'

Biddle looked uncomfortable. 'I don't believe I'm suited to this kind of operation.'

241

'Could you be more specific?' asked May, sensing what was coming.

'Mr May, my aim was to get inside the Home Office end of the London force, reach the important stuff, and I thought I'd hack it by working for an SIO. I knew Serious Crimes only handled murder cases. I was told how different this unit was to anything else currently available. I didn't realize working practices would be so – not how things are supposed to be.'

May peered at him in what he hoped was a manner of surprise. 'Would you care to give me an example?'

'Even the most basic procedures aren't followed. Take custody of evidence.' Biddle began to grow heated. 'I was taught to maintain continuous control over crime-scene evidence from signing and dating of possession to court introduction, keeping copious notes throughout the process. Mr Bryant walks into Dr Runcorn's lab and pokes about, and takes whatever he likes out of the property room. Half the time he doesn't even secure it as he leaves. When I remind him of protocol, he shouts at me, or he laughs.'

'So this is about Mr Bryant,' said May solemnly.

'Yes, sir. I was always warned that we would have to work reactively on suspects, eliminate or associate them according to the likelihood of their involvement in a crime. Mr Bryant doesn't do that, sir. He doesn't share information, and he starts with the unlikeliest scenario. He won't cold-type fingerprints or correlate his data with colleagues. He starts writing up reports before he even receives blood-typing results. Mr Finch should have run epithelial cell checks on the lift doors, the globe cable and the balcony seat backs by now, but Mr Bryant doesn't even seem interested. It's like he thinks he's above the law.'

'I understand your concerns. You must bear in mind that no fingerprints other than the victims' have been found at any of the three crime scenes. Still, sometimes Mr Bryant fails to respect the fact that criminology is a modern science.'

Bryant was keeping quiet. He had known this moment was coming, had seen it in the boy's disillusioned eyes.

'I'm sure Mr Bryant does not consider himself above the law,' May continued. 'His mind just takes him off the beaten track.'

'Think about why this case came to us,' suggested Bryant, relishing Biddle's discomfort. 'Does it appear to involve any of the elements present in your college case histories? Domestic violence, burglary, spousal assault, alcohol-related crime, pick-pocketing, grand larceny?'

'No, sir.'

'You see, Biddle, our cases get prioritized for the wrong reasons: they have a higher profile, meaning there's an influential relative somewhere in the background, or there's a more complex political element involved, or they're a publicity risk, or they're against the public mood. Most importantly, they're cases that can cause damage to public morale during a time of conflict. Thanks to Hitler, we are no longer living in a world that cares about the death of someone because they were loved in the past. It cares only if that death can do damage to the future. It's a grim truth, Sidney. Like Orpheus leaving Hades, we are rushing headlong into the light of a terrible new world.

'There is a way of providing accountability, though. You get a grant from the Home Office to run an autonomous unit like this, one that siphons off the publicly embarrassing cases during wartime and takes the heat, and you head it up with men whose operations run so contrary to traditional methodology that once in a while they produce the goods. That's what everyone's baying for now, the press, the state, they're only interested in culpability. Take a look at the witch-hunting that's going on out there, most of it whipped up by rumour and conjecture. We lump everyone we don't like in with the Germans, most of whom are probably as decent as you or me, and God help you if you disagree, because you'll be tarred and feathered along with them.' Bryant fumbled about

243

in his waistcoat for some matches. 'Tell me, Sidney, are you aware of the recent troubles in Greece?'

'Greece?' Biddle looked thrown. 'No, sir.'

'Last week some British soldiers got into a fight on a border checkpoint that they had no right to be on in the first place. It ended up with a local man being tortured and killed. The man was a Greek national suspected of collaborating with the Italians. When that happened, his family was shipped off and his private property was seized. The victim was probably innocent, but he was travelling without the right papers, and had bribed our boys to let him through. The British ambassador to Greece extradited the men, and the blame for the death was placed on an extremist Turkish national group. There have been quite a few violent incidents in Greece inspired by Turkish national activity, and relations between the two countries are poor. Meanwhile, we have a British building programme going on in Istanbul. Is this starting to make sense to you?'

Biddle stared furiously at his hands. 'No, it isn't.'

'Let me spell it out. The *Orpheus* production company is owned by the son of a Greek shipping magnate, and has its headquarters in Athens. The closest thing we have to a suspect is an illegal immigrant who happens to be a Turk. What will the Foreign Office's position be if it can be proved that a powerful Greek company deliberately framed an innocent Turk for murder?'

'You're telling me that this is about keeping building contracts in Istanbul?' asked Biddle.

'Add to this mix a powerful Austrian with Mosleyite connections in London, a man whose only daughter has died in mysterious circumstances, and a theatrical production, of all things, that simultaneously demonstrates international solidarity and co-operation while challenging the nation's moral dignity. Is it any wonder that the matter is attracting attention in high places? You see, Biddle, you have to look at the broader picture. Four days and three murders on, we're no further forward than when we started, so I'm going to handle the case in the manner I think fit. I know I'm an unlikely looking subversive, but it's people like me you have to watch out for. I won't toe the party line and I don't have to cover my back against losing a court case over technical irregularities—'

'You're talking about contaminated evidence, failure to observe—'

'—because', Bryant cut across him, 'our cases get solved before they ever reach a public court, something you'd have realized if you'd studied the unit's history a little more thoroughly instead of worrying about logging procedures on trace evidence.'

He rose, bringing the meeting to an end. 'Now you may want to reconsider your transfer. You seem like a smart chap. Put your talents to good use. Check out the spot where Darvell was butchered. Ask Runcorn about the blood patterns in the aisle. Forget the paperwork and get stuck in. That's where you'll be best used. Don't let your ambitions pull you in the wrong direction. I know you asked Davenport down here today. But think about what I've said. You can let me have your answer by tomorrow morning.'

'Thank you, sir,' said Biddle, looking at Bryant as if he was mad, 'but my mind is made up. I'm requesting a transfer from the unit at the first available opportunity.'

He's angry that John saw action and he didn't, thought Bryant suddenly. He wants to be out there rugby-tackling the villains. It was all he needed to understand to get Biddle back on track.

37

THE VOICE OF THE ABYSSINIAN

Arthur Bryant stood outside the café lost in thought as the rainwater slipped through its blast-damaged canopy, dripping onto the shoulders of his gaberdine. Some office girls dashed across the road with newspapers held over their heads. A taxi splashed past with a dirt-smudged child sitting on the running board. A tramp in a torn cardboard hat was carefully stepping in and out of a large puddle at the kerb, his head bowed in concentration. The safe canopy of inclement weather had brought life back to the night streets. Bryant checked his watch again, and decided to give Elspeth five more minutes.

Like Geoffrey Whittaker, Harry, Stan Lowe and Mr Mack, Elspeth belonged to a brigade of workers whose lives were lived in darkness, a perpetual night divided into sections that ran concurrently from one production to the next. Bryant was surprised how little they knew of the world beyond their own circle. They were the real theatre angels, happy to remain in the shadows beyond the footlights, only tangentially attached to the stage, essential to its survival.

He checked his watch again. She must have known that she'd be too busy to break for supper; that was why she had insisted on meeting him outside the café. She had not wanted to hurt his feelings by refusing him outright. He pulled his scarf a little tighter round his neck and sniffed the cold air. For a brief moment he thought he had been given a shot at finding himself a new girl. But it was clear where Elspeth's loyalties lay. After repeatedly choosing work over women, he felt as though he was getting a taste of his own medicine.

At moments like this, the memory of Nathalie returned. He missed her so badly that he wanted to cry. As he stepped back into the foggy drizzle, he decided to avoid the theatre in order to spare Elspeth embarrassment, and walked off into Soho to buy himself a mug of cocoa.

When he reached the corner, something made him stop and glance back at the theatre. He looked up at the pairs of mullioned windows, and had the briefest impression of being watched through the mist. A pale twisted face, a fleeting presence, like the fading heat of a handprint on glass. It dipped back from the window, and the thought of his aberrant imagination chilled him. He was starting to believe that buildings held ghosts.

'There's something in there I don't understand,' he told May later. 'I want to take someone in with me after dark.'

'Don't say it,' warned May. 'Don't tell me you want to go ghost-hunting in a theatre at midnight with one of your clairvoyant pals.'

'That's exactly what I'm going to do, how did you know?' asked Bryant innocently. 'Edna has a good sense for these things.'

'Not your alternative theologian, the woman with the cats,' groaned May. DS Forthright had told May about the eerie afternoon she had once spent with Bryant and Edna Wagstaff in a rundown slum flat filled with feline familiars.

'We're lucky she's had a cancellation and can fit us in so soon. She doesn't normally make house calls.'

'You've already spoken to her? What have you arranged?'

'She's meeting us outside the stage door at midnight tonight.'

'No, Arthur, you promised Davenport you wouldn't. No mumbo-jumbo, he said.'

'I think she might be able to do some good. Sensations of pain and harm are as visible to her as the walls around us. She doesn't charge, but I usually drop her something. Mrs Wagstaff is tormented by her gift. Past, present and future are all the same. Everything crosses over. The only way she can relieve the pain her gift causes is by using it to help others.'

'And you really believe this?' asked May.

'With all my heart.' Bryant's pale blue eyes were so wide, so honest that he had to be telling the truth.

'I'm sorry I'm late. The blackout and the fog. I had to follow a tramline to get here, and then I followed it too far.' Tall and ascetic, wrapped in a frayed black coat and carrying a cat box, the old lady looked considerably more frail than when Bryant had last seen her.

'Hello, Edna,' he said jovially, 'I hear you're still living on the Isle of Dogs.'

'Oh yes, Arthur, one of the last. I've been bombed out twice now, and I lost my Billy, my proud boy, at Dunkirk. At least he saw service.'

'I'm so sorry,' said Bryant, taking her hand.

'He was happy to be mobilized. The air force and the navy have no chance to stop and think because they stay on duty around the clock. My boy spent so much time confined to barracks, he was so terribly bored with the endless drills. At least it was an active end.'

'But how are you?'

'Oh, they keep trying to rehouse me. I had people round from the council, telling me my cats were insanitary. I explained they were all dead, what harm could they do? How could you catch fleas from them? They were sprayed for parasites when they were stuffed. They want me to go to a home in Stepney. That's miles away.'

'Can't your daughter take you in?'

'She's gone to the WRNS. I'm very proud. I wouldn't want to bother her.' She made her way up the stairs with awkward slowness. 'You know, I haven't been to the theatre in years.'

'Edna, this is my new partner, Mr May.'

She reached over and shook his hand, then hastily released it.

'I do beg your pardon, Mr May. What a jolt. I get very strong feelings from some of the people I come into physical contact with, mostly the young ones.'

'Oh, really?' said May, rubbing the static shock from his fingers with some embarrassment. 'What did you get from me?'

'Best not to say, just in case I'm wrong,' said Edna mysteriously. 'Let's not dwell on what hasn't happened yet. I brought Rothschild with me. He's an Abyssinian, the lion of cats.' She raised the cat box high.

'Are you sure this is a good idea?' whispered May.

'Edna sees things.'

'And I can smell something.' May grimaced. 'I think it's her.'

'I just need to pick up the psychic scent,' she called over her shoulder.

'I don't know how she'll do it, she's wearing so much of her own. She needs a bath, Arthur. And she's got her wig on back to front.'

'You're a sceptic, Mr May. I don't mind.' Edna gave a throaty chuckle. 'The world will need sceptics after the war is over. Too many people are ready to believe anything they're told. Where do you want me?'

Bryant led the way up the painted concrete staircase until they reached a set of red double doors. 'The dress circle will do,' he told her, 'there are—'

'Four floors, yes, I know, upper circle and balcony above us, stalls below.'

'You can sense the building's layout?' asked May.

'No. I saw *No, No, Nanette* here. I'll go down to the

249

front, if I may. Perhaps one of you could carry Rothschild.'

May reluctantly took the cat box and waited as Bryant showed the old lady to the front of the balcony. He raised the box to eye level and peered inside. Something glittered blackly back at him.

'Do you still have your familiars, Evening Echo and Squadron Leader Smethwick?' asked Bryant, seating her on the aisle.

'Sadly no.' Edna arranged the folds of her coat about her. 'The German bombers come right over my house and interfere with the signals.'

'You make it sound like tuning in a wireless, Mrs Wagstaff,' said May.

'Well, it's not dissimilar,' said Edna. If she detected the scepticism in his voice she gave no sign of it. 'Ever since they put a barrage balloon at the end of the street I've been getting terrible reception.'

'From your spirit guides?'

'No, on my wireless. I keep missing *Gert and Daisy*.' She leaned forward and looked about. 'Of course, London theatres are filled with ghosts.' She smiled, patting Bryant's arm. 'Mostly just echoes of emotional experiences, drawn out by the intensity of performance in such buildings. Any actor will tell you. They're terribly vulnerable to mental distress, you know. Unstable pathologies so often lead to cruelty and suicide. You know about the "Man in Grey", I suppose.'

'He appears in the Theatre Royal, Drury Lane, just before the run of a successful production, doesn't he?'

'That's right, dressed in a three-cornered hat, a powdered periwig and a grey riding cloak. He always follows the same route along the back of the upper circle, starting from the bar and vanishing into the far wall. Even the firewatchers have seen him, and they're not as prone to nerves as theatre folk. Workmen supposedly found his corpse bricked into a wall on the Russell Street side of the theatre. He had a dagger in his ribs. You can read about him in any cheap guidebook. I don't suppose there's much truth to the story, but there's no denying the fact that such houses attract collective hysteria and magnify the emotions. After all, that's what they're intended to do.

'There are lots of lesser-known spirits, though. The Haymarket has the ghost of the dramatist John Buckstone. Margaret Rutherford had to spend the night there once during a rail strike, and found him in the wardrobe. Or hasn't that happened yet? Time plays such tricks on me.' She thought for a moment, relaxing her watery green eyes.

'We're more interested in sensations, Edna.'

'I understand. Could there be another animal in the building apart from Rothschild? A tortoise, perhaps?'

'Yes, there is,' said May, looking at his partner in puzzlement.

'I thought so. I was getting a distress message.'

'He has insomnia,' explained Bryant.

Edna stroked her knuckles restlessly, anxious to help. 'There's so much humanity here. So many people have passed through. There are few public places left in London that are as psychically rich as its theatres. The interiors don't change. The walls absorb. I wonder if you'd get Rothschild for me?'

Bryant brought over the cat box and opened the wire door.

'I must be careful with him,' said Edna, 'he's getting rather fragile.' Her long, tapered fingers felt around the edges of the cat and pulled him out. Rothschild was a leonine sandstone-coloured Abyssinian, and had been stuffed in crouching position, as if watching a mouse. His ears were tattered with handling, one glass eye had sunk back into his skull and there was sand coming out of his bottom. She carefully set him on the edge of the balcony, facing stage.

'Is there any way of lowering the house lights a little?'

May had arranged to have them left up, mainly because he was worried about the old lady tripping over.

'I'll see what I can do,' he offered, heading back along the balcony.

'There are plenty of friendly spirits here, but then there should be,' she chattered on to Bryant. 'First-time performers are sensitive to them. Sometimes they help newcomers to forget their nerves and remember their lines, or they redirect them to better positions on the stage. Actors sometimes speak of being guided by unseen hands. Oh, there is something here.' She became silent, and seemed to fall into a light sleep. The house lights dimmed and May quietly returned, taking a seat behind the medium.

The detectives listened and waited. The faint, high voice that emerged from Rothschild startled them both. At first it seemed little more than the sound of a draught whistling under a door. Gradually they were able to make out a few words. 'Not the actors, the actors are adored.' The voice reverted to a thin wind. 'Someone has been ignored and forgotten. No hatred . . . only desperation . . . desperation. History repeats.'

May studied the old lady's face. She didn't appear to be throwing her voice. Something prickled the base of his neck.

'It's not his fault, you understand . . .' Now the voice was Edna's, so alone, so melancholy. 'Selfish and blind. Medea . . . Calliope . . . goddesses of the theatre, so very sad.' A tear ran down her left cheek and trembled on her chin. 'The poor tortured soul is here, right among us now. A painted world is so confining. There must be a way to set such a trapped spirit free. The cruelty of the moonlight, so far beyond reach.'

Just as May was peering into them, Edna's eyelids lifted, startling him. She sat up and wiped her chin. 'I'm sorry,' she apologized, 'I didn't mean to get so upset. It's being in a theatre. A house of the emotions. Did you hear the voice?'

'Yes,' said Bryant enthusiastically, nodding at his partner. 'Who was it?'

'I rather fancy it belonged to Dan Leno, the clown. This used to be a music hall, didn't it?'

'I believe so.'

252

'Dan's ghost often used to appear in the halls. There were many recorded sightings at Collins' Music Hall on Islington Green, and in Drury Lane. He would appear to give advice to the actors. Sometimes they heard him performing his clog-dancing routine. A very reliable source. What did he say?'

'Something about a forgotten tortured soul and a painted world, and history repeating,' said May irritably. 'Greeks. It could mean anything.'

'You're looking for a little child,' said Edna firmly. 'A child so desperate to be set free that it must hurt people. I feel that very strongly.'

'You make it sound as if we're supposed to be searching for a ghost.'

'I rather think not,' said Edna, lifting the cat back into its box. 'This is not someone reaching from beyond the grave. The person you seek is real, and dangerous when cornered. Medea murdered her sons to take revenge on their father.'

'But we're looking for a killer, not some Greek woman,' said May, exasperated. Edna did not appear to have heard. She looked up at the ceiling, listening to her inner voices. 'Edna?' He turned to Bryant with his palms outstretched. 'Look at her, she doesn't know if she's at the park or the pictures.'

'Come on, Edna,' said Bryant gently. 'Let's get you home.'

He helped her from her seat, and for a moment the house lights flickered out. They waited in the oppressive darkness, halted by the foot of the stairs, listening to the old woman's laboured breath. Then the auditorium filled with light. May wanted to complain that the visit had been a waste of time, but something stilled within him as he watched the balcony curtain lift and fall in the sighing draught that blew beneath the doors, as though the spirit of the theatre had departed with them.

38

RENALDA'S WAR

On Friday morning, the city awoke to the terrible news.

Despite the presence of a bombers' moon, as close and cold as death, London had passed the night unscathed, and instead, the city of Coventry, Luftwaffe target no. 53, had suffered the full force of Germany's squadrons in a devastating *Mondschein Serenade*, a 'Moonlight Serenade'.

Nearly five hundred bombers had delivered high explosives and incendiary bombs in eleven hours of dusk-to-dawn raids that had obliterated the heart of the city, destroyed its cathedral, killed over five hundred inhabitants, seriously wounded nine hundred more.

The night had been clear and frosty, providing perfect visibility. London was a metropolis large enough to weather such a disaster, but Coventry, with a population of just under a quarter of a million, had been almost eradicated. The residents who survived were dazed and terrified. Gas, water, electricity and transport systems stopped. Twenty-one of its factories – twelve of them tied to the aircraft industry – had been heavily hit. Radio reports made no attempt to make light of the attack; the news spread like bushfire. The lines to the city were down. It was impossible to discover if relatives were dead or alive.

Listening to the Home Service made John May late for work. He hurried to the unit and found his partner seated at the teleprinter, checking several yards of paper.

'You've heard?' May asked. 'Christ, we should be there instead of here.'

'There's nothing you or I can do for them,' muttered Bryant, barely raising his eyes. 'I want you to meet Andreas Renalda. He's the only Greek we know, and Edna mentioned Greeks. When I looked into his eyes I caught a glimpse of something.'

'He's probably upset about spending a fortune on a show that may never open. According to Helena Parole, updating *Orpheus* was all his idea. Anyway, didn't you already get everything you could out of him?' May was finding it increasingly hard to concentrate on Bryant's theories when, just a short distance from London, the bodies of so many innocent civilians were being dragged from the smoking ruins of a town. Their case seemed absurd and almost pointless by comparison.

'He might be different with you. Talk about whatever comes into your head. Keep him off guard. I want you to study him. You're better with people than I am. I'm still missing a link, and I keep wondering.' Bryant sucked at his pipe pensively. 'Suppose Renalda thinks he's betraying the ancient gods of his homeland by staging such a controversial production? He says his family is superstitious. What if they think he's going against the mythical protectors of Greece? He may have accidentally inspired someone to seek revenge. That would make him responsible for what's happened, wouldn't it?'

May gave a sigh of annoyance. Bryant's thinking seemed so far removed from his own, so unrelated to the cause-and-effect crimes of the real world, that he could not find a response. Instead, he went to see Andreas Renalda.

The tycoon was on his way to a board meeting but agreed to collect May at Piccadilly Circus and let him travel in his limousine as far as Hyde Park Corner. The sleek black Rolls-Royce was a vision of lost elegance. It glided to a stop beneath the vast 'Dig for Victory' banner that hung across the fascia of Swan and Edgar, and the chauffeur, liveried in black and red, the colours of the family guild, opened its passenger door to admit the detective. Renalda was sprawled across the back seat, his steel calipers holding his useless legs to one side.

'I have arranged a telephone call in order to speak to the board in Athens tonight,' Renalda explained, after introductions were made. 'My fellow directors have received news of our troubles, and require assurances. I was the one who convinced them that we should adopt such a high-risk venture. Our people, Mr May, are conservative individuals. They do not approve of my show, but they like the thought of the revenue it could generate. I have to assure them that we are not facing some kind of moral crusade. Harmful reports are appearing in your newspapers, suggesting that we have brought misfortune on ourselves, that we deserve what we get for bringing continental sex into venerable British theatreland. What your journalists are really saying, in their own charmingly circumspect manner, is that we are unwanted foreigners.'

'Not all of us share the views expressed by those newspapers,' May said, sinking back into the polished opulence of the leather seat. 'Since you've raised the subject, I was wondering about your enemies.'

Renalda peered at him coldly over the top of his rimless glasses. 'I don't recall discussing my enemies with your partner.'

'Forgive me, you're running a company that, according to *The Times*, is venturing into a market it knows nothing about. Your father was known to be a hard negotiator, and you told Mr Bryant that you take after him. You may well have offended someone. Your rivals have good reason to want to see you fail in this enterprise.'

'I am sure they do,' Renalda admitted evenly, 'but the wars

of my father are not mine. You might credit me with more sophistication. At the end of the nineteen twenties my father's company had few remaining assets. Its debts were converted into equity that is still held by the other trustees.'

'How do they feel about your plans to leave the world of shipping?'

'Most of them consider me foresighted.'

'Most but not all?'

Renalda folded away his glasses with a sigh. 'I have known the board's directors all my life. You are looking in the wrong place.' Something in his voice suggested this was not necessarily so.

'This is a very important week for you,' said May, watching the grey window-boards of Selfridge's drift past.

'It's the culmination of a lifelong project that has not been destroyed even by a world plunged into war. My mother was a free spirit, but my father's house was her prison. Sirius would not allow the curtains to be opened because the sunlight damaged his paintings. When I was a boy my mother used to play Offenbach's music and dance alone through the still, dark rooms. It was the only time she was ever really happy.' The Rolls-Royce pulled up at traffic lights. The red, amber and green lenses had been covered with black tape so that slits formed narrow luminous crosses. 'I cannot afford to make any mistakes, Mr May. There are too many people watching me.'

'Who, your directors? Your rivals?'

'There are others who are closer.' Renalda seemed about to speak further, but stopped himself.

'We may be able to find enemies you can't,' May suggested. 'But you have to tell us who you suspect.'

'These are family affairs,' said Renalda finally. 'If you cannot protect my company, I will have to take care of the problem myself. I do not trust the officials of your government. They happily take my money and make promises, then do something else.'

May wondered if Renalda had bribed civil servants connected with the Lord Chamberlain's office.

'I think you're right,' he told his partner later. 'Andreas Renalda isn't telling us the whole truth.'

'Perhaps we haven't asked him the right questions,' suggested Bryant. 'I need to know more about his family.'

'I can probably get the company records opened, but it'll take a few days.'

'I wasn't thinking about the official records. I'm more interested in where Renalda grew up, what the rest of the family was like, what his neighbours thought of him.'

'I don't see how that will help,' said May.

'You don't? No, I suppose you don't. I'm sure I read somewhere that Andreas Renalda was raised on one of the smaller islands to the south, Santorini, I think. Interesting, isn't it, that he chooses to honour his family with a play that mocks the mythology of his homeland? My uncle's friend at *The Times* wrote an article about the Renalda empire, but when war broke out the piece was spiked. I have a feeling Renalda has been generous with his war donations.'

'You still haven't told me what's on your mind.'

'Be patient for just a little longer.' Bryant knocked out his pipe and squinted into the bowl. 'I have to be absolutely sure.'

'Arthur, this has been an unusual week but even at the worst of times—'

Sidney Biddle put his head round the door. 'There's someone here to see you both.'

He pushed the door wide and DS Gladys Forthright walked in. Her hair had been dyed blond and cut in the style of the film star Alice Faye. Bryant leaped up from behind his desk and slapped his arms on the policewoman's shoulders.

'Forthright! Bless my old socks! What are you doing back here? You're supposed to be getting hitched and living with the land girls.'

The sergeant pulled off her jacket and gloves, and threw them into a corner. 'I had a bugger of a time getting here. The trains are up the spout. I slept on Chatham station last night.' She sighed. 'At least I didn't get around to posting a wedding list. It would have been embarrassing having to send gifts back.'

'What happened?'

'He didn't want to go through with it.'

'The absolute bastard,' cried Bryant, barely able to conceal the pleasure in his voice. 'What reason did he give, if I may be so bold?'

'Oh, the war, of course. He says it's not right to be thinking about ourselves when there are so many in difficulties all around us. We shouldn't bring babies into such uncertain times, et cetera. It was me who wanted to make us legal. I didn't want to risk dying a spinster. We drove down to his parents' on the last of his petrol, and I suppose I did talk about work quite a lot. We had a bit of a row, and finally came to an agreement. He promised not to mention his constabulary so long as I didn't talk about the unit. But I couldn't stay where I wasn't needed, like some kind of evacuee. I rang the unit to explain and spoke to Mr Biddle. I wanted to warn you that I was coming back.'

'He didn't tell me,' said Bryant indignantly.

'That's odd. How's he working out?'

'He's not. Look at this, I'm making my own tea from reused leaves.' He fished a half-dissolved sugar cube out of his mug with the pointy end of a dart. 'We have to make one lump go around the whole unit because it's against Biddle's principles to buy black-market demerara. His trial period ends today, thank God. He wants to leave us and go back to the Met, and the feeling's mutual. Here, I kept your mug just in case.' He poured her half his tea.

'Arthur, did you put him off?'

'I bent over backwards to make him feel welcome, the ungrateful little sod.'

'How's the case?' asked Forthright.

'I'll have to take you back, I suppose. Just until you can get yourself sorted out.' Having answered an entirely different question, he turned to the window and warmed his hands round his mug, smiling to himself.

'I thought you'd need me,' Forthright said, 'what with this latest development.'

He turned, the smile fading. 'What do you mean?'

'I picked up the call just as I was coming in. Something strange has happened again.'

39

THE ABDUCTION

The house in Lissom Grove was set back from the road and surrounded by battered birches. The hedge leading to the front door was so overgrown that it soaked May and Forthright as they passed. They were met by PC Crowhurst, who appeared from the shadowed porch and unlocked the front door for them.

'When was she last seen?' asked May, stepping into the gloomy Lincrusta-papered hall.

'The evening before last, sir. The girl she shares with was away for the night, but the next-door neighbour saw her coming in with shopping bags. She didn't turn up for rehearsals yesterday. They thought she was taking a day off sick, but when she failed to show again this morning, the other girl who boards here rang the police. I came round and found – well, you'll see.'

'Who is she?'

'A member of the chorus, name of Jan Petrovic. Sixteen years old. This is Phyllis.'

A slender girl held out her hand. She had ragged blond hair cut to her jawline, and was wearing a man's rowing sweater several sizes too large for her. 'Hello, you'd better come through.' She held open the door to a front room that was cluttered with the possessions of young girls living away from their parents for the first time: dinner plates, stockings, magazines, half-burned candles, a radiogram, some dance records out of their cardboard sleeves.

'In there, next door,' said Phyllis, wrapping her thin arms round herself. 'I can't bring myself to look.' Her voice had a soft Wiltshire burr. In the kitchen, a back door led to a small yard. The window above the sink had been shattered. There were several small drying spots of blood on the wooden draining board. May turned and found himself confronted by a shocking crimson smear that arced across the white-washed wall.

'When did you last see Jan?' asked Forthright.

Phyllis chewed her lip nervously and stayed in the door-way. 'Two days ago. In the morning. I went to visit my boyfriend in Brighton. He's studying at Sussex College. Jan was getting ready to leave for her rehearsal.'

'How did she seem to you?'

'Pretty much in the pink. We talked about what we were going to do this weekend. She was fed up, but that's because she's worried about performing in the show. She's talked about leaving it before the opening night.'

'Why would she do that?'

'The schedule's too hard on her. I mean, she's just a kid, and she bluffed her way into the part. She didn't think she could handle it. Then this week's goings-on have been the last straw for her.'

'Have you known her long?'

'No, only a few weeks. I don't think Petrovic is her real name. She doesn't like people to know where she's from. I wondered if she might be Jewish.'

'Do you have a photograph of her?'

'No, but I think they took some publicity shots at the theatre.'

'John, look at this.' Forthright pointed into the corner behind the sink. Two halves of a cup lay in shadow. Beside

262

them stood a short, wide-bladed knife, its tip stuck in the tiled floor, its handle darkly smeared. The DS stepped out of the kitchen, called the unit and asked to speak to Dr Runcorn. 'I'll get someone from FS over right now,' she told May, her hand over the mouthpiece. 'You'd better make sure Phyllis is all right.'

May gingerly stepped out of the kitchen's narrow corner and returned to the lounge.

'I've been calling her aunt's number, but there's been no answer,' said Phyllis, pacing along the edge of the carpet. 'She sometimes goes there when she gets fed up. I didn't know what else to do. Her mother rang to speak to her and I just couldn't say where she was.'

'When did you first think she was missing?' asked May.

'I tried calling her when I arrived in Brighton, but assumed she had gone to the theatre. Then when I got back and went into the kitchen I saw the mess.'

May took another look inside the kitchen. 'Odd. The break in the window isn't big enough to let anyone in, so why are there signs of a struggle? It's not near enough to the back door for anyone to be able to reach in and undo the latch.'

Forthright tested the lock. 'The door's still locked.' She carefully turned, studying the walls. 'Maybe he was already inside and she was trying to get out, away from him.'

May returned to the front room. Phyllis was seated with her hands pressed on her thighs, staring blankly at the floor. 'When you came in,' he asked, 'did you have to unlock the front door from the outside?'

'Yes. The latch is faulty, so you have to double-lock it as you leave or it comes open by itself.'

'What about the back door? Have you touched it?'

'No. I took one look at the kitchen and backed off. Then I called the police and was put through to your department.'

'When was this?'

'About two hours ago.'

'Hang on.' May called his constable in from the front garden: 'Crowhurst, come in here for a second.'

'Sir?'

'How did this get put through to us?'

'The station rang Miss Petrovic's work number, sir. As soon as they realized it was the theatre, the call was transferred to the unit.'

I bet it was, thought May. They couldn't get rid of it fast enough. He looked at the chaotic front room, at Phyllis, who seemed close to tears. 'Would you care to show me the other rooms?'

'Of course.'

Two small bedrooms, bathroom and toilet. An attempt had been made to brighten them up, the bedrooms painted a hopeful yellow, the bathroom pink, but the flat needed more than a lick of cheap paint to make it comfortable.

'Which one is Miss Petrovic's bedroom? No, just show me, don't touch anything.'

An unmade bed, socks and a sweater lay on the floor. A crumpled bath towel at the foot of the eiderdown. Stacks of books, undisturbed. If there had been violence, it hadn't reached here. He made a slow tour, checking the window frames and door handles. The flat reminded him of his own room.

'You think she's been abducted?' asked Phyllis, following behind him. 'Something terrible's happened to her, I'm sure of it.' She wiped her nose on the back of her hand. 'I should have been here.'

'We'll have to see what turns up from the kitchen,' May replied. 'We're going to have to take some items away with us.'

When he caught Forthright looking at him, he saw the same question in her eyes. If she's been abducted, her look said, how did he get her out of the house without opening any of the doors or windows?

The pattern, such as it was, had been broken, yet felt

264

strangely consistent. There was the same kind of arrogant theatricality; the evidence of the abduction reminded May of the blocking rehearsals he had witnessed. It's deception practised in public view, he thought as he left the house. The interpretation of gestures, wasn't that what acting was all about?

But who was providing the direction?

40

GROUND ZERO

The interpretation of gestures, May recalled as he unfolded the architectural plan from his pocket. It all happened so long ago, the other end of a lifetime. We've learned a lot since then. Then he remembered there was no more 'we'. He was alone now. He would never adjust to the awful singularity. There was no one else. His wife and daughter were dead. His son lived in a commune in southern France and refused to speak to him. April, his granddaughter, had suffered a nervous breakdown and could not bear to leave her house. Only Bryant had given him hope.

'John, are you all right?'

'Oh, I suppose so.'

'Then show me,' said Stanhope Beaufort, holding out a pudgy hand. The architect was uncomfortably perched on a glass stool at a glass bar with a glass counter, surrounded by glass walls, a glass floor and a glass ceiling. Hundreds of tiny silver bulbs reflected from hundreds of square mirrors. It was so bright that nobody could see a thing.

John May handed over the building plan he and Longbright had rescued from the debris of the burned-down unit and waited for his analysis. He had tracked Beaufort, one of Bryant's old contacts, to the new Hoxton bar, and was hoping that he could explain the meaning of the page. The roar of street traffic entered the bar and bounced off the vitrine walls, vibrating everything and making it difficult to hear. Dust sifted in and settled on the shining surfaces like radiation fallout.

'I'm sorry to hear about your poor partner.' Beaufort tipped the paper into shadow so that he could read it. 'Old Arthur was a bit of a one-off.'

'He was at that,' agreed May.

'What do you think of this place, by the way?' Beaufort asked, as a waiter blundered into an indiscernible column with a tray of drinks.

'It's very – glass,' said May diplomatically.

'Glass is the new steel,' Beaufort explained. 'They all want it, it's so seventies. I've lost count of the number of accidents we've had here so far. The staircase is glass, too. One of the waitresses went arse over tit down it this morning. Cracked a step and knocked out her front tooth. She's been locked in the bog all day, crying her eyes out. You can see her if you want. The toilets are transparent. The owner complained that it's like a hall of mirrors, and I said, "That's because it *is* a hall of fucking mirrors, it's what you asked for." Wanker.'

'But you must like it if you designed it,' said May, puzzled.

'No, mate, it's just a commission. The secret of design is re-interpreting what was popular thirty years ago. Everyone wants the things that remind them of childhood. I just re-imagine them with the materials of the present.'

'So this isn't your taste?'

'What, New Britain? Fuck off. I live in an unfucked-about-with Georgian house in Islington with nice big comfy sofas. I'm not going to split my shins on a chrome coffee table shaped like a fucking rocket. I've got three kids. I don't want them running around covered in dents. Same with the clothes. I don't dress like this at home, I wear jumpers. This is just for the clients.'

Beaufort was wearing black tracksuit bottoms and a

T-shirt that read: MUTHAFUCKA. 'It's like those singers who bang on about teen rebellion so they can buy homes in Hampstead. This is all wrong, by the way.' He turned the sheet of paper round and held it up. 'See the calibrations down the side? They're in feet and inches reading left to right. That tells us two things. Pre-metric, post-war. LCC stamp here, see? And it's not a ground plan, because the central corridor wouldn't be measured off from a single left-hand starting point, it would have a single width measurement.'

'So what are you saying? What is it?'

'A depth measurement, calibrated from ground zero going downwards. That's why it's shaded to indicate round walls. This isn't a corridor, it's a shaft.'

'What are the broken lines at the bottom?' May pointed at the base of the diagram.

Behind them, there was a small scream and a tinkle of glass.

'It's the architectural symbol used to indicate water. Looks to me like you've got yourself a well.'

'And the passageway off to the side?'

'Overflow escape. It's artesian; the water rises through natural pressure. If it rains heavily the excess drains off through the side passage and prevents the well from overflowing.'

'Where would the overflow pipe surface?'

'Oh, somewhere outside the building in the street, probably.'

'I need to get an indication of scale,' said May. 'Could a person fit down it?'

'Looking at this, the main shaft's got to be six feet across, so you can reckon the side vent is four feet, easily large enough to hold a grown man. The Victorians loved stuff like this. They built their drains big so they could shove children down them with brooms and shit shovels. They were great designers, but had no thought for the poor bastards who had to use their buildings.' Behind him, a waitress winced as she sponged blood from her sliced elbow with a cocktail napkin.

'Not like nowadays, then,' agreed May.

As he headed for Old Street tube, it began to rain. The area looked every bit as derelict as it had just after the war. How was that possible? May thought of the London that might have been, the abandoned plans, the failed dreams. Once, a causeway of buildings had been proposed for the centre of the Thames, a vast triumphal arch of Portland stone suggested for Euston Road, a grand national cemetery attempted on Primrose Hill, a Piranesian entry gate blue-printed for Kensington. Gothic towers, pyramid morgues, elevated railways, none had come to pass. The grand social schemes had collapsed in favour of piecemeal sale to private interests. It all could have been so beautiful, he thought sadly.

May pulled the backpack from his shoulder, removed his mobile phone and rang Longbright at home.

'You said there was no one left alive from the Palace,' he told her, 'but you're wrong. Believe me, I know how it sounds, but I think our killer is still around. Arthur recognized the diagram for what it was. A possible escape route.'

'It's a bit of a long shot, don't you think?'

'We know Arthur went to the theatre to research his memoirs. I think he discovered the blueprint and realized the implications at once. Then he did the most obvious thing. He ran a search. Combed the city's mental institutions and checked through hospital records looking for further signs of survival.'

'You're saying he traced this aged lunatic and found him in residence at the Wetherby? Why would he do that?' Longbright sounded sceptical.

'You know how Arthur always hated loose ends. He went galloping off to the clinic, made a nuisance of himself, questioned the nurses, poked about in their records and ended up with a shortlist of former patients.' May ducked through a grey wall of stalled trucks, heading for the tube. On the pavement ahead, a tangle of red and white plastic tape cordoned off a vast pile of roadwork rubble, more haphazardly arranged than any wartime bomb debris.

'He was only going to write up the story for his memoirs, but suddenly found himself back in the case. That's why he wanted me to go with him. He warned me he could get into trouble.' May was forced to shout into the cellphone. 'He found what he was looking for, then probably drove around to the poor bloke's house. You know how insensitive he could be.'

'The newspapers of the time called him the Phantom, didn't they? He was probably rather upset to be tracked down again.'

'Enough to follow Arthur back to the unit and plant a bomb,' May replied. 'From what we know of him, it would make perfect sense. A case of history repeating, a farewell performance. Finch said he thought the explosive material was old.'

'Yes, but sixty years old? Where on earth could he have been keeping it?'

'Who knows, he could have buried it in his back garden and returned to dig it up. I think seeing Arthur brought back everything that had happened, and ignited his desire for revenge.' May paused while the trucks juddered past. 'Listen,' he bellowed, sticking his finger in his ear, 'I need you to track someone down for me.'

'Of course, who do you need?' Longbright asked.

'Bryant's dentist. I know he's left the practice, but they must have a contact number. It's very important that you locate him.'

May snapped the phone shut and gave one final glance at the rain-filled sky before stepping into the clammy warmth of the tube station.

41

RUNNING TO DAYLIGHT

'You realize we're an hour away from tonight's dress rehearsal, and that we open tomorrow?' asked Helena Parole, lighting a cork-tipped De Rezske and fanning the smoke through the opened window in her office.

The young detectives were seated with her. Bryant listened as he cleaned out his pipe bowl with a pickle fork that he kept in his coat for just such a purpose.

'How am I expected to feel? I've got an under-rehearsed cast that's too panicked to concentrate on the score, a violinist who's more used to playing in Leicester Square for a hatful of pennies, a musical director who fights with the conductor over every note-change in the arrangements, fifty-year-old mechanical equipment that refuses to control several tons of lethal scenery, a replacement Jupiter who has never performed in the West End, a cleaning lady who's trying to scrub blood out of the balcony seats, and now some kind of women's temperance league is picketing the theatre. Stan and Mouse are spreading rumours about ghosts walking through walls. Benjamin got punched on the nose by a woman who says we're the spawn of Satan. I nearly broke my leg in the foyer after Elspeth's tortoise pulled rhubarb leaves all over the floor. And you're telling me we have an abduction on our hands.'

'How important is Jan Petrovic to the show?' asked May, attempting to look unfazed.

'She's just part of the chorus, not featured at all. I replaced her the minute she failed to show for the rehearsal. That's not the point. I have to be sure that you can protect my boys and girls, otherwise I can't go out there and convince them that everything's fine.'

'We're doing as much as we can. I'd prefer to see the production suspended rather than place anyone in danger, but Mr Renalda has every intention of ensuring the show goes on.'

Helena's voice rose a notch. 'This is no reflection on your abilities, Mr May, but in view of your *extreme* youth, I wonder if a senior officer might not be available now.'

'I'm afraid there is no one else available, Miss Parole,' he replied politely.

'They've spent a fortune on advance advertising and publicity. There's not a bomb site in London that's not been plastered with the posters. To Mr Renalda, a missing chorus girl is less important than an outraged review in the *Telegraph*.'

'Obviously we're all hoping that Miss Petrovic turns up safe and sound. We found signs of a struggle in her apartment, and several small spots of blood that may be hers, but no unaccounted-for fingerprints. What appeared to be a large smear of blood on a wall turns out, rather oddly, to be nail varnish. Beyond that, we know very little.'

'It seems to me you know very little about what's been happening at all. I suppose all the good detectives have been taken by the war effort. It's not your fault, you just lack experience. God knows who I'd blame. I certainly wouldn't listen to any of the cast.'

'Why not?'

'They're actors, for Christ's sake, they exaggerate everything. Have you talked to them all?'

272

'Pretty much.'

'What about those crazy women outside? Don't you think it could be someone who's taken the show as a personal affront to decency?'

'I think plenty of them are doing that. I just can't imagine anyone being so upset that they would break into a theatre and start murdering the performers.'

'Don't be so sure. The Nazis are on the lookout for signs of dissatisfaction and unrest. It said so in the paper. They're infiltrating groups and stirring up trouble, just like they did in the thirties.'

'I don't think we're under attack from German spies,' said Bryant firmly. 'My spiritualist mentioned Medea and Calliope.'

'Your spiritualist,' repeated Helena.

Bryant nodded, patting his pockets for a light.

'I'm surrounded by blithering idiots.' The artistic director rose to leave. 'If you'll excuse me, gentlemen, I've a show to rehearse.'

'Calliope was the mother of Orpheus,' Bryant explained once he and May had returned to their offices behind Bow Street. 'He got his musical talents from her. Perhaps we should take a look at the original legend, not Offenbach's version of it.'

'We're not looking for a mythical creature, Arthur, even your Mrs Wagstaff agreed about that.'

'We need to find a motive, John. Aristaeus tried to rape Eurydice, and she trod on a serpent as she fled. The poison killed her. Hemlock is a poison that was known to the ancient Greeks. Orpheus followed her down to Hades, and suspended the tortures of the damned with his music. Orpheus was instructed not to turn round to look at her until she had reached the light of the sun. Eurydice made her way through the darkness, guided by the sound of his lyre. As he reached the sunlight, he looked back and lost her for ever. Various reasons have been given for his behaviour. Some say he was frightened by a clap of thunder. Others reckon he was pushed in the back by Jupiter. Our Jupiter is dead, and can no longer stop the flight of Orpheus, running to daylight. Edna talked of ghosts, unseen hands guiding, pushing at the actors' backs. The girl, Jan, she's not been seen anywhere?'

'It's impossible to find out. The stations are still full of evacuees and servicemen, people moving around all over the place.'

Forthright looked in. 'Arthur, the article you requested from your journalist pal, Peregrine Summerfield. He's managed to find you a copy. He's sending a lad over with it right now.'

Several minutes later, a boy arrived with a brown envelope under his arm. May gave him sixpence from the petty-cash tin and tore open the accompanying letter.

'What appalling handwriting.'

'Give it to me, I'm used to reading his scrawl,' said Bryant, snatching away the letter.

Dear Arthur,
There was a lot of interest in this at the time, but the paper wouldn't run my article because Andreas Renalda got wind of it and threatened The Thunderer *with a lawsuit. The family was based in Calliste ('Most Beautiful'), also known as Santorini. I managed to locate his former home on the outskirts of Thira, but couldn't gain admittance to the estate. Everyone on the island knows the family, but nobody was very happy talking about them. I tried mentioning them in one of the local bars and the locals all clammed up, it was like one of those scenes in a cowboy film where the stranger comes into town. However . . .*

'Is there another page to this?'

'Sorry.' May handed the sheet to Bryant.

> ... *I wrote a profile and was even paid, but the damned*
> *thing never appeared in print. Andreas Renalda has made*
> *my life a living hell ever since, ringing up publishers and*
> *complaining about me. His old man employed half the*
> *island, and a lot of loyalties still survive. I suggest you read*
> *the article and form your own conclusions.*

For the next few minutes no sound was heard in the office, save for the familiar double clang of a distant tram.

'You wanted a motive,' Bryant said finally. 'It looks like we've got one. Listen to this.' He balanced his legs along the edge of the desk. 'Peregrine called his piece "Orpheus Ascending". Sirius, Renalda's father, lost an eye at the battle of Modder River, and was employed as a mercenary under General "Backbreaker" Gatacre during the Boer War.'

'That's not what I'd call a motive,' said May.

'Don't be so impatient. His wife, Diana, bore him two sons. Andreas came along in 1905, when his brother Minos was five. His legs were too brittle to support him, so Sirius had his workers build steel calipers that would enable him to walk. He had lost an eye before finding his own strength, so thought Andreas would also turn disability to his advantage. He gave Minos, his other son, an allowance, but reserved his empire for Andreas. He dismissed the missus to a wing of the house and took a series of mistresses. Diana stopped attending church and raised her son in pagan ways in order to afford him protection from enemies. Superstitious lot, eh? Andreas became the keyholder to a shipping fortune and Minos turned into an embittered drunk who couldn't touch his brother for fear of reprisals.

'Andreas married a young English girl called Elissa. He inherited the Renalda estate on his father's death, and it will be given to Minos only if his entire family dies.' Bryant swiped the papers with the back of his hand. 'Now *this* is where it gets interesting. A week after the old man's funeral, while Andreas was attending to business on the mainland, bad brother Minos told Elissa that he wanted to make amends for his behaviour. He took her out to a taverna, but only the brother came back. Nobody knows what happened. Elissa was seen with Minos on the jetty late that night. She supposedly slipped and fell into the water. It took a month for her body to wash up on the beach. Andreas took the case to the local magistrate, but no evidence of murder was found. The tycoon was convinced that his brother had killed his wife, but had no proof. Andreas moved to England, and Minos's whereabouts are unknown. Well, we wanted a suspect.'

'Andreas's brother. You think he could be here?'

'I suppose he could be using any name.' Bryant called in Forthright. 'We're going to need a recent photograph of Minos Renalda,' he explained. 'We have to talk to Andreas again. Have you got any tea rations left? We've used ours up.'

'Certainly.' Forthright paused in the doorway. 'Did you hear? The other army bike has turned up. No prints on it, though. I heard about Mr May's little adventure.'

'Where did they find it?' asked Bryant.

'Right outside the theatre, back with all the others.'

'I can't believe it. The audacity – he went right back. Gladys, what are you hovering about for?'

'May I just say that it's a pleasure to be working with you again?'

'No, you may not. Get on with your work.' Bryant smiled poisonously at his partner. 'I knew those two would never last,' he said.

42

MR MAY PRESENTS HIS THEORY

The follow-up to Coventry's night of terror was a bombing raid on London that proved almost as devastating as the attack of 15 October, when the city seemed to combust with over nine hundred fires. On that occasion all railway traffic had been halted, and the shattered Fleet sewer emptied its poisoned waters into the train tunnels at King's Cross.

On Saturday, those who survived the night arose to find great chunks of the city alight or simply gone. Hospitals, schools and stations had been hit, and doctors cut their way into unsafe buildings to administer morphine to the injured. Pumps and water towers were drained to fight the raging blazes spread by incendiary bombs. Because the city's water was routinely turned off at the weekend, the fire hoses had run dry, so riverside cranes were used to drop trailer pumps into the Thames from offshore barges.

Looters struck, risking their lives to pillage from the ruins of shops and houses while residents took cover, but most of the cases went unreported for fear of harming morale. A deep crater had been blown in the centre of Charing Cross Road, exposing the underground trains to daylight. In Farringdon, a fish shop was hit by a bomb that loosened a great girder, causing it to fall on a queue of housewives. Not even gangs of men could move the beam, and the women had to wait and die while a crane was sought.

Brick dust settled across the roads and buildings as thickly as falling snow, a pale cloak of mourning. All sounds were deadened. People moved quietly through the ashes like determined ghosts.

John May had spent the night under the stairs at his aunt's house in Camden. The noise had been deafening and almost constant, the explosions preceded by the droning of aircraft, the thunder of anti-aircraft guns and the ghostly wail of the sirens, one of which was mounted on the roof of the primary school opposite. The early fog was so dense, and the black-out still so effective, that May could see no more than a few feet ahead as he walked into Covent Garden, listening to the fall of masonry, accompanied by the chinking tumble of London bricks. The rescue squads were pulling down cracked chimney stacks and walls.

In Long Acre the atmosphere changed; the costermongers were still in fine voluble form, singing and bellowing jokes across their wicker stacks. Many offices asked their exhausted workers to handle extra shifts. With so many lines of communication cut, the daily push and pull of commerce slowed. But the size of London worked in favour of its population. No matter how much havoc had occurred in the night, it always seemed there was another way to get things done.

Bryant had spent the night in the office and needed to clear his head with a walk beside the river. He felt close to the truth and wanted to talk to Andreas Renalda, but nobody knew his whereabouts. There was no answer from the telephone at the tycoon's Highgate home, and his office was shut for the weekend.

The premiere of *Orpheus* was still planned for tonight, come incendiary bombs, hellfire murders or the Lord Chamberlain himself. The day was grey and dull, the skies louring with the threat of rain. Everyone was praying for a deluge to dampen the fires, and for clouds to hide the city.

An *Orpheus* lyric rattled around in Bryant's brain. 'The Metamorphoses Rondo', in which Cupid sings, 'What do these disguises prove? Only that you find yourself so ugly that whenever you want to be loved, you daren't show yourself as you really are.' If Andreas Renalda's brother was here, he could have adopted the identity of anyone. Tonight the theatre would open for the grand premiere, and the invited public would be admitted. How much harder would it be to spot a rogue face in the crowd?

Bryant studied the water, watching the chromatic petrol ripples of a passing boat blossom on the surface in diseased ziggurats. Then there was the matter of the missing girl, lost in a city of missing people. If Jan Petrovic had been kidnapped, why had no one heard from her abductor? What was to be gained from removing someone so unimportant to the production? He thought back to Edna Wagstaff's nervous chatter about the ghosts of the theatre, and how they walked through walls. How had someone been able to enter and leave the Palace unnoticed? When the building wasn't locked up, the two entrances had staff posted at them. There were two pass doors between the backstage area and the front of house, and one of those was kept permanently locked. The doors to Petrovic's flat were also locked from the inside. It was as if . . .

Edna had spoken of desperation, but someone desperate to do what? The police at Bow Street and West End Central were far too busy to help the unit. Sergeant Nasty-Basket Carfax next door had laughed in his face when he had requested assistance. Suppose Minos Renalda had infiltrated the staff of the theatre? He would be forty now, which eliminated quite a few members of the orchestra, about half of the cast and all but one of the house staff. Forthright was checking the ages of the backstage crew.

Bryant let his mind roam loose. In 1922, the Palace had premiered *The Four Horsemen of the Apocalypse*. Gilbert and Sullivan longed to trump Offenbach, and set *Thespis* among the gods of ancient Greece, but *Thespis* was now lost. The painting in the Palace Theatre's foyer was *The Concert*, a Greek revival subject. Offenbach's hero helped Jason to find the Golden Fleece. The brown interiors of the Palace were rubbed gold by the hands of patrons. Mythic links but also masonic links, the compass and the globe. Orpheus' mother was Calliope. The Maenads tore Orpheus limb from limb for preaching male love, and his head floated down the River Hebrus still singing. Which Greek goddess carried a scythe? Wasn't a scythe like a razor?

His mind was reeling with impossible associations. But there was a more prosaic possibility. The show was already being accused of blasphemy, indecency, blatantly unwholesome sexuality. Could some guardian of moral standards really have become so incensed by its perceived perversions that they were prepared to kill? The idea didn't sit well with him. The crimes felt passionless, almost accidental. It was as though anyone could have died in place of Capistrania and Senechal.

'I thought I'd find you here,' said May, laying a hand on his shoulder and passing him a silver flask. 'This'll warm you up.'

'I'm trying to think, old bean. Am I to be allowed no privacy?' Bryant grumbled, but unscrewed the cap and took a swig. 'This business is giving me the pip. If I had to paint a picture of the person we're looking for,' he said, passing the flask back, 'I'd reckon we were up against an older male, middle class, with some kind of grudge against the play itself.'

'Why do you say that?'

'Traditional theatre, by which I discount the music halls and picture palaces, is largely ignored by working-class youths. It's not really a public place but a sealed arena. Unless you're a paying customer or a member of the production, there's no easy way in or out of the building. Our killer acts with the kind of confidence that comes with experience. He's male because of the sense of distance from his victims. He's unemotional. Statistically, women make passionate murderers. He has a grudge against the play because the players themselves are unimportant to him. There's a plan, and we haven't seen its culmination yet.'

'Do you see any way of stopping it?'

'The theatre opens its doors tonight. The time for deciphering clues is over.'

'All we can do is be vigilant,' May agreed. 'Every attack points in a different direction.'

'Do they, though? Couldn't our killer be fulfilling a ritual? Orpheus faced the rigours of Hell before he was allowed to climb towards the light. I believe true evil is dispassionate, faceless, selfish. A game is being played out right before my eyes. Our perpetrator knows this and is unconcerned, or is so blinded by the need to take action that he's prepared to take risks.'

May had not seen his partner in this fugue state before. 'I think you're wasting your time with all this mythological stuff.'

'Oh?' Bryant turned to look at him. 'Do you have a better idea?'

'I wouldn't say it's better, but I do have a theory.'

'Would you care to share it with me?' Bryant jammed an absurdly large briar pipe in his mouth and waited for May to give him a light. He had misplaced his regular pipe. May would spend the next sixty years locating lost objects for his partner.

'Renalda's brother is implicated in the death of the tycoon's wife. Now he's missing, possibly here. Who would he want to strike at most? At Andreas himself. So he attacks the theatre to destroy his brother's empire.'

'But then he gains nothing financially.'

'What if it has nothing to do with financial benefit, but is simple revenge?' May leaned on the balustrade, watching the red fireboats pumping water.

281

'Why would he have waited until now to take action?' Bryant checked his watch. 'I have to find Andreas. He can't be far from the theatre. Let's have him removed directly to the unit for questioning, show him we mean business.'

'That's more like it.' May looked up at the dark, scudding sky. 'Listen.'

Bryant cocked an ear. 'What? I can't hear anything.'

'Neither can I.' May grinned. 'Wonderful, isn't it?'

43

MERRY HELL

'I have no time to talk to you,' said Helena Parole impatiently. 'When we hit our half-hour call in around one hundred and thirty minutes, the backstage area is sealed until the performance ends. Only the audience can enter and leave. Have you ever been backstage before the start of a first public performance? It's a nightmare, people running in every direction, and there's barely a corridor more than two feet wide in the entire building. You saw the understage area. Imagine it filled with actors waiting for their stage-lift cues. As far as I know, nobody's heard from Petrovic. Got a snout?'

John May dug a packet of Three Bells from his jacket and offered her one.

'We're not supposed to smoke back here either.' She flicked a cigarette between crimson lips. 'All these timber struts. But with buildings ablaze all around us these days, what's the difference? God knows there are enough fire buckets scattered about. Geoffrey fell over one by the grave trap and nearly broke his ankle. Quite how a bucket of sand is supposed to put out a raging fire is anyone's guess. The truth of the matter is, anyone caught understage would be fried alive. A theatre's no place for claustrophobics.' She rubbed smoke from her eye. 'This tastes like it's got vegetable shavings in it.'

'Mr Bryant got them for me.' He examined the strangely misregistered lettering on the packet. 'I don't think they're kosher, not at a shilling for twenty. He has a theory that Petrovic's abduction is somehow separate from the killings. You can't think of anything that would single her out?'

'She filled in the same employment forms as everyone else. We don't check their backgrounds. Right now, we're grateful to find anyone at all. I suppose it's possible she had another identity. Have you seen her rent book?'

'Yes, and I spoke to her landlord about her references. Nothing unusual there.'

'You know we have a full house tonight. How are you going to keep a check on the doors?'

'The only admittance to the auditorium is via the front of house. The ushers, bar staff and ticket tearers have to sign the book, and everyone else needs a ticket.'

'You've been around the building, you realize there are a thousand places to hide, and this maniac could be in any of them.'

'I know that,' admitted May. 'We can't search them all. We've only been allocated two extra PCs. Andreas Renalda insists that he's keeping the production open whatever happens.'

'I'd better get going. He'll be here soon.' Parole finished the cigarette and checked her watch. 'God, these things burn up fast. What do you make of him?'

'Seems very determined. A bit of a cold fish.'

'I just wish he'd keep his distance. He thinks we don't hear him, but we do. He gives me the creeps, thumping about in his leg-irons like the captain of an ancient vessel. This isn't just a financial enterprise for him, it's more personal.'

'What do you mean?'

'He's had one of the entresol dressing rooms converted

284

into a sort of chapel, and spends twenty minutes in it before he watches rehearsals. We're short of space here, John – may I call you John? – there's nowhere to put anything and there aren't enough dressing rooms, yet he's had one turned into a shrine. Doesn't count as normal behaviour in my book.'

'Is there bad feeling about that?'

'About that and everything else, Charles's death in particular. It was the one event witnessed by several people, and it's got everyone disturbed. You try standing in a dark corridor with ten other performers waiting to go on, and see if the atmosphere doesn't get to you. They fairly race out of here after rehearsals. No one wants to be the last to leave.'

'Who'll be last out once you start the run?'

'Elspeth, I suppose, although she's FOH, so actually it would be Stan Lowe at the stage door. He can't leave until the last of the backstage staff has gone. After the evening performances the actors invite friends up to the dressing rooms, but they're supposed to be out by eleven. Now that the run is starting, they'll go over to the Green Room, one of the actors' clubs off the Strand, or to Macready's in Covent Garden. You have to be an Equity member or working in a current production to get into such places. Absolute dens of vice, but I suppose they're a lot more convivial than staying here, drinking out of chipped mugs as the heating goes off.'

'Well, I'll let you get on,' said May. He stopped at the top of the stairs and turned. 'My colleague wanted me to ask you – the statue on top of the building, in the centre of the roof. You don't happen to know who it is?'

'I think she's a Greek goddess. There's some kind of odd story about her. She's holding a flaming torch, but she's not supposed to be, or something. There was an accident of some kind. I think she's bad luck.'

'You're superstitious, then?'

'Me? God, no. If you want to know about the statue you

285

could try the archivist, although I think he's moved out of London for the duration.'

'Do you know where I can find him?'

'Mr Cruickshank has a desk in the archive room, although you'll have trouble spotting it. It's buried under newspaper clippings and old building plans. You should speak to him before you start moving anything. Elspeth might have his new address.'

'Thanks.' He paused on the stair. 'And good—'

'Don't say it!' yelled Helena. 'No whistling, no well-wishing.'

'I thought you weren't superstitious.'

'I'm not,' she said defiantly, 'but obviously there are limits.'

'I'm glad we were able to run you to ground. Have a look at this.' Bryant smoothed the creases from the article Summerfield had penned for *The Times* and slid it across the table to Andreas Renalda. The tycoon was furious at being brought directly to the unit instead of being taken to his Highgate home to change for the theatre. He peered angrily out of the dusty windows as if searching for a means of escape. May called his attention to the document.

'What is this?' the tycoon asked, gingerly touching the edges of the pages.

'A history of your family,' Bryant explained. 'You were reluctant to talk about your background, so I took the liberty of digging it out.'

Renalda flicked the sheets aside in disgust. 'We sued over this damned article. There were dozens, and we took every one to court. They were appearing all over the world.'

'You won this battle without going to court. The piece was never published.'

'It was the last thing our shareholders would have needed to read about at that time, a public washing of dirty laundry. This man had no right to write about my father, but at least

286

he was one of the few to suggest my brother's guilt. Things were very difficult for me personally. I had lost my beloved wife, the light of my life.'

'You still believe she was murdered by your brother?'

'He said he took her out dancing as a gesture of reconciliation. My Elissa, out dancing, with her husband away on business! In our culture, this is not done. She did not know the island, and she had hardly ever had a drink in her life. They passed the evening in a taverna, and at midnight they walked along the harbour wall together. Ask anyone in the town and they will tell you that my wife was deliberately drowned. Every night, before I go to bed, I blame myself for being away in Athens on a trip that I could have easily delegated to one of my staff. Minos was waiting for me to leave.'

'But you have no proof.'

'There are some things in life you do not need proof to see.'

'You don't think that your wife—'

'Mr Bryant, I hope you are not about to suggest that she was in any way attracted to my brother. That would be an insult to her memory.'

'May I ask how your mother died?'

'In hospital, from cancer.'

'You've never feared for your own life?'

'Of course not.'

'I don't understand. If you're convinced that your brother is capable of murder, why are you so sure that you're safe?'

'My mother let everyone know that her religion protected me. Minos believed in the old gods enough to avoid angering them. Now I think I have answered all your questions.'

'But you,' persisted Bryant, 'do you really believe in the old gods?'

'It is how I was raised. I would sit in the cliff garden and see my ancient protectors seated all around myself and my mother.'

'And do they still protect you?'

'Of course. The events of my life are beyond my control, just as yours are. I must get to the theatre.'

'I'm sorry to have kept you.' Bryant rose to his feet. 'I was wondering . . .'

'Yes?'

'I'm fascinated by your mythological beliefs. I wonder if you'd care to take lunch with me tomorrow. The theatre has no performance, and you can tell me more about them.'

'I don't think that would be a good idea, Mr Bryant. I'm a little too old to fall for such obvious tricks, don't you think?'

'I assure you, I intended only to be sociable.' Bryant was flustered, mortified.

'It's all right, I suppose in your clumsy way you mean well.' He gave a sour laugh. 'You have a lot to learn, I think. I can take care of myself without the help of the damned police. I worry more for my friends at the Palace. My theatre is under attack, my staff are being killed and injured.' He struggled to his feet and swayed so violently that for a moment Bryant thought he was going to topple backwards. 'The Palace is being assaulted by Christian moralists, your courts are trying to close me down before we even open, and the press is denouncing me as a filthy foreign pervert out to corrupt the innocent, plucky islanders. This is no time to attack cherished national institutions. Well, we shall see who survives and who falls, but I know one thing, the show will go on, come hellfire, Blitz or the Lord Chamberlain. If people think I am the devil, we shall have a merry hell.'

And with that declaration of war, Andreas Renalda swept from the cluttered office with as much force as his crippled legs could muster.

'Interesting,' said Bryant after the magnate had been helped back into his car. 'He's hiding something about this brother of his. But he'll only answer direct questions, and I'm clearly not asking the right ones.'

'Then let's run with your instincts,' said May. 'Take a chance.'

Bryant shook the idea from his head. 'We have to uncover the truth about Minos before we start accusing anyone. Come on, it's time for curtain up.'

44

LOOKING OUTSIDE

'They've put together an e-fit of your culprit.' Liberty DuCaine waited for the printer to finish running off a hard copy of the monochrome JPEG, then passed it over to May and Longbright. The annexe of Kentish Town station was experiencing an eerie lull in the battle-stations activity that had been surging around them all day. Officers sat making quiet phone calls, wearily nursing plastic cups of coffee.

'What's it based on?' asked Longbright, examining the face on the desk.

'A couple of bouncers from the Camden Palace were walking past Mornington Crescent tube station, heading for their car. They saw this geezer come out of the door to the unit just before the bomb went off.'

'These things are about as much use as old Identikit posters,' May complained. 'He looks like a character from a video game. How can you identify someone from that?'

He studied the picture more carefully. It was the blurred face of an old man with staring alien eyes and abnormally large teeth. This wasn't Bryant's murderer. May was sure that the man seen loitering outside his flat had also stolen his partner's dental records. The infuriating part of it was, May knew his identity. But they had met only once, and had not seen each other in over sixty years. You could study the face of an old man and find no vestiges of his youth. DuCaine's e-fit bore no resemblance to that wartime killer. Time wrought great changes. How would he ever recognize such a person now?

'These two guys couldn't even agree on how he was dressed,' warned DuCaine. 'They'd been smoking a bit, and when I say a bit, I mean a lot.'

'This looks more like Arthur than our mad bomber. So much for technology. Did nobody see him turn up at the unit?'

'If they did, they haven't come forward.'

'What about the CCTV cameras?' asked Longbright.

'Nothing on that side of the road. We've got a shot from a supermarket camera further along the pavement, someone standing outside the entrance. Trouble is, the time lapse on the footage lets him simply disappear. All we've got is a distant figure in a grey coat.'

'You couldn't tell if he was carrying anything?'

'Not from the back. Nothing identifiable at all. I'm sorry.'

'That's all right,' sighed May, running his hands through his white hair. 'We weren't expecting a breakthrough. I'm told they want to use you here for a few days.'

'Yeah, I was going to ask you about that. I mean, the unit's got nowhere to work from, and they've got all this shit going on. Kids running around, taking each other out with activated replicas.' DuCaine felt guilty, but he was too valuable a resource to waste. His restless energy needed to be applied, and May wasn't about to hold him back.

'Someone around here is bringing Ingram Model 10 sub-machine guns in from the US and converting them into working firearms. It's the accessory of choice for would-be gangsta rappers. I've got some contacts, I can help—'

'There's no need to explain,' interrupted May. 'Do what you have to do. Longbright and I will figure this out.'

* * *

291

'Well, what do we do now?' asked Longbright as they walked towards the tube station.

'Something I should have done earlier,' May replied. 'I have to start thinking like Arthur. If he could do it, track down someone after six long decades, why can't I?'

'How do you propose to do that?' How much weight he's lost, she thought. This could be the last thing he ever does.

May thought for a minute. 'When I first met Arthur, he'd already suffered a tragedy. I didn't know it at the time, of course. It was your mother who told me what had happened. Later I realized it was what made him look beyond rational explanations. It drove him to solicit the advice of outsiders. In a way, it was what made him the man he became. It locked him out of the normal world.'

'You make it sound almost like a good thing,' said Longbright, stopping.

'Sometimes it almost was.' May gave a rueful smile. 'It could also be disastrous. That's why he needed me. To balance him.' He gave the detective sergeant a gentle pat on the elbow. 'I've been too sensible for too many years. It's time I learned the lesson he was always trying to teach me. Come on.'

45

IN THE DEVIL'S COMPANY

The audience was resplendent in evening dress, but most members were carrying gas-mask boxes. They were as Helena Parole had predicted, culturally more diverse, livelier and younger than the lethargic Home Counties brigade who usually attended operettas – perhaps reflecting that this was not in any sense a classical production. Eurydice's opening striptease and virtually naked seduction by an outrageously priapic Aristaeus saw to that.

The single intermission occurred between the second and third tableaux, and listening to the exhilarated hubbub in the building's bars, Bryant judged the production to be a hit – more, a sensation. The crowd made him feel claustrophobic. He descended the grand staircase and wandered out into the lobby. The bow tie he had donned for the occasion was strangling him. Few playgoers had ventured down here because the night was so cold. He nodded to PCs Atherton and Crowhurst, who were meant to be acting as security on the entrance but found themselves holding back a ragged line of irate demonstrators. Rain was falling hard from dark, low clouds, and that meant a cloak of safety for the theatre.

'We're going to need more men if this goes on every night, sir,' warned Crowhurst.

'They've got their own security people coming in on Monday.' Bryant studied the placards pinned to the steel barriers. BAN THIS PAGAN SHOW NOW. THOU SHALT HAVE NO OTHER GOD BUT ME. And more peculiarly, LESS LUST THROUGH LESS MEAT AND SITTING. This makeshift placard was displayed by a soaked young man in a corduroy cap who looked as though he would rather be somewhere else, preferably in a pub.

A mobile anti-aircraft gun had been placed on the opposite corner for the last two days, but now this reminder of danger from the skies had been moved away to higher ground. The theatre had been banned from spotlighting its exterior, and was forced to content itself with displaying a large OPENING TONIGHT! banner.

'They're all out this evening,' sighed Bryant. 'I'm surprised we haven't got any Band of Hope ladies.' Temperance women were known to turn up at any public event to extol the evils of alcoholism.

'There were a couple chucking eggs here earlier, sir,' said Atherton. 'One lady punched Mr Woolf on the nose and called him a dirty darkie. None of 'em has gone in to the show, they just heard that saucy bit about it on the wireless. You'd think they'd have something better to do with their time.'

Bryant strolled over to the box office, where Elspeth was closing up for the night.

'Have you heard from Miss Petrovic yet?' she asked anxiously, hauling a bagful of leeks from behind her counter. She had permed her hair into an unflattering helmet of Medusan curls for the occasion.

'Not a word.'

'I do hope she's all right. There's been talk about sea mines being dropped by parachute down the Old Kent Road. Sea mines! Apparently they blow up sideways and take out all the houses. I feel sorry for anyone over there tonight.'

'It seems quiet in town,' said Bryant, 'what with the rain.'

'I'm worried they'll shut the production down. The Archbishop of Canterbury says we're all going to go to Hell, and that the only practical solution is to pray.'

'Oh, he always says that,' said Bryant. 'The moment he finds something people enjoy, he's on the wireless faster than a cat up a Belgian, telling us all to stop doing it at once. Is everyone accounted for from your side of the house?'

'It would appear so, although I can only check the ushers and FOH staff. You'd have to go back to the stage door and see Stan about the sign-in book, but I think they've got a full complement.'

'No unfamiliar faces, then?'

'No, we know everyone. Mr Mack had to locate two more stagehands because a lot of the scenery has to be shifted manually. They're a father and son team who know the understage area well. He bribed them away from the Duke of York's.' She locked the box office and pocketed the keys. 'We're having drinks up in the balcony green room after the performance. You're welcome to join us.'

'I thought everybody had to be out quickly.'

'Yes, but it's traditional on opening night.'

'You know, I've walked around this place for a week now,' said Bryant, 'and the running of it is still a mystery to me.'

'Some people never get used to it. I've been at the Palace most of my life and I still get lost. I never venture down to the lower levels because the lights are scattered all over. You have to keep trying different switches as you make your way across, but half of them don't work, and you need to know where they are in the first place. Then of course there's the well. Everyone knows it's hazardous so they just stay away from the area.'

'Are there any parts of the building you haven't visited?'

'I've never been to the upper gantry levels, and certainly not to the grid. You can only access that via a drop-ladder, and I've no head for heights. Hardly anyone has been up there in years, but a couple of the stagehands had to get up there to refurbish the block and tackle system. You forget how big the Palace is. It's hemmed by three roads and a circus, all exactly as it was when Mr Sullivan was here.' A bell sounded above them. 'That's my signal. I'm not keeping the box office open once the second act starts, no matter what Mr Renalda says.'

'He wanted you to keep it open?'

'Until the end of the performance and for twenty minutes beyond. I told him absolutely not. We never have in the past, and he has no authority to change my hours because we work for different companies.'

'Of course, you're with the theatre management, not the company production,' remembered Bryant. 'Tell me about the pass doors again. You said there are two of them.'

'Yes, but as I explained, we lost the keys to the left-hand one. The right side still works, but not many people use it. There's no need, when you can go around to the stage door and access the backstage area that way.'

'But you'd have to pass at least one permanently posted member of staff to do so,' said Bryant thoughtfully. 'Who has a key to the pass door?'

'There are two, but they have to be signed out by Geoffrey Whittaker. He keeps hold of both of them.'

'Are you aware of him signing them out at all?'

'Not to my knowledge, but you'd better check with him. Are you going to watch the rest of the show?'

'Thank you, I saw it earlier in the week.'

'Yes,' Elspeth agreed, 'but you haven't seen it with the applause in.'

'My partner's prowling around the building with his henchmen, so I suppose I could spend a little time in the devil's company after seeing Mr Whittaker.'

'You can slip into the rear stalls box,' she said, leading the way. 'It used to be a cigar booth before it was converted to hold chairs. The sightlines are pretty poor because the ceiling of the dress circle cuts so low. We didn't open it tonight because Geoffrey's storing stuff from dressing room 2 in it. We'll have to, though, if *Orpheus* proves popular.'

'I think that's a pretty safe bet, don't you?'

'It's bad luck to discuss it before the reviews appear, but yes, I have a feeling we're in for a very long run indeed. Mr Renalda will be able to make good on his promise.'

'What promise is that?'

'Why, to run on right through the war.' Elspeth looked at him oddly. 'I thought you knew. He came round to tell us that he's done a deal with someone in the Home Office, not to let the bombs close us down. It's going to be good for public morale. "Britain Can Take It" and all that. That's why the Lord Chamberlain won't touch us. Apparently, Miss Parole will cover up a couple of the girls, take out some of the ruder lines, but we'll stay open right through to the bitter end, barring a direct hit.' She smiled nervously. 'You could say it's the first time theatre folk have ever prayed not to have a hit.'

46

FALSE IDOL

'As you can imagine, I'm rather busy,' said Geoffrey Whittaker, unsnagging his cardigan from a nail and racing ahead. 'Can't Madeline help you?'

'It's you I need to talk to,' said May, ducking beneath a low pipe as they passed along the narrow corridor at the head of the orchestra pit.

'It's the assistant stage manager's job to know everything I know,' Whittaker called over his shoulder. 'Mind out.' They passed a set of ten vicious-looking steel costume hooks, part of a quick-change area that had not been altered since the theatre's construction.

'This won't take a minute. I was wondering about the keys to the pass doors. I understand you're the only person who gives them out.'

'That's right. The left door got painted over, and then the lock broke. It was never much used because the company office and the stalls-level dressing rooms are to the right.'

'I need to know who you've given the keys out to this week.'

'That's easy enough. I can tell you from memory. Miles Stone asked for one a couple of days ago.'

The day the boy fell from the balcony, Bryant noted. 'How long did he have it?'

'A couple of hours. He wanted to store a suitcase, and it was too heavy to take the long way around. Helena borrowed the other one because she was shifting stuff out of dressing room 2 to make room for Mr Renalda's memorial thing. Sometimes it's quicker to do a job yourself than wait for the stagehands to do it.'

'How long did she have the key?' asked Bryant.

'She's still got it, as far as I know,' Whittaker replied as he vanished through an arch. 'She wears the trousers around here.'

Bryant stepped back and trod on Biddle's foot. 'Do you need me here, Mr Bryant?' Biddle asked. He looked very fed up.

'While you're still under the unit's jurisdiction, Mr Biddle, you remain on duty until we're through. Do we understand each other?'

'How can I help when you haven't told us what we're looking for?' asked Biddle angrily. 'I'd be more use filing DS Forthright's interview slips.'

'I realize it's boring for you.' The boy's attitude exasperated Bryant. 'Perhaps you'd rather be sitting in front of a nice big pile of paperwork. A lot of our tasks are the same as you get in any police unit, foot-slog stuff, standing around and waiting. It requires a sharp eye for detail, a good memory and an ability to judge character. But we have the power to leap off the rails of traditional thought and head into darkness. Once you've done it a few times you'll be hooked. Now go down to the floor below and watch out for anything unusual.' Considering there was a ten-foot-high three-headed purple dog god growling on the stage above their heads, it was a little like asking a clown to keep an eye out for any funny business.

Eurydice was imprisoned in Pluto's palace with her gaoler, John Styx. Jupiter had called for the three judges of Hades, and set about questioning Cerberus, Hell's doorkeeper. The gigantic six-eyed dog owned by Hecate was a mechanical device winched up onto the stage in three sections that slotted together as they met. It was a feat of engineering to rival the construction of a Spitfire, but with less practical purpose.

John May scanned the darkened auditorium through the velvet curtains and spotted Andreas Renalda seated in the royal box with several middle-aged men in smart black suits, who were busy ogling the chorus girls' exposed thighs. The front rows were filled with corpulent broadsheet critics taking notes, writing without removing their eyes from the stage. The orchestra performed beneath their steel mesh cage, a precautionary measure taken because the apron had been brought out to the edge of the pit, and some of the dancers came very close to the edge, much to the pleasure of the woodwind section.

May left the corridor and made his way to the rear of the stalls. He could see Bryant's tufted head poking over the parapet of the converted cigar kiosk.

'I thought you were keeping an eye on the backstage area,' Bryant whispered.

'There's nowhere to stand without being in the way. Did somebody check the fly wires on Senechal's replacement?' In the next part of the tableau, Jupiter was due to turn himself into a bluebottle in order to squeeze through the keyhole into Eurydice's cell. This involved him being swung out over the heads of the audience on a rig.

'I mentioned it to Geoffrey Whittaker this morning. They're using a double rig with a second set of cables attached. Did you hear about Senechal's wife suing the company for negligence?'

'Can't say I blame her. Gladys said she'd get in touch if she had any news on Petrovic. The girl Phyllis is adamant that she's been abducted. I'd like to know how her kidnapper got in and out of the house.'

'The same way he got in and out of here,' Bryant muttered. 'Maybe he's a magician.'

Onstage, there was a fiery explosion as Jupiter vanished through the floor and reappeared as a rather overweight insect. He rose from the ground and gracefully swung out across the front row of the audience, his wires glimpsed in the beam of the spotlights. Bryant held his breath, half expecting something terrible to happen, but the god made it safely back, flapping across to down right in order to duet with his lover. Bryant watched John Styx exiting the stage left centre with a silver hoop of prison keys in his hand.

'Tell me, who's got the keys to the top-floor offices?'

May thought for a moment. 'You'll probably find them in the box in the company manager's office. Why?'

'Something I've been meaning to do,' Bryant whispered, bypassing May's question. 'I'll use the pass door to the lift, I'm not facing all those stairs with my ticker.'

'Can't you get Biddle to run up for you?'

'No, I have to find it myself. Hang on here and enjoy the show. It's nearly the end of the scene.' Bryant felt his way out of the booth as a swarm of human flies invaded the stage and buzzed into a sprightly chorus.

The curtain fell at the close of the tableau, and reopened as the applause died down. Now they were at Pluto's orgy on the banks of the Styx, and once again the stage had filled with cavorting golden-breasted women. There were worse things, May decided, than guarding a theatre on a cold winter's night.

Bryant tried the lights, but nothing worked on the top floor. The oppressive darkness increased his heart rate. He pushed open the door to the archive and shone his torch inside. Beneath the photographs and programmes he found Cruickshank's desk. Beside it were piled damp-swollen books of building plans, blueprints filled with intricate arabesques of the understage structures, technical designs for a mechanized age too complex and cluttered for practical use. Bryant wedged the torch between his knees and flipped through the volumes, setting them aside one after the other. Finally he came to the volume he had been hoping to find, the one containing details of the building's exterior.

There, at the pinnacle of the roof, was the statue and a set of accompanying notes. Her designation, the name that had eluded everyone, was Euterpe, and suddenly everything began to fall into place.

He had been fooled – who wouldn't have been? – by the flaming torch she held aloft, because it wasn't supposed to be there at all.

According to the typescript pinned beside the picture, the statue was a copy. The original figure had been removed by the impresario Émile Littler, who had wanted it for his garden, but it had been smashed to pieces on its journey. A replacement statue had been commissioned, but a mistake was made. Euterpe was holding a flaming torch instead of her traditional double flute. Bryant shook his head in wonder.

Euterpe, the Muse of lyric poetry. He found himself a sheet of paper and began hastily scribbling notes in the torchlight.

47

DEADLY DEPARTED

Euterpe and the flaming torch.

He recalled Bryant's theory about the statue as he made his way through the crowded Camden streets. Euterpe had survived the war and was still cemented in place on the roof of the Palace Theatre, over half a century later. Not much else was, when you looked around the city. The Palladian stucco, the elaborate wrought-iron railings, the secluded courtyards and mysterious alleyways in permanent shadow, the absurd flourishes that gave the metropolis its character had mostly been removed, demolished, stolen. Developers had reinvented the future so ruthlessly that the London of his youth had disappeared. Offices were revealed behind glass walls, as though they had to offer proof of their profitability to pedestrians. There was no room in the modern world for anything unnecessary. At least Camden hadn't changed as much as people said. The layout of the streets was exactly as he had always remembered it.

The rain had eased, but the damp air invaded his leg muscles and made walking a chore. May wondered if he was being followed by the fanged man. He checked the pavement behind him. Camden was filled with students and tourists wandering between the market stalls. Every tribe and fashion was represented; nose-rings, navel piercings, velvet hats, leather jackets, Goths and God-Squaders, skinheads and Sex Pistolettes. A permanent carnival atmosphere had settled across the area. May was the oldest person on the street. Outsized sculptures of a spacecraft, a tank, a Dr Marten's boot, a rocking chair were suspended from the first floors of the high-street shops like toys discarded by a giant child. Camden Lock survived as a polyglot arrangement of stalls selling clothing, jewellery, incense, noodles and furniture. The pavements were dirty, noisy, chaotic, but alive in a way that the poplar-lined avenues of the suburbs could never be.

May felt bad about dismissing Longbright, but this had to be done alone. He stopped in front of the door leading to the flat above the World's End pub. A chunk of floorboard had been nailed over the letter box, giving the entrance an air of dereliction. A scuffed steel plaque on the lintel read:

COVEN OF ST JAMES THE ELDER
North London Division
No Hawkers or Circulars

Below this, a photocopied sheet read:

Suppliers of Equipment to the Spiritualism Trade
Wholesale Only

The woman who answered his knock had a square, friendly face framed by ragged curls of bleached hair. She appeared to have missed when applying her lipstick, and missed again with her eye shadow, so that she looked more like a confused plump poodle than a white witch.

'John, thank God, I was beginning to worry,' Maggie Armitage cried, propelling herself into his arms and hugging him fiercely. 'I'm sorry I didn't come to Arthur's funeral but the vibrations would have overpowered me. Isn't it awful? I mean, I know it's a great adventure for him, navigating a pathway into the celestial beyond, but I'll miss our monthly piss-ups. Sorry about the front door. Drunks kept being sick through the letter box. Don't talk to me about care in the community. Come on up.' She led the way into a tilting dark passage. 'Neema wanted to host a leave-taking ceremony for Arthur, but I couldn't bear the idea. She's a Muslim and I like to use dry sherry in the ritual, so we fell out.'

May followed the little witch into her front room, a riot of busy purple seventies wallpaper, battered Formica counters and plastic orange lamps. The thunder of a heavy metal band playing in the pub below was shaking the crockery in the kitchenette.

'What exactly is a leave-taking?'

'The idea is you summon the departing spirit with madrigals and conduct a ceremony to send it on its journey, but Neema's Yamaha badly needs a service.'

'She rides a motorbike?'

'No, her electric organ. It sounds so awful that decent spirits won't answer its call any more. The last time she performed the ritual she summoned an Icelandic incubus, and we had to burn incense-soaked cloths to clear it out. Unfortunately, she also set fire to the sofa and we all nearly wound up on the other side. Flammable kapok, I called *Watchdog* and lodged a complaint.'

Maggie's amber necklaces rattled as she threw herself down into a broken-backed orange armchair. 'There are only five of us left, you know. We had a membership drive for the new millennium but it's dropped off.' She waved a dismissive hand in the direction of the street. 'You'd think that lot out there would be curious about spiritualism, but they're more interested in shopping. Olive, the lady who used to conduct our seances, had to pack it in because she can't get up the stairs. She only attends the Hendon branch now because they have a ramp. Nigel and Doris have both passed over, and unless I use a spirit guide I never get to see them.'

'Do you still have Edna Wagstaff's cat?' asked May, looking around for the Abyssinian.

'I use it as a doorstop,' Maggie admitted. 'I fear its days as a source of spiritual succour ended when it got the moth. Of course I can't throw it out, because I have nothing else to remember Edna by, and she doesn't answer the Call' – Maggie pointed at the cracked Tibetan bell that hung above the fireplace – 'because she's a lost soul. Either that or she's gone deaf. You've lost a bit of weight. Are you dying?'

'God, I hope not.'

'God's not got much to do with it any more. You're not coping well without Arthur, are you?'

'I'll manage,' May replied wearily. 'Do you have anything to drink?'

'I just made tea. You can have a shot of whisky in it.'

'What brand?'

'PG Tips.' She made her way to the kitchenette and rinsed a mug. 'I suppose you want "closure". That's the buzzword these days, isn't it? When will people learn that there's no such thing? Life and death are open-ended. Everything begins and ends in the middle.'

'Not this time,' said May, accepting the mug. 'I know who killed Arthur. I just don't know where he is.'

'Perhaps I can help you there. Hang on a minute.' Maggie crossed to the window and shut the curtains. 'Did you remember what I asked for?'

'Here.' May withdrew a plastic bag from his overcoat pocket and emptied the contents onto the coffee table before him. 'You said bring something that belonged to him.'

'What is it?'

'A souvenir of our first case together. It belonged to a tortoise called Nijinsky.'

Maggie picked up the tortoise shell and peered through its leg holes. 'What did you do with the body?'

'I guess it just, you know, decomposed or something. Bryant was given the tortoise because it wouldn't hibernate

306

in the theatre. It lived right through the war, although its nerves went towards the end.'

'It's a bit Steptoe-ish, but it'll have to do.' She lit a pair of candles and set them at either end of the tortoise's earthly remains. 'Rest your fingertips on one end of the shell.'

'Which end?'

'It doesn't matter.' She seated herself opposite and extended her fingers to touch the tortoise, then began breathing deeply through her nose.

'You think you can really contact him?' May could hardly believe that he was doing this, after all the times he had given his partner grief about believing in the afterlife.

'As long as it's an object he touched many times in the past.'

'Oh, he had many happy years with Nijinsky.'

'Good. Now shut up and let me concentrate.'

May watched in the half-light of the front room as Maggie rolled back her head and fell into a light trance. After a few minutes, she started snoring. May wondered whether he should wake her. He leaned forward and reached out his hand, but just as he was about to touch her, she spoke. 'Do you remember the first time we met, John? What a sceptic you were in those days?'

'I still am,' he whispered.

'I can't be right all the time.' Her eyes remained closed. 'But you – I was right about you. You always did have a very powerful aura.'

'That's what Edna Wagstaff once told me.'

'So you do, and it's that which enables the sensitively gifted to read from you. You're a bit of a tuning fork.'

The wind breathed around the sashed windows, pulsing them in their casements. The sound faded from the street, and time was gently suspended. He remembered his first visit to the flat in 1942, when Maggie had just passed her nineteenth birthday. The surroundings were more elegant; she had fallen on hard times since then. But the flickering candles were the same, and so were the oddly shadowed corners of the room. He remembered the settling silence of the street outside, the suspiration of the wind, and the strange visions she had described to him.

'Oh, we're like hypnotists,' said Maggie, her slack mouth barely moving. 'Nobody believes in our effectiveness until some time later. You and I have known each other for over sixty years, and you still don't really have faith in me.'

'I wouldn't say—'

'There's no point in pretending, John. We're both far too old for that.' She drew a long breath, her trance state deepening. 'I am speaking now to the owner of this shell.' She tightened her eyelids, focusing her thoughts. 'He is dead, but present,' she explained casually, 'here in the room with us, right now. He is standing between us, silently watching.'

A chill lifted the hairs on May's arms as he shifted uncomfortably in his seat. 'Arthur?' he called, searching the shadows.

'He can't speak, poor man, he's dead. His injuries are terrible to behold. I can barely bring myself to look. He's put on quite a bit of weight. There is something he must communicate, but it's so difficult, so painful . . .'

I must be daft, thought May, sitting in darkness above a London pub, listening to the ramblings of a mad old woman. This is doing neither of us any good.

'He wants to show you what he feels, but to do so he must cross the divide between the spiritual and physical worlds.' Maggie raised her arms in a creaky gesture of prestidigitation, like an elderly magician's assistant. May had started to rise from his armchair when, to the surprise of both, a low rumble shook the room. There was a sheen of metal in the kitchenette, and something shiny shot between them. When May glanced down, he realized he was looking at a kitchen knife, and that it was sticking out of his calf. He sat down sharply in shock.

'Why on earth would he become violent?' asked Maggie,

examining the cut on May's leg. 'That's not like him at all.' She found a length of crêpe bandage and unrolled it over the cut. 'It's not deep,' she consoled, 'but I'm surprised by his behaviour. It's rare for spirits to react so violently.'

'It was the underground,' said May, wincing. 'Just a passing train. The vibration made your breadboard fall over and it flipped the knife from your drying rack, that's all. This bandage isn't very clean.'

'Well, you can choose a rational explanation if it makes you more comfortable.' Maggie poured herself a generous tot of Scotch. 'You never were much of a believer.'

'Not when the alternative is believing that my dead partner just tried to kill me. This is crazy. I'm being trailed by a man with werewolf fangs, and now this.' May rose and collected his coat. He saw what a mistake it had been to come here. 'Thanks for the drink.'

'But how are you going to find Arthur's killer?' Standing in the middle of the faded rug she suddenly looked lost and frail. This was how it would end for her, he realized, alone and bewildered, stranded by the world racing ever faster past her window.

'I'll think of a way,' he promised, taking a card from his wallet and handing it to her. 'That's my new address. If you need me, please call.'

It was the least Arthur would have done, he thought as he headed back down the stairs to daylight.

48

FALLING INTO HADES

'Hymn to Bacchus, we're missing someone, who's late?' Helena Parole checked behind her as she strained to hear the commentary on the backstage speaker. Pluto's party girls were arriving onstage in a hail of artificial flowers while the gods of Olympus and Hades caroused around them in various stages of undress.

'Goddesses are all on, Helena.' Harry checked the clipboard he kept on a string round his neck. 'The rest of the chorus are at the traps.' There were five narrow iron staircases on the first understage level leading to hatches on the stage, the centre of which was known as the grave trap because Hamlet had jumped into it during his graveyard scene. 'Everyone's present, they're just bunched up,' he explained.

'It's going to look awkward if the ends of UR and UL have to duck their heads exiting.' Helena checked the peephole at the rear of the stage, but the image it presented was so confusing that she could not tell who to move.

'Why didn't we see that in the technical?' she whispered over her shoulder to Madeline Penn, the ASM, who was trailing behind her with a pad and pencil, keeping notes on all the changes that would have to be made after the first night. 'Go and see if they've got the same problem over the other side, because there are a lot of flats coming down in a minute.'

The final tableau was long, and the full cast remained onstage throughout. Before they reached the cancan, additional chunks of scenery were to be brought up from under the stage and flown down from the flies. This left only a narrow strip for the girls to dance in, but the cancan was performed in a series of lines, with the girls yelling and pushing through each other, their ruffled dresses covering any awkward motions. It was a highly disciplined routine that was designed to give a look of wild, spontaneous sexuality.

Helena knew which of her dancers were weak, and had placed them in the second line. She was hoping that the attention of the audience would be focused on the bare white thighs of the girls and the high-cut French knickers they were wearing instead of traditional British bloomers. She knew that the reception accorded Offenbach's finale at the Gaîté-Lyrique in 1874 had never been topped, but she was hoping to beat it tonight.

Now Cupid, Eurydice, Jupiter, Diana, Orpheus and Pluto were onstage with assorted gods, goddesses and chorus members as the fiery crimson walls of Hades, great tilting shards of fractured glass, rose in panels, segmenting them off into different parts of the stage, ready for the revolve to begin its rotation as Orpheus commenced his ascent.

Sidney Biddle had started his tour of the building, working from the roof downwards. He pointed his torch up at the ladders leading to the grid, but could see little apart from a confusion of ironwork, suspended steel girders and cable drums. A pair of stagehands were balanced on rails in the gloom, listening for their cue beside the drum and shaft mechanism. Several more were waiting on the sides of the carpenter's bridge at the top of the three gantry levels, uplit in yellow and pink, like characters from a French Impressionist painting.

At this height the combined sound of the singers and orchestra passed upwards through the distorting baffles of the theatre's fifty-year-old mechanisms, creating strange discords that vibrated the cablework and hummed forlornly in the grid, dislodging ancient cobwebs.

Biddle walked down a floor to the area behind the balcony, past the offices to the fly and loading galleries. The scene was the same here: staff waited for cues, immobile, then burst into sudden movement for a few seconds before returning smartly to their positions. It surprised him that the backstage personnel were as disciplined and concentrated as the performers. He stayed out of the main backstage area, away from the gantries; he had no designated position to occupy, and was in the way wherever he stood. Consequently, he found himself relegated to the corridors and passages, unable to see much of the stage or the audience. He longed to be away from the whole rigmarole, to be useful somewhere, in an office of order and precedence.

To the right-hand side of the balcony, he could see the floor's electrical engineer watching for cues, and, for want of something better to do, went to join him.

'How much longer to the end of the act?' Biddle whispered.

The engineer held his forefinger to his lips, checked the stage and counted off fifteen minutes. 'Including encores,' he mouthed.

Sidney sighed and leaned back against the wall, frustrated.

Arthur Bryant pushed his unruly fringe from his eyes and folded the paper into the top pocket of his overcoat. He re-directed the torch and shoved the catalogues of drawings back in their places. After the death of Orpheus at the hands of the Maenads, his severed head prophesied until it became an oracle more famous than that of Apollo at Delphi, at which point the sun god bade him stop. His limbs were gathered up and buried by his mother's sisters, and his lyre was placed in the heavens as a constellation, so that his life began and ended at the same point in a great cycle.

Bryant was angry with himself for failing to recognize the symbolism earlier. He reached the door of the archive room and tried to open it. As he attempted to do so, he caught a glimpse of an angry white face in the gap. Someone on the other side wrenched the door shut and turned the great brass key. Footsteps thumped away along the hall. He pulled on the door, but the lock was set in thick oak and remained immovable.

He ran through to the adjoining chamber, but it contained no exit, only a half-boarded window that looked down to the street four floors below. With his heart thudding erratically in his chest, he watched as the torch beam flickered and began to fade.

John Styx took Eurydice's hand as Orpheus led them through the labyrinth of Hell. In front of the group, the earth's surface beckoned in the form of the single piercing beam of a par lamp, a lighting effect used to simulate daylight. At their head stood Public Opinion, Valerie Marchmont's face concealed behind a grotesque mask of tragedy. The procession walked forward against the revolve, appearing to climb towards the surface, as Public Opinion warned Orpheus not to look back for fear of losing his wife for ever.

To John May's mind, Eve Noriac was looking worried. He was not familiar with this part of the production, but even from the side of the stalls he could tell that something was going wrong. Eurydice stopped and nervously tried to pull free of John Styx's hand. May followed her eyeline up to the flies, but the gantries were concealed by the lurid decorative border that stood in for a proscenium arch.

At that moment, Jupiter was goaded into action, and sent a thunderbolt, in the form of an electrically ignited flash, across the stage. Orpheus looked back and Eurydice, now on her mark above the grave trap, vanished in a mushroom of white smoke. The scene changed as Eurydice – in fact a life-sized puppet cast from her nude body – was seen falling back to Hell, and a pair of great curving skycloths were flown down by the same drum and shaft device that hauled up the backcloths.

As he watched it swing lower, May realized that not all of Orpheus' group had moved clear of the revolve. Public Opinion, with her great trailing skirt, was still on the turning disc. The edge of the skycloth, weighted with a steel rod, dropped down sharply, moving towards Valerie Marchmont. Before May could do anything, it had swung down to her face, shattering the china tragedy mask she wore and yanking her off the stage like Eurydice's doll, but the audience noticed nothing because now the long-awaited cancan dancers were pouring on, screaming and high-kicking their way onto the extended runway of the stage.

May ducked out of the stalls' side entrance and ran towards the pass door, but it was shut tight. He hammered on it until someone pulled the handle on the other side, then pushed his way through to the rear of the stage. Behind the fallen skycloth, Marchmont lay on her back, her skull smashed through by the iron pole. Blood pumped from her severed carotid artery across the floor to the rear wall, pouring down into the run-offs that led to the main drain.

May looked around for Sidney Biddle and saw the young officer scaling his way along the iron-rung ladders that led between the first and second gantry levels above the stage.

Sidney had seen something from the corner of his eye, a blurred bluish figure strobing beneath the coloured lenses of the lights, but as he scrambled across one of the stage bridges, feeling it sway beneath his weight, he suddenly lost his sense of direction. The stage lighting distorted shadows, throwing them at mad angles across the scrims.

The dancers were screaming and whooping beneath him, a shimmering mass of white flesh and crimson silk. Above his head a shape shifted, knocking over a coil of cable, sending it unravelling down the side of the wing. Biddle ran forward, but the end of the bridge was blocked with equipment. There was no way of reaching the far side. He lowered himself over the bridge and swung his feet out until they touched the next gantry. Once he had established a foothold, he threw the upper half of his body forward and stretched out his arms, but even as he did so he felt the bridge beneath his feet kick away beneath his police-issue boots.

His right hand seized the railing of the gantry, but his left missed. He swung violently out above the stage.

As he hung from the bridge, his fingers slipping slowly from the rusty iron rail, the figure above him disappeared, a wraith returning to a realm of prismatic red and blue shadows.

The muscles in Sidney's arm betrayed him, and with a cry he fell to the level below.

49

THE PROTECTION OF THE GODS

The house lights were fully turned up in the stalls, giving the auditorium a shabby, melancholic air. Runcorn had taped off the rear of the stage. Wyman, a photographer from West End Central, was testing his flashgun on the blood spatters covering the backstage floor. The two halves of Public Opinion's white mask lay cracked in a coagulated crimson pool. It was now five minutes past midnight, and all unnecessary members of staff had been dismissed.

In true theatrical tradition the show had not been interrupted by the death of Public Opinion. The main purpose of the continuation was to buy the unit time before the news spread through the audience. Valerie Marchmont's body had been removed from the royal entrance on Shaftesbury Avenue and taken to University College Hospital in an unmarked van, the fourth they had used in a week.

'Has anybody heard from Arthur yet?' asked May anxiously.

'We've got him, John. He says somebody shut him in one of the rooms upstairs.' Gladys Forthright had slipped PC Crowhurst's rubber police cloak over her sweater. She had put her own coat down in the rush to help Biddle, and had lost it among the racks of costumes that hung like shucked carapaces behind the stage. Biddle had fallen onto a pile of folded backcloths but had split the cartilage in his left ankle, the tissue swelling so quickly that the theatre's medical officer had been forced to cut off his sock and boot with the blade of a pocket knife.

Arthur Bryant appeared to be in a state of great anxiety. 'I got locked in the archive room,' he said excitedly. 'He struck again, didn't he?'

May pointed to the rear of the stage. 'Public Opinion. Surprise meeting with a steel pole, fractured skull, killed instantly.'

'In front of everyone? How could that have happened?'

'One of the backdrops – dropped.'

'It came down right on cue,' said Mr Mack. 'Weren't our fault.'

Helena looked distraught and ready to sink a bottle of Scotch. 'The revolve should have carried her clear, but it halted suddenly. She was the last one off the stage.'

'One of the skycloth rods slipped out of its mooring,' May explained. 'It went right through her head, like a spoon hitting a soft-boiled egg, punched her backwards into the wall behind. Most of her brains are still on the bricks.'

'She must have felt the revolve stop. Why didn't she move forward?'

'Because the procession had to file offstage in a single column,' Harry explained.

'It's not my bloody fault,' exclaimed Helena, furiously digging through her bag for cigarettes. 'There wasn't enough room to take everyone off any faster. Getting into the wings is a tricky business. You have to wait your turn. Bloody, *bloody* hell, who's got a cigarette?'

'What happened to our cuckoo?' Bryant indicated Biddle, who was lying across two stalls seats having his ankle fitted into a wooden splint.

'Fell off the blooming gantry,' said Biddle. 'I saw someone

standing near the drum cable looking down, and tried to reach him.'

May turned to his partner. 'What were you doing in the archive room?'

'I had an idea,' said Bryant conspiratorially. 'I need to discuss it with you in private. I think I have enough to make an arrest.'

'You found someone up there?'

'In a manner of speaking. Greek legends percolate through our lives and live in our collective subconscious. You'd think knowing about the misfortunes of the gods would keep us from repeating their mistakes and go some way towards protecting us, but we're too blind.'

'What in God's name are you talking about?' May exploded, shocking everyone. 'We've just had another death, that's four to date, with one more missing presumed dead and one of our men injured, and you're lecturing me on Greek mythology?'

'You know my conclusions are, ah, well, tangentially approached,' stammered Bryant, taken aback by his partner's outburst. 'I can't follow your operational procedures, I warned you about that.' He blinked steadily, as though facing bright daylight for the first time, and scrunched his hat onto his head.

'Where are you going?' May demanded to know.

'To talk to – to – find out if I'm – I know who's on the list, the death list. There are still another four to die, they must die before the thing can be broken, that's the whole point.' He turned, holding on to the back of the seat in front of him. 'I can't believe you have no faith in me.'

'I didn't say that, but if you knew then why the hell didn't you do something?'

'How could I?' cried Bryant. 'I was locked in the blasted room upstairs. I couldn't get to the stage.'

'Wait,' said May, 'let me get someone to go with you.'

'No, leave me alone, I'll be fine.' Bryant turned, stopped in confusion, then walked off up the aisle.

'John, go after him,' urged Forthright. 'Just call in when you get to wherever he's going. I'll clear up here and get the archive door dusted for prints.'

May caught up with his partner on the steps outside. The rain had stopped and the night had turned bitter. Their breath distilled in the frozen air. 'I'm sorry I shouted at you, Arthur, it's just that . . .' He tried to give shape to his frustration. 'How can I be expected to help if you don't tell me what's inside your brain? Do you appreciate how dangerous things have become around here?'

'You'll think I'm mad,' said Bryant quietly, leading the way across Cambridge Circus, 'but I've got proof. If you believe in evil, you have to believe in devils. I mean the kind that live in your mind, the ones that are put there by people with the best intentions.' He unlocked the door of the Wolseley from the Bow Street car pool and levered himself inside, reaching across to pull open the passenger handle.

'I'll come with you, but let me drive,' May insisted. He could hear his partner's chest wheezing. Bryant was sweating hard, wincing in pain. 'Come on, out. You've had a shock. Sit back and get your breath. Then you can tell me where we're going.'

Tottenham Court Road was in total darkness. Someone had hit the traffic lights by the police station opposite Heal and Son and had knocked the pole to a forty-five-degree angle. Bryant prised open a window and drew in some cold night air. 'We have to get to Andreas Renalda.'

May spun the wheel to avoid the damaged post. 'You think his life's in danger?'

'No, not at all,' said Bryant, peering sadly through the smeared windscreen of the Wolseley. 'We have to arrest him before he kills anyone else.'

50

GRECIAN MOCKERY

The Wolseley pulled up outside the sandbagged gates of Andreas Renalda's Highgate house just as it began to rain again. May tried to use the windscreen wipers, but the Bakelite control knob came off in his hand. He chucked it onto the back seat and stared out of the window, impotent and furious.

'Helena says Renalda's Rolls left immediately after the performance to bring him back here,' Bryant explained anxiously. 'If he's innocent he shouldn't know what's happened yet, unless someone's managed to telegraph him.'

May pulled up the handbrake and climbed out. Bryant loosened his tie and fumbled with the passenger door until May yanked it open. 'I'm rather nervous about doing this,' he admitted. 'You know – accusing someone.'

'I suppose I'll have to support you,' May sighed. Being angry wasn't going to solve anything. 'How's your chest?'

'A little better, thank you.'

'Renalda has a very good reason for wanting to sabotage his own production.' Bryant clutched at his partner's sleeve. 'Wait, before we go in, listen to me. The whole thing starts with his brother Minos. Something bothered me when I read Summerfield's article: if Minos murdered Andreas's wife, why did he stop there? Because their mother had made him believe that Andreas was protected. She wanted Minos to think that he couldn't harm Andreas without hurting himself.'

'I'm with you so far,' said May, turning up his collar.

'To do this, she had to make her crippled son believe it, otherwise he would have made them both vulnerable. From the day Sirius decided that this child would own his empire, Diana filled the boy's head with tales of old gods, and Andreas grew up believing in his protectors. He's even built a shrine to them in the Palace Theatre. That's why he chose the Palace, because of the statue of Euterpe on the roof. It was a sign to him. The building was guarded by a Muse.

'I hadn't realized who the statue represented at first, because nobody in the theatre could remember, and I was misled because the statue is wrong. Euterpe has a flaming torch in her hand instead of a flute. The original figure had been smashed, so it had to be rebuilt from scratch, but the delicate instrument she held, hard to see from the ground, and much less dramatic, was replaced with a burning brand. This much I know. But now I see how everything fits together.'

'For God's sake, let's get back in the car until you've finished. It's falling like stair rods out here.' May settled back into his seat and turned on the Wolseley's heater. 'Come on then, give me the rest of your hypothesis.'

'Which gods did Renalda's mother believe in?' There was excitement in Bryant's voice. 'Euterpe was one of the nine Muses of Greek mythology. Diana summoned the Muses to protect her son. These nine sacred goddesses nurture and inspire, bringing continued wealth and good fortune. But if you've ever studied mythology, you'll know that every request made to the gods exacts a price. The price for this protection was losing Elissa, Andreas's wife. Andreas believes that everything in his life has been decided by the Muses his mother invoked. Now that Diana is dead, Renalda is exorcizing his guardian spirits, getting rid of them one by one. He no longer has need of them. Worse, they've become his gaolers.'

'What do you mean, his gaolers? I thought they were helping him.'

'My guess is he doesn't want their help any more. He wants to prove himself, to make his own way, just as his father did. So what does he do? First he negates Euterpe's power by daring to stage a sacrilegious play in her temple, the building over which she presides in the form of a debased statue.

'Then he chooses Offenbach's version of the Orpheus legend, because it's a cruel mockery, and because it will give him access to all the representatives of the Muse. The mother of Orpheus was Calliope, one of the Muses, remember?

'After this, the removal of his gods begins in earnest. He drugs Tanya Capistrania with hemlock, a poison his mother would have taught him how to use, but panics when he can't tell whether the drug has worked. He isn't sure the dancer is dead, so he drags Capistrania's feet through the trellis of the lift to make certain. Tanya, a representative of Terpsichore, the Muse of dance, loses her feet, you see?

'Next, Renalda impales Charles Senechal, a perfect living example of Urania, Muse of astronomy. How better to kill him than with a giant planet? Urania is usually depicted carrying a globe and compasses.'

May shook his head, trying to free it from the clouds of Bryant's madness. 'But surely Senechal was the wrong sex to represent a Muse.'

'Come on, John, gender is virtually interchangeable in Greek legend. So, where are we? Ah, yes.' Bryant nodded vigorously. 'Andreas watches and waits for his next opportunity. Nobody knows when he's in the theatre, he told us that himself. He spots Zachary Darvell, the son of the performer representing the Muse Clio, proclaimer of history, smoking up in the gods. He waits until Darvell is alone and attacks him with a razor he has taken from one of the dressing rooms, pushing the body over the balcony.

'Why Darvell? Because in ancient mythology, Clio's son was murdered. Renalda nearly got two for the price of one, because the real-life mother of the stage Orpheus – Calliope, the chief of the nine Muses, represented by Miles Stone's mother Rachel – was seated in the dress circle underneath. But Zachary yelled as he fell, enough for her to look up and get out of the way.'

'Do you have proof for any of this?' asked May, shaking his head sadly.

'I bet you anything that we'll find out Zachary is, you know, a confirmed bachelor. Clio's son was murdered by his male lover, and a flower sprang up in the blood he shed. The blood-spattered silk carnation in Darvell's buttonhole, remember? Whoever gave it to him is implicated in the murder, but we don't know where he got it. Which brings me to the woman he missed, Stone's mother. She had time to get clear, and it's ironic that she was alerted by the shrill blast of a flute, because it's the sound that always accompanies Calliope in Greek mythology.

'Andreas partially failed this time, but he can't allow himself to stop, so he must go on removing the power of each Muse, moving towards the day when he will be free of them all. Thalia, one of the three Graces, represented by Jan Petrovic, is missing presumed dead, then Melpomene, in her mask of tragedy, represented by the figure of Valerie Marchmont, Public Opinion, gets flattened. Five Muses down, four more – Erato, Polyhymnia, Clio and Calliope – still to go. Then he'll finally be liberated from his mother, and free to act for himself.'

'He's a cripple, Arthur. He can barely manage to get out of a chair.'

'For a man who makes a noise like a pile of saucepans falling downstairs when he walks, we still had no idea he was attending rehearsals. He knows every inch of the

323

theatre. Everyone keeps telling you the building is filled with hiding places. It's a mechanical hall of mirrors.'

'I don't know – he doesn't sound like the person Betty Trammel saw when she stayed overnight in the theatre. How could he have vanished from the roof right in front of the fire-watcher? And how could he have got in and out of Jan Petrovic's flat without being seen? Anyway, why is it so damned important for Andreas Renalda to be free of his protectors?'

'Because they prevent him from doing the one thing he longs for most of all.'

'Which is what?'

'To take revenge on his brother for the death of his wife. Revenge, John – that most classic of all motives in mythology. He can't do it so long as he thinks the Muses guard him. So he's showing them who's boss. He's humiliated them and now he's sacrificing them. The whole play has been set up just to do that.'

'And the Muses will let him without striking him dead with a thunderbolt? What about the creature? The terrible face? Others have seen it at night in the theatre.'

'Masks and make-up. The prop room is filled with disguises. They're used in virtually every scene of the production. They must be lying around all over the place. A Greek tragedy mask? Bit of an obvious touch, that.'

'Do you know what I think?' said May, his voice cracking with anger. 'You're deranged. In a week of utter lunacies, you've finally lost your mind. Do you have any idea how insane all of this sounds?'

Bryant's eyes widened even further. 'That's why I didn't want to tell you, not until I was sure my theory was watertight.'

'I think *you're* tight.'

'No, no. I have you to thank for seeing clearly. You're part of the maieutic process.'

'The *what*?'

'Socratic midwifery.' He shook out his fingers in frustration. 'You know, the easing out of ideas. You help things out of my head, things that were already there but unformed. It's because you're so sensible, you're like the control part of an experiment.'

'All right, let's confront Andreas Renalda and you'll see how crazy this – delusion of yours is.'

At the top of the drive, the magnate's housekeeper had heard the car doors slamming and now stood in the doorway to the entrance hall. 'Mr Renalda is getting ready for bed,' she warned as they approached. 'He won't want to see anyone.'

'We'll wait downstairs while he dresses,' said Bryant, loosening his scarf and walking into the hall. 'Can we get some strong tea? It's been a long night.'

After a few minutes Andreas Renalda entered the lounge. He was dressed in a blue silk dressing gown, and was drying his neck with a towel. The steel calipers were still fitted to his legs, and May saw now that they were bolted through the flesh of his shins, deep into the twisted bones.

'It's late and I'm very tired,' he warned. 'I thought we had finished speaking.' Renalda's housekeeper helped him into a seat opposite the detectives. He looked thunderously from one face to the other. 'Good Jesus in Hell. What has happened now?'

'Public Opinion. The stage revolve jammed and she was hit in the head.'

'Is she hurt?'

'Um, actually she's dead.'

Renalda swore in Greek. It sounded as though he said 'God in a gondola'. 'Did anybody see her die?'

'Quite a few people. The stage was full—'

'I mean in the audience. Did the audience see anything wrong?'

'No, the cancan number covered it.'

He thought for a moment. 'I am not without heart, you understand, but I must think of the show.'

'I think I understand very well,' said Bryant.

'There have been mechanical problems with the traps and flies ever since my company moved into the theatre. The equipment had not been touched in half a century. We cannot get any new parts. The company that made them is now making armaments. Every spare scrap of metal is going to the war effort.'

'Whatever caused Miss Marchmont's death, the theatre is closed as of this moment,' Bryant warned.

Renalda's face set. 'I think not.' He hurled his towel aside. 'Until you come up with proof that these misfortunes are the result of negligence, I can promise you that I have the necessary paperwork to keep the show open.'

'You're insured, so what difference does it make?' asked Bryant. 'I'll let the press in and turn the case over to Westminster Council. At that point, your personal involvement in this will surface.'

'What do you mean?' asked Renalda, his anger growing. 'You know I have nothing to do with these tragedies.'

'Arthur, are you sure you want to do this?' asked May, wincing.

'I'm fine, John.' Bryant drew a deep breath. 'Andreas Ares Renalda, I am arresting you for the murders of Tanya Capistrania, Charles Senechal, Zachary Darvell and Valerie Marchmont, and for the abduction of Jan Petrovic.'

Renalda's face transformed from anger to amazement. A nerve in his neck blew some kind of synaptic fuse and started making his mouth twitch.

Breathing ever more deeply, Bryant explained his hypothesis. It took him a quarter of an hour to do so, and when he finished he sat back, exhausted from the effort. He waited for Renalda to explode.

'All right,' said the tycoon, in a suspiciously affable tone. 'This is most amusing.' He wagged tanned fingers at Bryant as though he was pointing a loaded revolver. 'The true part of your – what shall we call it? – fable is how my mother protected me from my brother. He was not a bright man, Mr Bryant, no sharper than the average police detective. He believed he could not touch me for fear of something terrible happening to him.'

'And that's why you're taking revenge on him now.' Bryant was sticking to his guns, May had to give him that. It took guts for a 22-year-old detective to accuse a middle-aged millionaire of multiple murder and abduction.

'No.' Renalda laughed politely. 'Of course not.'

'Can you prove that?'

'I do not have to prove it.' He stared defiantly at Bryant, and a slow, terrible smile spread across his gaunt face. 'Even if I wanted to take revenge on Minos, I have no way of carrying it out.'

'Oh, why not?' asked Bryant.

'It is common knowledge. Even the most stupid Greek policeman knows about it.' Andreas Renalda shrugged theatrically. 'Minos, my brother, is dead. I buried him myself.'

51

THE END OF THE ROAD

'You honestly thought I would destroy the *Orpheus* production and ruin my company's reputation to take some kind of warped revenge against my dead brother?' said Renalda. 'British police. Too much Agatha Christie, no?'

Bryant wasn't about to give up without a fight. 'Can you tell me how you know that Minos is dead?'

'Well, I saw his eyelids and mouth stitched shut with catgut, and I saw him nailed into a coffin and placed in the ground, then the earth put over the top of him, and the shovels flattening down the earth, if you think that's proof enough.'

'How did he die?'

'He was killed in a car accident near Athens two months before the war started. He had been drinking all day. He lost control of the car and went off the road into a canal. He drowned, and so my wife, in some strange way, is avenged. I saw his body pulled from the wreck and buried in the family cemetery.'

'It doesn't make sense that Minos is dead,' said Bryant, staring down at the floor in confusion.

'I'm sorry it doesn't fit your theories. I suppose you can arrange to have his grave reopened if you like – you wouldn't be able to make yourself any more foolish. My brother's death is well documented.'

'Why didn't you tell me?'

'Why should I? If you had any connection with your police friends in Europe instead of keeping to yourselves on your funny little island, you would know how many times the press has told the story.'

'I thought you said you sued them all.'

'All the ones I knew about, but there were plenty of others. "The cursed family, the child protected by ancient gods." Journalists scaled the walls of the house to take my picture, they tried to bribe me, harassed me so much that I moved here, where I thought things would be different. The English, so private, so aloof, so secretive. They would leave the memory of my family alone. But no, along come you two, the music-hall comedians. Yes, I am sure that Minos killed my wife, but I am not glad that he suffocated in the filthy waters of a drainage ditch. He was blood of my blood. And I will not allow his memory to be defiled by young men who think too much about the wrong things.'

'I didn't mean to imply—'

'I know exactly what you meant. In your own clumsy way you suggest we are nothing but ignorant pagans. Our private beliefs have been raked over in your *News of the World*. You think I would slaughter my own cast and wreck my production, you arrogant little boy?' The veins were pulsing in his temples, and he began to shout. 'You pious English Christians, always so right, what do you know of the world that you have not read from your precious books? Do you know how many times I have heard these idiocies since my wife died? Her death was a godsend to your journalists, another tragedy in a rich family, and you believe it just because you read some news clippings? Get out of this house now, before I have you thrown out. Get out!'

* * *

329

'Well, that went well,' said May, stepping out into the pouring rain.

'I thought I'd discovered something new. I was sure Renalda was setting himself free from his past.'

'No, Arthur, you believed what you wanted to believe, no matter how demented the notion was. You squeezed the facts to fit your theory.'

Bryant was indignant. 'I did not!'

'Of course you did. That thing about the high note warning Miles Stone's mother. The flautist was late that day, remember? There was no high note from a flute, just somebody scraping a violin in the orchestra. And another thing. Edna bloody Wagstaff and her chatty cat. She couldn't have heard Dan Leno in the Palace, because he never came to the Palace. He died in 1904 without once performing there. She's just a crazy, lonely old woman. Andreas Renalda's story appealed to your romantic notions of classical literature and myths, that's all. Maybe Biddle was right when he asked to leave. You don't share information and you don't listen to reason. I'm not sure I'm cut out for the unit any more than he is.'

'What are you talking about?'

'You, Arthur. I'll never get used to working like this. Just sitting in your room is enough, all those volumes on clairvoyants, astrologers, white witches, spiritualism, covens. While everyone else is reading the *Daily Mail*, you're studying the *Apocryphal Books of the Dead*. All the stories they laugh about over at Bow Street while you look for a vampire that preys on foreigners in Leicester Square. Running down alleyways in the dead of night, trying to catch some kind of shapeshifting wraith that sucks the blood out of Norwegians. How do you talk people into believing stuff like that? Why did DS Forthright spend her New Year's Eve in a King's Cross goods yard waiting for a priest to mark out crucifix patterns in holy water? And did you ever catch him? According to her, you're the only one who saw him dash into that cul-de-sac. He must have run up the wall, you told her, they can do that in moments of stress. You have us all mesmerized under the spell of your insanity.

'Well, no more. I've just not got that turn of mind. It's the effect you have on people, you mean well but you get everyone caught up in these ridiculous fantasies. Why can't you just face the truth and admit you've not got the right experience for the job? You should be curating in a museum or something, lecturing on ghosts and goblins, digging out Egyptian tombs. It was good enough for Howard Carter, he didn't decide to be a policeman, did he?'

'May I remind you,' said Bryant, trying to muster some dignity, 'that this is called the Peculiar Crimes Unit?'

'The day we met, you told me that their definition of peculiar and yours were different. You just didn't warn me how different. I know you're a bit older than me, but I'd like a chance to handle things another way, before Davenport hears what you've done and nails boards across the entrance to the office. I should have put my foot down when you brought in the clairvoyant, then perhaps none of this would have happened. Why don't you take a break, go and give the ARP boys a hand, make use of yourself, and try not to think so much?'

'I'll admit that as a team we've been having a few teething troubles.'

'*Teething troubles?* You just accused a man who has the ear of the Home Office of practising witchcraft! Christ on a bike.'

'John, at least let's leave it until the morning,' Bryant pleaded. 'You might feel differently then.'

John raised his hands defiantly. 'No, because in the morning you'll try to convince me that Renalda is part of a satanic sect, or that the theatre is built on an ancient Saxon burial ground. Besides, it has nothing to do with me. Renalda – and Biddle, come to think of it – will be on the phone to Davenport right now, and he'll have taken you off the case before dawn. I'm prepared to go a long way with you, Arthur. I even see some demented sense in what you say. The killer is a psychopath driven by desperation, fine, yes, I agree with that. But Muses, curses, protective spells? That's where we part company.'

He stopped when he realized that his partner was no longer following him. Looking back, he saw Bryant standing in the rain, his head dropped forward onto his chest. He looked close to tears, but May knew he couldn't be because nothing ever seemed to upset him.

'Where are you going now?' asked May.

'I promised my mother I'd look in on her,' Bryant replied miserably.

'I'll drive you. There won't be any buses running at this hour. Then you must try to get some sleep. At least it's a quiet night. I'll go back to the theatre and make sure Forthright has everything she needs.'

'You're right,' Bryant said softly. 'I thought it was – I don't know what I thought. I'm so sorry.'

'Don't be, just get some rest. Leave it to me. You won't have to do anything. I'll sort everything out with Davenport. Just accept that things didn't work out with us, that's all.'

Bryant suddenly looked so pale and fragile that May felt a rush of pity for him.

He drove his distraught partner slowly back through the smouldering ruins of Hackney and Bow, past a makeshift hospital set up on the broken pavements. There were patients lying on brass beds outside McFisheries and Woolworths. A woman was sitting on the steps of a church with her head in her hands. When a nurse tried to comfort her, she pushed her away.

As they drove on, the devastation grew. The house where Bryant asked to be dropped was in a bomb-scarred terrace of slum dwellings long due for demolition. May was shocked to find that his partner hailed from such a rough neighbourhood.

Embarrassed by the events of the night and by his own impoverished circumstances, Bryant stood awkwardly in the entrance to the alley beside his mother's house and waited until the Wolseley had pulled out into the deserted road, its tail-lights fading in the thickening drizzle.

As he watched John May drive away, he knew that the unit's last chance for survival was leaving with him.

52

TAKING LEAVE

Early on Sunday morning Londoners once more awoke to the drone of the bombers, but the drizzle had persisted through the night, and only a few aircraft had managed to drop their loads. Several fires were started, and their smoke added to the city's dawning pallor of eye-watering gloom. After the RAF released two thousand bombs on Hamburg as a reprisal for Coventry, Germany turned its attention to the Southampton docks, steadily bombing them for the rest of the day. Attack, reprisal; the process continued in a depressing rhythm of retaliation.

Sidney Biddle sat on the bench near the tea stall with his hands stuffed deep in his overcoat, watching the oily water surge back and forth around the barricaded pillars of Waterloo Bridge like the action of some vast diseased lung. Daylight had begun to creep across the sky, and now he could see the silver barrage balloons following the shoreline. One of them was tied to the top of Bank power station's chimney. Another had partially deflated, and hung amorphously over the river like a creature in a Salvador Dali painting. Biddle's foot was throbbing, but it was strapped up with splints and bandages and he was able to walk with the aid of a crutch.

'Your char's getting cold, love,' said Gladys Forthright, churning the contents of her mug with the end of a pencil. 'They never leave enough chain on the teaspoon to give you a good stir, do they?'

Neither of them had slept. Biddle was angry and confused, but invigorated by the action of the night before, newly hooked on the case and on the unit. 'I mean, you outrank him,' he said finally. 'Can't you do something?'

'It may have escaped your notice, Sidney, but although I have the rank, I'm still a woman. Davenport won't even talk to me. He acts as if I'm not there. My appointment was approved because women have to be drafted into the force. We're fine for driving fire engines and ambulances, tracking aircraft and manning switchboards, but they don't want to give us jobs that involve strategic decisions. You won't find policewomen in positions of power. The men want to keep those for themselves.'

Biddle took a sip of his tea. 'Why does Bryant always come here? PC Crowhurst told me he sits at this spot nearly every day at sunset.'

So that's it, thought Forthright, he wants to understand.

'You don't know the story?' she asked, surprised. 'I thought someone would have told you by now. I know it's hard to believe, but our Mr Bryant was once a man in love. Back then he was still training out of Bramshill on a one-year intensive. So many were pushed through the courses because of the approaching war. He was very young, of course. Boys leave school at fourteen in the East End, and they marry early. By the time I came up from Hendon as a DC he had met the love of his life and become engaged to her.'

'Bryant had a fiancée?'

'Nathalie was from France, Marseille, I think. She was dark and rather beautiful. Not easy, mind you – very independent. When they met, she was working in ground command, co-ordinating air-support units. There were so many rehearsals for war that I was relieved when it finally happened.'

Forthright warmed her hands round her enamel mug. 'This is where she died, on the evening of her eighteenth birthday, May nineteen thirty-seven. She fell from the bridge, just in front of us. She'd climbed up onto the balustrade and was walking along it. They'd been out drinking, celebrating, and were both a bit tipsy. He'd asked her to marry him. She would probably have been fine, but at that moment a bus horn sounded behind them, and it made her start. She lost her balance, and when he turned round to grab her, she'd gone. Arthur jumped into the water and tried to save her, but the tide was going out, and the current was too strong. He was wearing his overcoat and hobnailed police boots. He nearly drowned as well. Underwater search teams dragged the river for weeks, but they never did find her body. The river widens here. There's nothing between us and the sea.'

She rested the mug on her strong, shapely knees and sighed. 'He was taken very bad for a while, tried to enlist when war was declared, but the War Office looked at his mental health record and wouldn't take him. They marked him down as unstable. He was training to spend his life helping others but hadn't found a way to save the girl he loved. She was the point of his life, the one he felt fated to be with for ever.

'That was three years ago, and although he never talks about her, he never looks at anyone else either, not in a serious way. Oh, he thought he'd fallen in love with me for a while, but I could see it was just a crush, and put him straight. As far as he's concerned, he was given his chance for happiness and buggered it up. It's something he'll never find a way to make amends for. That's why none of this touches him.'

'I wish someone had told me.'

'We all have our private tragedies. You can't change the past. You keep going.'

Biddle swallowed from his mug. 'I'm not part of your past.

336

You all seem suited to each other. I don't think I'm the right person for your kind of operation.'

'That's where you're wrong. We're all so different. They say all the good men have gone to war, that only the unemployables are left. That's why we were lucky to find Mr May. He's practical, he'll give Arthur the grounding he needs. We've no permanent staff over the age of twenty-five. I'm the oldest person in the unit. The Home Office will close us down as soon as the war ends. Davenport hates us, thinks we're a bunch of academic pansies. Now he's got all the ammunition he needs.'

'I don't see what I can do.'

'You've got Davenport's ear. You can protect us if you stay.'

'I already told Bryant I was going.'

'Then eat your words. No one will think less of you. Tell him you'll stay.' Forthright followed his gaze to the river beyond the railing. 'I came back, didn't I? Swallowed my pride. I was supposed to get married. I could have kept away, but I didn't.'

Biddle looked at her. 'Why not?'

'Mr Bryant needs me.' She checked her watch. 'God, I can't remember the last time I ate. You must be starving.'

'There's a decent workman's café near Coin Street.'

'I need sausages. You're allowed a hearty breakfast on the morning of your execution, aren't you? I'm in charge of the unit's petty cash, and you won't shop me, will you? You can tell me more about this monster you saw in the rafters.'

They passed a skinny brown nag drinking noisily from a corporation horse trough. Forthright paused to give its milkman a cigarette. The poor man looked on his uppers, as thin as his horse and the empty wire crates on his cart. It was the first animal she had seen in days; she wondered if they were being taken out of the city.

Biddle waited for her, then they resumed walking in comfortable silence through the miasmic mist that ebbed over the

337

Embankment, down to the roads where daylight and life were returning to the city.

Arthur Bryant gently placed the framed photograph of Nathalie, the one he had taken by the river that terrible afternoon, into a cardboard box, added his carved Tibetan skull, tossed in some incense sticks, some mystical diagrams of Solomon's Temple, several beeswax candles, a gramophone record of Sir Arthur Sullivan's *Te Deum*, two volumes of criminal records from Newgate Gaol, a three-dimensional bronze model of the Kabalistic Pentagram of the Absolute, a rare limited edition of Seymour's *British Witchcraft and Demonology* and a paperback copy of *RAF Slang Made Easy*, then closed the lid and bound it with thick brown tape. Set beside each other, the three crates contained almost everything he owned. It's not a lot to show for my life so far, he thought gloomily.

He propped the letter of resignation, addressed to Davenport, against May's desk lamp. He wanted to leave before his partner arrived. He felt that he had passed the point beyond which no amount of apology and retraction could return him, and he did not wish to place John in the embarrassing situation of having to defend him to their superior.

Perhaps it was for the best. He wasn't cut out to be a politician. It was clear now that the unit was little more than a public relations exercise. For a while he had believed that the old-money occupants of the HO could be superseded by a new breed of experimentalists for whom the past held no loyalties, that brave new rules would operate throughout British government, from the lowliest town council to the offices of Whitehall. Now he doubted that the war would make any difference to government at all.

Bryant loved London. He had been born in Whitechapel, in the lowliest of circumstances, and had grown up on the streets of Wapping and Borough and Mile End. He was proud of having got this far. But now the city was changing.

338

Its sense of good cheer was being chipped away by bombardment in a war that Neville Chamberlain had insisted would never happen.

He was going to load the boxes into a cab if he could find one, but remembered that he had packed some hefty mementos, including a paving stone that held the burned-in handprint of Jack the Ripper, and decided to have them delivered instead.

There was no place for his arcane studies in the police force of the future. He thought of his friends in the Camden Town Coven, and their arch-rivals, the Southwark Supernaturals. He gathered together the scrawled addresses of the Mystic Savoyards and the Prometheus League, the emergency numbers of the Insomnia Squad's sleepless academics, the diary that contained lists of assorted primitives, paranormalists, idiot savants, mind-readers and madmen, all available to the unit if someone only trusted him enough to use them wisely.

All for the best, he told himself. John was young and bright. He might be able to modernize the unit and bring fresh technology into their casework once Bryant himself was out of the way. They were clearly doing something wrong if they couldn't keep lads like Sidney Biddle interested enough to stay on.

He unclipped a small glass case of poisonous caterpillars from the wall behind his desk and emptied it into the bin. There was a time when he would have taken them out of their case and dropped them in Oswald Finch's teapot, but the spirit had gone out of him.

Bryant saw now that he had willed a culprit into existence because he wanted to be challenged. The real solution would doubtless prove to be rather ordinary, not peculiar or paradoxical at all, a disgruntled employee, a youth filled with such directionless anger that he could equally have decided to attack the staff of a bus depot or an insurance office. Grey crimes for a grey nation.

It was the second time he had failed. Overcoming his guilt about Nathalie's death had been tough, and just when the world was starting to make sense again he saw that he hadn't made sense of it at all. He knew he would have to write a formal apology to Renalda.

He looked about the desktop to see if there was anything he had forgotten, and saw that the drawing of the statue he had deciphered as the key to a mythological conundrum was just another memento. He carefully folded it into a square, tucked it into his tattered briefcase and snapped the lock shut.

Pausing in the doorway, he took one last look around the room he and May had shared for the past few days, and wondered about the cases they might have solved together.

Then he quietly pulled the door shut behind him.

53

TOUCHING THE TORTOISE

Mementos and conundrums, all the cases we solved together, thought May. It was always Bryant who had set the puzzles. He himself had just been the faithful sidekick, an anchor of reason to his partner's flights of fancy. We solved our first case together. I'll solve our last one if it kills me.

His bandaged leg was swollen and sore. He looked along the crowded platform of the tube station, unpleasantly sweaty even though the day was cold, and waited for the approaching train. He felt his coat pockets. The tortoise; he had left the damned shell in Maggie's flat, but he wasn't going back for it now. I'm old, I'm tired and I've been stabbed by a ghost, he thought angrily.

Not that he remotely believed in such things. The breadboard had fallen, hitting the handle of the knife. More accidents happened at home than anywhere else. Besides, even if he was a believer it would have made no sense. Why would his best friend return from the grave to hurt him? The only person who could do that now was very much alive.

Except that it wasn't him ... unless he had grown fangs ...

And then he saw the error he had made. He saw how badly he had misread the situation, just as Arthur had all those years before. How guilty he had been of jumping to the same mistaken conclusion.

May pushed his way back up the stairs of Camden Town tube station, fighting the onrushing flow of travellers. He needed to obtain a signal for his mobile. Outside, wedged into a litter-strewn corner, he punched out Alma Sorrowbridge's number. He waited for fourteen rings, but there was no answer. The shadow of the buildings opposite had begun to reach this side of the street. He looked at the keypad of his mobile, and was about to try her again when it rang.

'Grandad, is that you?'

'April?'

His granddaughter couldn't have picked a worse time to call, but it was good to hear her voice.

'I've been meaning to ring you for days. I was so sorry to hear about Mr Bryant. He was always nice to me. You must be—'

'Listen,' May cut across her, 'I'm more sorry than you could ever be. Arthur asked me to call you and I didn't. I've been too wrapped up in my own problems. How are you? Have you been able to get out at all?'

'A little. It's tough. Open spaces still do my head in, but I'm handling it.'

'Remember what the doctor said, one step at a time.'

'I know, but I want to go back to work,' April complained. 'I've seen enough of these walls to last a lifetime. I could do with some advice.'

'Sure. I'll come and see you.'

He wanted to tell her he was ashamed, that he would make up the time they had lost. Instead he could only promise to ring her again in a day or so. It wasn't much, but it was a start.

'It's funny speaking to you at this hour. It's the time I always think of you.'

May was puzzled. 'Why?' he asked.

'Oh, you know. You always took a walk with Mr Bryant at sunset. It was the only real ritual you had.'

'I suppose it was a ritual, wasn't it?' May was amazed he hadn't thought of it earlier. 'I'll call you tomorrow, sweetheart. There's something I have to put right.'

And he was off along the pavement, moving around the crowds and into the road, the pain in his leg forgotten, breaking into a run as he speed-dialled Janice Longbright's number, praying that she would pick up the phone.

54

FULL DARK HOUSE

'There's nothing to report that a layman can't see with a cursory examination of the body,' said young Oswald Finch, rinsing his hands at the deep ceramic sink. The remains of Valerie Marchmont, Public Opinion, lay under an ordinary bedsheet; the army had requisitioned the pathology unit's entire supply of rubberized covers.

'It's the same as the others. There are no second-agent marks on the skin or clothing, just a few fragments of corroded metal at the contact point. I presume the iron rod that passed through her head was slightly rusted. Some of the rust was scraped off by the edges of the skull. Not much point in making a toxicological examination, but I'll do one if you want. The damage is consistent with what you'd expect to find in an accident of this kind. You see wounds like this all over London these days.'

'Dr Runcorn has been over the stage equipment but he's come up with nothing,' said May, leaning against the sink with his hands thrust into his pockets. 'The skycloth came down a fraction later and slightly further over to centre stage than it was supposed to, and the revolve stuck for a moment. The stagehands reckon they oiled the revolve before the performance but say it still judders occasionally.'

'An unfortunate combination of factors. Although I daresay young Mr Bryant would have us believe something different if he was here.' Finch rubbed a lotion into his fingers that was supposed to remove the smell of chemicals. 'To be honest, it surprises me that Bryant could be so *completely* wrong. I mean, we've had our disagreements, and he's certainly going to make mistakes during a time like this when you can't get your hands on basic equipment, but there's usually something vaguely right about his thinking. Are we having a farewell party?'

'I don't think any of us could stand it,' said May despondently. 'His landlady hasn't seen him, only his boxes. He's not been home for a change of clothes. It's been two days now. I wondered if he might have gone to stay with relatives.'

'He could be at his mother's in Bethnal Green Road. Forthright tells me the house next door to Mrs Bryant's got bombed out and she's worried about her walls falling in. I know he wanted to help her move somewhere safer. She's not on the telephone but I daresay someone in the local nick could run round.' Finch leaned back on a stool and administered drops to his right pupil. The atmosphere of formaldehyde left him with perpetually red-rimmed eyelids.

'Do you think Davenport will keep us open with Bryant gone?' asked May.

'That's a tough one, seeing as he set you chaps up in the first place. It could be construed as failure on his part. He'll probably merge you with one of the other divisions: fraud or this special squad that's been set up to deal with looters. At least it'll keep you afloat. Did Forthright mention that your Mr Biddle has had a change of heart? He's decided to stay on after all.'

'That's good,' May said. 'Arthur thought he might come round. What happened to the tree he gave you?'

'Bit of a sore point, that. It was too big for the bureau

345

so I took it home, and now the wife won't talk to me.'

'Why?'

'Her cat ate one of the leaves and died. She tried to chop it down with a kitchen knife and it leaked some kind of poisonous sap on her. The doctor reckons her arm should stay bandaged for at least a week, which is inconvenient because she plays the organ. I have a suspicion', he said, blinking the drops from his left eye, 'that it was one of Bryant's pranks. He really was the most impossible man.'

'He's not dead,' said May.

'Well, he is missing,' responded Finch, dabbing his eyes on a flannel and blinking.

May was surprised by the way his partner had responded to failure, but his first duty was to the case. 'He'll turn up,' he said unsurely. 'You might try liaising a little more with Dr Runcorn rather than telling me you can't find anything. Four dead, one vanished, a few near misses. I need physical proof fast, or we'll all be out of a job. A couple of heel marks, no fingerprints, no real murder weapons to speak of, it's not much to go on. You'd think we were dealing with someone who doesn't exist in the real world.'

The annoying thing was that, although he had not believed Bryant's explanation, his partner was still the only one to come up with any suggestions at all.

He looked in on Forthright and Biddle, who were continuing to check customs information from air, sea and freight terminals for the whereabouts of Jan Petrovic. At dusk he walked through brown smoke billowing across Lincoln's Inn Fields, searching the darkness of the unsettled trees as he tried to work out how they had gone so wrong. Crows called loudly from the lower branches as he passed beneath them, their old eyes glittering between the leaves. An elderly man was hoeing a muddy trough through an allotment, one of many that had been dug across the once-perfect lawns.

Just when he was free to follow traditional procedures,

346

May tried to imagine how Bryant would consider the evidence. Minos Renalda was dead, and with him died a motive for revenge. Forthright had confirmed that Andreas was a witness to his brother's burial. The body had also been identified by close friends and relatives.

But what of Elissa Renalda? Her body had been too long in the water for proper identification. Suppose it hadn't been her, and she had survived somehow? What if she had returned and disguised herself as a member of the cast, and was trying to destroy her husband for – what? Failing to save her from his brother? May angrily kicked a stone into the bushes. That was the trouble with thinking like Bryant, it made absolutely no sense.

When he reached his aunt's house in Camden Town, he opened his briefcase and pulled out a stack of the unit's files. Bryant had perversely embedded his private notes into illustrated cryptograms representing Offenbach's theatre posters. To provide the reader with clues, he had painted sections of the posters in the wrong colours to their originals. He had taken Davenport's precautionary measures to a ludicrous degree, without disobeying his orders. Codes, encryptions, puzzles, everything was a game to him, thought May as he began to sort through the material, wondering if Bryant, wherever he might be, was thinking of the files and chuckling at his partner's confusion.

He sat on the candlewick bedspread and laid the posters before him, trying to plot a new direction through the details of the case. He could hear his aunt on the landing outside, polishing the lino for the third time in a week. Perhaps as a response to the chaos outside, she had become obsessed with keeping the house immaculate. She made her own cleaning fluid from Castile soap, saltpetre and ammonia, and mixed up polishes and linaments from turpentine and vinegar until the entire house stank. He felt trapped in the dark little terrace, too broke to be able to take a girl anywhere, unable to get away from the blighted city, unwilling to knock mugs with the sanctimonious doomsayers and patriots who gathered around the piano in the corner pub.

His best bet, he knew, was to sort out the mess at the Palace and get a recommendation out of the unit. He thought of the way he had arrived at Bow Street the previous Monday, full of expectation for the days ahead. Instead he felt lost and abandoned. Arthur Bryant was the most annoying man he had ever met, but at least he was fun to be around. May lacked the confidence to continue without him. Now all he saw in the days ahead was failure and shame.

The door of Helena's office burst open, and Harry ran in. 'Can you come quickly?' he gasped. 'The Phantom, we've got him cornered.'

It was the middle of Monday morning, and the first rehearsal after the start of the run was in as good a shape as could be expected. Reviews were in, a combination of outrage and ecstasy in equal measure. Sandwiched between cheering articles about opera singers becoming train drivers and church wardens who had narrowly missed being hit by bombs were the sexy photographs that Helena Parole had approved for use. The scantily clothed chorus girls were already being nicknamed 'Dante's Infernettes', and had prompted outraged calls to the Public Morality Council. This august body already had its in-trays full, thanks to the problem of 'undesirable women' approaching servicemen in the West End, and had formally asked the Provost Marshal for military police to help close London's illegal gambling and drinking dens. Without the Lord Chamberlain to back them, the council could only acknowledge complaints against the theatre and suggest that it was carrying out investigations into the matter of public indecency.

Harry excitedly led Helena up the central staircase and down through the upper circle. 'Look over there,' he cried, pointing up into the gantry that ran along the right side of the stage. 'One of the profile spots came loose and fell onto the stage, missed Eve by inches. Luckily she'd just been called back by Ben Woolf.'

'What was he doing up onstage?'

'I don't know, giving her some kind of legal advice, I think. The stagehands saw someone up on the rear gantry, moving about by the lights. He's trapped against that far wall.' A dark shape could be discerned caught in the crossbeams of torches.

'He's making weird noises,' said Harry. 'Nobody's had the nerve to go and challenge him because the walkspace is very narrow, and the rails are low.'

'Can't you get more light on him?' asked John May, beckoning to Biddle.

'We can put the house lights up and all the backstage ones, but it'll take a few minutes. Half the areas near the top of the house will still be in darkness,' warned Biddle.

'All right, let me think. Sidney, how's your foot?'

'I can be pretty sharp on it if I have to be.'

'Then you can give me a hand. Get Crowhurst off the stage door. You go up to the balcony.'

Sidney hobbled forward as the others approached the figure behind the torchlights.

'I know who it is,' Harry announced as they stepped onto the gantry. 'It's that rude critic who wrote about us being cursed and snored through the second half on opening night. He trod on my foot at the intermission, rushing to get to the bar, without so much as a by your leave.'

'Gilbert Riley?' asked Helena Parole. 'Are you sure? What's he doing up here? Mr Riley, is that you?'

'Dear lady,' called a wavering voice. 'I was making some notes, but I'm stuck. My trousers are caught on something.' His arrogant tone had vanished. As more torch beams pinpointed him, they could see the goateed critic splayed above the stage like a Savile Row-suited barrage balloon.

'Sidney, see if you can get him free,' directed May.

'Maybe we should just leave him there.'

'Don't tempt me. What *are* you doing here, Mr Riley? You know it's off-limits.'

'That's the problem,' whined Riley. 'No one will talk to me about what's going on. I'm trying to do a feature and no one will tell me the truth. I'm doing your show a favour, bringing it the oxygen of publicity. The least anyone could do is return my calls.'

'So you thought you'd break in and nose around.'

'It's hardly breaking in. I know the boys on the stage door.'

'You mean you bribed them. And you nearly killed someone.'

The critic raised his hands in a gesture of horror. 'I leaned on one of the lights to get a better view and it came loose. Everything is held together with clips and ropes up here.'

'You're not supposed to be here at all, Riley,' said Biddle, reaching over and tugging at his trousers. 'There you go.' There was a tearing sound, and the critic fell forward with a yelp. The officers helped him back onto the balcony.

'For this I thank you, dear fellow,' said Riley shakily. He dusted down the knees of his trousers, regaining his composure. 'It was ghastly. There was someone else back there with me, breathing heavily through his nose. It sounded like he was wearing a gas mask. I could hear him moving around, jumping between the gantries. He stopped right in front of me, watching, then moved away.'

'You didn't get a good look at him?' asked May.

'Only enough to see that he was barely human, hulking and hunched over, a giant dwarf or some kind of large animal, great big teeth. I'm sure he meant to do me harm.'

'He's not alone there,' muttered Parole. 'And I'm not sure what you mean by a giant dwarf.'

'I think you should go down to the stalls and apologize to the cast for nearly wiping out the star of the show,' Biddle told him. 'Then we'll go and write up your report while Mr May decides what to charge you with.'

'Charge me?' Riley looked shocked.

'Unlawful entry and trespass,' agreed May, taking his cue from Biddle, 'circumstances of *actus reus*, some broken by-laws because this is a public building, several causation and situational offences, and anything else the lads can think of, the precedent of the Crown *v.* Woolmington nineteen thirty-five springs to mind. Then Miss Noriac will probably want to press charges for invasion of privacy and attempted assault, and sue you and your paper, assuming you were acting under its auspices, for causing her undue distress.'

'Please, no! Think of the publicity!' Riley wheezed.

'I imagine her attitude could be mitigated by the level of contrition you show her.'

'And you might want to pin yourself up, seeing as your arse is hanging out of your trousers and there are ladies below,' added Biddle, leading the horrified critic downstairs. Parole and May followed at a polite distance.

'Are you really going to press all those charges?' asked Helena as they descended to the stalls.

'No, I was talking absolute rubbish. So, another false alarm.'

'It's wearing down my cast. They're seeing things in every dark corner. We're all spooked, but of course nobody wants the show to close. I think I preferred it when there was just a murderer loose. Now all they talk about is this – creature.'

'You shouldn't believe everything you read in the papers,' said May.

'No, other people have seen things. Corinne says she glimpsed it again in the upper circle. Says it was running on its hands like a monkey. Madeline, my ASM, was understage and heard something hooting, or crying, near the orchestra. She reckons it sounded like an animal in pain. Your Betty still hasn't got over her nasty turn.'

That's a point, thought May. We were supposed to see each other at the weekend. He suddenly realized that he had been too preoccupied by the investigation to call her.

'They can't all be imagining things,' Helena continued, 'but what on earth could it be? It's not like anybody's keeping a noisy pet tucked away backstage. Stan Lowe was the only one in last night, and said he was just about to lock up when he saw the shadow of something swinging back and forth on the underside of the dress circle. I know they're very artistic people but this is a kind of collective madness. It's a dilemma: do we stay open for business and hope to catch this thing, or close and never discover the truth? Have you heard anything from the council?'

'Still no word from Westminster on the safety ruling,' said May, 'and the Lord Chamberlain's office is suspiciously silent, so I think it's safe to assume that Renalda nobbled them.'

Helena stopped as they reached the landing. 'I hear your partner accused Andreas of sabotaging his own production, and that he's been chucked off the case.' She smiled ominously at him. 'Don't look so surprised. Everyone talks around here. You should hear some of the rumours. I even heard that he was having an affair with poor Elspeth, but I know that's not true.'

'Why are you so sure?'

'Darling, she's a professional virgin. Married to the theatre. It takes some people like that. They get like nuns, very vocational.'

'What else are your cast discussing in their dressing rooms?'

'They're saying the Phantom will attack again tomorrow night, during the show. It's a gala charity benefit and we have a lot of celebrities attending, including Vera Lynn, half of the Crazy Gang and Mr Claude Rains, if you please, so if the Phantom does appear perhaps the two of them can have it out on one of the electroliers.'

'You don't sound very worried.'

'At this point, Eurydice would have to explode into flames and burn to death in front of a thousand people before anything could surprise me. Although of course poor old Valerie did get her brains knocked out in front of a full house.' Helena examined the end of her cigarette. 'And to think she was always so worried about being upstaged.'

55

ENGLISH CRUELTY

The front door was locked and barred with planks.

For added emphasis, a DO NOT ENTER poster had been glued across it. This was how May found the Peculiar Crimes Unit when he returned to it in the afternoon. He walked round to the Bow Street duty desk, where Sergeant Carfax could barely suppress the smile on his face.

'Ain't you heard?' he asked May. 'Davenport's closed you lot down, pending an official inquiry. You and your weedy book-reading chum are for the high jump, mate.'

May was shocked, but wasn't going to let Carfax see how upset he was.

'Then I'll set up a base at the theatre,' he told the sergeant. 'If Mr Davenport has anything to say to me, he can do it to my face.' There was a typewriter in the company office at the Palace, and a telephone. That was all he needed. With Bryant gone and Forthright's position hingeing on her undecided marriage, he was now in charge, and determined to make sure that everyone knew it.

At 5 p.m. the Westminster Council ruling came in. The envelope arrived by messenger and was taken to Andreas Renalda's office. The tycoon summoned May, who was in the process of taking up residence on the ground floor. May found Renalda sprawled on his leather couch, resting the steel calipers that caused him so much pain.

'We have been granted a stay of execution,' he said, indicating that May should pour whisky into a pair of glasses. 'You will join me? "The council was not presented with any proof that these deaths could have been avoided by better safety regulations within the theatre." I told you. Their inspectors found only minor infringements. We must open the second pass door to comply with fire regulations, then we get a clean bill of health. The exact word they use to describe recent events is "unfortunate". So we go on, and unless you can come up with any positive evidence for nightly turning away over one and a half thousand people, your job here is over.'

'I'll still be close by,' threatened May.

'Your partner behaved in an irresponsible manner.'

'Mr Bryant voluntarily tendered his resignation. Our director endorsed his decision for a transfer, and has closed down the unit. He'll probably take me off the case as soon as he can find me.'

'One would hope to discover friends in adversity, Mr May, but I suspect this makes us enemies.' Renalda smiled knowingly. 'Your people are famous for supporting each other against the rest of us, even when you're not in agreement.'

'I have no quarrel with you. I was trained to believe that the case is always greater than the officer.'

'Well, that is very diplomatic of you, but I come from a long line of grudge-bearers. I know how the world works. Business decisions are not made for the good of the people, but for the sake of profit, loyalty and expedience. Why do you think I am financing this production? You think I am honouring my wife, paying a debt to my Muses, giving something back to the world of theatre?'

'I imagine your motives are the same as anyone's in business.'

'I go where I see the money going next. There's no future

in manufacturing during peacetime. Once we have rebuilt the cities, people will have more time on their hands. They'll have money to spend.'

'They're turning the theatres into boxing rings, Mr Renalda.'

'Only while the war lasts.' He knocked back the rest of his whisky. 'Afterwards they will pay fortunes to see spectacle. There will be many more young people. We are killing off the older generation. Shows like this are just the start. What humanity wants most is crude sensation.'

'Really? I thought what humanity wanted most was dignity.'

'He was a shrewd man,' May told his biographer decades later. 'But someone else beat him to his big idea. Two years after *Orpheus*, a play called *Oklahoma!* opened, spawning over thirty thousand different productions. It is one of the highest-earning entertainments of all time. Then popular television programmes arrived. Renalda hailed from a ship-building family, but he missed the boat. It's not enough to have vision, you need foresight. I often wonder what happened to him and his dream of entertaining the masses. He was in it for money, not pleasure. That was why success eluded him.'

'Let's get back to the murders,' said the biographer.

'Tell me something.' May turned to the tycoon, watching as Renalda's broad hands absently massaged the steel pins in his knees. 'Where did we go wrong?'

The magnate sipped his whisky. Drinking dulled the pain of his strapped-up legs. 'By looking for someone foreign,' he said at last. 'I suppose it's only natural during a time of war. You don't see it, do you? The English cruelty. That is what your crimes stink of. The culprit is English. You are a cold race. You don't beat your animals, you're subtler, less human. This killer does not think of others, he cares only about himself. You could not find him because you, too, are English.'

'It seems to me that you care only about your company, and the City's faith in it.'

'Faith is a fragile thing these days. A good businessman takes nothing personally. It is unfortunate that lives have been lost. This whole war is unfortunate.'

'Thank you for the advice,' said May, buttoning his coat. 'I'll see you this evening at the theatre, and I will bring the violence to an end. The unit may have been shut down, but it will not stop operating until justice has been served.'

He only wished he was as confident as he sounded.

He left Renalda's office and walked into the dimly lit corridor, where his eye was caught by the ornate gilt-framed wall mirror that stood there. The glass was cracked, and something had been scrawled across it with a blood-red stick of greasepaint. The letters were six inches high: GET OUT OF OUR HOUSE.

I'll get out, thought May grimly, but I'm taking you with me.

'I have a terrible feeling about tonight. He should be here,' said May fretfully. 'It doesn't seem right without him.'

'I understand how you feel, John, but you have to give him some breathing space.' Forthright hooked back the dusty brown drapery and studied the edge of the stage. 'They're running late again. The curtain should have gone up five minutes ago.'

'We're starting it late because the trains are disrupted again,' said Harry, listening for the backstage sounds that told him things were running to schedule. 'There's hardly any service from the east. A church steeple fell on the line outside Fenchurch Street. They reckon Winchester's going to cop it next, after Southampton. Trouble is, it's all getting back to Hitler.'

'What is?' asked Forthright.

'The air-raid damage reports. Franco gets them in code

from the Spanish ambassador in Whitehall. That's what Lord Haw Haw reckons.'

'Things have come to a pretty pass if you're believing *him*,' said Forthright indignantly.

'There's a lot of coughing and sneezing in the audience this evening. My mum says it's because everyone stands around outside at night watching the planes circling. Right, there goes the signal.' Harry darted off through the narrow corridor leading to the left wing just as applause broke out across the auditorium. The conductor was taking his place at the podium.

'Where's Biddle?' May checked the area behind him. 'I thought I told him to keep in the backstage area. I have a suspicion he's rather enjoying his new role.' May had spread his constables around the theatre, but with tickets changing hands for high prices on the black market, they had been refused seat allocations and were forced to stand conspicuously at the rear of the stalls.

'He wanted to write up his report, so I gave him permission to use the company office. He said he's expecting some news.'

May sniffed the air and looked at the sergeant suspiciously. 'Are you wearing eau de Cologne?'

'Why, yes.' Forthright blushed. 'I thought, well, it's a night out at the theatre.'

'You're not worried about Davenport closing us down, then?'

'I have confidence in you, Mr May.' Her hand squeezed his shoulder. 'You'll see us through.'

'I wish I had your faith.'

'Oh, it comes from being around Arthur. It'll rub off on you, don't worry.'

The orchestra launched itself into an *allegro* version of Offenbach's overture, and May was forced to raise his voice. 'I don't know which area to watch first,' he confessed. 'A murderer operating in an area the size of a football pitch, and we can't find a damned thing.'

358

'More like eight football pitches, with all the other levels,' said Forthright. 'If someone wanted to stay hidden, what chance would you have of finding them?'

'Everyone backstage is signed for. It would have to be someone in the audience.' The music thundered to a crescendo. 'Or someone we haven't thought of,' mused May.

'I missed that,' shouted Forthright.

'Forget it.' He realized he was following the same mental patterns as Arthur Bryant. He'd been about to wonder if it could be someone they had dismissed as dead. But all the victims were accounted for. There was no one else.

Slowly the realization dawned. 'Blimey.'

'What is it?'

'We've overlooked something. You'd better come with me.'

A tidal wave of applause broke over the theatre as the conductor took his bow. May pushed Forthright back towards the right-hand pass door. 'I was thinking the other day – suppose she's not dead.'

'Who?' asked the sergeant, trying to keep up with him. 'What are you talking about?'

'Elissa Renalda. I've had a chance to go through some of the other clippings, and there's been a fair amount of speculation since her death. They never properly identified her body. What if she didn't drown? Suppose she *was* the gold-digger that Minos had always suspected her to be? She could have married Andreas for his money. Sources agree that Sirius liked her, she managed to wrap him round her little finger. But she lost everything when Minos warned her to get off the island. Imagine. She has to flee before dawn, while her husband is away. She has nothing but the clothes she's standing in, and maybe her passage on a fishing boat. Minos tells the police she accidentally drowned. He protects her memory for the sake of his brother. Only Andreas believes she was killed. Elissa comes back to England, her home country, and bitterly follows the business exploits of the

Renaldas in the newspapers. She waits for an opportunity to exact revenge. She returns to Athens and tracks down Minos, who's killed in a car crash after a day of heavy drinking. But we don't know the details of that event.'

'So Minos is killed by Andreas's wife. For what motive?' asked Forthright.

'Elissa was in the line of succession, but her "death" cut her out of the will.'

'You realize you're sounding like Arthur.'

'I know,' May admitted. 'Once she was declared dead, she was free but penniless. Mere revenge isn't enough for the way she's been treated. She stages an attack on Renalda's empire, to ensure that his credibility is destroyed for ever. She'll back off, though, if he gives her a cut. Who is she? She could be anyone. None of us has even seen a decent picture of her. She could be operating here, inside the company.'

Forthright struggled with this new idea. 'You think Renalda knows who she is now?'

'I think he was lying the night Arthur accused him.'

'But why wouldn't he have told the truth?'

'Because . . .' May clutched at the air, trying to make sense of his idea, 'he would have been forced to admit that he was still married. If Elissa is alive, she's still an heir, and the case would have to go to court.'

They had reached the musty company office, where Sidney Biddle was working.

'Sidney, I need you to check whether there was another vehicle involved in the crash that killed Minos Renalda. If there was, find out whatever you can about who was driving. Bryant left all the relevent phone numbers in his work folder. I don't care who you have to disturb to do it.'

Biddle's smile broadened at the thought of upsetting people in the name of the law. 'Right away, sir,' he cried, only just resisting the temptation to salute.

Andreas Renalda was watching the performance from the

sealed-off royal box. The divider between the two sections had been restored. In one half sat a group of noisily enthusiastic businessmen. On the other side of the brown partition, the millionaire sat in the shadows, absently chewing his thumb. When the door opened a crack it threw a shaft of light across his pale, angry face. 'You cannot possibly wish to see me now,' he hissed at May. 'The American investors are here. It is the time of Orpheus' big duet. We have the *Times* critic sitting in the front row.'

'Fine,' whispered May. 'I'll come in and tell you why I think your wife is in this theatre. Then you can try to convince me that you're not an accessory to murder.'

Even in the dim light of the box, he could see Renalda blanch. 'Help me up, damn it,' he hissed. May opened the door wider, ushering him out into the corridor. For the first time since they had met, Renalda looked unsure of himself. May wondered if he was deciding whether to lie again.

'Can we talk where your clients can't hear us?' May asked as he pulled the box door shut behind them.

'Here, this is the eviction staircase, nobody uses it any more.' Renalda unlocked a door on their right and led the way onto a concrete landing faced by damp-tainted ochre walls. 'What do you need to know about Elissa?'

'You could start by telling me how long you've known she's alive.'

The millionaire rubbed at his broad forehead, as if afflicted by a migraine. 'You're saying that—'

'Any delay now risks everything you've worked for.'

Renalda sighed heavily. 'She contacted me about eighteen months ago. A phone call out of the blue. At first I did not believe her.'

'But you arranged to see her.'

'We met for a drink at the Savoy. She told me that she had been ordered off the island by my brother. Minos had acted in good faith. It is the way of our family, to protect one another. She was very beautiful, very young, and I was blind,

361

a cripple bewitched by a girl who tricked me into marriage. Minos scared her away for my sake. The police found the body of a drowned swimmer a month later, and after I spoke to them, they conveniently decided that it was my wife's. It suited us for her to appear dead. No loss of face, you understand.

'But she was alive. Elissa timed our meeting well. I was about to sign the deal with the theatre. She asked me to sign half of my holdings in Three Hundred International over to her. If I did not agree to do so, she said she would go to the press, tell everyone that she was still legally my wife, that I had conspired to have her killed and that she had survived the attempt. Me, who had only ever loved her! I could not allow an ugly court case, just when I was fighting to make a name for myself in London. I was not prepared to risk losing the confidence of our shareholders. But I would not sign over my father's empire. We drank, and I let her talk until she talked too much. She said she had heard about Minos's death.'

'She caused his accident, didn't she?'

'She was in the other car, the one that ran him off the road. I saw in her eyes that I had won. She had only one card to play, you see. Any accusation from her would bring a far more serious accusation from me. How the press would have loved that! We had reached an impasse.'

'So she followed you here, and the trouble began. Do you know where she is now?'

'Of course. She is here all the time, where I can keep an eye on her at every single performance.'

'Who is she?'

'Who do you think? That girl in the chorus, the one you spent the night with.'

May's jaw fell open. 'Betty Trammel?'

'Elissa. Elissabetta. Betty. You see? She is a little older and more experienced than she looks. What could I do, tell Helena not to hire her because she was my wife?'

'She's not only your wife, she's a murderess,' said May, horrified that he could have been such a poor judge of character.

'She followed Minos in a state of frustration and anger, and ran him off the road. She did not mean to kill him. And I don't think she's harmed anyone in this theatre.' Renalda gave a sour smile. 'Although she's broken a few hearts. I imagine she found it exciting to seduce a boy who could have her arrested.'

'Where is she now?'

'Backstage, I suppose, waiting to go on. She's a natural performer, as I'm sure you have discovered.'

Andreas Renalda pressed his hands against the sides of his calipers to steady himself. 'God spare me from the designs of angry women.'

56

A DEATH FORETOLD

If John was now thinking like Arthur, the reverse was also true.

Bryant was pursuing a more logical line of enquiry. Forget mythology, he told himself. Don't be misled by the intrigues of the Renalda family. The feud is a red herring. Start afresh, follow a new path. How, he asked himself, would a sensible, methodical man like John May interpret the facts?

After his humiliating experience at Renalda's house, the young detective had carefully rethought his strategy. Seated on his favourite bench by the river, as close as he could get to the memory of his fiancée, armed with the blue crystal fountain pen that Detective Sergeant Forthright had given him on his twenty-second birthday, he mapped out the personal details of the Palace's victims.

Immediately, one name separated itself from the others. One of the two key factors, he felt sure, was Jan Petrovic. Phyllis, her housemate, had told May that Petrovic wanted to leave the show because she wasn't up to the part. Two days later she had gone missing.

The other key was the fact that, however much you allowed for coincidence or fate, the deaths were patterned exactly on Renalda's family mythology. It followed that the murderer not only knew about his past, but was attempting to shift the focus of blame onto him. But why? To take revenge on him for some perceived slight? Possibly. Surely it was more likely to have been arranged out of convenience? The killer was going to commit acts of violence whatever happened, and it made sense to deflect suspicion by implicating an innocent man.

Bryant raised his head and looked across the sluggish brown river, out towards the open sea, the breeze lifting his fringe from his eyes. Two further possibilities presented themselves. Either the person he was looking for had read about Renalda's background – according to the tycoon, it wouldn't have been difficult – or Renalda himself had provided the information. Which meant that it was someone he trusted, somebody close to him in the production.

Petrovic's flatmate said she had lied her way into the job, and was unable to handle it. Suppose she had used the murders as a way of disappearing? She fitted Renalda's mythological beliefs perfectly – almost any chorus girl would have done so – and it was easy to fake her own abduction. But in her haste she had made a mistake, failing to allow her 'abductor' any method of entering the flat. The doors had been shut from the inside, and the neighbours had seen only Petrovic herself entering and leaving the house.

Bryant gently shook ink into the nib of the pen, and drew a series of connecting lines on his pad. Petrovic had wanted to break her contract. Her fellow performers at the Palace were mysteriously disappearing, so she used it as a chance to vanish, to set herself free from a contract she didn't feel capable of honouring. She couldn't provide a body, of course, just a few tiny drops of blood, and a smear of crimson nail polish when they didn't look enough. The rest was easy. When someone had a little money in their pocket and didn't want to be found, Bryant knew, it was difficult to track them down. With the war on, it seemed that everyone was on the move.

Bryant studied the missing section of his diagram. Who knew about Petrovic's problem, and had been able to provide her with a solution? Who told her about Andreas Renalda's Muses, and could explain how her own vanishing act might work?

It had to be the same person the tycoon had confided in. One person linked them both together. Bryant stared at the blue question mark he had scored on the pad, and pensively scratched at his unshaven chin.

What puzzled him most of all was why someone would go to so much trouble. Why was it in their interests to make it look as if Petrovic had also been attacked by the Palace Phantom?

He assumed he had been locked in the archive room by the killer, but at the very same moment Valerie Marchmont had been murdered onstage. How could her attacker have been in two places at once?

The odder pieces of the puzzle sharpened into focus. The picture of the statue in the archive room. The canopy that hung over the east face of the theatre. The reason why the murders had been made to look like accidents.

Actors, damned actors, covering up their secrets, hiding behind their masks.

He had been lied to, again and again and again. He was young and eager, blinded and sidetracked by the mythology of a famous family, all because their story so perfectly matched the opera they were presenting.

Bryant released a groan as he realized the truth. Something far simpler, far more apparent, something that had been staring him in the face for the past week. He needed to get back to the theatre, to check the paintwork on the other pass door – the door that Stan Lowe's boy was supposed to be jemmying open to comply with the safety regulations.

There was only an hour to go before the curtain went up on Monday night's performance of *Orpheus*. It took him nearly twenty minutes to locate a working telephone in the

Aldwych, and then, in his haste to find someone who could help him, he managed to call the woman who was most likely to make his mission more difficult.

'Who is this?' shouted Maggie Armitage, practising white witch and founder member of the Camden Town Coven.

'Who have I called?' Bryant asked himself aloud.

'Don't you know, you silly man?' she shouted more loudly. 'If this is Trevor Bannister from the Southwark Bridge Supernaturals, I've already told you, we don't want your South London call-outs, thank you. Five shillings for spirit clearance, it's not worth the taxi fare. I'm not wiping up other people's ectoplasm for less than seven and six.'

'Maggie, I'm sorry, I seem to have dialled without concentrating . . .' Bryant had been staying with the spiritualist for the past two days. He had felt the need to be away from people who knew about the case, and his landlady was in daily contact with DS Forthright.

'Arthur? Is that you? Your dinner's ruined, I'd give it to the dog but turnips give him wind. I had a feeling you were going to call. It's about the Palace, isn't it? You think you know who's behind the murders.'

'I, er, ah . . .'

'Your timing is spot on, we just finished a seance. We were going to have a few madrigals, but my harpsichord has suffered some minor bomb damage. I used to be able to slice hardboiled eggs through the top chords, but of course it's all powdered stuff now. Do you want me down there? The auspices are very good tonight. Fog always helps the ectoplasmic manifestations. I hear the show is absolutely disgusting, can you get comps?'

'I'm on my way there. I think I'm going to make an arrest,' he foolishly admitted.

'I can do you a quick reading on the telephone if you like. I get the vibrations from the tone of your voice.'

'That's clever,' said Bryant. 'What do you know about fear of open spaces?'

'That's psychology, dear, not spiritualism. It can set in when a susceptible person doesn't get out of the house for a long time, especially if they're undergoing some kind of personal crisis. You think your murderer is agoraphobic?'

'I'm sure of it.'

'Be careful, though, won't you? Phobics can be very nasty when they get into a state of panic. Phobias are powerful vehicles for aggressive feelings. They condense anxiety. Intrusive phobias aren't part of general personalities, they just kick in at key moments. They're a defence against intense trauma, fear of intimacy, stuff like that.'

'You seem to know a lot about it.'

'I once performed an exorcism for a bonce doctor. He was broke and paid me off in therapy. Oh, I'm sensing something very dangerous.'

'In what way?'

'The war. An unexploded bomb. I'm seeing fire and screaming. An explosion, Arthur, a terrible explosion that I'm rather afraid causes the death of one of you.'

'Are you sure?'

'Absolutely, as sure as if it has already happened. In a way, of course, it already has. I don't think you should go to the theatre tonight.'

'I have no choice.'

With the witch's warning words ringing in his ears, Bryant hung up and ran grimly on towards the Palace. When he arrived there, he immediately headed for the right-hand backstage area.

He knew he would find the proof he needed on the lintel of the second pass door.

57

A LIFE IN THE THEATRE

'Because I need you to help us,' said Sergeant Forthright, pausing at the top of the stairs and making sure that the coast was clear.

'I don't know anything about detective work,' Alma Sorrowbridge complained. 'I'm a landlady, for heaven's sake. I'm better on beds.'

'Mr Bryant reckons that any respected person with common sense and an analytical mind could be recruited, so I'm recruiting you.'

'I thought you'd resigned.'

'I never technically left. Although I'm still hoping they'll throw me a party.'

'But why me?'

'Because you're the most enormous person we know. You weigh what, about seventeen stone, don't you?'

'Sixteen and a half. There's nothing wrong with my weight. It's my height, I'm too short.'

'The point is, Alma, you're strong.'

'I'm not that strong.'

'How do you clean behind your mangle?'

'I lift it out.'

'Exactly. What I want you to do is wait at the top of

these stairs and don't let anyone – *anyone* – get past you.'

'What if the audience starts leaving? How can I stop them?'

'They won't be turning out for a while yet. I think you'd better have this, though.' The sergeant handed her Bryant's swordstick and showed her how to unscrew the pewter top.

'I've never used a sword before,' said Alma hopelessly. 'I'm more at home with a mop.'

'Hopefully you won't have to run anyone through.' Forthright struck a pose with the sword, then resheathed it. For a moment she looked like Douglas Fairbanks in drag. 'If anyone comes this way, just sort of – spread out. And scream blue murder. Someone will come to assist you.'

'This is beyond the call of my duties,' sighed Alma, practising with the stick. 'Wait a minute, how did you get this?'

'Arthur.' Forthright grinned. 'He's back.'

'You mean he's here?'

'Right here in the theatre. He's been staying up in North London with that mad girl from the Camden Town Coven, the one who came to dinner and got poltergeists everywhere. She insisted on saying grace, only she read from the wrong book and we had manifestations. She told him someone's going to die tonight in a UXB explosion. Mr Bryant reckons that whatever happens, he'll make an arrest before the end of the show.'

'Nice of him to tell me where he's been living. He didn't even take a change of underpants.'

'I'm sure Maggie Armitage has been taking good care of our boy.'

'Well, I never did.'

Forthright gave her an old-fashioned look. 'No, but you wish you had.'

'I've got a soft spot for him, that's all.' She waved the stick. 'OK, bring on this phantom of yours. I'm ready for anything.'

370

'What do you mean, he's here?' whispered May. He was wedged in his usual position at the side of the stage, in a black-painted brick inlet provided for quick changes. 'You're telling me he's back?'

'He's figured it all out and is going to make an arrest,' said Biddle excitedly. 'I can help. I was a boxing champion at school.' He took an experimental swing with his left fist. 'I put my geography teacher in the hospital. He shouted at me about alluvial deposits so I decked him.'

'Really? I'm seeing another side to you,' May replied, alarmed. 'I hope violence won't be necessary. We're the police, we don't thump people.'

'It's funny, isn't it? I thought I was more interested in the paperwork side of the job, but it turns out I much prefer the chase.'

'What does he want us to do?' asked May.

'Who?' Biddle took another practice swing.

'Mr Bryant, you idiot.'

'Oh. He said to go to the foyer of the theatre at exactly half past the hour.'

'What time do you make it?'

Biddle tilted his watch to the light. 'Twenty-nine minutes past.'

May shoved at him. 'Well, let's go then!'

They filed through to the end of the corridor and dropped down to the pass door, making their way along the dark tiled halls to the front-of-house area.

'I don't suppose Bryant told you who he was planning to arrest, did he?'

'He didn't want anyone to know in advance.' Biddle hobbled on ahead. 'He told me to tell you no mythology this time. He said he needed our help because it wasn't one person.'

'What do you mean?' asked May.

Biddle shrugged. 'He said there are two of them.'

Arthur Bryant checked the buttons on his smart scarlet waistcoat and straightened his scarf. Forthright was bound to have put some constables in the auditorium. If things turned nasty, he hoped they would get here in time.

He checked his watch again. There could be no more mistakes. His nervousness receded as he walked confidently forward to the box-office window. His knock on the glass echoed in the eerily empty foyer.

Elspeth Wynter suddenly appeared from behind the counter. She was holding Nijinsky, her tortoise. 'Oh, it's you, Arthur.'

'I wonder if I could have a word with you, Elspeth.'

'Of course.' She smiled sadly, then set the tortoise back in its box. 'Look, Arthur, I know what you're going to say, and I'm flattered by the attention you've given me, but I don't think it would work out between us.'

For a moment Bryant was flummoxed. This wasn't what he had come to discuss.

'I thought you were – lonely.' He knew by the look on her face that he had chosen the wrong word.

'Whatever you thought we had in common, I don't – I mean to say, I'm not as free as you. I can't leave this place.'

'I realize that.'

'No. I mean I really can't leave.'

'Elspeth, I have to talk to you about Jan Petrovic.'

'Oh, I see.' He heard the relief in her voice. 'Have you found her?'

'No, but I have a good idea where she is.' Bryant tried to sound nonchalant.

'You do? Where is she? Is she safe?'

'She's fine. She's in Dublin.'

'Dublin? I don't understand.'

'Petrovic wanted to get out of the show but had an unbreakable contract, so someone suggested a way that she could escape. That was you, wasn't it?'

Her shoulders slumped wearily, and she placed a hand over her face. For a moment he thought she was going to cry.

'I know the truth, Elspeth. I'm sorry. I spoke to Phyllis, her flatmate. She told me Jan came to see you. She didn't think anything of it at the time, because Jan told her you worked at the theatre.'

Wynter raised her head and studied his eyes intently. 'I just suggested that with these murders going on, there was a way she could easily leave. I told her, it's just a bit of theatre, that's all. Break a window, give yourself a little nick on the thumb, leave a drop of blood and people will think that the Palace has claimed another victim. She's a Hungarian Jew, Arthur. Her parents are waiting for her in Ireland before the family heads for America. She desperately wanted to go and join them.'

'But why would you do that?' asked Bryant. 'Why would you give the police even more cause for concern?' He held her gaze steadily, and in that moment, she knew that he knew. 'I've never made an arrest before, Elspeth. I'm afraid you're going to be my first. You see, this time, I know I've got the right person. I know it's you.'

'Arthur, please—'

'I know you've spent your whole life in the theatre,' said Bryant quietly. 'Raising him and looking after yourself. I can't blame you for wanting to be free. But you chose the wrong way to do it.'

She unlocked the box-office door and closed it behind her with infinite care. 'So you really do know.'

'The other pass door,' he explained. 'There are no coats of paint holding it shut, just a lock. Nobody ever thought to check it. You told Stan it was sealed, and he told everyone else. I knew that if it could be opened, somebody must have a key. I found it in your tortoise box.'

'So you unlocked the door and discovered the room. I wonder if we could sit down.' She looked around, her hands knotted together.

'Of course.' Bryant ushered her to a small alcove with a velvet-covered bench seat.

'I thought we were fine,' Elspeth explained. 'It was such a big building, that was the thing. Nobody even knew he was there. Oh, one or two of the girls sat with him when he was small, but they all moved on. I hadn't even realized I was pregnant, Arthur. I was fifteen years old. Nobody told me the facts of life. A painful two-minute act in the dark of a dressing room with a man I had never seen out of villainous stage make-up. I was frightened out of my wits. The show closed and he left with it. I gave birth just as my grandmother had, here in the theatre. The difference was I was unmarried. There was no one I could go to for help.'

A look of overwhelming misery settled on her. 'I knew I would have to raise the boy alone. They wouldn't let me stay in my lodgings, not in my condition. It was a respectable boarding house. So I moved in here with him. Nobody knew – why would they? There are whole floors barely used. That's when I found the other storeroom behind the pass door. We slept there and were happy enough. My boy stayed quiet. He was as good as gold. There were members of staff in whom I confided. They all moved on. The shows came and went, just as they always had. We would still have been in lodgings, sharing a room. There was so much homelessness. You started to see people sleeping in the parks. We were better off here. Then my boy began to grow restive. He spent too much time alone. Something went wrong in his head.'

'What did you expect?' asked Bryant. 'You can't lock a child up, away from the real world, away from light and friends, no matter how much love you give him.'

Elspeth appeared not to have heard. 'He was always playing with the costumes and props, you see. Trying on the masks. He especially loved the Greek ones, but the comedy face got broken and he was left with the mask of tragedy. It got so I couldn't get him to take it off. He seemed happier behind it. We would eat together, and I would leave him

374

playing or asleep while I went to work, just as always. But he kept the mask on more and more. I tried to pretend that things were normal. Then he became ill and started acting oddly, and I finally took the mask off.' She bit her knuckle, tears welling in her eyes. 'At first I couldn't remove it. He'd cut himself, you see, and the cut was infected. The mask was papier mâché. It was damp from his face all the time. It went rotten. It did something awful to his flesh. I treated it as best I could, but there were terrible scars. It was too late for a doctor. I knew they would send me to gaol. My poor boy. The skin dried all shiny and stretched. He started to remind me of men who'd been in the Great War, the ones who'd been burned, who stand on street corners selling matches. I didn't know what to do. I decided it was time to leave. This place had become our prison. But when I went to go—'

'You found you couldn't leave.'

'I couldn't even set a foot outside the door.' She shook the memory from her head. 'I looked up at the sky and felt sick. Had to sit on the step to stop myself from vomiting. The sun burned my eyes. The cars, the traffic, the noise. I didn't know there was a word for it.'

'Agoraphobia. It's hardly surprising, the amount of time you spent in this dimly lit building.'

'Then the war started. The blackouts. Everything went quiet. Everything was dark. I felt it more with each passing performance, the pressure to leave, it stalked me through the building like a living thing, daring me to go outside. I took my first steps out of the Palace in seventeen years, and was violently sick. Everyone else was in the shelters. The bombers passed overhead but they kept on going. You'll think this is strange, but it was so peaceful.' She exhaled sadly. 'Then they sounded the all-clear and people came out onto the streets again. But the lights stayed off. I knew that if I was ever going to get out of the Palace and back into the world, I would have to leave soon, before the war ended and all the lights came back on.'

She looked at Bryant pleadingly. 'But I couldn't go. How could I go? A new show starting, I'd never missed a performance, never let anyone down in my life. The rehearsals were beginning, they were relying on me. There was no one to take my place. I'm the only one who knows where everything is. There's Stan Lowe, of course, he's been here as long as me, but he's fond of a drink, the place could burn down and he wouldn't notice. So long as the show stays open, I have to be here.'

'So you decided to close the show.'

'It was my boy, Todd. I called him that after Todd Slaughter, the star of *Maria Marten – The Murders in the Red Barn*. That was the show his father had been in. Todd was growing up fast. He took a shine to Tanya Capistrania, watching her from the wings while she practised. I thought he might try to do something cruel, something bad. I thought, history's going to repeat itself if I don't do something, he'll become like his father, and I won't be able to control him. He's too big for me now. He's seventeen. He's already started to slip out during the air-raid warnings, moving under cover of the dark, while everyone's off the streets. I didn't want to see Tanya raped and left pregnant with some awful— I thought, if she dies, there'll be a scandal. They'll shut the place down and I'll have to go. I'll be forced out. It was the only way I'd ever be able to leave.

'No one liked her, no one was close. I didn't want her to suffer, so I poisoned her. I thought it would just put her to sleep. The hemlock was the easiest thing to get hold of. It grows on the bomb sites, you see. I put it in a sandwich and gave it to her. I thought she'd be able to tell if there was something funny about the flavour, so I got quail, something she'd never eaten before. She trusted me. Everyone trusts me. The hemlock made her fall down, but she wouldn't die. Todd saw she was sick and got very angry. He tried to pull her out of the lift, and, God forgive me, in my panic I pressed the call button.

'He went crazy when he saw what the lift did to her. He threw the severed parts out of the window in a rage. He wanted me to be caught. They rolled off the canopy and landed somewhere below. When I went to look for them they were gone. Tanya's body was discovered, and I thought the show would be shut down at once. But no, Mr Renalda kept it going. I'd met Mr Renalda at the start of rehearsals, and instantly disliked him. I read about his family in the papers, all that stuff about him being raised to believe in Greek myths, and I thought, this is perfect.

'A theatrical mind, you see. Plot mechanics. I see them every day of my life. Plots and puzzles and murder mysteries. Faking the way things look, it was second nature to me. I thought, I'll just keep going until they close us down and someone puts the blame on him. Todd had helped me once, so I got him to help me again. I'm his world, Arthur, he'd do anything for me. I told him to watch certain people and to look for opportunities, things he could do that would make everyone get out of our house.

'I made him wear gloves, the same gloves his father had worn on the stage in his role as a murderer. He knows the theatre better than anyone. He cut through the cable holding the globe, and he pushed the boy over the balcony, and he jammed the stage revolve so that Valerie Marchmont died. I knew if he acted during the raids, no outsiders could come into the theatre and discover him. But whatever he did, it seemed that everyone just became more determined to stay. The Blitz mentality, it's infected everything.'

'It was you who locked me in the archive room,' exclaimed Bryant. 'Why, because you wanted to keep me away from the site of Valerie Marchmont's murder?'

'No, I was just really annoyed with you.'

'Oh.'

'I thought I was leaving such an obvious pattern, using symbols of the Muses. You were supposed to go and arrest Mr Renalda. The show couldn't continue without him. But you made it so much more complicated. He slipped out of your hands, the show went on, and I was still *stuck* here, with Todd upstairs, threatening to expose us, becoming more disturbed with every passing hour.' She wiped her eyes with the sleeve of her cardigan. 'Now you'll have to take me out of here, won't you?'

'Yes,' Bryant admitted, 'but you'll be swapping one claustrophobic building for another, I'm afraid.' He looked at his watch. Half past eight. Biddle was supposed to have brought May here by now.

'Where is Todd?' he asked. 'What's planned for tonight?'

'He's under the stage right now,' said Wynter. 'You may already be too late.'

'Bryant! You're back! So Biddle wasn't pulling a fast one!' May rushed forward across the foyer, followed by Sidney. He clapped his partner on the shoulder, then looked at Elspeth Wynter and saw that she had been crying. 'What's going on?'

'Come with me,' said Bryant. 'There's not a moment to lose. Sidney, whatever you do, don't let Miss Wynter out of your sight.'

May fell into step as they headed off along the corridor. 'Where are we going?'

'Do you have a torch?'

'Yes, I always carry my Valiant.'

'Good,' said Bryant, pulling his scarf tighter. 'Where we're going, we'll need it.'

58

LIVING LEGEND

'What's going on?' asked Janice Longbright, trying to catch
her breath. An absurdly long McDonald's truck had nearly
run them down on the Strand. 'Where are we heading?'

'There's not a moment to lose,' May warned. Longbright
strode beside him as they raced off along the pavement. May
was forced to push his way through a slow-moving crowd of
backpacked tourists, and for a moment the detective
sergeant was worried that she would lose him.

'What have you got there?' She pointed at the bulky plastic
Sony bag slung over May's shoulder.

'Something I thought we might need. Keep up with me,
the sun's nearly set,' May called back. Lorries and vans
chugged sluggishly onto the bridge, their exhaust fumes
obscuring the kerbs with grey waste. Longbright caught up
with her former boss as he waited for the pedestrian signal
to change.

She pushed her hair out of her eyes, turning to face the
stale breeze from the river. 'Tell me what happened. Did you
have any luck with the dentist?'

'He's in Sydney, Australia. I woke him in the middle of the
night. Arthur had an appointment with him just before he
left. He'd cracked the top plate of his false teeth and wanted

them replaced. The dentist didn't have time to cast new moulds before he left, and typically Arthur had lost the old mould he was supposed to keep safely stored away for just such an event, so he had to make do with a pair that didn't fit. They were far too big.'

'I don't understand,' said Longbright. 'Why does it matter how big his teeth were?'

'According to my next-door neighbour, the intruder who she thought was trying to break into my apartment had beady eyes and abnormally large teeth. Do you know anyone with beadier eyes than Arthur? Alma Sorrowbridge said that someone had been in Arthur's room, but the front-door lock hadn't been forced. There are few things more personal than your dental records. Who else would take them?'

'Wait a minute. You're telling me Arthur's alive?' shouted Longbright.

'Oh, he's alive all right, but I think he's suffering from amnesia. Over sixty years ago, Elspeth Wynter's deranged son climbed out of the well at the Palace via its drainage tunnel. Bryant recently tracked him down to the Wetherby clinic. He disturbed a forgotten history, even added a footnote to his memoir before changing his mind and hiding it. Todd followed him back to the unit with the intention of attacking him.

'I think Todd took some kind of explosive device along, but it went off at the wrong time, and Todd was killed. He was only five years younger than Bryant. We found the remains of Todd's body, and Bryant's old teeth. Bryant had been placed at the site, and we weren't looking for anyone else. I think he survived, but he's confused, or concussed or something. He went home, but didn't stay. He came to me, but couldn't get in. I've been stalked by Arthur, not Todd. And if there's anywhere in the world that he does still remember, it's here, on Waterloo Bridge at sunset, where he's walked every night for most of his life.' He pointed across the dual carriageway. A blood-red sun shimmered through exhaust fumes behind the Houses of Parliament. 'You take one side, I'll take the other.'

It was May who saw him first.

Bryant was standing at the spot where his fiancée had died, peering over the edge of the balustrade into the opalescent brown water. He was wearing his favourite gaberdine coat, several filthy scarves and a torn hat. He looked – and, as May got closer, smelled – like a very tired tramp.

'Arthur, it's you. It's really you. I thought you were dead.'

May grabbed his arm and twirled him round for a better look. Bryant had a raw-looking gash on his head which he had tried to bandage with an old tie. He was sporting a set of ridiculous ill-fitting teeth that looked as though they had been made for someone with a much bigger head.

'Look at me.' May grabbed his empty face and tilted it up. 'It's me, John May. You're here on the bridge, on Waterloo Bridge where we always go, where Nathalie died. You're Arthur Bryant of the Peculiar Crimes Unit and you're my best friend. Look at me.' He held Bryant's face steady in his strong hands, but the old detective's eyes remained impassive.

'For God's sake, Arthur,' May shouted, 'you'd remember Edna bloody Wagstaff well enough if she was still alive. Well, take a look at this.' He dumped the carrier bag on the pavement and pulled the stuffed cat from it. Time had not been kind to the Abyssinian. Most of its fur had been eaten away with mange, its remaining eye had fallen out and one of its back legs was missing.

'You remember Rothschild?' May thrust the deformed cat carcass in his partner's face. 'It was her familiar. Squadron Leader Smethwick used to send messages through it. Edna left it to Maggie Armitage in her will.'

It was the only thing he had been able to lay his hands on that Bryant might recognize. Rothschild had sat on his desk like a moulting familiar for over twenty years. Slowly, very slowly, the light of recognition began to return to the elderly detective's eyes. Finally, he opened his dry, cracked lips.

'John, what are you doing here?'

'It lives! It speaks!' He turned excitedly to Longbright, who had reached them. 'Look who this is – Janice is here!'

'Why are you talking to me as if I'm a child?' Bryant complained. 'Is there something wrong with you? Hello, Janice. Have you got anything to eat?'

Then he fainted.

May caught him and sat him against the balustrade while Longbright rang for an ambulance.

59

THE CRUELTY OF THE MOON

'Sergeant Forthright has got your landlady stationed across the stairs,' May explained.

'What on earth for?'

'She thought we might need reinforcements. We've only got Crowhurst and Atherton in the auditorium.'

'The White Witch of Camden gave me a warning about tonight,' Bryant cautioned. 'The killer can't go back to his lair because I took the key to his room out of the tortoise box.'

'I think it's this one.' May pointed out the brown door that led to the first of the understage areas. 'What's been going on?'

'Well, it struck me that if you removed Jan Petrovic from the victim list, all of the deaths took place in the theatre. Why? I asked myself, knowing there could only be one answer. They happened here because the murderer hardly ever leaves the building. Elspeth Wynter has been trying to close down the show because she needs to be free of this house. But she's become agoraphobic. I remember her sweating in the restaurant when we went out to lunch. She can't bear to be trapped in here any longer, but on that day she couldn't wait to get back. Hiding her boy all these years was

383

easier than hiding her own feelings, but she managed that as well. Hardly surprising, seeing as she's spent her life in the theatre watching people fake emotions. In a way, she's more talented than any of them.'

Bryant pulled the door shut behind them and flicked on his torch. Ahead lay a maze of bare wooden walls. Makeshift timber railings prevented them from falling to the lower levels.

'She couldn't have killed anyone,' May pointed out. 'You only have to look at her, she's tiny.'

'She staged the murders for her son to carry out. He's getting too big for her to take care of any longer, creeping around the theatre frightening the ladies in their dressing rooms. He's down here somewhere. Elspeth can never have a life, never be close to anyone, never ever leave so long as a production continues. She needs the show to close so she can finally escape. And now it's all too late.'

He led the way along the wooden bridge that ran round the central dark square. 'We're nearly under the orchestra. Look up.' Above them was the dust-caked wire mesh that indicated the start of the orchestra pit.

'So you were right, in a way. It was about the assassination of theatre gods – just not the ones you thought. Mind your head.' The corridor was lower now. They passed several rusted iron-rung ladders leading to the star traps, segmented doors through which an actor could be catapulted onto the stage under cover of smoke. At the downstage centre point stood the grave trap. Light from the spots above the dancers shone down through the grille.

'I don't like this, Arthur. He could be hiding anywhere.'

Bryant pulled something metallic from his pocket. The click of a ratchet sounded.

'Are you armed?' asked May.

'It's a service revolver that belonged to my brother.'

'I didn't know you had a brother. Do you know how to use it?'

384

'The principle's not hard to grasp. Trigger here, bullets come out of the end. It's my understanding that he kept it loaded. I don't think the boy is on this level.' Bryant peered over the side of the rickety balustrade and shone his torch into the darkness below. 'We're going to have to go further down.'

'I don't like this at all,' May complained, feeling for the steps ahead. From the stage above their heads came the sound of the orchestra launching into the show's grand finale set piece, the cancan.

The stamping of the dancers dislodged showers of dirt. Sawdust sifted past their faces. Bryant pulled out a handkerchief and discreetly coughed into it.

'Are you sure he's down here?' May shifted uncomfortably. He was starting to feel shut in.

'Listen.' They stopped as they reached the middle of the three floors constructed beneath the theatre. The music was distorted by the gurgling steam pipes that ran all around them. Bryant shone his torch beam over the walls. The shadows of the stage props, a dozen twisted demon heads, stretched and fell away. The giant eyes of Cerberus, the watchdog of Hell, gleamed wetly at them from a corner. Spiders and mice scuttled from the light. Ahead, just out of the beam, something moved.

'I think that's him.' Bryant's eyes widened. 'Stone the crows.'

The boy caught in the torchlight seemed more frightened than angry. His pale, fleshy face was cicatrized with the marks of a badly healed infection, the skin pulled taut and shiny across his skull, his right eye milky with cataracts. His chin was sunk into the bulky mass of his chest, so that he appeared to have no neck at all. Having never left the confines of the theatre, he had the typical deficiencies of a human deprived of sunlight and nutrition. His bones were twisted with the effects of rickets.

'The light's hurting his eyes, keep the torch trained on him,' Bryant called over his shoulder as they advanced.

'Go away from me. I know she sent you,' cried Todd suddenly, throwing his hands across his eyes and edging from the circle of brilliance cast by May's torch. The voice was as dry and dead as the air in the theatre, no louder than the rasp of a scrim sliding in its oiled wooden groove, and yet its tone was clear and cultured. He had spent his life listening to actors' declamations.

'Todd, we don't mean you any harm, we want to help you, but you'll have to come with us.' Bryant took a step closer.

'She intends to leave me here, all alone here.' The boy backed away with his arms still raised.

'No, she doesn't, your mother is going to take you with her,' Bryant promised.

'I've seen you, both of you. I did it for her, so we can get out. But I know she's not taking me.'

'Where did he get this idea from?' whispered May.

'I hear everything through the grilles and traps. I heard her telling you.' Todd thrust an accusing finger. 'You, the short one.'

'I'm not short,' said Bryant indignantly.

Todd suddenly broke free from the light and dropped down the wooden staircase leading to the lowest level of the theatre. The detectives were forced to move forward over the narrow footbridge, one behind the other. Far above them, thirty dancers bared their thighs and hammered out the steps of the cancan.

Beneath the three great turbine engines, the steam pipes and oiled cables that led to the flies, Todd darted along the open corridors, loping from side to side like an ape, dislodging props and items of clothing that hung along the walls, a half-wild creature at home in a penumbral world of brick and iron.

'Keep away from me.' They heard him before May could shift the torchlight onto his face. He was on the far side of the understage. The ground beneath the detectives' feet had turned from planks to stone and earth.

386

'Keep the torch trained on him, John.'

May picked out the boy's twisted features with his beam. Todd released a despairing bellow of pain as the light seared his eyes.

'All right, wait.' May moved the circle of light lower, over the boy's chest, until he had grown calmer.

'I didn't want to hurt her,' he called back, 'the dancer, she was so beautiful, but mother poisoned her. Then she started the lift and it ruined everything. She wanted to shock the outsiders. Poor precious feet, I threw them from the window of the smoking salon, hoping someone would see. But outside was all black, there was no one about.'

'The air raid,' murmured Bryant. 'You weren't to know.'

'My mother says it is too dangerous to go outside, there are bombs falling from the sky. But I've been out. I know how to drive a bike.'

Todd reached down and picked up something that looked like a length of oak. May lowered the torch and saw that it was a sledgehammer.

'She'll leave me, and I will have to stay here alone in Hell, with Eurydice.' He shifted his weight until he was standing astride something grey and heavy, and raised the sledgehammer in his broad fists.

'Don't go any closer, Arthur.' May's torch picked out the object at Todd's feet, an absurdly bomb-like thing with tail fins, spattered in white dust, in a round steel case as tall as a man, tapering to a point. How it had reached the basement was a mystery; the ceiling above it was intact.

May had seen enough photographs of unexploded bombs in the *Evening News*, with proud ARP men standing beside them. By the end of the war, fifty thousand would have been defused in streets, factories, shops and homes. Sixty years later, they would still be discovered and deactivated.

'We'll all go together, to the real Hell, not one made of paint and plaster,' said Todd sadly. 'It's for the best.' He raised the sledgehammer higher over his head.

'No' – Bryant threw up his hands – 'don't do it, Todd. Remember all the girls above us, the young dancers, like the one you didn't want to hurt.'

'None of them will have me. Who would want me? I'm a man, not a child. I have no face. I have no life. Can't go. Can't stay. And now I am a murderer.'

'Todd, please.' A sense of dread flooded over Bryant. He was horribly aware of Maggie's warning, that death would come from an unexploded bomb. He held out his hands. 'Please,' he begged the boy again. May was standing right in its path.

The muscles in Todd's arms flexed, and he swung the sledgehammer down into the bomb with all his might. Bryant and May threw themselves down onto the floor.

The only sound that followed was a violent splintering of wood. May groped for the fallen torch and twisted its beam back towards the boy. The head of the sledgehammer was lodged firmly inside the bomb case.

'It's a prop, a bloody balsa-wood stage prop,' cried May.

'Blimey.' Bryant rose clumsily to his feet as May ran past him. He saw his partner wrestling with the boy, then watched as they fell with a crash that jolted aside the torch beam. Grunts and shouts filled the enveloping darkness. A few moments later came a terrible cry. Bryant thought of Maggie's death warning again.

'John!' he shouted, but there was no reply. Nothing but silence in the turgid claustrophobia of the darkened underworld.

60

THE MOON IN A BOX

Biddle pulled a Woodbine from behind his ear and kept his eyes on Elspeth Wynter as he dug around for a light. He didn't like the look of her. Panic was flickering in her eyes. She was searching for a way out. From the street outside came the familiar whine of the siren mounted on the roof of St Anne's Church. For a moment he thought she was going to drop in her tracks.

'It's all right, Mrs Wynter, our lads will find your son. Everything's going to be fine.' It was the reassurance everyone gave each other throughout the war.

'He's very strong,' she warned. 'I feel a little faint. Do you mind if I sit down over there, where it's cooler?'

'Here.' He took her arm and helped her to the stool in the box-office booth. 'They timed the raid well tonight. The show's just turning out.'

Behind them, the ushers opened the auditorium doors as the sound of applause billowed into the foyer. Moments later, they were engulfed by members of the audience, leaving quickly to obey the warning of the air-raid siren. Biddle took his eyes off her for only a second. When he looked back at the booth, Elspeth Wynter had gone.

* * *

'John, where are you?' called Bryant. 'Shine your torch.' He heard a strangled grunt in the dark. Water was dripping somewhere.

'Over here.' May was coughing, trying to catch his breath. He grappled for the Valiant and pointed its beam up once more. Bryant saw that he was sitting beside the mouth of the artesian well. He limped over and joined May at the glistening ring of stone.

'Down there.' May shone the torch over the side and saw Todd hanging by one claw-like hand from the slippery green brickwork.

'Good Lord, look how deep it is.' Bryant got onto his knees and leaned as far over the well mouth as he dared. 'Todd, give us your hand. We can get you out of there.' He turned to May. 'You're taller than me, you can reach further.'

The boy was shaking his head rhythmically, scraping the damaged skin of his forehead along the brickwork until a dark caul of blood veiled his eyes. 'No,' he called up. 'I come from deep inside the Palace. This is where I belong. I see the stars from the skylight, lying up on the grid, just under the roof. The moon is always in a box, and the box is only full of tricks. I want something to be real. Death is real.'

As the detectives cried out in unison, Todd opened the fingers of his left hand and dropped down the centre of the well, a fall of almost seventy feet before he hit the black water below. There was nothing either of them could do. For a moment they lost him from view. Then they turned the torch on the distant oily surface until it settled once more into an unbroken mirror, the remaining effect of a vanishing act.

Biddle pushed through the crowds, shoving his way out of the congested theatre foyer. His one chance to make good, to do something positive, and he had messed up. He threw his cigarette aside and looked around desperately as the theatre-goers began making their way towards the shelters. There was no sense of urgency on the street, no rush or panic. Couples crowded the narrow pavement outside the Palace as ARP wardens directed them to the nearest shelter. He couldn't see her. There were people everywhere. As Biddle searched the faces, the detectives arrived beside him.

'Where's Elspeth?' asked Bryant, wheezing badly. 'What have you done with her?'

'It's my fault,' Biddle admitted. 'She ran out as the stalls started emptying into the hall. My eyes were off her only for a second.' He looked at Bryant's dirt-covered clothes. 'What happened to you?'

'We have to find her, Sidney.'

'She can't have got far. Here, give us a hand up.' Biddle leaned on the detective's shoulders and hoisted himself onto the edge of a stone horse trough. On the other side of Cambridge Circus he saw the back of a woman in a brown cardigan and skirt, fleeing in the direction of the British Museum. 'I can see her. Come on.'

The detectives lost precious seconds extricating themselves from the crowds. When they managed to catch sight of Elspeth Wynter again, she was running blindly across the intersection beside the Shaftesbury Theatre.

'Where's she heading?' asked Biddle.

From somewhere near the river came the dull drone of a bomber squadron.

'Out,' said Bryant, 'just out into the open, away from the theatre, but the more open it gets, the more frightened she'll be.'

They were fifty yards behind her when she turned into Museum Street and froze, standing in the middle of the road, looking up.

Overhead, the thick grey clouds had parted to reveal a midnight-blue sky glittering with stars as bright and sharp as knives. As the gap grew larger, the oval of the moon appeared, flooding the street with silvered light.

Bryant, May and Biddle came to a stop some way back,

amazed by the sight of the buildings' dark recesses melting away beneath the lunar brightness. 'She's reached it,' said Bryant, 'she's reached the light. If she can survive this, she'll be free.'

'She's still going to gaol,' said Biddle indignantly.

'Freedom will be inside her head.'

They could hear Elspeth sobbing in awe and relief as she looked up, transfixed by the quiescence of the moon. The droning of the bombers was fading now, growing quieter and quieter until the four of them were standing in unshadowed silence.

Bryant knew he could not compete with the world that beckoned to her. He watched as she took a faltering step away from him, then another. Part of him wanted Elspeth to run and keep on running, until she was liberated from the city's life-crushing influence, free to live a normal life. Go, he thought, don't look back. Whatever you do, keep going.

'Look, are we just going to stand here and let her get away?' asked Biddle impatiently.

'No, I suppose not,' said Bryant with a sigh as they walked forward. 'Elspeth,' he called gently. 'Please. Let us help you.'

She stopped in her tracks and looked back over her shoulder with sad deliberation. She saw Bryant and held his eye, unable to move any further, and in that moment she was lost.

Up ahead there was a muffled thump, and the road vibrated sharply beneath their feet.

'What the bloody hell was that?' asked Biddle.

Elspeth had heard the noise too.

'Oh no,' was all Bryant managed to say before the two-storey front of the antiquarian bookshop lazily divorced itself from the rest of the terrace and fell forward in an explosion of dust and bricks.

As the airborne sediment settled, they saw the neat rooms inside the bookshop exposed like a child's cutaway drawing. The building's frontage lay collapsed across the road, virtually unbroken. As a fresh wind picked up, the entire street was scattered with the pages of rare books. Colour plates of herons, butterflies, monkeys, warriors and emperors drifted lazily past them. There were diamond shards of glass everywhere. The detectives' clothes were pin-cushioned with sparkling slivers.

'Bloody hell,' said Biddle, scratching his head in wonder.

Of Elspeth Wynter, there was no sign at all.

61

SPIRITS OF THE CITY

Margaret Armitage sipped the glass of vervain tea made from leaves she had specially shipped to her from a French necromancer in the town of Carcassonne. Beside her, Arthur Bryant and John May dangled their legs over the ancient wall of the riverbank, nursing foamy pint mugs of bitter. Above the pub door was a large blackboard that read: HITLER WILL SEND NO WARNING – ALWAYS CARRY YOUR GAS MASK.

The waitress of the Anchor had looked at Maggie as if she was mad when she asked for a glass of freshly boiled water. It did not help that the teenage leader of the Camden Town Coven, an organization that had counted Sir Arthur Conan Doyle and Edgar Allan Poe among its members, was wearing a purple and gold kaftan belonging to an African tribal chief, topped with a peacock-feather hat and half a dozen amber necklaces inscribed with carvings representing the souls of the dead.

'I'm a bit disappointed about there not being an actual phantom at the Palace, just a poor tortured boy,' said Maggie, looking out across the placid grey water at the bend in the river, where it widened to the docks. 'Let me get under your overcoat, it's big enough.'

'Yes, that was rather an intriguing aspect,' Bryant agreed as he extended his gaberdine. 'Of course, Todd Wynter was never at Jan Petrovic's house, so there were no walls to walk through, so to speak. But when he vanished from the top-floor corridor, and again from the roof, he had me fooled for a while. John, you remember I asked you about the wind that night?'

'Yes, I wondered what you were on about.'

'We found Todd's jacket,' he told Maggie. 'The one his mother had made for him, just a hood and cloak stitched out of blackout curtain, but it was absolutely huge, rolled up like a sheet. When I ran after him, I imagine he simply remained still at the end of the passageway and unfurled the cloak. It was too dark for me to see him. An old magician's trick; he'd witnessed plenty of those at the Palace. He threw it off the roof when he was finished with it, and waited until he could return to his private quarters. We found it hanging from the steeple of St Anne's Church in Dean Street. The wind had carried it like a sail.'

'What a pity,' said Maggie. 'I had hoped you might be able to give us proof of the spirit world.'

'Oh, I've no doubt Andreas Renalda is possessed, but he's possessed by the spirits of his childhood.' Bryant swallowed some of his bitter, savouring the pungent taste of hops. 'In her own way, so was Elspeth Wynter. Her life was shaped by the ghosts of the theatre. She was a woman forced to survive in a world of harmful magic.'

'That's what witches are. Do you think she was a witch?'

'Well, someone dropped a house on her,' said Bryant, 'so she might have been.'

'You can't fool me. You were keen on her.'

'I was only ever keen, as you quaintly put it, on one girl. Once you've met the one, all the others are just phantasms.'

Maggie lightly stroked his hand. 'Perhaps it's time to let her memory go, Arthur.'

Bryant looked out at a pair of swans settling on the oily

water. 'It's not a matter of choice. I have to wait for her to do that.' He took a ruminative swig of beer. The evening's chill had blanched his cheeks and knuckles.

'Did you hear about your landlady?' May was anxious to change the mood. 'She stabbed the editor of *Country Life* in the foot with your swordstick.'

'Serves him right,' said Bryant, cheering up. 'He has no business being in London.'

'And Davenport's very pleased. He came into the unit this morning and wandered around for a while, shifting pieces of paper about, looking into drawers, fiddling with things. Turned out he'd come to congratulate us formally, and was having trouble uttering the words.'

'Perhaps he could jot it on a postcard,' offered Bryant. 'He means well but he's such an awful clot. Fancy ordering our front door to be barred.'

'I think he was a bit embarrassed about that. You should have seen his face when Biddle stood up for you. He looked as if he'd been stabbed in the back.'

'I don't suppose Davenport's good mood will last. The Lord Chamberlain has changed his mind about the show. Says it's indecent and has to come off. I think somebody higher up must have had a word with him.'

'So all of Elspeth Wynter's efforts were wasted. The production would have closed anyway. How sad. God, we're such a lot of hypocritical prudes.'

'You didn't sleep with her, did you?' asked Maggie. 'You didn't get your conkers polished by a murderess?'

Bryant looked horrified. 'No I did not, thank you,' he said, as though the thought had never even occurred to him. 'For a spiritualist, you can be very crude.' He suddenly brightened. 'Mind you, *he* did, our Mr May, he made love to a murderess.' He pointed at John May.

'Unproven,' said May hastily. 'I mean Betty's involvement in the death of Minos Renalda. There's nothing on record, only the conversation I had with Andreas.'

'I thought her real name was Elissa.'

'That's right, abbreviated to Betty. She has a sister in the Wrens. I should introduce you.'

'I don't think so. Once bitten and so on.' Bryant raised his trilby and shook out his floppy auburn fringe.

'I should be going.' Maggie Armitage set down her tea glass. 'I'll be late.'

'What have you got tonight?' asked May. 'Druid ceremony? Seance? Psychic materialization?'

'No, Tommy Handley on the radio at eight thirty. I never miss him.' She thrust a lethal-looking pin through her hat. 'I was listening when Bruce Belfrage got bombed. We hadn't laughed so much in ages.' Belfrage was a BBC news announcer who became a national hero after carrying on his live radio broadcast even though the studio had received a direct hit and several people were killed. 'I actually think I'm going to miss the war when it's over.'

'Don't be obscene, Margaret,' said Bryant hotly, swinging his legs down from the weed-riven embankment wall. 'Death is stalking the streets, death made terrifying by its utter lack of meaning.'

'The closer you are to death, the more attached you become to life,' the coven leader reminded him. 'The city is filled with strengthening spirits.'

'The city is filled with brave people, that's all,' said May, and took a long drink of his beer.

'If people ever stop thinking about the ones they leave behind, Mr May, your job will cease to exist. All that you see – all this' – she gestured around her, 'is about generations yet to be born.'

'Don't take her too seriously,' Bryant warned his partner. 'You were wrong about one of us dying in an explosion, Maggie.'

'It's never a dead cert, otherwise I'd make my fortune on the gee-gees instead of helping the police with their inquiries,' she snapped at him, stung.

'You told me you once copped a monkey on a nag called Suffragette racing at Kempton Park because he was possessed by the spirit of Emmeline Pankhurst,' complained Bryant.

Maggie saw more than she ever dared to tell anyone. Time compressing, days blurring into nights, speeding skies, great buildings whirling into life, wheels of steel and circles of glass. She saw a girl her age but half a century away, a girl too afraid of life to leave her house.

She saw the future of John May's grandchild.

'I'm sorry,' she apologized suddenly. 'I have to go. Don't be downhearted, Mr May. And don't worry about the future. Things have a way of working out. The song of the city will live on, so long as there is someone to sing it.'

'Well, I wonder what got into her?' exclaimed Bryant. The detectives watched as she walked off down the street, pausing to stroke a tortoiseshell cat on a doorstep, listening to it for a moment, then moving on.

'You know some very peculiar people, Arthur,' May pointed out.

'Oh, you haven't seen the half of it. I intend to bring many more of them into the unit. I have a friend who can read people's minds by observing insects. He'd be useful. And I know a girl who's a ventophonist.'

'What's that?'

'She can throw her voice down the phone.'

'Now you're teasing me.'

'Our work is far from finished. I think I've finally found a purpose to my life. Something I can dedicate myself to. Thanks to you.'

Bryant looked over at his partner and grinned as the sun came out above them, transforming the river into a shining ribbon of light. He rubbed his hands together briskly.

'But where to start? We have yet to discover the lair of the Leicester Square Vampire. He's still got my shoes, you know. And that poor girl he snatched, buried alive with all those rabid bats and someone else's head. There are other cases starting to come in. We've got a 21-year-old Hurricane pilot accused of a brutal stabbing in Argyll Street, several witnesses, his bloody fingerprints on the body, and a cast-iron alibi that places him in the middle of Regent's Park, tied to the back of a cow. He's one of the Channel heroes, so it's in everyone's interests to exonerate him, but how? No, our labours here are only just beginning. This city is a veritable repository of the wonderful and the extraordinary. Isn't that right, Mr May?'

'I couldn't agree with you more, Mr Bryant,' replied May with a lift of his glass, and this time he really meant it.

Bryant looked over his friend's shoulder, in the direction of Waterloo Bridge. Something drew his eye to the centre of the bridge. There was a coruscating flash of dark sunlight, a spear of greenish yellow, and for the briefest moment two elderly men could be seen leaning on the white stone parapet. Then the light settled, and they were gone.

Far above them, the silver-grey barrage balloons that protected the city turned lazily in the early evening air, like old whales searching for the spawning grounds of their youth.

62

SLEIGHT OF HAND

'What time is it?'

'Almost sunset.' May came away from the hospital window. 'You can see the river from here.'

'Look, John, I've still got the mobile phone you bought me.' Arthur Bryant pulled the silver Nokia out from under the bedclothes and waved it at his visitor, waiting for a compliment. The hospital room was awash with garish flowers and get-well cards.

'I thought you'd lost it,' said May, tearing off a grape and eating it.

'No, I'd accidentally switched it with the television remote. Every time Alma changed channels to watch QVC she speed-dialled the Berlin headquarters of Interpol.'

'Well, why didn't you use the speed-dial to call me?'

'I wasn't thinking very clearly. I'd been hit on the head,' Bryant complained.

'How is the old noggin?' May peered at the top of his partner's skull. A row of neat stitches extended from his right ear to the middle of his left eyebrow. 'You're going to have a scar there. Can you remember what happened that night after I left you?'

'Only bits,' Bryant admitted. 'I went downstairs to get my paperweight back.'

'What paperweight?'

'The one I threw at the lads from Holmes Road when they came by to make fun of me. It must have been around six in the morning when I went out. I thought I'd better get the thing back because it was a souvenir from the war. I was just coming up the stairs when I saw him. The top door was wide open, and Elspeth Wynter's son was standing there. He had a green metal cylinder in his fist. He started accusing me of persecuting him, and said he was going to kill me. I should never have sought him out at the Wetherby. I'd upset him when I reminded him how his mother had died. It's funny the way little things can trigger memories. Give me those, for God's sake.' He reached forward and emptied grape pips from May's cupped palm. 'Ow.' He clutched at the top of his head and fell back onto the pillow.

'You shouldn't move about,' warned May. 'The nurse says you have to lie still for a few days. What happened after you saw Todd standing there at the unit?'

'What do you think? He hit me, and there was an explosion. I'd just nipped out in my shirt sleeves, I had no ID on me, no wallet. I woke up in a hostel off the Charing Cross Road. A very nice lady kept feeding me mushroom soup. I went back home but my teeth were hurting, so I picked up my dental records.'

'You also took the blueprints covered with your notes from the Palace.'

'Yes, but I couldn't remember why I'd taken them. I went to see you but I couldn't get in, so I thought I'd wait. Some hideous monkey-like woman appeared from nowhere and started screaming at me.'

'You missed your own funeral.'

'Was it a good turnout?'

'Excellent, lots of wailing and gnashing of teeth, really miserable. You'd have loved it.'

'How did you figure out what had happened?'

'I must admit you had me going for a while. Maggie suggested we try to get in touch with you on the other side—'

'Don't tell me you've become a believer,' interrupted Bryant.

'—and she needed something you'd touched, so I took her Nijinsky's shell. She reached the person who'd been killed in the explosion, just as she'd promised. But she'd made contact with Todd, not you. He'd touched the tortoise too. It had probably been his only childhood friend.' May tucked the blanket around his partner's pyjama'd chest. 'I think you'd better come and stay with me for a while, just until you're a hundred per cent.'

'God, no, you have the television on all the time, it would drive me mad. This one's bad enough.' He pointed to the wall-mounted TV, tuned to a silent news broadcast.

'We'll discuss it later. What would you most like to do when you're better?'

'Oh, I don't know, take tango lessons, do a bit of sky-diving, the usual stuff.' He thought for a moment and smiled. 'Or perhaps we could just go to the river and watch the tide going out.'

'Why not?' May agreed. 'There aren't too many of the old rituals left. It seems a pity to break this one. We'd better get your choppers sorted out as well.' He looked at the bedside table, where Bryant's gruesomely enormous false teeth sat grinning at him. 'If it wasn't for those horrible things I'd never have thought of searching for you.'

'Then I'd like you to keep them.' Bryant grinned tooth-lessly, then the smile faded. 'He'd not had much of a life, you know, Elspeth's son. In and out of institutions and halfway houses. He was registered under his mother's name, Wynter. Yet he seemed not to remember her when we spoke.'

'He remembered enough to follow you back to the unit and wait there until the next night. We were wondering where he got the incendiary device from.'

'Ah, um, I'm rather afraid that was my fault.' Bryant looked sheepish.

'What do you mean?'

'It was mine. I'd kept it as a souvenir from the war.'

'Kept it, all this time? Where?'

'On my desk.'

'I don't remember anything like that on your desk.'

'The paperweight, the one I chucked at the lads from Holmes Road that night.'

'You're telling me that was a *bomb*?'

'I thought it had been defused. I painted it yellow in the sixties – it was the sort of thing you did back then. I must have destabilized it when I threw it out of the window. I got back to the room and found Todd there. He threatened me.'

'So this green metal cylinder he was carrying wasn't a bomb?'

'No, it was his thermos flask. He hit me over the head with it.' Bryant gingerly touched his scar. 'That's how I got this. He was trying to kill me. I didn't know what to do, but the paperweight was still in my hand so I chucked it at him. I didn't expect it to explode.'

May buried his face in his hands. 'I can't believe you blew us up. We thought you were the victim, not the bomber.'

'Try to look on the positive side,' said Bryant brightly. 'Maybe now they'll give us some decent offices.'

'We are in so much trouble,' moaned May. 'Do you realize we've buried someone else in your grave? Why can't you be like regular old people and put irresponsibility behind you?'

'I know there have been some inconsistencies in my past behaviour, John, but from now on I'll try to be exactly the same.' Bryant's watery blue eyes looked hopefully towards a more certain future.

'Oh, before I forget,' said May, emptying the contents of his nylon backpack onto the end of the bed, 'I know how much you hate staying in bed and I thought you might like something to occupy your mind while you're lying here, so I brought you the job applications Sam Biddle forwarded to the unit. You can go through them and select a few of these "ordinary civilians" for interviews.'

Bryant eyed the pile of letters suspiciously. 'Do I get paid for working overtime?'

'You merely receive the thanks of a grateful nation.'

'Huh.' He lifted the letters up by their corners, examining them as though they were dead animals. When he reached one handwritten envelope, his brow furrowed even more deeply than usual. He opened its flap with a theatrical flourish.

'Hmmp.' He waved at his bifocals. 'Pass me those, would you?' He unfolded the letter. 'Aha. Hmph.'

'I assume you are making those cartoonish noises to attract my attention,' said May wearily.

Bryant tossed the letter at him. 'How about this one? We'll give her an interview, shall we?'

May read for a moment, then raised his eyes. 'This is a formal application to join the unit from April, my granddaughter.'

'And you thought there wasn't anyone in your family willing to carry on the tradition.' Bryant smirked. 'Shows how much you know about people.'

'Wait, did you put her up to this?' asked May.

Bryant's eyes widened with indignant surprise.

'No, of course you didn't. You couldn't have, because when I told you last week that the Chief Association of Police Officers was inviting non-professionals to train alongside detectives, you acted as though you didn't know anything about it.'

'Oh, well then, I don't. You ought to see her, though.' He licked his lips. 'Blimey, I'm starving. It must be nearly time for them to bring the mince trolley round. You'd better be off before it arrives.'

As May slipped the note back in its envelope, he couldn't keep himself from grinning. 'Perhaps I should get Longbright to fix up an appointment.'

'I think you'll find she already has. Next Tuesday at eleven.'

He was going to ask how Bryant could possibly know, but his partner was already starting to feign sleep.

'You missed your vocation, Arthur,' he said softly. 'You really should have been on the stage.'

'The city is my theatre,' murmured Bryant. 'I never want to leave it.' He closed his eyes and allowed himself to sink into vast white pillows. 'The war.' His voice became a faint whisper. 'How little we knew about people then. How little we ever really learn.'

Above the foot of the bed, the silent television replayed footage of guns and men, and a distant battle that could never be won.

THE END

Appendix

NOTATIONS MADE BY MR ARTHUR BRYANT IN AN
ACCOUNT OF HIS FIRST CASE WITH MR JOHN MAY

Abyssinians, uses of when stuffed
  For purposes of ventriloquism
  Possession of by squadron leaders

Actors, unreliable behaviour of

Agoraphobia, dangers of

Airships, German, poor performance of

Amateurs, abilities of encouraged by Home Office

Architect, incomprehensible explanation by

Armitage, Maggie
  Psychic powers of
  Price charges for ectoplasm clearance
  Link between horseracing and women's suffrage
  Ability to use harpsichord as boiled-egg slicer

Astaire, Fred, appearance at Palace

Bananas, as weapon against Hitler

BBC, hilarity caused by bombing of

Bengal tiger, as shameless plug for other published Bryant and May cases

Betts, Corinne, as murder witness
   As stand-up comic

Biddle, Sidney
   Bovine addiction to law and order
   Enjoyment of complicated paperwork
   Pleasure derived from hitting geography teacher

Bombs, used in destruction of police stations
   Falling on London like jellyfish
   Exploding in tube stations
   For use as stage props

Bridge, Waterloo, as conduit for rumination
   Psychic phenomena on

Bryant, Arthur, displays of temperament against constables
   Addiction to illegal narcotics
   Insensitivity
   Rudeness
   Uselessness with opposite sex
   Poor dress sense of
   Comparison to tortoise
   Inability to read flags
   Love of tachygraphy

Hopelessness with technology
Association with tontine, Savoyards, butterfly-covered corpse etc.
Possibility of being mistaken for mental patient
Preference for wood carving to having sex
Unflattering description of

Capistrania, Tanya, thankless role in tale as unloved murder victim

Carfax, Sergeant, similarity of wife's face to witch doctor's rattle

Caterpillars, poisonous, use of in teapots

Cats, ginger, arrival through kebab shop windows of
Stuffed, as conduit for dead squadron leader

Cheese, *see* Skittles

Chorus girls, unlikeliness of wearing knickers

Davenport, Farley, highly unflattering description of
Emotional constipation of

Dental records, pertinence in murder investigations
Likelihood of use in identifying werewolves

Dwarves, gigantism amongst

Finch, Oswald, inflexibility in humorous situations
As butt of cruel practical jokes
Under attack by dangerous vegetation

Forthright, Gladys, desire for assonance of
Peculiar taste in role models
Unsuitability of choices where men are concerned

Ginger people, use of by Germans during blackouts

Greeks, shipbuilding and theatrical enterprises

Incendiary devices, inadvisability of using as paperweights
    Mistaken for thermos flasks

Jack the Ripper, ability to melt pavement slabs

Landladies, unlikely swordsmanship abilities of

Lift, as device for removing feet

Lithuanian botanists, incidence of vampirism amongst

London, bus standing on end in

Matthews, Jesse, eerie power to drive men mad

May, John, predictability of female dinner dates
    Peculiar ability to turn women's knees to jelly
    Last chance to have sex of
    Stoic qualities of
    Claustrophobia suffered by

Memory, lost
Memory, revived
Memory, regained

Muses, as template for murder spree

Norwegians, anaemic condition of
Norwegian painter, similarity to medical officer

Offenbach, Jacques
  As progenitor of Gilbert and Sullivan
  As inspiration for deranged serial killer

Opinion, Public, violent death of

Orpheus mythology, as motive for murder

Palace Theatre, resemblance of to Borley Rectory

Paperweight, use of for incendiary purposes

Parole, Helena
  Heartlessness of
  Alcoholism of
  Medusa-like qualities of

Pepys, Samuel, talent for tachygraphy

Petri dishes, mysterious existence of under Bryant's bed

Phantoms, ability to walk through walls of
  Likelihood of picking a fight with Claude Rains

Planet, as symbol of freemasonry
  As murder weapon

Plants, tropical, propensity for sickening cats, wives, etc.

Poltergeist, dangers of intrusions by while saying grace

Pope, violation of with roofing tiles
  As condom spokesman

411

Pork, as substitute for human feet

Senechal, Charles, clouted by planet

Skittles, as a boring esoteric hobby for aged detectives

Statuary, as esoteric clue in criminal investigation

Stone, Miles, unfortunate choice of pseudonym by
    Inability to be faithful with women

Technology, peculiar backfiring of when confronted by technophobes

Teeth, as clue in criminal investigations. *see* Dental records

Theatre critics, climbing abilities of

Thwaite, Olivia, floral solution to prominent nipples by

Tortoises, life-threatening habits of
    Uses of in spiritualist rituals

Trammel, Betty, mysterious true identity of

Traps, star
Traps, grave

Turk, body parts found in chestnut brazier by

Varisich, Anton, orchestra conductor forced to work with buskers

Wagstaff, Edna, psychic sensitivity of with dead pets

Whittaker, Geoffrey, unorthodox sexual arrangements of

THE WATER ROOM
By Christopher Fowler

The new Bryant & May mystery.

Originally built to house the workers of Victorian London,
Balaklava Street is now an oasis in the heart of Kentish Town
and ripe for gentrification. But then the body of an elderly
woman is found at Number 5. Her death would appear to have
been peaceful but for the fact that her lungs are full of river
water. It falls to the Met's Peculiar Crimes Unit, led by
London's longest-serving detectives, Arthur Bryant and John
May, to search for something resembling a logical solution.

Their initial investigations draw a blank and Bryant's attention
is diverted into strange and arcane new territory, while May finds
himself in hot water when he attempts to save the reputation of
an academic whose knowledge of the city's forgotten underground
rivers looks set to ruin his career. In the meantime, the new
owner of Number 5 is increasingly unsettled by the damp in
the basement of her home, the particularly resilient spiders and
the ghostly sound of rushing water . . .

Pooling their information to investigate hitherto undiscovered
secrets of the city, Bryant and May make some sinister
connections and realize that, in a London filled with the rich,
the poor and the dispossessed, there's still something a
desperate individual is willing to kill for – and kill again to
protect. With the PCU facing an uncertain future, the death toll
mounts and two of British fiction's most enigmatic detectives
must face madness, greed and revenge, armed only with their
wits, their own idiosyncratic practices and a plentiful supply of
boiled sweets, in a wickedly sinuous mystery that goes to the
heart of every London home.

0 385 60554 4

NOW AVAILABLE FROM DOUBLEDAY

THE FIG EATER
Jody Shields

'AUTHENTICALLY EERIE AND EROTIC – A VIENNESE DANCE
OF DEATH'
Victoria Glendinning

*He watches her eating one fig, then two more, grinding the seeds
between her teeth, the sound echoing in her head, perhaps the
last sound Dora heard before there was the thunder of blood in
her ears . . .*

Vienna, 1910. On a warm August night, the body of a young girl
is discovered in the city's celebrated Volksgarten. She has been
strangled. Using the latest forensic methods, the Chief Inspector
of Police begins his painstaking search for the killer. He is not
alone, however. His wife Erszébet – a woman steeped in the folk
tales and Gypsy lore of her native Hungary – becomes obsessed
with the dead girl. In secret, she conducts her own investigation
of the murder, guided by intuition, instinct and superstition.

Set against the brooding backdrop of *fin-de-siècle* Vienna. *The Fig
Eater* is a mesmerizing novel of suspense and latent eroticism.

'A GRIPPING PSYCHOLOGICAL THRILLER . . . CAPTURING
THE NERVOUS MOOD OF A CITY PRE-OCCUPIED, LIKE ONE
OF ITS MOST FAMOUS RESIDENTS, WITH SEX AND DEATH'
The New York Times

'SHIELDS' GRASP OF TIME AND PLACE IS WHOLLY
CONVINCING AND THE WRITING RICHLY POETIC'
Guardian

'AN INTENSELY POWERFUL SENSE OF TIME AND PLACE IN
THIS ATMOSPHERIC AND ACCOMPLISHED PERIOD
WHODUNIT'
Harpers & Queen

0 552 99865 6

BLACK SWAN

WIDE EYED
Ruaridh Nicoll

'A QUIETLY SPOOKY TALE . . . BOTH UNSETTLING AND
ODDLY EXHILARATING'
Sunday Telegraph

A remote fishing village in Scotland seems the perfect place for
Betsy Gillander to abscond for a few days with her fiancé. There,
in a landscape marred only by a vast MoD range away to the west,
the pale winter sun lights up this next step in her happy and
structured life.

But then a violent storm wraps itself around the village and for
three days the couple are trapped in their hotel. The enforced
intimacy opens Betsy's eyes to the indolent cruelty of the man
she's agreed to marry, while in the hotel bar the locals gather,
increasingly anxious for news of a boat still out at sea.

By the time the sun reappears, Betsy's fiancé has left her and she
is adrift in a community shattered by the loss of the boat and
seven of its sons. The pain of her break-up in the face of such
tragedy produces in her a terrible guilt and Betsy finds herself
drawn into a cloistered, close-knit community with a morality far
beyond her understanding . . .

'AN ABSORBING YARN . . . WHILE THE NARRATIVE IS WELL-
CRAFTED AND BUILDS TO A BRAVURA CLIMAX, IT IS IN THE
EVOCATION OF ATMOSPHERE, THAT ELUSIVE ART, THAT
NICOLL REALLY EARNS HIS SPURS'
Sunday Telegraph

'LYRICAL AND COMPELLING . . . NICOLL'S PORTRAYAL OF
GRIEF, AND THE NEED TO MAKE SENSE OF CALAMITY IS
NEVER LESS THAN CONVINCING. ANOTHER TRIUMPH'
The List

'NICOLL WRITES INTRICATE, ACCURATE PROSE AND OFFERS
ALLURING DESCRIPTIONS OF THE SCOTTISH LANDSCAPE . . .
THE LANDSCAPE OF *WIDE EYED* IS BEAUTIFUL AND THE
SITUATION IS FASCINATING'
Guardian

'EMOTIONALLY-WROUGHT . . . IN TURN LYRICAL AND
VIOLENT, FABLE-LIKE AND GUTSY'
Sunday Herald

0 552 99904 0

BLACK SWAN

A SELECTED LIST OF FINE WRITING AVAILABLE FROM BLACK SWAN AND BANTAM BOOKS

99863 X	MARLENE DIETRICH LIVED HERE	Eleanor Bailey	£6.99
99824 9	THE DANDELION CLOCK	Guy Burt	£6.99
99979 2	GATES OF EDEN	Ethan Coen	£7.99
99686 6	BEACH MUSIC	Pat Conroy	£8.99
99925 3	THE BOOK OF THE HEATHEN	Robert Edric	£6.99
81416 8	THE CRUSADER	Michael Eisner	£6.99
99935 0	PEACE LIKE A RIVER	Leif Enger	£6.99
77125 2	TRICKS OF THE LIGHT	Alison Fell	£6.99
81429 X	THE SURGEON	Tess Gerritsen	£6.99
81389 7	THE GRENADILLO BOX	Janet Gleeson	£6.99
77080 9	FINDING HELEN	Colin Greenland	£6.99
81384 6	A CARESS OF TWILIGHT	Laurell K. Hamilton	£6.99
99966 0	WHILE THE SUN SHINES	John Harding	£6.99
77001 9	HOLY FOOLS	Joanne Harris	£6.99
77082 5	THE WISDOM OF CROCODILES	Paul Hoffman	£7.99
77109 0	THE FOURTH HAND	John Irving	£6.99
77005 1	IN THE KINGDOM OF MISTS	Jane Jakeman	£6.99
99996 2	EVA'S COUSIN	Sibylle Knauss	£6.99
99807 9	MONTENEGRO	Starling Lawrence	£6.99
81222 X	MYSTIC RIVER	Dennis Lehane	£6.99
81350 1	A CALL TO ARMS	Allan Mallinson	£6.99
99904 0	WIDE EYED	Ruaridh Nicoll	£6.99
81386 2	LAST OF THE AMAZONS	Steven Pressfield	£6.99
77088 4	NECTAR	Lily Prior	£6.99
99810 9	THE JUKEBOX QUEEN OF MALTA	Nicholas Rinaldi	£6.99
81406 0	BOUDICA: DREAMING THE EAGLE	Manda Scott	£6.99
99865 6	THE FIG EATER	Jody Shields	£6.99
81404 4	THE LOST ARMY OF CAMBYSES	Paul Sussman	£6.99
99864 8	A DESERT IN BOHEMIA	Jill Paton Walsh	£6.99
77107 4	SPELLING MISSISSIPPI	Marnie Woodrow	£6.99